Yeshu

Yeshu

A Novel for the Open-Hearted

Charles David Kleymeyer

Quaker Heron Press

Yeshu

A Novel for the Open-Hearted

by Charles David Kleymeyer, PhD

The persons and events in this work of fiction have representations in history; nevertheless, this novel's story is the author's creation and should not be construed as historical fact.

ISBN # 978-1490353005 (paper)
Library of Congress Control Number: 2013912393

Published by
Quaker Heron Press
Columbia, Maryland

Cover art by Marsha Lederman

www.YeshuNovel.com

www.facebook.com/YeshuNovel

Written for my children

Ana Maria

Joshua David

&

Lily Delorey

Acknowledgements

For his gifted editing skills, his dedication, and his belief in this book, I thank my editor, Ron Weber. Without him, this novel would be a shadow of what it is today.

For her many years of unflagging moral support and her broad theological insight, I lovingly thank my spiritual soul mate and wife, Ann Kathleen Delorey.

For her striking pastel cover art, I wish to recognize the artist, Marsha Lederman. I also thank my diligent proofreader, Susan Kaul.

For their extensive and constructive feedback and support, I would like to express my gratitude to the following people:

Evelyn Bence
Anne Berry
Pat Breslin
Bill Barbieri
Ann Delorey
Bernard Delorey
Bob Dockhorn
Joe Elder
Guli Fager
Dianne Greenley
Jim Greenley
Jim Hall
George Holliday
Marsha Holliday
Evelyn Jadin
Leslie Jadin
Ana Maria Kleymeyer
Joshua David Kleymeyer
Lily Delorey Kleymeyer
Ruth Mueller Kleymeyer
Ylene Larsen
Mindee Laumann
Anne Lindbergh
Sarah Payne Naylor
Kate Oberg
Mary O'Brien
Richey Sharrett
Susan Shaughnessy
Naomi Thiers
Luke Greenley Stone
Lilian Weber
Jill Weiler
John Yungblut

I also want to express my appreciation to others who, though they may not have been acquainted with the actual text of this novel, directly influenced my writing skills, thinking, and growth in ways that enabled me to create my story:

Clifford Alfred Kleymeyer, Sr., my father

Reverend Ruben J. Bierbaum, pastor, Bethel United Church of Christ, 1947–1960

Members of Friends Meetings (Quakers) of McLean, VA, Washington, DC, and Madison, WI

Wallace Stegner, my teacher and friend

The following creative persons and works helped build the foundations of thought and imagination upon which this book stands, and I am forever indebted to them:

The *Gospels* according to John, Luke, Mark, and Matthew (1st and 2nd Century, CE)

Hermann Hesse, *Siddhartha* (1922)

Pier Paolo Pasolini, *The Gospel According to St. Matthew* (1964)

Michelangelo Buonarroti, *La Pietà* (1499)

Sainte-Chapelle stained-glass windows, Paris, France (1239–1248)

Kurt Vonnegut, Jr., *Cat's Cradle* (1963)

Nikos Kazantzakis, *The Last Temptation of Christ* (1960)

Folk masses: Fr. Guido Haazen, *Missa Luba* (1958); Los Padres Oblatos y el Coro de la Parroquia de Llallagua, *Misa Incaica* (1960); Ariel Ramirez, *Misa Criolla* (1964)

Matsuo Basho, Yosa Buson, Kobayashi Issa (17th to 19th centuries) and other haiku poets

Vincent van Gogh, oil paintings (1886–1890)

Martin Luther King, Jr., *Letter from a Birmingham Jail* (1963) and other writings

Rabbi Abraham Joshua Heschel, public lectures at Stanford University (1965–1966)

Alan Watts, public lectures at Stanford University (1965)

Thich Nhat Hanh, *Living Buddha, Living Christ* (1995), plus other books and Dharma talks

Krzysztof Kieslowski, *The Decalogue* (1989)

Credits

Biblical passages in this book, frequently revised for reasons of literary style and composition, are from *The New English Bible (The Standard Edition; with the Apocrypha)*. New York: Oxford University Press, 1961/72; and *The New English Bible: The Old Testament*. New York: Oxford University Press/Cambridge University Press, 1970.

The characterization of Yeshu was inspired by repeated listening to *Symphony No. 7 in A major, Op. 92*, by Ludwig van Beethoven (1811–12)

The process of imagining Yeshu was enriched by countless hours of meditation on the monumental woodcarving of Jesus, placed slightly in front of a wooden cross—not crucified on it, but standing with arms outstretched to welcome and embrace—which is located on the wall behind the altar of Bethel United Church of Christ, Evansville, Indiana. This piece was designed by P. John Hoener of Hoener, Baum, and Frese architectural firm of Saint Louis, Missouri; it was carved by craftsmen employed by the Ossit Church Furniture Co., Janesville, Wisconsin (1937).

The historical context in this book was enhanced by a course offered by the Smithsonian Institution, entitled "The Historical Jesus" (Winter, 1995), as well as numerous other lectures and readings.

The characterization of Yohanan was shaped by frequent viewing of the sculpture of John the Baptist by Pablo Gargallo, entitled *The Prophet* (1933).

The story of the man who was once a thief was sparked by the passage about the bishop's candlesticks in *Les Misérables* by Victor Hugo (first American publication—Hugo, Victor. *Les Misérables*. New York: Carleton Publishing Company, 1862).

The chapter entitled "Star Sign" was influenced by a program at The Arlington Planetarium in Arlington, Virginia, entitled "Star of Bethlehem" (ca. 1985; by permission from Steven Smith, Director).

The story of the frog in the well was heard in the course of numerous storyteller open swaps, 1976 to 2000, and elaborated upon by the author.

The chapter entitled "Stones to Fruit" is based on a spoken message given by Leon Kanegis in a Quaker meeting for worship, Friends Meeting of Washington, October 5, 1986 (permission given by Leon Kanegis).

Shoshana's lullaby was sparked by "The Hobo's Lullaby" as sung by Utah Phillips, who attributed it to Goebel Reeves (1961). Reeves' melody is in turn almost identical to George F. Root's popular Civil War era song, "Just before the Battle, Mother." "The Hobo's Lullaby" has also been performed by Woody Guthrie, Pete Seeger, The Kingston Trio, Arlo Guthrie, and Emmylou Harris, and is available on the Internet. The lyrics of Shoshana's lullaby, with the exception of the first three words, were composed by the author:

> Go to sleep my little wanderer.
> Travel safely through your dreams.
> Come back home at tomorrow's dawning,
> A wiser and more loving being.

The chapter title "Nothing Is So Like God As Stillness" is a paraphrase of a statement by the 13th Century mystic, Meister Eckhart (see Woods, Richard. *Meister Eckhart: Master of Mystics*. London: Bloomsbury Publishing, 2011).

The chapter entitled "God is in the Mouth of the Wolf" resulted from a friendly challenge from a mentor—Quaker theologian John Yungblut—to introduce spiritual paradox into the storyline (conversation in Round Hill, Virginia, 1993).

The chapter entitled "The Goose Girl" is an adaptation of a Chinese folktale in the public domain, heard in the course of numerous storyteller open swaps, 1976 to 2000, and elaborated upon by the author.

The chapter entitled "Heaven and Hell" is an adaptation of a Japanese folktale in the public domain, heard in the course of numerous storyteller open swaps, 1976 to 2000, and elaborated upon by the author.

(Note: the author is not familiar with any published versions of the stories or folktales that are referred to above as having been heard in open settings.)

The chapter entitled "Disobedience" was inspired by "Letter from a Birmingham Jail" by Dr. Martin Luther King, Jr. (April 16, 1963), as published in various sources.

The chapters entitled "She is the Wisest" and "Gospel According to Maria" were influenced by observations about Mary Magdalene made by Elaine Pagels in her book, *The Gnostic Gospels* (New York: Vintage Books, 1979.

The description of an "Ethiopian" helping Yeshu carry the cross stems from Bible study classes taken at Shiloh Baptist Church, Washington, D.C. entitled "Blacks in the Old Testament" and "Blacks in the New Testament" (1988).

The chapter entitled "Powered by Love" was inspired in part by the striking woodcarving of Jesus that is described in the third item in this list of credits.

The story of the injured bear and the compassionate rabbit was shaped by the story of "Androcles and the Lion" in *Aesop's Fables,* by Aesop (ca. 620–560 BCE).

The description of Mama Maria holding Yeshu after his execution, in the chapter entitled "Hill of Sorrow, Wellspring of Joy," is based on Michelangelo Buonarroti's sculpture, *La Pietá* (1499).

Various other stories and elements in this book are autobiographical in origin (shepherd girl; blankets from home; rebuilding of Ludum; my own father's wooden workbench; fogged-over hillside; giant trees; storytelling with kids; lakes, campfires, celestial drama). In such cases, the names of people and places have been changed. The one exception is the character "Mama Maria" who is named for a Quichua-speaking Indigenous woman from the Ecuadorian highlands (her paternal and maternal last names will remain confidential).

Several passages in this book are extensively revised versions of free-standing short stories that were adapted from the author's manuscript and published prior to this novel:

"A Parable of Stones into Fruit," *Quaker Life,* Series 30, No. 2, March 1989, p. 20.

"God Is in the Mouth of the Wolf," *Friends Journal: Quaker Thought and Life Today,* Volume 50, No. 4, April 2004, pp. 12–15, 39.

"Unclean!" *Friends Journal: Quaker Thought and Life Today,* Volume 52, No. 3, March 2006, pp. 6–9, 29.

"When I Was Thirsty...Flowers Bloomed," *Quaker Life,* Series 47, No. 6, November/December 2006, pp. 14–15.

"Heaven and Hell," *Friends Journal: Quaker Thought and Life Today,* Volume 53, No. 6, June 2007, pp. 10–13, 29.

"Away in a Manger: A Quaker Midrash," *Friends Journal: Quaker Thought and Life Today,* Volume 56, No. 12, December 2010, pp. 6-7, 36. [For this story, Friends Journal received a "Seasonal Article" Award of Merit in 2011 from the Associated Church Press.]

Other Books by Charles David Kleymeyer

Padre Sol, Madre Luna: Cuentos del Desarrollo de Base Pluricultural; Inti Tayta, Killa Mama: Runallaktakunapak Tauka Yachaykuna; Father Sun, Mother Moon: Stories of Pluricultural Grassroots Development

Cultural Expression and Grassroots Development: Cases from Latin America and the Caribbean

La Expresión Cultural y el Desarrollo de Base

¡Imashi! ¡Imashi! Adivinanzas Poéticas de los Campesinos Indígenas del Mundo Andino: Ecuador, Perú y Bolivia (tercera edición)

Poder y Dependencia Entre Quechuas y Criollos: Dominación y Defensa en la Sierra Sur del Perú

Table of Contents

I. Beginnings

Starpath

I loved Yeshu. And Yeshu loved me.

This is the heart of my story, and it could easily fit into the palm of my outstretched hand. It's the story I yearn to tell forever.

It always begins the same way: I have just turned seven years old, so Yeshu must be twenty-three. He is standing waist-deep in a field of wheat, gazing at the full moon rising as the sun sets behind him.

"Why are you looking at the moon?" I ask.

"Because it marks the path to the stars," he replies.

"Is there a path," I say in a near whisper, "to the stars? Can you really travel there?"

"Yes," he insists. "And so can you, Daavi."

I smile. And he laughs.

For me, that moment is the brightening dawn of our friendship.

The last time I saw him—years later—there was no moon in the sky. And no stars.

The sky was dark as night.

But it's not night.

Yeshu's fire is going out like a dying ember in a shepherd's hearth.

In spite of the danger, I cannot leave him. His deep, dark eyes hold mine. And mine his.

The three Marias and Joanna are beside me, and this protects me from the soldiers. Otherwise I might lack the courage to stay while the unspeakable proceeds.

Our gentle carpenter, the teacher of love, the peacemaker, is being put to death. And nothing I do can stop it.

I am barely seventeen.
It's the most terrible day of my life.
Yet despite the darkness without, I know now that light was within.

Storyteller

A relentlessly curious seven-year-old, I eagerly joined the crowd of kids outside the open door of the carpenter's workshop to listen to the man inside singing. The voice was compelling and melodious like wind moving through tall trees. At first the words were just sounds till we realized that the carpenter wasn't singing at all. He was telling a story, and by the way he looked up from his work now and then, we soon figured out he was talking to *us*.

One by one we edged into the room, which was light and airy despite the numerous logs and boards stacked against the walls. The floor was covered with sawdust and wood curls that made you want to dig your toes down until your feet disappeared. Just the way we seemed to disappear into his story. I remember few words that were spoken that morning. What lingers to this day is the scent of freshly cut cedar and pine.

In the months and years that followed, as Yeshu seemed to just get better and better at storytelling, and when we had no pressing chores to do, that abiding freshness drew me and the other village kids back to his workshop.

To encourage us to come in and stay, he built a collection of small stools out of spindly sycamore limbs and set them along a wall he had cleared for us to lean our backs against. Each morning whoever could do so would fill those seats, sometimes locking arms at the elbows, and Yeshu would fill our heads with stories.

Some of these stories he had learned from his maternal grandmother, whom everyone called "Mama Ana," and some from the Temple rabbis in Jerusalem. Other times, he made up his own. Those stories were my favorites. Whenever I got the chance, I'd ask him for one.

Yeshu always worked while he told his tales. His hands and eyes stayed fixed on the plow handle or table or door that he was making, but the rest of him belonged to the story and to us.

Between stories—and sometimes within them—there were stretches of silence. Yeshu would labor on, while we struggled to sit still. If we started whispering about who was fastest or who could jump the farthest, or if we giggled from the strain of keeping a straight face, Yeshu would quietly look up in a way that made you sit back and think again about the story he had just finished.

Sometimes, of course, he joined in when the joking was irresistible. Once, my little brother Aaron fell asleep, his chin sinking slowly to his chest, and Yeshu leaned over and poured sawdust on his palms and feet until the tickling, mixed with our laughter, woke him up.

Aaron's eyes darted around the room and then peered up at Yeshu, who was now on one knee, smiling down at him. I could tell by the broad grin on Aaron's face how very important he felt right then.

~ ~ ~

There were always *lots* of people visiting Yeshu to talk and listen about everything from the Prophet Elijah to the dreadful Roman occupation of our land. Most of the visitors were local elders. If we weren't already sitting on the stools that Yeshu had made for us, the grownups would pick them up, carry them over by the workbench, and sit down in a semicircle to hold forth on the topic of the day, their knees sticking up to their ears like a choir of wrinkled frogs.

The first time we stepped into the workshop to find our seats taken, we hung around a while, but it was like being at the back of a crowd trying to peer through a forest of big people's legs to watch a procession. After that we would steal a look at the doorway, and if Yeshu had company, just turn around and leave.

So one night Yeshu stayed late, lit an oil lamp, and added curving backs and armrests to each stool so that only a child could fit. And in we came again.

The storytelling only happened in the morning because Yeshu said the afternoon heat muffled his words. It was so. As the warm morning sun climbed higher and higher, sometimes you couldn't help but feel drowsy like Aaron had, and your attention would roam far from what was being said.

During the storytelling, time stopped. I would watch the carpenter's beard moving gently as words flew from his lips like breezes through a springtime meadow. My eyes would glide over the tall grasses covering the lower half of his face, searching the tangles of light and shadow below his cheekbones for some small surprise—maybe a bumblebee looking for clover. I wondered what it would be like to sink my fingers into the brush and give that beard a strong tug. But I didn't dare.

As Yeshu's story rolled on, my eyes would wander from his mouth and beard to his hair. Like the other men of our town, his hair was ebony-colored: shiny and curly when just washed, streaked with dust after hot days of long work. It was thick and loose, tumbling down freely; not like Roman hair, which was always cut short and groomed in military style.

When the sun finished climbing its ladder at noon, out we would file from Yeshu's workshop and go home for something to eat. Often, I would return alone later on and watch Yeshu work. Soon I was almost his second shadow, sitting for hours on end while he patiently turned wood into wonders. Wordlessly his warm, brown eyes told me I was welcome any time I happened by.

I was as certain of this as of my next breath, even though I lacked the words to say why. I believe it's because I already understood something about the power of silence. It's what I picked up spending lots of time alone in the fields, first with my family's small flock of sheep, later on with the flocks of others. Sheep don't have words either, but I learned a lot from watching and listening to them carefully. It was my job to look after them, yet they were also my teachers—until that winter day later on when Roman soldiers would take them all away.

But that's another story, one that could be told by countless others in the towns and villages of Galilee and Judea. And though the shadow of Rome was everywhere, it isn't time to talk about that yet.

It's better to talk about a particular quality of silence. At the time of the loss of our flock, my father put it like this, beginning with what it's not.

Wiping his lips and placing the cup of goat's milk he was drinking back on the table, he turned his head to look straight inside the angry shell in which I was stewing.

"Daavi," he said, "Whatever would become of the eagle and its young if the great bird passed its time on the bare snag of a treetop limb, thinking about the mice it had failed to catch? Behind the brooding silence that devours us is the watchful silence from which action springs."

~ ~ ~

Quietly keeping Yeshu company during the long hours he toiled, I increasingly tried to make myself useful in any way I could. Partly, I just wanted to help. My parents had explained to me that Yeshu had precious little time for his own pursuits since losing his father and taking over the family carpentry shop to support his mother, whom we all called "Mama Maria," and his brothers and sisters. Work had to come first. Becoming a rabbi or starting a family were hopes that had to be postponed or set aside. Maybe that was why his eyes could seem so far away, even when he was making the kids or grownups laugh who'd come by to visit. Sometimes a really exciting story would be tinged with an unspoken sadness.

It struck a chord with my own loneliness. Just months before, my older sister Shoshana—who had often joined me in Yeshu's workshop—had vanished without a trace. No one could tell me where she was. Even her name was lost from my parents' lips. The more it wasn't spoken in our house, the louder it sounded in my ears.

Doing things for Yeshu reminded me of helping Shoshana with her chores, and that brought her nearer.

Whatever tool Yeshu needed, I'd fetch it. After a while I could jump up and get it even before he pointed. From the well I brought cool drinking water that we would share. I did whatever I could, so his hands could do their magic. And so his thoughts could soar.

In return he told me stories, and he made things for my family. That made my mother and father happy. He made sturdy shelves for our clay plates, a new door for the courtyard, a toy fishing boat for Aaron, and lots of things we could not otherwise afford. But of all these things, what pleased Father and Mother most was how Yeshu made a friend of me. They could see me blossoming in his presence.

Gradually I learned not just how to watch but how to listen. And doing so let me soar along with Yeshu.

One day after years of stories, my friends and I got too big for the chairs, but that was okay. Others took our place. My friends and I began to do our part for our families, while our younger brothers and sisters went on listening to Yeshu's singing.

I still dropped by whenever there was a spare moment, of course, and the stories were just as good, maybe even better. I took them with me when I left and soon the sheep were hearing about King David and about the grasshopper and the ant.

Yeshu's shop was like another part of my home, and I thought little about time or growing up. But still something was missing that I couldn't quite put my finger on. Then came the day that he brought the toy boat over to our house for Aaron. While my brother gleefully sailed the little boat across his lap, I felt odd and wiped my cheeks with my arm, wondering if I had dirt on my face. When I looked around, Yeshu was watching me.

Every day for the next week I had to tend a neighbor's herd of sheep. Early one evening Yeshu found me at the well and asked me to come to his workshop the next morning. When I walked in, he reached behind his back and then held out a closed fist, which he slowly turned over and opened.

"I heard this calling out from a small block of cedar," he said. "And after freeing it, I knew it belonged to you."

In his palm stood a miniature sheepdog, with a tail of real camel's hair and floppy ears made from leather scraps rescued from the pile in my father's workshop. The dog's coat shone from being burnished and oiled, and its eyes and mouth and nostrils had been carefully carved in.

How I loved him. Each morning he leapt into my pocket to keep guard, and each night I took him into bed and told him stories about my day. While he listened, ears cocked, I would fall gently asleep into a night brightened by the sharp smell of cedar.

I named him *Shalom* because of the peace he brought when I pressed him close to my heart in the dark.

Now, whenever I headed over to Yeshu's, Shalom went along. Watching the carpenter work made me wonder when he had found time to make Shalom so perfectly. It had to be after evening prayers, or before the morning ones, because the rest of his days were full to the rafters.

As I grew, I began to listen to Yeshu's stories more carefully and noticed the care with which they, too, were made. How much thought they contained. How much of his daily life was spent reflecting. While he worked on his wood with hammer and saw, chisel and draw knife, planer and marking awl, he was also turning over in his mind what was going on in our village and the larger world outside.

He talked to himself, and to me too I suppose, about the Roman armies occupying our land and keeping its people pressed to the ground. He mulled over where we Jews were headed; what our relationship was to the peoples of the world. Who are our neighbors: Are they only the nearby Samaritans? Or also those farther away with whom we traveled and traded, like the Egyptians and the Greeks and the Ethiopians. But however far his mind wandered, sooner or later his attention would come back home to our own people and the priests and legal authorities that ran our affairs.

"Things must change," he said to me one afternoon, "if we are to draw closer to God."

Glancing up from the board he was planing smooth, he paused to explain, "We are like lost sheep and goats that have strayed from God's path. You see that, Daavi, don't you?"

I looked back and nodded, hoping that I saw it.

"But how?" he wondered, as if he too were puzzled. "What do we do if the people in charge are blind or afraid?

"Someone needs to wake them up. Help us better discover God's will for our people. Show us how to carry it out!" he concluded.

His draw knife attacked the board, sending thin wisps of wood flying. Absently, I gathered a few of the springiest curls to take home for Aaron to play with.

Yeshu didn't notice. He had stopped working and was staring out the window, down the sunlit road.

I followed his gaze, but no one was there. After a while, his hands resumed working, but without a word being spoken. Hours seemed to drift by.

Watching the wrinkle creasing his brow just above the bridge of his nose, I could tell his mind was still racing. I wanted to ask him—"Where are you now?"—But something told me not to break the flow of his thoughts.

All I could do was hope that one day the world inside of him would become clearer to me, like finding a spot on a grassy hillside to watch the morning mist lift from the valley below.

But not today. Dusk was already spreading its purple cloak over the room, the gloaming gently enveloping us. Soon it would be too dark to work without burning oil Yeshu could not afford to waste. Motioning to me, he headed out the door and we walked down the road and out of town to the river. In the dying light we washed the day's dust off our hands and feet and said our evening prayers together.

~ ~ ~

Rarely was Yeshu hesitant about sharing his beliefs. With groups, he always spoke freely. In private he was more mysterious. It was quietness dancing with words as he talked and listened and pondered and spoke. It was like watching the moon moving from fullness to absence to fullness again, until suddenly a new season was there. It was always surprising but somehow familiar.

When Yeshu mused out loud, you felt like a mouse in a moon-drenched field sniffing for clues, tasting the wind and watching the clouds streaming by overhead and conversing with their shadows below. You could feel the subtle shifts in light as the sound of his voice moved from thought to thought.

Trying to figure out where those thoughts came from or were going was like figuring out where the moon had come from or was headed toward. Its presence was just there. Even in its momentary absence, I felt it nearby and didn't want it to be anywhere else.

Listening to Yeshu this way taught me one thing about him for certain.

The urgency in his voice when he talked about his father always caught my attention. Yosef had passed on before I was born, under circumstances I didn't fully grasp, but he was still in Yeshu's life.

"He prepared not just my hands but the rest of me," Yeshu explained one afternoon, turning his palms to face upward, then lifting his right forefinger to his eye, before settling the hand down over his heart.

Picking up a wooden mallet, he carefully tapped the wooden dowel of a leg into the seat of the chair he was fashioning.

"My father—I always called him Abba—could have been a famous rabbi," he said. He knew *that* much, Daavi. But we were poor, like all our neighbors, and he had to work hard to support us. Families we knew lost half their children to sickness or hunger or terrible accidents. In our family, thanks be to God, all but one child survived.

"Carpentry isn't always steady work," Yeshu said. "It's like traveling from oasis to oasis. But even when his caravan was crossing the desert, my Abba found opportunities to learn.

"'Teachers are all around us,' he would say to me, 'in the most humble things.'

"He welcomed everyone: his family and neighbors in Nazareth and the surrounding villages, plus the countless travelers passing through on their way to and from Jerusalem and beyond. He treated all as though they were angels of God in disguise.

"'Everyone has a gift to share,' he would say, 'and we owe them our concern in return.'

"Abba also taught himself to read, and he spent hours at a time studying the scrolls in the synagogue. No mental task was too hard for him," Yeshu said, turning the wooden mallet over and over in his hands.

"He soon taught me to read as well, and he taught me that life, too, was a scripture. I learned from him that people often become like ladders for others, especially during personal troubles such as an early death in the family. Or a calamity that affects several communities, like a terrible harvest that yields only hunger.

"Once he took me to the mountain village of Ludum, near Nain, where day after day of heavy spring rains had finally triggered a landslide, sweeping all the houses away in a torrent of mud. We traveled there to help those who survived restore their homes, accepting the small meals and makeshift bedding they could offer as our only payment.

"The morning we left to return home, the oldest man in Ludum approached my father, embraced him, and then leaned back, holding him by the shoulders.

"'Some men tear down,' he declared so that everyone in earshot could hear. 'But you, Yosef of Nazareth, you are a builder!'"

Yeshu paused to drink from the cup of water I had brought him earlier.

Then he continued, "We walked for a while before my father spoke.

"'Yeshu,' Abba said, 'What do you think about the elder's compliment?'

"'It made me proud,' I answered. 'One day I hope to be as fine of a carpenter as you.'

"My father smiled and said, 'But son, are the people of Ludum not builders also? Did we not work together side by side? And wouldn't Nathan, their master carpenter, have come to Nazareth with his neighbors to help us if our houses had washed away?'

"'This is one of the oldest stories of our people,' Abba went on, 'and this week we added our names to the scroll.'"

Yeshu could take your breath away. Life, his life, was full of such stories. And I listened to him tell them all. Over time the stories got better, hinting at something bigger than any of us could see. They lit the landscape of our village like the moon on a long night.

Mulling that over one day I asked Yeshu, "Where does the moon dwell when it's dark and why does it go away? Could it one day disappear forever?"

He stared at me with a distant look in his eyes. The thought struck me that maybe that wasn't the right question. Or maybe the answer I wanted was hidden inside the question I'd asked, and the problem was knowing how to dig it out.

Then out of the blue, Yeshu replied. "Every time the moon returns from the dark as a crescent, we celebrate it by observing *Rosh Hodesh*. Another month has passed.

"One of my favorite Psalms in the scrolls," he said, "is found in the Book of *Tehillim*." And Yeshu recited a passage from it:

> You have made the moon to measure the year
>   and taught the sun where to set.
> When you make darkness and it is night,
>   all the beasts of the forest come forth;
>   the young lions roar for prey,
>   seeking their food from God.

Yeshu became quiet. Finally he said, "When the moon's light vanishes, you begin to notice the other stars and planets in the night sky."

This puzzled me, but later I realized he had been referring to his father coming and going. After Yosef died was when Yeshu's grandmother had stepped in as his teacher. Yeshu had many teachers who helped hone his other skills, but his grandmother, Mama Ana, was perhaps the best storyteller Nazareth ever had. Before her grandson came into his own, that is. She picked up where Yosef had left off, teaching Yeshu the secrets of making stories come alive, making them ring true.

One thing she repeatedly told Yeshu was that a story is unconvincing if the storyteller herself is not convinced. The teller has to believe the story with a full heart.

This is why the Yeshu stories I loved most were the ones that were *his* favorites. Like the one about the landslide in Ludum.

I have to admit that I often couldn't follow the twists and turns of a story of his the first time I heard him tell it. But the words would paint a picture so vivid that I just drifted along, hovering like a minnow in the sheltered pool of a stream, moving my tail only enough to keep distracting eddies from carrying me away. I would carefully watch Yeshu's face and the faces of other listeners, waiting for some word or gesture, some hovering dragonfly of a thought to approach close enough to make the purpose of the telling clear.

Sometimes the story took me to a place where I wasn't sure I wanted to be. Yeshu's tale about a man afraid of not getting into heaven, for instance, left me suspended in midair.

I blurted out, "Yeshu! That man wanted into heaven so badly, but what if I get to heaven one day and don't like it, can I just turn around and head back home?"

He looked at me steadily, a smile playing at the corners of his mouth. He said nothing, suggesting I needed to rethink my question in a new way. After a bit, I tried a different lure.

"What if I see God's face," I said, a little nervous about sounding silly, "and it scares me?"

Yeshu neither laughed nor made me feel dumb. His eyes warmed. "Many have been frightened by the face of God," he said gently and seriously.

"But I know you, Daavi. I know your heart. When the time comes, God's face will not scare you."

Shoshana, Our Lily Flower

Trying to figure out these puzzles was such hard work. I wanted to know *all* the answers, right away! If I couldn't, I'd wonder why the adults were holding back. When one of them caught the eye of another, but not mine, that was my clue.

The problem is this: I didn't quite grasp yet that stories are mirrors, and questions breed more questions, and answers cannot be transplanted like saplings from someone else's orchard, but must grow up from seeds within you. I had yet to discover how to live the question so as to grow the answer.

It's easy to believe that truth is something readymade that a person can pluck out of his pocket, like a coin or a tool, in a time of need; maybe even hand over to someone else who is asking the same question.

But the mystery that scared me most no one seemed willing to talk about at all. I tried not to think about it either, but then it would pop up in the middle of something totally unrelated.

One day Yeshu was walking by when we kids were playing tag in a field, and he joined in. That made us happy as it always did because we all secretly wanted Yeshu to be "it" so we could receive his hugs when he caught us. Lots of us would rush to get past him, but make sure to run close enough so we wound up in his arms anyway.

When Yeshu hugged me, I hugged back, and he smelled like pine shavings and the good sweat of a hard day's work. Once when I pretended to dodge past him, he caught me up in the hug I was hoping for. I returned the hug the way I always did, but this time I forgot where I was.

Suddenly it felt as if I were a toddler being lifted into the air by my big sister, Shoshana. With my head buried in Yeshu's robes, tears spilled out noiselessly and wouldn't stop. There are no words for what I felt. Before Yeshu could discover that my heaving body was sobbing not giggling, I broke away and ran home.

I was left embarrassed and ashamed by a torrent that had caught me unawares. Shoshana was lost, and no one was doing anything about it. One day she was with us; the next she was not; and my parents went mute. She had simply disappeared into some invisible mist along with her name. I was the only one who ever spoke it, and when I did, people just looked downward or away.

It was incomprehensible. Why weren't we all out searching for her? If a lamb goes missing, a shepherd must hunt for it till it's found, scared but alive or merely a broken body.

I couldn't forget that my sister's name, Shoshana, means "lily" in Hebrew. Should a family allow a lovely lily flower to be erased from its midst?

In the middle of the night I would wake up and ask myself barbed questions. Was it my fault? Had I done something to drive her away, or somehow put her in danger? Maybe that's why no one would tell me what had happened. Sometimes I even wondered if she was dead. But the dead have names, don't they?

She had not been gone even a week when late one afternoon, as twilight slipped into darkness, I resolved to find her. I combed the streets of our small town and haunted the lanes winding through the countryside, looking for Shoshana. Wouldn't I be the hero if I found her!

Finally, one day I went to Yeshu's grandmother. Mama Ana knew the stories of every family in Nazareth, going way back before anyone now living was born. Surely she could tell me what had happened.

She looked at me carefully, trying to see something, measure something—exactly what I couldn't tell—but she, too, finally looked away.

Shaking her head slowly, she whispered, "I gave my word."

Now I was really confused. Then hurt and angry. What was everyone in charge hiding? My parents were people of respect and others took their opinions into account. Maybe they didn't want Shoshana back. If so, what would happen if somehow *I* got lost?

The only person I never asked about Shoshana was Yeshu. It's odd because Yeshu was the one person I knew who never lied. He would say that any question asked in earnest deserved an honest answer. In his stories though, the answers often came as riddles. When I asked him about that, he replied that at first some truths are too big for us; we must wear them for as long as it takes to grow into their fit.

Some part of me must have been afraid that if the news was bad, only Yeshu would have the courage to tell me. Despite my wanting to be strong and brave, bad news was something I could not bear to hear.

Here's something else that disturbed me. For a long time I could still see Shoshana's laughing face clearly, framed by the thick wavy hair that tumbled down to her waist. But gradually its sharpness began to dim.

However hard I thought and searched, I couldn't bring my sister back. I felt I would never be whole again until she was home again. The only way I could endure being without her was to forget, but that felt like betrayal. Still, little by little I found myself caught up in other things. Life went better when I was busy.

Some of the other things were my chores, but mostly it entailed following Yeshu's footsteps. He had an enormous stride, his arms swinging loosely at his side, sending his robes billowing out like sails in the wind, his head thrust forward like the prow of a fishing boat.

Time and again, after finishing his last tale of the day, Yeshu would suddenly put down his tools and step to the doorway of his workshop. I can still see him staring intently straight ahead as he sets off for the river to bathe. Racing behind, I am panting, pleading for him to slow down.

Glancing back over his shoulder, his eyes laughing, the storyteller picks up the pace!

Hearing the call in that laughter, each time I find the strength to take off running, shedding my tiredness quicker than an eyeblink. Suddenly we are at the river again, and I am leaping and yipping in circles around his bent-over waist and smiling face.

The Family Next Door

Our small house stood right beside Mama Maria's and Mama Ana's. Father's leather-goods workshop was out back, in a rickety lean-to, whereas Yeshu's carpentry workshop faced onto the road in the front of their house. Father's shop was much smaller—no need to store all those wooden planks for turning into objects built to order, or the broken tables and plows hauled in by villagers for repair. In Father's rather cramped corner, he toiled every day but *Shabbat*, our holy Sabbath. And under that overhanging thatched roof he patiently taught me his trade whenever a bit of free time was available.

There were moments when I was sure I'd never learn all the skills I needed, and he probably thought so too, though he didn't show it. There were other times when I wished I could be with my friends, or learning another trade like taking care of donkeys. I loved their perky ears and insistent voices. But we were too poor to own a donkey, and besides, I had no choice. Boys learn to do what their fathers do; girls learn skills from their mothers. That's just how it is.

My father could make anything out of leather, even plates and cups if someone wanted them. Which they usually didn't—preferring ceramic or wood or even stone—but he could still do it. When my sister Shoshana was small, he made a full set of tiny kitchen pots and platters out of scraps of leather, for her to play with. I hid them in the rafters after she went missing, so no one would throw them out before her return.

What my father usually made, because people actually did want to buy them, were practical items: sandals, bridles, saddles and saddlebags, even leather door hinges. My mother helped with the finishing work: oiling and polishing, braiding tie-strings, and occasionally engraving and dyeing a design or symbol, like a rising sun or an olive tree.

As we got old enough, first I, and then Aaron, took on much of this work, except for the symbol making. That was Mother's specialty, and it was the reason Father had so many customers. People would come from all over, just to have my mama's designs worked into their leather belongings.

In my opinion, the best thing my parents ever made was Yeshu's carpentry tool-bag. He had been traveling around, searching out work, with a shabby old bag woven from sheep's wool. But the problem was that the sharpest tools kept working their way through seams and holes and falling onto the road.

One day my mother saw him coming home, dropping tools, and she ran out and told him, "Yeshu, that's enough! We're going to make you a nice new leather bag for your journeys."

And they did. It was oiled and burnished to the color of mahogany. It had a broad, woven strap that fit over his shoulder and across his chest, and separate compartments inside so the tools wouldn't jumble around, one against the other, and go dull. On the outside, my mother engraved a large, Lake Galilee fish. The fish design was made with one continuous curving line that crossed itself in the back to form the tail. For the colors, she used a dye made of mica slivers ground to a powder with a stone mortar and pestle and then mixed with red wine.

Yeshu loved his new bag and showed it off all over town. He soon struck out on another working journey, from village to village, after loading his carpentry tools in that leather bag. I was maybe eight years old at the time, and it made me *very* proud of my parents.

Another of my early memories seems like a dark forest covered in fog: Two Roman soldiers arrive at my father's workshop. They try to force him to make leather manacles to bind the arms of Jewish prisoners tightly behind their backs. I guess the army had taken so many wretched souls prisoner lately that the supply of straps at the regional garrison had run out.

My father refuses, politely at first. But then I can hear voices rising.

The soldiers are growling; and Father is firmly repeating over and over, "No. No. No."

Next I hear a body slamming against the wooden wall of the workshop, and the gasp of breath rushing from someone's lungs. Father's "no's" cease, but I assume he continues to shake his head because the next thing we know they are dragging him away, my mother pleading for them to let her husband go.

We didn't see my father for seven whole months. All of us were torn apart by his absence, and I felt vexed by our bad luck that Yeshu was traveling when the soldiers came. I was sure he would have known what to do. He would have stopped them somehow.

It seemed like forever, waiting for Father to return home. Day after day, I sat in our doorway staring down the road, eyes wide open like a fledgling bird in his nest, high up in a wind-tossed treetop. I clung to my faith that in the end, all would be well.

Mother seemed less certain, probably as I now know, because she knew things that I didn't. At twilight I would slowly enter the house again, and watch her grim face as she went about her evening duties in the soft lamplight.

Every day, either Mama Ana or Mama Maria brought us bread. Other people brought us a fish or two, a bit of meat, a fistful of dates. When Yeshu returned from his working journey, he came over and fixed our roof and talked in low tones out by the road, to my poor mama. I couldn't hear, but I could see her nodding. When he left, she smiled for the first time since Father was abducted.

The day he came home was the most joyful day of my childhood: I am the first to see him, walking slowly up the road, pushing his chest against an uncaring wind. Each foot rising, and then falling again, like the relentless spokes of an oxcart. Dust swirls past him, and large drops of luminous rain begin to fall from the sky onto the road and adjacent fields. On and on my father trudges as if dragging some unbearable load, his dark-rimmed eyes fixed on our doorway.

As soon as I spot him, I rise to my feet and begin running. It seems that I will never reach him, but my young legs eventually win out over the distance. When I get there, he looks down and smiles wanly through a scraggly, dust-covered beard that makes him almost unrecognizable.

I long for him to lean down and pick me up, but I can tell by his sagging shoulders that he hasn't the strength. So I reach out, clutch his hand, and begin pulling him toward the door, screaming, "Mama! Mama!" with all my might.

As I tug on his arm, his sleeve rides up toward the elbow, and I stare in horror at the deep, red welts encircling his wrist. What have they done to my gentle father just for refusing to make leather bindings!

My brother Aaron springs through the door, followed closely by my mother. They wrap Father in a dual embrace, one high, one low. Then, with me supporting one arm and my mother the other, we walk him to the door while Aaron rushes ahead to spread out his blanket. When we've eased him over the threshold and let go, he stands for a few moments, looking around, before sinking to the floor in a heap.

At last, his hands seek out one another for prayer and we all help him, ending up with eight hands clasped together in jubilation. My father is saved! Suddenly I see what Mother has feared the whole time he was gone. He has escaped being hung on a cross like the countless men I'd heard Yeshu and others speak about, men who had stood fast for what they believed was right. And against what was wrong.

Foremost in my mind, though, was the sense of deep relief that Father was home, safe and sound, at last.

With any luck, our dear Shoshana would be next.

Wandering Carpenter

Long after his father died, Yeshu helped his mother—whom all of Nazareth called Mama Maria—take care of his many younger sisters and brothers. He did this out of love and duty, till eventually one by one they left to start lives of their own.

Even so, during those years there were other matters on Yeshu's mind. Those closest to him knew he was preparing for something far in the future. This isn't so surprising when you think about it. It's how the best stories work, too. In the middle of the telling you believe you know what it's all about; then you learn it's a building block for a much larger saga.

Yeshu knew he had to put first things first, but that didn't mean standing still. It's not at all uncommon for carpenters in our region, in order to support their families, to need to leave home and wander the countryside in search of work. They pack their tools on their backs and offer their services to whoever might be in need of them.

Hence, Yeshu spent many months of the year walking from town to town, supervising a roof raising here, fixing a broken oxcart or yoke there. Someone's family furniture always needed repairing, or their farm animals needed a stable, with a wooden manger for their feed.

That's how Yeshu got to know so many people, some of them from distant lands. In addition to those he worked for, there were those he traveled next to—many of them men, who like him were also looking for jobs, or were transporting goods. All of them valued good company and entertaining talk to shorten the journey. These were qualities this tall carpenter had in abundance.

He was full of stories that could lull like a soft breeze or roar like a thundering river. In return, he received sagas back from these travelers, many of whom later played a part in some of his best stories. Back in Nazareth, Yeshu would tell us all tale after tale about people he had met from Jerusalem, Samaria, Greece, and beyond. He described the powerful armies that occupied our land and the rebellions that rose up. And those that were brutally put down. He heard of how every month, hundreds of Jewish men, sometimes women, were hung on wooden crosses to die.

He could tell you about the next village over from Nazareth, or faraway places like Lebanon. Some of the people he talked about were ancient holy men like Moses and Elijah, and holy women like the prophetess and judge Deborah, and Queen Abigail, married to King David. Others were from our own time, like Joanna, a compassionate woman of prominence from Jerusalem; he had done construction work for her. Then there was the great Rabbi Hillel, and Yeshu's own second cousin, Yohanan.

As for Yohanan, Yeshu made sure he always kept up on his latest whereabouts, and especially his teachings and other activities. It was said that the closeness between them predated their births. Mama Maria had her own story about this that she loved to tell.

Here it is just as she told it to Aaron and me, one lazy afternoon in her courtyard.

"Having just learned that I was expecting my very first child—and you know who that was!—I decided to visit my dear cousin Elisheva.

"Elisheva was already six months along in waiting for *her* first baby. That would be Yohanan, of course."

Maria gave a toss of her head to clear the hair from her eyes. "At the time, Cousin Elisheva lived a full day's walk away, in a windy hill town, with her husband Zachariah.

"Well, imagine this: just as I crossed the threshold of the door, Elisheva felt her baby move for the first time—leaping with joy in her womb. From then on she would always remark about how the quickening of her child at that very moment revealed that Yohanan had sensed the presence of Yeshu growing inside of me! And this was even before Elisheva herself had learned my own happy news."

Shaking her head, Maria clapped her hands down on her knees and drew in a quick breath to show us how surprised she had been.

Years later Mama Maria told us that on that particular occasion, having only recently reached womanhood, she stayed several months with her much older, and much admired cousin. She learned many things about the unexpected ways that life unfolds; how we can set off on paths that only later reveal their twists and turns.

What is certain is that the two women opened their hearts to one another about their hopes for their coming firstborns. They became much more than kin. Now they were kindred souls, their lives bonded forever.

Yeshu loved this story, and he loved telling it to us, too, as well as many others that he had heard over the years from his mother and Elisheva. He wove bits and pieces of yarn from those early years into many of his tales. I would try to pluck and comb through the loose fibers till they glowed in my mind like the dust floating in the sunlight that filtered into his workshop. I would follow their dance up through the softened rays until they reached the window, keeping time with the lines of the stories as they worked their way into my heart.

Oh, and I can still hear Yeshu's voice changing in timbre whenever he spoke of Yohanan. Within the melody of the telling there was a clear ringing, sonorous but insistent as a bell.

Yohanan had left his hillside home to live in the wilderness when he was scarcely more than a boy. Now he was walking the length of the River Jordan as a man, baptizing seekers of the spirit. He poured over them the cool, clear, living waters from the mighty stream. This was to cleanse their minds of doubt and suffering, while purifying their bodies and souls. Then he taught them—one fist gripping his staff held high in the air—about how to live rightly with the plants and animals, and with all people.

And thereby, with God.

Yeshu and Yohanan saw each other often when they were boys. They were together every year during Passover in Jerusalem, plus there were frequent weddings and funerals and other celebrations, like the High Holy Days. During these times when their families were reunited, the two boys were absolutely inseparable.

Later, when Yohanan was preaching and baptizing, they sought one another out whenever they could. They were like the two wings of an ascending bird, wings that touched above and below when flapped.

~ ~ ~

Of course, most of the people that Yeshu met during his travels lived in the very places through which he wandered and toiled, and they were complete strangers before becoming his friends. He opened himself to people of all kinds: shepherds and midwives, tax collectors and road builders in the Roman army, blind musicians and well diggers. There were also bread bakers and new mothers, woodchoppers and spiritual teachers, especially those we call rabbis. Yeshu talked to everyone and worked for anyone. He slept in their spare beds and on their floors. Or even in their stables. And he sat down to eat beside them.

"In Cana," Yeshu once told me, "a rich village merchant hired me to make him a table, adorning it with ebony inlays he had brought home from Ethiopia. When it was done, he exclaimed, 'You, master carpenter Yeshu, you will be the first guest to sit at my fine new table!' And he ran to the kitchen, snatched a pot of mutton stew from where it hung over the fire, brought it to the table, and ladled generous portions into two wooden bowls."

Yeshu paused to laugh with pleasure, recalling the merchant transforming himself into a servant.

"Joining in the fun," Yeshu went on, "I said, 'and you, esteemed merchant of Cana, will be the first to eat from this new table I have just crafted for you!'

"Then I rushed to my pack, pulled out a loaf of bread, and brought *it* to the table. Sitting across from the merchant, I bowed my head over the bread in silence, then tore the loaf in half and handed him the larger piece.

"The merchant's eyes now sparkled as he pushed across the table toward me one of the bowls brimming over with the fragrant stew that he had just ladled in. The two of us were men of many journeys—one a wealthy merchant and the other a poor carpenter—and here we sat, breaking bread together and eating and talking deep into the night."

Not all nights were so merry. I also learned from Yeshu that trudging along the roads of Galilee can be quite solitary. Sometimes it can even be dangerous, too, which is one more reason why he found it prudent to seek out other travelers going his way, and walk with them.

There were more of these folks than I had imagined. Yeshu drew on the ground for me with a stick how Nazareth lies very near important caravan routes leading to and from lands far to the east. In the opposite direction he sketched out other such routes that continue on to Ethiopia and to Egypt, and eventually across the great sea to Rome itself. Even to the farthest northern and western corners of Caesar's Empire.

Pointing with his stick, Yeshu told me, "Many kinds of spiritual pilgrims also walk the roads, back and forth from the holy city of Jerusalem. Merchants and traders lead strings of camels or donkeys to and from Syria, Phoenicia, and as far away as Greece. Or they head south to Jerusalem and on to the splendid Egyptian port of Alexandria.

"All sorts of wares were stuffed in their packs. But even more alluring to me," his eyes brightened, "was all the news of the world, and the many personal stories that these folks carried tucked away in their heads.

"Nazareth may be just a tiny town that few outsiders know or care about. But from here, roads lead to the ends of the earth!"

I learned from Yeshu that on those roads were people who had set out on every kind of journey you can imagine. Besides the merchants and pilgrims, he met people on the way to visit distant family members. They travelled to mark a birth, celebrate a wedding, or maybe arrange a loan. Others were fleeing a crime, the Roman Army, or a nameless personal failure. Yeshu traveled with them all, learning from each.

But those who seemed to move him most were the ones on some pursuit or quest of the spirit, seeking peace for their wandering souls and answers to deep-rooted questions about their lives. Or they had suffered grievous loss from the death of a loved one or from illness, and had hopes of finding solace or a cure. He told story after story about searchers and seekers, about human suffering and longing. Some people were sliding downward...even as others were rising up.

Hearing these stories, I wished with my whole heart to someday go on the road with Yeshu. To see and learn. Maybe find Shoshana.

How I longed for that!

~ ~ ~

One traveler who had captivated Yeshu was a man without sisters or brothers, who had lost his parents in childhood and had struggled for many years to find his way. Long before Yeshu met him, the man had begun stealing from his neighbors, people he knew well. He told Yeshu that it was because his children were hungry and he had no relatives to whom to turn. Whatever the reason, he became a skilled thief. He took food, cattle, money, anything he wanted. The more he stole, the bolder he got. Finally he was entering his neighbors' homes while they slept and taking away as much as he could carry, from new clothes to goatskins of wine!

He was bound to be caught, and sure enough, his neighbors figured him out and set a trap. When they caught him, they stripped him half-naked and beat him, then ran him out of town in the middle of the night. His wife and children wept loudly and begged the neighbors for mercy, but they would not listen.

The man ran for his life and kept running until he came upon two sleeping travelers. Did he wake them and ask for help? No, he stole their bulging packs, scrambled into a cave and put on their clothes, then ate and ate until he was sick.

From that moment on he became a thief of the road, preying on anyone he came upon. He hit them with a club if need be, leaving broken heads and limbs behind him.

One night he fell upon an old man wearing a fine robe. Not needing his club, he just tore the robe off and started to run.

Suddenly, he heard the old man call out, "Come back, you've dropped the belt!"

The thief halted in his tracks and turned around. The old man was holding out his braided belt, a silver buckle reflecting the moonlight. He was offering it up freely.

"To steal like you have from a defenseless person, you must need these clothes far more than I," said the old man, as the thief's mouth fell open.

"I have some coins, too, if you are even worse off than you seem. For a long time, I've had far more than I need."

He smiled softly, looking at the thief. "I've decided only recently that my final years will be dedicated to sharing with those who have less. You seem like you might be a good one to start with."

The thief was so stunned he could not move. Finally, he sputtered, "This is a trick isn't it? You are killing time until your sons come back and tie me up and leave me here to die."

"No," said the old man, beginning to walk slowly toward the thief. "I have no sons or daughters. But if you have no father, I could adopt *you* as my son."

He looked down at his weathered hands and clasped them together. "A life unshared has very little spark for me."

"But I stole from you," the younger man interrupted, "and besides, you don't even know me! You have no idea *who* I am or what I've done in my life, how low I've sunk. Just think what I did to you."

"That's all right. I forgive you," the man said, coming still closer. "And now I want to know who you really are."

He reached out and touched the younger man's arm.

In an instant the thief—who had once, long ago, been a human being like any other—fell to the ground and began to shake uncontrollably. When he was finally able to clamber back to his feet again, he knew his life had changed forever.

He went home with the old man and worked as his apprentice, trading fine clothing from distant lands. Following the merchant's example, he dealt with everyone with impeccable honesty. To his amazement, people gave him their trust and respect in return.

After one year, the transformed thief had saved enough to be able to secretly send money to his wife and children, who had in the meantime become desperately poor. Not long thereafter he headed back home himself to observe *Yom Kippur*: that time of year when all Jews everywhere focus their attention on repentance and atonement. He was determined to make things right by repaying his former neighbors and bringing his family back to his new home.

At first, no one but his wife recognized him. But his identity was soon clear to the others, as he repaid each family, with gold and silver coins, for what he had long ago stolen. Then he gathered up his wife and children and returned to the home of the old man, who greeted them joyously. He had no family of his own and longed for someone to care for him in the future when he might be too infirm to work. He had first found in a stranger, a son. And now an entire family.

The adopted son told his new father, "I've learned that any living creature, no matter how great or small, can pull himself out of the cavernous hole into which he has fallen—worse yet, that he has dug for himself—to stand in the sun again!"

The older man beamed and the younger man added, "I've also learned it helps to have a friendly hand reach down into that hole."

The older man bowed his head.

Then he slowly looked up into the eyes of his adopted son and said, "One day you will want to know the deeper reason why I reached out to you that night, long ago, when our paths first crossed."

He smiled faintly. "So why don't I tell you right now!"

The son's eyes brightened.

"The prophet Micah puts his finger on that reason," the old man said, "when he speaks to us across the ages, from the Book of Mîkhāh.

> What is required of you?
> To do justice and to love kindness
> and to walk humbly with your God.

"That's why, my son. That passage has been the star that has guided me and lit my path, throughout my life."

And so, the man who had once been a thief had found his life's calling, not in taking whatever he wanted from others, but in giving aid and comfort to his family and neighbors whenever possible. He would choose compassion and honesty over greed.

Yeshu always finished the story with these words: "Both aging father and adopted son had discovered that the more they gave, the more they got back. Try as they might, they could never get ahead. They became enriched within, beyond their wildest dreams."

Many times, growing up, I heard Yeshu tell this story. It was never exactly the same. Each time, the story journeyed over new ground, and like spring rains, soaked in to new depths.

One day, in my own way, I started telling it myself.

~ ~ ~

Although it took a while, I figured out that stories were also a kind of traveling. A storyteller was like a shepherd following his herds and the seasons where they took him. They go up in the hills in summer and return to the valleys below in winter, each place revealing something new, each season different from the previous one.

Yet how was it that farmers, who almost never leave home, also have stories from other places? As a wandering carpenter, Yeshu—a man of the village *and* a man on the move—offered a clue.

While journeying, Yeshu met many people. So that part was obvious. But even when he was home, he found ways to keep on the move. Just like his father, he searched out the travelers passing through town and offered them lodging. In return, he got long evenings of conversation about their lives, and more news of distant places. It was a matter of keeping a door open, and a mind open, as well.

Of course, in addition to the travelers, there were all the people of Nazareth and its surrounding villages. Scores of Yeshu's relatives, and even more friends and neighbors, were drawn to him to share their lives and drink from the well of an expansive mind and a singing heart. He knew their deepest hopes and fears, and their life stories from swaddling clothes to burial wraps. He seemed to be everyone's brother.

Yeshu truly liked people, you see. All people. It didn't seem to matter if someone was poor or rich, female or male, Samaritan or Ethiopian, sinner or saint, or in between.

He was a great listener, too, good at getting people to talk about themselves: their troubles and qualms, their dreams and strongest beliefs. Even if he had only one life, and time to journey to only a few places, he had learned how to share in many lives and how to travel the whole world by listening to other people tell their stories, many of them in their own houses or his.

So during these years, Yeshu had two homesteads and two schools: Nazareth and the open road. Each taught him invaluable lessons. In Nazareth he learned both a trade and a way of looking at the world, from his father. He also learned legends and tales of his ancestors, spun by his mother and grandmother. Plus he learned Jewish law and history from all the villagers, woven into everyday life from dawn to bedtime.

On the road he learned about the world beyond his home, about the Promised Land and how it was part of an even larger quilt. There he heard talk of uprisings and hopes for liberation, and of the meanings revealed by the stars that covered the heavens. He heard accounts of holy men and women, such as the great prophet Elisha, the faithful and loyal Ruth, and Isaiah with his poetic heart. And of course there was also the dark-skinned, Egyptian-born Hagar, cast out by Abraham and Sarah into the wilderness, where God sustained her. Time and again, the insightful Hagar exclaimed she had been protected by "the God that sees."

These stories moved Yeshu to head straight for the synagogue whenever he returned home to Nazareth, to study even more from the sacred books written down in the scrolls that were kept in that place. There he read about the astute and judicious Solomon and the wise peacemaker Abigail, and others whose names I had never heard, but all of whom left me enthralled and wanting more.

Later I would realize he was measuring all these stories against one question—how should we live; how should *he* live? This was even harder than it seems, because a person's life swims in the currents that twist and turn far beneath the surface of time's ceaselessly flowing waters.

And a person's life also unfolds and unwinds gradually, just like those ancient and vast scrolls that I so often saw him standing before, tracing line by line with a finger.

Blankets from Home

My family also traveled when I was young, but nowhere as far away or as exotic as the journeys that Yeshu took. Mostly it was weddings or funerals, or Passover in Jerusalem, and on almost every trip we saw our grandmother Ruth, my mother's mama. The best thing about her was that she liked kids more than adults. We knew that because she told us so, but also because she spent all of her time playing with us and sitting with us during meals. Shoshana and Aaron and I saw her only a few times a year, but we loved her madly.

Sometimes Yeshu was at the same weddings as we were, and he and Gramma Ruth really hit it off. They joked with one another other and danced the line dances together.

Yeshu always ended up telling stories in a circle, and Gramma Ruth grabbed the seat nearest to him, pulling us along with her. I was used to hearing his stories with a group of kids, but when he shared his tales at weddings or other festive gatherings, everyone wanted to listen, from the youngest to the eldest.

He would tell every kind of story you could imagine: ones he made up and ones that had been passed down for generations. Funny ones, sad ones, simple ones, mysterious ones. In most all of them, the spirit was present. And usually a lesson, whether obvious or hidden.

Many times, Gramma Ruth said that she never met a man who could be funnier than Yeshu, or more serious. Or one who was more able to mix wisdom with laughter. Her favorite witty riddle of Yeshu's was the one where he declares, "It's easier for a camel to go through the eye of the needle than for a rich man to get into heaven."

Gramma Ruth found just the thought of that to be so hilarious she would hoot loudly. Once she told us, "Other people try to make a point with a serious story and two hours later no one remembers what it was even about. But Yeshu, he shakes you with laughter and years later you still remember every word!"

She clapped her hands a single time and kept right on speaking. "Even more important, lots of people can bring you to yawning with all their plodding talk. Yeshu tells you a story or riddle and it may puzzle you so, that days after you heard it, you are still trying to untie the knot! Or like the camel story, it tickles you right away and either at that very moment, or a while later, you realize why you're laughing.

"The best ones are when you laugh not just once, but again later when a deeper meaning hits you like a hard walnut in its mushy, ripening rind, one that falls from the tree and crowns you on the head," she chortled.

"Take that line about the camel and the rich man. Now first of all there's the hilarity of imagining a camel trying to get through a needle's eye. My thread has a hard enough time passing through, even when my hand isn't shaking like a palm frond in the breeze.

"But then I'm reminded that the main gate in the walls of Jerusalem has two massive double doors, the right one of which has a smaller door in its lower-left corner. At sundown, the gate guards swing the giant doors closed to keep out unwanted intruders, who could be thieves or kidnappers. This happens to block the entry of late-arriving camel caravans. Anyone approaching the gate between dusk and dawn has to go through the smaller door, which is only big enough for one person at a time. Local folks call the small door 'the eye of the needle' and just thinking about trying to squeeze a camel through it, or worse yet, an entire caravan of camels, makes me laugh till I cry."

We immediately made a gate out of two chairs and pretended the space between the rungs was the smaller door. I had Shoshana drop to her hands and knees and then tried to coax her through the tiny space, as if she were my camel. We all laughed knowingly and nodded our heads.

Next Gramma Ruth fashioned a crown out of a cooking pot and robes out of bed clothes. Dressed up like a rich man, she tried to squeeze into heaven. First, there was more chuckling; then guffaws.

After that fun, she sat us down around her and told us about wealthy people she had known or observed in her long life. Some had become greedier, the more riches they amassed, stuffing themselves and their children with expensive foods from faraway lands while their servants put their own children to bed hungry.

But other wealthy people she knew about never failed to use some of their riches to help their neighbors who were needy. And they were fair with the wages they paid the people they hired, and with the terms of trade when they bought from those who were less fortunate.

Shoshana asked her, "Why do some people treat others badly, and other people treat them well?"

Gramma Ruth put her pointer finger up beside her chin.

"That is sometimes a great mystery, child," she said. "Yet I believe it's got to do with how they saw their own parents treat people, and how that caused their hearts to grow. Or to shrink. But it also has to do with whether they take time to truly listen to God during their prayers, instead of doing all the talking and asking!"

While Shoshana was still with us, our dear Gramma died of old age in the village of her birth. Walking to the funeral, I stared down at my tunic, which was torn across the chest in our way of practicing *keriah* when someone passes away. I felt lost in my loss.

All I could think about was the other times we visited her when she was still alive. She always headed straight for us when we arrived at her house; and while my parents unpacked, she would teach us hand games with pieces of bone or old twine.

We kids would make up the most ridiculous jokes we could think of, and after each howler she laughed and exclaimed, "That's the best one yet!"

Then she would try to top us, which she nearly always did.

Once she asked me, "If you got closed up inside the house and everyone went away, how would you get out?"

I thought for a while, desperate to dig up an answer that would really crackle. Finally, I found it: "I would knock myself out!"

Gramma Ruth laughed for a long time, coughing and gasping, and finally she said, "Cleverest idea I ever heard! You know how I would get out?"

I shook my head rapidly, almost bursting with anticipation. She paused so long, I nearly toppled off my stool.

Suddenly she hollered, "I would kick open the door and jump out the window!"

We all three roared.

Not only was it silly, we could picture her doing it.

Then Aaron said with a straight face, "You couldn't do that."

And we roared even louder. Aaron laughed with us since the joke was his.

So then I asked him, "Why couldn't she?"

He quickly answered, "Because windows are only for letting things in, like sunlight and breezes. They never let anything out, now *do* they?"

We all got giddy and breathless on that one, and our parents just rolled their eyes at the roof.

~ ~ ~

When our grandmother was lowered into her grave, Shoshana, Aaron, and I hugged one another and wept and wept.

Our sobbing blended with the mourning prayer that the adults were chanting, the one called *Kaddish*. This prayer does not mention the word death, not even once. It simply lauds the greatness of God and expresses our yearning for peace—peace inside each person, and peace between people and between nations. That's because God and peace are the two sources of comfort to us when a loved one is lost.

When night fell, we slept in the home of relatives we barely knew. I had only a thin blanket or two and fell asleep shivering. In the middle of the night, I had a vivid nightmare in which I tumbled into my Gramma's grave as I leaned over it to watch the diggers lower her down. No one noticed my absence. I woke up screaming to be rescued, and Shoshana softly sang me back to sleep.

To my dismay, the dream resumed. But now it was totally changed.

This time I didn't fall in. It was a moonlit night and I stole out of the house to trudge back to the burial site, dragging my blankets from home behind me. When I got there I lay down beside Gramma's grave to keep her company, covering both of us with the blankets.

I was warm now. I could sense her there smiling, and I knew she was happy with me for coming.

It felt as if I had lost her and found her all at once.

Crafted in a Carpentry Workshop

Sitting in Yeshu's workshop, listening to him hour after hour, I never once dreamt that years later I might hear him tell some of those same stories in front of thousands of people. Had he been practicing on us all that time? Or would he have been just as surprised as any of us, had he been able to see into his future?

I can only say with certainty that Mama Ana and Mama Maria knew. I believe they were preparing him from the very start. Preparing him to teach and heal, with his voice and his hands. If those two women had been men, they could have become village rabbis or even priests in the Temple in Jerusalem. I never met a rabbi who knew more than they did.

Once, Mama Ana came into the workshop with some bread and goat cheese for Yeshu and found him telling the bunch of us there a story. She put the plate down on the workbench, and brushing silvery hair back from her handsome, craggy face, she listened for a while. At first she was absolutely still, but then she began to rustle her skirt. Yeshu was coming to the end of the story when he paused a moment, in midsentence, searching for a word. Without missing a beat, Mama Ana stepped into the story and carried on with the telling.

Her voice was quieter than his, shimmering slightly as is common with someone of her age. But the strength was there. She paused at the most exciting moment...until we were all about to fall on our noses.

Then she pressed on to the story's surprising finish, and we clapped our hands together and let out a shout. But she ignored us completely and just looked at Yeshu. She held his eyes as he looked back at her, nodding his head ever so slightly, a smile tugging at the corners of his mouth.

With that she swept out the door, a song on her lips that the women of Nazareth sing together when they are kneading dough for baking bread:

> Well, the loaf is round, and the family encircles it.
> Oven's made of mud bricks baked in the sun.
> Dough starts as seeds, laid in the warm earth.
> And the hands of women shape it all...
> And the hands of women shape it all.

The next day I saw Yeshu at the well, learning a lullaby from one of the oldest women of Nazareth. She was laughing with toothless delight at the attempts of this fine-looking young man to sing a woman's song.

I asked him later why he was doing that, and he replied, "Well, if you have a skill, it's good to keep in practice. I may have never told you, but years ago whenever Mama Maria went on a journey to visit relatives—usually to see her cousin Elisheva—I stayed home with my younger sisters and brothers. It fell to me to sing them lullabies."

"What a fledgling I was!" he laughed, "Maybe not much older than you are now."

Then his face grew serious and his hand settled on my shoulder. It was a large hand: squared-off and muscular; scarred and calloused by years of handling chisels, mallets, and draw knives.

"You want to know something else," he said, "about singing lullabies?"

He was looking into my eyes.

"I take every chance that comes along to find out what it feels like to be someone else, especially someone different. Usually only a woman gets to hold a child and sing it to sleep. For me, learning what others feel and do makes my life larger."

Puzzled, I stood peering up at him wordlessly, blinking hard. He gently squeezed my shoulder and then turned and strode off toward his workshop, leaving me there in the road.

I began walking slowly, pondering what it would be like to be someone else. What was it like to be my father? Maybe I *would* be him someday, laboring in his leather-goods workshop, my head bent down day after day, year after year.

Being my mother was harder to imagine. I contemplated her giving birth to me, and caring for my brother Aaron when he was a baby a few years back.

And what about Yeshu—what would it be like to be him? Suddenly, I felt warm as the sun. But thinking about it some more brought on an evening chill. So, what was that all about?

As I continued to walk down the road, kicking up dust with my sandals, I lost myself deeper and deeper in thought. I revisited the day that Yeshu had lifted up a great cedar log when no grown-up was there to help, and then carried it into his workshop.

It had gotten me thinking: I'll bet he could have fought Goliath *without* a sling.

At first I felt proud, but that soon turned into anxiety. I realized right off that it wasn't Yeshu's physical strength that was unsettling. Every village had its strongman, after all, and there were contests on various feast days to see who that man was. Yeshu didn't even join in these competitions. He only called on his strength if work or some emergency required it, or if we were playing and the game was to see how many kids could climb Mount Yeshu at once.

Furthermore, never had I seen or heard of him striking a person, or using force of any kind against someone. So what was making me anxious?

Looking back, I guess the scary thing to me was considering what could happen to a man who was gentle and tender, but at the same time strong and powerful. People could misunderstand that.

Besides, I had seen him always so unafraid to speak his mind. Unafraid to condemn wrongs and point to what was right. Could being like this put him in danger? Maybe even provoke others to mindless fury?

With all my might I didn't want my storytelling carpenter friend to be harmed in any way. Losing Shoshana and her lullabies was already more than I could bear.

Lost

During the spring of my ninth year, my family was invited to a wedding in a village a few hour's walk from Nazareth. We left at dawn and arrived at midmorning when the festivities were just beginning. The bride was related to Yosef's family, and Mama Maria and Mama Ana had traveled the day before, accompanied by Yeshu and his brothers and sisters, to help with preparations.

As we walked into the center of the village, I heard lively music and saw a crowd of people standing in a circle, so I went over to find out what was happening. Unable to see anything, I squeezed my way in sideways and plopped down at the foot of the front row to get a good view. Directly in front of me was a line of dancers, with Yeshu right in the middle! His feet stepped swiftly and lightly. His head was high, and he was smiling broadly.

My eyes grew wide—could Yeshu ever dance! He circled round and round, gracefully swinging his arms in front of his body, his head inscribing a long and steady arc above all the others. This was a side of him I'd never seen before. Nearly everyone else's eyes were on him, too, especially those of the young women watching him spinning and turning like some great eagle gliding above a lush, green meadow. I couldn't remember ever having seen him so lighthearted and blissful.

A line from the Psalms wafted through my head. It was one my Gramma Ruth used to melodiously chant from memory to us, from the Book of Tehillim, when we were toddlers:

> Sing to God a new song...
> Let them praise his name in the dance,
> and sing him Psalms with tambourine and harp!

I wasn't able to watch the dancing for long. Aaron pulled me away to play with him and some other children who were spinning a top in a courtyard. We kids called this top a singing *s'veevon,* and no one could best Aaron at it, once he got going.

For reasons I didn't understand, our family left the wedding feast before it was over. I noticed my mother and father off to one side discussing something, and the next thing I knew we were heading home.

That evening at bedtime I began searching for Shalom, the wooden dog Yeshu had so carefully carved for me. With a sickening feeling in my stomach, I realized I had left him on the windowsill of a house back in the wedding village. It was when I was playing games with the other kids.

I was inconsolable. That night and the next day, whenever I thought about Shalom, I sobbed. With Shalom lost, my peace was gone also. When my family figured out what was going on, they tried to distract me. My mother promised to bake my favorite fig and honey cake.

Aaron ran to check on his toy boat, to make sure it was still there, before coming back and trying to get me to play games. Only because he was trying so hard did I play along, but half-heartedly.

When Yeshu heard what had happened, he offered to make me a new cedar dog, that very day, but I shook my head no and fought off more tears. He looked closely, then nodded, knowing what I was feeling. It would be another dog, not *my* dog. Not Shalom.

Finally, seeing how forlorn I was, my father came up with something he had to do in the wedding village. Off he went at dawn, returning just before twilight with Shalom.

I ran to meet him. As he pulled his hand out of his pocket, he leaned over and said softly, "You see, what is lost *can* be found!"

I grabbed my little wooden friend and ran out the door into a nearby field to play until darkness, feeling closer than ever to Shalom. I was so excited, I didn't even tell my father thank you, but hopefully he knew how grateful I was. Now, of course, I wonder how it made him feel. Certainly, I don't think either of us knew how much the example of his good deed would mean to me in the years to come.

That evening just after going to bed, I felt the sleeve of Father's robe sweeping softly over me as he bent down close to my face. I waited in anticipation for what he would say.

He quickly whispered into my ear, before spinning off into the night to secure the gate, "Finding Shalom gave me peace, too."

Tell Us!

Whenever Yeshu was on the road doing carpentry for weeks at a time, the kids who most missed his storytelling would seek out Mama Ana. The first place we went was her small room next to Yeshu's workshop. Mama Ana liked living there, close to Mama Maria, Yeshu, and her other grandchildren. I speak only of those who were too young yet to have married and moved into their in-laws' larger and less-crowded houses. Mama Ana's first grandson, plus her second granddaughter, had each left home to start families of their own. And already, children from both new families were old enough to be regular participants in our story group at their Uncle Yeshu's workshop.

If Mama Ana happened to be out somewhere, Yeshu's youngest sister, Shaani, would tell us where to look. She was named after Mama Maria's favorite flower and Yeshu's too: the *shoshana*, the lily of the field.

Shaani had the same birth name as my sister, which shows the great admiration my mother and father had for the family next door. The only difference was that Maria and Yeshu used the shortened version of her name out of affection, since she was the baby of the family. And our family used the full name Shoshana for my sister, the oldest child, who was born just one month after Shaani.

Mother and Mama Maria used to laugh as they mimicked the two babies toddling around together holding hands as if they were teaching one another to walk. So this pair of lily flowers grew closer as they grew up.

Often they would take me to the meadow, hand in hand, when I was still small. Once there they would weave clover blooms into my hair until I pulled them out and tried to put them in *their* hair. The three of us always ended up laughing, which further brightened my day.

Shaani's laughter was like a spring shower in an orchard that left everything sparkly. Since she had been so close to my sister, she was special to me after Shoshana's sudden absence. We didn't talk about it, but each of us recognized the look of sadness in the other's eyes.

Sometimes, with Shaani's help we kids found Mama Ana washing clothes at the river or standing by the well, talking to other women. She always knew by the way we looked at her that we wanted stories, and sooner or later we would end up around the cooking fire at her place, sitting on benches Yosef had made for the family to use at mealtimes. If there were too many kids, some of us sat on the wood-plank bed nearby. Like all humble families in Nazareth—craftspeople, field laborers, herders, and farmers—this home had just one main room that served all purposes.

So, there we would wait, encircling the stone hearth, trying to control our whispering and fidgeting, because we knew Mama Ana wouldn't start the storytelling until all of us were still and the quiet had settled into true silence. She always sat with her feet apart, hands on knees covered by a great flowing skirt, leaning forward. Waiting.

Many times, she explained to us how a story requires stillness, and finding it can be hard. Listening profoundly is really challenging. It's like walking through a forest on a moonless night and trying not to bump into any trees. Just where are you, and where is everything else?

"You can practice," she would tell us. "Close your eyes and feel your feet touching the earth. Try listening for the presence of whatever is in the room. All things around us are speaking, and you have to listen carefully for a calling of your name. There are already paths through that moonless forest for you to follow, and the whisperings are alerting you to the gaping pitfalls and the serene clearings ahead. Listen deeply now...."

When the mood was right, Mama Ana always began by speaking directly to each of us, one at a time. Usually she started off with a story she had heard from her own mother, or maybe one about something she had lived through, or one pieced together from other people's accounts. Without a doubt, my favorite Mama Ana story has always been the one about Yeshu's birth. She told it to us every time we asked.

I can still see her sitting there with her hair going white, spilling like a waterfall to her shoulders, her face crisscrossed by time as if it were a rocky cliff.

This time, fixing her gaze on me, she asked, "What will it be today, Daavi?"

I was always thrilled when I was the one chosen. "Tell us about when Yeshu was born!" I answered immediately.

She continued to look into my eyes. I was warm as if I were outside sitting under the noon sun.

Then she leaned back slightly and asked, "Don't you already know that story by heart?"

"Almost," I replied.

She smiled, lifting her gaze above my head as if she were searching for something in the distance. "All right, then," she said.

We knew she loved to tell this tale. As we waited for her words to flow, we all watched her sip water from an old clay cup that always sat on top of the small barrel next to her knee.

Finally she set the cup down, cleared her throat, and began to speak.

Away in a Manger

This is what Mama Ana told us. "Twenty-five years ago, before any of you were present on this earth, my daughter Maria and my new son-in-law Yosef were required to journey to Bethlehem, in the distant land of Judea, for the Roman census. Caesar Augustus was then emperor of Rome, and he had decreed that each family must be counted in the father's place of origin. So, I had to go my way and they went theirs.

"I was not at all happy about this. But there was no getting around it. Especially since the Romans use the census for collecting taxes and for recruiting men into their army. Of course, in the countries they occupy, it's the taxes they are really after. Romans wouldn't have Jews in their army; and Jews wouldn't want to be there.

"Now, the name Bethlehem means "house of bread" in Hebrew, the language of the Torah. How would you like to live in a house made of bread?" We all giggled at the thought, and licked our lips.

"It's in the scrolls that we are told King David was born in Bethlehem a very long time ago, three generations after his dirt-poor great-grandmother Ruth had gleaned in the nearby wheat fields for a bit of food."

My ears perked up when I heard my birth name, David, plus the name of my Grandmother Ruth.

Mama Ana looked out the door and across the road, then back again before continuing. "Many, many years after King David passed on, Yeshu's father was born in Bethlehem, too. That's why the family had to travel there all the way from Nazareth.

"Unfortunately, it was lambing season, which is not a good time of the year to be gone from home for a poor carpenter who also had a few sheep.

But even more troubling, Maria was expecting a baby any day. Yet Rome made no exceptions, so they had no choice but to make the journey.

"Yosef borrowed a donkey from my Uncle Lukas, who lived at the edge of Nazareth and had lots of animals. And off the young couple went.

"Maria was upset about traveling at this stage of her pregnancy. How could she give birth alone, safely, without the presence of her midwife from Nazareth? What if there were complications? She and the baby could be at risk, and like any first-time mother, she longed to have by her side the comforting hand and voice of the woman who had carried her into this world."

Mama Ana paused to stare at the folded hands gripping one another in her lap. "And I wanted to be there with her!" She shook her head. "But since my father was not from Bethlehem, there was nothing to be done about it. Except to pray, and trust in God that all would go well.

"The journey was demanding, Maria riding on the donkey and Yosef keeping pace on foot by her side. All along the way, Maria fretted that she might have the baby while they were on the road. Yosef did what he could to reassure her. His mother had been a midwife, he reminded her, and he'd grown up surrounded by conversations between his mother and visitors to his boyhood home about what to do and not do during a birthing.

"Rising on the fourth day of travel, Maria sensed that her time was near, so they decided to set out before daybreak, chewing on a few crusts of bread along the way. Hardly resting at all, they raced the sun across the sky to reach their destination.

"Maria felt like a ship lost at sea. At one point she wondered aloud, 'With no port in sight, upon what island will we land?'

"When the weary couple crested the final hill, they could see the houses of the town nestled together on the slope below. The walls of each house were lit by the crimson glow from the sinking sun, their corners etched by the lengthening shadows they cast.

"As they reached the edge of town, Yosef stared at the people bustling through the streets and along footpaths, and he was troubled. Where would he and Maria find lodging for the night?

"The two of them went from inn to inn with no luck—all of Bethlehem was full of visitors."

Hearing this, my brother Aaron couldn't stay quiet a moment longer. He was only four or so, less than half my age. "Did they have to sleep outside," he asked, "in the cold night?" He gulped. "*That* would be scary."

Mama Ana leaned toward him, looking gravely into his eyes, and shook her head very slowly. "No," she said. "You will see how God works." And a faint smile crossed her lips.

I glanced at Aaron. His eyes were big and round, and he was biting on his lower lip. Mama Ana returned to her story. "Finally, Yosef and Maria knocked on the door of a small, sad-looking inn at the far edge of town. When the owner slowly shoved the door partway open on its creaking, broken hinges, he took just one look at the bedraggled couple, wagged a finger, and shook his head, saying, 'Move along. Move along.'

"He was tired of people rousing him to ask for a bed he could not give because he had not a single one left to offer.

"As the weary innkeeper was shaking his head no and pulling the door shut, Maria fixed her liquid eyes on his face. Meanwhile, Yosef's heart sank and his gaze dropped to the ground. Immediately he saw something at his feet and knelt to pick it up. The innkeeper's *mezuzah* had fallen from its place on the right doorpost."

Mama Ana scanned the circle to see if we all knew the word. "Each of our families has a mezuzah on our doorway," she paused to point to her own door, "holding a tiny parchment scroll. As many of you know, the scroll contains two passages from the *Debhārîm*, the book of Deuteronomy in the Torah. Those words call for us Jews to do as follows: love God with all our hearts and all our souls, and all our strength and all our minds; teach this to our children; and place these words on our doorways and gates."

Without missing a beat, Mama Ana continued, "Yosef quickly stood up and handed the mezuzah to the innkeeper. Then he gestured toward Maria whose condition as an expectant mother was unmistakable, and the voice of God flew straight through the innkeeper's head like a nighthawk crossing the sky at dusk.

"Stunned, the man looked the two strangers over. He noted their exhaustion, and even a fool could see that Maria's time was near. With that, he let out a bewildered sigh.

"'Look,' he said, 'there's no more room in my inn.' He blinked twice, then resumed. "'But I do have a stable. You can spend the night there, if you want.'

"He wiped his forehead with one sleeve. 'I laid down new hay in the mangers just this morning, and the straw on the floor is clean and dry.'

"Yosef caught Maria's eye. Her face was drawn, and her lips had lost their color. Her look said she was in agreement.

"The innkeeper stepped outside and led them to the back where a stable was built in a shallow cave in a steep hillside. It was full of cows and goats, plus the donkeys of guests lodging at the inn.

"'Sleep here,' he grumbled. 'Just be sure you're on your way by morning.'

"Maria and Yosef sighed, mouths slightly agape, and nodded almost imperceptibly to each other.

"Then the innkeeper turned on his heel and strode away. The couple took one another by the hand and stepped into the cave. The man was right; the space was warm and dry. Exhausted, Maria lay down on a pile of hay.

"It was golden-green and smelled newly cut, just like they'd been told. And the scent it gave off was just as sweet as it is here in Nazareth," added Mama Ana, "right after we finish the first scythe-cutting of the springtime."

My little brother chimed in again, "Did Mama Maria fall right to sleep?"

I turned and hushed him, but when I looked back at Mama Ana, she was staring at *me*, not at Aaron. Pointing at him with her chin, while shrugging and lifting both hands palms up, she said, "He's listening..."

Mama Ana picked up her story where she left off. "Maria heard a cow shifting its weight and breathing heavily. As she turned her head to look, a tawny calf awkwardly pushed its nose up under its mother and began suckling. That was when Maria felt her labor pains begin.

"It was a difficult birthing, being her first. She tried hard to remember all the advice our local midwife gave her before the journey. And she found sustenance in reciting verses from the Book of Psalms that I had chosen for her, searching my memory for passages from the scrolls. One of my favorites was:

> I lift up my eyes to the mountains;
>   where shall I find help?
> Help comes from God
>   who will not let your foot stumble.
> God will be by your side to protect you.

"When the sharp pains came, Yosef held Maria's hands; and when she rested, he wiped her forehead and cheeks with a damp cloth. He did whatever he could to calm her when she began gasping in shallow breaths. He tried to recall what he had watched his mother do while helping so many babies into the world. When there was no other suitable place, his mother had brought women into the carpentry shop to give birth on a bed of pine and cedar shavings.

"But simply being within earshot while someone else's child is entering the world did not prepare him for the birth of his own. If only his mother could have been there with them now—but sadly she had passed away the year before. So he did his best, rubbing Maria's shoulders and bringing her water to drink. He even cleared a space near the mouth of the cave and made a small fire just beyond the doorway. This gave them a bit of smokeless warmth and some light to see by.

"The world outside shrank into the deepest hollow of the night. Bethlehem was fast asleep, even the shadows. Everyone except for Maria and Yosef, and the animals keeping watch.

"Before long Maria felt her labor pains getting stronger and closer together. A small inner voice pleaded, 'Can I bear this? Will I crumple?'

"Breathing rhythmically, she reached inside for strength and found a pool of resolve fed by a spring so powerful that its waters never seemed to flag. It was then she knew they were not facing this challenge alone.

"Still it was not easy. Each wave of wrenching pain shook her down to the ring of fire below her midriff, threatening to wipe her away. Just when she was on the edge of faltering, she felt a breeze from what seemed to be a large bird alighting beside her and gently wrapping her in its wings. She gratefully surrendered to it and in doing so was herself delivered."

Mama Ana fell silent. One hand rose till the fingertips lightly touched her cheek. Then she continued. "Maria noticed her hand relaxing in Yosef's, which had turned white from her grip. He was dazed after so much hard walking and struggled to keep his eyelids open. Once he actually dozed, before sitting up with a jerk, believing he heard the roof of the cave crash in. Just then he felt Maria's hand squeezing his again as another searing swell crested and broke.

"As the time between pains shortened, Maria felt her strength fading. A sob escaped her lips, and her mind called upon another Psalm I had given her from the Tehillim:

> Hear my prayer, oh God,
>   and listen to my cry.
> Come to my aid when I weep,
>   for I find shelter with you.

"The voice inside Maria's head stopped reciting, while she paused to catch her breath and push again. Then it went on.

> The sun will not strike you by day
>   nor the moon by night.
> God will protect you from all danger
>   and keep you safe.
> God will guard your going and your coming,
>   now and for evermore.

"Aloud she repeated in a whisper, 'now and for evermore,' gathering her strength for a final strong push. With that, the baby's head crowned and next the shoulders appeared. In one sudden motion, the child slid into Yosef's waiting hands.

"'Dear heaven!' he gasped. 'Yes, a boy!'

"'We knew,' Maria whispered. 'Yosef, we knew!'

"Tears streamed down their faces while they laughed and laughed. The oddness of laughing and crying all at once never even occurred to them. There was too much to do.

"Quickly Yosef began wiping the tiny body with a cloth. Maria reached out to receive the wriggling baby from her husband. 'In my dream I was told it would be a boy,' she said. 'Remember?' Too tired to sit up, she eased her son down onto her chest.

"'Yes, a boy for our first child,' Yosef said with wonder. Then he blurted out: 'How many more shall we have, Maria? How many sisters and brothers shall we give him?'

"'You want me to think about that *now*? You have the pride of a lion,' Maria laughed hoarsely. Besides,' she added, 'that's not for us to say. God will know.'

"Yosef chuckled, wiping the tears from his eyes with one worn sleeve, followed by the other. Seeing that Maria's mouth was dry from the hard breathing, he went over to the large clay jar that stood by the door and brought back a gourd full of water. He held it to her lips as she drank and drank.

"Maria felt the coolness gliding all the way down her throat to her belly. She pictured the bird that had visited her earlier now landing in a pond and folding its wings. That's when she became certain, without knowing why, that all was well.

"Reaching a hand out to let Yosef know, she felt him shiver and realized how chilly the night air had gotten. He had stood to fetch the wrappings they had packed for the child. Before bundling him up, Maria carefully inspected each tiny finger and toe of the baby. His small, waving hands reminded her of sycamore leaves when they first unfold from their buds in springtime.

"Meanwhile, Yosef looked for a way to keep a newborn safe and sound till morning. All he could find was a small, wooden manger. Usually packed with hay, it was empty since the animals had already fed.

"Maria handed the baby to Yosef while she carefully lined the manger with new hay. He offered to do this, but she waved him away. As her hands worked, her mind sifted through the many reflections and feelings she'd had regarding this child during the months of waiting for his arrival.

"She'd been long enough in the world to know that every infant stirs the yearning hearts of its parents and family, but something about this baby was special. She knew in her bones that someday he would touch lives far beyond Nazareth.

"Her hands trembled as they patted the last sprigs of hay into place. After pausing to draw in the sweet aroma and settle her churning thoughts, she rose to her feet.

"Yosef stood in the middle of the stable, holding his son in his arms, right over his heart. Feeling the warmth of that little baby spread across his chest, and then all through his body, brought more tears to the new father's eyes.

"Time seemed to stop."

Mama Ana paused to smile at each of us in the room. We were all leaning forward. At last she resumed, "Years later, no matter how cold it got, Yosef could still feel the glow from that baby whenever he crossed his arms over his chest.

"Of course Yosef wasn't thinking about cold days ahead. He was basking in the warmth of Maria's smile as she knelt beside the manger and reached out for her baby. Yosef carefully lowered the gurgling child into the cradle of her arms. Touching her lips to the baby's head, Maria began humming a wordless lullaby passed down from my mother to me to her.

"At that moment a mouse poked its head out of the hay and scurried fearlessly to the top of the manger, hardly an arm's length away. Craning its neck, the mouse seemed to be sizing up the strange new creature so recently arrived in the stable.

"The mouse wasn't alone. Nearby could be heard the stirrings of a cow and calf and Uncle Lukas' ash-gray donkey as they edged closer to share the new family's warmth.

"'Do you think he's ready to sleep?' asked Yosef.

"Maria looked over at the manger, with its nest of hay, and nodded. The mouse had scurried away.

"Then Yosef touched Maria's shoulder. 'He needs a good name. We have the one from our dreams. It's a very large robe for a child to grow into.

Will his life be different if we choose another name? Will it be easier?'

"'Yeshua,' Maria said firmly. 'We are to call him Yeshua. The name is only a promise; his life will tell us what it will mean for him.'"

Mama Ana noticed that a young girl who was hearing the story for the first time looked puzzled. So she stopped to explain, leaning tenderly toward the small child.

"It's a name shaped from the word *Yehoshua,*" she said. "That's Hebrew for 'God is salvation.'"

A smile brushed across the child's face.

Returning her attention to the rest of us, Mama Ana resumed her story.

"Many parents call their firstborn sons Yeshua because of the prophecies that say the Messiah will carry this name. Maria and Yosef knew the oracles well. What mother and father wouldn't be thrilled to bring to our people the savior who would deliver us? Nevertheless, they would not have picked that name on their own. During the pregnancy, both of them had been left shaken by hearing the name 'Yeshua' in their dreams.

"I'll tell you about it," Mama Ana said. "One morning months earlier Maria awoke and began talking to Yosef about a strange vision she had just had, in which their baby would be called...and before she could finish, he answered, 'Yeshua.' They looked at each other quietly, trying to get used to the idea that their firstborn son belonged not only to God, which is custom, but perhaps to the Jewish people, as well.

"Of course every newborn child is a sign of hope," Mama Ana continued. "And gazing down at that precious baby boy convinced Maria and Yosef that the name Yeshua fit."

Again she halted her telling, her gaze brushing across our faces one by one. As I watched everyone mouthing the name, trying it on, I thought to myself: but all of us use the shorter version. We just call him Yeshu. And that's okay, too. It felt so good to say it. "Yeshu. Yeshu."

Then I noticed Mama Ana was still talking: "Yosef liked the name of his son, and he spoke it softly to the child. 'Yeshua.'

Mama Ana laughed. "But baby Yeshu showed no interest in his name. He just wanted to be held."

I felt goose bumps, hearing Mama Ana call him Yeshu like the rest of us did.

She moved on with her story. "Soon, a large family of shepherds arrived from the camp they had pitched beside the stone corral just beyond the inn. The mother and grandfather had both awakened from dreams of a special child being born. The visions were so strong and similar that the excitement lifted up their voices as they talked about it, and the entire family awoke. During a lull in the chatter, they heard the crying of an infant and immediately glanced around at one another.

"In a heartbeat, they made sure the corral was secure and guarded by their dog. Then they headed toward the sound of the baby's cries and a man's joyous laughter. To their surprise, they soon found themselves in the doorway of the stable behind the inn. There they hung back, shyly knotted together, the scent of sheep and goats in their hair and clothing, burrs stuck to the ragged hems.

"When the matriarch of the family saw the couple huddled inside and again heard a baby's whimper, she turned everyone around and they rushed back to their camp, their ragged cloaks flapping around their knees like the wings of ravens.

"Then they hustled back to the stable again with cheese wrapped in palm leaves, a clay pitcher of goat's milk, and flat bread that had just been baked over the open fire. It resembled the *Pesakh* bread everyone eats at Passover, which was only a few months off.

"Maria and Yosef beckoned the humble strangers to enter. First came a boy carrying a newborn lamb, looking just as pleased with his own good fortune as Yosef did with his. Next, an old woman entered, bent over from the waist, supporting herself with a crooked cedar staff and smiling broadly. She was the matriarch and she bowed her head again and again at everyone in the small stable, including the cows and the donkey. She seemed intent on blessing all who were present.

"Finally, nudged forward by her mother, a shy shepherd girl stepped in, followed by all the others. The mother handed Yosef the pitcher and a wicker basket. He peered inside and saw the cheese and bread.

"Yosef and Maria thanked everyone profusely and dug into the food, realizing at last how famished they were. They had gone with nothing to eat since early that morning. And this repast was especially welcome, served to them by the shepherd family that stood quietly watching them begin to devour the fragrant meal.

"While swallowing his second mouthful, Yosef peered up at them and slapped his forehead. 'Ah, but you're all probably hungry, too, aren't you?' he asked.

"The shepherds all laughed and gestured in protest, but Yosef noticed each head lean forward slightly. Spreading the food out, he motioned for them to move in closer and share in the meal. Eagerly, they crowded around as Maria broke the large round loaf of bread into pieces, handing one to each person. All smiled and whispered their thanks.

"With bright eyes, Baby Yeshu watched as both families ate together gratefully, in a silence that was itself a feast. The shepherds chuckled, looking around as they munched on their bread together. The circle of giving was unbroken."

Mama Ana paused to study each one of us. Then she continued spinning her tale. "Shortly, the shepherds said their good-byes, turned, and walked back to their blankets, gathering tightly round the fire they had built at their campsite. And Yosef and Maria curled up next to the manger that held their slumbering newborn. Though they tried to stay awake, weariness from the long journey, plus Maria's labor, soon tugged their eyelids downward and carried them off into a brief slumber.

"The body heat and the exhaling of the animals kept the small family warm. The lowing of the cows sounded like distant lullabies, and this soothed Baby Yeshu.

"Wanting him closer, Maria moved the small bundle from the manger to a place between herself and Yosef. This would keep the baby warmer. Several times during the short stretch of night that remained, Maria gave him her breast so that he might become familiar with nursing.

"At those moments, Yosef awoke and knelt beside his wife and child, holding his son's tiny feet in his massive carpenter's hands, scarred from years of hard labor with sharp tools. And again his eyes brimmed with tears of joy.

"'I will teach him many lessons,' he whispered to Maria just before dawn, gathering his thoughts like kindling for the fire. 'I can teach him to use his hands and his head to build good things. People know me for making strong tables and roofs. I will teach him to do that and to build doors and bridges, as well.'

"Yosef was quiet for a few moments, then he went on. 'I can teach him to use his head, also. To always be open to life and ready to learn. And I can follow the same advice my grandfather gave my father Yakob about me. 'Show his heart how to lead his head and his hands,' he said, 'so our world can have more love and less hatred and suffering.'

"'These lessons are my wish for him. They will be his inheritance from me. I'm a poor man. My tools and my guidance are what I have to give.' With that, Yosef fell quiet and the two new parents edged a bit closer to the baby lying between them.

"Sleep was fitful because under the sparse straw the ground was hard, and the swarming worries were as incessant as biting flies. Where would the three of them go tomorrow once they had registered for the census? What would they eat? Should a new mother journey again, so soon? And what about their child who has just been born? Nazareth was four long days away. The open road could be a cruel nursery.

"Dawn opened like a rose, and soon the first rays of the sun ventured through the doorway and illuminated the face of Baby Yeshu. The anxious new parents heard footsteps approaching. The innkeeper entered, sleepy and frowning, to do his morning chores. Seeing that a baby had indeed been born during the night seemed to make him even more irritated. Maria and Yosef waited quietly to be told they should pack up and vacate the stable.

"That's when Maria's face brightened, and it wasn't from the sun's rays. Scooping up Yeshu in one arm, she reached down to tug at Yosef's sleeve, urging him to his feet. Then she strode the three steps across the stable floor to where the innkeeper was standing and thrust the baby into the arms of the speechless man.

"Turning and reaching for Yosef's cloak, Maria hurried through the stable door, pulling this *other* speechless man behind her.

"Once outside, Yosef found his voice and blurted out, 'What on earth are you doing, handing off our son like that to a complete stranger!'

"Placing a fingertip on his lips, she replied softly, 'Have faith, husband.'

"For a long moment they stood completely still, hearing nothing coming from the stable, other than a few animals stirring. Then they heard what sounded like gurgling and chuckling. They peeked around the door jamb and there stood the innkeeper, his face aglow. He was staring down at the creature in his arms, as astonished as if he held the sunrise. Man and child had locked eyes together fitting the whole world into the space between their two foreheads.

"Quietly reentering the stable, Maria gingerly took the baby back into her arms. Yosef followed and waited quietly beside her. The innkeeper seemed reluctant to leave, but now it was *his* turn to pull Yosef outside.

"Maria could hear them talking in low voices, punctuated by Yosef saying 'Yes, of course!' every few moments, and then, 'I thank you, good man. God will know your generosity.'

"Maria heard the innkeeper walking away as Yosef stepped back into the stable. The words tumbled out of his mouth as he recounted what the transformed fellow had said. 'We can stay as long as we like! We can eat with the servants in the kitchen. All I have to do is fix that creaking front door and find some other carpentry chores to do around the inn.'

"'You see?' said Maria. 'That of God in our child spoke to that of God in this man—without a single word being uttered.'

"She smiled at him. 'Our problem is solved.'"

~ ~ ~

In a low voice, almost a whisper, Mama Ana said, "So, imagine that. Our Yeshu—less than one day old—had already succeeded in turning his first heart. Leading it back onto a path of compassion."

Then she fell silent and we all sat quietly with her, turning the images of the story over and over in our minds like a treasure. After a bit, she once again looked around the room at each of us in turn.

"Now, I have work to do," she said suddenly, her eyes shining.

She held her arms out, and one by one we go went to her, gave her a hug, then walked out into the sun-drenched patio, humming and kicking up our heels.

Star Sign

Even the best story, endlessly repeated, couldn't sate our appetites. We wanted to hear more about Yeshu's coming into the world. So after leaving Mama Ana we all scuttled up the road in search of Mama Maria. She could tell us what happened when the three really smart and mysterious men—she called them the "Magi"—came looking for Baby Yeshu. That story was another of my favorites, because the characters in it stirred such wonder in me.

On our way, several of us passed the time by stepping on nearly every ant we discovered in the road, trying to see who could find the most. And squash them. Eagerly we peered into each courtyard searching for Mama Maria. We weren't being very patient, or very thoughtful, either, especially given the person to whom we wanted to listen.

According to my mother, Mama Maria was the town peacemaker, the person called upon to solve quarrels among neighbors or even inside families. Life had taught her how to endure, how to have patience, until it was time to act. It was she who taught Yeshu how to struggle without fighting.

The mother of seven children, married as a young girl to a much older man, and widowed in her mid-twenties, she died an old woman with a young woman's face. Mama Maria was a quiet person who lived to see many wonders, survive many tragedies, and discover many secrets. All of these experiences were seasonings for her stories.

On this day we didn't have to search very far to find her. She was sitting quietly in the courtyard of the home of Yosef's aged Aunt Naomi, waiting for loaves of bread to finish baking in the large mud-brick oven. Yeshu's family had no oven at home because they were too poor and had no room to build one. So Maria came to her in-laws' house one afternoon a week, carrying enough bread dough to bake seven loaves for her large family, and one for Aunt Naomi.

We all crowded around her, begging, "Mama Maria, tell us the Magi story! Tell us about the star sign."

She looked at us sideways and smiled. "You've been with Mama Ana, haven't you?" We all nodded.

"You remind me of a flock of flitting sparrows forever hopeful for bread crumbs," she said with a laugh. "Okay, then," she nodded. "Fold your wings and find a place to perch!"

Each of us flitted about the cobblestone courtyard to find a mud brick or a log to sit on. We pulled them up close to where Mama Maria sat on a low bench, her arms wrapped around her knees. And we waited.

For a few moments, she stared through the stoke hole at the burning coals in the oven. Without taking her eyes from the flames, she began to speak in a soft voice that carried you far away but held you close at the same time.

"After Baby Yeshua fell asleep that night and the shepherds left," she began, "Yosef and I talked. Following so closely upon our journey from Nazareth, the delivery of my first child had worn me out. Just sitting up all night nursing the baby was exhausting. We would register for the census in the morning, but Yosef was afraid of what might happen on the road if we left for home too soon. On the other hand, with no money, what else were we to do?

"I knew that God would help somehow. And sure enough, the next morning a grumpy voice sounded at the door of the stable.

"'May I come in?'

"Looking over, I saw the innkeeper's head peering around the doorjamb."

When Mama Maria mentioned the innkeeper, it struck me that *her* version of the familiar story might differ from Mama Ana's. I brightened inside as she went on.

"Yosef seemed apprehensive," she said, "but I had faith. 'Please enter,' I said to the innkeeper.

"So he entered, bending down as he stepped through the low door. Yosef sprang to his feet.

"'Come closer,' I said, putting a smile in my voice.

"As he approached, I shifted Yeshua in my arms. The innkeeper stared into those big, dark baby eyes, and he melted. His smile got so broad it pushed his beard toward his ears. First his fingers and then his hands emerged from his sleeves and they danced over Yeshua in an attempt to indicate how small and perfect the baby was. Before long he grew serious again.

"'Here,' I said impulsively, handing Yeshua over. Now it was the innkeeper who seemed apprehensive, trying to hold something so vibrant but fragile. Yosef started to speak, but I shushed him by glancing over and pressing my lips tightly together. The innkeeper cradled Yeshua in his arms and stared, open mouthed, into his tiny face. Yeshua stared back, hardly blinking those deep eyes of his.

"The two of them locked gazes for the longest time. When the innkeeper finally looked up again, I knew from his face that our problem was solved, even though it wasn't clear yet exactly how."

Mama Maria paused, the fingers of both hands wrapped around one knee. She sniffed the air to see if the bread was done, then went on.

"The innkeeper handed Yeshua back to me and motioned for Yosef to follow him. They went into the courtyard. I could hear them talking a while, then nothing, then talking some more.

"Finally Yosef came back inside, smiling. They had agreed that he would do carpentry work around the inn for a few weeks in return for food and lodging.

"So in no time at all, our problem had turned to dawn mist and blown away! And just think," Mama Maria said, shaking her head, "if Yosef and I had been forced to leave immediately for Nazareth, we would have missed the Magi! And just think how disappointed *they* would have been, having journeyed so long from a land that lay far beyond the eastern horizon."

With her chin Mama Maria pointed toward the spot where the sun rises each morning.

"The Magi are used to traveling of course, but mostly they journey with their minds. They are scholars who study the stars, night after night, to help people try to fathom what is happening here on earth. Some people believe that what they do is magic since they seem to pull out answers to baffling questions, like doves from a tightly wrapped turban. But mere magicians are usually interested in little more than the show. Rarely do they ponder mysteries beyond the grasp of us common people.

"These Magi were from wealthy and privileged families and were able to take year-long journeys by camel train, wherever their quest for knowledge led them. The innkeeper was thrilled to receive them, and he laid out a special meal for all of us. He and his wife even offered their own bedroom for the three august travelers to stay in, expecting of course to be rewarded royally.

"You can imagine how awed Yosef and I were when these three men, dressed like kings, entered the stable and placed gifts at the foot of a manger in which lay the child of a lowly carpenter and his young wife. Our lives had become one surprise after another ever since we had been promised in marriage. But little did we know what was coming!"

Rising to her feet, Mama Maria went to the woodpile. She carried two logs to the oven and thrust them through the stoke hole. The hungry fire roared its approval. Returning to her seat, she picked up the thread of her story.

"Unfortunately, the Magi also brought with them disturbing news from King Herod's Court in Jerusalem. They had gone there first to pay respect and deference to the sovereign ruler, as was their custom. They assumed that Herod would surely know of the newborn child, whom their calculations had revealed was to become the next Jewish king.

"When they asked about it, Herod spit out through clenched teeth, 'I am the only King of the Jews! There will be no new king while I live! And only *I* can choose my successor.'

"Then Herod grew quiet, aware that his court had many ears and afraid that dangerous ideas might take root in some of them. Slowly a shrewd smile creased his lips. Maybe these Magi knew something that would be of use to him. And if not, he could use them to find out more.

"With feigned politeness, he ushered them into his private quarters and asked in a voice as smooth as oil, 'How is it that you come here searching for a child who will be king?'

"'We saw signs in the stars,' they answered.

"'Oh? What signs?' he pressed on, as if he were a student, not the king.

"'A rare meeting of three wandering stars,' answered one of the Magi, 'in the House of the Jews! It all began when, three times, the great Jupiter took his leave only to return again!'

"'I asked for clarity,' Herod snapped, 'not confusion.'

"He knew little about the stars, you see, and cared even less. Herod looked up to nothing, and no one. He was interested only in himself and his place right here on earth.

"Nevertheless, he had decided to pry loose from these men what they knew, which meant acting as if he too was a man of learning who wanted to discover even more. He appealed to the teacher in them, knowing all the while that it was he not they who would decide what was important."

Mama Maria studied our faces and then continued, "Here is what the Magi told King Herod, first one of them speaking, then another. 'Besides the constellations," they said, "and the thousands of common stars that accompany them every night, there are other kinds of heavenly bodies. For example, racing stars flash across the sky in a second and then vanish, occasionally dozens and dozens of them streaking by in a single night.

"'Bearded stars, on the other hand, pass very slowly, and very rarely. Years can go by between appearances. When one finally comes, its long white beard precedes it, and it can take several phases of the moon for it to cross the sky just once. As you can imagine, these bearded stars are very ancient. And they bring bad news: of war, famine, and plague.

"'Finally, there are a handful of wandering stars that are nearly always with us, journeying nightly as they will through the Twelve Houses of the Nations, those dozen constellations of the nocturnal sky that make up the Zodiac. These wandering stars go wherever their business takes them; whereas the common stars, the ones that make up the constellations, must travel together in a set order.'

"The king in Herod had begun to fidget," said Mama Maria, "but the Magi were true scholars, lost in the vastness of their learning and intent upon explaining all they could about the blackened skies between dusk and dawn.

"'According to the Greeks, who have spent generations studying the heavens,' they said, 'these wandering stars total five. Jupiter is considered by all nations to be a lucky and royal star. Saturn is the ruler and protector of the House of the Jews. Not unlike yourself.'

"Herod covered a smile with his fist—best not to reveal that one liked this kind of stroking.

"Without missing a beat, the Magi continued: 'Mars is the God of War and maker of great changes. Venus is the Goddess of Love. And Mercury? Mercury is the most hurried traveler of them all.

"'Last year, while mapping the skies as we always do, often laboring from dusk to dawn, we saw Jupiter meeting with his father Saturn in the fish constellation Pisces. As you know, Pisces is the House of the Jews and the sign of Israel.'

"Herod dipped his chin once and sighed deeply. It was clear to him that these strange men were not stupid.

"'Those two wandering stars,' the Magi went on, continuing to take turns speaking, 'were closer than the width of your pointer finger held at arm's length against the sky. And Jupiter stood directly above Saturn!

"'Now, this may seem of little consequence to those who seek wisdom by daylight. But mind you, these two great stars meet like that just once a century. It can only mean that something very significant will happen for your people.'

"Herod broke in impatiently, 'Soon the daylight you mention will be gone and you still haven't answered my question. Step aside from your tedious lessons,' he growled. 'Get on with it!'

"Then he turned his head toward one of his attendants and sniffed, 'It isn't right that he who makes things happen for his people should be left in the dark.'

"The attendant nodded nervously, all too aware of how conditionally his head was attached to his neck.

"All three Magi stared at the king as if he were a dunce," said Mama Maria. "But this didn't stop them from describing precisely the extraordinary event they had witnessed. And besides, by now they knew Herod would not let them go before hearing the entire story, so on they rolled.

"'Well, Jupiter took his leave. For half a year he and Saturn went their separate ways. Then Jupiter reversed course and, to our total amazement, returned to stand again directly above Saturn! Surely it was an omen of a truly great event about to occur.

"'Now, with help from several of your learned rabbis, we have studied your scrolls and learned much about these predictions. So, we know there are countless Hebrew prophecies concerning a Messiah.'

"With that, they had Herod's full attention. His lips twitched ever so slightly, while his head nodded slowly. The Magi hardly noticed. They were by now so excited, they were stumbling over one another's words, each trying to speak next.

"'But this second meeting was *nothing* compared to what then happened—something we had never heard of, even from the white-haired teachers who taught us as boys. The two wandering stars parted once more only to back up for a *third* meeting. Not in a dozen centuries of records could we discover a similar occurrence!

"'And not only that, as soon as they met for the third time, Mars entered the sky and approached his father, Jupiter, and his grandfather, Saturn. Mars crept steadily nearer until he stood squarely between them, burning as red as a hot ember in ashes.

"'Imagine that—the three of them standing there together in the night sky, in a line shorter than the space between your eyes.'

"Herod was on the edge of his seat. 'So, what were they meeting about?' he asked, one eyebrow arching.

"'Perhaps Mars had been summoned to announce the coming of great change,' they responded 'of a magnitude that only he has been known to accomplish. Finding the explanation is precisely why we left at once on this long journey that has lasted several complete phases of the moon. We were afraid of missing something important, and so here we are searching for more clues in this land we have never before visited.'

"The Magi were speaking faster and faster now," said Mama Maria, leaning forward. "At times they all spoke the same phrase.

"'Your ancient religious scrolls,' said the Magi, 'tell us of a savior to be born in a place called Bethlehem. This very event may be what drew the three, powerful wandering stars together. We ask your blessing to visit this place within your kingdom, so that we can see for ourselves. We concluded the child might be your son or grandson. And if a newborn is already there who fits the predictions, we want to give him gifts.'

"King Herod's eyes narrowed to slits as he finalized his plan. Yes, he would give these three fools safe passage; let them do his snooping for him. When they reported back, he would deal with any upstart they had uncovered—in that dung-hill village of Bethlehem—anyone who might threaten his reign! His hands gripped the armrests of his throne.

"And so," said Maria, "Herod let the Magi hurry off for Bethlehem, provided that they return and tell him what they discovered. That's how they came to visit us, bringing wonderful gifts the likes of which Yosef and I had never seen. At the time, I couldn't even name two of the presents they brought! Besides gold, they held out to us 'frankincense' and 'myrrh.' How should I have known about such costly things?" She looked at us, wide-eyed.

"And the clothing they wore!" she continued. "I had never even imagined someone wearing such garments. Beautiful flowing robes, with jeweled clasps holding them closed, and strange wraps on their heads, made of woven cloth with designs and colors that seemed to shimmer and change the way sunlight dances with clouds. Even their sandals were astonishing, covering their feet from heel to toe and ending in an upcurving point."

"Were they scary?" asked Aaron. "Did they have bushy eyebrows and long noses and stuff like that?"

Mama Maria laughed. "No, that was what struck me the most. Foreigners can be strangely kind and gentle, and curious about everything. Just like you, Aaron!"

My brother quickly buried his face in his shoulder, to hide a large smile.

"They asked question after question," she went on. "Even Yosef's tools interested them. And when he pulled out an interlocking wooden puzzle he had made to sell in the Bethlehem market, oh, they went wild, trying to solve it. Scratching and pulling on their ears, they called it a 'head twister,' and all three laughed liked ten-year-olds when Yosef finally had to show them how it worked."

Then Maria's face went dark. "But, as I said earlier, these three kind travelers also brought bad news. The more they mulled it over, the more they were worried by Herod's reaction to their quest. An angry tongue sheathed in a smile of cold marble made them uneasy. They had concluded that it was likely that Baby Yeshua was in danger."

Mama Maria bit her lower lip. "They advised us to hide for a while. At least a year!"

Her brow furrowed and she sighed. "But where could a poor carpenter hide for that long with his wife and newborn child? We couldn't stay in Bethlehem, and the census takers and innkeeper knew we were from Nazareth, so going home wasn't safe either. In fact, anywhere we went in Galilee or Judea, we would eventually be spotted, and Jews are not popular in Samaria among the Samaritans, who predominate there.

"That's not all. We wondered *how* we would live. With the gifts from the Magi we could pay for food and lodging for a good while, but trying to explain how a family of meager means had come by such expensive things wouldn't be easy. And if people know you're running, things can get knotty; some might try to take advantage of us. So where and how was safety to be found in this precarious world?"

Escape to Egypt

One story leads to another, the way one camel follows the next across the desert. Unwilling to stop there on the edge of a cliff, we let our wide eyes and open mouths prod and nudge Mama Maria until finally she gave us a glimpse into the secret hideaway she and Yosef eventually settled on.

"That night," she resumed. "Yosef had another dream. He was told we must flee far away, across a broad river, first heading out of Bethlehem past the Salt Sea—a lake as dead as a wooden trough of stagnant water—and then turning to follow the setting sun for as many days as there are grains on a stalk of wheat.

"The Magi had advised us to pay particularly close attention to what our dreams might reveal. So, using the gold they had given us, we left at once for the ancient land of Egypt. You've all heard of it in the stories about Moses and how our people were once enslaved there."

We nodded our heads.

"Well, it was odd to return to the place our people had fled from, odder yet to think that this would be our salvation," she continued.

"There in Egypt we set up shop and lived for several years. Yosef supported us with his carpentry, and Yeshua grew into a strong toddler and then a quick young child. And soon we began to learn the answer to the question Yosef had asked the night Yeshua was born, about how many sisters and brothers our son would have. First came our daughter, Netanya, which means 'gift from God' in Hebrew. Next came our second son, Yehuda.

"While Yosef worked, sometimes traveling, Yeshua helped take care of our babies like a little daddy! He played handclapping games with them for hours on end, and he taught them how to eat piping-hot food safely at mealtimes, how to say morning and evening prayers, and how to prepare for bed at night. He was a great help to me.

"One day at dawn, Yosef awoke with a start. Yet another dream had come, with a clear message that it was safe to return home to Nazareth. We had recently heard from travelers that King Herod had died, and we reasoned that the newly installed king—who had succeeded his father—would be no threat to Yeshua."

Mama Maria slowly wiped her forehead with the back of her hand while tilting her head in thought. "It seemed to me that with the grace of God upon us, we would make it safely through the thicket of perils."

She breathed deeply. "Several days later," she went on, "we left Egypt in a caravan, crossing the River Nile on a log barge. We then walked through the desert far north of the Red Sea and along the route Moses had taken as he led our people out of slavery all those years ago.

"We worked to pay our way. I cooked and washed for the merchants and the camel drivers, and Yosef watered the camels and made repairs to the cargo racks that these grand animals carried up top.

"Those camel drivers were hard as sun-baked clay, having spent their entire adult lives on what must have seemed like one endless caravan. They would journey northward from Ethiopia to Egypt and on through Galilee to Phoenicia, then eastward to Persia and beyond, before turning back to begin again. All along, suffering every hardship imaginable: aching with hunger, following mirages of water, hunkering down in sandstorms, fighting off illness and attacks by thieves and marauders.

"But these hard-bitten men were enchanted by Yeshua. They hoisted him up on one of their camels and strapped him to the cargo pack, where he rode like a prince. And they told him stories in the evenings, twisting and turning tales about Nasrudeen Hodja the witty and wise Arab, and about strange night creatures that jumped from the stars dotting the skies, to prowl the desert wilderness.

"All day long, I would watch this tiny boy, wearing a red head-wrap to protect him from the throbbing-hot sun, rocking to and fro and side to side with the camel's steps. He would stare over the heads of these majestic beasts, gazing into the distance as if he could see for a thousand miles. Captain Yeshua, navigating his fleet of camels across the great rolling waves of sand!"

Mama Maria shook her head as if such a sight was simply too fantastic to believe.

"But the camel drivers were not the only storytellers on that trip," she continued. "Around the campfire at night, we were beseeched to tell *our* stories, too. Unfortunately, Yosef and I spoke only a little of their tongue, and haltingly. So, while I held baby Yehuda in one arm and little Netanya in the other, Yosef would sit five-year-old Yeshua in his lap and tell the ancient Jewish tales that he had told his son countless times in Aramaic, the language you and I are using right now.

"For us to share these stories, Yeshua had to carry over his father's words into a tongue his audience understood. Just as a camel's shadow follows it across a sand dune, Yeshua took those merchants and camel drivers through the stories line for line, using the words he had quickly picked up playing with local kids in Egypt. Each phrase from Yosef was followed by the same phrase from Yeshua—but in the other language—matching stride with stride, just like that shadow does."

Mama Maria clapped her hands in delight.

"The drivers prized those double performances more than anything. They would roar with laughter when Yeshua hopped out of his father's lap to act out a word he didn't know. Or a part of the story too complicated for the words he knew how to use.

"Their favorite tale was about the Great Flood, perhaps because rainwater in the desert was like liquid gold, and the idea of all those animals on the ark, floating around with Noah and his family, well, it just tickled them. It lifted them out of their sandals and took them on a journey unlike any they'd ever been on before.

"Once, right when Yosef and Yeshua were finishing that particular shadow act, up jumped the most imposing of all the camel drivers. 'Hah!' he said. 'Were there two camels on that wooden boat?'

"Yeshua turned his head and whispered up to Yosef, who nodded. Then

Yeshua turned back and pronounced authoritatively: 'Yes, there were.'

"'And two donkeys, as well?' asked the driver.

"Yeshua checked again with Yosef, and then he nodded vigorously in affirmation.

"'Hmmph!' exclaimed the driver. 'And what poor soul had to clean up afterwards?' He paused to look around dramatically at all of us.

"Yeshua laughed so hard he tumbled from his father's lap."

We all laughed, too, when Mama Maria recounted it. And so did she.

Then she went on, "A few days later we arrived in Jerusalem, purifying ourselves with living water, as is the custom, before entering the city gates. This immersion in the stone-lined *mikveh* was not only vital, but joyfully welcomed by us. During all our years in Egypt, we had been unable to participate in such a ritual purification because the local customs were not ours. So, now we felt at peace again, both with ourselves and with the teachings of the scrolls.

"Just before our mikveh bath, we said our good-byes, because we had to leave the caravan to fulfill an important obligation before returning to Nazareth. As you all know, it is written in the Law of Moses that every first-born male shall be taken to the Temple in Jerusalem and dedicated to God. This is supposed to be done within forty days of birth, but we were fleeing Herod long before then. Now, more than five years later, we were determined to fulfill our obligation.

"We went straight to the Temple and were met right off by the joyful gaze of an ancient woman, sitting in the corner of the doorway. Later we learned she was a renowned prophetess named Annot who lived in the Temple, never leaving its grounds but praying and fasting for days on end. '*Annot*' is the name we give to a type of lamp that gives off much light. We could see the bright glow in her eyes reflecting for all to see, the immense light that filled her heart.

"Annot was over a hundred years old, having been married seven years and widowed for eighty-four. To our great surprise, the prophetess seemed to know who we were because she struggled to her feet and hurried up to us with the help of a gnarled and well-worn walking stick.

"Smiling broadly, Annot gestured that she wished to touch our Yeshua on the forehead, her eyes alternately searching our faces and looking up to the heavens. After she blessed him, she began stopping anyone who walked by, telling them that this child was going to set Jerusalem free. He was going to be a light in which our people would forever be held.

"I was so young—not even twenty years old—and I just stood there staring at her. Of course I hadn't forgotten the dream about naming my child, but hearing such statements spoken aloud by someone I did not know made me shiver. After all, Yeshua was but a boy. Our boy.

"Before parting, we gave her a bag of Egyptian figs and a woven shawl for her shoulders.

"Delighted, the prophetess Annot counseled us, 'Go home and nurture Yeshua so that he may grow straight and strong and tall, like a cedar of Lebanon! And teach him the Torah and the Nevi'im: every word of every passage. He must become a master of Hebrew, our beloved language of the synagogue.'

"She stared hard at Yosef, who nodded his agreement to take charge of that task.

"Yeshua then hugged her and kissed her on both cheeks.

"She beamed. 'I've been waiting a long time,' she said in a near whisper. Then she fell serious. 'Now, I too can go home.'

"Having done our duty by God, the very next day we set out for Nazareth. Our homecoming was both joyous and heartbreaking. Before leaving Bethlehem for Egypt, we had sent word to no one but our parents that we had to go into hiding. To protect them, we gave no details about how to find us. And only they knew that Yeshua had been born in Bethlehem, so that neither Herod nor his heir would be able to trace our son if they endeavored to do so.

"Now all of you are in on the secret." She winked at us. "Yeshua of Nazareth, son of Yosef and Maria, is really Yeshua of Bethlehem. And even though the danger has passed, I know that none of you will tell."

We all shook our heads solemnly.

"Because we were so out of touch with everyone," Mama Maria continued, "we hadn't heard what had happened in our absence."

I watched her closely. She seemed to be struggling to find the right words. This was something new, and what followed was a part of the story that was new to me, maybe because in the past she had considered some of us to be too young. But now she carried the story forward.

"The very day after our return to Nazareth," she said, "our parents told us of something truly dreadful that had taken place just after we fled for Egypt.

"When the Magi did not return to Jerusalem after visiting Bethlehem," she said, "Herod decided they must have learned, by treason or by some mystical device, of his scheme to change the prophecies and remove any rival from his path."

She covered her eyes with a hand and shook her head.

"Probably Herod felt contempt for star gazers and their predictions. And yet, deep down he was a coward, afraid to risk anything, so he gave a tyrant's order. He decreed that every Jewish baby boy in Bethlehem, from newborn..." she hesitated, "up to two years of age..." her voice faltered again, "must be put to death."

Mama Maria sat, staring mutely. After a very long time, she sucked in a jagged breath and pushed out the words. "And so it was *done*."

She stood up quickly and herded the lot of us out of the courtyard. But not before I caught a glimpse of her eyes. They were dark as the sky just before a thunderstorm.

Storm Born

The next morning Mama Maria was over at our house visiting my mother. Suddenly a real storm came up. Mama Maria shrank back from the doorway where she had been sitting on a stool, to find a new place near the hearth.

"I abhor thunderstorms," she said hoarsely.

My mother looked at her with soft eyes and continued her mending.

"I get a bad feeling," Mama Maria went on, "when the sky goes suddenly dark and all grows quiet. Have you ever noticed how even the birds stop flying?"

Mother nodded and broke a thread off with her teeth.

"It makes me feel that something terrible is about to take place."

My mother gently interrupted, "I've never known why you feel that way, Maria. Your family is blessed by God." On the word God she gestured with her forehead for emphasis.

"And remember when Daavi was born? Remember?" She glanced over at me.

Mama Maria looked, too, and slowly nodded.

I waited.

"It was during the most dreadful storm of the year," my mother continued. You were sitting with me during my labor. "Suddenly thunder began rolling from horizon to horizon like stampeding horses. Lightning flashed like sparks from their hooves until I feared our houses would all burst into flames."

I felt my eyes growing wider and wider.

"And what happened next?" Mother laughed aloud. "You rushed home to fetch the herbs you had forgotten, for the tea that would calm my back aches.

"After helping the midwife deliver Daavi, you looked up to see Yeshu dashing through torrents of rain to see our baby, only moments after he heard Daavi cry out between two great claps of thunder.

"Yeshu was laughing and clapping his hands, as well, rain water streaming off his beard as if he were a sopping-wet willow tree.

"And you, Maria? I couldn't tell whether the lines around your eyes and mouth were from concern...or joy! "

Glancing into the fire in our hearth, Mama Maria murmured, "Mmm, that's so."

Soon after, she went home to prepare the evening meal.

That evening I lay in bed wondering why Yeshu and Mama Maria ran back and forth through the storm to see me. I was just one more yelping baby among scores born in Nazareth that year. I promised myself to ask Yeshu when he returned from his traveling what *he* thought of thunderstorms, and why he had raced over. But I promptly fell sound asleep and by dawn I'd forgotten about it.

Nevertheless, beginning with family stories about my birth, I developed a fascination for storms. I've forever been drawn to thunder—the first sounds of my life—after my mother's heartbeats, that is. Unlike Mama Maria who would scoot indoors and shutter the windows and bolt the door whenever she heard thunder approaching, I would stay outside as long as I could, standing under an eave of our roof, feeling my chest swell with the grand and furious drumming. And though thunder's drumming was a source of power and peace to me as a child, it later became more complex and weighty.

In my mother's case, what followed the storm that accompanied me into the world proved to be tangled. It brought her neither power nor peace. For unknown reasons, she fell ill soon after my birth and was confined to bed for seven months. Shoshana had to take over raising me until Mother was back on her feet.

Shoshana was only five or so, but it wasn't unusual for a girl that age in Nazareth to help out with her younger brothers and sisters. And yet it must be scary, wondering if your mother's going to get well, and knowing the well-being of a toddler depends on you when you're barely starting to grow up yourself.

Maybe that's why Shoshana learned to sing.

Morning Star to Lion of Judah

In telling and retelling the story of her family's return from Egypt, Mama Maria had tried to protect us from the hard news of the slaughter of innocents in faraway Bethlehem, until at last she felt we were ready to hear it. She seemed as taken aback as we were by the infinite sorrow that enveloped her, as if she were hearing the story for the very first time, even though she was the one who had lived it.

Stories are like that. One day you hear a tale that you already know like the back of your hand, and suddenly it *is* the back of your hand. You start to laugh or cry without fully knowing why.

I think we instinctively knew that Mama Maria was mourning the boy babies who had died as well as grieving for her son who was meant to be among them. And what might she and Yosef have done had they known what would happen after they fled Bethlehem?

Or what if they had *not* had prior warning that they must leave?

Those of us who begged her hardest for more stories felt it was our fault that those memories had swept her into a place of such aching sadness. We decided we had best return to Mama Ana to hear more stories about Yeshu growing up.

After searching Nazareth in vain, we finally found her near the stream just outside of town, gathering wild herbs. As always, she let us interrupt her work.

"At my age," she said, "it seems at times that the past is more present than when it first happened. I find myself walking slowly through a forest of memories, seeing plants and birds I once walked by without noticing.

"Nowadays I stop and carefully turn over the recollections of my own growing up, and of Maria's and Yeshu's, too. I turn them over like stones, weighing them in my hand and searching for meaning."

"Have I guessed right, that you all want to hear more about Yeshu?"

She brushed a wisp of gray hair away from her face as we all nodded in unison.

Mama Ana closed her eyes and began.

"For me, Yeshu began with a bright star I saw in the morning sky, the very day that Maria told me she was expecting. I must say I was surprised. But also very happy. I liked Yosef as a person and loved him for loving Maria. And until the day he left us, bless his soul, he was a devoted husband and father.

"I myself was widowed soon after Yeshu was born," Mama Ana went on, opening her eyes again.

"Like so many other things, Maria and Yosef didn't find out about our shared loss till they returned from Egypt. Though they had a growing family, they insisted I live with them. You can never have too many eyes, ears, and hands when it comes to raising children, and I welcomed the chance to walk beside Yeshu and his sisters and brothers from that day to this. It has kept my heart young."

She laughed.

"Yeshu was above all a curious, talkative little boy, with shining dark eyes, always seeking adventure or falling into some kind of harmless mischief. He was forever testing his world: full of questions and jokes, and brimming over with affection. Sometimes, especially as he got older, he would hug so hard, I thought my last breath was being squeezed out."

Hearing that, I smiled inwardly.

"Now," she said, "Yeshu is my magic carpet from the East. We embrace and he carefully lifts me into the air where I hover until I demand to be set back down on earth!

"As a young boy, half the time he was a day dreamer, lying on that hillside just over there," she said, pointing with her upraised chin.

I perked up, hearing that.

"And the rest of the time? Well, Yeshu was a whir of motion, at the center of every game. He would insist on fair play, taking care to look out for the smallest child, the one who might be run over by the others if she got in their way.

"From the time he was, oh, I don't know how young, he considered it wrong for the other boys to keep the girls out of their games, especially his sisters Netanya and Shaani.

"And if the boys were not to be moved, he'd take anyone who agreed with him to another part of the field and play. Often as not, when the unrelenting ones heard Yeshu and the others laughing and horsing around, they would give up and come on down to ask if they could join in.

"And look at him now," she said, her voice ringing like a bell, "a lion of Judah, carrying his family on one shoulder and our village of Nazareth on the other."

Mama Ana's face glowed as she spoke of her grandson.

"My favorite story," she continued, "is about Yeshu in the Temple in Jerusalem. That was not long before Yosef, bless his soul, left us forever.

"Yeshu had just turned twelve, and as usual we journeyed to Jerusalem for Passover. That year we went with many relatives and neighbors from Nazareth.

"'Nearly the whole village,' Yeshu teased us, 'except for the houses!'

"We celebrated our Pesakh meal as if *we* were the ones who had been delivered from Egypt. The food was laid out on our Seder table that year until first the table groaned, later followed by more groaning—by us and by our guests after the meal was over!

"Oh, yes, and we ate lots of lamb sprinkled with spring greens, sopping up the juices with flat pieces of *matzah* bread, followed by a dish made of pomegranates and melted goat cheese that I had never even imagined existed, much less eaten.

"Then from sundown that evening until sundown the next, we spent our day of Shabbat at the Temple. That night we slept like a pride of engorged lions after a long hunt. The following morning, we made a final visit to the Temple, then gathered up our belongings and promptly set off for Nazareth.

"Our group was so large that to our great surprise it was nearly nightfall, after we had stopped to set up camp, when we realized that Yeshu was missing. The entire time each of us was certain he must have been walking with someone else, strung out as we were along the dusty, winding road."

Mama Ana gave a small shrug of her shoulders.

"There was no moon that night," she continued, "and it was too dark to travel. But early the next morning, Yosef, Maria, and I headed back to Jerusalem to find Yeshu. My creaky knees were bothering me, so we stopped frequently to take breaks.

"At midday we sat resting, with our backs against a stone wall, when suddenly a shadow passed rapidly over us. When I looked up, I caught sight of a great white bird gliding in an upward spiral high above our heads.

"I clambered to my feet and sputtered, 'Time to move on,' and began walking with renewed spring in my step.

"Still, it was late afternoon before we arrived. We immediately began looking for Yeshu, returning to where we had celebrated our Seder meal, then to where we had slept at night, and even to the central marketplace. But there was no sign of a solitary young village boy anywhere.

"Finally, we went to the Temple to ask the priests if they'd heard anything."

Mama Ana shook her head several times.

"Imagine our astonishment to find Yeshu sitting among a crowd of rabbis, peppering them with questions and answering theirs in kind.

"I wasn't as surprised as Yosef and Maria, but it soon became clear we were not the only ones who were taken aback.

"The rabbis were exclaiming to one another, 'Listen to his answers! Who in the world has taught him all this?'

"Maria ran straight up to Yeshu and exclaimed, 'Why have you done this to us? Don't you realize the scare you've given your family? We thought you were lost, and we've been searching for you everywhere.'

"Yeshu gazed back calmly and asked, 'But why did you even have to look? Didn't you know I would be here, tending to God's errands?'

"Maria shook her head, then sighed. Yosef merely shrugged his shoulders.

After all, they had dedicated this son of theirs to God, in this very Temple.

"As for the rabbis, they wanted to continue quizzing the boy whose surprising responses bloomed like roses from the thorniest questions. They found him clever and quick, and with a little practice he would make a powerful debater, someone who could humble the doubters.

They urged us to leave him with them in Jerusalem so they could train him to be a rabbi. But Yosef and Maria were intent on returning with Yeshu to Nazareth. It was their understanding of God's will that they and only they were the ones to bring him up.

"I locked elbows with the two of them," added Mama Ana. "And I reminded them that it was also here in this very Temple that the prophetess Annot had told them to take him home and nurture him. Did she not have special knowledge and understanding?

And so we took our lion cub back to Nazareth with us to grow among ordinary people and to learn how one can change lives without using tooth and claw, sword and dagger.

"Not long after that, Yosef died," she said, her voice catching. "Our family was wounded in ways that still show, like a tree scarred where the largest limb has broken off.

"Yeshu hardly spoke for a year. Thank God he hadn't remained in Jerusalem when he was younger because we really needed him here. He quickly took up Yosef's carpentry tools and shouldered the load. When work ran out in Nazareth, he went on the road, but unlike other young men, he always came back.

"Any other plan he may have had for his life, he put at the back of the bottom shelf. For sure, there would be no thoughts of a new family for him while his father and mother's young brood was still growing toward adulthood."

Momentarily, my aching from Shoshana's loss smothered the story of the unbearable hurt Yeshu had suffered. Then I blinked hard.

Mama Ana was saying, "Yeshu's shift from son to family head came as quickly as a storm flying off the sea. To meet such a challenge, he learned to become as wide as a sky that holds both the storm and the sun in the same embrace."

Mama Ana had been watching me. She was gazing straight into my eyes, boring deep inside me, and her voice dropped almost to a whisper.

"The cloth that is torn *can* be mended," she said, "the broken wagon wheel repaired.

"Loss is not the same as emptiness." She smiled softly. "And *not now* is very different from *never*." Her eyes moved on to the others in the circle.

"For many years after," she continued, her voice rising to its normal level, "to earn the money that we desperately needed, Yeshu worked as patiently as an ox that lowers its shoulders to pull the plow through parched and rocky fields.

"One day, the last of his sisters and brothers will be ready to stand on their own," she said. "And that part of Yeshu's work will be over.

"But our Yeshu has more to do in this life," Mama Ana insisted.

Her eyes shone brightly.

"*Much* more."

II. Quest

The Torah and the Nevi'im

I think I must have been born searching for God. People have told me that just as my head crowned during my mother's labor, there was a clap of thunder and she shouted out God's name. You're never supposed to speak that name aloud, of course; it's too holy. So maybe she burst out with something else. No matter, my mother couldn't help herself, with the room shaking around the searing pain.

In any case, that very first utterance spoken in my presence seems to have ignited my imagination like the dazzling flash of lightning that preceded it. Maybe that's why I started so young with all my questions.

"Where can I find God?"

"What does God look like?"

And a big one for me: "When I finally see God's face, will I be afraid?"

Yeshu told me once he'd never known a young person so intent on searching for God. And he knew *lots* of kids from all those hours spent in his workshop telling his stories. I can still see him in my mind's eye, as clearly as if it were this morning. Yeshu planing the rough edges from a door or chiseling a wooden saddle, his dark eyes intent on the job his hands are doing, his beard flowing down from cheekbones like hillsides full of wildflowers.

And there I am, listening like a wolf pup as the pack leader sings the moon up through the sky of glistening ebony. Listening like a sapling on the forest floor as an ancient cedar of Lebanon lifts its branches to the heavens and chants its wind song.

On many occasions, before evening prayers, I passed by the synagogue door and saw Yeshu standing there alone. He would always be reading from the great scrolls that contain the books of the Laws and the Prophets. There lay the Torah and the Nevi'im: more than two dozen books of religious rules and practice, history and wisdom. As we all know, these beloved scrolls hold the spiritual heritage of the Jewish people, going back beyond our beginning to the very beginning.

These scrolls in our synagogue are the very same writings that Yeshu's father and his grandfather Yakob had studied, and all the other men of the village. They were all shades of brown, worn and softened and oiled by years of handling. When the older men moved in somber procession carrying the Torah and the Nevi'im slowly around the synagogue on their shoulders, they seemed to grow younger under the burden of time and the centuries.

It was a sight to see, these elders, bent from years of work and study, standing straight as pillars as they bore the weight of the ages.

The first time I kissed the Torah, I was just a boy. It was during our weekly Shabbat services. The Torah smelled familiar: something like a reed breadbasket; something like dusty footpaths and my father's hands.

I hoped—with more strength than the grip of my fist—that one day I would be able to read what was written there. First, I would have to learn Hebrew, the language of the synagogues and the Temple in Jerusalem. My father had begun teaching me a few phrases, showing me how similar the language of the scrolls is to the Aramaic we speak every day. But also how different the two ways of speaking are, especially certain important words.

Whenever I passed by the synagogue and saw Yeshu inside reading the scrolls to himself, I would pause for a moment and study him standing there with his head down, one hand idly fingering his beard, while the forefinger of his other hand glided over the words, right to left, right to left. Lost in thought, he never lifted his gaze from the text, never noticed me watching.

I would go home content, reassured that the world was being made right because the words written so long ago were still being read. One afternoon, however, while walking by the synagogue shortly after Passover, I realized with a start that I hadn't seen Yeshu reading the scrolls for months.

I happened to be headed to my Aunt Sarah's house to deliver three freshly caught fish wrapped in large leaves and tied with a reed. It was a gift from my mother. When I handed her the package, I received a plump woven bag full of sweet dates in return, plus an extra one popped into my mouth. Mama Ana happened to be there visiting, so I asked her if she knew where Yeshu was. She motioned with her chin toward the olive grove at the edge of town.

There I found him sitting with his back against a tree trunk. He was braiding slender pieces of rope from cactus fibers, for tying thatch to a roof. His head swayed rhythmically as his hands danced from strand to strand. I crawled over the stone wall and dropped to the ground in front of him.

We exchanged brief greetings, and he continued with his work, his smile telling me he was pleased by my company. When I didn't say more, he raised his eyebrows and tilted his head back slightly, his fingers continuing to cavort among the fibers. He looked patiently at me down his nose until I spoke up.

"Yeshu," I finally said. "I never see you alone anymore in the synagogue, reading the scrolls." I cleared my throat...once...twice.

"Why have you stopped? Did you finally tire of them?"

His eyes held mine for a moment, and then he abruptly put his work aside and motioned his thumb toward the wall. Knowing him well, I climbed up and got as comfortable as I could, expecting a story. But somehow I knew that whatever followed, I was to stay put and listen until he was finished. Gazing into his face, the thought came to me that he was going to say something he would only tell a young friend like me.

It was early in the planting season, and the afternoon sun was already headed for the horizon. Yeshu looked back at me, his head cocked to one side and nodding faintly as though he were listening to a song and wondering if I could hear it too. I was reminded of those special moments just before sunrise when the birds start talking, calling the light back into the world. It was then I realized that Yeshu's lips were moving, that he was talking softly and not just to me.

I could feel the hairs standing up on my neck.

He closed his eyes and the murmuring became a stream of words that sounded like the wind might, if it could talk. It was like overhearing a conversation in another room without being able to tell what was being said.

All of a sudden my ears captured some of the words my father had been teaching me over the past year, and I realized that Yeshu was speaking in Hebrew. Even though I only partially understood him, I quickly recognized phrases.

Next, a realization struck me like a door opening up in the morning to let in the sunlight—he was reciting from the scrolls, starting at the very beginning of the Torah.

Berêšîth bara Elohim et hashamayim ve'et ha'arets,
(In the beginning of God's creation of heaven and earth,)
Veha'arets hayetah tohu vavohu vechoshech al-peney tehom.
(The earth was without form and empty,
with darkness on the face of the depths.)

Passage after passage, chapter after chapter, rolled off his tongue.

Veruach Elohim merachefet al-peney hamayim.
(The spirit wind of God moved over the water's surface.)
Vayomer Elohim yehi-or vayehi-or.
(God said, "There shall be light," and light came into existence.)

I listened, captivated as always by the tones and rhythms of his voice; by the way he paused, with his lips slightly apart.

Vayar Elohim et-ha'or ki-tov vayavdel,
(God saw that the light was good)
Elohim beyn ha'or uveyn hachoshech.
(and God divided between the light and the darkness.)

As he continued—finishing one book, beginning another—the sun sank slowly in the sky, burned red, and slipped below the horizon.

Still he spoke. At times it seemed as if he were chanting.

The shadows lengthened around us, and the sky gradually turned a darker and darker blue. Finally it reached a burnished ebony hue and countless stars sprang out. On and on Yeshu went as the moon began its climb.

And I fell off the wall deep in sleep.

~ ~ ~

I awoke to the sound of Yeshu laughing. His hands had caught me before my head hit the ground. I felt warm, and slightly ashamed.

He lifted me to his shoulder like a sack of meal and carried me home. Opening the door with his knee, he nodded to Mother and Father and gently dropped me into bed.

Now it was clear to me why I no longer saw him reading the scrolls in the synagogue.

Give Me Your Pain

When I was still that dreaming boy, one of my favorite games was to sit high in the ancient walnut tree in front of our house. As I surveyed the waves of wheat and grasses rolling over the nearby fields and pastures, I would pretend to be the captain of a grand ship on Lake Galilee.

Other times I was a camouflaged bird invisibly watching what people were up to beneath me. I would see Yeshu emerge from his workshop and head off down the road to the well for a drink of cool water. It seemed to me that he looked forward to chatting with the village mothers and grandmothers who gathered there daily without fail.

One afternoon around my tenth year, after listening to Mama Ana and Mama Maria tell us more stories about Yeshu's growing up, the two women swept us out of the house with their hands and skirts. They had been unexpectedly called to a home across town to assist with a birth. Nazareth had just one midwife, and she was rapidly aging, so Maria had been chosen several years earlier to learn everything this elderly matriarch knew. That way, when the time came, a new mid-wife could step into the old one's sandals. It seems the time had come.

Not anxious to begin my chores, I went immediately to my haven, the walnut tree. Quickly I climbed hand over hand, much higher than usual, and scooted far out on a limb. There I perched, passing the time deep in reverie, until suddenly I lost my grip and fell, twisting and turning through the tree limbs and crashing to the ground. Right away my leg throbbed so fiercely I cried out in misery, my head swinging back and forth as I felt the rushes of red hot pain.

In an instant, Yeshu burst from his workshop and came running to the base of the tree. He inspected my leg, probing with his fingers. Then he took my head in his hands.

"Look into my eyes, Daavi," he said quietly. "Take long, full breaths."

I did as he said. Every time my mind slipped back to my leg, his steady voice would insist, "Look into my eyes, little friend. Give *me* your pain."

As I stared into the calming pool of those eyes, the searing pain lost its bright color. A soothing warmth radiated from Yeshu's hands outward from my temples as he slowly rubbed them, all the while intoning verses from a Psalm in the book of the *Tehillim*.

> I have no food but tears, day and night.
> "Where is your God?" they ask me all day long.
> Deep calls to deep in the roar of your cataracts,
>   and all your waves, all your breakers, roll over me.

For a moment, my eyes glazed and the thought of God's face was carried by Yeshu's resonant voice reciting words that flowed over me like the River Jordan.

> As a deer yearns for the running streams,
>   so does my soul long for you, oh Yahweh.
> With my whole being I thirst for God, the living God.
> When shall I see the face of God?

As my eyes regained their focus, I realized it was Yeshu's face I was looking into. The pain kept getting smaller, like a bird flying toward a twilight hill, and yet Yeshu's voice held me close.

Sunk deep in my misery, groaning in distress,

I will wait for God...my refuge.

The last of the aching fell away like a stone from a mountain ledge. Another Psalm or two and all the throbbing had vanished. Yeshu helped me to my feet. Not once had his gaze left my eyes, nor had I even glanced away.

In the months and years following my tumble from the tree, Yeshu taught me many ways to lessen the pain from injury and illness, and then repair the damage. Although at first it was hard to believe, he revealed to me how we all have powers buried down inside that make it possible to heal ourselves. And one another. Yeshu said all it took was the trust to put your hand in God's hand.

But reaching out for that hand, without having any idea where it was, was not easy for me.

Many years later the terrible day would come when I tried to return that past comforting gaze to him. It would be all that I could do for him at that moment. For a long while thereafter, I would wonder if it had made a difference.

~ ~ ~

The next day Yeshu came over to my family's house in the early morning to see how I was coming along. I was still in bed, a little sore. He sat down next to me and pulled a handful of dried figs from his pocket. For a long time the only sound was our chewing as we ate them one by one.

Finally I broke the silence, "Yeshu, how did you come to love so much? Were you always this way?" I peered into his face. "I want to be just like you."

He laughed softly. "Mama Maria tells me that I was the warmest, most affectionate baby she ever held. And of course she plays no favorites!"

This time I was the one who giggled.

"The truth is," he continued, "beyond those days of our baby warmth, we all have to learn how to love. I learned from Mama Maria and Mama Ana, and from my father and my grandfather, too."

Then, after a long pause, he said something really surprising, "And I learned from listening to God's stillness."

Before I could ask what that meant, he turned his head to stare out the open door of our house toward his own, and then he finished, saying, "I also learned to love from helping raise my sisters and brothers after our father..." he hesitated, "was no longer with us."

He became quiet again.

"You can't feed and dress and put to bed that many kids, nurse them when they're sick or hurt, and teach them control when they act badly," he looked back at me, "without discovering many lessons about love. That's just one of the reasons why it can be easier for women than for men to enter the doors of heaven."

He locked his fingers together and studied them carefully. "Yes, I believe that children teach you love."

"In that case," I said. "I'm going to spend more time with children."

He glanced over at me and this time he roared. Then he hugged me, stood up, and waving to my mother, was out the door and gone.

Question to Quest

The following week I saw Yeshu walking in the hills west of town with someone whom I didn't recognize from a distance. I ran to catch up with them. The air was heavy and hot. I arrived so winded that Yeshu stopped his friend, a spirited fellow named Judah. I remembered having seen them talking together once before.

Yeshu said, "What do you two say? Why don't we stretch out here and rest for a while?" I saw him wink at me.

And so, sitting on the grassy hillside, we began to play questions and answers.

"Yeshu?" I asked. "Where did I come from? Did I come straight from God? From heaven?"

"You are made of dust," he responded, "a blend of stardust and ancient water." I glimpsed a twinkle in his eye.

"Just like Adam."

It didn't take long for Judah to lose his patience. He stood up and walked over to where I sat.

"Stop asking so many silly questions," he told me, his bushy eyebrows rising and falling. "You are wasting Yeshu's time. He has better things to do than tend to your childish musings. We were talking about what the Roman army..."

Yeshu's head swung around, and he stared at Judah. His face went dark. "Never!" he said through a set jaw, "Never stop this boy from asking questions."

Though Yeshu was pointing at me, he continued looking straight at Judah. "Few of his age are searching like he is. He's on a quest—a quest for God. That's a good thing, no?"

Judah frowned, then nodded vigorously, causing a riot of black curls to spring into motion like swarming bees. "Well, of course it's good," he said. "And that's exactly why he needs to have more discipline. He should listen more and talk less."

He glanced back at me. "He needs to learn to follow."

"No, Judah, you're wrong," Yeshu responded. "He will find his way not by following but by searching. What he finds will be *his* God-given truth, not someone else's. To own it, he must have the freedom to carry out that search.

"The discipline he needs, Judah, is not found in blind obedience." Yeshu was smiling now. "It's found in the hard work of learning *how* to search out, how to find, how to know the truth when he comes upon it.

I felt my eyes grow wider. Sweat droplets ran down my brow and I diverted them with the back of my hand. Was I caught in the middle of a tug-of-war? It was as if I'd inadvertently stepped between two sand cats vying for the same golden hamster. Could it be my fault?

"Daavi is on a great pilgrimage," Yeshu went on. "He is a treasure of ours. This boy will go farther than others because he dares to question me on the path. And he listens to my responses."

Yeshu was looking at me again. "Do not block his way."

Wiping more perspiration from my face with my sleeve, I gazed into Yeshu's eyes. It seemed as if I might see all the way to the end of time. I felt a wave of gratitude wash over me. Yeshu understood me; he defended me.

I was just a boy, but to him it didn't seem to matter. He believed in me.

With that realization, an enormous happiness filled me to the brim. It made me feel light as a soap bubble lifting into the air. Staring into Yeshu's eyes, I floated gently up and up.

Then, turning to look back, I began to fall through his eyes. Slowly, head first, I tumbled deeper and deeper, past moon and stars and into blue space.

I fell beyond Yeshu's sight and into heaven.

What else can I call it? God was there though without a form that words can hold. But I knew it was God. It was a presence: like the promise of an empty cup. In it I heard music with no sound. Seeing and hearing were one. Time passed without heartbeats. A soft mist, of every color, swirled around me—swirled as if the robes of a thousand angels were dancing to a song played by musicians at a distant wedding.

Listening intently, I watched the mist dissolve into a flock of giant birds flapping their wings slowly, slowly, in time to the music. One by one they broke off to dive into a forest, gliding between majestic trees without touching a single trunk. As they turned to bank this way and that among the trees, the sun lit their wings from behind like apple blossoms wafted into the breeze by an unexpected gust.

I felt so tired. Heaviness pulled me down into the sweet-smelling, tall grass. The grass was supple, and it rustled this way and that in the warm breezes above me.

My eyelids closed and opened. Yeshu stood above me, chuckling. He was gazing steadily into my eyes. And I into his.

I had been to the dream world and back again.

Judah stood next to him, still as an oak tree.

Yeshu knelt beside me and placed his forefinger lightly on the center of my chest. "There's a lion-man way down inside you," he said, "a lion stalking truth. The person you will become, hunting and hunting for his path."

"Daavi," he said. "Don't ever let anything, or anyone, hold you back or stand in your way."

I looked up at him gravely. I felt so important.

And for the very first time in my life, I felt powerful.

Standing up, I threw myself into Yeshu's arms. As he hugged me, I breathed in slowly. This time he smelled of cedar sawdust and a shepherd's cloak and the Torah being rolled open in the synagogue.

My head was spinning. My eyes moved to Judah, who was smiling wryly and shaking his head.

As he turned to whisper something to Yeshu, my gaze wandered over him, from his tangled thicket of curls to his closed hands that revealed every vein and tendon, and then back up to his bobbing beard and inquisitive brow.

When Judah glanced back in my direction and saw me watching him, I momentarily caught sight of something in his eyes. In spite of my feeling intimidated by him, I couldn't restrain myself from peering deep inside. There in those flinty eyes I saw a faint, warm glow—like that of a tuft of tinder, just before it bursts into flame and licks at the kindling stacked above it.

Who, I wondered, is this friend of Yeshu's? Might his blaze flicker over me again someday?

If so, would it soothe me? Or maybe singe me. I swallowed hard.

Or perhaps by tomorrow, I thought, I would recall him as a mere passerby who simply disappeared like a rolling cloud in the sky, one that dissolves into the blue when you aren't watching.

Yeshu sat down again, then quickly scrambled back to his feet. "Come on, Daavi! Judah! Let's tramp up the hill to the village orchards and climb a pomegranate tree. We can take care of hunger and thirst all at once."

I trotted after them, puffing intensely. Merely thinking about splitting open and biting into the rich redness of a round, plump pomegranate, I could imagine the scent of the exploding juices and feel them running down my chin.

Tools

One morning a few weeks later, I slipped out of my house and headed over to Yeshu's workshop. I needed to get away. My mother was ordering me to do one thing; my father another. *What* was I to make of it?

People were always telling me: "Do this, do that. No, that's wrong, how about the right way!" I got totally confused from so many adults laying down rules, each with different ideas about how and who I should be. I knew I was supposed to obey. But some days the words buzzed in my head relentlessly, driving me crazier than horseflies down the back of my tunic. Soon it seemed I didn't know anymore what *I* thought.

Increasingly I felt lost in a dark forest. Everywhere I turned, a different path through the looming limbs cried out, "This way, follow me!"

It was nightmarish. I was so happy to find Yeshu in his workshop, sharpening his tools. After we greeted one another, I pulled up a small stool and plopped down.

Once again Yeshu appeared to know what I was thinking even before I did.

"I've been considering a notion in the Book of Mîkhāh," he said, "while preparing to begin my workday."

Putting down one tool and picking up another, he wondered aloud, "What *is* it that God asks of me?

"We all know the passage," he continued, "from attending synagogue. But lately I've been dwelling a lot on that question, sitting with it like a fisherman who casts his net on the water again and again, day after day, waiting for a shining fish to appear."

Yeshu paused, then inquired again, shifting the emphasis, his eyes on his row of tools. "What is it that God asks of *me*?"

He reached for a mallet, then withdrew his hand. "When we have a lingering question, Daavi, we can go back to the scrolls."

"Do you remember the story of the merchant who adopted the younger man that robbed him?" I nodded in anticipation.

"He was following the Prophet Micah's advice," Yeshu said, "which gives us a shimmering piece of the answer.

> What does God require of you?
> To do justice,
> and to love kindness,
> and to walk humbly with your God.

He reached out and lifted up the mallet this time, placing its head in the palm of his free hand. Then he leaned toward me. "Beautiful words," he said softly.

"In that passage I see three exquisite lanterns that aid our feet as they seek their way along the path of life." He paused, turning the mallet over and over in his hand.

"They guide me through life, just as they did the merchant and just like the stars guide the sailor at night." He raised the mallet head to his lips.

"And yet, I'm certain that something more is required of us, Daavi, don't you think? Something beyond Micah's words." He bit pensively on his lower lip. "But what?"

I watched his face. The expressions on his brow and around his eyes moved and changed ever so slightly, like the patterns of breezes on a still lake at twilight.

Then those eyes brightened. "Let me tell you something, my friend, something very important to me."

I leaned forward on my stool and felt my ears perk up. I was listening so closely I could hear my own breathing.

Yeshu looked straight into my eyes. "I want my entire existence to be described by one word. Love."

He paused, lifting the mallet high as if to use it. "Say this mallet were to strike a bell a single time...and the sound it intoned would never fade away."

"Love for my family, for my village, for the people of Galilee, for all people in all lands." The mallet bobbed.

"Oh, and all plants and animals, as well," he added with a smile.

I suppose he must have had Yohanan on his mind at that moment.

"That's how I want my life to ring out." He brought the mallet down against an imaginary bell.

"But, let's think this over," Yeshu said, "is there yet another lantern?"

We were quiet for a while. I dropped my eyes as I gnawed on the end of a thumbnail. Glancing sideways, I saw that Yeshu was cocking his head and staring at me, waiting.

"How about doing good things?" I said. "Helping people. Earning God's love."

Yeshu cocked his head in the other direction and kept studying at me as he pulled on his beard.

Finally, he spoke. "Helping is always important," he said. "But think it over carefully, Daavi. It's not for good works that God loves you. God loves you for you." He emphasized the final "you" with a shake of his head.

"Good works are what God *asks* of you. But they aren't you." He brushed a fly away from his face. "And they aren't why God loves you. What causes love to be showered down on you is God's grace, not your deeds."

He put his mallet down and leaned toward me. "Think about that the next time you're tending sheep. You love those little lambs no matter what they do or don't do; am I right?"

I nodded, and smiled at the idea. Then I decided to try again.

"One more lantern," I repeated his earlier words. "Well," I said, pulling on my fingers, "you always talk about how important it is to learn to forgive."

I checked his expression, which was unchanged. "How forgiveness can nurture peace and healing."

I hesitated. "So...could that be the fourth lantern?"

"Excellent!" said Yeshu, leaning back and beaming at me. "You've been listening, young lion. Listening *and* thinking about things."

"Yeshu, I want to learn the sacred Books like you have," I blurted out, surprising myself. "So I can be wise like you!"

"Ah," he replied quickly, considering my request out loud to himself as much as answering me. "That's a fine place to begin. But only knowing the Torah and the Nevi'im; that's not enough. No, it's only tinder for a bonfire before dawn. You also need to meditate and pray, so that you can understand how to use what's *in* the Books, apply the words to your life, Daavi, and to the lives of others.

"Just like my father's wood planer or your father's leather awl, the Books are tools," he said, nodding firmly for emphasis. "They lie as sightless and soundless as stones on a mountain path until our feet trip over the questions we need to ask. Out of our stumbling come the answers."

Surprised, I gave a start. Appearing not to notice, Yeshu fell silent, gazing out the window.

"Look at that tree," he said, "the way the light filters through the leaves, illuminating the edges, casting shadows. The laws handed down in our ancient texts need to be reread in the light of human suffering. How do these laws speak of the love, or lack of love, between people?"

He carefully rubbed the blade of his chisel against the heel of his hand, assessing its sharpness.

"How do they sound the bell of compassion?" he asked, turning the blade over to examine the other side. "How do they call us to ring out with forgiveness—the hardest task of all."

He stopped for a moment. "Yes, someone needs to do that reflection, Daavi," he said. "Do you agree?"

Not knowing what to say, I nodded...waiting.

He went over to the window and looked up at the sky. There he stood for a while, gazing at that intense and infinite blue; the blue beyond blue.

Then he stared down at his hands, brown and work-scarred, which he'd stretched out in front of him.

Addressing his hands as if they held the answer, he said, "This could be the life's work I've been given."

Time stopped. My eyes shut. The thought that anyone would consider trying to reassess or improve upon a single phrase in one of our ancient books completely overwhelmed me. That anyone would allow a cloud of dust or one lone doubt to fall upon even one word, one letter of the beloved Torah that guided our lives, well, such an idea was more than my mind could grasp hold of. The very thought of it blotted out the sun; trapped the breath in my chest.

On top of all this, what had truly stunned me was the fact that it was not the High Priest in the Temple in Jerusalem, but my friend the carpenter —my next-door neighbor—who had just uttered such a notion.

Yeshu had indeed said it, so now a seed of possibility had been sown in my head. I have to say that I would never see him exactly the same way after that revelation. He would be the same Yeshu, only different somehow.

This tale spinning carpenter of ours, it seemed, was getting ready to rebuild, and to retell.

I have no idea how much time passed, but gradually I became aware that I was staring at Yeshu's profiled face, and that my eyes had widened.

Yeshu had returned to his workbench and was sighting down the edge of a new door. He was making slight adjustments with a curved knife in one hand and a palm-sized pumice stone gripped in the other, lost in his work. I observed his total attention to detail as he shaved a tiny sliver of wood off here; made a rough spot smoother there.

Finally he stood the door against the wall next to him and surveyed it approvingly. Then he stepped back to the window and peered out. As if his thoughts had taken wing, he once more began to study his hands in the light that fell on the windowsill. I was relieved that he seemed unaware of my state of mind.

I knew enough to remain silent. Quietly I slipped down off my stool and went to join him by the elevated, rectangle of light. On tiptoes, I stretched up to peer over the sill. Far above, a large white bird was circling, its legs trailing behind its body. Once in a great while it slowly flapped its wings.

Yeshu was watching it, too.

I pressed my lips together tightly, sealing all questions in. We just stood there motionless, following the flight of the great bird until it shrank into a dot and vanished.

I heard Yeshu gradually breathe out. I reached up to touch his hand that now rested on the edge of the sill, but something held me back.

My hand had been there for a while when Yeshu turned and looked down at me. I returned my hand to my side. Staring up into his eyes, I thought I could still see the great white bird flying deep inside them.

Sadness momentarily clouded his face. He turned and stepped back to his workbench and began laying his tools out in a predetermined order, all of them newly sharpened and oiled. He lifted a large plank of cedar onto two sawhorses and swung himself into the rhythms of his next piece of work.

It was time for me to go. I swallowed my urge to say something, anything, as I headed for the door.

"Daavi," he called after me.

I turned and waited.

"We will see to it that you learn the Books."

I nodded my head once, smiling, and ran out into the burning sunlight.

Unclean!

It was nearly Yom Kippur, our Day of Atonement, when we're all expected to repent and seek forgiveness for wrongs against God and against people. The goal, my mother reminded me, is to actually improve upon our behavior, which can be a daunting task. I had already learned from her that saying you're sorry is easy compared to the harder undertaking of truly becoming different.

One morning I stood in the doorway of my house, leaning against its wooden frame, my head just below the mezuzah, and there I considered the day. The sun was pressing down as hard as it could on the earth, till it felt that my eyes might burst into flame.

When Mother asked me to get water from the town well, thoughts of a thousand better things to do buzzed in my head. Hauling heavy buckets in that heat would be no dip in the river! But then my stomach rumbled, anticipating the tasty soup my mother would make for dinner.

Besides, fetching water had been one of Shoshana's duties, and doing her tasks after she disappeared always made me feel as if she were walking next to me. So I ambled outside and slowly untangled the braided leather thongs on both of the goatskin water buckets.

Hanging one bucket on each end of the wooden yoke and hoisting it to my shoulders, I stood there a while, dipping this way and that, pretending I was a giant walking on a long rope stretched between the sun and the moon, using the yoke for balance as I crossed the sky.

To make it extra hard, I closed my eyes, and that's when a story popped into my mind.

I had heard this tale more than once from Mama Ana, and it was one of my very favorites. With the first scene floating in my head, the next one was already surfacing.

~ ~ ~

Once there was a frog that discovered a well that was so deep and dark, so cool and pleasant, that he decided to keep it just for himself. So he set about scaring all of the other animals away.

Sitting on a rock ledge way down inside the well, right at the water line, he would arch his long, sinewy legs, puff up his chest, and roar out a threat that echoed and swelled as it rose up the steep walls like a thunderhead in full voice.

I AM A MOST TERRIBLE MONSTER!
I MAKE THE LION TURN TAIL AND RUN!
I *CRUSH* THE CAMEL UNDER ONE FOOT!
I CLEAN MY *TEETH* WITH THE EAGLE'S BEAK!
I HAVE TAKEN POWER OF THIS WELL FOR MYSELF!
I...AM...IN-VINCE-ABLE!
BEGONE.
BEGONE.
BEGONE.

At first it seemed like the frog had miscalculated, since the commotion caused animals of all sorts to gather near this well that most of them had passed by many times without a thought.

Whenever an animal approached, the frog would slide into the water and bob up and down, causing the water's surface to ripple, turning the reflection of whoever was peering down, into the face of a fearsome creature gazing up. Hearing the bold assertion and seeing that terrible sight was enough to make anyone jump back in fright.

One by one, each animal found the courage to creep up to the wall of the well and peer over. The first to try his luck was a plucky rooster who hopped up onto the stony rim of the well to see what the fuss was all about. Before he could fold his wings he was greeted by a second salvo of the frog's booming challenge.

I AM A MOST TERRIBLE MONSTER!
I MAKE THE LION TURN TAIL AND RUN!
I *CRUSH* THE CAMEL UNDER ONE FOOT!
I CLEAN MY *TEETH* WITH THE EAGLE'S BEAK!
I HAVE TAKEN POWER OF THIS WELL FOR MYSELF!
I...AM...IN-VINCE-ABLE!
BEGONE.
BEGONE.
BEGONE.

Crowing as if he had landed on hot coals, the rooster sprang backwards, flapping his wings as he fell against the ground. When he scurried back to the other animals, they asked what he'd seen. He just stood there shaking, saying nothing—not a peep—like a ghost.

By and by, a cow, a dog, and a goat tried it in succession, and they, too, ran in panic back to the others. Finally a sweet, young donkey couldn't stand it anymore. She had to know what was causing all that bother. She clopped over, loud as she could, letting that water monster know *it* wasn't the only big thing in the world.

Peering into the shadowy well and hearing the reverberating threat rolling up once again, her ears stood on end and she, too, turned and ran. Braying, her tail stretched out straight behind, she crashed smack into a clump of bushes before turning to look back, only her trembling ears and wide eyes visible through the leaves.

This went on all morning. By noon nearly every animal who used the well, and many who normally didn't, had taken a turn. They huddled together nearby, trying to shake the sound of their own screams out of their ears, each reporting something more fearsome than the last.

The entire time, a small, walnut-brown monkey sat on a large stone at a safe distance watching the parade and observing the antics, scratching first her head, then her belly, then her head again. At last it was her turn to peer into the well, and she did so with great fanfare, striding up to the wall with enormous steps, then bounding up onto the ledge, and of course making her monkey faces at the water below.

With each funny face she laughed louder and louder, not so much at herself as at the foolish animals who had scared themselves half to death by seeing their own reflections in the glistening, dark water.

Then the monkey made a noose from a rope of woven vines, and she carefully fished out the frog—who sat blinking in the sunlight that bore down on the dusty clearing. Woefully he continued to proclaim his monstrous wrath.

> I am a...a most terrible...er, umm...
> I make the, the lion turn tail and...I, uh...

The monkey then called to the other animals to come closer and face the source of their fright.

"After all," the monkey laughed, "You weren't completely wrong. Had you taken the care to catch a good look at him, well then, his appearance *is* a teeny-tiny bit horrendous, isn't it?"

~ ~ ~

Chuckling as I always did at the end of this story, I adjusted the wooden yoke on my shoulders and turned to look down the road toward our village well. Now the midsummer sun beat down mercilessly like a hammer pounding on a spike. It hadn't rained in weeks, and the streams and waterholes were mostly bone dry.

The air shimmered up ahead, and my ears rang faintly with the sound of softly clanging bells and a low singsong chanting. I shook my head to clear my ears and realized with relief it wasn't me succumbing to the heat, but the dirge-like voices of people approaching the well from the other side. At first, I couldn't understand the words. So I took a few steps down the road, buckets swishing. As I began walking, the voices grew clearer.

"Unclean!" they wailed. "Unclean! Unclean!"

Fear stabbed me. What was unclean? The well! Could the water be polluted by some dead animal? We depended on that well. Especially in the dry season.

I walked faster. The chanting was growing louder. Passing Yeshu's workshop, I glanced in. My carpenter friend was looking up, his eyes wide. I stopped and waited as he put his tools down and came out.

He entered the road already walking fast, rushing right by me as I hurried to catch up. "What do they mean by 'unclean' Yeshu?" I yelled out to his back. "What's unclean? The water?"

He said nothing, but the set of his jaw told me how determined he felt. But about what? By now I was trotting. "Yeshu?" I repeated, puffing.

Glancing down, he reached over, without missing a step, and effortlessly took the yoke from my shoulder onto his. Freed from the weight, my heart gradually slowed as I caught my breath.

"They are calling themselves unclean," he said, walking and staring down the road toward the ragged group of strangers milling in front of the well.

"Yeshu, I don't understand."

He seemed to be thinking aloud as we advanced. "They have a disease called leprosy. No one knows what causes it. The sickness is terrible and the dread and rejection it brings makes the suffering even harder to bear.

"Fingers and toes rot on the body and fall off. Sometimes even a person's nose. Soon you'll see for yourself." He quickened his pace, and every few steps I had to break into a full trot, just to keep up.

"Everyone is afraid of them," Yeshu went on, "terrified of catching the sickness through touch or even by breathing the same air. These people have been cast out by their neighbors and some by their families, condemned to wander from village to village. No one will hire them, even the skilled ones. Homeless, they beg, picking through trash for a scrap of food or a rag to wrap round their wounds.

"On top of everything else, they've lost their names. People call these wretched souls 'lepers,' as if leprosy were their mother and father. Or their home village. Those lucky enough to have escaped this affliction have taken to forcing those who haven't to warn of their approach with bell and voice.

"Adding to their injury, these folks who already suffer unbearably must condemn themselves to live as outcasts. Those who choose to walk in silence, who do not loudly brand themselves, could be stoned to death.

"So that's what you hear, Daavi. That and the agony of blameless souls being shunned by others whom they have no wish to harm."

"What are you going to do?" I asked him.

"Whatever I can," he answered.

By then we were close. I could clearly see the strangers now, standing together facing us. I forgot to keep my eyes on the road and nearly tripped and fell. What I saw was more awful than anything Yeshu had described.

These homeless wanderers were painfully thin, like splinters of pine wood, and it hurt to look at them. Their hair was long and stringy, matted with dirt. Their clothing was threadbare and it was impossible to tell if the rotting smell came from their unwashed robes or from the open sores they couldn't hide. Many had crooked sticks to pair up with a good leg while they limped along dragging the stub of a foot bound in yellowish and blood-stained rags. Some carried others who were old or too crippled to walk. One had a face that resembled melted wax.

As I stared, they continued to slowly wail out their searing song, "Unclean! Unclean!"

I felt Yeshu wince as he gripped my arm.

Then I spotted a boy in the group, not much older than I, peering out from behind a woman's shoulder. I would not forget him because he had one blue eye and one brown, and I had never seen blue eyes before. He held a hand to his face, with one finger missing and half of another. I felt overwhelmed with guilt and pity. And, yes, horror.

That was when I became aware of a crowd forming. Our neighbors, folks I saw every day, were all screaming, "Go away! Shame on you for endangering innocent people. Get away from our well!"

Some even picked up stones and threw them. But the forlorn group would not fall back. They began pleading for water, and for food.

I looked around for Yeshu. He was gone. For a moment I thought to myself: Had he fled? Was he afraid like the others?

Then I saw him at the well, filling my buckets with water. He hefted the dripping vessels to his shoulders and began walking toward the band of outcasts.

I frowned, torn in half. A voice in one ear whispered, "How could you have doubted him?" In the other ear I heard, "But what will Mother and Father say when they learn I let Yeshu use our buckets for this?"

The townspeople were aghast, but no one dared challenge the tall, willful carpenter. As Yeshu approached, the outcasts began backing away. Stones and taunts would not move them, but fear of physical contact with a "clean" person did.

"Put the water down over there!" one shouted out. "Don't touch us!"

"I was touched by you the moment I saw you," Yeshu answered, smiling wryly. "If someday I must share the burden you bear so bravely, so be it."

He nodded his head firmly, sighed, then exclaimed, as if the thought were forming on his lips, "Doing nothing would scar me far worse."

They stared back blankly, befuddled.

Then Yeshu brightened. What he said next revealed he'd found, in his mind, a middle ground where it was safe for these forlorn souls to approach.

"Do you have water pots?" he asked.

Quickly, they produced partially broken pots and weathered gourds from inside their ragged packs. Yeshu walked from person to person, filling the outstretched containers to the brim. All of them drank as though they had not tasted water for a week.

Yeshu filled their containers again.

After he finished, he turned to the townspeople. "Bring me bread," he asked of them. "Please. Even if it's a week old."

No one moved.

"For the love of God, lend a hand. These people are starving," he implored. "How many of us haven't struggled through a famine? Or a bad harvest? We have all known hunger."

He waited, then said, "The Jubilee Year is coming. We can start early—today!"

Still no one moved. Most just stared at the ground.

Yeshu's face began to color. I could tell by the way people were standing that if he yelled at them they would all run.

"Yeshu," I called to him. "I'll round up your story group."

He understood instantly and relaxed, nodding slightly.

I ran through the town, rallying kids to bring Yeshu all the bread they could find. A mob of children soon formed at the well. We knew where every scrap of bread was, including pieces that had sat on a shelf for an entire phase of the moon. Many of us would have less to eat that night than we usually did, but it would be worth it.

Yeshu set down my water buckets and began handing out the bread, dropping the hardest pieces into bowls of water that the outcasts extended to him. As soon as the bread softened, they snatched it up with cupped hands and slurped it down. Yeshu laughed, and they laughed back.

Some had no teeth at all.

Then I saw his shoulders rise and settle as he took a deeper breath and let it out. People in the crowd probably concluded he'd been standing out in the sun too long when, one by one, he went up to each person in that group of lost souls and gave them something worth more than bread and water.

He touched each one.

This man on the shoulder; that woman on the hand. The young boy whose eyes had met mine—one eye brown, the other blue—received a stroke on the cheek. The boy smiled broadly and leaned his head back, showing his face to the sky.

"God bless you!" declared an old woman after Yeshu had embraced her tenderly and moved on to the next.

Yeshu returned and took her by the shoulders. "God continually blesses all of us," he said. "The question is will *you* bless me?"

She stared at him for a moment, her mouth agape. Then she reached out and touched her fingertips to his forehead. The entire group of outcasts cheered, and we kids joined in. Yeshu smiled broadly.

Turning my head, I stole a fleeting look back at the crowd of neighbors, who now seemed like strangers to me. It was then I saw my father. He was standing behind everyone else, his back against a wall. His face was gray, and his shoulders slumped. He seemed anxious, as if cornered, and there was a look in his eyes that I had never seen before. Pain too sad to bear. I twisted round to check on Yeshu, and when I turned back to see what was happening with my father, he was gone.

Scrutinizing the crowd, I could see people I had known my whole life. They seemed like strangers to me now. As I searched their faces for a hint of compassion, I suddenly thought I heard an owl cry out in the distance, but I knew that was not possible. It was broad daylight.

Shaking the sound from my ears, I returned my attention to the crowd. The people continued to stand rigidly silent, their eyes hard as stones. They seemed farther away now, smaller.

That silence lifted soon enough. Many townspeople would complain for days afterward about Yeshu's foolhardiness. A delegation was even sent to talk to Mama Maria. Those who came believed that she, as the new town midwife, should know better when it came to keeping things clean and safeguarding our children.

"Your son shows no respect for rules," they said. "Now we will be overrun by every filthy leper for miles around."

Mama Maria would have none of it. "Unclean is in our minds," she replied, her jaw set firmly. "It's a way of *seeing*, not being. None of us gets through life without illness. Illness is not a mark of sin." She shook her head adamantly. "It's a sign of bad fortune.

"You know my son has his own way of approaching life and human suffering. Why not ask him to explain?"

She looked each one in the eye. "And remember, tomorrow begins Yom Kippur, our time for atonement. Are you ready to repent your wrongs against others? Have you earned forgiveness by changing your hearts?"

The townspeople just went away grumbling. Who did she think she was? A rabbi?

As for me, I walked home that afternoon feeling like the hero of the Great Bread Raid. But that bravado soon faded. Late that night, falling asleep in bed, all I could think of was the boy I had seen, holding his disfigured hand to his face, and looking at me with his striking eyes.

I wondered if he was sleeping now. If so, where? What kind of life would he have?

I wished I had gone up and hugged him.

When sleep finally rolled over me, I dreamt I was lost in that dark forest that had enveloped me more than once in the past.

The darkness was so profound, I could not even catch sight of my own hands, or touch my face to reassure myself that I was still there.

All around me, I could hear people milling aimlessly about. But when I called out for help, the only response I heard back was their footsteps hurrying away.

Rage to Love

The next morning I went to visit Yeshu in his workshop to share with him what I felt about the people at the well the day before; and to recount the dream that followed. After I finished, he looked into my eyes for a long time, saying nothing. Finally, he stood up and went to the door. He pointed to the remains of a goat carcass across the road.

"Guilt and pity," he said, "are as useless as that rotting heap. They are feelings that will paralyze us, leaving those they sting as lifeless as that poor old goat with its bloated belly and its legs stuck out stiffly."

"But I feel terrible," I said. "That boy with one blue eye and one brown, why didn't I go up and hug him, or give him my cloak or a new bowl or something?

"I felt bad for him. Now I feel like I failed him," I wiped my brow, "and myself."

Yeshu tilted his head slightly to the side, thinking about what I'd said.

"It's good that you feel so dissatisfied," he finally said, still facing the doorway. "It's easy to believe that guilt and pity prove our worth, and leave it at that. But if we truly feel bad for someone who's in trouble, we must gather up all our understanding and compassion so as to push beyond guilt to another level of feeling that actually leads to something useful."

He paused again and turned back toward me.

"In order to accomplish that," he went on carefully, "sometimes we have to look within ourselves and ask our hearts to muster the compassion that can leaven our outrage and our terror."

I flinched when he said that. Yeshu had seen what I had been unable to see, that my guilt and pity were covering the gripping anger and fear

I had felt at seeing that boy and his companions in such misery. Misery that could touch me, or my family.

"But how?" I asked. "How can I do that?"

Yeshu tugged at his beard with one hand while he lifted the other. His lips moved slightly, as if he were testing different words. Then his eyes returned to mine.

"It isn't easy. But it *is* possible."

He pointed at me abruptly with a single thumb. "First, learn to recognize injustice. You did that yesterday. Don't turn away! Feel the anger and fear that come like hungry wolves. Watch them carefully so they cannot devour you. If they do, the flock will also be in danger. But if you keep still and do not strike out, the wolves will also wait."

He pointed his other thumb at me. "Then let your heart reach out to ask the wolf what it truly wants. Within that white-hot rage you will find love yearning to answer in a language you didn't know you could speak.

"Soon thereafter, you'll know what to do in order to mold rage into love, and love into action."

He walked back to his workbench and picked up a freshly cut cedar board. I watched and waited. He held the reddish-hued plank straight out and inspected each face and edge for flaws or blemishes.

"It's a path that first changes you, Daavi, so that you can in turn change something you sense is wrong in the world. It's like using a blazing oven to make dough into bread. Or to fire clay into durable water pots."

Summer storms swept across his eyes. "Rage is a lot like heat. Both of these can be tempered and directed, in order to make something new."

I strained to understand, while Yeshu thought aloud a bit longer.

"But never forget," he said, "that the love whose voice we hear has to lead us to act. And the action must be constructive. You cannot fool yourself into believing that destruction is justified by what you will build after destroying. That's a false path that will lead you backward like a crazed animal fleeing into a burning building.

"Keep your eyes on love and compassion, so they can reshape that which begins as burning rage. So that in the end, the rage will be of value.

"Do you see, Daavi?"

I listened hard, but the words were ants swarming around something that seemed just a bit too big for me to grasp.

Yeshu noticed the perplexed expression on my face, and setting the board down on his workbench, he picked up a chisel and a wooden mallet. At times like this, when he was searching for words, he often took up a tool and began using it.

For a long while he worked in silence, shaping the board so that it would fit flawlessly into the other pieces of the door he was making. Occasionally he glanced up at me and then returned to his work. I felt my mind calming.

After a good while, Yeshu leaned on the workbench, still holding the tools, and stared at the scarred surface of the bench top.

Then he looked intently back at the tools and said, "When I was growing up, my father, my Abba Yosef, taught me that life is a craft just like woodworking. What I'm talking to you about doing is very hard, Daavi, much harder than making this cedar door. Harder even than building a temple for God.

"Turning rage to love and love to action is a skill one learns by doing. And it helps to have a good teacher, don't you agree? Someone who can guide you along your path."

I nodded at him, a smile pushing its way across my compressed lips.

His eyes brightened. "I've had many!"

I blinked.

"All of us are still learning," he went on, "learning how to craft acts of love from rage. It hasn't been done perfectly yet. Or only rarely, here and there.

"But when we get it right, it will be like the most beautiful door you've ever seen. Like a door to an inn that opens when you are tired and weary, and rather than turning you away the owner welcomes you in. Like a door that is opened when you knock on it; a door into the heaven that is within us all, right here on this earth."

I sat without speaking as I pondered how skillful Yeshu was at explaining one thing by describing another. Each time was like hearing a small story with a quick, clear point.

Yeshu was quiet, as well, for a long time. Finally he lay his mallet and chisel down again, side by side, and he began pacing back and forth through the wood chips on the workshop floor, raising a small cloud of sawdust each time he pivoted. It was a cloud that the sunlight spilling through the door briefly turned into a small burst of sparks.

"Those people we met yesterday—what they really need is fairness," he insisted, "not charity." His jaw was set firmly.

"They need wells of their own rather than a few sips from ours to wet parched lips. Worse yet, drops of water that had to be begged for. And at great risk."

He locked his fingers together in front of his chest. "Until the day comes when they can return home and live among their own people, they must have not just wells, but land and the tools to work it so that they can live decently together and feed themselves."

Yeshu stared out the door to the spot where I had stood just the day before, the spot from which you could look down the road and see our town well.

"One day we will help them do this, you and I." He shifted his gaze back to me.

When Yeshu said that, whenever he said anything like that to me, I felt pleased and special—the way he always made me feel. I was ready to set off down the road that had been laid out; able to fly almost. At first I could see us striding toward that well together, full of purpose. Then a moment later it seemed impossibly out of my reach—like I was alone and walking over a cliff.

If only I could have seen into the future.

~ ~ ~

Slowly I ambled back home, turning a notion over and over in my head: When I was with Yeshu, it always felt like I was on a journey of some kind. Or about to leave on one. But I had rarely been out of Nazareth, except to take sheep up to the pasture above town, or to visit my Gramma Ruth. Would I ever go anywhere else? Yeshu had traveled afar, would I?

Staring at the plate, I hardly spoke while I chewed my dinner. Out of the corner of my eye, I could see my mother watching me.

That night I had a second dream. It was twilight, and I was all alone in the desert. I felt intense hunger and thirst, so deeply I wanted to weep, but I had no tears.

Suddenly a lone figure stood before me and I tasted bread in my mouth. And cool water on my lips.

I closed my eyes and opened them again.

Wide.

A sob escaped me as the tears streamed down my cheeks.

It was the carpenter.

Stones to Fruit

The day following Yom Kippur, Mama Maria headed over to our house with a newly baked loaf of bread for my mother. Smelling the scent of the warm bread as she passed underneath my perch in the walnut tree, I closed my eyes and saw my sister's lovely face rejoicing over a big, round bread loaf being pulled fresh from an oven. Shoshana loved baking day and always took me along. For a moment I smiled on the inside.

When Mama Maria looked up and saw several of us boys high above her, pretending we were Michael's angels keeping watch from the ancient tree, she lured us down with that sweet-smelling bread. Then she sat herself under the tree with her back against the trunk, and we all crowded around her.

We were hoping not only for a snack, but maybe a story as well. Mama Maria had learned storytelling at her mother's knee, which is only one of the reasons why she was so good at it. She didn't much like talking to large groups, as did her mother Mama Ana until advancing age kept her from traveling to weddings or funerals. Or as Yeshu would do one day, and perhaps till the end of time. No, Mama Maria preferred just a handful of listeners, and the younger the better.

After passing around warm chunks of bread that she tore from the newly baked loaf, Mama Maria suddenly reached over and picked up two small stones, dropping them in her lap. She started speaking just softly enough that all of us kids stopped giggling and tussling with one another, so we could listen.

Two older girls climbed down from the mulberry tree across the road, where they had been eating the ripe fruit. They hurried over and flopped on the ground, their hands and lips purple from the juicy berries.

Mama Maria began. "This is a story about changing stones into fruit!"

There were startled faces all around the circle.

"When we are out, looking around at the world as it is," she went on, "stones can be seen everywhere. They lie along the roadside, among the roots of forest trees, on the bottoms of streams. In all different shapes, sizes, and colors."

From her lap she lifted up a round greenish stone, which fit perfectly in the well of her cupped hand.

"It doesn't seem like much does it? A larger stone can be used to pound a tent stake in before a wedding feast. Or if you were strong enough, like Samson, you could even lift one big enough to hurl in fury through a closed wooden door or a window.

"A palm-sized stone can be cracked against another one, to see which one chips first. Or it can be aimed at a person."

She drew back her hand as if preparing to throw a missile. We all just laughed at her.

"David killed the giant Goliath with a single stone no larger than this one," she said, opening her hand and displaying it between her thumb and forefinger.

We suddenly became quiet and the youngest children stared, wide-eyed.

"But what is it that *we* would do with stones?"

She looked round the circle at every face.

"We could pick up a stone in each hand." She showed us the second one, in her other palm, "and rub them together, and scrape them, and work on them like this...." She rubbed the two stones against one another, scrunching up her face in the process.

"As long as it takes us to turn them into a small mound of dust." Unknitting her brow, she stopped grinding the stones.

"Next we search for a seed, and we plant the seed in the pile of dust. We sprinkle it with water, and we wait.

"The seed sprouts. And soon it dies. The dust is lacking in richness.

"We plant another seed, and again we water it. We make sure that it gets enough warm sunlight.

"That seed sprouts. And *it* dies." She paused.

"Once again we plant a seed. We give it water and sun. And we wonder how it's going to do this time.

"And once again the seed sprouts. And it dies."

For a second time she scanned the faces in the circle.

"This doesn't stop us! We keep rubbing stones, planting new seeds, and nurturing them, and one after another they die.

"One day there is enough fertile soil formed from the stone dust and all the tiny lifeless seedlings. We carefully gather this soil, and we lay it on a large stone with a bowl-shaped center. We mix the soil with our fingers, and then we stir in a little water.

"Again we plant a seed and put it in the sunlight, and we give it water every day. This time it grows and takes root!"

She leaned forward. So did we.

"We plant another seed. And another. Nearly all sprout and grow. And each one eventually dies and is transformed back into soil.

"Finally, we have enough of that soil for a tree. We plant a tree seed and give it all the care it needs. As we nurture it, the young seedling sends down roots, and it becomes a sapling. We transplant this small tree to a place in front of our house, where we can tend it daily. Its branches grow toward the sky."

Mama Maria raised her hands above her face. We all looked up, mouths open.

"Like the rhythms and verses of a song," she went on, "the seasons change and the years pass by. Eventually our tree flowers, and that very year, after the petals fall, it bears fruit!

"We share the fruit with our family, our friends, our neighbors, and those who have very little and would otherwise go hungry.

"And we enjoy our fruit together, in quiet moments, savoring each bite as those around us do. Basking in the closeness.

"If our companions ask where the fruit came from, we tell them the story of how it fell from a tree...that grew from a seed...that was planted in stones.

"There are many such stones that lie around us." Mama Maria brought the story back to its beginning. "And *you* know what to do with them."

Smiling, she reached out with both hands, and glancing up at us now and again, she gathered up handfuls of stones and put them in her lap. She stood and held the front of her skirt out to form a cloth basket for the stones. Walking among us, she let each of us pick two of them for rubbing together.

I promised her I would take mine with me the very next day to make them sing as I did my chores, minding our neighbors' sheep.

A Voice Cries Out from the Wilderness

As I got older, this shepherding for my uncles and the occasional neighbor kept me busier and busier. It was well known that I was skilled as a shepherd and would tend the herd of anyone who would give me a coin for my efforts; which I then turned over to my mother. It made me feel like I was pulling my weight in the family, but it also left me less time for stories. Still, I never stopped visiting Yeshu during spare moments.

One day when I was about ten, a local well digger—one of the village men who were always meeting together at night—ran into Yeshu's workshop while I was there, and implored him to come to the river. Yeshu hurried out the door.

I started home, but then my curiosity stopped my feet, and I turned on a heel and followed behind them to the bend in the stream at the outskirts of Nazareth.

Yohanan was there!

Kids were crazy about Yohanan, and I was no different. He always played and danced with us when he came to Nazareth. He wore animal skins and a camel's hair cloak. And he looked just like the descriptions in the scrolls of the great prophet Elijah.

Yohanan ate locusts and never cut his hair or beard, but that didn't scare us. It just made him all the more fascinating. We couldn't understand why the soldiers were always after him. What threat to Rome was this wild man, eating his insects and honey?

More than once, though, my father insisted, "Yohanan's voice is going to change the world."

But being with Yohanan was too exciting for me to think twice about all that. We would sit around him for hours to hear what it was like to live alone in the hills, and how bad King Herod was acting. And though we listened and nodded our heads in agreement, what we were really intent on doing was weaving wildflowers into his great, tangled beard and sticking shafts of wheat into his hair.

Eventually he would sneeze and the spell would snap. With that he would grab at us with his hairy hands and let out a lion's roar as we scattered across the field like wild pheasants, flapping our arms and squealing.

But even if his words floated past us, his life made us think. Lying in bed at night I would picture Yohanan when he was still quite young, trekking deep into the wilderness to live as a man of the spirit. To listen to swaying tree branches and field mice feet and moonlit sky, all commenting about life; and in their murmuring, to overhear God's thoughts. For Yohanan, journeying into the desert in search of solitude was just like Moses going to his mountaintop.

Yeshu took even greater interest in all of this. He was always talking about Yohanan's purpose in life and quoting to us from his teachings. He told us how he and Yohanan traded stories and debated about God's plan for humankind, and about whether our world would ever change. As Yeshu looked at us one by one, to see if we had listened, he would smile broadly as though he were gazing out over the Promised Land.

That day at the river, I saw Yeshu and Yohanan embracing like lost brothers. It had been nearly half a year since they had seen one another, and they had much to share. They sat on the bank talking the morning away, their voices mingling with the sounds of rippling water.

Yeshu had told me time and again how he and Yohanan had known each other for many years—ever since they were toddlers. I already knew that they were related through their mothers. Yeshu said that as they were growing up, they saw each other regularly, especially when Yohanan's mother Elisheva came to Nazareth to visit her much-loved relatives, Mama Ana and Mama Maria. And then, of course, there was every spring when Yosef and Mama Maria took the family to Jerusalem for Passover. Yohanan's father, Zachariah was a priest in the Temple there, and Elisheva was also from a priestly family, so this was a special time for all of them.

Before Shoshana vanished and our family conversations went cold, my father loved to talk to me about Yohanan and Yeshu. He told me, "Since their mothers were cousins, and the births were around the same time, those two played together like twin brothers. As babies, they were always crawling off in different directions but finally arriving in the same spot, laughing like bigger children playing hide and seek with their shadows.

"Even now," he went on, "it seems to me they are taking separate paths toward similar ends. And those paths will be forever entwined, crisscrossing into eternity.

"Take Yohanan," he said. "He was born of aging parents. His mother Elisheva seemed much too old to have a child, whereas Cousin Maria was barely out of childhood herself when the two baby boys were born.

"The way I see it, Daavi," my father went on, "Yohanan comes in out of the wilderness to bring its voice to people who cannot hear it; anointing us with the living waters of the earth. But just like a storm, he can't be still and soon moves on. Yeshu immerses himself in the heart of the people he lives and works among, and when he faces a crisis or feels that he is drying up inside, he journeys back into the wilderness in search of the cool healing hand of the natural world.

"Reflect on them closely, Daavi. Yeshu has the moon and the stars in his eyes. Yohanan's eyes burn with sun fire. He speaks straight from his heart, without considering what is prudent. The temple police chased him out of Jerusalem. Their bosses, the chief priests and the High Priest," my father explained, "want Yohanan silenced for good." Father shook his head.

"The aging Zachariah and a few other older priests stuck up for Yohanan," he went on, "but no one listened. The higher authorities only wanted to hear that someone, anyone, could get this ragged, disloyal agitator to shut up."

I frowned, thinking about what this could mean, but my father didn't notice, he just pushed on. "Without Yohanan, Yeshu might simply live out his life as a carpenter," my father concluded, looking off into space, "and die in bed surrounded by grandchildren stroking his beard and asking for another story."

He paused to stare at his feet.

"But I'm convinced that will not be."

~ ~ ~

Watching the two of them laughing by the river that day, conspiring like kids, I was worried about Yohanan, but glad that nobody was angry with my friend and neighbor, Yeshu.

Abba

One day at noon, fetching water from the well, I ran into three of Yeshu's close friends: Martha and Miriam, who were sisters, and Joanna. I knew from Yeshu that he had been close to the two sisters since he was a boy, after he and his parents returned home from Egypt. They had all been neighbors and had often run errands together when their mothers needed fresh herbs from the fields or kindling from the forests for the cooking fire. That was before Martha and Miriam's family moved home to Bethany to take care of their elderly grandparents. Now they were back in Nazareth for the high holidays.

Joanna had come from Jerusalem a few months before on her annual visit to relatives in Nazareth. Her husband Chuza had served for many years as the man who managed the household of Herod Antipas, the Jewish King of Galilee. Chuza died suddenly one day, clutching his chest. Having also been steward of the King's estates for many years, he had done quite well—both for the king and for his own family.

Joanna had always found court life tiresome and frivolous. She had first become fascinated by what Yohanan was saying about how we should live, and what our rules should be for relating to all other living things, human and otherwise. Now that she was widowed and childless, she was free to live as she pleased. And what pleased her most was to use her wealth for what she believed in.

I began telling the three women about my special friendship with Yeshu: how I helped out in his carpentry shop; what great fun all of us kids had listening to him tell us stories; how we sought out accounts of his childhood from anyone who knew him back then.

Martha and Miriam just nodded while I burbled on. Finally they asked if I had known Yeshu's father before he died. He had been like a second father to them they said, and to all the children in the village. They suggested that perhaps I should ask Yeshu what his beloved "Abba" was like.

So I did. I went straight to his workshop, plunked myself down on a stool, and after waiting a bit, asked him, "Yeshu, tell me about your daddy, your Abba."

Yeshu had been planing a board when I walked in, and he kept right on doing so, the wood curls flying through the air and dropping softly to the floor among countless others. For a long time, he said nothing. I looked at his eyes and saw storms brewing there.

I got scared. Maybe I had said the wrong thing.

I stood up.

"Sit down," he said softly.

I sat down.

Still he did not talk, but continued to work. Furrows appeared on his brow, and I saw his chest rise.

Then he smiled gently and stopped working.

"Do you see this smoothing plane?" he asked.

I nodded.

"My Abba's."

I waited.

"And this workbench?" I nodded again.

"My Abba worked here. And here he taught me to be a craftsman, to pay attention to detail and beauty. Not just usefulness."

His fingertips traveled lightly across the grooves and other markings of history that crisscrossed the bench.

My eyes followed his hands over the surface and along the grain of the workbench. It shone like mahogany from decades, no, from generations of use. It gleamed through the thin layer of sawdust, with a deep finish made of body oils and sweat from long days of labor.

"And these hands," Yeshu asked, "Do you see them?"

Setting the plane down on the board, he raised his arms high until the sleeves of his cloak slid to his elbows as I watched.

"My father's hands."

My eyes moved to Yeshu's hands. They were very striking—dark brown and marked with scars like a wall of sheer sandstone etched by wind and rain. The sinews and veins and muscles pushed through the skin on the back of each hand.

Yeshu closed one, then the other, and bringing them together until they touched, he looked upward.

"May fathers and sons forever stand side by side, like this," he said.

Then he put his hands back down on the surface of the workbench.

"When I was a boy," Yeshu went on, "even younger than you, my father's friends called me his *tsel*. In Hebrew that means 'shadow.'"

Yeshu laughed heartily, the sound thundering up out of his chest.

"Everywhere my Abba Yosef went, I tagged along. When he headed out on an errand, his tsel was at his hip, matching each step of his with two of mine."

I nodded.

Yeshu pushed his hair away from his forehead. "I remember my father would touch my head and answer his friends, 'One day I will be in my tsel's shadow.' This would spark a knowing smile in the older ones.

"We were inseparable, my Abba and I. When he sat in the sun talking to my Grandfather Yakob, I sat in Abba's lap, hanging on every word they spoke."

Yeshu's eyes had drifted and were looking far away.

"I would listen for hours while they talked," Yeshu said. "My grandfather's hair and beard were white as an egret, and he always wore a dark robe. People called him 'Rabbi,' but his only training was as a carpenter and builder."

Yeshu's eyes brightened as if he had just found something precious, or maybe amusing, long forgotten. "I used to call him my 'Abba-Abba'—even after being corrected. Someone would say, 'No one can be a Daddy-Daddy. The proper term is '*Sabbah*.'

"I would just smile and say, 'That's right! Abba-Abba Yakob.'

I knew that would always get a laugh and squeeze out of my Abba Yosef and *his* father, my Abba-Abba Yakob."

I chuckled with Yeshu. I wished I had known my own grandfather, to be able to call him Abba-Abba, too.

Then Yeshu became serious.

"The more I grew up, the less I needed to be my Abba's shadow."

He pointed at the tools on the bench.

"We worked together and traveled together, and he taught me all he knew about shaping wood to fit people's needs."

Yeshu went back to his planing.

After a while, I asked, "Yeshu, what happened to your Abba?"

He stopped abruptly, a wood curl arching up, trembling just above the plane's blade. He was quiet for what seemed like ages, gazing down at his hands gripping the tool. I held my breath until finally he cleared his throat and spoke.

"I had just turned thirteen. It was the winter following the Passover when I remained in the Temple in Jerusalem for three days, talking to the rabbis."

Yeshu paused. "My father didn't look so good all that season. His face was gray and his walk had slowed. He dropped tools in the workshop."

I stared at Yeshu's tools, knowing he spoke of these very ones.

He went on. "One evening Abba went to bed very early, just after the sun had gone down. Mama Maria and Mama Ana had gone to the synagogue with my brothers and sisters, so Abba and I were alone. He called me over to the side of the bed, saying he had something important to tell me. I sat still on the edge and our eyes met. Lying in the deepening shadow that was purplish as a bruise, Abba suddenly seemed very, very old."

Yeshu's voice sounded old too, at that moment, almost gravelly. "Abba took hold of my hands and he looked up at me for a long time. Then he smiled softly and whispered, 'My work with you is done, but you will not be alone. Others will step in.'"

Yeshu's gaze dropped to the tools on the bench. He picked up a smooth whetstone, started to sharpen a chisel, and stopped.

"His last words to me were, 'Take care of your mother. Keep the family together. Always be true to yourself and others.'

"My eyes were locked on Abba's, and I gave my promise with a nod.

"Then he squeezed my hands. 'God is near!'"

Taking a long, slow breath, Yeshu straightened all the tools on the bench, wiping the sawdust off lightly, rearranging them again, slowly letting the breath out.

For a long while, he stared down at the tools. Then he said, "I'm always struck by how Abba continues to lead me, long after he has gone."

I looked into Yeshu's eyes. They were brimming with tears that pierced my heart like the brightest stars of a winter sky.

"You really miss your Abba, don't you, Yeshu," I said.

He bowed his head, silent.

Finally he said, "I miss him every day—even though I know he is next to God."

He paused and raised his face slowly. "Sometimes I think of him as part of God."

Quiet again.

"Other times he's the touch of God's hand."

I touched Yeshu's hand and then slipped outside, not knowing what more to say, leaving him there in the workshop with his God and his Abba.

~ ~ ~

I also knew how it felt to really miss someone cherished. At first it's like being kicked in the chest so you can't breathe. When that passes, you still can't bear being touched. It's as if the lost embrace has scraped away skin, leaving you wounded and haunted.

The numbing ache for my sister Shoshana had become my constant companion. It tailed me like my shadow. Shoshana had been swallowed up before I had a chance to come into my own. At night I cried out in my sleep and during the day broke into tears for no reason.

Then finally, one day, I just closed up. I couldn't stand my parents looking away from each other, and from me, whenever I said her name.

Sometimes my mother would shut her eyes tight and whisper, "Lost," and I'd wonder whom she was talking about, Shoshana or herself or me. Maybe it was all of us.

The house would be hushed and sad for the rest of the day.

But deep inside I couldn't stop asking what had happened. Was Shoshana dead? Or abducted by robbers, perhaps to sell her into slavery? Maybe she ran off with travelers. Did spirits come during the night and carry her away? Did a leopard drag her off to a cave, or did eagles drop down and carry her into the clouds?

Why would no one tell me?

It was crazy of me, but I peered carefully into every cavern and hollow place I came across, and I couldn't stop searching for her face in the sky.

I vowed to someday uncover the truth. And if she were still alive, I would find her and ask who had taken her away, why she had left. Whatever could have caused her to part from those who knew and loved her best?

Shoshana and I had such a special bond. She was the firstborn and I was the second. When barely old enough to stop playing with dolls, she was entrusted with a flesh-and-blood baby to take care of, as Mother struggled for years to regain her health. Though just a girl, Shoshana became—there's no other way to describe it—my second mother for a good long while.

In many ways it was even better, because she didn't have to discipline me or see that there was food in the house to feed me or feel responsible for how I turned out.

She just taught me games and told me funny stories and sang me songs. Oh how she could sing! Even now I can close my eyes and hear her voice on the wind.

She would sit with me for hours, in front of the house or in the cool shade of a tree, singing songs of our people or ballads about the life of someone special. Sometimes her voice was like a cloudless sky, other times it was laced with enthralling shadows. Those feelings stayed with me, and eventually I would associate them with other matters like love and privation.

And then there were the silly songs, full of rhymes and not much reason. They were as irresistible as a brook playing tag with stones.

But there was one song above all the others that took root inside me. It was a lullaby that Shoshana made up herself, perhaps just for me. When she sang it, I felt she was singing me into being. In the song a brave child journeys into sleep, to wander through dreams from which the child always returns home, a day older, with some shining new treasure of wisdom or love.

How did she know how much I longed to travel? Or did her lullaby stoke the fires of that yearning?

She sang it to me night after night, even when I was too old for lullabies. But I would beg for it, and we would sing it together. Her voice was not the kind that lulled you to forgetfulness, making you snuggle up into blankets that you pulled over your head to shut out the darkness. No, her voice opened doors and windows to the dreaming promised by the song. Often it made me feel awake and asleep all at once.

With Shoshana, I felt warm, happy, and calm. And yet a part of me also grew adventuresome. After she was gone, a dry well opened deep inside me that no other voice could fill.

Surely this is one reason I later joined Yeshu on his journeys. "Seek and you shall find," he would say. "Knock and it will be opened to you."

In my ensuing travels, I never gave up hope of hearing a passing word, however small, about my sister. I believed that if I just kept searching and searching, one day a clue would turn up that would lead me to her.

Listening to Butterflies

Later that afternoon, I was back in Yeshu's workshop, delivering his drinking water. I put down the full water bucket next to the empty pitcher, then wrapped both arms around it and lifted it up so I could pour the luminous, cool well water into the empty vessel. Setting the leather bucket down again, I peered into the full pitcher, then turned my head and spoke.

"Yeshu, I have a question for you." He looked straight back at me with those dark eyes that could see so deep into a person.

"Ask," he said simply.

"Okay," I went on, swallowing twice to gain some thinking time. "When you pray to God..." Yeshu nodded gently. I started again, "When you pray to God, what do you say?"

I paused. "Do you do most of the talking? Or do you mainly listen?"

Yeshu's eyes widened ever so slightly, as if in surprise. He raised his hand to his beard; one finger aside his cheekbone.

Shaking his head gently, he said, "Daavi, I know many people, even some elders, who could not have phrased that question better than you have done."

He stared down at his workbench.

"In fact," he went on, "I'm going to ask you for a bit of time for me to think about this. I don't want to answer too quickly."

He reached over and picked up a mallet and chisel.

"But I can say right now, that if you ever have a question, about anything—prayer, compassion, love, death—there is a place you can always go to first, in your search for an answer."

I sat up straight, thinking he was making me an offer.

"Do you know where that first place is?" he asked. Not waiting for me to answer, he said, "It's not the synagogue, or the Temple in Jerusalem. And it's not the Torah or the Nevi'im. Sometimes an answer will lie in those places, but it's not every day that you can find a Torah or a synagogue nearby when a question buzzes into your mind, and it just won't settle down or fly away.

"Like right now," he said.

I looked up at him and blinked in anticipation.

"Even so, there is a place where you can *always* go for an answer," he repeated. "That place is inside yourself—in your thoughts; and especially in your heart. God is in there waiting, and if you go deep enough, with God's help you'll find an answer."

I smiled, and Yeshu smiled back, knowing he had tossed me an idea and I had caught it.

Then he turned back to his task, setting down the mallet and beginning to sharpen and oil his chisel. He was preparing to start on the inlaid tabletop he had agreed that very morning to make. For quite a while, his head bent over his work, carefully readying one tool after the other, so that each would function at their very best.

I watched him work. His movements were quick and certain in the way he deftly turned a tool with the fingers of one hand and sharpened it with a whetstone grasped in the other, making a rhythmic, circular motion.

After what seemed like an hour, Yeshu surprised me by suddenly speaking without the slightest warning. "Often I spend my time in prayer just listening."

He flipped a tool over and leaning forward on his stool, inspected the newly sharpened blade in a ray of sunlight. "Listening and waiting in silence for the voice of God to come to me." He leaned back again. "Or to emerge out of me, from deep within."

I imagined myself listening closely, intent on capturing God's words as if each one were a diaphanous, golden butterfly flitting just beyond my fingertips.

"At other times," Yeshu went on, "my prayer contains no words at all, and no waiting. At those moments, my prayer is action." His brow creased.

"I see a child fall and skin her knee, and her shrieks call me closer, and I hold her and rock her to quietness. I meet a person on the road who has no place to sleep, no cloak, no food or water. And I provide what I can, with prayerfulness in my heart.

"*Doing* steps in and replaces speaking. Later on, reflection can kindle new thoughts, even answers.

"So, let's imagine I enter a home, and crouching in the misty shadows is a forlorn soul, lost at sea, storm-tossed, with twisted face, and hands pulling hair. I go straight to that creature and try to throw her a rope to pull her out of the waves. Or I look into her eyes to see if I can spot demons there that I can stare down and force to leave. In living prayer.

"Once, just such a crouching soul was completely deaf. I recognized immediately that she could not hear my greeting. But I could see in her flashing eyes that she was very aware I was reaching out to her, especially in the way those eyes sparkled when I sat on the floor in front of her and began to play hand games.

"Remember when I've showed you how my father taught me to make it appear that I had just removed my thumb from my hand? And then put it back where it belonged?"

I smiled broadly recalling that deft trick.

"Most children are totally baffled by that, throwing looks around the room at one another, or stifling their astonished squeals with the backs of their fists.

"But this child observed me very closely, as a smile spread slowly across her face. Then she signaled with a flip of her wrist that she wanted to see the maneuver again. I complied, and she immediately replicated the trick! Now it was my turn to laugh.

"Laughing was not enough. I stood and motioned to her parents to step outside with me. I told them what a smart daughter they had, and I urged them to have her trained to work with her hands, perhaps to make twine and rope out of cactus fibers.

"To my delight, they agreed. They were pleased to see new possibilities for their—until then—lost child."

"Hooray!" I cried out.

"Hooray for her," he answered. "And for her loving parents."

Yeshu grew quiet. He lifted one last tool off the workbench and began to sharpen it. "And then there are the times," he said, "when I hear a child crying desperately in the night under some neighbor's roof, and I know there is nothing I can do. The mother and father's muffled voices are audible alongside the child's."

He drew in a breath. "So, I simply press my hands together and pray.

> Dear God, Amen.
> Dear God, Amen.

"There's no need for more."

Yeshu looked at me and he could read on my face that my question had been answered.

For now.

My God Is in Wildness

The following morning at the edge of Nazareth, I came upon Yohanan sitting on a slab of rock in a field of wild grasses, wide-eyed and very still like a great predatory bird. I called and waved to him. At first he seemed startled, but then he motioned me over with a quick dip of his beard. I ran to him and stood right in front of where he sat, so that we were looking eye to eye.

Our faces said hello, but neither of us spoke. I surmised he had arrived in the night.

With a long, crooked finger, Yohanan pointed, sweeping his hand from right to left, and stopping at a flowering crab-apple tree. As I turned, my eyes soared across the field like a falcon swooping down to a waiting branch. I stood poised for further flight, glancing over my shoulder at him.

Mouth open, Yohanan at first seemed speechless, but then he leapt to his feet and cried out.

> Praise God, my soul,
>   from the heavens and the heights!
> Praise God, sun and moon;
>   praise God, all you shining stars.
> Praise God, you heaven of heavens,
>   and you waters above the heavens!

Breathless, I stood staring at him. Suddenly he took off, striding over the swaying, bending grasses with his long, sinewy legs. I had to run to catch what he was saying.

His voice sang on.

Praise God from the earth,
you sea monsters and ocean depths;
fire and hail, snow and frost,
stormy winds obeying God's voice;
all mountains and hills,
all fruit trees and all cedars!

Back he strode through the wildflowers with me tailing him, his skins and camel's hair cloak flapping in the breeze, still holding forth.

Wild animals and cattle,
creeping things and winged birds!
Young men and women alike,
elders and youth together;
let all praise the name of God!

I was certain Yohanan was making all this up, right on the spot, but I discovered months later he was reciting poetry from the Tehillim, the Book of Psalms. He loved those old verses. They really got him singing!

And I loved the songs. They moved me to rejoice along with him.

Yohanan sat back down, staring at me and smiling, a single eyebrow raised. He was waiting for me to speak. So I did, with the first thing that came into my mind.

"Yohanan, you hardly sleep at all. You eat honey and insects. No meat, no bread. Where do you get the strength you need to keep going like you do?"

Yohanan looked puzzled as though this had never occurred to him before. He gave several vigorous shakes to his head and beard. Dried blades of grass took to the wind. Even a dragonfly flew out to see what the disturbance was.

"Well," he said, "God feeds me with power whenever I need it." He crossed his arms and sat staring at the sky.

Then he opened his mouth, head thrust back as if to shout, and I could see every one of his teeth. But he didn't shout. He sucked in a lungful of air and exhaled.

"That's why my soul overflows with the power of the spirit!"

For a while he was very quiet. With a downward glance as if to confirm that I was still there, he took in another long, slow breath, and this time let it out slowly through his lips. Finally, he spoke.

"Daavi, my young friend," he said. "God gives me more strength than I can hold." He smiled broadly, lots of teeth again down in that tangled beard. Even his eyes smiled.

I had never seen Yohanan having such trouble expressing himself.

"But *how* does God give it to you?" I asked. "Where does it come from? When..."

Suddenly, he burst out, "From the desert winds. From the mouth of the wolf. From the great rising moon, red and round. From the eagle's wingtips when they touch. From the dusting of stars in the vast dome of night sky. From the dreams I have as I fall asleep. As I roll over in the dark. As I wake up at dawn and stare at the translucent clouds blowing over me."

On and on he went, hardly pausing for air, "From the sight of a young mother fox feeding her first litter of kits. From the sound of my own heart beating like a drum when I see water shimmering at sunset. From the scent of a field of red poppies stitched together by the flight of countless bees seeking *their* power."

He was on his feet.

"From the unfettered laughter of you children at play. From the cry of the hawk as it hunts the vole. From the wing of the butterfly as it climbs the petal's edge. From the leopard's loping..."

"Yohanan!" I yelled out, then took a breath. "Yohanan, stop. No more. That's all I can take in at one time."

I held my head with both hands, as I shook it. "These are mostly things I know nothing about."

He sat back down, pulled on his beard, nodded, then took hold of me by the shoulders.

I looked deep into his eyes, and there I saw flames. I could feel the warmth of his chest radiating against mine, as soothing as the midmorning sun. He smelled like deerskin and honeycombs and wildflowers.

He spoke firmly now and deliberately. "He who comes after me will find God in humankind." He paused briefly.

"My God is in wildness."

I could tell he was finished.

"Yohanan," I said to him, "show me this God of yours! I want to see God like you do."

"That's not as easy as you may think," he replied. Then he went on slowly, "It's not exactly seeing."

"Why not?" I asked. "You see God everywhere. I want to as well."

He looked at me for a long time, silent as an owl inspecting its fledgling in the hollow of an aging sycamore. His gaze moved from my eyes to my mouth, the top of my head, my shoulders, and back to my eyes again.

He reached out and took hold of my hands and lifted them toward his face, turning them over to study my palms. Then he let them fall back to my sides. I guessed that my feathers were just too short for flight. His chin dropped to his chest; his mouth lost in his beard. Perhaps he was done with me for now.

But I was wrong. He opened his eyes wide and I could see that he was more interested than ever.

Slowly, steadfastly, he spoke under his breath, "Daavi, my friend, if you truly want to see God, come into the wilderness."

At that, he sprang to his feet and strode off.

I stood stock still where he had left me, immobilized. How could I go away with him just like that? My mother and father would be worried; they would come looking for me. With one lost child already, how could they survive another?

Or on the other hand...*would* they look? Why would they turn over every stone to find *me* if they hadn't done so for Shoshana?

Our house was already too quiet; wouldn't it then seem like a tomb?

I shrank away from all this questioning, but my thoughts just wouldn't stay still. That's when the conundrum snuck up behind me and tapped me smartly on the back of the head: Just who is this man who is to come after Yohanan? And did it mean Yohanan himself would not be returning? It occurred to me I should have walked along with him part way. Maybe I could have discovered what he meant.

But Yohanan never looked back. I stared at him as he disappeared over a hill.

Had I just lost my chance to see God?

Tiny Lamb, Great Cat

Soon after Yohanan left, I was helping Yeshu in his workshop one windy afternoon when he turned to me, put down the tool in his hand, and said, "Daavi, I've been thinking. I want you to teach me everything you know about shepherding."

"Sure," I said, feeling flattered. "But why, Yeshu? You're a carpenter."

He paused for a moment and then said, "I'll always carry with me the stories that Mama Maria told me about the shepherds who came to see us just after I was born. They brought us food for our very first family meal. Caring for life came so naturally to them. And my Mama welcomed them in to share that first meal with us.

Yeshu's eyes brightened. "That visit from the shepherd family left as forceful an impression on my parents as the arrival later of the three Magi. Neither of those visits feels accidental. And yet I'm still trying to understand just what they mean in my life."

Yeshu paused, then went on. "That's one reason I want to know more about shepherds. After all, during my time here in Nazareth and on the road, I've probably talked to at least seven traveling traders for every *one* shepherd. The other day it suddenly struck me—I'm living next door to one!"

I hid a smile behind my sleeve. I couldn't believe I had a skill to offer Yeshu; something he had decided he needed.

"Aw," I shrugged, "it's usually only a day or two a week. Except when my blind uncle suddenly needs an extra person." Yeshu cocked his head and smiled wryly. He wasn't going to accept my disclaimer.

"In fact," I suddenly remembered, "Uncle Bartholomaios told my mother that he wants me to tend his sheep tomorrow. I leave at dawn."

"Me, too!" Yeshu responded.

And so the next day, as dawn gradually warmed into pale pink over the eastern horizon and then fired half the sky with streaks of crimson, Yeshu and I walked quietly toward my uncle's house. Once there we lowered the posts that blocked the entrance to the stonewall corral, and this awakened the three sheep dogs that were curled together in one corner. With their help, we drove the herd into the lane. Separately we carefully counted each of the wooly animals as they bleated and pushed through the narrow opening. Then we compared numbers—there were exactly twenty.

At that, my uncle appeared in the doorway of his house, and a look of sleepy surprise crossed his face as his head moved to and fro. All but totally blind, he was trying to detect my shadow against the barely brightening sky. He was also trying to identify the second voice and shadow.

When he realized who it was, he raised both hands in protest, saying "Yeshua, don't embarrass me and yourself like this, going off to do a boy's job in the hills!"

Yeshu feigned indignation. "Go back to sleep, Bartholomaios, and do the work of babies on a mound of blankets."

He laughed gently and continued. "Daavi here, on the other hand, will be doing a grown man's labor by protecting half of your worldly wealth. Wouldn't you agree?"

Uncle Bartholomaios just sighed and shook his head as he turned and disappeared back into the house.

We headed deep into the hills, Yeshu and I, because my uncle's regular shepherd, who had taught me everything I knew up to then about tending sheep, had forewarned me that all the hillsides close to town had long been overgrazed. We must go farther away.

When we arrived an hour later at a nice grassy spot, I left the sheep with the dogs and trotted around until I found a steep ravine with no way out, one that could serve as a natural corral in case we needed it for any reason.

We let the sheep scatter themselves over the hillside and eat to their hearts' content. Yeshu and I settled down on a large boulder uphill from the herd, allowing us to keep watch on all of them at once. We stretched our legs out in front of us and spent some time just looking around, observing the lay of the land.

Yeshu posed a few basic questions about shepherding, and I answered as best I could. He then assured me that he was mostly interested in just watching me work.

During a lull in the conversation, I cleared my throat, staring at our four feet that stuck up before us, his twice the size and twice as far away as mine.

"Yeshu?"

He turned his head toward me.

"One of the other kids told me..." I hesitated. "She told me..." I was apprehensive that Yeshu might be displeased by my question. "That her grandfather said you might be the Messiah."

I threw a quick look at Yeshu to check his reaction. His face was impassive, so I went on.

"Well, I asked that girl, 'What exactly is a Messiah?' and she said, 'It's sort of like being God on earth.'" I stopped and waited.

"And?" said Yeshu, continuing to look right at me.

"Well..." I asked him tentatively, "are you God on earth?"

"Yes. You could say that," he answered, still looking at me.

I felt my eyes widening and my voice stuck in my throat. But it didn't really matter, because I realized I had no idea what to say next. Fortunately, Yeshu spoke instead.

"God is in me. I am *of* God."

He kept his gaze fixed on me.

"And God is in *you*, Daavi," Yeshu went on.

I blinked, hard.

"I am God. You are God, too," he said. "And we are God."

He clasped his two hands together, interlocking the fingers.

"All of us have that of God within us. And among us."

Yeshu studied his right hand, then his left.

"That's why, that's precisely why we cannot, *must* not, take anyone's life.

Not as an act of what some would call 'justice.'" He shook his head. "Nor as an act of vengeance, nor honor, nor war."

He continued shaking his head. "Think about it—if we did that, we would be killing God!"

He gave me a moment to ponder his words, still looking straight at me.

"And that's why we forgive someone for striking us, hurting us. Instead of attacking back in retribution, we reach out to touch that of God in the other person. We do so, knowing full well that person is capable of becoming a better human being. We trust that the God within will flower."

He paused again.

"By forgiving them, and expecting the best from them, we make it possible for them to open up. To find, and embrace, the God deep inside."

Finally, I found my voice again. "Even the Emperor of Rome?" I asked in amazement. "Or what about King Herod?"

"*Especially* those two," Yeshu responded with a hoot. "It's easy to forgive your best friends. And it's easy to see that of God within your grandparents. But forgiving your enemies, or someone who has done you real harm, and seeing God in such people...now, that's really tough."

I was searching for my next question because I knew my understanding didn't square up, when suddenly I thought I heard a distant bleating. I sprang to my feet and Yeshu stood with me.

"Yeshu!" I said with alarm. "We must count the sheep!"

Leaning toward the sound, I hollered out to my uncle's three dogs and gave them the sweep-around arm signal that told them to gather the sheep together. Both of us scrambled down from the large boulder.

"You start on that side," I pointed to my far left and Yeshu nodded, "and I'll start over here."

Yeshu strode away and I took off at a trot as the dogs ran a large circle around the sheep, barking and yipping at their heels. Next they made smaller and smaller circles until all the sheep were packed together, shoulder-to-shoulder and hindquarter-to-hindquarter.

Yeshu and I began walking toward one another, counting sheep and pushing them behind us as we went.

When we met in the middle, I looked up at him and said, "Nine!"

"Eight!" he answered.

Quickly I added the numbers in my head, plus two strays I had just seen the dogs round up.

"Oh no, we're one short. Go back. Let's count again!"

We counted again, and Yeshu called out to me, "Same number."

"Me too!" I countered, adding the two extras on top.

I felt the chill on my face and neck where the breeze touched the perspiration that had formed there.

"Search! Search!" I shouted to the dogs.

And off they took in a frenzy, circling the herd in ever widening arcs, wriggling under low bushes, scrambling behind rocks and under ledges, pushing their noses along the ground as they ran.

Meanwhile I instructed Yeshu to help me count only the lambs. Perhaps it was a young one that was missing. When he gave me his count and I added my own, I knew that was it. A baby lamb had wandered away, or fallen into a crevice. Or worse.

It was well known that there were hyenas and golden jackals about, and all kinds of wild marauding cats like leopards and even lions—any one of which might crave a tender little lamb for supper. I tried to control my panic. I loved each of those tiny lambs. And my uncle prized them. Two reasons to worry.

"We have to corral the herd so we can help the dogs search!" I yelled over my shoulder as I scrambled back up onto the large boulder.

Thrusting two fingers into my mouth, I whistled four or five times to the dogs, and they immediately turned and raced toward me. Before they reached the milling sheep, which were now bleating nervously, I pointed toward the closed ravine and began shouting to them, "Corral! Corral!"

Out of the corner of my eye, I caught Yeshu watching me closely, but I had no time to find out what was going through his mind. The dogs had the sheep moving again now, barking and barking at their tails and legs. I held my arms wide and hollered at the slowly moving animals, glancing over at Yeshu who quickly mimicked me.

Soon we had them all in the makeshift corral, after which I instructed two of the dogs to stay at the mouth of the ravine. This would keep the sheep in, and any predators out. With that I stepped toward the dog that I knew had the keenest sense of smell, grasped her by the scruff of her neck, and pulled her firmly away from the other two, rubbing her ears and muzzle affectionately.

I commanded her to come with me. She yipped and leapt into the air with joy at being chosen, and off we raced up the hill to get a vantage point that allowed her to sniff the wind. Yeshu followed along behind.

At that, we heard the cry again, and the keen-nosed dog ran straight for a path that headed up the slope. Yeshu and I were right behind her. On we pushed as the cries became louder, mixed with the dog's barking. Finally we rounded a bend to see the dog lying on her stomach—legs straight out, tongue lolling and laughing—staring at an opening in the rocks.

I dropped to my knees, spotted a ball of wool, and reaching down as far as I possibly could, grabbed the baby lamb by its rear end, and pulled it up to safety. Our lost sheep was found. I felt a wave of elation sweep over me, leaving my eyes brimming.

Yeshu and I let out a cheer, which the dog added to with a rapid string of wild yipping. I rubbed the lamb's tiny ears and received a hand-lick in return.

On the way back to the corral, with the small lamb tucked under my arm, I suddenly stopped abruptly, and Yeshu almost fell right over my shoulders. Crouching down, I carefully studied a footprint on the path.

"What do you see?" Yeshu asked.

"Large cat tracks," I answered. "Maybe a leopard!"

I stood up. "I can't tell if it was stalking the lamb—or *us*. Or it could have been heading up the hill so as to circle down to the corral. We'd better hurry back."

At that I heard the two dogs we had left with the sheep break into a chorus of frenzied barking. Yeshu and I took one look at each other and began running down the hill. As we arrived at the corral, our eyes flew swiftly over the scene. The sheep were skittishly moving first one way, then another. The two dogs circled us, yipping and whining, and they greeted their companion with nose nuzzles and high-pitched yelps.

Suddenly my eyes caught a slight stirring in the low bushes uphill from us and off to the right. It appeared to be the flitting of a tufted tail. Maybe there *was* a leopard or some other great cat stalking the sheep. Pointing, I let out a yell, and the dogs went crazy. They raced straight for the right side of the ravine and attempted to run up it, each time sliding back.

It was then I saw the two yellow eyes—a pair of quarter moons gazing at me calmly.

I glanced over at Yeshu and gestured soundlessly with my chin. When I looked back, the moons had vanished.

Both of us stared into the bushes, sweeping our eyes back and forth. If the big cat attacked, what would we do?

I searched the ground for loose stones and saw none. There were only tufts of grass encircled by sandy soil. When I raised my eyes again, I noticed the flicking tail once more. It was circling the ravine ever so methodically.

And then, without a sound, it disappeared, not to be seen again.

~ ~ ~

On the way back home, tired and a little hungry, I did my best to keep up with Yeshu's long strides. It was getting easier than it used to be. The sheep were moving quickly, too, eager to be safely home in their stone corral after the encounter with the big cat.

"Yeshu, can I tell you something?" I asked him as we walked.

"Sure," he answered, "any time. Whenever you wish."

I chose my words carefully. "Remember what we were talking about earlier?" He nodded.

"I can always see that of God in you, Yeshu...." I wavered. "But I don't really see God in myself."

"Oh, *I* do!" said Yeshu without hesitation.

My eyes grew wide for the second time that day.

"God is like a shepherd," he said. "Don't you think?"

He looked back at me, then answered his own question. "I think so. God loves each of us so much that whoever is lost is searched for, no matter what it takes."

Yeshu's eyes swept over the flock of sheep.

"However far we wander," he went on, "God searches for us, never giving up until we are found again and returned to the fold."

He paused to let the words sink in.

"Just like you did today, Daavi, with the baby lamb.

"And that's only a hint of it," he went on. "I have known you since the day of your birth, Daavi. I see God in you all the time. One day you'll see what I do. Trust me. You just have to figure out how to look."

I could only smile and nod, raising a hand to my brow. Well, it must be so. How could Yeshu of all people be wrong about such a thing?

When we arrived home, my mother met us at the door and after hearing the story of the lost lamb and the big cat, she turned to Yeshu. "Thank you for bringing my boy home safely."

Yeshu shook his head, saying, "The truth is, your Daavi brought himself *and* the herd home safely." He glanced down at me, smiling.

"In some ways he's still a boy, and rightly so. But in other ways—like caring for those precious creatures in his charge—he's already a man!"

I felt taller than the house.

Nothing Is So Like God As Stillness

Several months later, Yohanan was back in Nazareth again. I caught sight of him as I went by Yeshu's workshop. Yohanan was jabbing his finger toward Yeshu, again and again, and Yeshu was laughing and shaking his head.

Sensing that it was better to let them talk alone, I didn't go in.

Later I saw Yohanan collecting roots and berries in the meadow at the edge of town where I often found him. His hands were full and he was squatting on his haunches, emptying his treasure into a goatskin shoulder bag.

I raced through the tall grass and flopped down next to him. He immediately stopped what he was doing and grabbed my hand. I grabbed his elbow in return. We smiled broadly at one another.

He was the first to let go, and he peered at me sideways. When he saw me flinch, he reassured me. "It's all right. Ask."

So I did. "Yohanan, the last time you were here, you talked about, 'he who comes after me.' But who is that? And does it mean you're planning to go away forever? Or...are you thinking of maybe having a son?"

Yohanan grinned and then chuckled. "No," he said, "I'm waiting on a brother. And he's already here."

He gazed over the swaying grasses and wildflowers.

"The rest of you folks just don't know it yet. But you will, someday soon," he said. "Stick with me. I'm the one running ahead to open the gate."

Very often Yohanan left me confused. It reminded me of when someone carrying a bright lantern steps into the pitch-dark room in which you are sleeping at night. When you first open your eyes, your vision is worse rather than better.

Yohanan drew in a breath and began quoting the Prophet Isaiah. It was a passage I had heard recited before from the Book of *Yesha'ayahû*.

> A voice cried out in the wilderness:
> Get the Lord's road ready for him.
> Make a straight path for him to travel.
> All low places must be filled in;
> all high mountains leveled off.
> The winding road must be made straight,
> and rough paths made smooth.
> And then *all* God's children will be saved.

That's fine, I thought. But though I felt lifted up, it still didn't explain just who it was that Yohanan was talking about. Still, it was stirring, hearing his voice ring with Isaiah's words.

Since I wasn't getting a straight answer, maybe it was time to switch subjects.

"Yohanan," I said, "do you hear God? Does God speak to you?"

His eyes grew wide. "Without a doubt," he said. "God speaks to me."

I waited for him to continue.

"God speaks to me out of the silence. Out of the stillness of a windless night...a mountaintop at dawn...a lioness gazing across the plains and into the distance as she nurses her young."

He paused to refill his lungs. This time he spoke more slowly than before, perhaps to give me time to absorb his words.

"God speaks to me from the quiet of a deepening, starry sky; from the still surface of a morning lake when a breeze scurries softly across it. God speaks from the quiet of a slowly growing smile on a young woman's face; from the rhythmic breathing of that same woman sleeping beside her baby in the shade.

"There is nothing so like God as stillness," he finished, closing his eyes. "Nothing so like God as silence."

"But wait, Yohanan," I said impatiently. "Does God speak to you with words? I mean..." and here I scrunched up my eyes trying to find the right question to pin him down, "does God tell you what to do?"

His eyes reopened. "With *words*?"

"*Words*," I repeated firmly.

"Well, now and then I've been praying in the forest, or tramping the ridge tops in the desert," he said. "Or sitting in silence with my mind poised like a spider on a web suspended between two tree branches. And yes, some of those times I get a message from God."

He tilted his head as if to lift an ear skyward. "I don't necessarily hear things," he said. "I'm no madman, my friend. Not yet!"

With that he laughed as a bear might, or a mountain when the earth shook: his face to the sky and his beard bobbing up and down. It was almost frightening.

But for a moment I thought I could see petals between his teeth, and I smiled. I guess he had been nibbling flowers again.

This wasn't his noiseless laugh, when he rocked to and fro, holding his midsection with his arms while you tried to figure out if perhaps the joke was on you. No, this was the roaring laugh that erupted from inside when the joke was on himself.

I laughed with him. Who wouldn't?

"But, oh yes, Daavi," he said, scratching his head and blinking furiously, "there's a clear message." Suddenly, he beamed and the whole world seemed to change.

My thoughts had to scurry, just to keep up with Yohanan. One moment my head was full of thunder, and then the sun was out and burning brightly and I was blinking.

"Sometimes..." he rushed on, then paused, his voice trailing off. "Sometimes," he resumed, speaking very deliberately, almost whispering, "I just...*know*...what I'm supposed to do."

His voice sounded sure of itself, but his face revealed a hint of surprise. It was as if he were listening to himself think out loud: about something he'd known without realizing it.

"And when that happens, a small clear voice forms inside me that says: I will do this because God has told me so." He shook his head affirmatively.

It's not God's voice the way we might imagine it. You know, accented by Gabriel's trumpet. And it isn't like being handed a list of orders either," he said, speaking soothingly now. "It comes out of the feeling of having spent hours meditating in the palm of a vast open hand."

He was looking straight at me.

"In a moment so still that it rings, a thought arrives that glistens like noon sunlight on a single droplet of water falling from a suspended bucket. Falling back into the dark well from which it was lifted. I *feel* spoken to. I feel a bright, shimmering message passing out of God...and into me."

He raised his hands shoulder high, palms upward. "In filling me up—as drop upon drop of water become a cup of pure light—God has told me what to do!"

I nodded, yet in a daze, as I continued to watch the single droplet fall out of sight.

Yohanan must have noticed, because he quickly said, "So, Daavi, now you know how it is that *I* hear God. Others hear God in the scrolls, in dreams, in thoughts, in actions. I know that's so because they tell me. And because I observe closely how they've been changed."

Now he gazed at me pensively.

"God, it turns out, speaks in as many tongues as there are ears to hear with. I am at peace with that because, when all's said and done, I hear God the way *I* hear God."

Jumping to my feet, I clapped my hands together. "Yohanan!" I cried out. "Finally, you've said something understandable!"

He rolled off his rock, and this time I received the silent laugh.

When he was finished, he stretched out flat on his back before lifting his head and saying, "Better stated, finally I've made sense to you," he smiled contentedly. "At last we're getting somewhere!"

It felt good to have him say that. I smiled back broadly and started to head home, but he sat up and raised a hand to stop me.

"Daavi," he said.

"Yes?"

"Above all, never forget what is written in the Book of Psalms."

I stopped breathing, poised....

When at last he spoke, it was in a near whisper. "The voice singing to us from the Tehillim instructs us." He paused.

> Be still,
>
> and know that I am God.

My breath returned in a rush.

Wordlessly, our wilderness walker looked away. Again his gaze brushed slowly over the flowering meadow. I sat slowly back down in the greening grass, and for a long time neither of us uttered a sound.

Then he closed up his sack full of roots and berries. We got to our feet, and remaining totally quiet, walked back to town together.

Lullaby

Stillness was fine for me, up to a point. Then thoughts would begin to circle and buzz inside me like locusts, whirling around until it felt as if I were an entire wheat field under attack. Pretty soon I could stay quiet no longer. I absolutely had to get up, walk around, do something different.

At moments like that, I needed someone to talk to, someone to help me put these thoughts of mine in order. If no one else was around, or if it were nighttime and all the lamps were out, I would think of a story and whisper it to my cedar dog Shalom, and to myself. Usually it was one I had heard from Mama Ana or Mama Maria or Yeshu, but sometimes I just made a story up.

Or I would sing myself a song. Although I didn't know very many by heart, one in particular, was all that I usually needed. For years and years at times like that, especially in the dark of night, I sang my sister Shoshana's lullaby to myself. This was often when I was intensely missing her, or when something had happened that day that reminded me of her.

I also sang it when I was tending sheep, lying there in the grass gazing at the sky. Doing so would sometimes make me ache even more with longing, but sadness can be affirming. It can be warm like a hug.

Occasionally a pair of the long-necked storks that Shoshana loved so much soared overhead as I sang. When that happened, I felt calmed, as if I had company. Sometimes it seemed like it was my singing that actually called the great birds in. I wondered if that were really possible.

I would promise myself that when I was grown and married, I would sing Shoshana's lullaby to my own children before they went to sleep. It would remind me of what Yeshu had said about a man walking in a woman's world.

Happily, over the coming years, I often heard my own children singing their aunt's lullaby to theirs, before these little ones sank down into slumber.

Even when I was a young boy, I began teaching the lullaby to my little brother Aaron, and to the rest of the children in our neighborhood. Gradually a number of other families picked it up until nearly all of Nazareth could be heard singing it. Men sang it almost as much as women, probably because they liked the traveling part.

Whenever I passed a house at night and heard Shoshana's lullaby, I felt all warm inside. It was almost like hearing her sing it again.

> Go to sleep my little wanderer.
> Travel safely through your dreams.
> Come back home at tomorrow's dawning,
> A wiser and more loving being.

Taste of the Raspberry, Tongue of the Mouse... All Things Are Sacred

Yohanan was a true wanderer. He ceaselessly moved in and out of the wilderness. Perhaps he was someone who could only relate to people in small measures—a ladleful at a time. With all his coming and going, he would usually pass through Nazareth once or twice a year.

His mother had been so old when he was born, that by the time he was twenty she was no longer living. So Yohanan would come visit Mama Maria and Mama Ana "to get a family love bath," as he would put it. I found that to be pretty funny because I had never seen him take any other kind of bath.

And of course he also came to see Yeshu. I know, because they would spend hours together walking in the fields, talking and talking.

One summer day Yohanan showed up early in the morning. The ancient hides he wore were full of sprigs of grass and burrs. I was sure he had spent the night sleeping on the ground.

As always, Mama Ana and Mama Maria made him eat a big meal of what they called "people's food"—fresh bread and cheese curds and stewed figs, simmered with spices.

But no goat meat or mutton. They knew he would say, "How can I truly love my brothers and sisters? And also eat them!"

Late that afternoon, I saw Yohanan sitting on a bench in the lengthening shadows of the courtyard next door. His own shadow sat against the wall beside him like a plump twin.

I ran up to say hello, and he clapped his hands and gestured to me to have a seat next to him. It was a hot day, so I sat in his shadow. I'd been thinking a lot about our last conversation, so I launched in, "Yohanan..."

Suddenly his hand leapt to my knee, and I closed my mouth on my question. Out of the corner of my eye, I could see he was staring intently at something.

He stood up, and glancing down at me, smiled and said, “Come.”

He walked straight toward a corner of the courtyard, and I hurried after. Kneeling, he reached out his hands toward a tiny flower emerging from the spot on the ground where the two mud walls met. The last rays of the sun lit the petals.

I knelt beside him. He clasped his hands and began to speak.

“Daavi, look at this lovely flower. Cast your gaze down within the folds of these lucent, veined leaves. Go deep—past the yellow petals. Draw near.”

He gave me time.

“That’s it. Now peer inside the gilded cup.”

He pointed with a single long finger. “Do you see the tiny fronds all covered with golden dust?”

I edged ever closer, nodded my head, and waited.

“If God has a Torah, friend Daavi, this is what it looks like.”

The parched air moved slowly in and out of Yohanan’s chest. I listened while waiting for him to go on.

“See the rounded paunch, just under the bloom, where the seeds lie hidden?”

I nodded again.

“Think about it, Daavi. From every single flower springs creation!” A smile danced on his lips.

“God’s work has only just begun.”

He looked over at me, the sun in his eyes warming my face. Then he turned back to the buttery flower, bending down even nearer. His fingers reached toward the petals, and they trembled almost imperceptibly.

When he spoke, it might have been directed at me, but it sounded as if his voice had turned inward.

“And in each and every flower...lie the beginnings...of eternity.”

I dared not utter a word. His words echoed in my ears. I tried hard to expand my thoughts so that I could encircle both creation *and* eternity.

It seemed at first as if I had just been tossed off a precipice and knew

I had but two possibilities: either I would soar—or I would fall. But where to begin?

A sideways glance from Yohanan signaled that I was to hold my mind in check, and just observe. So I did, noticing how each petal quivered as my breath, and his, brushed over it.

"And the great dome of night sky, Daavi?" He waited patiently.

"Just like this flower—creation and eternity!"

I sucked in a lungful of air through open lips that were no longer pressed together to grasp and hold all of these ideas at once. I felt a sweet happiness expanding in my chest, like a turtledove lost in song.

Gradually, my mind went clear as a pool of water with no breeze to ruffle its surface. When finally I turned my eyes toward Yohanan, I saw him gazing gently down at me.

He knew.

Slowly we both stood and walked back to the bench and took our old seats. Yohanan looked at me like my father did the first time I stitched a piece of leather correctly.

We sat there together for a long while, wordless, until at last I rose to go.

Yohanan put his arm in front of me and said, "I believe you came here with a question. Well, it still clings to the end of your tongue like a tree frog waiting for rain."

I sat back down and settled into a slight hollowing in the wall.

Then I spoke, my voice growing stronger with each word. "Yohanan, how far into the wilderness will I have to go to find God? Does God live deep, deep in the forests and deserts, far away from everyone?"

He laughed, tilting his head only slightly skyward.

"You only have to go in," he said, "as far as it takes to leave the jumbled thoughts and noise of this world behind you. And to open yourself up.

"It might take only a single step. Or two. Like it did just now."

He paused, watching me. "Or you can choose to go further in."

I peered up at him.

Then he said, almost gravely, "Some day I will accompany you there."

My breath caught in my throat.

"But no matter what, Daavi, you won't find God only with your feet! You'll find God with your eyes. And your ears. And your mouth and nose. And the tips of your fingers. And most of all, with your heart.

"You'll find God in tiny blossoms in the mountain frost. In the clear water running over your shoulders as you lie in a streambed." His eyes widened. "In the taste of the wild raspberry. In the tongue of the mouse as it licks honey from the palm of your motionless hand.

"Many people look for God only in the Temple and in the Torah and the Nevi'im. They search through the past, or deep in their heads, but nowhere else. I believe that's not enough. God is out in the wild places. Right now. In sunbeams and breezes and starlight.

"The only *inside* places where I find God every time I look," he said, "are the human heart and soul. And human hearts and souls open up in the wilderness!"

Shaking his great mane, Yohanan went on, "Daavi, my young friend, you must go there and see for yourself."

Nodding again, I silently promised myself that some day I would.

We sat for a while longer, both of us lost in thought, our eyes closed.

I stood up again to go.

"Sit back down," Yohanan said softly, his eyes still shut. "I think there is more."

I sat down.

"You're right," I said. "I have another question." I began scratching the back of my head and clearing my throat.

"Ask anything, Daavi."

Yohanan opened his eyes. There were smile lines emanating from the outer corners of each one.

"I'm at your beck and call."

I took my time.

"Yohanan, just the other day you told me that God sometimes speaks to you."

I glanced at him and he nodded, cocking his head.

"The times when you hear God's voice, *where* does it come from? From way far away in the sky? From some giant boulder in the desert sand? From a cave in the mountainside? Where..."

"No, Daavi," he broke in, "the voice does not come from anywhere outside, but from deep within me."

"But how, Yohanan? How does the voice get inside you? How do you hear it?"

"I go into the well," he said.

I felt my jaw drop and my eyes bug out. "You *what*?"

This time he spoke slower and louder, the final word emerging with more force than the first ones.

"I go into the well."

Then Yohanan looked at me and winked, saying, "Close your mouth before it fills up with bees."

He lowered his gaze toward the ground, sighing and smiling faintly as if he realized how he had just confused me. How I was probably imagining him lowering himself down into a well with a thick rope.

"Daavi?" He raised his eyes again.

I finished closing my mouth and nodded in anticipation.

Certain that he had my full attention, Yohanan placed his pointer finger between his eyebrows and drew it deliberately down his nose, his chin, his chest; stopping at the breastbone, where he gave a single tap.

"Into the well," he said once more.

In a flash it came so clear to me that a slight shudder shook my shoulders and even my head. The image of Yohanan going way down inside himself opened my mind like two window shutters swung wide apart in the morning, the daylight suddenly pouring in.

"God is inside you, Daavi. God is inside all of us. Inside all living things."

He paused, chewing slowly on his lower lip. Then he tapped his chest a few more times.

"Go into your well, young friend...deep, deep in...to hear what God would say to you."

I nodded my head once again. Then twice more. Suddenly I realized that I felt larger than only a few moments before. And my thoughts seemed clear as a sky swept clean by a swift breeze of all troubling clouds.

~ ~ ~

The next day, after I finished my chores, I saw Yohanan kneeling down in the middle of the road that led into town. He appeared to be working on something. But in the middle of a dusty old road?

I went up and peered over his shoulder. With a crooked twig in his hand, he was waiting patiently while a black-and-orange-striped caterpillar crawled slowly up onto it.

"Yohanan, what in the world are you doing?" I asked.

He turned his head to look at me, without moving his hand.

"I'm saving this caterpillar from certain death," he said. "Lots of people walk this road. Oxcarts pass by, too. This little fellow is sure to get crushed."

His eyes widened, and then his lips parted in a smile.

By then the caterpillar was straddling the twig. Carefully, Yohanan stood up, lifting his load into the air. The caterpillar hung there, its rear end drooping off to one side and its head to the other. Two slender antennae wriggled as its head moved back and forth, back and forth, searching for where to go next. Yohanan carefully walked with it to the stone wall by the road. Leaning over, he deposited it gently on the other side.

Then he turned and peered down the road. Steadily, I followed his gaze. And my mouth dropped open. As far as the eye could see, there were caterpillars. Every few paces. Some crossing to the left, some to the right. A few heading away from us, others approaching.

Yohanan strode over to the closest one. I ran along behind him, trying to catch his sleeve.

"Yohanan, have you gone crazy?" I asked. "You could be here until the sun sets."

I grabbed hold of his rope belt, and he stopped abruptly and bent over. I almost ran into his backside.

"You could be at this task until the sycamore leaves fall," I went on. "Until the storks fly back from the north, next fall."

He looked at me with flashes of sparks in his eyes.

"Yes, I'm crazy," he said. "Crazy for life!"

He was already on his knees waiting for the next caterpillar to mount the bend in the twig.

"All life is sacred, friend. The lion cub is sacred, and so is the furry little caterpillar. Your sister and brother are sacred. And so are the mice in the cupboard."

I blinked.

"The cedars of Lebanon are sacred, Daavi. And the people who walk the earth shouting, 'Unclean!'—they are also sacred.

"The gnarled old tree with its roots exposed is sacred. The rivers are, too, even when they flood or run dry. The child that falls into the cooking fire is sacred. And the earthworms in the soil of your mother's garden, they are just as sacred as all the rest."

He had another caterpillar by now and was heading for the stone wall.

"Once you learn this," he spoke over his shoulder. "Once you begin to live in sacred friendship with all living things, then you will be powerful! You will no longer be trapped in the misery of others. You will be free from torment. No more risk of being death while you are still full of life!"

Back he went to save another one.

"That love for all living beings will fill you up," he continued talking from his knees again. "It will fill you up and *propel* you into doing what is right. You can even face the Emperor of Rome or his entire army if you want!"

He was at the wall again.

"Any one of us can do it, you see. We can care for birds and animals and children and elders." He nodded firmly. "And if others notice us doing this, especially if young people see us, then maybe they will stop what they're doing and watch more closely. Perhaps even follow our example." He clapped his free hand against a thigh.

I suddenly remembered the ants my friends and I had stepped on in town, more than once, and my face burned with shame.

"Maybe they will never learn," Yohanan continued. "But if they try it, and begin to understand by watching and listening to the creatures they've helped, then the day *could* come when they, too, will know that all living things on this earth are sacred.

"All things. Sacred!"

Standing in the Light

Every time I thought I finally understood what it meant for something to be sacred, and how God and love could be one and the same, I found I had more to learn. In fact, I was a full-grown man before I finally realized that in matters of the soul, one never stops learning. Unlike your bodily self, inner growth never has to cease. You can keep growing forever. And truth be told, you really need to do just that.

One afternoon, after herding the local tax collector's sheep back to his corral, I suddenly realized that somewhere along the way I had dropped my pouch of leatherworking tools that my father had given to me on my twelfth birthday. So I trudged back to the hillside where I had last been working on a pair of sandals.

The money I earned for my mother and father by herding other families' animals was not enough to buy even an extra loaf of bread, at the end of each day I worked. I had to fix broken sandals as well, in order to bring my share to the table, and it had taken my father half a year to save the money to buy those secondhand tools. They weren't much—an awl, a punch, a cutting blade—the whole lot fit in the palm of my hand. But I could not even imagine how awful it would be to lose them.

Halfway up the hill I found my pouch lying under the bush I had crawled beneath to escape the midafternoon sun. After reaching in to fetch the pouch, I stood back up, and instantly my heart felt lighter. Taking a gasping breath, I let it out with a burst, "Eureka!"

That's what the Greeks say when they discover something. Once my father and I journeyed beyond the River Jordan to Dekapolis, to sell leather goods. Dekapolis is where there are ten Greek-built towns, one right after another. On market day I made friends with a boy who taught me more than a dozen words in his language. After that, I loved to run around exclaiming all the time, "Eureka! Eureka!"

Finally, people started answering me back, "You be quiet! You be quiet!" But I still say it when I'm alone.

The day I found my no-longer-lost, Eureka! tool pouch, I stuffed it deep into the pocket of my cloak and just happened to look down the hill toward the lake.

There was Yeshu.

He was standing, totally still, facing the lake. I began trotting down the path toward him, a smile already on my face. I loved having time alone with Yeshu. Without fail, something would happen worth pondering later.

When I ran up to him, he turned his head and smiled a greeting. The light in his eyes seemed as if it might explode at any moment into a thousand shooting stars. He turned back to the lake.

"Yeshu, what are you doing?"

"Looking. I'm looking at the water."

"Why are you looking at the water?"

"To take the light in."

"Why?" I asked. "Why do that?"

"To fill my soul up with light," he said.

"Okay, so how do you fill your soul?"

"Well, I open my eyes, wide. I hold my palms toward the lake." He showed me, his arms at his side. "Then I open up my chest, my heart, my mind. And the light pours in."

"Can I try it?"

"Sure. Stand over here. Next to me. That's it."

And so, as the sun bled slowly into the lake, we stood side by side, Yeshu and I, staring across the still waters, palms turned slightly outward, letting the diaphanous colors and the warm light soak into us. The colors, intertwined in all their brilliance, flowed through our eyes and our chests and our hands. And into our souls.

We stood in a silence so profound I could hear my heart beating in my breast. I could hear the wings of the swallows beating also, as they skimmed the smooth surface of the lake, scooping up tiny mouthfuls of water.

After a long while, I slowly turned and looked up at Yeshu.

His face was afire. His eyes were in flames. His hair and beard glowed and pulsated like a ring of red-hot embers.

Yeshu was in the light.

And the light was in Yeshu.

It was then that I knew, in the batting of an eye, that the same force that had created the sun and the shimmering blood-red lake, had also created Yeshu.

And I knew that this same force maybe...no, *certainly*, had created me, too. From then on I felt linked forever through Yeshu and the late-afternoon and early-morning lakes, and the sun and the moon and the stars, to the heaven and the creator beyond; the heaven and creator deep within me.

And in one huge leap, I thrust beyond love itself, and into a thrilling, embracing bond for which as yet I had no name.

Soul Walk

It was Yohanan's idea to walk to Lebanon. He said that all his life he had heard stories of grand cedar forests in the Lebanese highlands that were full of giant trees, trees that covered the rolling slopes farther than an eagle's eye could see. Trees that stood so tall it made your neck ache to search the sky for their tops. Yohanan wanted to travel there with Yeshu and a few others—to see God together.

This was my chance.

I wanted to go with them so badly I could taste it all the way down my throat. I could hear inside me one of my favorite passages from the Book of Psalms. It was among the many Tehillim passages Yeshu recited that day, long before, when I fell out of the walnut tree.

> The voice of our God
> that thundered over the waters...
> that cracked the cedars of Lebanon....

The fresh, sharp smell of cedar was already curling in my nostrils.

Most of all, I could imagine what fun we would have, journeying together. As soon as I heard, I ran straight to Yeshu's carpentry shop and asked if I could go along. He smiled and said, "Just a moment ago, I was thinking we should invite you!"

He hefted a board from the floor to his workbench, "Would you like me to speak with your parents?"

My heart leapt with joy. If anyone could talk my parents into it, Yeshu could. That was especially true for my father, who thought Yeshu and Yohanan could make walls out of wind and roofs out of rain. Then cut a doorway through with a single shaft of sunlight.

Once, of an early morning, my father told me about a dream he'd just had in which Yeshu and Yohanan had bent a rainbow into a circle and then together had flung it to the top of Mt. Sinai where it melted into sunset.

People tell me I get my imagination from my father.

That very evening Yeshu showed up at our house and convinced my parents to put me under his care for the journey. He said just the right things. He told them that the group would need someone to fix their sandals and pack-straps, not to mention the goatskin water bags. He commended my father for how well I had been taught the craft and reminded him that the demand was slow for craftsmen in Nazareth right then. So it wasn't like my hands were going to be sorely missed. And of course Mother and Father were well acquainted with how much I longed to travel the roads that led to and from the exciting places I'd been hearing about for years.

But what clinched it was when Yeshu told them he wanted me along because I was special. He said I knew how to dream things and to live in my imagination. He said I had a lion cub's spirit that would just grow and grow all my life, and that traveling was one of the best ways to nurture the soul.

I felt larger when he said such things. Maybe too large.

When I glanced at my father, I saw a faraway look in his eyes. And suddenly he said yes!

Now, Yohanan had a different way of looking at my going along that really got me thinking.

He said to me, "Daavi, wildness is the best teacher. You will learn things from the great cedars that no wise man or scroll can ever teach you."

Those words brought me up short. Would I understand? Would I even notice?

Yohanan went on. "I've told you God speaks through wild things. You'll encounter clouds of butterflies soaring in the breeze and tiny mice scurrying through lilies of the field, searching for God's bounty. And you'll see many of the eight-legged creatures we call *akkabishim*. These are the 'swift weavers' that suspend their rainbow-tinted, silken webbing overnight, catching drops of dew at dawn and creating visions that delight our eyes and feed our dreams. And of course, there are those majestic trees that carry the earth and the streams up to heaven. Daavi, at last you will see all this for yourself."

I felt my heart begin to tremble deep in my chest.

Then Yohanan looked at me sideways. "You've been to the Temple in Jerusalem."

I nodded.

"When wise King Solomon built that magnificent place, do you know what he chose for pillars to hold up the great, arching dome?"

I shook my head.

"Cedars of Lebanon!" he said. "Carried by seven ships to a specially built port on the coast near Jerusalem. Unloaded and hauled by wagons bound together, one behind another, for the final journey to the gates of the city."

Grasping my shoulders, he said, "You can go to the synagogue and find it all described in verse in the *M'lakhim,* the combined Book of Kings."

> And the cedar of the house within
> was carved with knobs and open flowers:
> all was cedar; there was no stone seen.

Yohanan always knew how to connect the natural world to God. For him they were one and the same. And he talked about it to whoever would listen.

Yeshu told me after our journey to the cedars that Yohanan had urged him over and over to go into the desert wilderness to fast and meditate. There, Yeshu was to talk with God and examine his own soul, seeking purity through intense privation. Allowing silence and solitude to burn the brush away.

~ ~ ~

But that would come later. The day we left for the cedars of Lebanon, Yohanan gathered us all at the main well: Yeshu, Joanna, and Martha; two of Yeshu's fishermen friends, John and James—the ones he called the *Boanerges,* the "Sons of Thunder"—and a leatherworking shepherd boy.

Yohanan started by giving each of us a gourd full of water and told us to drink. Then he had us fill our goatskin bags, saying, "We come from this water, and we will return to this water."

And off he strode toward the edge of town, with all of us trailing behind.

The Boanerges, these two sons of Zebedee whom the rest of us came to call the "Thunder Brothers" were close on Yohanan's heals. Each of them always wanted to be first—that is, when they weren't joking, which was most of the time.

Yohanan didn't even notice. Suddenly he stopped, bent down, and picked up a small stone. He observed each of us until we followed suit.

"We will each carry a stone to the giant cedar forests and leave a bit of Nazareth there."

He held his up, then swiftly pocketed it. "You'll learn why when we arrive."

I got such a kick out of Yohanan.

Of course, as I look back on that journey, I realize the wilderness walker had dead-serious reasons for dreaming up this trek. He was gathering strength and forming ideas for his return to preaching to crowds at the edge of wildness, where forest and desert met fields surrounding villages.

Beyond that, I believe he was also drawing a group of people together that would later, along with others, accompany Yeshu on *his* mission.

I think Yeshu was not certain at the time what his path would be. But Yohanan had a clear vision of his own. He knew that he was breaking the ground for Yeshu to till and sow. I feel certain he knew it.

As we seven friends walked along that first morning, Yohanan told us a story that he had heard as a boy from Rabbi Abraham in Jerusalem. Rabbi Abraham was Yohanan's favorite. Yeshu said he had a white beard that was twice as long and twice as wide as Yohanan's. It seems that it reached his shoulders and waist and was never completely still.

Rabbi Abraham used to make up his own stories about ancient times, starting with some bit of thread from the scrolls and weaving it into a larger fabric. He did this especially when he found what he believed was a hole in an existing text—something missing that he felt needed to be filled in. The rabbis who imagined such a mended and expanded story called it a *midrash*, and Abraham was famous for his.

In the midrash that Yohanan wove for us from Rabbi Abraham's story that morning, God had created the first two people, Adam and Eve. Right away God took them on a walk.

"Consider the meadow all around us," God said, "full of wildflowers and birds, with every color of the rainbow on their faces and backs."

Adam and Eve looked around at each of these and nodded.

"Just ahead is a tall forest," God continued, "with a stream running out of it. Do you see?"

The two human beings, who had only their own hair to cover themselves, turned and faced where God pointed.

"Well," said God, "take a walk through the woods, eat nuts from the trees and collect the healing bark. Find the stream and follow it back to this meadow, stroll across it, and fill your mouths with handfuls of the blue and red berries.

"When your stomachs are full, go back to the stream, step in and cool your feet. Lie down and let the clear water run over your bodies and wash you off. Be sure to take a long drink to quench your thirst.

"And when you're finished bathing, find a large slab of rock and stretch out there in the sun for a while to dry off and warm yourselves. Throw your hands toward the sky so that drops of water fly into the air and form a momentary rainbow. Whenever such a rainbow arcs across the heavens, you are to remember the everlasting covenant of caretaking between me and you and every living creature on earth. This is the covenant that will commit you to acting as stewards of all life!

Lastly, as you lie there close your eyes and recall all that has passed before you. Contemplate for a while just how lovely and clean it is; how it refreshes and fills up your body and soul.

"Consider everything you've seen, and respect it. Don't ever desecrate or misuse this bounteous garden I've given you. Learn to love and nurture it as it nurtures you. If you're selfish and greedy and despoil this thriving heritage, you will regret it. Because if it withers, so will you, and there will be no one to come after you who can put things back the way they were.

"Then you'll have brought death into being. You'll have brought death to yourselves, and to me in you and in the world.

"All life is hallowed.

"Revere it.

"Care for it!"

Humming to Our Heels

That's how it went, day after day. We did nothing but walk and talk. Oh, how we talked! We discussed everything imaginable. These conversations were often started and led by Yeshu or Yohanan. But not always, and without fail everyone got their say. No opinion or idea was seen as less worthy of consideration than any other. Always the women were listened to, which was not always the case back home in Nazareth. And even the only young person—I'm referring to me!—was welcomed into the thick of things.

Our discussions ranged across every sort of subject, back and forth and then back again, like swallows building a nest. Usually Yeshu would get things going, tossing out a question like a twig, sometimes starting by saying, "So, let's see what kind of a dwelling we can construct with a notion like *this*."

A typical to-and-fro began the morning we felt the road starting to ascend, our legs and backs telling us we were now climbing ever so gradually.

Yeshu lofted the first pebble into the pond by asking, "Friends, how should we live our lives, every day, to be one with God and at peace with our own souls?"

Much of the time I kept quiet, but sometimes something jumped out and surprised me. This time I blurted out, "I've seen Yohanan kneeling in the dust to help one caterpillar after another safely across the road."

I took several more steps, collecting my thoughts all the while.

"I think that bonds him with the God that is in the lowest of creatures."

With a vigorous shake of his head, he signaled his agreement.

Meanwhile, Yeshu touched his forehead, thinking. At last, he broke the silence. "My beloved cousin wears only tattered clothing, but his life is like a seamless cloak, each part blending perfectly with all the others. He has nothing in the way of worldly wealth, but he is anything but poor in spirit. He has great stature, but he never hesitates to kneel before the lesser ones among us. Even those that crawl on their bellies across the surface of the earth."

He glanced toward Yohanan who seemed to be examining his feet, as if counting his toes. His face was flushed with the color of a Damascan woodpecker's topnotch.

Noticing that Yohanan, who sang so eloquently about the marvels of creation, was embarrassed to find himself being praised, Yeshu swerved away in another direction, tossing out, "Do you believe that a rich man can get into heaven?"

"Not very easily!" Joanna cried out. "But a rich woman can, as long as during every Jubilee Year she frees her debtors from their obligation to repay, and shares her wealth with the poor."

Yeshu laughed and nodded, but he wouldn't let Joanna off the hook easily with such a jaunty comeback.

"And how is it that a rich woman is in less peril than a rich man?" he asked her.

Joanna grew serious. "Perhaps because men amass their wealth by shaping the world around them in ways that harden their hearts. On the other hand, most women of wealth have inherited theirs and believe it should continue to be shared with others."

"Nice footwork," Yeshu answered, with a wink. "You have had more than one eye open, haven't you?"

Joanna's blush was even more pronounced than Yohanan's.

Yeshu noticed her discomfort, and just as he had with his cousin, he found in her answer the fleece for spinning another question. Looking pointedly at the rest of us, he asked, "All right, then, what should a woman's role be in the synagogue? Have we Jews squandered a treasure by keeping women at the doorway rather than see them sit close by the flame?"

That kept us going for several more miles.

Sometimes Yeshu's questions got really tricky. One I remember was this. "Is it okay to break a holy law, if there's a sound reason? Especially one thrust forward by the spirit?"

He kept his eye on the rest of us as he walked.

"For example, can a healer care for someone who falls ill on the Sabbath, even though the Books say it is the lawful day of rest when one may do no work?"

Questions like that one made you think not just about what words meant when you heard them, but what happened when they were actually applied in real life. Was it truly honoring God to let someone suffer—or die—on God's day, when that was totally unnecessary? If so, just how would this be honoring God?

Sometimes the path to answers seemed well lit. Other times, fog and darkness obscured the way. But always the back and forth was stimulating.

Many times, I heard about things I had rarely if ever come across before. At one point, when all that could be heard was footsteps, Joanna said, "Kindness and compassion can tame a wild and furious young colt. In the same way, love and forgiveness can soften vengeance and fear in neighbors and in strangers—any or all of whom might feel rivalry toward us."

She turned toward Yeshu.

His eyes met hers and he responded, "This is so true. I remember from my travels how love can give rise to changes in the human heart. And more changes in the actions of people who feel love or who receive its warmth."

He said nothing for a few steps. Nor did anyone else. All were waiting.

"Once, on the road, I worked for a man whose neighbor hated him so," Yeshu recalled, "that years before, he had tried to poison my host's cow, by giving it snakeroot. The ill feeling was reciprocated with gusto.

"Eventually both men married and had sons and the sons became fast friends as young playmates. A bit uncomfortably, the fathers watched their sons playing together, day after day.

"By chance, on a sunny morning one of the boys, fascinated by a viper hanging from a low tree limb, reached out to capture it. The other boy knew the viper was poisonous, and he snatched his friend's hand away before he could be bitten.

"Both fathers saw this near tragedy unfolding and were so shocked and relieved that they looked toward one another, their eyes locking together. Each one loved his own son and recognized how his son loved the other boy. The fathers' capacity for hate broke up into pieces, fell to the ground, and scattered.

"Tentatively the two men walked toward one another, jabbering excitedly about the deadly bite that never struck flesh. Their wives rushed out to see what the ruckus was all about, only to find the two men laughing in relief. Quickly returning to their houses the women brought out apples and date honey, and the four parents sat together in the olive grove, sharing a mid-morning bite to eat as the boys climbed snakeless trees.

"Soon after, the two men were helping one another with planting and harvesting, turning over the hardened soil of years past."

We all walked on without talking, over a rise and down into a small valley. Joanna seemed pleased with the story that cast light on her earlier observation.

Finally she said, "I've seen how one heart can join with others, perhaps many others, to peacefully oppose hatred and evil and eventually transform the world into a better home for God's children.

Make that for *all* creatures," Yohanan chimed in, and Yeshu turned his head to toss a smile at his cousin.

Joanna's "hmm" signaled her concurrence.

Several dozen more steps were taken in silence.

Then Yeshu added, "It's also true that things we take for granted right now are the result of victories emerging from the timeless struggle of people long gone, people whose names we don't even know any more.

"For example, who invented the community work day? And who were the first people to dig a village well? Had they not, each family might still be forced to walk a long way to carry back water for drinking and cooking and washing.

Additional wordless steps. "And chew on this one," Yeshu went on. "Some villages are full of folks giving one another a hand. In contrast—sometimes inexplicably—there are other villages where people seem full of spite and slander."

I noticed Martha watching Yeshu closely, hanging on every word he spoke.

"Is this due to bad luck? I think not."

More steps were taken.

"Some believe love is nothing but a feeling, but it's also a choice. You can learn to love, and you can will yourself to be loving. One person can decide to change, or an entire village can. Sometimes it happens in that order.

"Folks can even show love toward a person or a group without very much liking them. Or even while being angry with them.

"We humans are complicated aren't we?" We all joined him in his bemused chuckling.

"But know that there's always hope. And that's especially true where love is present."

No more steps. Abruptly Yeshu had stopped walking.

"Time to eat!" he shouted. And we all cheered.

Sharing our meager repast of strips of dried goat meat, we were brought back to Joanna's favorite thread. She had dangled it before us earlier: namely the coming Jubilee. Because it arrives every seventh year, one could not wait too long to begin preparing.

As we Jews all know, Jubilee is the celebration when we're urged to share our surpluses with the hungry and homeless and excuse any debts that were burdening others. There on the road, we could easily imagine what it was like to feel hunger and have no home.

We finished our chewing and swallowing, except for Yohanan, of course, who had amiably abstained, busying himself with a handful of nuts and berries fished out of a deep pocket. Suddenly, as if we were a flock of birds all leaving our perches at once, we stood and began moving on. Again, each of us fell silent and there was only the sound of our sandals on the dusty road. I wanted to put my spoon into the pot too, and stir it, but I was having trouble finding the right words for my query.

Feeling a tightening in my throat, I swallowed carefully and then ventured, "I have something..." Heads turned in my direction, and this gave me courage. "Yohanan, why do you save the lives of caterpillars but eat locusts with honey?"

I said nothing while I took several more steps. "Just a few months ago you said to Mama Ana and Mama Maria, "How can I truly love my brothers and sisters, and also eat them?"

Yohanan nodded, his mane of hair bouncing.

"Aren't the locusts your kin, too?" I asked, biting my upper lip with trepidation. All heads turned toward Yohanan.

Yohanan raked his fingers through his beard several times, then exclaimed, "Fair question! Why hasn't anyone else asked it?"

Thunder John quickly shot back, "Because we were afraid you would bite our heads off." He put a hand to the nape of his neck. "And pull our wings off, too."

There was chortling all around, joined in on by Yohanan. I relaxed.

"Well," said Yohanan after the jocularity had died down, "the locusts that I eat have reached their time to give themselves up. And I am always careful to say to them, 'Thank you, brother locust, for surrendering yourself to me.'

"But the caterpillars crawling across the road, or chewing holes in the leaves of the lemon tree, they are different. It's not their time yet. They still have to be transformed into butterflies in order to bring their lives to fruition."

He shifted his bedroll on his back and lowered his head, to signal that he was done talking.

I wanted to ask, "And the old ram? The aging cow? Have they not reached their time?" But I held my tongue.

I knew that brotherhood was not an easy knot to untie. And I knew that it wasn't my role to disrobe or trip another in mid-path. It felt right to give up my turn now and give others an opening to speak, or not.

They chose the latter, and all of us tramped on for some time, lost in our thoughts. Contented to listen to inner voices for a while.

If our road-walking discussions sound stuffy, well, they weren't. Maybe because we talked about lots of other things, too: such as hair-raising, storm-ravaged fishing expeditions that Thunder James and Thunder John had hired themselves out for; and weddings Yohanan and Yeshu remember dancing madly at when they were boys.

As I grew more comfortable speaking, I shared my stories of my sister Shoshana's thwarted attempts to get the older men to teach her Hebrew, and how she took care of me like a little mother and was later lost and had still not been found.

I learned during those long conversations that being serious was not the same as being grim. Many hard things have lighter sides. And the exact opposite is also true, which is one reason people can laugh so hard that they cry.

For sure, we were always laughing at something or other. Laughing because it was hilarious, or because it was delightful. Sometimes because it was just plain fun and nonsense, all of us guffawing together to be silly.

One of our very favorite topics was to talk about *other* journeys each of us had taken. It was a bit like sitting at a feast and topping things off by trading memories of past meals that had still more savory tastes and smells to offer.

I hadn't traveled nearly as much or as far as the others, of course. In fact, this was my first long journey. But they loved my story about my family's trips to see Gramma Ruth. They howled and back-slapped when I recounted her best jokes and word games.

And when I told them my dream about dragging my blankets to her gravesite to lie down beside her, I heard several people suck in their breath. Thunder John wiped his eyes with the backs of his huge fists, and then threw an arm around me and gave me a firm squeeze on the shoulder.

Truth be told, I had never imagined traveling in such company, even when I'd lain awake at night wishing I were on the road. During much of our trip, I could feel myself climbing high up in storm clouds—my chest filling with the rolling thunder, my eyes flashing and glowing with lightning.

Sometimes it seemed like more than I could contain, more than I could carry. I doubted that I had much to offer the others. And yet it became clear to me as the journey progressed, that each of us gave something and got back even more.

Take Joanna, for example, who often sang to us as we walked. She had a rich, strong voice that stopped all conversation. She had had plenty of free time to learn to sing when her husband had been perpetually busy, as one of the more powerful men in Herod's court. She could sing almost like my sister.

Joanna liked to drop to the rear of the group as we walked. There she would begin humming wordlessly to the rhythm of our footsteps until one by one we ceased talking. Only then, when she had found just the right tempo, just the right mood, would she begin to sing behind our heels. Invariably making our feet feel lighter and our tramping easier.

And every time she sang, I knew she would speak to us afterward. She used melody to center our attention and attune our ears and minds.

Once she belted out an anthem she said came from the times when we Jews were enslaved in Egypt. It was all about the human spirit being like a great river, flowing and rolling. Each person was like a stream coursing into that river, joining forces the way fingers come together to form a strong and agile hand. And the swelling river was the accumulation of countless human spirits combined into one open hand reaching out to eternity.

By the end, all of us were singing the chorus, "flowing, rolling...like a river...to the sea."

As the last notes died out, Joanna began speaking. "The way I see it, a person's spiritual journey begins the moment life is received. Life *is* spirit. And the spirit of each life begins growing, becoming fuller, as soon as it enters the world.

"This journey starts with the baby floating inside its mother, listening in rapture to its mama's heartbeat. Attached by the cord to her lifeblood and unaware of being connected through her to the family and community that formed them both."

She paused and smiled.

"There waits the baby, dreaming of God perhaps; or of life before life. Water dreaming of water. Who can remember?" she shrugged.

"What matters is that another journey of the spirit has begun its endless quest for a true home—all the way to the final step of life, and beyond!

"For some, that voyage may pause in midstride, one foot motionless in the air, like this..." And she stopped just so.

"Although the journey has halted, the possibility of journeying has not ended. It will simply stay suspended in midair, no movement in any direction, perhaps until the last breath is gone."

She started walking again.

"Many travelers grow in the course of their journey. Some become smaller. A few take great strides, pressing their own footprints into the earth as they tread, exploring this vast world under an even vaster firmament. In this way they forge a path where there was none before. Sometimes it's a path that only a mountain goat or a tiny, iridescent serpent could follow.

"Others follow the well-worn trail, taking care to step gingerly in the footsteps of the multitude of seekers who have gone that way before." Joanna stayed quiet for at least ten paces.

"And some will do both, straying from the route travelled by the many to find sweet orchards and meadows and clear streams that the weary can rest by and drink from as they journey home, sometimes creating new paths for others to explore.

"I gaze into the eyes of every woman and man I meet," Joanna paused, "and I try to guess where they are in *their* spiritual journey. Are they wide-awake while dreaming, or snoring softly when they speak? Have they truly begun traveling yet? Are they stuck, one foot suspended in the air? Are they struggling uphill like a donkey laden with stones...or gliding down the slope like a gazelle with the wind at its back?

"But most of all: are they aware of how exhilarating this kind of travel can be?"

Joanna clapped her hands together and whooped so loud that a clutch of quail leapt from a nearby bush and sped straight up into the sky.

Maria Magdalena Set Free

One sunny morning, early in our trip, we trooped into the village of Magdala and met an amazing person. Here's what happened: We were heading down the road to the well in the town plaza to fill our goatskins with water. Suddenly a mad woman flew out an open doorway and hurled herself at Yeshu. Her hair was a matted tangle and her clothing hung in shreds. From the stains and smudges on her face, it appeared as if she hadn't bathed in ten years or more. The smell rolling off her body confirmed it.

She fell upon Yeshu with such ferociousness that it carried him off the road and onto his back in a field of clover. Sitting on his chest she flailed at him with both fists, screaming more profanities than I had heard in my whole life.

We all leapt to Yeshu's defense, and it took Thunder James and Thunder John—two of the strongest men I'd ever known besides Yeshu—to pull her off. When they managed to do so, they could hardly control her. Their faces were etched with looks of barely contained anger alternating with utter disbelief.

Soon a crowd of villagers formed and began bellowing insults at the mad woman, words that were almost as crazy as the things she had been yelling. They called her names that no one should ever be called.

Yeshu, back on his feet, smacked his open palms together like a crack of thunder and ordered the villagers to cease their flinging of barbed words. Startled by the commands of this tall stranger, the crowd became still.

Then Yeshu said softly, "Have you no pity?"

His eyes turned to the madwoman whom he looked upon with such compassion that the crowd seemed to swallow its insults. Still, you could tell that some wanted to go on spitting them out.

At that, to my great shock, Yeshu himself began shouting at the madwoman, "Get out! Do you hear me? Begone! Go, now!" he barked out, moving toward her, one hand outstretched, pointing at her chest.

"Get out!" he thundered even louder.

By now he was face to face with the madwoman, staring into her eyes. Then he lowered his voice.

"I will tell you seven times to get out, and seven times you will leave."

He put his hands on her shoulders and began intoning, with ever-increasing force, "Out, out, out!" And again, "Out, out, out, out!"

I watched with astonishment as the contortions melted from the woman's face. Her entire body gradually relaxed and her head sank onto her chest. I had never seen Yeshu, or anyone else, do anything like this.

He then gestured to the Thunder Brothers to let her go, which they did, slowly lowering her to the clover. She lay there weeping like a baby.

Yeshu turned to the crowd and explained that this woman was not evil, but was an unfortunate soul who had been possessed by seven inner demons.

"Even *one* demon is overpowering," he said. It takes someone very strong to survive the suffering inflicted by seven. Now they have taken their leave and so should you," he finished, bidding them good day.

One by one the townspeople headed homeward. Some looked over their shoulders as they went, making sure the excitement was really over. Others stared at the ground.

Then Yeshu knelt down and picked the woman up, cradling her in his arms like a child. Turning to Joanna and Martha, he requested of them, "Come to the river with me."

When they arrived at the riverbank, Yeshu set the woman down and left. Joanna and Martha stripped off her rags and flung them into the woods. They bathed her, washed her hair, and dressed her in Joanna's finest cloak.

An hour or so later the three of them walked into the clearing where we were setting up camp. The rest of us just stopped what we were doing and stood there, rooted to the ground.

The crazy woman was a brand new person! Her deep-set eyes were alert, framed by long, flowing hair. Her face was covered with scabs and open wounds where she had scratched herself in her madness, but we could tell she would soon be quite pleasing to look at.

She ran to Yeshu, threw her arms around him, and begged him to take her with us wherever we were going. "You've saved my life," she said. "Please don't leave me here to lose it again. I cannot remain in this place any longer. I have no family; I don't belong."

Clinging to Yeshu's robe with one hand, she pointed the other toward the town. "These people despise me and call me names and accuse me of crimes and worse."

She was crying again, tears streaming down her face.

"Who are the criminals, I ask you, and who the victims? Is it the sane, or the mad?"

"Come, break bread with us," Yeshu responded gently. "We'll talk about your wish, and we'll decide together with you."

I already knew what my vote would be. Maria of Magdala should come with us!

And she did.

Cloud of Dust

We left the fields of Magdala behind us directly after eating, with Maria Magdalena near the front of our group. I was still feeling stunned by Yeshu's deft healing that morning. How was it possible that I had never known about these powers? It seemed like every time I thought I knew the carpenter from next door, some completely new side of him would be revealed.

I did recall that my mother had once said to me, "This craftsman Yeshu is a gifted healer." But I thought she was talking about his skill at getting people to patch up their differences and forgive one another.

I also remembered with great clarity that day I fell from the walnut tree, but I was only in pain then, not gravely injured or crazed. And Yeshu was my comforter.

These notions buzzed my head like bees as we tramped the road out of Magdala. We had gone less than half a mile when I looked back to get a final glimpse of the village where I had seen my old friend, with new eyes. What I got was another surprise.

Midway between the edge of town and where we now stood, I saw a small figure surrounded by a cloud of dust, with only a head sticking out. Without thinking, I yelled, "Whoa!" in amazement, stopping everyone in their tracks.

Soon the entire group had turned to watch the figure scurrying toward us. The Thunder Brothers quickly fell into spirited debate over whether it was someone on a small camel or on a large donkey, agreeing only that the mount was galloping and not trotting. My vision being much better than theirs, I could make out that it was a man running with long loping strides and pounding the road with two of the biggest feet I'd ever seen since I began sandal making.

When this baffling runner finally reached us, he collapsed in the tall grass on the roadside and lay there panting on top of his pack, completely speechless. We all sat down around him and waited for his breathing to return to normal.

After his gasping stopped, he spent many more breaths apologizing for his unannounced arrival, his unkempt appearance, and his delay of our departure. He described in detail how difficult it had been to fit this thing and that into his pack, and then adjust it just right so it wouldn't strain his back, while also saying his proper if hasty good-byes to the friends he had been visiting with in Magdala.

We nodded, waiting for him to finally get to the point. Any point. He seemed not to notice our impatience. Eventually, however, he introduced himself.

"I am Philippos the tailor's son, from Bethsaida," he said, staring straight at Yeshu as he spoke. "I detest sewing as much as eating bitter herbs. My eyes are just fine for counting the leaves on a distant tree, but when I examine my hands, I see three thumbs and eleven fingers. Once I sewed the arm holes shut on my cloak, when I thought I was only hemming them."

He stopped to draw the back of his hand across his forehead.

At that, I caught sight of the Thunder Brothers, who were grinning like two foxes that had just spotted a cotton-tailed rabbit, dozing.

Completely oblivious, Philippos chattered on. "When I was born, my great-grandmother gave me the Greek name for horse lover—Philippos—and throughout my entire childhood I longed to work with animals. But my father would have none of that. We had no animals and couldn't afford any."

My ears perked up. Philippos continued speaking, intently and without a hint of a smile.

"Complicating matters, there were too many tailors in town for me to simply follow in my father's footsteps, so he arranged an apprenticeship with a physician. Three weeks after I began, the doctor choked on a fishbone and died in front of us all. I had learned two, interlocking facts during that short time with him: that I loved curing people, but I could not stand the sight of blood."

By now, his eyebrows were scrunched together like a couple of competitive caterpillars. "I would pass out on the spot, every single time."

Joanna and I threw glances at one another.

"You are a gifted healer," Philippos said to Yeshu, pressing his hands together. "And there is no blood involved. I was in the crowd back there and saw it all. Please, please." He pumped his clasped hands up and down. "Please let me travel with you and learn your trade. I promise to be your hardest working apprentice. I'll practice diligently every day. I'll never yawn...."

Philippos had run out of breath. His eyes were locked on Yeshu's, and they had not blinked once since he began his speech. I couldn't help thinking how much he resembled a leggy water bird intently eyeballing a nearby fish, then losing sight of it among rocks and reeds, but continuing to stare.

I looked first at Yeshu and next at the others in the group. Many of them were quietly shaking their heads in disbelief.

Yeshu responded at once. "Yes, Philippos. You have chosen me, and therefore us," he emphasized. "In a like manner, so will we choose you. Does anyone disagree?"

No one uttered a word.

Philippos, the horse lover and tailor's son, did not smile even now. He stood up immediately, bowing his head and speaking earnestly, "I assure everyone here, you'll never be sorry."

Yeshu stood also and clapped him on the shoulder. Glancing around at all of us, one by one, he read the approval, even if a bit wary, in our eyes. At that he turned to Yohanan, who jumped to his feet and swung back onto the road, the rest of us following like goslings behind the mother goose.

Yeshu hung back for a moment, watching the parade with amusement. Reaching down he picked up the pack Philippos had forgotten and swung it onto his free shoulder. He was content to bring up the rear, at peace with his thoughts.

Shepherd Girl

Continuing on our way to the renowned cedar forests, we had to cross a high, sloping plateau. We ascended a steady incline, all eyes on the trail, breathing heavily, trudging up and up and up. It seemed as if our path might end in the distant clouds.

Far above us, an enormous white bird glided on the wind.

Around midmorning we began to hear water rushing in the distance further up the trail: a mountain stream maybe.

Suddenly Yeshu stopped and cocked his head, then held his hand out parallel to the trail to draw our attention. We all halted and listened with him. Woven into the low roar of the water was a high-pitched sound, rising and falling. Was it an animal? Maybe the wind? What on earth could it be?

We resumed our climb. I could now hear, intermixed with the mysterious sound up ahead, our breathing getting more ragged. My chest was damp and chilled, and the leather pack on my back made my tunic stick to my skin with sweat. At last we reached the top of the hill, where the path curved abruptly to the left. We walked on around the bend, and in an instant the roar became so loud it drowned out our gasps of surprise.

There she was. A tiny figure, clad in a patched cloak that hung almost to her ankles and a shapeless shepherd's hat made of felt. The girl stood on a flat stone in the middle of the rushing stream. Her back was toward us, with a loosely braided plait of thick hair tumbling down to her waist. She faced a wall of falling water several times her height. Her head thrown back, she was singing at the top of her voice into the thundering waters.

Clenching her small hands by her side, the shepherd girl swung her head slowly left to right with the rhythm of her song. Once, when her head turned more than usual, I saw that her eyes were shut tight. She was in her own world, singing and singing, oblivious to anyone around her.

Yeshu raised his arm to stop us from advancing and disturbing her. For a long time we stood and watched and listened. I hoped no one was in a hurry to move on.

The girl's voice was high and sweet in tone, yet surprisingly strong coming from such a diminutive body. The water fell with such ferocity that we couldn't make out the lyrics of her song, but it didn't matter. The feelings in the melody held us and spoke to something deep inside. I turned slightly, to look at the others. Everyone was staring, transfixed, at the little shepherdess.

The whole universe had closed in and centered around the girl's tiny body, and in the water's roar, I could hear God laughing with loving delight.

It caused me to tremble with awe and compassion.

My attention returned to my companions. Their eyes were shining, and several had raised both hands to heart level, fingertips lightly touching. Maria Magdalena's face shone like the sun reflecting from a dew-drenched flower. We were all stunned by the force of the falls and the answering sound of a soul reaching out to God.

Every time a cross-breeze blew the watery mist sideways, it struck the morning sun and faint rainbows appeared, only to disappear as the mist wafted away. Not one of us made even the slightest move to leave.

A moment later the tiny singing shepherdess turned her head further than usual, and I saw that her eyes had opened. Catching sight of us, she spun around nearly toppling into the rushing water. In an instant, Thunder John jumped in up to his waist to swoop her up if need be. Her face was frozen in fear, and her voice had promptly trailed off into muteness.

Thunder John climbed, dripping, back onto the bank, and Yeshu waved and smiled warmly at the girl. Her body relaxed.

Yeshu then motioned us to move on. We had broken in on a private rapture.

Maria Magdalena started off, stopped, and looked back as if wishing to return. Then she tilted her head, pursed her lips, and blew a kiss to the shepherd girl, whose face brightened almost imperceptibly.

The last to leave was Thunder James. I saw him thrust his hand down into a large pocket of his cloak to retrieve a half-loaf of bread left over from our breakfast. He held it high in the air, his shadow dwarfing the small shepherd girl, and then he laid it on top of a rock ledge beside the path. And we were gone.

~ ~ ~

As we rested that evening after our meager dinner, Thunder John asked Yeshu to teach us how to pray. "Not so much what to pray, Yeshu, but *how*."

Yeshu became quiet for a moment.

Then he said, "There are many ways to pray, all of them good: Talking alone with God. Praying in unison with family, or with friends or strangers. Chanted prayers. Even being absolutely silent. *Especially* being silent—alone or with others.

"We Jews pray in myriad ways. So do other people, those who follow their own prophets, such as Greeks and Ethiopians. Romans pray, too, even the military officers. People are at their best when they are praying."

He paused.

"Except for false prayers such as those that ask for victory over others. Or harm to others. But of course that has to do with what people are praying *for*. Not how they pray.

"So, Thunder John, your request does not have a single answer," Yeshu said, "or a simple one."

He paused once more. I could see in his eyes he had momentarily gone away.

Then he was back. "But always, *always* you should strive to pray—even if it's in total silence—like that little shepherd girl today singing into her wall of falling water."

Later, as we laid out our bedrolls, Yeshu called us back together around the fire. Foregoing any small talk, he spoke to us.

"When you want to center yourself in spoken prayer," he said, looking at us one by one, "use these words," and he lifted up his hands, "Our God in heaven, hallowed be your name...your will be done, on earth as it is..."

I realized Yeshu was teaching us a prayer I had not heard before.

On he prayed, his eyes closed, his voice rolling forward like a hillside rivulet in the springtime.

In the middle of his prayer he said, "Give us this day our daily bread..."

And then, "Forgive us the wrongs we have done, as we forgive those who wrong us..."

Yeshu had often given us bread. Now he was giving us a special gift: his own personal prayer. I noted how he once again placed acts of forgiveness in the center of the table. And I thought about how grudges held can spin into violence, and how forgiving can be an act of embracing life.

When he finished, we were all very quiet. Then he simply said, "Amen," which we softly echoed and crawled into our bedrolls to embrace sleep.

That night I lay awake for a while staring up at the starry heavens and thinking about Yeshu's prayer. And the singing of the tiny shepherdess.

I listened to the breathing of those sleeping all around me and tried to harmonize my inhaling and exhaling with theirs. That was when I heard a low voice; I was sure it was Maria's.

In a barely audible murmur it said, "That little shepherd girl? Not so long ago, I was that child." The voice went quiet. "Though I called not into falling water but into darkness."

I wondered to whom she was speaking. To Yeshu? Yohanan? Or perhaps to all of us who were listening. I waited for more, but the voice had gone still.

The only whispers now were the night breezes in the grass, speaking an unknown language.

Finally, my eyelids got so heavy I no longer had the strength to hold them up. I entered into the dream world, falling deeply asleep holding onto only the earth upon which I lay.

Cedars of Lebanon, Legs of God

Looking back at that young lad curled into a question mark as he slumbered, I know that each day of our journey to Lebanon—to walk among the giant cedars—seemed like the answer to the prayer the boy had whispered as he fell gently asleep. How could anyone know it was the calm before a storm?

Just because your eyes see a mountain peak doesn't mean there are no clouds behind it; and it doesn't mean your feet can walk straight up to the top.

At that moment, I hoped fervently there would be other trips with Yeshu and the Thunder Brothers and Maria Magdalena and Johanna and many others. And of course, I also wanted more journeys with Yohanan, whose spirit was so bright that no cloud touched our sky.

One day poured into the next like water from a leather bucket into a clay pitcher, and the pitcher into a bowl. Yeshu was still just a village carpenter, with no reason to fear priest or soldier or anyone at all. Easy and free and unafraid, we could go wherever we liked, and say and do whatever we pleased.

To put food into our lean stomachs, we worked whatever odd jobs turned up, and when we found none, we walked some more. Sometimes villagers put us up in their homes or stables, either in exchange for work, or because they were simply good people, eager to help some hungry pilgrims and to hear the stories we had gathered from far and wide. When no one offered us shelter, we slept under the stars.

As the days and nights tramped by, the moon brightened and then darkened. Getting to the cedar forests was always in our heads, especially in mine. I couldn't wait to see this place that had inspired so much talk.

Every day brought us closer to those ancient trees that loomed larger and larger in my mind.

One morning, following a day of gentle rain, we woke up enveloped in fog. A giant cloud must have lain down for the night beside us and fallen asleep. The fog was so thick, we couldn't see forwards or backwards. Even the trail our feet had trudged upon the afternoon before had vanished.

I heard the others searching for the path, calling out to one another, and then I detected Maria Magdalena's calming voice suggesting that we should simply rest right where we were and wait for the fog to lift.

"The fog was our friend during the night, so why not this morning?" she asked. "Perhaps it's merely wrapping us in a soft embrace before it glides away."

I imagined the others sitting down on the spot from which they had stood calling only moments before, so that's what I did.

Before long, I heard Yohanan's voice sing out to all of us.

> I will come to you in a thick cloud,
> so that the people will hear me speaking to you
> and will believe you unfailingly.

I recognized those words from the *Shemot*, the Book of Exodus in the Torah, when Moses climbs Mount Sinai to receive the Ten Commandments, and God reassures him.

In spite of Maria and Yohanan's soothing words, I gradually felt a foreboding growing deep inside. It seemed as if the earth had been reduced to the spot where we waited, leaving us in a silvered netherland. Lost to the world and the world to us—as if a giant eagle had lifted us up into some far-off cloudbank.

It reminded me of the phrase from the Shemot that recounts God's role in the exodus of the Jews when we were liberated from Egyptian bondage.

> You have seen how I bore you
> on eagles' wings
> and brought you to myself.

But who knew where our small band would be set down? Or if we would be set down at all. My chest tightened and my breath grew short the more I thought about it.

Then a long while went by in which I could hear no voices. Nor could I see a single person in our group. I sat there on a rock hugging my knees. Even on pitch-dark nights, I had never felt such solitude and isolation. I didn't dare call out to my friends, for fear they would hear panic in my voice. Or worse yet, only a squeak would come out, betraying me. I knew they weren't going anywhere—just like I wasn't.

After what seemed forever, a soft breeze arose, and the fog slowly wafted away. I looked around, squinting in the bright sunlight. Our group was scattered all over the hillside, leaning against tree trunks or stretched out on the ground, waiting and napping.

I leapt to my feet and ran to the others. The world appeared to be clearer and friendlier than ever, and I blushed with embarrassment at having been knotted up with dread only moments before. Maybe my case wasn't so different though: it seemed that many of the others, especially Philippos, were talking just a little louder and laughing a bit more easily than usual.

Not Yeshu and Yohanan. They were still lost in conversation, too far away for me to hear a word of what was being said.

Quickly the group gathered together, hailed the two cousins, and as one, we swung our belongings up onto our backs. Soon we were walking again, surprisingly subdued compared to previous days. Except for Yeshu and Yohanan, who kept right on talking.

Only Maria was smiling.

Now that the fog cloud had lifted, most of our band had their eyes fixed upon the great cedars looming in the distance. They covered the mountains ahead of us, the tallest of the trees silhouetted against the sky on the horizon. Not a single head turned aside.

~ ~ ~

We finally arrived at the edge of the forest just at sunset, said our evening prayers, and pitched camp beside a tiny brook. No one spoke. We were bone-tired from the daylong trek, and from the weeks of walking and working. Nonetheless, keen anticipation was bubbling up inside me and, from the looks of the others, inside them too.

Our eyes were scanning the dark trunks up ahead as dusk spread its cloak, and we sought a way into the place we had imagined for so long. It seemed that each of us was gradually descending inside ourselves in the waning light, till soon it would no longer be clear just what was inside and what was out.

Yohanan broke the spell by reminding us we had things to finish before the last of the daylight vanished. By the time the campsite and fire were ready, water boiling, it was too dark to enter the forest for a good look. Walking toward the nearest cedar, Yohanan thrust his hand deep down into his goatskin pack and pulled out his small rock from Nazareth. He let it fall at the base of the tree, and one by one we followed suit.

I was last, and letting go of my stone, I could feel my tiredness melt away by the time the pebble hit the earth. The relief that had brushed over me just this morning—when the fog lifted and that great eagle carrying us off, put us safely down—came flooding back. How amazing, I thought, that the burdens of the body and the soul, which felt like the weight of the world one moment, could be gone the next.

Looking back at Yohanan, I saw that he had raised his eyes skyward, and I heard him softly quoting the Prophet Isaiah, from the Book of Yesha'ayahû.

> Those who hope in God will regain their strength.
> They will sprout wings like eagles.
> Though they run they will not grow weary.
> Though they walk they will never tire.

We ate a few handfuls of dried berries, drank herbal tea to warm our insides, and crawled into our blankets. There was very little night talk that evening, and soon we were all asleep.

When I awoke, it was still dark. In the cool air it sounded like the stars were singing, but I realized it was birds high in the cedars greeting the first light of dawn that had not yet reached us.

Well, most of us. I could hear someone stirring and I sat up to see who it could be. Yohanan was kneeling on his blanket, sitting back on his heels, his hands together in his lap. He was praying along with the winged creatures invisible on their branches.

Soon Yeshu turned over and sat up. Pushing his hair aside with the back of his hand, he rubbed his eyes and combed his tangled beard with his fingers. He looked over at Yohanan. Without first standing, Yeshu rolled to his knees. Gazing down at his hands and then up at the sky, he too began praying.

I tossed aside my blanket and carefully crawled through the sleeping bodies to find a spot between Yohanan and Yeshu where I could join in.

Imagine that. A former shepherd boy, now a sandal maker, becoming aware of his voice rising softly up on the words intoned by Yeshu and Yohanan.

One by one, other members of the group awoke. We were joined by Maria Magdalena and Martha, then Joanna and the Thunder Brothers. Soon the sound of a small chorus wafted up, as most prayed on their blankets that were still warm from sleep.

By the time the sun thrust over the horizon, the forest birds were in full throat and so were we. Soon, the chirping was muted, as the feathered scavengers went about their search for seeds and berries and tiny bugs.

Yohanan jumped to his feet and exclaimed, "Let's go!" almost tripping over a slumbering body. It was Philippos.

The Thunder Brothers took one look at one another, winked, and bent down on opposite sides of the sleeper. Carefully thrusting their hands under his back and hips, they quickly lifted him upright, still snoring. When the brothers let him go, Philippos fell awake the way others fall asleep. He was saying good morning even before hitting the ground, and he nimbly sprung back to his feet as if he had only been pretending. His face turned red, however, even as he joined in the friendly laughter.

Thunder James and Thunder John both hugged him, and he broke into smiles. I could see in his eyes that he was basking in the warmth of being part of the group.

Eager to see and be touched by what we had traveled such a distance for, we all headed into the forest, following the first rays of morning sunlight through the giant trees. Walking slowly across the woodland floor, our group fell silent, allowing the hush of the forest to settle steadily into us like a gentle rain, centering our souls.

Soon we were filled to the brim and everyone stood still. One after the other, we peered up and up at the soaring treetops that seemed to brush the newly blue sky with ancient fingertips.

Yohanan was the first to sink to his knees. We all followed and remained for a long time kneeling in a loose circle on the soft needles. I was just behind Yohanan and Yeshu. They were side by side, their shoulders touching, their backs gently rising and falling as they breathed together. I wanted to jump up and hug them both, but dared not break the spell.

Instead, I reached out and carefully took hold of a corner of each of their cloaks and held fast, as if I were in a chariot behind two powerful horses standing stock-still, waiting to carry me to glory.

I looked around at the faces of the others. All of them were smiling, several with their mouths open. Eyes glistened. The only sound was that of our breathing.

I caught Maria Magdalena's eye and we beamed at one another and nodded slightly, each knowing that no words could describe what we were seeing, and that there was no need to do so.

She continued to stare into my eyes with such warmth that I began to feel giddy. The joy bubbled up into a glee I barely stifled behind my hand. She smiled back, her head tilting slightly to one side.

Embarrassed and on the verge of laughing aloud, I cast my eyes about the great cedar forest for something to anchor my feelings. The gently rolling floor was covered with lacey ferns of every shade of green. The morning sun that streamed down over the delicate fronds as they swayed in an almost imperceptible breeze, cast a shifting kaleidoscope of shadow and light across them.

I imagined that the sunlight and the moving air of the warming earth were being guided by an invisible hand that was inscribing our story on the scroll of the forest floor. Not in words, of course, but in the unique language of souls on fire, stoked by the power of rising chests and beating hearts. It felt so clear and yet the inscriptions vanished before the mind could read them.

We knelt there enveloped in profound stillness for a long, long while.

Finally, Thunder John stood up and said, "I'm hungry. Let's go back to camp and eat."

Several others began to rise.

Without looking directly at John, Yohanan gazed out across the forest floor and spoke as if he were addressing the creatures that lived there.

"I wonder how long Elijah would have knelt here, and what knowledge he would have found gradually opening from bud to bloom."

Thunder John sank back down with a sheepish look on his face. So did the others. We stayed until the sun was above our heads. Had we not, we would have missed the turtle that crept slowly by, laboring over logs and around rocks and under swaying ferns.

Its journey reminded me of ours.

When it had finally disappeared around a giant cedar, Yohanan softly quoted our beloved Rabbi Abraham, "And every time I see a turtle walk...I've never seen a turtle walk before."

A brightening passed over Yohanan's face like the sky at sunbreak.

In my mind's eye, I could still see the turtle crawling along, toes turned slightly inward, powerful legs straining to carry the weight on its back onward by pushing the earth down and away, underneath its scraping belly.

And all the while, its head thrust forward resolutely, like a bridge builder hauling a large rock up a creek bank on broad shoulders, carrying a load that seems impossibly heavy, but will soon begin to create a way across the chasm.

Yohanan spoke again, breaking into my thoughts. "I find my spiritual home in the natural world. At the same time, I find my natural home in the spiritual world. The two have become one, like two hands clasping," he said, slowly bringing his hands together above his head.

Another nagging question flew through my mind, darting like a cliff swallow through a stand of saplings: This man keeps telling all who will listen that the one coming after him will be far greater. But who could that be? Will it be a new prophet or prophetess? Maybe even the Messiah.

Yohanan had hinted back in Nazareth that Yeshu had a special mission. Could he be the one? There were always rumors, this way and that.

It was Yeshu who suggested, on that day months back when we were tending sheep together, that the Messiah was to be found inside each of us. How could the Messiah be outside and inside us at the same time?

Whenever I tried to pry more out of Yeshu about this mystery, he just smiled and watched me as if I had the answer. At times he could be so exasperating. I mean, he was the teacher, right?

Still, at this moment of spellbinding peace in the cedars, I felt so close to Yohanan and Yeshu, and to everyone in our band of wanderers—it was as if we were all rooted to this place like the trees towering above us.

How could I begin to explain any of this to my mother and father? Or to my sister if ever I found her? I didn't have the words yet to fully understand it myself.

Yet even though I wasn't very old and the world was very big, I knew for sure that no king or high priest in all of history had ever built a palace or temple equal to this, the cedars of Lebanon.

And so my thoughts flitted from needle to leaf to petal and back again, like a meandering butterfly. Tugging on my mind to return it to the present, I looked at Yohanan once again, closely: at the cedar needles tangled in his beard from the night's sleep and at the flowers that Martha had put in his hair only yesterday. Last of all, at the eyes full of fire.

If one of these trees could speak, I silently reflected, it would sound like Yohanan. Closing my eyes, I paid heed to the wind moving through the tall cedars, and I strained to hear what they were saying. The breathy refrain was so sonorous, so lilting. Was it the hidden name of this place? Or perhaps it was the name of the one who would come after.

As I listened even more intently, I started to feel warm, as if I were being watched. I was sure it was Yohanan, with his head cocked, his lips moving along with the wind. He seemed to be whispering: yes, do you hear,

Daavi, this is what God sounds like.

Suddenly, I found myself descending into the well. I had no recollection that I had ever been there before, though it was just like Yohanan had described. I was far down in the center of my soul, and I could sense my inner eye focusing on the surface of a luminous pool of still water.

Listening closely I was certain I was hearing God's voice. I couldn't distinguish actual words, but that didn't concern me. All I wanted to do in this, my first journey into the well, was to hear that voice. Listen to the breezes encircling my soul, like majestic owls flying invisibly through the night. Hear the tears falling from clouds and wafting fog, falling like stars into the pool, playing their celestial music as they sequentially penetrated the water's pristine surface.

Most surprising to me was that the well felt like home. It seemed completely familiar, not alien. Without a doubt it was a place I would return to often—now that I knew the way.

All at once there was a loud crack, like thunder out of a clear sky. I jumped to my feet, rubbing my eyes, finding that all the others were looking upward. I seemed to have dozed off, and now I heard the Thunder Brothers whistle softly. I thought maybe it was at me, but no, it was in wonder. Seed cones were dropping from far up above.

It was then that I noticed Maria Magdalena had not moved at the sound. My legs lowered me back to the forest floor as I observed her face. It was so radiant it seemed as if there were fires inside her. Her eyes were staring into the forest and they were brimming.

I threw a quick glance at Yeshu and Yohanan. They were both watching Maria, too, each with a hint of a smile in his eyes.

They knew.

We all sat in stillness until finally Maria brushed her sleeve across her eyes, and drawing in a lengthy breath, let it out audibly. She then rose to her feet and steadied herself, followed by Yeshu and Yohanan. The rest of us followed suit. Together, we began strolling again through the magnificent old trees.

When the Thunder Brothers found a really huge one, they walked up to the trunk and joined hands to see how far around the trunk they could reach. They laughed in astonishment when they saw how much of the girth they were lacking and waved the rest of us over. I ran, arriving first.

Soon all nine of us were encircling what must have been the most commanding cedar in the forest. We stood with our arms and legs outstretched, hands clasped in a ring, faces raised to the sky. I felt sure I was going to fly to the crown.

I continued staring up and up into the treetops.

Suddenly, Thunder John leaned as close to me as he could without losing his balance, and nodding skyward, whispered near the back of my head, "Legs of God!"

I could not remember ever feeling such joy.

And All the Trees of the Wild Will Clap Their Hands

Everything that I was feeling in the cedars, I never wanted to end. And in many ways, for me the journey that brought us to that place keeps rolling on, just like the river to the sea from Joanna's song. Many moments still seem so vivid that I have to shake my head to realize they aren't happening right now.

My outer eye peers at what is before me: a bowl of mutton stew or a piece of leather I am laboring over. But my inner eye—the eye that sees the farthest—focuses upon those visions of light and shadow dancing over the ferns and moss of the forest floor, and on the arching canopy of ancient branches with their curving needles, high above me.

In the forest of cedars, as my mind sorted through all that had happened on that awe-filled journey, my heart raced from notion to notion like a stone skipping across water. At other times, there were moments of utter and profound peace. Lightning bolts without the thunder.

And then it hit me. Just think how far back these lofty trees went in *their* journey through time. When they were mere saplings, pushing up out of the ground, Moses was leading our people out from their slavery to the pharaohs of Egypt!

Unlike those ancient Jews, being in no hurry to leave we spent many days there in the forest, deep in silence and deep in conversation. We walked together and alone, our eyes searching all the live things that surrounded us. We lay in our bedrolls at night, engaged in discussions that probed our beliefs and our world of struggle, until the sinking moon finally pushed our eyelids shut. And often we simply sat by ourselves in favorite, leafy nooks, lost in dreaming and meditation. Always to be found again.

More and more frequently, I saw Maria Magdalena walking with Yohanan, or with Yeshu, or both of them. The three always seemed locked into their talking, and I felt good about that rather than wishing I could be right there in the middle of it. What surprised me was how much Yohanan and Yeshu listened to *her*. She didn't appear to be even remotely like a student of theirs. Neither did she seem like a mere newcomer to our group.

Once, in particular, the three of them were standing together conversing next to a colossal cedar that stood directly across a large clearing from where I sat. I saw Yeshu suddenly glance toward Yohanan and they both shrugged, then each turned to Maria and nodded as if they were agreeing with her. She grasped the two of them by the elbow, and they strolled off again, clucking and chirping like a covey of quail.

Other times, our band stuck together, joking and playing games.

Maria kept reminding us, "Too much seriousness will turn us into old crusts of bread on a dusty shelf."

And Yeshu was always the first to agree, with the Thunder Brothers rolling in right behind, it should be added.

I had brought some pieces of bone and leather thong on our journey, and I taught everyone all the games my grandmother used to play with Shoshana and Aaron and me. It was funny how Thunder James and Thunder John always wanted to win. So much so, that sometimes we let one or the other of them get the best of us, just so as to hear the end of it.

Finally it was time to go home. Our food was running out, berry season was ending, and we needed to work again and to see our families. Yohanan gathered us on the final morning. We stood silently in a circle, for a long while.

Then Yohanan leaned down, plucked a stone from the ground, and pocketed it. We all followed suit.

On the long walk back to Nazareth, I mulled over what I knew for sure now: that God is in wildness and that this aspect of God is deep inside each of us, if we would only look there, and listen.

I had also discovered how God could be present in a group of close friends. This was as clear to me as a shining Jupiter racing through patches of clouds in the night sky.

Now I wanted to know if that were only true for this special group or could God also be found, say, in my family. Even though a terrible thing must have happened to Shoshana, maybe God was there, too, poised for something to be resolved.

I also wondered whether God could be in a larger group of people, like a neighborhood or a whole town. Or what about a band of thieves or a detail of soldiers? I wasn't sure of this. Maybe I would find the right moment to ask Yeshu. I could start with a small village like ours.

Or perhaps I should just try to puzzle this out myself...

At that, Thunder John broke into my thoughts with his favorite game. "Point to the moon!" he suddenly yelled out. Everyone rushed to point their finger, most peering up at the sky, but I pointed at the ground.

"Daavi wins!" he proclaimed, clapping his hands together.

"How can that be?" protested Philippos. "The moon can't be underground." It was his first time playing the game.

"Sure it can," said John. "The moon circles us, just like the sun, and so half the time it is beneath the earth."

He was enjoying lecturing that studious old Philippos.

"The trick is to always be so aware of just where the moon is on its journey, even in the daytime, that you don't have to search for it. You just know."

He threw me a sideways glance.

"If you need help, ask Daavi." And he hooted loudly.

Philippos merely shook his head and concentrated on the trail. A proud smile crept across my face, so I lowered my gaze and studied my sandals. After a dozen or so steps, I picked up my pace to catch up with Philippos. He looked down at me and I touched him on the shoulder. We both grinned and wrinkled our noses.

~ ~ ~

On the last day of our journey, as we got closer and closer to Nazareth, I walked for hours not talking. My mind was traveling more rapidly than my feet. I felt like I was somewhere far away, looking back.

Just think, I told myself silently, even if nothing else remarkable happens in my life, I made it to the cedars of Lebanon!

Walking along I felt an inner clarity that I had never experienced before. It was different from the peace I'd found encircling the giant cedar. Everything seemed sharper and brighter: The dusty road just ahead; the honeybees tugging an invisible blanket over the meadow; the trees moving in slow motion like hands waving farewell, or was it hello, as we passed them by.

I'm not the same person, I reflected, who left home several crescent moons ago, am I? I see differently. I hear differently. I am different. Even my thoughts and feelings seem deeper and broader.

I listened to my footsteps for a while as I walked. Before, I resumed my unvoiced musing, my feelings kept swirling together, all jumbled and murky, like a muddy stream after a spring thunderstorm.

I kept my eyes on the path, so as not to stumble.

But now, I went on ruminating, things seem more lucid, like that same stream when it's running clear. Full of rocks of all colors sparkling like jewels on the bottom, and fish darting this way and that, nosing in and out of holes, while the stream just goes on flowing.

I promised myself I wouldn't forget a single detail, so that if I ever saw Shoshana again, I could tell her everything that had happened to me on this journey. Especially the currents that swept along down inside.

For a while, I listened to my footsteps again, as they kept time with the feet around me, creating a music that made you want to dance.

Then my mind turned inward once more, spiraling like a fish diving to the bottom. I scarcely watched my feet walking along, while meanwhile I was far, far away.

Of course, I thought to myself, not everything is clear. Probably never will be, I chuckled. New thunderstorms will muddy up the stream again. Nights will fall when nothing can be seen till dawn. Those holes at the river bottom will always be there for fish to pop into and out of.

But at least I know the difference now between clear and murky.

I let my eyes roam over the nearby hills and the brilliant white clouds lying beyond them.

How easy it was to be lost in thought when nearly everyone around you had stopped talking. Just before mid-day, Maria Magdalena broke the silence.

"I have watched many a flower bloom," she said suddenly, "but until now I have not known what it must feel like to be a seed lying dormant underground, passing through a winter with little rain and only chill permeating from up above.

"And at last to feel the first rains soaking in and surrounding you, softening you and opening you up.

"Then experiencing your head and your hands gradually thrusting upward toward an unnamed warmth coming from on high. Finally pushing through the surface of what was pressing you down, and you feel a splash of sunlight illuminate your face, your eyes, your mouth.

"Reaching upward until all you want to do is stretch everything you have to the heavens: your arms and fingers; your chest, shoulders, and neck; your chin and mouth. Thrusting upward until shouts of color blossom from your throat to your tongue, to praise the heavens above. Praise God who has made us all."

Everyone listened to her intently, faces turned in her direction.

She looked toward Yohanan, saying, "Thank you gardener, for tending me with such care."

Then to Yeshu, "Thank you, harvester, for setting my soul free."

And finally to the rest of us, "Thank you all for welcoming me in. And lifting me up."

As one, Yohanan and Yeshu raised both hands, palms toward the sky, and lowered them back down.

We all had smiles on our faces. And we strode on, our feet beating out a single rhythm, as the scent of the sweet fruits of the journey wafted through our minds.

~ ~ ~

A fortnight later, deep in the afternoon, we didn't merely walk into Nazareth, we floated in. People stepping out of their houses just stared at us. Small children ran behind us, laughing and cutting up. We must have been a real spectacle after so many months on the road, this ragtag group of men and women, dusty and dog-tired.

Besides that, we knew well that it was unheard of for women to travel with men unless they were married to them. But with Yeshu that simply didn't matter. He believed strongly in including *every*one in whatever he did, and he once told me he was willing to face any consequences that this brought him. It was exciting knowing we were part of this spring ground-breaking, and all our eyes were lit up. So I suppose we seemed like a meteor shower streaking into town.

Yohanan led us straight to the town well, where he gave us all what he called, "a last and a first drink of water."

We each dug into pockets and shoulder bags to fish out the small stones from the cedars of Lebanon. Wordlessly we placed our stones by the well.

Before the last stone hit the ground, Yeshu stepped forward and spoke, "The Prophet Isaiah gives us just the right words to brighten our return."

> You shall go out in joy and be led back in peace;
> the mountains and the hills before you will burst into song,
> and all the trees of the wild will clap their hands.

With that we all clapped *our* hands as one, hugged each other, and then headed off to see our families and seek lodging for our friends. I lingered, not wanting the trip to be over, staring into the well, then gazing back out of town in the direction from which we had come, into the sunset.

That's when I realized that something else in me had changed. Before my travels to the cedars of Lebanon, I had heard people talk about the soul, but I wasn't sure what they meant. I'd nod my head in agreement. Or if I were feeling uneasy, which I sometimes was, I'd look about or just slip away. But now that I was home, here by this well that I knew like the palm of my hand, I could feel something new stirring far down inside, like one of those fish that I had imagined nosing about, as I pondered matters on the road.

It reminded me of that time I've talked about, when Yohanan's mother first felt him stirring inside her. It was when Mama Maria had just walked through Elisheva's doorway, bringing news that she was carrying Yeshu inside of *her*, and before Maria could utter a word, Elisheva felt the quickening—tiny Yohanan leaping with joy within her.

If this cedars voyage was the quickening of my soul, I couldn't wait to find out what life might be like, growing and being birthed through other quest journeys with Yohanan and Yeshu. I could feel something awakening deep within: pulsating, thirsting for more. I didn't know where these two travelers were heading next, but I knew that somehow I had to be right there placing my feet in their footprints.

Rainbows

Following our return to Nazareth, Yohanan hinted that he might not be staying long. Meanwhile, Maria Magdalena left for Bethany with Martha, who needed to tend to family, and Joanna struck out for Jerusalem. The Thunder Brothers said they had a fishing boat to repair. Philippos received word that his mother was ailing, and he left in the night.

Yeshu went back to his carpentry the very next morning to take care of the crowd of people lined up at the door of his workshop, each of whom had been patiently awaiting his return. It seemed as if half the families in Nazareth had broken a bench leg or had a door crack in two, while we were walking.

My father put me straight to work, as well. There was plenty to be done in the leather shop, and the local tax collector was once again short a shepherd. Both my parents gave the impression that they were put out with me for being gone so long. They didn't seem to understand how important it had been for me, nor were they very interested in lingering at dinnertime to hear my stories. Only my brother Aaron wanted to listen.

The next day, in the late afternoon, Yohanan and Yeshu took a walk to say their sundown prayers at the small lake just outside of town. As they passed my house, they saw me and waved. After they tossed glances at one another, they both motioned that I should come along. My father noticed the exchange and gestured his reluctant approval with a shrug of the shoulders.

I had to sprint to catch up with them. My breath didn't return to normal until we arrived at the lake. At least for some time now I was big enough that I could keep up with them without walking a few steps, running a few more, walking, running, as in the days when I was just a kid.

On a whim, I went off to pick berries for the three of us. By the time I got back, I found Yohanan and Yeshu standing, shoulder to shoulder, as still as two herons, mesmerized by a thin young moon descending through the sunfire, like a silvery fish. Rosh Hodesh!

I joined them and we stood gazing out over the smooth surface of the lake as twilight cast color changes across the water again and again. It went from crimson on blue to magenta, sparkling purple, and beyond.

The air was calm. Not even the faintest breeze touched my hair.

All during the gloaming, swallows skimmed the water, turning left, turning right, to snatch their evening meal. Their reflections in the still lake looked like images from another world just below the lake's surface.

I listened while Yohanan and Yeshu talked quietly, with sometimes lengthy stretches of stillness in between exchanges. Not once did they mention the High Priest, or the court lawyers, or King Herod, or the Roman Army commanders. Nor did they speak of any other problem they knew was waiting for them, and I didn't.

Instead, they talked about a favorite waterhole they had known as boys; and a tall red-legged stork that fished there, walking slowly, deliberately, just like an old man stepping carefully through high grass. And they raved about the taste of figs early in the season when they were still slightly green; and later in the season when they were ripe and mushy and falling off the tree. Oh, and sun-dried and stored in your pocket in the winter, to chew on after dark.

They remembered variations in the tone of voice their mothers used when calling them to the evening meal; the slippery feeling of wet wood on the bottoms of fishing boats turned over in the sand; and the night they stood watching a shadowy arc glide slowly over the moon—this same moon, only full—darkening it bit by bit until all that was left was a red ring that resembled a slender crown hanging in the sky.

They spoke of two gently billowing tents, one of them with a single candle inside, casting the shadow of a young family preparing for sleep. The other tent dark, sighing.

Meanwhile, the sky turned a deeper and deeper blue until finally it became black and the stars began popping out. To keep our necks from aching, we lay down on our backs on the narrow, sandy beach, lying close together so that each one of us warmed the other.

I was the first to discover Venus, my favorite wandering star, shining brilliantly just to the left of the crescent moon. These two travelers were descending slowly together toward the horizon—Venus seeming to peer into the mouth of a cave.

"I can't believe it's Rosh Hodesh again," I said. "The past month went by so fast!"

"And can you see the seven sisters?" I added, pointing. I was quickly rewarded with a double-voiced, "Ahh."

Out of the corner of my eye, I could barely make out Yeshu and Yohanan, their chests rising and falling.

At that moment, I thought to myself, "If the other thirteen-year-olds in Galilee knew about this, every one of them would want to be me."

~ ~ ~

After our return from the cedars of Lebanon, we learned that the local area had suffered for months without rain. The air was dry and hot, and everything had browned. The trees drooped their heads, and their leaves began to curl, as if to hide themselves from the burning sun.

The people in our village stayed indoors most of the day, working only from first light until midmorning and from late afternoon until dusk. The rest of the time, the heat crushed them into the ground, sucking out any interest in exertion.

One afternoon I joined Yohanan who was sitting with four or five kids in a covered gateway that led into the cattleyard of a house down the road from ours. Two cows were lying on the ground against the mud walls, trying to find the spot of most shade, their bones pushing out like tent poles. We could hear their labored breathing, and we watched their tails incessantly whisking the same hundred biting flies off their shanks. There was one solitary puff of cloud hanging in the sky near the horizon.

Yohanan stroked his great, shaggy beard and began describing all the ways that animals in the wild survive heat and droughts. He told us how the skinks and lizards knew which plants collected moisture down in the folds where leaves emerged from thick stalks. They proceeded even if there were only a few dewdrops that had slid downward in the night and formed a miniscule pool that could be reached by a pointed, carefully probing tongue.

He told how tortoises would bury themselves in the ground with only their nostrils sticking out. And how most animals kept still for hours during the highest arc of the sun. No birds in the white sky. No field-mice scurrying across the burning sand.

He told us he had discovered all this by mimicking the animals in order to survive. "I thirsted for knowledge," he laughed.

And so did we.

Then he was quiet for a while as each of us looked around, noticing even the slightest movement.

When he spoke again, he said, "When there's been no rain for a long time, do you know what I miss the most?"

We all turned our heads toward him.

"I don't miss bathing in the waterholes. You can do that twice a day during the rainy season, though I don't know who would want to." He rolled his eyes to make us laugh.

"I don't miss picking wild fruit. There are always nuts and roots and honey, or bark for seasoning a tepid drink.

"What I miss most..." he paused and gazed out over the brown hilltop in the distance. All eyes were on his mouth that we could see at the end of that tunnel of beard. "What I miss most are the rainbows." He was still for a moment.

Eyebrows popped up all around.

"I'm being very serious now. Heat can be hidden from. Moisture is there to be found. If you lack a lizard's tongue, there are always blades of grass to chew on, or chances for searching out a trickle of stream underneath the rocks. And as for fancy food and drink? You know I do best without them. Some of my happiest times have come from fasting, from meditating during days of going without.

"But no rainbows?" he exclaimed. "No thin arc of flower petals thrust against the sky? No tinted mist floating in space, dancing through time?" He looked around at each of us, with a glint in his eyes.

"I'd much rather be filled with the wonder of seeing things shimmering in their infinite hues than be weighed down and sluggish with much wine and spiced fruit." Yohanan waggled his head, and his hair and beard settled slowly on his shoulders and chest.

"Cakes and wine aren't enough to keep a person alive and certainly aren't worth living for," he said, shaking his head. "Our deepest hunger and thirst is for something more, wouldn't you say? I know this when my eyes feast on the reds and yellows, the greens, blues and violets, arching across the sky. Suspended in air...gliding before my eyes...filling my heart with hope."

His lips were firmly set, down inside his beard.

"And don't ever forget what is reported in the *Berêšîth*, the Book of Genesis in the Torah, about God's message to Noah and his sons concerning the rainbow.

> Here is the sign of the covenant
> I make between myself and you
> and every living creature on earth with you,
> for all future generations.

Yohanan took a breath, held it, then let it out. Drawing himself up, he began softly quoting more of God's words.

> Whenever the rainbow appears in the clouds,
> I shall see it and call to mind
> the everlasting covenant between myself
> and all earth's creatures.

"God is present in the rainbow," he said, "reminding us to be devoted caretakers. This is our sacred duty."

So, whenever I see a rainbow," Yohanan spoke firmly now, "I feel called forth and inspired to push on. Energy flows out from somewhere down inside me as if I were feeding nectar to a probing bee."

He grew quiet, but we could tell he wasn't finished, so we were quiet, too.

"Now, as you know, a rainbow is not the only dish at the feast. Out here in God's house you can hold up a broad sycamore leaf to the sunlight and dance along each of its veins spreading rhythmically outwards. Or picture a lion's massive paw, slightly bent in sleep like a kitten."

He bent his leathery hand and laid his forehead across it.

"You can rise up with the furious flight of a startled mourning dove. Or feel yourself floating like a kite made of thin bark as you run breathlessly down a hill, vainly trying to catch up with your laughter."

Yohanan finally paused to take several mouthfuls of air himself.

"But rainbows are for me the best food of all. They give me what manna must have given for our ancestors wandering in the wilderness, because they fill me up to the brim with the promise of God's covenant. They fill me with God's pledge to provide for us for as long as we care for the earth."

Yohanan slept in my house that evening, which always made me proud that we had so earned his trust. When he came to town these days, he usually passed the night in the fields or pastures, or someone's barn, so the soldiers could not find him. There were still orders out for his detention.

I awoke at dawn, folded the covers back and slipped my sandals on. Because I had spent much of the previous day listening to Yohanan, I had totally forgotten to gather the firewood my mother had asked me to bring home, and we had run out just after our evening meal. If we were to have a warm drink for breakfast with our bread and honey, I had to rise before the others to find wood.

I stole noiselessly out of the house just as the curtain between night and day was lifting and parting. The air felt exquisite, with a deliciously balmy and moist breeze blowing gently from the direction of Lake Galilee. I could smell iris petals and freshly cut hay on the wind. A rose-colored glow slowly crept up the cloudless sky above the distant fields. Soon the sun's chariot would hurtle over the horizon.

Leaving the village, I struck off down a path through a lightly wooded area, gathering twigs and branches from the ground. When I had an armful, I continued out into a small meadow nestled between rolling hills. Suddenly, the sun broke over the rise behind me. I stopped and stared at the grasses, barely believing my eyes.

Gripped by excitement, I turned on my heel and raced all the way home. Dropping my meager haul of kindling at the door, I headed straight to my father's workshop where Yohanan was lodged, and I knelt beside him as he lay stretched out on the floor on a stiff old cowhide, slumbering.

"Yohanan!" I whispered close to his ear, placing my hand on his shoulder and gently shaking him.

His eyes sprung open like a frightened deer's, and his entire body clenched.

Seeing me, he released his breath and moaned, "What is it?"

"Don't be cross with me for disturbing you, Yohanan, but there's something you *must* see in the meadow."

He stared at me. I could see him trying to decide behind his half-open eyes whether to just roll over and fall back asleep.

"Rainbows!" I whispered. "Thousands of rainbows."

For a moment, while he lay motionless I wondered whether he might have been pulling my leg the day before. An instant later he sprang up and was out the door before I could regain my feet. I ran down the road after him.

Catching up to him, I gasped, "Not this way. The other way."

Without missing a step, he pivoted on one foot and took off in the opposite direction. I had to run to stay ahead of him, so he wouldn't miss the turn just beyond the orchard of ancient fig trees.

When Yohanan came to the edge of the meadow, he fell to his knees, flashed me a quick look with eyes blazing and bearded mouth wide open, and then knelt there motionless, just staring straight ahead, his hands outstretched with fingertips quivering.

"Look at them all!" he cried out. "So many—a *minyan* on each clump."

Our eyes were fixed on the meadow. On each blade of grass clung one or more tiny drops of beaded dew. Each dewdrop reflected miniature slivers of rose or orange or lemon. There were countless fragments of rainbow as far as we could see.

We stayed there kneeling on the carpet of grasses for a long while, soaking up the colors, with the new sun gently warming our backs. We were faced that way because rainbows only reveal their wonders when the sun is behind you, peering over your shoulder and hurling its rays.

When Yohanan finally turned to me again, his forehead and cheekbones shone. His mouth was outlined with lime and blueberry, his beard streaked with indigo and violet. And in his eyes were reflected flashes of rainbow shards.

"Isn't God beautiful?" He shook his head in wonder as he spoke.

Then his voice dropped, quavering just a bit, "Thank you, Daavi, thank you." He paused to put a hand on my shoulder. "You understand me."

Yohanan's eyes had now misted over like the seashore at daybreak, and the mist shone bright with all the rainbow hues. Wordlessly, he helped me gather more wood and deposit it next to my mother's cooking yard.

Then, refusing any food or drink, he left town before the others awoke. It was not in Yohanan's nature to ever say goodbye. This time he grasped me by the shoulders and leaned over until his forehead touched mine.

"Go to Yeshu and wake him if he still sleeps," he said. "Tell him I'm gone. I've seen a sign. The time has come to return to my preaching."

My mouth wanted to ask him when he would be back again, but my head knew the question was unanswerable.

And anyway, he always came back—when the time was ripe.

So why did my breath catch tight in my chest?

God Is in the Mouth of the Wolf

One day a few weeks later, I was helping Mama Ana with carding a bag of raw wool she had just gotten by bartering for it with a dozen packets of herbal remedies. Combing and combing the wool with a dried thistle head left lots of time for talking and soon the conversation turned to God: How Yeshu spoke of God; and how that differed from what Yohanan said. They seemed like two different Gods!

"Yeshu says God is love," I started out.

I was speaking evenly as if I were drawing the shape of a foot on a piece of leather to make a sandal. That's something I had done a hundred times or more. The reasoning I was laying out was similar. Footwear has to fit right, and even the same person can have two different sizes or shapes to their two feet.

Does God vary to fit each soul? Or perhaps the soul must conform to a single way of knowing God. It was a confusing stone I'd been kicking around in my mind since we'd gotten back from the cedars. Or maybe it was more like a pebble lodged inside my sandal as I walked.

I went on, "Yeshu also teaches me that God is inside every one of us."

Mama Ana nodded, letting me talk it out.

"Even the Roman Centurion and the spiteful murderer must have God inside of them, though that's hard for me to see."

She nodded again and waited for me to continue.

"And God occupies the spaces between people," I said. "So God must exist in our communities. In Nazareth and Bethlehem. Even in Magdala where so many people were cruel to Maria Magdalena. I think God must have been there too, working with those people." I paused.

"After all, for years Maria was one of them, so it seems to me that they had some of her goodness inside themselves.

"But could God exist in a new village of people with no history? Or must it be made up of folks who have been friends practically forever, or family for countless generations?"

Mama Ana let me pose question after question without batting an eye... or trying to jump in and answer.

I gulped more air and continued. "So Yeshu talks about the God of humankind. Yohanan, on the other hand, says God is in wilderness. God is in silence, and eagles' wings, and the mouth of the wolf.

"After he told me that," I went on, "I spent a whole night dreaming of a wolf in front of my face with its jaws wide open. Each time it lunged at me, I'd push my fist into its steaming mouth to keep those rows of long, yellowing teeth away from my throat.

"How could that be God?"

Mama Ana waited to see if I was finished. She looked at me for a long time before she finally spoke.

"Let me tell you a story," she said, leaning toward me with her hands on her knees, elbows akimbo.

"Once a woman and a she-wolf," she began, "found themselves on a narrow island in the middle of a flood-swollen river, just after a storm. The woman had a baby boy in her arms, and the mother wolf had three pups."

I felt my brow furrowing as I puzzled over where this story was heading. And where it had come from.

Mama Ana was undeterred by my expression.

"The two mothers locked eyes," she said. "The baby's mother, perhaps having heard the same overblown stories that you have heard about wolves, was afraid the panting creature would attack her and her child. She clutched her baby to her breast and plunged into the water to try to make it to shore. In an instant she was up to her neck, and the raging current tore the infant from her arms!

"Twisting her body, she caught a root that extended from the island and pulled herself back ashore. Desperately she clambered to her feet and ran down the shoreline, searching the water sweeping past for a sign of her child. But the only moving body she saw was that of the she-wolf streaking past her and throwing itself into the river. A few moments later the wolf surfaced, swimming relentlessly against the current to return to land at the far tip of the island. The baby boy was gripped firmly in the wolf's mouth by his clothing.

"Crawling ashore, the mother wolf gently laid the tiny infant on its back.

"The baby's mother raced down the island toward her child.

"While the mother ran, the wolf noticed the baby was coughing up water, so she turned him face down with her muzzle and forepaw and put her mouth around his chest. She squeezed gently until the infant spit up water and bits of leaves and then gasped for breath.

"By then the mother had arrived. She stood frozen, an arm's length away, staring into the eyes of the wolf until finally the wolf released her hold and trotted off up the shoreline to check on her pups, any one of which could have been the baby she had plunged into the water to save.

"The mother knelt down and bent over her coughing child, patting his back and gently opening up his clothes. She found not a single tooth mark on his skin. Her shoulders shook as she wept."

I looked up at Mama Ana, and raised one hand to my open mouth, the other one touching her knee.

"So," I said, "God is in the mouth of the wolf..."

Mama Ana smiled back at me, brushing away a wisp of hair that had fallen over one eye. "Daavi, before you think you understand God so easily," she said, "I'm going to tell you another story.

"My Uncle Danyel once traveled far to the west and north, across the great sea that the Romans call Mare Nostrum."

With a wry smile, she added, "I guess if you control an empire, you can name an ocean 'Our Sea.'"

She went on. "Uncle Danyel journeyed twenty days walk beyond Rome, in search of famous mines he had heard about from a traveler. They were said to be full of gold and silver and salt.

"He came to a land where the mountaintops are higher than the clouds and covered with snow all year. The winters are so cold, the lakes become solid as rock.

"One clear-blue winter day, late in the afternoon, Uncle Danyel sat wrapped in blankets in the doorway of an abandoned woodcutter's hut, high up on a mountainside overlooking a great white lake. Below him he suddenly saw a lone elk burst onto the solid surface of the lake, running like fury with its head and antlers thrown back, its tail flitting from side to side.

"A few moments later, five wolves raced onto the frigid lake, fanning out in a tight semicircle quite a ways behind the elk. Every time the elk turned, the wolves turned in unison, a breath later. Tenaciously, the five wolves gained on the fleeing elk, its antlers flashing fire as they caught the final rays of the sinking sun.

"The elk was running for its life, and the wolves were running for theirs.

"One wolf, the color of charred firewood, ran faster than the others, his ears and tail flat out in the wind. As the elk tired and its hard hooves slipped and churned wildly on the rock-white lake surface, the charcoal wolf steadily closed in.

"Instead of leaping on the running elk's back, or biting its hindquarters, this lead wolf suddenly threw its body down, and sliding in a sharp curve hit the elk's legs broadside, sweeping it off its feet like a hand would sweep breadcrumbs from a tabletop. The elk fell heavily, its antlers inscribing a curving scar on the lake's surface.

"The next two wolves to reach the downed elk bit through the tendons on the backs of its rear legs, and the final two tore open the elk's throat. It took all five of them to drag the carcass back to shore, where a jumble of thin pups awaited their supper. Hungrily they fell upon the fresh kill. On the hardened lake behind them, a long streak of glistening blood stretched toward the setting sun.

"The charcoal wolf stood, head down, its legs apart and shoulders heaving as it got its breath back. Then it arched its back...raised its muzzle to the sky...and opened its great mouth to sing."

Mama Ana stopped talking.

I stared at her in stunned silence. Now I was confused again.

"Are people like wolves?" I finally asked.

She waited for me to go on.

"And are wolves like people?"

"That's only a part of it," she answered. Noting my distress, she spoke in steady tones, "Daavi, you've been told that God is in the butterfly wing and in the mouth of the wolf."

She was looking into my eyes. In her voice I caught a sliver of Yohanan's.

"Think about God with your heart—and in your dreaming—not just with your head. You seek answers where there are only questions. You will not find God by looking straight ahead, but out of the corner of your eye."

She stopped for a moment, giving me time to reflect on her words. I could see she was not going to make this easy for me. Her pause signaled there is no easy way to understand something so vast and ancient as God.

Then she went on softly, "Daavi, the human spirit is a wanderer. Knowing God is a journey; an unwalked path across the desert sand. It's a path for you to make for yourself each step of the way—sometimes alone and sometimes with others.

"Close your eyes, open your heart, and walk!"

Torch Passing

Stories began to reach us about what Yohanan was saying, now that he was preaching again. He was telling people that things were not right in our world, that Rome was corrupt, and that the king of our people was an immoral person who needed to repent for his behavior.

My Uncle Bartholomaios came for a visit one day, with his little daughter Sara leading him through his private darkness.

I listened as he stared blankly up at the rafters and told my father, "Your friend Yohanan and his kinsman Yeshu are revolutionary fools. They just distract the people from what really needs doing." He shook his head in exasperation.

"This time next year," he said, wagging his finger, "they'll both be gone and forgotten. What good are speeches about repentance and love and justice? The only way to free enslaved people is with a sword!" His face shook as he spoke. "We Jews must meet might with might. We must not collaborate or capitulate. When the Messiah comes, he will be a great general, like David."

When I heard my birth name, my ears perked up. As a young boy, I had wanted to learn everything there was to know about King David and his prowess as a warrior. But now that I had gotten to know people like Yeshu and Yohanan and Mama Maria, I had formed a very different notion of what the savior of our people would be like. After all, Moses raised no sword.

And yet my Uncle Bartholomaios could be so convincing. Sometimes I believed he could see far better than the rest of us.

On top of that, I could not forget the terrible things I had heard from neighbors and travelers: of people being dragged from their homes to do forced labor in mines that most would never come home from, and of soldiers coming in the night to put others to the sword, or arresting them and hanging them on crosses, so as to terrorize the rest of us and crush our spirits.

I knew in my heart that Yohanan, and perhaps even Yeshu, might be taken from us. The thought made me tremble. So seeing them together, the day that Yohanan passed his fire to Yeshu, is one of my most vivid memories.

My father must have gotten word that something was going to happen, because early one morning, he woke me up and told me to pack some things.

"We are walking to the River Jordan," he said.

And walk we did, all day long. When we reached the river, the sun was low in the sky.

There stood Yeshu and Yohanan, facing one another in the river. Living water was dripping from Yohanan's hands back into the Jordan. All around, the river sang as it spilled over the rocks. Yohanan seemed made out of stone. He didn't bat an eye, even when a white dove fluttered down and lit upon Yeshu's shoulder, the same shoulder that could lift a cypress log.

The dove spread its wings and folded them into its body, spread its wings and folded them again.

Suddenly a memory flew through my mind like a bat in the night. It was of the day that Yohanan and I had sat quietly on a hill above town until finally I broke the silence.

"Yohanan," I had asked, "I keep looking for God. I search where you tell me to. But so far I can't find what really seems to be God."

Yohanan's eyes softened with affection, and then he pointed at the beating wings of a single swallow flitting across the sky.

As I followed its flight, he leaned over and spoke into my ear, "God is not the bird. Nor the wing in motion. But the flight of your heart as you watch that bird and then turn to face this world."

However, on this shining afternoon by the River Jordan with my father, the bird did not fly across the sky but straight to Yeshu—no sooner than Yohanan had poured the living water over his cousin's brow. I watched the white dove settling down calmly on the carpenter's shoulder. Now the dove looked back at Yohanan, and so did I.

For the first time ever, I saw that the sun in Yohanan's eyes was setting. His cheekbones were sparkling with tears.

For a moment, I wondered if he was afraid for Yeshu. Or maybe for himself?

Many years later I understood what those tears meant. They were the tears that well up from your soul when you know that your work is nearly done and it's time to go in peace.

I know. One day I would feel just that myself.

The Sweet Voice of Wildness Is Silenced

Whenever the soldiers carried out their searches for Yohanan, Yeshu and my father and I were among those who sent out warnings. If he was in Nazareth, we hid him and we made every effort to sidetrack the search parties.

Ever since Yohanan had returned to preaching from the edge of the wilderness, and baptizing people in the living waters of the Jordan, his spiritual message had grown sharper, more focused. He stared straight at those in power, and described what he saw, and it wasn't pretty. Not at all how they saw themselves.

He continued to urge the common people to strive toward perfecting themselves, by acting justly and humbly, and being loving stewards of the earth and all its creatures. But now he was applying these same principles to the Romans and to our authorities, too. Those with earthly power should also strive for such moral perfection. And they, too, should care for the natural world, in keeping with God's rainbow covenant with us, the earth's people. After all, the strong were examples for everyone else. Each action they took affected thousands, maybe tens of thousands.

Yohanan wanted his message to fly as far as the falcon, and as high, too.

People began to say that his most biting words he saved for Herod Antipas, our Jewish king. He was a monarch whom the Romans deftly used to justify their rule and make it easier for them to control us. Antipas was the son of the same tyrant, Herod, who after Yeshu was born, had ordered every male baby in Bethlehem to be put to the sword.

One day Yohanan ended any doubts that remained in people's minds about his preaching. He publicly denounced King Herod Antipas by name.

He accused him of being an adulterer who had thrown out his own wife to marry Herodias, the wife of his brother, who still lived. Herod Antipas had broken the Laws of Moses, and Yohanan stood in front of crowds of people and said so. And he called on Antipas to repent.

When these stories reached us, people argued about whether Yohanan was being brave or reckless. Yeshu was often silent, listening, but in the end he always stood up strongly for Yohanan.

Yeshu had a way with words and he could have taken either side to win everyone over. And yet he himself was still trying to figure out just how and where the spiritual world met and changed the world of power.

Yohanan didn't hesitate. He scolded and hectored and denounced Herod Antipas relentlessly. The king's spies were everywhere, mingling in the crowds thronging around Yohanan, so Antipas had to have known all that was going on. But it seems that at first he was puzzled. Before the talk had turned personal, he found this man with his animal skins and odd teachings something new and fascinating. Now he felt the sting of the hornet. And it wasn't just wounded pride, he told himself; maybe this brash huckster would turn the huge crowds he was attracting into an angry mob.

If Herod Antipas was displeased, his new wife Herodias was livid. How dare some rowdy beggar call the new queen immoral! Finally, Herod had to quiet his wife's voice, which had a way of festering in his ear like a broken-off thorn. On top of that, he was growing frightened by the whispering he sensed was rising up the moment he left a room of people. So, he ordered his swarming band of guards to mount an all-out effort to capture Yohanan and throw him in the dungeon of Machaerus, that cruel mountain fortress. The very next day, an entire regiment surrounded the spot where Yohanan was teaching. This time there was no escaping.

Try to imagine so many armed men being required to imprison a single, ragged, wilderness-walking preacher armed only with words.

During a drunken party a few nights later, Herod Antipas asked Salomé, the fourteen-year-old daughter of Herodias, to dance for him. Salomé was virtually a woman, and she dazzled Antipas with her flashing hands and swaying hips and swirling silk scarves. His senses were pulled this way and that like a dog being teased by a boy with a scrap of meat. He downed cupful after cupful of sweet red wine until finally he blurted out that Salomé could have any prize she wanted, even half his kingdom, if only she would not stop dancing.

When he finally motioned her to rest, she settled beside her mother who, with set jaw, whispered something in her ear.

Salomé turned slowly to Antipas and said, "What I want most is the head of that harping baptizer upon a silver platter."

And God help us all, Herod Antipas ordered it done.

~ ~ ~

The news raced around Galilee. I heard it in Nazareth at the well one morning. I dropped my buckets in disbelief and ran to Yeshu's workshop, stumbling, tears stinging my eyes, my chest aching.

But the workshop was empty, the door closed. That door was never closed, so I rushed to the house and found Mama Ana sitting at the table, mending clothes. Taking notice of the shock in her eyes, and hearing her tell me that Yeshu was gone, stopped the breath in my chest. The look on my face made her smile softly the way a mother will when softly touching a scab that makes you wince.

Quickly taking in my distress at learning Yeshu had left us during this terrible time, Mama Ana shook her head gently, saying word had come from Jerusalem at dawn. Yeshu had roared in pain. Then he'd stormed from the house, closed up his workshop, and had yet to return.

Burying my head in Mama Ana's lap, I sobbed and sobbed. When finally I turned to look up into her face for solace, her tears mixed with mine.

I spent the day waiting by the workshop door, working and reworking the same sandal thong that defied fixing. I lay all night in a pile of wood shavings and sawdust under Yeshu's workbench. I slept fitfully, waking from nightmares of Yohanan's ghostly face being tossed about like a ball by the savage beasts who ruled us.

In the fiery heat of my sorrow and desolation, I could find no way to turn rage into love, as Yeshu had long ago urged me to do.

"Perhaps I'll try tomorrow," I kept telling myself. "Maybe then I can do it."

In the morning I awoke to find Yeshu standing over me. Slowly he knelt down and then sat in the wood shavings, cross-legged. He wearily told me how he had walked aimlessly for hours before coming upon a small boat on the lakeshore. He rowed it out onto the water and spent the day and a night there, praying, fasting, and grieving.

"Finally, my arms rowed me back to shore," he said, "and my feet led me here again this morning."

It was then I saw that his cloak was torn near his heart. He was practicing keriah as part of his mourning.

And so was I.

Slowly he bowed his head. I reached out and touched his arm, and he buried his face in his hands.

Yeshu wept.

I joined him; we spoke no more.

In the days that followed, I could see that Yeshu was different, changed in ways I still find hard to describe. His head tilted slightly to one side, as if he were a wounded animal getting ready to howl. His jaw was set firmly at a new angle. His eyes had lost some of their silver sparkle; the boyishness was diminished in his laugh.

This wasn't Yeshu's first heavy loss, of course. Long before this he had lost his beloved Abba, whose workbench I had slept under just a few nights earlier.

Yeshu must have realized that he now faced a great struggle without the two strongest shoulders to lean upon that he had ever had. He must have also seen it was now his turn to somehow step into the void and take Yohanan's place.

As for me, my heart was like a broken clay pot. My whole inner being had shattered into so many pieces. The thinking part of me now lay at the bottom of a dry well, peering up at the narrow hole through which some uncaring monster had tossed me. I wondered fearfully what would become of us all.

I felt Yeshu's anguish as my own. After all, this was my second crushing loss, too. First Shoshana, then Yohanan. Would it ever stop?

Meanwhile Yeshu seemed to have buried himself in work. The sound of his saw and mallet began before daylight when I left the house to pasture sheep, and was still resounding at dusk when I returned. Day after day my anxiety grew as I waited for my chores to let up so I could visit him and see what he was building so furiously.

At last a free morning came and I headed over. Yeshu was bent over his workbench, sanding and sighting along a chestnut plank. Finished boards like it were propped around the shop.

Without looking up from what he was doing he mumbled, "Welcome, Daavi."

I replied in kind, the formality of our words ringing hollow, magnifying rather than dimming the sadness in the room. The bruising was so deep, both of us were wary of being touched. It was as if I'd fallen out of the mulberry tree to find Yeshu already flat on his face. Who was here now to take my pain? Or his.

Not knowing how to begin was scary. This was the first time with Yeshu that I felt there was something I just couldn't say. I'd lost Yohanan and I wanted Yeshu back.

Finally I stepped onto an easier path and asked, "Yeshu, what on earth have you been building?"

"A holy ark," he responded, showing me the piece he was burnishing.

The face-up side of it had been strikingly engraved using the carving tools that lay near it on the bench.

"It's for storing the Torah. I can't count the times Yohanan asked me why Nazareth didn't have an *aron kodesh*. Now there will be an answer. I'm hoping it will help my beloved brother find peace."

He paused.

"I have to finish it before doing what must be done."

I flinched hearing that. I wasn't sure I wanted to know what exactly had to be done. Saying nothing, I moved closer to study the ark taking shape. Yeshu was a master carver and this was the finest work I had ever seen him do. Etched in relief in the door panels was a stream of living water spilling from a single cupped hand to anoint an expectant forehead below.

A long sigh of recognition escaped me. "Ohhh."

I turned toward him. He was gently rocking forward and back, leaning with his hands on the bench. His eyes were closed.

~ ~ ~

Mama Maria was grieving also. Early one morning I saw her sitting in her doorway, neither in nor out. It was so unlike her.

I walked over and stood close by her side. She looked up and our eyes met.

Noticing her face, I nearly jumped back. It was the color of ashes, and she seemed to be peering out from behind a door far down inside. Her cheeks were streaked but dry. I imagined that she had no tears left.

Touching her shoulder, I asked how she was doing. For the longest time, she stared into my eyes, saying nothing.

Finally, she answered softly, "I feel like the mother who gave birth to twin sons, only to have one struck down by a plague not long after both had learned to walk and talk."

She paused, swallowing hard.

Then she said, "I now have two hearts. One is broken and I'm afraid the other may be breaking."

I reached out and stroked her cheek. She caught my hand and squeezed it. From inside, we heard Mama Ana calling for her daughter. I helped Mama Maria to her feet. The slash torn in her cloak met my eye as she disappeared through the doorway.

That afternoon I headed out in search of firewood for our hearth. Trudging home through the meadow that Yohanan had once run across singing the Psalms, I could feel the silence. Where were the bees? Even the butterflies were gone. Not a single creature was drinking nectar from the flowers.

How much, I wondered, do they know?

I felt a shudder. The executioner's knife had gashed us all: Yeshu and me, Mama Maria and Mama Ana, my father and mother, and everyone who had been touched by Yohanan. Even the plants and animals seemed diminished—the lilies of the field and the swallows soaring overhead, had they not also suffered mortal injury?

The world seemed pointless. My tears had burned away and I was turned round, bound tight in pain and anger.

And then one day I'd had enough. I was walking along the shore of the lake at the edge of Nazareth. Suddenly, I knelt down and scooped up as many rocks as my hands could hold. Standing, I began to throw them one by one at the water's impassive face.

I yelled through clenched teeth, one accusation per stone: "Yohanan is dead." (Throw.) "Murdered." (Throw again.) "A dozen Jews die on wooden crosses every day." (Throw another.) Thousands slain every year." (Throw. Throw.) "Life is unbelievably cruel. Would a just God let this happen?" (Throw all that are left.)

I stooped down to gather more rocks.

"Next, it will be *Yeshu* who is hounded." (Throw.) "Our Jewish authorities stand by and do nothing." (Throw.) "Is God deaf, blind, and speechless?" (Throw. Throw. Throw.) "When will God act to save us?" (Throw the rest.)

Other than my aching arm, I had no answers; no resolution.

~ ~ ~

Some weeks later, lost in thought on a hillside while tending sheep, I suddenly remembered Yohanan standing in a spot just like this one, wagging a finger at the sky and saying, almost singing, "When I die, wear flowers!"

I shivered. It felt like he was sitting right next to me, waiting for me to ask him what I should do next, how I could ever be healed. Rolling the questions around on my lips, I knew that only I could give answers.

Even so, I wondered what my friend Yohanan would have said to help me tease those answers out. What would he have expected of himself had it been I who was killed? To cry out in pain and protest? Take revenge? Or celebrate my life on earth by finding and nurturing it in the life that continued around him.

I knew, of course, what he would do. But I wasn't Yohanan. One answer that later seemed so obvious took many days on that hillside, many evenings walking the roads outside of town, many nights lying sleepless on my back in bed, before I found my way through the maze of thoughts and hurt to take one simple action.

After a hard winter, on a day in early spring when I noticed the clover seeds had pushed up their sprouts through the decaying leaves toward the sunlight above, I knew it was time to do it. So I did. That day I wore flowers for Yohanan.

At supper that evening, my father noticed the woven garland of iris blossoms around my neck. When we finished our meal, he asked me to join him outside. Looking up for the first stars and smiling faintly, he said with quiet resolution, "Yohanan's life was short but brilliant. He streaked across our cold sky like the racing stars we sometimes see."

I nodded in agreement though it didn't feel quite right. I can't say I understood how a streaking meteor can live in the world of men and women. A flesh and blood person is not merely a glowing ember momentarily bursting from a campfire. No matter how brightly his life blazes, there just has to be something more lasting than that.

Shutting my eyes tight, I pictured Yohanan's great hairy head roaring in laughter. I could feel the fierce love blazing in his gaze. How I wished that somehow he'd been more careful so that his burning convictions in life would not have been extinguished in the black, starless night of death. I longed fiercely to have spent more days basking in his light.

I know now that some things are beyond our control. But I still yearn to see him bent over, carefully lifting a caterpillar onto a stick to carry it to safety by the side of the road.

Moved by this longing, I would often say to Yeshu at good moments and bad, "Oh, if only Yohanan were here!"

One day, when Yeshu and I were resting by a spring during a long walk in the hills, he responded. Turning toward me, he said, "Yohanan *is* here."

"Where?" I asked.

For a moment I was confused. Fog settled over my mind, muffling any thoughts. Without hesitation, I peered into the tangle of bushes surrounding the pool of water, searching for my cherished Yohanan and not finding him.

"There," Yeshu whispered pointing down at my face reflected in the water. "See how it shines," he said. "Yohanan lives on inside you, Daavi."

He was quiet for a moment. "You and I are Yohanan."

I continued to look. But I was unable to really see.

Finally, all I could say was, "Yeshu, don't you miss him terribly? Doesn't it feel sometimes like part of you has died, too?"

He looked at me and didn't speak. Perhaps he couldn't speak.

I stared back. When his gaze returned to the water, he seemed so far away, wrapped in thoughts I couldn't fathom.

I pledged then and there that I would do everything in my power to keep Yeshu from harm. I would stand by his side as the fiercest guard dog any shepherd ever had. And with God's help, I would succeed.

~ ~ ~

Soon enough we would all find ourselves deep in wilderness. Journeying through the wilds but also through the heart of humankind. Crossing back and forth from campfire to hearth.

Although I could not have believed it at the time, my life was about to explode in a wondrous shower of sparks.

III. Mission

Yeshu in the Wilderness

No matter how hard I tried to heal—yet not to forget—losing Yohanan was like having my heart torn from my chest. And the pain would not go away, pain that sometimes made me want to scream, other times to hide, even from those I loved most. In spite of myself, I couldn't imagine looking Yeshu in the face without seeing Yohanan's face being gone.

At the same time, I wanted to link elbows with Yeshu, walk through the fields, and share Yohanan stories and nuggets of wisdom to do my part in keeping his spirit alive.

Yeshu, on the other hand, had a plan of his own. He kept it to himself, probably giving thought to little else. One morning, as I passed by his workshop, I saw that the door was again closed. Mama Maria was in front of her house and noticed me standing there, staring dazedly at the doorway.

She beckoned for me to come over, but before she could say anything, I blurted out, "Where's Yeshu? He's shut his door again. Why did he leave?"

My eyes must have been open really wide, because Mama Maria tilted her head and took hold of me gently by one shoulder.

"It's all right, Daavi," she said, "It's all right.

She gently stroked the back of my head.

"All will be well. Come sit a spell with me."

I followed her to the bench that rested against the front of their house. The morning sun and a gentle breeze wrapped me in a sublime embrace and my throbbing heart began to return to normal. How did she always know just what I needed? Just the right thing to say?

After some settling-in time, adjusting her skirts and scraping away a few rocks with her sandals, she turned her head toward me.

"Daavi, do you remember what Yohanan was always urging Yeshu to do?"

Letting out a great sigh, I knew instantly. Yeshu hadn't run off. He'd gone into the wilderness to fast and wait. To meet with God and face his own soul.

I nodded my head, more to myself than to Mama Maria.

Yohanan had wanted him to do this even before our journey to the cedars, and Yeshu had begun making plans in earnest to do so right after being baptized in the River Jordan. Yet, because of mounting obligations at home, he couldn't set out right away. Eventually he stopped talking about it, and it backed out of my mind and winged off like a carpenter bee leaving its hole in a roof beam.

But the thought never left Yeshu's mind, I'm sure of it. Now Yohanan's slaying had changed everything. The leather traces that had been tying Yeshu to his old life, like an ox to a plow, had already begun breaking and falling away. He had turned thirty; his youngest brother and sister had both married and left to set up their own households. Mama Maria and Mama Ana were now fixtures in the village and could support themselves as long as there were babies being born and ill people to nurse back to wellness with herbs and gentle counsel. At last Yeshu's vow to his Abba Yosef had been fulfilled. At last he was free to pursue his own calling.

When word came about Yohanan, Yeshu was at first spun round on his moorings. To reset his anchor and to honor his beloved cousin, he had crafted the Torah ark in Yohanan's honor and installed it in the synagogue. It became the pride of Nazareth. But for Yeshu it was a gift: homage, pure and simple.

As soon as the Torah was placed inside its striking new aron kodesh, the way opened up for Yeshu. Without telling anyone other than his mother and grandmother, he packed a few things, strode through the doorway, and headed into the desert.

In the days and weeks that followed, I visited Mama Maria regularly, partly to see if she needed anything, but also to check if Yeshu had returned. She assured me he would be back, and I counted the days, losing track after thirty-five or so. I couldn't wait to hear what he would say. To learn if he had found Yohanan's spirit in the desert, and what had passed between them.

Most of all, had he met with God?

Finally, late one afternoon, as I was finishing up a leather-covered stool seat that a neighbor had ordered from my father, I suddenly heard exuberant voices from next door. I knew immediately one of them was Yeshu. Running to the open window, I saw the two of them in the courtyard: mother and son, face-to-face, gripping one another's hands.

I wanted to rush over and join in, yet I knew I should wait. I told myself to give them time together; let him recover from his journey.

But that wasn't easy to do. All through the evening, I struggled to occupy myself at home. Sleep did not come easily. I arose at daybreak and marked time until I heard someone stirring next door.

Only moments later, I went over. Yeshu was standing by a large, ceramic water jar next to the door, head cocked to one side as if he were listening to what the morning breeze had to say before the heat of the day clamped its mouth shut.

I was shocked to see him up close. He was thin as a sapling. His cheekbones stuck out like the folded-in wings of a vulture perched on a limb. His sun-baked face was cracked and leathery, his beard a tangled thicket.

But his eyes glowed as if he had swallowed the sun.

After we hugged, I couldn't hold back my astonishment. "Yeshu, what has happened to you?"

He tugged his ear and reflected a bit, before responding with a question of his own. "Do you mean on the outside or the inside?"

I wasn't prepared for that, but it didn't matter. Before I could choose, he replied.

"Well, in a way it makes no difference," he said softly, "because the outside and inside of me became one."

He leaned over to scoop a cupful of water from the jar, sipping it slowly to clear the hoarseness from his still parched throat. Then he resumed his telling.

"By searching and searching, I strove to place my footsteps in Yohanan's so I could follow his path.

"Time thinned each morning and evening, as I walked and walked, matching my steps with my breath. I halted when the heat rose or the light failed, and sat down wherever I found myself, to meditate and pray."

Minding his feet, Yeshu slowly made his way to the bench by the doorway and sat back against the wall. I plopped beside him, turning my head so that I could see his face.

"The first few days I was hungrier than I've ever been. What I wouldn't have done for a crust of bread soaked in goat's milk! But after eating nothing for nearly a week, the hunger fell away like a snake sliding out of its skin."

He cocked his head again, as if distracted by someone calling in the distance. Or perhaps a recollection was softly tapping at the door. A moment later, he went on.

"It was strange, since no one else was around, but for the first time since the moon last went dark, I didn't feel alone. I called up memories of Yohanan telling stories about being in the wilds. Only this time the story was happening to me.

"As I wandered, Yohanan's voice welled up inside my head, ringing like a bell.

"'Meditation is wilderness,' it rang.

"'Prayer is wilderness,' it tolled.

"'*You* are wilderness!'"

Grasping the bony elbows of his crossed arms with his hands, Yeshu whispered, "And so I became."

"'Embrace the wildness,' the voice intoned, 'let its beating heart guide your own. Follow the path it traces through your soul.'"

Yeshu's hands crept up to his shoulders.

"That night, eyes closed, I watched a cloud form till it surrounded me. I slept soundly. At dawn I opened my eyes and lay there while the cloud, seeming to sense I was awake, broke up and drifted away."

I waited for Yeshu to go on. The quiet lingered with the kind of stillness that makes the hair on your arms stand on end, not because of fright but because something really big is gathering.

I examined the back of Yeshu's work-scarred hands. The veins stood out like crisscrossing ridges of rock on the desert floor. When I looked closer, it seemed that I could see his heart beating there.

"What happened after that," he continued, gazing far away, "I have no specific words for."

I said nothing, trying to imagine my body ringing like a bell with Yohanan's voice—Still here!

After a long while, Yeshu resumed. "Do you remember when I told you about meeting with the rabbis in the Temple as a child?"

I nodded.

"It was a little like that." His eyes stared straight ahead.

"I stood there in that vast sanctuary, empty except for the voices talking, mine conversing with itself and with people I've known. Yet occasionally it was joined by another deeper voice that I knew from somewhere but could not name.

"At first I thought it must be the wind in the canyons. Yet this voice warmed me however cold the night air got, and cooled me however hot the sun pressed down.

"It kept insisting there was something important I had to do. But what that was, I couldn't quite make out, because other voices rose up promising me all kinds of things if I would just do whatever caught my fancy.

"Anything was possible they said: The world was my orchard. Whatever my hands or eyes or tongue desired was there for the taking.

"'You don't have to be hungry, ever again,' one voice said. 'Or thirsty, or poor, or a nobody,' the others echoed. 'People are lost without your orders. A better world is waiting to serve your purpose. To serve *you*.'

"It was very strange because these voices all sounded like mine, only there was a shrillness to them that made me think of tin being polished to pass for silver."

He gazed out the doorway and sighed. "The entire time I listened, that other wind kept blowing softly, reminding me that wilderness is within us as well as without, and that everyone needs to hear it speak, not only me. Still, I loved just being there, cradled in its arms like a child."

He filled his lungs with air and slowly let it out.

"Day after day I listened to the conversations inside me. I sensed the voice of the wilderness becoming stronger. I decided to come home when I understood that my new task is to walk the wilderness *here*, in the hearts and souls of our people. To call out until others, taking note of their shadows, waken to the light that cast them."

Yeshu glanced sideways at me, then away again.

"As I said, some things I found I have no words for yet. Maybe the words don't exist. What happened was too personal to be shared that way, Daavi."

He smiled softly.

"Even with you."

There was a time when hearing "even you" would have made me feel smaller. But that day I heard I had his trust. Seeing how pleased I was, Yeshu's eyes sparkled.

I felt he was telling me something; acknowledging something I had said without my knowing I'd said it.

But I was speechless.

"Is there anything else?" he asked, tilting his head.

Without thinking, I blurted out, "Weren't you ever scared?"

He looked at me the way the moon must look down at the earth. "In the end," he said, "there is nothing to fear in wilderness, whether it's the desert outside or your soul inside.

"We need to know wildness," he said, his eyes locking with mine, his eyebrows arching. "The wildness that tames us," he laughed.

After a long pause, he noted my bewilderment and went on. "Be patient, Daavi, and remember that one day you, too, will go into the wilderness to find yourself and meet your God."

He held back.

"Either that, or wilderness will come to you when you are ready to welcome it."

I could only stare at him and wonder how he knew such things. As always, he didn't avert his gaze.

Looking into Yeshu's eyes, I saw Yohanan's. Although I was grateful, it made me shiver.

~ ~ ~

For the next week I saw little of Yeshu. There was a sudden and inexplicable cascade of requests for my shepherding, and I was gone each day from daylight till nightfall.

When I asked at supper, my father assured me he had heard Yeshu laboring every day, all day. Later, I realized he was finishing up the jobs still to be done before he took on his mission journeys.

As for my own work, it gave me ample time while watching the flocks to mull over Yeshu's recounting of his time away. I knew there was more to hear; I just didn't know when.

And though I was comforted by his return, my moods swung back and forth. Still haunted by Yohanan's loss, little did I know that my release from such buffeting would result from another story about wilderness.

And it would not come from the carpenter.

Fox Paws In Living Water

We Jews who live in villages have a custom that is more than just a habit. It's a part of the bedrock of our lives. Here's the tradition: in a farming village like Nazareth where I grew up, in years when the harvest is bountiful, everyone, even visitors, pours out into the fields to help the farmers bring in their crops.

This was one of those years. I was a shepherd, my father a leatherworker, Yeshu a carpenter. None of that mattered. We all pitched in with our neighbors—women and men, children and elders—to do our part in gathering the barley and wheat before the ravens or the rains took it.

As soon as the reaping in a field was done and the oxcarts and donkeys were led away, then the poorest among us, those with little hope of feeding their families with their labor alone, swarmed over the stubble and gleaned every last kernel of grain that had fallen to the ground.

The first fields to be visited by those whose cupboards were empty were always my Great Uncle Moishe's. This is because he invariably instructed his harvesters to leave every tenth furrow untouched.

When I once asked Uncle Moishe why he always left some of his grain standing, he winked at me and answered, "Because I don't want to be alone at my funeral."

Well, my great uncle got his wish. The day he died there was no room in the synagogue or the courtyard in front of it for even one more mourner to stand. Most wore clothing torn at the chest, as called for by the same keriah tradition we followed with Gramma Ruth and Yohanan. And all the voices singing the Kaddish prayer rose up together, in a swelling chant that carried to the farthest reaches of his fields.

Uncle Moishe, rest his soul, even got a laugh when I told that story the other day. How many of us can bring laughter to others long *after* we have passed on?

Nowadays around Nazareth, it's not unusual to leave grain unharvested for the needy. After he died, whenever I saw that I smiled inside, pleased that dear Uncle Moishe was still walking among us.

Of course, during the year of which I am speaking, in the weeks after Yeshu had returned from journeying alone in the wilderness, Uncle Moishe was still very much around. One day, near the end of the harvesting, he hobbled with his cane out to the fields to bring news to Mother and me. Martha had just arrived from Bethany, her home village on the slopes of the Mount of Olives above Jerusalem. Best of all, Maria Magdalena had come with her and both would join the harvest tomorrow.

Although my whole body ached from cutting and sheaving wheat, my fatigue melted away like candle wax at *Hanukkah*, the Festival of Lights, which we would soon be celebrating. Walking home, I knew I could not wait until morning, so I rushed straight to where they were staying.

Martha and Maria greeted me with warm hugs. The three of us all choked back our tears, preferring to face up to that later. I saw that they were practicing keriah, too, with ripped shawls across their chests covering their hearts. I knew our *shiva* for Yohanan would not end after the usual twelve months of mourning. No, I feared it would be with us forever.

The two friends sat me down and filled me with warm biscuits stuffed with chopped olives, followed by two plump pomegranates.

Martha reminded me, "Don't forget that the pomegranate is a symbol of righteousness, and you know why, don't you?"

Then she answered her own question, which lots of adults like to do, "Because tradition says it has 613 seeds, the same as the 613 *mitzvot*, our holy commandments of the Torah. This is why we eat pomegranates on *Rosh Hashanah*. It's the best way of remembering the obligations that we carry into the New Year."

Peering up at her and leaning over my plate, I nodded my agreement as I slurped up the sweet juices. While I continued to eat, the two of them brought me up to date on their lives. Martha was thrilled with her first niece and couldn't stop talking about her. I smiled but felt something dark gathering inside.

I set my jaw, thinking to myself it was better to keep one's heart fixed if at all possible on a new baby's laughter, rather than to dwell on Yohanan being put to death in a brutal ending to a vibrant life.

The proud new grandmother barely noticed the cloud I was under. Soon she was off to run errands, carrying a basket as large as a donkey saddle. This gave Maria Magdalena and me the chance to talk alone. I never tired of that, partly because it caused me to reflect on how it might be to talk with Shoshana, now that I was old enough to have something that seemed important enough to say.

Although I was probably half Maria's age, not once did she make me feel like a kid. I could share feelings about anything, like friends do, and not worry that she would cluck dismissively, smooth my feathers, maybe pat me on the head and send me on my way.

The first words out of both our mouths were of Yohanan. What had happened was so painful that I had hardly been able to talk about it clearly with anyone. This made it all the worse because Yohanan in life sparked amazement and joy, and now I could barely say his name without sobbing.

I could see the same agony in Maria's eyes, feel it in the slump of her shoulders, hear it in the way she said his name. Talking about it was like walking to the well and back on a broken foot, but both of us knew how much we needed water.

With a lump in my throat the size of a stone, I told her how the wounding felt like it would never heal.

"It's been months since they murdered him," I said, "and the hole in my chest has hardly shrunk at all." I placed my closed fist over my heart.

She nodded, and gripped my hand firmly. Then, with her voice catching as the words tumbled out, she told me what the news of Yohanan's death had led her to do.

"When we heard about the slaying," she began, "Martha and her sister Miriam and I just held one another tight and wept. We wept all day. I would struggle to regain control and comfort the two of them, but as soon as I did and they calmed a bit, then I'd lose control all over again. Next Martha would comfort Miriam and me till we stopped weeping and it was safe for her to begin sobbing once more. I didn't know so many tears could fit inside three people.

"Finally we were able to speak. And all we could talk about was what Yohanan had taught us. In particular, this entailed his lessons about the wilderness within and how journeying through the forests and valleys of our souls could feel like coming home. We were lifted up by again recalling the phrases that took flight from his mouth and flew into hearts, especially when he baptized people in the River Jordan. Or in whatever flowing water was at hand.

"Miriam recalled how his left arm would gradually lift his staff higher and higher into the air as he preached. And how we watched as each point he made was punctuated by another shake of his staff. Our Yohanan was as fearless as any guard dog facing a leopard."

Maria wiped her eyes with the backs of her hands. "But of course a leopard doesn't kill for the pleasure of it. Nor does it kill for revenge. Yohanan knew that even the great cat has something to teach us.

"With that the three of us gleefully began to share the countless acts of kindness he showed to animals. This ranged from a dung beetle skittering on its belly across a pasture, his sandal protecting it, to the rowdiest camel in a caravan charmed by a dried raisin he pulled out of his beard."

Mimicking the camel squinting to get a clear view of what was in the outstretched hand, Maria rocked her head forward and back, while I slapped my thigh and snorted.

"But best of all, we shared what he told us when no one else was present, as he pressed his words, like bright flower petals, into our open palms.

"Next we started re-telling his stories, finding ourselves jumping like mountain sheep from rock to rock up a twisting path, trying to keep up, until we arrived at a pool so clear we couldn't tell if the creature gazing back at us was a ewe or a me."

Maria held the sides of her head with both hands, while I sputtered helplessly. I knew exactly what all the brittle hilarity was for. In the jaws of the weasel, the rabbit stares up at the moon.

I noticed Maria had stopped speaking.

"Mostly though," she said when she finally resumed, "Martha and Miriam and I just ached." She bit on her lip.

"Then the dull constant throbbing of him having been lost would give way to the stabbing fear of who might be next?"

Maria went quiet again—really quiet. Her shoulders shook with each breath, her eyes tight shut. As we sat there wordless, I squeezed her hand to signal we were both still present.

Finally, she opened her eyes and spoke through the trembling.

> I have no food but tears, day and night...
> Deep calls to deep in the roar of your cataracts,
>   and all your waves, all your breakers, roll over me.

She struggled to keep her voice from breaking as she continued.

> Sunk deep in my misery, groaning in distress,
>   I will wait for God...my refuge.

How well I knew those words! Yeshu had quoted them to me from our beloved Psalms the day I plummeted to the ground from the gnarled old walnut tree.

Maria paused for a moment and then spoke again.

"Soon I knew I had to do more than talk about how I felt. I had to find an act of healing. Above all, I had to do something to honor Yohanan; something to keep my sense of him alive, like a shepherdess in her hillside lean-to who keeps a campfire burning through the stormiest night, even when rain threatens to smother it out.

"Recently, I had been deliberating on all the times that Yohanan had admonished us. 'Go into the wilderness,' he would say firmly. 'Find your God and have a long conversation. And above all, open yourself up to listen—really listen.'

"So I did.

"Early one morning, I rolled up a few loaves of bread and some dried figs and dates in my blanket and tied it off with a braided leather rope to sling over my shoulder. I filled a goatskin with water from the well, and as the dawn washed the stars from the great night sky, I struck off into the most desolate and untamed place I could find near Bethany.

"Had anyone seen me heading out, and asked where I was going or why, I would have simply said: 'I'm searching for the wilderness walker.'"

She smiled wanly, and I gripped her arm with my free hand. "And did you find him?" I asked.

"I did," she whispered.

My jaw dropped and I leaned closer.

"I found him in the unrelenting lizard's tongue," she said softly, recalling his words, "and in the cry of the osprey signaling to its young."

She followed with her own words. "I found him in the weeping of my heart in darkness, and in the longing of my dreams just before daybreak."

Maria slipped into a contemplative hush while I waited patiently, letting Yohanan's familiar litany echo in my head.

"Daavi," she broke in, "do you recall what he told us in the forest of cedars?" She raised her eyebrows. "He said that God dwells in stillness."

As I nodded, she continued, "He said we could find God in wildness. We need only go and seek."

She paused. "Yohanan told me I could find *him* in wildness, too. He promised he would meet me there."

"Maria," I said, laying a hand on her shoulder, "I'm so glad you went. You must know that Yeshu took Yohanan's advice and journeyed into the wilderness, too."

She nodded. "Except that my going was but the *dawning* of my search," she answered.

I swallowed hard, and before she could ask, I told her, "I don't feel that I'm ready yet."

She tilted her chin to one side and looked over at me.

I shook my head, back and forth. "Sometimes I feel like I can't take another step. It's as if I were a baby again who's forgotten how to walk. How can I go on without him? He was going to take me into the wilderness with him when I was ready. He said so."

Maria set her jaw and spoke firmly. "Daavi, Yohanan will always be with you. Right here," she said, reaching out to touch the center of my chest with two fingers.

I flinched as if stung, then sensed a feeling of warmth spreading through me like the calm that follows a wind gust dying down. Fleetingly I recalled Yeshu telling me the same; placing his hand on that very spot.

"Be patient, Daavi. Listen for his voice. It's in you and in the voices of everyone he touched. If you allow it, he will continue teaching you, wherever you are."

I nodded hesitantly, then firmly. I could do this. I knew I could: By using my memory and my imagination. Waiting for the right moments. Recognizing them when they appeared. Paying attention to my dreams.

"Daavi, You know how to wait in silence for the voice of God, how to wait for the way to open up in front of you."

My face signaled my agreement.

"In that case," she said, "you don't *need* Yohanan anymore."

I stared at her in disbelief and felt anger welling up.

Again cocking her head at me, she said just the right words. "You aren't abandoning him...it's your time to walk alone. Just the way you learned to cross the room without the arm of your father holding you up."

She stopped for a moment and seemed to be searching for words. Furrowing her brow, she looked at the open door and then back at me.

"Come," she said, rising to her feet abruptly. "Let's go for a stroll."

I stood and she waved me through the door first. Without tarrying, we set off side by side. I had no idea where we were going, and I don't think either of us cared.

Neither spoke until we were on the outskirts of the village, when Maria suddenly asked, "Did you just hear something?"

"Only the river," I said.

"You know," she replied, "it's strange. When I was really tired after walking for days in the wilderness, I kept hearing that sound even though the ground was as dry as the stone before Moses tapped it with his staff.

"It wasn't until the end of my stay that I figured it out. All I had to do was be completely still and I could hear the sound of running water. If I listened closely as it rolled over stones, I would gradually hear the flow of Yohanan's voice rubbing words smooth as he spoke, words that the spirit was polishing into gems."

I felt my breath catch in my chest. So as not to miss a word or an expression, I twisted my shoulders toward her.

"And it wasn't just water that was the carrier, either. One day I sat from dawn to dusk," she continued, "my back pressed against a great boulder, listening to the breeze that whispered through the canyon and laughed across the tips of the broom grass.

"The sun sailed from one side of the sky to the other, and when it began to glide back to earth, I could hear Yohanan."

> Get the Lord's road ready for him.
> Make a straight path for him to travel.
> All low places must be filled in...
> and rough paths made smooth.

Watching the expressions dancing over Maria's face as she spoke, I was convinced that she had heard Yohanan. Certainly with her heart, if not her ears.

I shivered. Although it was a different time of year, in a field very much like the one in which we now stood, I had heard that same voice cry out above a sea of wildflowers, speaking to me those very words of the Prophet Isaiah.

Grasping Maria's elbow I begged her to tell me more about her time in the wilderness. And she did. I was thrilled, but also anguished. Yohanan seemed so close and yet so far away. When I told Maria this, she resumed her story in earnest.

"After a week of wandering, I finally squeezed the last drop of water from my goatskin, so I badly needed to find more. The streambeds were all dry and there wasn't a spring in any crevice. Not even a mudhole in sight. I hadn't seen any water in days. After so short a time, my quest for Yohanan's voice had turned into a struggle to stay alive.

"I was so thirsty my tongue began to swell up and it was hard to breathe," she recounted. "My legs were wobbly; I felt light-headed. It seemed as if I were floating, but also like I was stuck in the same place. I wanted to lie down and sleep, except that I knew I had to keep going. I didn't have time or strength enough to walk back to Bethany where water was plentiful. It would take two full days to get there had I been starting out strong and rested. But in my weakened state, it was likely to be more.

"That night I had crazy dreams—of bathing in dust and eating dried leaves—and I awoke the next morning feeling feverish. Everything around me seemed blurry. I knew I had to find water that day or I would perish without anyone knowing what had become of me."

My chest tightened as Maria rolled on.

"I was too weak to carry the blanket so I let it drop from my hand. Slinging the empty goatskin over my shoulder I set off with purpose but was soon meandering aimlessly through the brush. I began to stagger along, lurching like a tipsy wedding dancer, but without the merriness.

"At the bottom of a slope, I tripped over dead tree roots and stumbled forward but caught myself. More than once I fell, my hands stretched out to cushion the blow. I knew that before long I would not be able to get up again. My head was cut, my hands bloodied. I was a fright.

"Suddenly I broke through a small stand of nearly leafless bushes and staggered into a clearing, where I confronted a silver fox. It stood warily, sizing me up, its long sleek tail twitching this way and that.

"I stared at the fox dumbly, wondering if it were really there. Maybe my eyes were seeing a specter. Why wasn't it running away? I would have.

"The fox returned my look with a gaze so penetrating I felt turned inside out. When it was ready to let loose, it swung round and commenced to slink off through the brush where it stopped to sniff the ground.

"It did this sniffing more than once, each time scratching at the earth before looking back over its shoulder to where I stood transfixed. Maybe this was what Lot's motionless wife felt like as she left the earth.

"Even so, I could still move, and with the first step I knew I should follow this fox. Strangely, it didn't seem to mind.

"I was afraid I'd lose it in the brush, but it trotted along a narrow trail that must have been made by deer, and soon we were out onto open ground strewn with rocks and boulders. The fox began to pick its way through, pausing here and there to sniff and scratch at the ground. It occurred to me that it might have left food somewhere and was trying to find it, but from the way it kept looking back at me I began to wonder if it was slowing down so I could keep up.

"Finally the fox arrived at a large slab of rock. It leapt up and walked slowly in a circle, sniffing, searching for something. Then, seemingly satisfied, as if it had all the time in the world, it curled up and went to sleep.

"I was tired, too, and didn't see any point in going on, especially not without the fox. So I edged forward as quietly as I could until I was near the rock, maybe three strides from where the fox dozed. I lay on my side, facing the slumbering animal, and closed my eyes. Each time I did so, I had the feeling I was being observed. I'd snap my eyes open but the fox was still there slumbering. Then it occurred to me that when I shut my eyes, the fox opened its. I felt suddenly at peace, knowing that at all times someone was keeping watch.

"Lying there near the warm stone, I began to drift off. As during so many times in the past few days, my reflective center turned toward Yohanan, and I longed to wash myself in the clear sound of living water. Soon I was at one with the murmuring; bathing in its glory. I felt myself dissolving into the flow, searching with it for cracks in the stone until at last we both disappeared.

"But before I could discover to where, I heard a rustling sound.

"It must be the fox stirring, I thought, but what I pictured was Yohanan combing his fingers through his beard when he was concentrating really hard on a thought puzzle. One that Yeshu or you, Daavi, would have posed to him."

I blinked, and Maria looked back at me with a twinkle in her eye.

She went on. "I opened my eyes only to see the fox was gone. All that was left was a set of damp footprints: from the edge of the rock where it had been sleeping...and then back again.

"As I watched, the tracks slowly faded, and I decided the bright sun was either driving me mad or I was imagining things.

"The soft laughter I heard was not reassuring. It wasn't from me; my cracked lips were shut tight.

"Suddenly, I *was* laughing. Laughing because—Praise God!—I was hearing the sound of real water.

"But where was it? All I could see was the flat slab and the boulders strewn around it. I followed the now faint trail the fox had made, over to the edge of the rock, and I peered down. Below, I could see a narrow furrow where sand had been scraped away to show a glint of silver.

"With that, a quake shook my whole being. Water had been running under us the entire time—I was standing just above an underground stream!

"Now praising the fox for the gift its nose had brought us, and Yohanan for his love of the wildness of foxes, I stepped down and fell to my knees. Grabbing hold of a flat piece of stone, I began to attack the spot where the fox had dug. Good thing I had seen the wet pawprints when I did; minutes later they would have vanished into the air.

"The more I dug, the stronger I got. When I hit damp sand, it was hard not to just scoop up a large handful of it to fill my mouth with the moisture. But I managed to keep working until the small hole the fox had cleared was unplugged again and flowing. Cackling softly like the mad woman I once was, I sat and stared while the small basin I had carved out gradually filled with enough water to drink.

"Then I lowered my head like a she-wolf and drank and drank. Cupping my hands together, I raised my face and sloshed torrents of water on my brow. The streaming liquid mixed with the tears running down my cheeks."

Maria paused to look away and then slowly back at me. "Yohanan, not the fox, had vanished...and remained present."

~ ~ ~

We had stopped walking; I'm not sure when. For a while, neither of us spoke. I was still caught up in the twists and turns of all that I had just heard. My thoughts were washing back and forth in my mind like waves rolling up on a rocky lakeshore.

Frankly, it felt like I was stuck fast several steps behind Maria, trying to find words for my own feelings after hearing hers in the story. If Yohanan were still here among us, I wondered, just what would he advise me?

A lone whippoorwill called out in the dusk, saying more than ever I could about what it felt like to be lost and found, all at once.

Looking at Maria, I wanted to ask whether Yohanan had left her any signs about what she might do next. Or whether she had shared all this with Yeshu.

"You know," she said, as if she were listening in on my inner voice, "Yeshu has decided on another long journey. This time he'll go to Jerusalem. And beyond. He wants company."

My head snapped to attention.

"He says that Yohanan usually traveled and taught alone, but that he wants to form a group to accompany him. He asked Martha and me if we wanted to come along."

Even in the dim light, Maria could see the hurt in my eyes. She let me struggle with it, there on my own.

Why hadn't Yeshu mentioned this trip to me? He knows how much I yearn, how much the wanderlust enthralls me. My breath caught in my chest. So...wasn't I welcome?

Just then I was startled by a sound at the back of my mind of Yohanan clucking his tongue. I could feel his gaze measuring me for size and me coming up smaller than I wanted. Hadn't I been crouching on a slab of stone since his murder, dying of thirst, avoiding Yeshu because I was afraid water was only tears?

Yeshu had returned from the wilderness to fulfill his life in the company of others. He needed friends who loved him, companions who could protect him.

"Do you think he'd let me come, too?" I asked softly. "I really want to. I *need* to..." Maria put her hand on my shoulder. Nearly whispering, she said, "You're asking the wrong person. You should be saying this to him."

The Vessel Is Formed and Fired

Like a sleeping deer startled awake, I leapt to my feet and ran, shouting goodbye to Maria over my shoulder as I bolted off. I headed for the other side of town, dodging animals and people trudging home for the evening, thinking furiously how I could persuade Yeshu to take me along.

When I found him, sitting on a bench in front of his workshop, all my good arguments were forgotten. I blurted out the truth plain and simple.

"Yeshu, Maria says you're gathering people to travel again, and I really want to go with you."

"Sit down Daavi, catch your breath."

I sat. He flashed me his welcoming smile.

"I was wondering if you would ask."

He looked away and back again. "You are your own person now, able to pick your own road. I was hoping you would choose to walk with me."

I felt my spine straighten, and I smiled at him. We leaned toward one another and clasped all four hands. Just that quickly it was settled. Everything, that is, except what would come to pass.

Deep down, underneath the exhilaration, my life felt like it was hurtling out of control. Once again I was tumbling from a high branch of the old walnut tree. Only this time I hadn't lost my grip and fallen; I had jumped.

Where I would land was someplace far beyond my imagination. And I took comfort from the thought that wherever the ground was, Yeshu would be there waiting.

Sensing my uncertainty, he began to speak, putting firmness underneath my feet.

"*Sukkot*, the Festival of Shelters begins in three days," he said. "And the book of Deuteronomy tells us how we must celebrate it."

> You must observe the Pilgrim-Feast of Shelters
> for seven days at the end of the harvest season,
> when you bring in the produce
> from your threshing floor
> and your grape press,
> to honor the Lord your God
> who blesses you with bountiful harvests
> and gives you success in all your work.

Yeshu stopped, threw a glance in my direction, and went on.

> This feast will be a time of rejoicing and celebrating
> with your sons and daughters,
> your male and female servants,
> the Levites from your towns,
> and the foreigners, orphans, and widows
> who live among you.

Making a fist and pressing it into his other hand for emphasis, Yeshu added, "And we are further instructed to observe the festival where God *wills* us to be. That's why I am going to Jerusalem for Sukkot. Much needs to be done there. Many truths must be spoken that need to be heard.

"Afterwards we'll walk from village to village like Yohanan did, teaching people wherever they gather, on hillsides or by wells, calling them to serve God and one another. We will speak to the basic goodness in their hearts, appealing to them to greet each person who stands before us, whether a stranger or a neighbor, and embrace them like members of our own family.

"We'll bid them to love others as if these others were themselves. And by doing so, to stand firmly behind peace and life, not violence and death.

"We'll beseech them: rather than turning aside, they should feed the hungry, clothe the poor, care for the ill and the aged.

"In this way, we'll harvest their souls, just as the farmer harvests his wheat by bringing in the sheaves."

I held my gaze on Yeshu as he turned his head to stare out the window; the same window that had lit his shop for so many long years of labor.

His eyes turned back to the room. "For those who come in search of healing, we'll minister to each one. We'll give them comfort and soothe them. We'll show them the power of the human spirit, and their own capacity to heal themselves."

The timbre of Yeshu's voice lowered.

"All of this I've been told to do," he said, nodding resolutely.

"It wasn't so clear at first. For years—nearly twenty of them now—these thoughts have been swirling inside me, taking shape. I've turned them this way and that during the day, as if planing a cedar plank until smooth, or squaring a log with an adz. And the thoughts have turned *me* at night as I tossed and rolled in bed.

"Looking back I can see how these notions were always with me. Every door I've hung for a family, every roof beam I've set, every bridge I've built to narrow the distance between two neighbors or two villages, has been a step along the way. While my hands kept busy, my head and heart were working their way through a forest of doubt and uncertainty. There is so much suffering in our world, and it isn't easy to be a good son, a good brother, a good neighbor."

Yeshu paused, giving the words time to surface.

"By the time I met up with Yohanan on the banks of the River Jordan and he opened me to the water of life, I knew what I had to do, but I didn't yet know when I would start or exactly how. Because you see, it wasn't just about me, or my path.

"*Now* I know." Yeshu's gaze caught mine. "The desert showed me the way."

He stopped abruptly, forming two fists this time, and bringing them carefully together, knuckle against knuckle.

"On the darkest night out there," he said, his voice flint-like, "a bright light burned inside me. I've brought that light back with me. Yohanan's fire must never be allowed to die out. While I can, I will carry it forward, carry the torch high with *both* hands if need be." He opened his hands wide.

"I know I won't stand alone. I'll have you and my other friends beside me."

Once more he glanced away, then back again. "And each one of us will be standing on Yohanan's shoulders."

From one moment to the next, the tempo of Yeshu's voice picked up. "Yohanan and I have been soul brothers since we swam at the same time in our mothers' wombs.

"When a great tree is cut down, the sapling that once knelt under its canopy must stand and grow to fill the space that's opened.

"When the sun sets, the moon must rise to take its place. I'll not allow the light of my beloved brother to disappear—like a snuffed-out candle at the end of the day, that plunges us into darkness.

"Those who executed him will discover that killing a man will never kill the spirit and vision he shared with others while walking over this earth beside them."

Yeshu grew quiet. But his eyes were still flashing, and he was leaning forward as if preparing to run a dash.

Glimpsing the spark of Yohanan in Yeshu's eyes made me shiver.

Who was this man? It was not just the young carpenter who had lifted me to his shoulders as we strode home through a field of wheat when I was a child. Not even the same man I'd walked beside to the cedars of Lebanon. Somewhere deep inside him, bedrock had shifted.

And yet he seemed to still be the storytelling carpenter, still be my friend and neighbor. I felt awe without feeling distance, as if I were standing next to a whirlwind without being harmed.

Later, I would call that moment back to my mind and see that Yeshu was like a sturdy vessel that had just been pulled from the potter's kiln. Far more than the clay from which he had been molded and shaped by so many loving hands, he was now fully formed and fired—ready to carry water to the parched mouths of humankind.

I Learn the Truth

Sitting on a hillside the next day, tending Uncle Moishe's sheep, I had second thoughts. I'd made my decision to leave for Jerusalem without talking to my parents about it. The decision felt right, so why was I feeling guilty? It wasn't fair. I was fourteen now, a man in the eyes of everyone in Nazareth, except my own family evidently.

Losing Yohanan had been nightmarish. Whenever I talked to Yeshu about it, I became afraid of hurting him more than he already was. The next thing I knew he had gone off. By the time he'd returned from the wilderness, I didn't know where to begin. Finally, Maria had helped me sort my feelings out. But why was it so easy talking to her and nearly impossible to talk about loss with my own mother and father?

My heart stopped. There again were those memories rising up: Hushed voices in the night waking me. Shadowed silhouettes leaning over Shoshana. Clothes rustling. The next morning finding her gone, perhaps forever.

I could easily believe that Maria and Yeshu had rediscovered Yohanan again, partly because my sister was still alive inside me. But for how long? It was distressing being the only one keeping her alive. Why was her name never heard in our house?

In the days after I'd come of age according to custom—my father pronouncing his blessing over me before God—I'd hoped my parents would finally tell me what they knew. I tried to be patient. I really did. I would drop a crumb hoping a bird would land. One day I'd mention how my mother's comb reminded me of Shoshana's and I'd wait for her response. Anything. Any place to begin. Another time I'd tell father about a lamb that had gone lame and then ask if that had ever happened when Shoshana was tending sheep. Nothing.

It was as if they had sealed their ears with wax to keep from hearing in my voice the answering echo of Shoshana stirring in their hearts. The silence of these moments was louder than screaming. Months went by this way, and I was no closer to the truth.

This couldn't last any longer. That night, I told myself, the silence would end.

After supper, Aaron went to bed in the loft, but I stayed up with my parents. My mother was mending clothes, and my father sat beside her, braiding strips of hide into a bridle. We talked about the heat and lack of rain, the price of leather, how tasty the stew had been, the chores that needed doing the next day, everything imaginable except what I really wanted to talk about.

Until finally I just blurted out, "Has there been any news of Shoshana?"

Quickly they shook their heads.

All right, I'd thrown one pebble into a bottomless well and gotten a faint splash. Now I'd throw in another.

"Listen to me," I said. "She's my sister. I have a right to know what happened to her."

My mother looked away while my father studied the bridle intently, seeming to be searching for a hidden flaw. The stillness was smothering. It was as if a black curtain had fallen over us in open sunlight.

I pictured myself shouting out, "This must be what it feels like to be a traveler buried at a crossroads under a pile of stones, far from home!"

From the startled looks on my parents' faces I saw that the shout had been real.

My mother caught sight of my father's widened eyes, and their shoulders sagged. At last, I thought, I'm going to learn the truth.

But still they said nothing.

"I'm waiting," I said. "And if necessary, I'll wait till the rooster crows."

I stared at the ripped garments that each of them wore for Yohanan. Was the fact that they never tore keriah for Shoshana a bad sign or a good one? The next thing I knew, my teeth were pressing so intensely into my lower lip that my shoulders jumped with pain. With a shake of my head I tried my best to send my mind elsewhere.

Finally, mother breathed long and haltingly, and in a low voice, began talking. "She wasn't well."

Mother halted; spoke again.

"She had not been well for a long time. We were told she could not be cured and she could pass her sickness on to you and Aaron and..." After a lengthy pause, my father picked up the thread. "People came in the night and took her away."

I sat speechless. It wasn't enough, the details were all missing, but I was too stunned to absorb even this after knowing nothing at all for so long. For an eternity I stared straight at both of them, just waiting, waiting to discover what words would come next out of their mouths. Or out of *my* mouth.

Perhaps the silence made my mother afraid of how I might break it. Staring at her hands, she spoke again. We didn't tell you when you were small," she pleaded, "so you wouldn't be afraid. Afraid for yourself; afraid for your sister."

She paused again, for another eternity.

Bitterly, I thought to myself: who knew two eternities could sit side by side and never touch?

She went on, "And so you wouldn't blame us before you were old enough to understand."

A red cloud swelled up inside me. I pushed it down to press her for more information. "But *where* did they take her?"

She spread her hands wide and shrugged her shoulders, "We don't know. We just don't. They were wanderers passing through. Believe me: they were good souls; special people who knew about her ailment. They had no home I know of. We hoped we could somehow stay in touch with them. Who can say where they ended up? I wish with all my heart I knew."

Covering her mouth with the back of her hand, she struggled to her feet and rushed out the doorway.

My father sat staring after her into the darkness. Finally, he looked over at me. He started to say something, but whatever he saw in my face made him stop. Sighing heavily, he began reworking the bridle, fumbling with the straps, dropping one after another and leaning down yet again to scoop up the errant piece from the floor and into his lap.

Days later, when it was too late to do anything about it, I would berate myself for not asking *who* had taken my sister away, what were their names? What illness?

I consoled myself that I'd held back because telling the truth was tearing my parents to pieces. Then a whip-like voice at the back of my mind wondered: was it because I was afraid of the answers?

In any event, that night I packed but a few belongings: only my leatherworking tools and an extra tunic. I ached all over and wanted to leave behind as much as I could. I even left Shalom, the dog that Yeshu had carved for me years before, the friend who had never left my side. Perhaps Aaron needed someone to watch over him the way Shoshana had watched over me.

~ ~ ~

The next day I rose before dawn, dressed, grabbed my pack, and tiptoed to the door. Hearing a stirring behind me, I turned to look. My parents had gotten up and stood side by side in the shadows of the room, watching.

"Yeshu asked me to join him on his journey," I said, not quite accurately. And then I added, "I accepted."

I didn't say so, but I was thinking: I'm my own man now, old enough not to have to ask your permission. And besides, what authority do parents have who let strangers take their eldest daughter away?

"I can't say when I'll be back," I added without blinking, clipping each word so they would know I meant "if" not "when."

My mother and father said nothing, their eyes lowering. It's hard to explain, but that made me furious. It was as if they were confessing guilt; but at the same time, not admitting it. They had betrayed Shoshana on that night years ago. And me ever since.

Watching their mouths frozen open, a dark image flashed through my head of a hawk pouncing on a nest of mice. For all I cared, they could be scooped up and dropped down a hole in the rocks of a faraway desert.

The room felt cold and silent as a tomb. My father and mother seemed to have both stopped breathing. Slowly their eyes lifted to face me.

"May God go with you," they said together.

I stared at the wall behind them and nodded to the shadows.

Then I walked out the door and into the rose dawn of my new life.

A Whirlwind of Doves

A few hours later I had joined the meandering line of pilgrims—each of us with a torn garment—trudging along the road with Yeshu, from Nazareth to Jerusalem. We were ready to begin our mission of teaching and healing.

Up front were Martha and Maria Magdalena, talking quietly with Yeshu. I kept company with the Thunder Brothers, James and John, those giant, rambunctious fishermen whom Yeshu loved so dearly. They seemed to know without being told, when he was about to travel, the way storks find their way across the great sea when the seasons change.

Philippos tagged close behind. He had shown up a few days before, looking to apprentice himself with Yeshu in the healing art.

Mama Maria was along for the first leg of the journey. She carried in her pack medicines to ease childbirth. She hoped to sell them to midwives in the Jerusalem market. As soon as that was done, she planned to return home to Mama Ana and Nazareth. And I suppose, after what had happened to Yohanan, she wanted to be certain her firstborn made it through the festival without incident.

When someone asked after Mama Ana, she said in a voice meant to reach all of our ears, "She was feeling poorly this morning. Ever since the night air began creeping in with a chill on it, her legs have kept her lying in bed much of the time."

Yeshu's friend Judah joined the procession outside of Nazareth. He quickly worked his way to Yeshu's side, which made me curious, so I picked up my pace and joined them for a bit. Judah was already holding forth when I got there, the tangle of ebony locks that covered his head bobbing like the crest of a woodpecker chasing down termites, his eyes flashing as he poked this way and that to find advantage.

I doubt that he noticed he was mostly arguing with himself. Yeshu just smiled as if a thunderstorm were passing by some distance away. I listened as carefully as I could, but Judah was tossing out so many contradictory ideas, with such absolute certainty, I marveled that he had somehow managed to escape their thicket to find and join us.

On we walked, small groups of two or three carrying on quiet conversations, sometimes punctuated by laughter, a brief protest, or some other exclamation.

After we had covered a mile or two, I happened to catch a glimpse of Judah staring out of the sides of his eyes at Yeshu with what appeared to be childlike adoration.

What was it, I wondered, that this fiery fellow wanted from our carpenter and storyteller?

My eyes ran over his protruding brow and set jaw, then down his arm to a fisted hand. And what did Yeshu see in him?

Perhaps if I could practice more patience, I would find out. Judah was certainly a rabbit warren of opinions that popped out of burrows and darted across clearings, zigging this way, zagging that.

At other times, those thoughts of his were more like the swift and relentless cheetahs out on the plains beyond the Negev desert; the ones that hunters say run down those hapless hares.

Our three-day trek to Jerusalem was otherwise uneventful. When the walls of the great city appeared in the distance, Martha went ahead to make arrangements for our lodging in Joanna's home. Meanwhile, the rest of us stretched out by the roadside to take a break. There we lay munching on this and that from our packs and talking about what we would do once we entered the city gates.

Yeshu said nothing, but I could see by his face he was chewing on more than the stale bread rolls we were all sharing. From his quietness I was guessing it must be something to do with Yohanan, who had himself made this journey only a few months before—perhaps even stopping to rest by these same two trees. After a while, I moved over to sit by Yeshu's side and asked what he was thinking about.

Taking his time, he swallowed the bread in his mouth and then said, "Well, lately, the Prophet Jeremiah has been on my mind. Especially the image of him walking back and forth in front of King Zedekiah's palace, with an ox yoke on his shoulders that was fastened to his neck by leather straps."

"Why on earth would he do that?" I asked.

"He was telling a story with action," Yeshu answered, "declaring to the king and the leaders who had gathered from other lands, that God had willed that their necks be bent under the King of Babylon's yoke. They must not listen to prophets predicting a successful revolt that was not destined to take place."

Yeshu thrust his hand under his chin and rubbed his beard pensively with a forefinger. "Jeremiah tells us in the Book of *Yirmy hû* that he had a vision in which God gave him instructions."

> Brace yourself, Jeremiah!
> Stand up and speak to them.
> Tell them everything I bid you.
> Do not let your spirit break at the sight of them.
> This day I make you a fortified city,
> a pillar of iron, a wall of bronze,
> to stand fast against the whole land –
> against the kings and princes of the Judean Kingdom,
> its priests and its people.
> They will fight you but will not overcome you,
> for I am with you and will keep you safe.

Yeshu extended his hand, palm open and pointing skyward. "So Jeremiah followed his vision. He found a way to demonstrate outwardly the unwelcome news circling around inside of him."

Yeshu's hand sunk back down to his lap. "That's what I've been ruminating on, my friend—stories in action."

Out of the corner of my eye, I noticed Judah nodding vigorously. I suspected he might have missed the point. But before he could speak up, Martha suddenly appeared on the road, hurrying along with Joanna herself. Leaping up, I called out a greeting, and all conversation ended as everyone rose to meet the two of them.

Joanna embraced each of us warmly but saved her biggest hug for Yeshu. Right off, the words tumbled from her mouth as she began telling us of Yohanan's last hours.

When she came to a break in her account, Yeshu touched her lips gently with his hand, brushed the tears from her cheek, and said, "Let's walk."

We gathered our things and set off as Joanna recounted what she had heard from several men who had been at Herod's Court the night of the execution. These fellows had been her late husband's aides at the Court, when he was still living. What they said was at first unsettling. But knowing Yohanan like she did, what they did not realize they were saying was much more important.

"They told me people in the Court boasted how this great wild boar, for all his public ranting, went to the slaughter like a lamb. And a crazy lamb at that, bleating how it wasn't only he who was accusing Herod of betraying the Jewish people, for all Herod had to do was put down his wine goblet and look calmly into the pool of water in his palace and ask what *it* saw.

"Disgustingly, when Herod had Yohanan's head cut off and delivered on a platter to his wife and daughter, every so often he would raise his cup and ask what Yohanan was observing now."

A notion penetrated my mind: it's a good thing for Herod that Yohanan's eyes were closed, or the tyrant would have been blinded by what he saw reflected there.

It was then I heard Yohanan's voice at the back of my mind chuckling, "But Daavi, Herod was already blind don't you see?"

Joanna went on, "Others said they were glad to be rid of 'that unruly preacher of myths and tales.' They dismissed him as 'just another crazy ne'er-do-well with a grudge against the King: a wild man who was on a futile jeremiad.'"

I kicked at the road, kicked it hard. How could people be so thickheaded and brutish? Especially ones who neither planted nor harvested, nor did any other kind of labor themselves. Did they even have their own thoughts? Hadn't many of them joined the crowds that had gathered when Yohanan first began preaching and later told their friends all the intriguing things he had to say? And now it was good riddance, as if none of that had ever happened.

Joanna saw I was upset and said, "What kind of host am I being? Let's not chew these bitter herbs anymore today. They taste too much of tears."

She wiped her face with a sleeve. "Please, be my guests. You will honor me by staying at my home. Once there, we'll share a meal together like old times. We'll remember Yohanan as he was, until we've laughed and roared ourselves to sleep. In the morning you can tell me what your plans are."

We quickly agreed and stepped up our pace, pausing only for the ritual cleansing required before entering the massive gates of Jerusalem. One by one we reverently touched the prominent mezuzah on the wall, and I stared at the smaller door that formed the corner of one of the majestic ones.

This was that man-sized door that was popularly known as the "Eye of the Needle." I smiled inwardly, recognizing it immediately as the crux of Yeshu's favorite comical riddle, about the difficulty of a rich man getting into heaven.

Without tarrying, we plunged into the city where King David and his son, King Solomon, and so many others had walked. We wound through more streets than Judah had arguments. At last we arrived at Joanna's spacious house. Supper was followed by story after story, until weariness bent us over and sent us wriggling into cozily blanketed beds.

The next morning Yeshu spoke to Joanna privately. Knowing about her husband's past position in Herod's Court, he told her he had a thorny matter to take care of at the Temple and it might be most prudent for her if she were to remain back at home. With a lone hand motion and a wisp of a smile, she signaled her agreement and we headed out.

~ ~ ~

What happened that first day in Jerusalem, I have never forgotten. When we entered the Temple grounds, I paused just inside the arched entryway and took a sweeping look around. The noise was deafening. Lined against the walls of the courtyard were row upon row of tables. Behind each one sat a moneychanger or someone selling live cattle, sheep, or doves for sacrifices in the Temple. I had heard they deftly cheated travelers carrying foreign coins. More than a place of worship, this place had the looks of a bazaar.

I studied the expressions of the horde of merchants, then searched for Yeshu's face to see what he thought. But where was he?

Suddenly he emerged from behind a knot of strangers milling around one of the tables. The muscles of his back and shoulders quivered in a way I had never seen before. His head was tipped downward and to one side as though he was about to leap across a wide ravine. Something was terribly wrong.

Yeshu slowly swung round—his right arm pointed at each table as he completed a circle—and he roared like a lion.

"The scrolls say, 'My house shall be called a house of prayer,'" he cried out. "And yet you have made it a den of thieves!"

The words echoed like a mighty drum in the stone courtyard. The din of bronze, silver, and gold changing hands, and of people haggling and animals being trussed and bagged, all fell away like the wind going suddenly still in the treetops before a torrential cloudburst.

Everyone had frozen in place. The whole world closed in tight around Yeshu. All I saw was his face, the face of a stranger. Fury had turned it dark as a thunderhead, blocking out the moon and stars from his eyes. Lightning flashed there even more fiercely than the blazing sun I had so often seen in the eyes of Yohanan.

And yet he seemed perfectly balanced on the balls of his feet. The muscles of his face were not twisted into something ugly as I had seen in others who were enraged. His eyebrows were like doors propped above a roaring oven as he fixed his silent gaze on the nearest moneychanger. His lips stayed as tight as the seams of a ship on a tempest-tossed sea.

Yeshu was at war.

He bore down on the first moneychanger's table, and with one sudden sweep of his outstretched arm sent stacks of coins spilling across the smooth stone floor.

Among the scramble of bystanders who dropped to their knees to pick up what they could, other voices cried out in protest and fear. People were running everywhere as Yeshu pushed on, sending whole tables tumbling and splintering. Then he yanked off his rope belt and swung it round and round in a great, humming spiral, cracking it so that smoke snaked from the free end.

The smell bit so strongly my nostrils twitched.

The crowd of sellers and moneychangers, paralyzed at first, then bellowing in protest, suddenly turned and fled as one person, rushing for the doorway to escape Yeshu's wrath. I barely stepped aside in time, or the flood would have swept me away.

On and on Yeshu strode, table by table, until they all lay at his feet. Straightaway, he untied the sheep and cattle and sent them running toward the great portal leading to the streets. Next he tore open each birdcage, and soon the air was thick with a whirlwind of white doves, ecstatic in their liberation.

When the doves' wing-beats finally subsided, Yeshu stood motionless in the middle of the hushed yard. Patches of dampness marked his robe on the chest and arms. A single feather floated past his cheek as it descended toward the cobblestones at his feet.

One by one he looked at the few of us who remained. As his cooling eyes touched each one of our faces, we quietly let out our breath.

After his eyes met mine, I stared past the ruins that lay strewn about us, whispering under my breath, "Yet he struck *no* man."

Slowly, Yeshu knelt and held his hands out in front of him, palms facing upward.

He stared into those hands for a long time, as if trying to understand their purpose. He was as still as the marble columns around us. Momentarily he looked up at the sky, then down again, his eyes glistening.

For a long time he held his gaze on his hands, and one by one, those of us with him knelt down, too. I saw his lips move, and I strained forward to hear him speaking with a voice as clear as a rabbi reading from the scrolls.

For where your treasure is,
there will your heart be also.

We all fell silent together, peering deeply into that heart. We may have been kneeling on stone, but it felt soft as a cloud.

~ ~ ~

Over the years, I would find myself dwelling again and again upon Yeshu's raging storm that far off morning, and the calm that followed. It made his other moments of waging peace all the more striking.

He had chosen the uphill path for his life—steeling himself for a mighty struggle. His goal was not to harm or conquer; no, it was to meet might with love. And in doing so, he called out to others to bear witness to which of the two is stronger.

That day in the temple, as I knelt watching the carpenter, my thoughts were tangled and unruly, flitting in and out of my head like the newly freed doves that were picking seeds from between the pavement stones of the courtyard.

And just like a dove that's found a seed it can't quite tease out, I kept returning to something Yeshu had said years ago. He was in his workshop, patiently explaining how important it was to not just blindly read the laws that have been handed down to us in our ancient scrolls.

"We have to learn to read what is written between the words," he'd insisted.

"That's where the water collects," he added. "Stone is the vessel, and the spirit is water. And law that invites reflection, rewards us with wisdom."

And yet, was reflection what I had just witnessed in the Temple courtyard? It seemed more like hammering a bell to sound an alarm. But what were we being told to flee from or run toward?

Was Yeshu calling out for something new? Or was it for a return to something we'd lost? After all, these moneychangers were following the laws of men, not those of the God of Moses and the other prophets.

I tried to shake my head clear. Maybe he was as clouded by grief as I still was, and he'd momentarily lost his way. Or perhaps it was simply honest anger. Yohanan would have been outraged, too. Yet I couldn't shake the feeling that what Yeshu had done had been filled with purpose.

It was like Jeremiah acting out his story, I thought.

In the end, I didn't know for sure. And that's how life sometimes is. Something utterly transforming happens, but it takes your entire lifetime to figure out what it means.

Next, out of the corner of my eye, I saw Maria Magdalena rise and walk over to where Yeshu knelt. She stood next to him and laid her hand on his shoulder. His head turned to look at the hand resting there. I saw his chest rise and slowly fall. His eyes closed, and his brow smoothed out like a lake gone flat after a rainstorm has passed.

Meanwhile, Mama Maria was smiling. She had stood up along with the younger Maria but had knelt back down when she saw the Magdalena walk toward Yeshu. There are times, after all, when it's better to have someone other than your parent giving comfort.

Mama Maria sat quietly, perhaps recalling another time, long ago, when Yeshu's voice made its mark in this very Temple.

From where it perched atop its cage, a final dove took flight, its shadow winging across the stones of the courtyard floor.

Slowly, Mama Maria stood and walked to Yeshu's other shoulder. I saw his eyes open again, and I realized how fortunate he was to have a pillar on each side of him.

Finally he rose to his feet, and we all followed suit. One by one we went over to reach out to him and clasp his hand, a forearm, an elbow. Then all of us turned and exited the temple grounds together.

The Lost Sheep and Other Stories

The next morning we left Jerusalem. After poking the sleeping cobra, one is wise to back away quietly and choose another path. So that's what we did. By early afternoon, as the heat was rising, we came to a quiet village that seemed a good place to stop for a while.

Since there was no synagogue, we found an ancient chestnut tree near the community well and Yeshu suggested we sit and wait for people to come. Leaning against the thick trunk, he began telling stories in the cool shade that covered the ground beneath the outspread branches.

Some of the stories I had heard before; a few of them, many times. Others felt completely new. The burning sun had ended most work in the fields for the day, so it wasn't long before word skipped around the village that a storytelling preacher was in town. At least one person had recognized him as a man who used to wander the countryside as an itinerant carpenter, a fact that further pricked people's curiosity. Soon a large crowd was sitting around Yeshu.

The children in the crowd gathered closer when the storyteller pointed to the nearest child and motioned with his hands that everyone no taller than his rope belt should move forward.

The village women sat to Yeshu's right, with their water urns on the ground next to them. Many had babies on their backs or in their arms or at the breast, and their hands never stopped working: spinning wool, making prayer shawls with long needles carved from bone, gesturing soundlessly at a rowdy child who hadn't gone forward, until the young miscreant noticed and quieted down.

The men stood to the left, conversing in low voices about this and that but keeping an ear cocked to catch the storyline. When Yeshu finished a tale, the men would drop whatever else they had been talking about and argue among themselves about who had best captured the story's meaning.

The story that made me sit up sounded oddly familiar from the beginning, but I didn't recall ever hearing it before.

"A man worked hard for many years till he finally owned a vast flock of more than a hundred sheep," Yeshu began. "He tended the animals himself, aided by two loyal sheepdogs. One summer, in pasturelands farther from home than he had ever gone, the shepherd was counting his flock, just as he regularly did several times a day, and he came up one short.

"He counted again, and then again to make certain the number was right. Always it was the same. Somehow a sheep had gotten lost. Quickly, he whistled and motioned with his hand for one dog to stay and watch the ninety-nine sheep, while he and the second dog set out to find the stray."

Yeshu glanced at me and then back to his audience.

"The man was concerned because that very morning he'd seen lion tracks, no more than a day old. He couldn't be sure whether the lion was still around or if it had roamed onward, but he knew this meant it hunted in these parts.

"After a long search the wayward sheep turned up, bleating frantically from a thicket of brambles. The man rejoiced as if he had found his own son, carefully cutting away the thorny tangle with a long knife.

Lifting the freed sheep and cradling it in his arms, he said, 'I love you more than the ninety-nine back there on the hillside. You were lost, but now you are found!'"

Then Yeshu turned to the group and asked, "What lessons can we glean from this story?"

My thoughts had drifted back to the day he and I had gone shepherding, but I said nothing, waiting to see what others would answer.

Standing suddenly, a youth with a slingshot piped up, "The man was a fool. He loved his money and his dogs more than his own wife and children. That's why he lost all his other sheep while he hunted for the stray."

The crowd burst into laughter. Yeshu joined in, before asking, "But what about you? Do you love your tongue more than your slingshot? I suppose those stones in your hand are your only contribution to spicing up the stew tonight for your family's evening meal."

The crowd roared even louder, tickled by the give and take that was customary in small villages where everyone knew everyone else. The boy sat back down, proud to have provided such entertainment, while Yeshu's eyes sparkled with the certainty that he was accepted and the teaching could really begin. The boy and Yeshu traded smiles.

Then Yeshu turned to Maria Magdalena, and asked, "What does this story tell you about God?"

The men stopped their kibitzing and stared in astonishment at Yeshu and Maria. What kind of teacher lets children answer first? And when they cannot, then turns to a woman? How preposterous is that!

Maria stood but said nothing. Several of the men began to smirk. Turning her head toward them, she answered Yeshu, "Your story means that God loves the sinner who has strayed off, even more than he loves those of us who have remained with the flock."

As quick as thunder follows lightning, Yeshu sang out, "Well done!"

At this, more than a few mouths dropped open. One man scuffed his feet and asked a friend, a bit too loudly, "Why is this so-called teacher making a long afternoon longer, playing women's and children's games with us? His story makes no sense."

"Does a good riddle ever make sense when you first hear it?" countered Yeshu. "At times it does, but you only know that after your mind pares the nonsense away."

The man stared at his sandals. Yeshu waited for the man's gaze to lift and when their eyes met, he smiled.

Nodding his head slightly at the man, Yeshu added, "Some teachers give straight answers all day long even when the road is crooked, and so no one listens to them because the life we lead always takes us on a winding path."

The man conceded the point with a quick hand gesture and a begrudging smile.

Yeshu raised both arms and returned his gaze to the rest of the crowd.

"I can see that you good people can figure out how you will find your way to your own destinations. You don't need me to tell you where the hidden spring can be found."

He lowered his arms back to his side. "Now, it's your turn to quiz *me*." His eye skipped around. "Anyone have a question?"

From the center of the gathering came the voice of a young woman.

"Teacher, how do we know what God would have us do?"

Yeshu smiled again and nodded in her direction, saying, "That question is as important to us as a mother's milk is to her hungry baby."

Several women glanced up from their work.

Yeshu continued, "Let's turn our thoughts to the scrolls known as the combined Book of Kings, what we call the M'lakhim in Hebrew."

> Elijah was told to go to the top of Mount Horeb
>   to receive a message from God.
> As he waited, a great strong wind came up,
>   shattering rocks,
>   but God was not in the wind.
> And after the wind an earthquake,
>   but God was not in the earthquake.
> And after the earthquake a fire,
>   but God was not in the fire, either.
> And after the fire, a still small voice...
>   and that was the voice of God.

Yeshu raised an open hand and cupped it just behind an ear. Not even a rustle came from the gathering. He allowed time for the passage to soak into parched ground. When he spoke again, it was with a quiet, steady voice.

"So, my friends, your first task is to always listen for that still, small voice of God. Listen for it in the dark of night under the stars, or at home as you draw the blanket up to your chin for sleep. Listen for it in the shimmering sunlight as you head out to the fields in the morning. Listen for it in your heart and in the hearts of your loved ones, and even in the hearts of those who seem to be your enemies.

"God is continually speaking to us," Yeshu said, "often in ways that may seem mysterious but only because we don't always know how to listen.

"Listening is hard when you are doing all the talking, drowning out the still, small voice. That voice is even more easily lost when you are scolding your child or shouting down your neighbor.

He leaned forward and turned his head slightly, as if straining to catch the sound of a voice. "So if you want to truly hear," he said, "practice silence. Go deep within yourself, and wait. Wait for the voice to reveal itself like a hidden wren singing in a thicket. You will hear it rising up from the tangle of your thoughts, or from words someone else is speaking, maybe even without knowing it.

"And the way will open." Yeshu's eyes lit up. His cupped hand returned to his side.

"It will open as surely as a swinging door. As certainly as a cloud of fog lifting at dawn to reveal the path."

Standing back and to one side, I could see Yeshu's face and also those of many of the villagers, young and old. Yeshu's was glowing and so were theirs. These faces seemed like sunflowers turning as the sun journeys across the sky; turning as they attended to every nuance in this humble teacher's voice, his gestures, his expressions.

Sighing, I felt a boundless peace, as if all of us were being held in the palm of God's broad hand.

"What else puzzles you?" Yeshu asked out of the blue, his eyes moving around the circle.

One of the better-dressed villagers stepped forward and cleared his throat. All faces turned toward him. He presented his question with the assured voice of someone important.

"Teacher," he said, "how much of what we own should be shared with others, to be certain we are being generous enough?"

Yeshu replied, "I can tell your mind has been occupied with the Jubilee Year that is fast approaching. My response to you is wrapped within another story."

I sensed the crowd edging toward him, desiring more. After taking a drink from a goatskin that lay at his feet, Yeshu began.

"Several years ago, standing near the Temple treasury in Jerusalem, I watched people placing their offerings into an ornate chest of burnished cedar. The finest-dressed benefactors held their hands high and dropped several large coins with a flourish, waiting to hear the ring of metal against metal as their gift cascaded down the pile of contributions below. Others reached out and let their more modest coins fall just beyond the edge of the chest as they hurried by.

"Then I saw a tiny, grey-haired lady," Yeshu said, "steadfastly making her way down the corridor. As she approached, she threaded deftly through the crushing throng of priests and congregants that pushed by her, threatening to sweep her away.

"Noticing her worn clothing and bent back I guessed she was an elderly widow struggling to make ends meet during the last years of a long life. With small, quick steps, she made straight for the chest, all the while digging down into a modest pouch on her waistband. Finally reaching the chest, she pulled her hand from the pouch and stared into her cupped palm. There lay two tiny bronze coins, each as thin as the down on a sparrow's breast." Yeshu peered into his own palm.

"Shaking her head at the meagerness of her offering," he went on, "she lifted her eyes heavenward, closed them, and dropped her feathery coins into the coffer. They fell soundlessly onto the pile.

"But the roll of thunder in my soul was great.

"Why? Because a poor widow with next to nothing had given more generously than those who had more than enough to spare."

Yeshu became still, and soon a woman's voice protested, "But teacher, you haven't answered my husband's question."

"I have not come to offer answers," responded Yeshu, smiling, "that do not stir up new questions. You must wrestle with the answers by living out your questions."

I could see that the shepherds and fieldhands in the crowd liked the story far better than the people whose appearance gave sure signs that they were wealthy. While the second group fidgeted uncomfortably, the first group lifted their chins with assurance and murmured to one another.

One emboldened shepherd spoke out, "My children implore me to tell them the one thing God is most like. To me this is a riddle with multiple answers. How should I respond to my little ones?"

Yeshu wrinkled his brow and nodded toward the man, showing how pleased the question made him. He took in a long breath.

Then he began speaking. "Most simply stated, God is love," he said. "Those who dwell in love dwell in God. And God dwells in them."

The shepherd nodded in affirmation, and many others did too. This answer rang true to them.

"Allow me to add mint leaves and dates to the stew," Yeshu continued, scanning the many faces, one by one.

"My dear friends let us love one another, because love is from God. Everyone who loves is a child of God and knows God, but the unloving know nothing of God, for God *is* love."

Yeshu looked once more at the shepherd who had posed the question.

"As long as we love one another, God dwells in us, and God's love comes to its perfection in us. This is the proof that we live in God and God in us."

I saw that some brows were furrowed in thought, as people attempted to grasp the meaning in Yeshu's circling words.

"God is a mystery we are born into," he added, raising one hand horizontally to his forehead. He looked like a man shading his eyes when facing the sun and peering at something far away.

"By loving one another," he continued, "you will come to know God without searching for images and descriptions."

Yeshu's hand fell back to his side as he affectionately scanned the faces in front of him. He was finished and waiting to discover what subject might open up next.

When no one spoke, but all watched him with expressions that seemed ready to hear more, he complied.

"I find in my travels that people talk a lot about what goes on in the kingdom of men. Such kingdoms are very imperfect, and bring about much suffering."

I noticed a number of folks gesturing in agreement.

"But with you, I would rather talk about God's kingdom," said Yeshu. "What do you know about it?"

All eyes watched him in anticipation, until a grandmother spoke up.

"Rabbis go on and on about the Kingdom of God, but no one tells us what it looks like."

She lifted her chin to point it at Yeshu. "Are you any different? You brought it up. You tell *us* what it is."

Yeshu smiled broadly at his challenger's spunk. In an instant he became solemn, rubbing his forehead and then tugging at his beard. It was clear he was mulling the question over carefully. All present were suspended like spiders in a breeze.

Suddenly, out of the deepening silence Yeshu declared, "God's kingdom is like a grain of mustard seed. A mustard seed that a man has sowed in his field."

His gaze swept over the crowd. "Does that surprise you?"

From the looks on faces, it obviously did.

"As you well know," he went on, "the mustard is the least of all the seeds. But when cast on prepared ground, it is the greatest of the herbs. It grows like a tree, so large that the birds of the air arrive and nest in its branches. All this from a tiny seed that can be blown from the palm of your hand with a faint puff of breath."

A young girl in the front row clapped her hands together smartly upon hearing Yeshu's answer. She blew and blew, first on one palm, then on the other. But some of the elders glanced around at one another, shaking their heads.

At that, a man stepped forward who seemed young enough to have just struck off on his own. With a frown, he said, "Last year, my brother who lives far from here did me a terrible wrong and then never asked for forgiveness on Yom Kippur. Last week he sent a message seeking help with the roof of his house that had caved in when a dead tree fell on it, a tree he should have cleared away long ago. Should I help him, no matter how he's treated me, or should I teach him a lesson by refusing him any aid?"

Yeshu studied the young man for a while. Then he said, "How can you say to your brother, 'Let me take that speck of sawdust out of your eye,' when all the time there is a great cedar plank in your own?

"First take the plank out of your own eye, and then you will see clearly to take the speck out of your brother's."

All eyes were on the young man as he stood chewing on his upper lip and staring at the ground in front of him. It was difficult to tell whether he was being resistant or just pensive.

Thunder John broke the silence by leaping to his feet and crying out, "Ha! A carpentry joke told by a carpenter!"

Once again the crowd burst into laughter, and the young man smiled at last, most likely with relief at being lifted so gently off the hook.

Meanwhile, Yeshu glared at John and threw up his hands in mock exasperation. John just looked around like he was pretty darned proud of himself. One more ripple of laughter traveled through the gathering.

And that's the way it went all afternoon, until finally dark blue evening shadows began to stretch across the clearing surrounding the great chestnut tree, and Yeshu bid his farewell and turned to leave.

Many in the crowd ran up to hug him and thank him for sharing his stories. Others shrugged, shook their heads, and meandered off, talking and laughing among themselves. The man in the fine cloak who asked the question about generosity stepped over and invited us all to spend the night in his home.

We happily accepted, following behind our host, most of us linking elbows to walk together, arm in arm.

Tale Weaving

The next evening around the campfire, after a day of walking the open road, Yeshu talked about why he used stories and riddles to teach lessons. "If I simply told people what to do without involving them in the story," he said frowning faintly, "they might readily agree but soon forget it."

He appeared to be brooding for a moment.

"Or it might make no impression on them one way or the other: as if a fluffy milkweed seed had floated onto the surface of a puddle of mud and vanished." He smiled.

"It's easy to say that the Kingdom of God is like a mighty cedar of Lebanon. But looking up into the clouds around its canopy, people might forget about their own lives here on the earth. I prefer to challenge them to search through what's right in front of them. More often than not, what we need lies not in some far distant land. It's here; it's now.

"Just think of it," Yeshu went on, "the doorway to God's Kingdom can be lodged in a tiny mustard seed that falls from one of the countless plants growing everywhere like weeds. Even along the roadside."

He paused to examine our faces and see if we were following his train of thought.

"A good story, well told, will reach out and grip people by the tunic," he said. "Young or old, rich or poor, it doesn't matter. It's all the better when the point of the story isn't given, but must be found. Working through the dense foliage, following a forest trail of twisting paths not easily traversed, this allows people to find themselves in the story and make it their own."

Once more Yeshu paused.

"So," he said with a twinkle in his eye, "the story's meaning shouldn't be as easy to find as a cow's hoof in a bowl of soup."

Knowing chuckles rippled through the group.

"Not if it's to be savory enough to eat."

Judah, however, who had been staring at the heel of his hand the whole time, was not amused. Shaking his curly head as if to clear away a cloud of deerflies, he turned and spoke sharply to Yeshu.

"But why confuse people who are already lost? They need answers, not more doubt. Just give them the truth up front, all of it, without the honey of children's tales. Give them the vinegar too, so they will know exactly why they must do what you tell them to."

He pounded a fist into an open hand—just like Yeshu sometimes did—only when Judah did it, it sounded like two blocks of wood being slammed together in the night. And it made people jump.

"The only point of stories," Judah said, "is to pass on history: our people need to know all about the hard facts of the tyranny we have suffered for centuries. No one must ever forget. Ever. That's what stories are for; that and nothing more."

Thunder John broke in, "Well, in my opinion, Yeshu has split the log with the ax, right down the middle." He looked sideways at Judah. "And yet it's not trunks and limbs that I want to talk about. It's clothing."

John cleared his throat. "For me," he said, "a strong tale is like a fine weaving."

His voice turned wistful. "James, my dear brother, do you remember the textiles our mother wove? Their intricate patterns were so surprising that you'd never be able to imagine them if you hadn't seen them. Don't you agree? Even when we were just knee-high, we'd spend hours following those designs with our fingers and then go off to invent new ones of our own with a stick in the dust."

James was nodding in agreement even before John had finished, and he added a touch of his own for punctuation.

"My beloved Brother John, I recall this scene even more clearly than all those mornings you poured water on my slumbering head to wake me up."

John grinned broadly while James took up the cudgel.

"If our friend Judah had his way, everyone would wear the same cloth, dyed the same color—something a good Roman wouldn't be caught dead in, although I suppose Judah would wish that all of them *were* caught dead."

All eyes turned to Judah, who sniffed and looked away. But John jumped in again before Judah could recover to lead us back up his usual blind alley.

"Well, then," said John, glancing at Yeshu, "allow me to demonstrate, with a not-so-good story.

"Once upon a time a man kicked his neighbor's dog for sniffing at the clay pot of milk in his doorway. That very night, the man's wife became ill. So he went to that same neighbor's house in search of herbs to make his wife a healing tea. Halfway there, the dog bit him on the leg, and chased him back home."

Thunder John paused and pointed his nose toward the sky, wrinkling it up like a dried-out lemon.

"Way too easy," he said, before any of us could comment. "Sooner or later your kick will come back to bite you because meanness breeds in a vicious circle. No need to crack your noggin with my brother's cane to be able to figure that one out."

He held one hand high in the air for dramatic effect. "After all, only Abel would fall victim to *that* Cain!"

I glanced over at Yeshu and caught him lifting his eyebrows wryly. But I just knew that inside he was laughing heartily.

Not to be outdone, Thunder James swiftly retorted. "Excellent, my brother; excellent re-caning of a sagging old chair seat.

"Unfortunately," he pontificated, "your tale did nothing but wag that flea-bitten dog! The afore-mentioned notwithstanding, I have a *much* better story, of the challenging kind that our dearly venerated Yeshu suggests we tell.

"Once upon a time," proclaimed James, "a man kicked his neighbor for sniffing his tea with honey. That very night the neighbor's wife became ill, and the neighbor sent his dog to steal a clay pot of milk from the man's doorway. Halfway there, the man saw the hound, who turned tail to run back home. But the man pursued the pooch doggedly and bit it on the leg to hound it into submission. Without paws, the righteous man rushed howling back to his house and clumsily kicked the pot of milk. The herbs fit nowhere in this tale, so I'll save them for my next one. How did I do?"

We were so weak with laughter we couldn't say, lost in our own howling from the moment the dog was chased down and bitten by his two-legged neighbor.

I made it a point to remember to ask the Thunder Brothers if they were somehow related to my Gramma Ruth. They weren't, of course, and yet they refused to say if the pup in question was family, and if so, on which side of the family tree.

Judah was standing now, looking like he wanted to strangle the Boanerges, these interminably pesky Sons of Thunder, if only they weren't half again as big as he was.

And for sure, Thunder John was not ready to quit.

"Yes, I can see, Brother James," he intoned dramatically, that *your* tale also goes on wagging. Just like your tongue.

"Oh yes, and that wooly story you wove is far more threadbare than mine. It has many more dead ends to lead us astray (or was the dog a stray?), until at long last we find ourselves confronted with that most tantalizing of questions. It's the one you hold out to us at the tail end, like a date on a ponderous and pointed stick; or sticking point. And you ask us to swallow them both.

"The *point* being, of course that laughter is painful, and if you don't believe it's so, you're free to backtrack along your crooked trail all the way to the beginning, to start the story over again at either end, and to end up, if fate would have it, in the middle."

Any more serious discussion that night was hopeless. The brothers had accomplished their mission, to drive us all under the covers. It was bedtime, with no more squabbling or cogitating until tomorrow.

Goose Girl

By now, it will come as no surprise that over the years Yeshu's voice never left me. It was so rich and warm, the sound penetrated my chest and lifted my soul like a wave. From the time I was a young child, I could listen to him endlessly, even if he were merely counting boards in his carpentry shop.

But it was in speaking to an audience that his voice was truly unforgettable. It seemed able to travel any distance over the heads of the gathered crowd, all the way to the last person in the rear. And yet Yeshu never resorted to shouting. Each word was distinct and resonant, like the sure beat of a small, tight-headed drum.

When it was a message he really wanted you to hear, his voice rang out like a bell.

Once when we were picking berries for sweetening the barley cakes, Maria Magdalena told me, "Here is a voice that can penetrate the walls of the palace chambers of Caiaphas the High Priest, and Pontius Pilatus the Roman Governor. "In time," she continued, "Yeshu's voice will travel to every corner of the world. It will turn over rocks and blow down trees, and then turn them all right again."

Maria smiled, looking at me out of the corner of her eyes, her head cocked in my direction. When she saw I was in step with her, she kept going.

"It can even sweep the stars from the great night sky, echo off the full moon, fly circles round the rising sun!"

We were both giggling uncontrollably by the time she bounced Yeshu's voice off the moon. Maria had a way of describing things that made you laugh and want to listen even more closely.

"Here on earth," she grew very serious now, "this voice will change history. I am certain of it.

"Yohanan's was a voice crying out from the wilderness: a solitary owl calling to us to hold on through the night.

"At other times," she added, "he was a leopard ordering its young out of the den into the morning light.

"Yeshu's voice is thunder and falling rain," she said. "It has power *and* gentleness. It rings with wrath at injustice; and compassion for the vulnerable."

Her eyes danced. "Yeshu coos to us like a dove to its mate. But he also makes himself heard with the fierce urgency of a wolf pack calling to a lost pup in a windstorm.

"When he speaks, Yeshu is the living word. Peace on earth. Love, pure and simple."

She smiled again. "But don't tell him I said so...we have to keep him humble!" And she burst into laughter.

Smiling at her, I responded, "Most important to me, Yeshu's voice is all of that and more when he's telling stories."

"Mmm-hm," she answered, pressing her lips together.

~ ~ ~

Some months after the Thunder Brothers regaled us with their contrasting styles of storytelling, Mama Maria rejoined our wandering band in a village near Nazareth that was ringed by date palms. Somehow she invariably knew where we were. And we were always happy when she tracked us down.

That very afternoon, Yeshu stood teaching to a crowd of palm cultivators and shepherds in a meadow up the road from where we were lodged. Word had arrived of a young girl, perhaps eight years old, being carried there by her father to be healed. It seems the news had been traveling ahead of us, announcing a teacher with special wisdom and powers, so the father had sought Yeshu out. At last he found us.

Yeshu asked to see the girl. But the crowd was so tightly packed, the father had difficulty coming closer. So he lifted his daughter over the heads of the people, whereupon hand after hand reached up to receive and pass her forward, her shining black hair hanging down around her like a curtain in the Temple.

It only took one quick look to see what the small girl's problem was: she had been brought there because she had no legs below the knees. Yeshu let out a long breath, and his shoulders sank. He turned his face away from the crowd.

After a few moments, I made my way over to see what was wrong. I wanted to let him know that people had backed up to make an open space, and that the girl was waiting there, in the arms of Philippos.

When I reached Yeshu, I saw that his eyes were clouded. Mama Maria stood beside him, and she had quietly taken hold of his hands.

Yeshu looked at her and shook his head almost imperceptibly.

I heard him saying softly but emphatically, "I cannot put her legs back. You know that. This can't do the child or her father any good. I don't wish to rob them of hope."

Mama Maria gripped his hands tightly. "Yeshua, go to her. Heal her soul."

Yeshu raised his mother's hands to his forehead and held them there for a moment. Then he nodded, straightened, and made his way to the girl's side.

The crowd surrounding us fell quiet. Everyone was expecting a miracle.

Yeshu lifted the little girl up in his arms and smiled at her. She was trembling with nervous excitement.

"Hi, I'm Yeshu," he said.

She giggled. "Hi, I'm Rebekah!"

Her eyes flashed, lighting up the sweet beauty of her face. It was an image that would stay with me for years.

Yeshu looked out at the crowd. "Thank you all for bringing me Rebekah."

The eager response picked up volume as it rolled toward us. All present were closely watching Yeshu, anticipation animating their faces.

Yeshu closed his eyes, and murmured something, almost soundlessly.

Then he looked directly into the little girl's eyes. "Rebekah, no one can bring back your lost legs. But you are so bright. So lovable," he said, loudly enough that all could hear.

"See how devoted your father is to you? He must have risen before dawn and carried you for hours on his shoulders to get here."

The tall carpenter sighted over the heads of the crowd to where her father was.

"Rebekah," Yeshu's eyes returned to her, "you have received gifts that not all children have. Nurture them so that they grow, for your good and for others."

Then, still holding Rebekah in his arms, Yeshu addressed the gathering.

"I'm going to tell our treasured Rebekah, and all of you, a story about a little girl very much like her.

"This little girl lived in a village not far from here," Yeshu said, in a voice loud enough for everyone to hear. "She was the only child in a very poor family, and first one parent, then the other took ill and died. This town had no rabbi who might have taken the girl under his wing and perhaps would have found a family to adopt her. So, one thing led to another until she was finally taken in by a man and his wife who set her to work tending geese. The couple had no children of their own, and yet they didn't want the orphaned girl for their daughter. It seemed they only wanted someone to take care of their flock.

"All day long she had to stay in the yard with the geese. She did nothing but sleep at night and watch those geese during the day. After a while, people began to call her 'Goose Girl.'

"Now, the goose girl was convinced that she would never leave the old couple's house, never be married and have her own family, never make anything of her life. She felt sorry for herself and was sure that no one cared about what happened to her. Often, just before falling asleep at night, she let loose a single sob. And she greeted the morning with another just like it after waking up. Nothing ever seemed to change for her."

Yeshu looked out at the crowd and back at Rebecca.

"One day, however, a magical goose flew out of the dawn and joined the girl's flock. She knew it was magical, not because it looked any different but because that evening, as she was bedding her flock down, and twilight welled up to touch the sky, much to her surprise the goose batted its eyes three times and began to speak.

"On that first occasion the goose just chattered idly: about the warmth of the breeze and the afternoon rain shower and the amount of grit in the grain. But as night deepened, it beckoned to the goose girl to come closer. With one wing extended, it pointed up at the large swan constellation flying along the *Via Lactea*—that wide band of stars that looks like a milky stream, high above our heads.

"'That swan is Cygnus, my great grandmother,' the magical goose said, with a twinkle in its eye.

"'You know, when I was young, ages ago,' it went on, 'I wished as hard as I could to be a grand swan with a long slender neck and shimmering white feathers. And I wished that everyone would notice my beauty and want to be around me all the time.'

"Then, lowering its voice to a whisper, 'I wasn't at all proud of being a very round and very plain,' it bowed its head, 'goose.'

"'One breezy night I fell asleep and dreamt till dawn of soaring through the clouds with two majestic and graceful birds, one on each side of me, our wingtips brushing.

"'And I woke up like this. You know...well...magical.'

"'It isn't just speaking I do. I can look into someone's thoughts—yours for instance—through their eyes,' the magical goose said. 'I know you feel sorry for yourself and think you're stuck in this forsaken place forever.'

"'Now, it's true that you will live your whole life right here in this tiny hut, first taking care of that aging couple as long as they live. But then later, there will be a family of your own.'

"The Goose Girl smiled and blushed.

"'However, you will indeed go somewhere. This I can assure you.'

"'But,' the goose girl protested, 'you just said I would never leave this wretched house and yard.'

"'Did I?' said the magical goose. 'Well, perhaps I did. But I thought I said you would live here all your life. That doesn't mean you won't go away and come back many times.'

"Before the goose girl could put the question that was in her eyes into words, the magical goose answered it. 'Because...since you have been so good to my young nieces and nephews here, I am going to repay your kindness by teaching you to fly!'

"The magical goose ruffled its wing feathers several times and then folded the wings against its body again.

"'If you're in agreement, we begin tonight.'

"And so, that very night and the next and the next and the next, the magical goose gave the goose girl lessons in how to fly.

"First it taught her how to move her arms. Not beating them down against the wind, like threshing sticks on barley, but moving them smoothly and rhythmically like fish tails, until they truly glided upon the wind."

Rebekah, by now was moving her arms up and down in a gentle curving motion, watching first one soaring hand and then the other. Yeshu smiled at her and nodded in approval.

"Then the goose girl learned to arch her back ever so slightly," Yeshu went on, "so as to float on each rising breeze."

Rebekah arched her back and lifted her chin.

"Finally, she learned to stretch her head forward, slicing through the air like the lofted spear of an Ethiopian hunter. Never looking down. Never looking back."

Rebekah stretched forward, her hands reaching out.

"And finally the magical goose kissed the goose girl on the nose and released her into flight.

"And she flew. Away she flew!"

Yeshu held little Rebekah high in the air, and she moved her arms as gracefully as if she were actually flying. Everyone laughed and cheered, waving their arms too and wiping their eyes.

They had forgotten their impossible wishes to see new legs sprout like winter wheat.

Then Yeshu passed Rebekah back to her father, over the heads of the crowd. As myriad hands reached up to send her along, she rhythmically flapped her arms in imaginary flight, her face shining with joy and self-assurance, all the way to her father's embrace.

The people cheered again, clapping their hands.

Yeshu spoke to her over the crowd that stretched between the two of them. "You are splendid, Rebekah. There's no one else like you, and your soul shines," he said. "That's what each one of us aspires to."

Waving, he turned and walked back to where our group was standing.

As the crowd broke up and people started off for their homes, Yeshu asked Joanna to talk to Rebekah's father. Joanna located the father straight-away and told him to send the girl to her house in Jerusalem when Rebekah was ten years old, and an artisan would be found to teach her a craft that would help her make her way in the world.

Rebekah and her father followed after Yeshu to thank him and ask what they owed in payment.

Yeshu just laughed and responded, "Another Rebekah smile!"

Payment was instant, of course, and then Yeshu gave Rebekah a bracelet he had made of polished ebony, but not before he pulled out his knife and with several flicks of the wrist, carved two geese flying along the center of its dark band.

"You and the magical goose," he whispered in her ear.

Mama Maria reached out and took Rebekah's hands, turning them over to inspect them closely.

"They're broad and strong," she said. "These are the hands of a potter or a weaver."

Rebekah's father listened closely with a look of wide-eyed appreciation on his face. Then he shifted the girl's weight on his shoulders and gripped her knees firmly, ready for the trek home. As they left, I waved good-bye to Rebekah, and she waved back smartly, holding her hand high above her head.

~ ~ ~

That evening, we were invited to stay in the country house of a wealthy man who had been present at the day's gathering. Just after we arrived, a young fellow, short and slightly chubby, came looking for Philippos. It turned out to be his very own brother, Nathanyel, wanting to join up with us. I believe that was the first time I saw Philippos' face break into a broad smile. We all joined in, especially Yeshu. Nathanyel was now one of our band.

Before seating us for dinner, the rich man's wife put out a bowl of warm water for rinsing our hands. This was a treat for those of us who came from poor homes because water was always scarce, and warming it required precious firewood.

Then our hosts served us a meal like we hadn't seen in a long time: mutton shanks turned on a spit, along with roasted carrots and onions. All of it was soon washed down with brass goblets brimming with wine. Huge loaves of warm, spicy bread, just out of the oven, were piled high on the table. The bread smelled so sweet that no sooner had a servant girl glided with it through the kitchen doorway, than my mouth began to water.

We sat together with our hosts at a long table as broad as the backs of two oxen. It was made of split cedar logs that had been planed and oiled until they glistened. I glanced at Yeshu and saw him eyeing the table closely, as people settled into their places on the single-plank benches.

Yeshu extended his arms in front of his chest, turned the palms of his hands upward, and prepared to lead us in prayer. He waited to begin until the couple took note that he was looking toward the three servants in the kitchen. Finally, with an embarrassed laugh, the rich man called the servants in and we all scooted aside and made room for them to join us for Yeshu's blessing and the meal to follow.

After we finished eating, the family and their servants retired to their respective sleeping quarters, leaving each of us with a wooden bowl brimming with purple and green grapes. We remained at the table far into the night, eating the juicy grapes and talking with Yeshu about that afternoon's gathering, and what people were expecting from him. It was clear their hopes were rising day by day, and he was feeling increasingly distressed.

"Consider what happened today," he said. "I couldn't give little Rebekah much more than a story."

"But that was a great gift," Mama Maria broke in. "Healing is not just a matter of the body." She spoke more to the rest of us than to him.

"Healing either the body or the spirit does not send us down separate paths," she shook her head firmly. "The two go side by side, working in tandem—just like our feet!"

I nodded my agreement and recounted the story of how Yeshu had eased my pain the day I fell from the ancient chestnut tree in front of my house.

"But that was body pain," said Philippos. He turned to Yeshu. "How can you heal sickness in the soul?"

Before Yeshu could answer, Maria Magdalena weighed in.

"My friend, I suffered for years from just such a sickness. Seven inner demons had taken hold of me, and Yeshu drove all of them out! He set me free. Am I not cured?"

She looked steadily at Philippos, who could not question her assertion, since he had been there to see it happen.

At that I noticed how quiet Yeshu was. We had all been deliberating among ourselves like cawing crows. Gradually, we stopped talking and turned our faces toward him. For a long while he sat with his elbows propped on the burnished tabletop and his chin resting on his two, broad fists. His gaze was fixed on the breadbasket that still sat in the middle of the table.

Finally he spoke. "If the bread is the body, the soul is the basket. The basket holds the bread, sheltering it and giving it purpose."

He reached for the lone remaining loaf of bread and began breaking it into pieces and passing it around the table. "Just as I give you this bread of life, our God, like a good Abba, has given you the strength to heal your body and your soul...and those of others."

Yeshu kept one piece of bread for himself, which he ate slowly but not before looking around the table at each of us to be sure we had all taken a bite.

Then he went on. "Our first task is to uncover the strength inside ourselves and nurture it."

His eyes met ours, one by one.

"Our second task is to learn to help others to discover and unlock their strengths and be healed."

He slowly brushed the fingertips of one hand in a circular motion over his forehead. Then he added, "But in doing so, don't confuse who you are with what you are doing. *You* are not healing anyone. You're merely the rope and bucket others can use to draw water from God's deep well."

Yeshu fell silent, and no one else spoke. We stayed sitting together for a long while. I allowed his words to settle slowly into my center, like rain-water seeping into a limestone cave.

Finally, Yeshu stood and so did we. We hugged one another wordlessly, laid out our bedrolls on the floor of the warm room, crawled into them, and fell asleep.

A Mighty Stream

Maria Magdalena and I became fast friends on the treasured journeys our small band took together during those three years of Yeshu's teaching and healing. Few people are aware that much later, an unnamed person wrote down a gospel about Maria's time with Yeshu. It's true, and everyone needs to know what's in it. It's her own account of a story I was fortunate enough to experience myself.

I'm sure she and I didn't see everything the same way. After all, when we started out, Maria was a lot older than I—much closer to Yeshu's thirty years than to my fourteen. Yet unlike some of the other members of our band, she always treated me as an equal. When I told her how much I appreciated that, she beamed.

Maria dealt with everyone she met warmly, just like Yeshu. And like him, she made me feel special. I had always assumed she simply had that gift, so I was surprised to learn it wasn't something she was born with.

"I wasn't always open with people," she explained one day as we sat talking. "Yeshu taught me how, by word and example."

She looked at a place on the horizon before adding, softly at first, then with her voice rising, "I had been treated so badly by so many, especially my family, it made me wildly angry with nearly everyone.

"But every time I told Yeshu about this as we walked to and from the cedars of Lebanon, he'd just smile back with all his warmth. He listened very carefully but his response was not what I wanted. Nodding ever so slightly, he would insist: 'Turn your heart toward these people, just as you might wish them to turn their hearts toward you.'"

She shook her head. "For a long time that really got under my skin because I wanted him to understand how badly *I'd* been wounded, and here he was telling me to reach out to my tormentors. People who had hurt me."

Drawing her hands up to her cheeks, she told me, "Finally I got the point. One day he asked me a question I never wanted to hear. 'Where,' he said, 'do you think the demons that possessed you came from?'

"Certain that he was blaming me, I snapped back, 'How should I know?'

"I started to cry because I couldn't stand the thought of how he must be seeing me.

"At the sight of my tears, he touched me softly on the cheek and said, 'Maria, I'm sorry. I wasn't suggesting the demons came from you. I should have worded this differently. What I meant to ask you was, what were they feeding on?'

"I didn't answer him; I don't believe he wanted me to respond right away. But his question kept tugging at me like a small child who wants what I have in my hand.

"That's when I began watching him closely: how he was with you and the others, with strangers, even with those people who seemed to cultivate enmity with him. It became clear that I couldn't feel better, be better, until I'd pulled the thorn out that had lodged inside, festering for longer than I could remember, blinding me to all the love hidden by anger.

"Yeshu got me to face the fact that anger drives the thorn in deeper, breeding even more anger. And love pries the thorn out, releasing more love. He told me not to fret about it. Bad wounds take time to heal. But they can be cured if properly cleaned and tended to day after day."

She looked down at her palms that lay side by side in her lap.

"He encouraged me to soothe and smooth the hurt with soft touches, rather than hardening it with fists. I began, step by step, letting go of blame."

"And it worked!" she said, looking back up. "Yeshu showed me a new way to see the world. And living with Martha in Bethany, on the slopes of the Mount of Olives, brought the world up close.

"There are so many different kinds of people, Daavi. Finally I understood that each one is a blade of grass in God's field, a blade like all others and unlike all others. God's light shines down on all of us, whether a newborn like Yeshu's youngest nephew or someone seasoned like your Great Uncle Moishe.

"It shines on the wealthy merchant and the hungry beggar who just happen to stroll side by side in the market, yet are worlds apart. God's light shines on Greek, Ethiopian, and Samaritan. It shines on the Roman soldier and the Jewish seamstress alike. And if God watches over *all* people, who are we to look down on anyone?"

When she shared insights like that, it occurred to me that Maria Magdalena was someone who could easily have made most of us appear foolish and slow-witted, but she never did so. Some members of our band, like Shimón Petros, resented her anyway, believing that women should listen a lot and say little.

It seems to me that what put some people off was exactly what I found most admirable about Maria: her courage to learn by keenly examining her own way of being. Plus her always staying open to what this new life brought her, rather than just crossing her arms and accepting her lot.

"Everyone is my teacher," she would tell me. "I have learned something from each person I've gotten to know."

And it's true; I saw it with my own eyes. Maria found time for anyone who crossed her path. Sometimes it was an old widow with an aching back; other times, a sniffling child. Even the rabbis were disarmed. They opened up to her steady gaze like flowers in sunlight.

Maria knew how to listen. When she listened, you felt as if nothing more important existed in the world than what you were saying. One day, our group had to wait several hours to cross a river engorged by a flash flood from sudden rains. Maria and I sat together under a weeping willow, and I told her the story of the frog in the well; following it with what happened when the handful of folks suffering from leprosy paraded into Nazareth crying out, "Unclean! Unclean!"

As I spun out my tales that day, it felt as though she were right there in the story, first as a neighbor in the crowd feeling scared, then standing in line, abject and thirsty with the ragged band of outcasts. For a moment I even wondered if she had one brown eye and one blue.

Gazing into those eyes I forgot I was telling a tale and began reliving it. The spell was broken not when I stopped speaking, but a moment later when she clapped her hands once and wiped her eyes with her sleeves.

"Those are true stories, she said, "so true it's going to take two crescent moons, two full rounds of Rosh Hodesh, for me to pull out all the lessons."

And suddenly I felt the same way. Stories that I knew like the back of my hand, ones that had helped define me, got wider and wider as I told them to another person. Those stories broadened out as I realized that what happened that day at the well could also be told from the point of view of the other people who were there to experience it, not the least of whom was Yeshu.

These tales weren't just mine, you see, they belonged to everyone: those present and those hearing them later. They lived outside me as well as within. This all became clear as I watched my stories unfold in the eyes of one person, under a tree, immersing herself in them for the very first time.

I felt proud and humbled all at once. But above all I was grateful. Just imagine, a young person like me offering insight to a person whom Yeshu treated like one of his principal followers. And then discovering that what I had to give was not only welcomed by her but returned twofold.

This back and forth took other paths, as well. One day a few months later, Yeshu was telling tales to a group of children and elders in a village not unlike Nazareth, though half a country away. Maria Magdalena sat with me, listening until he was done.

Leaning slightly, she turned and whispered near my ear, "Of all the teachers in my life, he's the best. He shows me the way."

Yeshu, who had just received a tiny bouquet of wildflowers from the crowd of laughing children, somehow overheard her and joked, "So I'm just another stuffy old teacher?"

She responded without cracking a smile, "Well, sometimes you do go on too long, but no, you're never stuffy about it."

Yeshu laughed, raising the flowers to his nose.

Then, relenting, Maria smiled and leaned forward so we knew she was serious. "Yeshu, you are a master teacher—whether it's with preaching, or storytelling, or action."

She was looking straight into his face. "Of the many teachers in my life, you are in first place." She punctuated the statement by nodding.

"In second place is no one." Another nod of the head.

"And in third place are all the rest." The final nod ended the discussion.

Yeshu laughed out loud and pretended he was going to throw the flowers at her.

~ ~ ~

I believe that Maria was closest to Yeshu because he saw her in a way that no one else did. He saw her only for who she was, on the inside. In contrast, her beauty blinded others, with craving or envy. This made it hard for them to see her other qualities. It had been that way since she was a girl.

And it wasn't just the deep jet eyes or the long ebony hair spilling down her shoulders that made her so striking. Her voice was like the low notes of a flute; a blind man hearing it was as captivated by the tone as the sighted were by the easy grace of her walk.

When we entered a village, people would stop and stare. You could see how the men wanted to reach out and touch her, and how their women experienced that as a slap. Had she not been an outsider and unmarried, the reaction might have been different. Who knows?

As it was, comments were made, sometimes within our hearing and not always nice. When she glided by, unreachable as a cloud, you could watch some peoples' faces hardening.

What surprised me was her total lack of either aloofness or conceit in such situations. Or irritation. On the contrary, she was warm and kind with friends and strangers alike. She had time for everyone and always stopped to give comfort.

But most important to me, Maria was fearless and devoted to Yeshu. Just as he was to her. It wasn't that he held her above the rest of us. Among us there were no captains, no priests; we all ministered to others and to one another and we made decisions together. Yet Maria stood out in our company like a bonfire in the night. She became Yeshu's best friend after Yohanan's death. And to his dismay, she suffered the envy of others because of it.

More than once he told me, "Maria's soul and mine flow from the same source. The valley of life brought us together like converging currents in a wide river."

I would be forever grateful for that mighty stream.

The Sword and the Cheek

Planting season came and went and soon it was time for another harvest. Sukkah huts of branches and leaves were springing up all over, people ducking in and out of them carrying things and making small improvements. We were all preparing again for Sukkot, the Feast of Shelters, and I for one found it hard to believe how long it seemed since our band's very first Sukkot together, in Jerusalem.

We were still traveling, day after day, village after village. One afternoon our group was resting by the roadside, not far from a fortified Roman garrison. Lying back in the grasses of the cool meadow, we passed the time away by watching hundreds of swallows swoop and dart overhead. As they fished the air for bugs and mosquitoes, we tried to guess what they might be writing invisibly on the sky.

Meanwhile, stray soldiers occasionally walked along the road. When it was a pack of them you could hear them coming, laughing and rowdy. I suppose we must have been the object of some of their jokes because you could feel the soldiers' stares as they looked us up and down. All afternoon they traveled by like storm clouds cutting off the sun.

Maria Magdalena was clearly a focus of their attention. Pointing at where she sat against a rock, clearing the knots from her hair with long sinuous strokes of her comb that made her bare arms flash in the sunlight, the legionnaires could not tear their eyes away.

It made me feel uncomfortable and after a while, I got up and walked across the road to a tree stump that I could lean against as I sat working. Pulling out my leather tool pouch from under my cloak, I fished around for my knife and awl and began to repair Thunder John's sandals. One of the cross-straps had pulled loose during the day's trek. For the last few hours it had been flapping back and forth like a cow's tail futilely swatting at flies. He hadn't even noticed until I pointed it out to him.

The air was hot where I sat. I was tired, and as I said before, the soldiers' banter was getting on my nerves. Why should they be so cocky and smug? Perhaps because they had been fed so well after putting down a disturbance the day before—by torching a village in the valley we had just passed through.

A twig snapped at the very moment that I was muttering, "Some day...." And a shadow fell over me. I glanced up to see a figure towering above me, and it made me jump. It was a Roman soldier.

"Look at my sandal," the man barked. "It's much worse off than that one you're working on. Fix mine first."

I glared up at him. The sun behind his head made me squint. I could see the thicker, more elaborate sandal thrust out at me, but pretended I couldn't.

"Are you deaf or just stupid," he snapped. "Take it and get to work, or you'll feel the smack of my good sandal on your backside."

I said nothing. For an instant, I saw not my own hands in my lap, but my father's—the wrists with deep red welts encircling them from being bound tightly together. Staring down at Thunder John's sandal, I shook my head *no* ever so slightly.

"Why you dumb pup," he growled, leaning so close his hot breath touched my face. "Let's see if you have some clever excuse to keep me from thrashing you."

Setting my jaw tight, I studied him carefully for as long as I dared. For the first time I could see his face. His nose, broken in some past battle, bore a resemblance to Mount Tabor rising above the rolling hills. I sat still, defiant as one of those hills.

Suddenly, he placed a foot under John's sandal in my lap, and with a flip of his ankle, kicked it out of my sight."Speak up, you insolent snot!"

At that point, I lost control of my tongue. "Maybe with a flapping sandal, you will march one mile less, and one Jew less will be dragged from his bed and put to death on two crossed trees!"

With a quick motion the soldier drew his sword. You could hear the awful sound it made leaving its scabbard. I felt a faint breeze brush my cheek.

A torrent of words exploded from the soldier's flushed face like lava from a volcano. "Jewish donkey! I'll teach you a lesson, you stubborn little mongrel!"

The sword rose. I shrunk into the ground, hoping to somehow avoid the blow. Out of nowhere, Yeshu stepped between us.

He spoke to the soldier, pouring forth soothing words to put out the fire. "We want no violence. Let him go in peace; he's young like you were once. We know none of this is your fault. It wasn't your idea to crucify anyone."

The soldier would not look Yeshu in the eye. "You'll all see where Roman-hating gets you!" he sputtered as he paced to one side and then the other, trying to slide around the tall man in his way.

I sprang to my feet, prepared to flee.

"I, for one, hate no Roman," Yeshu replied. "I dislike the harm I've seen inflicted and the injustices I've heard about elsewhere. But those are the acts of an empire you are not responsible for. I'm sure you would rather be home with your family."

For just an instant, the soldier paused, but he quickly resumed his yelling while trying to shoulder by Yeshu to hack at me with his sword.

From a distance it must have looked comical. Yeshu was even taller than the Roman, and nimbler. Plus we all knew that no one had stronger hands than the carpenter. He had strength enough to seize the soldier's upraised arm, immobilize him, and snatch the sword away like it was a toy.

But Yeshu continued to reason quietly. He never stopped speaking, steady and persistent as a brook working at stone. By this time, a crowd was forming around us. Lots of Jews were gathered on one side, a handful of Roman legionnaires on the other.

The Romans left plenty of space between themselves and us. None of them wanted to be hit by a flying rock or a wildly swinging sword yielded by a comrade. But there they stood, menacing with their mere presence.

Steadily, the soldier's face was getting redder, his voice reedier. He probably dreaded backing down, now that his comrades were able to witness just how he would deal with this challenge to his authority by a plucky Jewish youth and his tall, unruffled protector.

The soldier kept flexing his muscles, raising and lowering his shoulders, and rocking back on his heels and then up again on his toes. He seemed furious yet also defensive, like a wild animal suddenly caged.

I could tell Yeshu's words were beginning to soak in, because the soldier would turn to leave, then spin around abruptly, and raise his sword again to demand an apology from me. Yeshu's voice was working like the string pulling a spinning top.

Meanwhile, my voice was frozen. I could not have apologized had I wanted to. But it didn't matter because Yeshu was shielding me, his left hand reaching back to grasp my arm above the elbow to keep me from showing myself.

The soldier was caught between what he knew a good legionnaire should do in the face of insolence and insult, and how his heart responded to this ragged preacher with the calm voice, offering a way out.

Finally, as the soldier vacillated yet again, Yeshu began withdrawing, guiding me backward with his hand. Peeking around his side, I saw the Roman advancing.

Just when I was sure the gyrating sword had taken on a life of its own and would swing the man who wielded it, Maria Magdalena pushed through the wide-eyed crowd and strode toward us. Reaching me first, she grabbed my collar, spun me around, and propelled me toward the throng of Jewish onlookers.

I ran, peering back over my shoulder and stumbling. But I caught a glimpse of the soldier's face that has stayed with me forever.

His blank look seemed to say, "And now a woman! What next?"

That wasn't the only surprise. Maria gripped Yeshu's sleeve at the shoulder, and digging her feet in, gave him such a yank that he nearly fell onto his back. In an instant, she was between him and the soldier. She looked the man squarely in the eye while motioning behind her back for Yeshu to leave. Trusting her, he turned toward the crowd and gestured for everyone to begin moving away.

Maria laid one hand gently on the center of the Roman soldier's chest, letting its warmth penetrate as she spoke softly. He seemed surprised at being touched and addressed this way, as though an arrow had pierced him. Gradually his body relaxed and his sword lowered.

Later, she told me she had simply said several times in different ways, and as gently as she could, "Please. We want no trouble. A clash will only make things worse—for you and for us. Your friends might join in, ours too. People each of us cares about could be badly hurt. And for what? You saw the sandal maker. He's a kid, no match for a seasoned warrior.

"And besides, the lad has nothing against you personally. He has a father and you probably have children, or you will one day. Think it through. What is there to gain from hurting him? And if you do, for a moment's satisfaction, won't his eyes follow you forever, gazing out whenever you look into your own child's eyes?"

Speechless, the soldier simply stared back at her, immobilized.

She smiled up at him. "*Your* eyes tell me now you are a good man and you agree with what I'm saying. I'm going to walk away now; please don't follow me."

Finally the soldier groaned, shaking his head dramatically as though he had shooed away pesky children trying to filch pomegranates from an army commander's expropriated orchard. We all saw the relief on his face. Glancing around at his companions, he could see that no one found Maria to be a threat to him. She was smaller, unarmed, a woman. He could honor her plea and keep his own honor.

Just that quickly, the duel tirade was over.

Maria approached those of us who remained, her eyes scanning the faces of strangers and friends. She walked resolutely, holding the palm of one hand outward at chest level for us to see. Not a soul flung a barbed word, much less a stone, toward the back of the departing Roman.

~ ~ ~

That evening, Maria had stern words for me.

"You could have gotten yourself badly hurt, and Yeshu as well!"

She paused to allow the enormity of that to penetrate.

"Don't forget. Our enemy is not the other person. A good peacemaker struggles against unjust *actions*. And against the laws, the beliefs, the practices, that produce those wrong actions.

I nodded, mentally kicking myself for forgetting, in my moments of ire, all the lessons I assumed I had learned from Yeshu. They seemed to have blown away in the wind like goose down, when tested by an unexpected gust.

Maria was not done with me.

"And Daavi, we can't attack every symbol that offends us or every misdeed we encounter on our path. We must choose carefully where to direct our efforts, and when. And we must take time to prepare not only our minds but our spirits, for the struggle we have chosen.

"That man's sandal shoved into your face was not worth *your* life *or* his. Certainly not Yeshu's, for heaven's sake."

That night I crawled like a worm into my bedroll feeling pretty lousy about myself. I fell asleep with the image in my mind of Thunder James and Thunder John standing shoulder to shoulder in front of the crowd that afternoon, prepared to defend me if necessary, when Maria sent me hustling back to disappear into the crowd.

The next morning, I sought out Yeshu to ask his forgiveness for putting him in danger. He sat cross-legged, his elbows resting on his knees, his fingers interlocked just below his chin.

Smiling softly, he said, "Don't fret about it, my friend. Learn from it."

He looked up at me, as if holding onto a thought.

Then he said, "Besides, my time has not yet come."

I felt a shiver hearing that, but before I could ask what he meant, the Thunder Brothers came storming up, pushing and jostling one another in playful competition, each trying to be the first to speak to Yeshu. And nearly falling on top of me.

"Yeshu!" they bellowed, in unison.

"We've been *invited* to Emmaus," spouted John.

"They want you to *teach*," added James.

"The crowd could be *huge,*" exclaimed John.

Yeshu answered immediately, "Then let's go. But..." he said stopping short.

The Thunder Brothers froze, tipping forward onto their toes in their eagerness to learn exactly what the holdup could be. Yeshu just stared at them until they were about to topple into our laps.

"You two will stay behind until you learn to stop your ridiculous competing." He glared at them.

The two brothers threw astonished looks at one another and then back at Yeshu, who was biting his lip to bury his laughter. Realizing they'd been tricked by the quick-witted teacher, the brothers tried to cover their chagrin by hugging one another and dishing out syrupy politeness as they ambled away.

"Can I get you a nice, sweet cup of milk, my dear brother?" asked Thunder John, bowing slightly and pressing his large hands together.

"Oh, you are so kind, but no thank you," said Thunder James. "And yet, John, my most precious brother, please take my cloak. You appear to be a bit chilly this morning."

James tried to force it onto John's broad back as they continued down the path.

"That's quite all right, James, my sweet," countered John. "You need it more than I, you being the *thinner* one."

"Oh, John, how gallant you are," shot back James. "Now I know why Mother preferred you over the rest of us, you with your large heart and handsome face—both of them the same size as the place you sit on."

Yeshu rolled his eyes and motioned to me.

"Come on, let's take a walk."

We strolled along a winding brook for a while, discussing what had happened the day before, carefully going over how I had felt at each turn of events and weighing all that against what might have happened had things gone really wrong.

Then we ceased talking and my thoughts swung to how menacing the legionnaires seemed to ordinary people like us who have no shields or armaments. I pictured falcons circling above spring rabbits in an open meadow. I presumed Yeshu was thinking along the same lines.

I was wrong.

Without warning, Yeshu turned to me and said, "Daavi, there is a great difference between resisting evil," he paused, "and impulsively losing your temper with someone you resent."

He gave me ample reflection time. Suddenly my father's face flashed in my mind. But why? Then I saw again the red welts around his wrists and recalled the prisons full of Jews just like him. It struck me that I had learned half a lesson and muddled up the other half, confusing justice with vengeance.

I realized that my boyhood vow to shield my father, and others like him, was completely beyond my means. Facing up to that made me feel small, and then angry. I watched as that anger hardened into a fist-sized stone and began throbbing, beating like a drum inside my chest and causing me to walk faster.

Soon a white heat flamed in my midriff and spread upward to my face, making me feel large—so big I was no longer scared; so unafraid because I was no longer there. Yet I saw in an instant that the anger wasn't just in me, I *was* the anger, and the furnace fueling it was my own heart. The fire was on the verge of blazing out of control.

I peered up at Yeshu and found him still watching and waiting as he kept pace beside me. When I slowed down, he spoke again.

"Anger is like a hot blast of air. It can easily turn a spark into a whirlwind of retribution that can burn down a house and everyone in it."

He stopped and put his hand on my shoulder, letting the words sink in. "As we move on later today, think about how you can keep that from happening to you and to those for whom you are responsible. How you can break the hammer-forged chain of violence and hatred before it can entangle you. Maybe strangle you."

He took up my hands, cradling them in his, and looked straight into my eyes.

"Daavi, here is what I believe: Love your enemies. Be good to those who hate you. Bless those who curse you. And pray for those who do you wrong."

Speechless, I gazed into Yeshu's face. It was radiant.

"Do not take revenge on those who wrong you," he continued. "If someone slaps you on the cheek, well then, don't be afraid to turn the other cheek toward them. If your neighbors sue you over a tunic, remember the story of the old man who befriended the thief and made him his son. Give those folks your cloak and belt as well."

His eyes widened and he smiled slightly.

"And if an occupation soldier demands that you carry his pack a mile down the road, carry it two. If he asks you to repair a sandal, offer to repair them both. Not because you are his or anyone else's servant. But because you are each the other's neighbor."

Yeshu raised my hands to the level of my heart as he spoke the last word.

"By doing these things, taking that extra step, you may open up that person to see himself more clearly, and to weigh what it is he is about to do or has already done. This is one way hearts are changed."

He dropped my hands back to my sides.

"And besides," he asked, "What's so great about only loving the people who love you? Or only being good to those who reward you? That's easy!" He made a quick twist of the wrist and snapped his finger with his thumb.

"Daavi, I feel I must say it again: Love your neighbors, your enemies, and those who are different from you. Be merciful, as God is. Treat everyone just as you want to be treated."

"In the end you'll be rewarded," he said, "in ways you cannot yet imagine. But even when it seems you aren't rewarded, it makes no difference; you will have done the right thing. You will respect yourself for that, and your life will be enlarged and deepened.

"Mull over all of this for a while, friend Daavi, and we'll talk some more."

I nodded yes, uncertainly. His words were well meant, I knew, but they felt like a yoke.

Then much to my surprise, Yeshu swung his right arm straight at my head, as if he were going to slap me sharply on the cheek, stopping his hand right before contact.

"Just testing," he said, with a twinkle in his eye.

I turned and pointed to my other cheek.

"You forgot this one," I retorted.

We both laughed heartily, and all the huffing puffed our cheeks out like two frogs.

The Soldier Among Us

That night we were sitting around the campfire in a field outside a village just a short distance up the valley. We were listening contentedly to Mama Ana telling stories. She had joined up with us that evening and would be accompanying us for a few weeks.

When she finished her tale about the feisty child who forgot who his parents were, Yeshu said, "Just listen to her! Some call me a preacher, but I'm really a storyteller. And Mama Ana taught me most of what I know."

She gave him a wry smile, saying nothing. She just sat as she always did when telling her stories: leaning forward with her hands on her knees, her feet wide apart as they peeked out from beneath her long flowing skirts. When she started up again, I looked around the circle and for a while felt as if I were in the background, overhearing her speak to the others one at a time.

Thunder James and Thunder John sat like two cedars of Lebanon rooted in the ground, heads barely swaying in the clouds. Even Judah was paying close attention, not attempting once to change the subject.

Martha and Joanna, Yeshu's old friends, were listening particularly intently. Every time Mama Ana said something they liked, they nodded their heads and intoned, "Mmm-hmm. Mmm-hmm."

When Mama Ana's story took an unsettling turn, their hands flew to their mouths, as each sharply sucked in her breath. Funny lines got them giggling, which soon had the rest of us tittering, too.

At one point, Martha leaned over and whispered in my ear, "Have you ever seen two old ninnies giggle like us?"

Naively, I shot back—way too loud—"You and Joanna aren't such old ninnies!" That sent them nearly toppling off their logs, and everyone else joined in their laughter.

Feigning offense, Mama Ana said, "Is it okay if I break in here? Are the crackpots ready for me to go on?"

Like little children, the three of us sat on our hands in the middle of an enveloping hush. Martha faked a glare at me, her eyes twinkling in the firelight.

Then suddenly from out of the quiet we heard a rustling noise just beyond the fire ring. Everyone stiffened, and several faces clenched in fear. I noticed, because as the youngest in the group, I always checked my companion's faces to see what people might be feeling when something new was going on.

I also had the sharpest eyes in the group. "Keen as a desert owl's," Yohanan had once said. And just like that owl hunting through his darkness, I saw someone standing back in the shadows behind Mama Maria and Thunder John, head cocked like he was listening in.

Without thinking, I cried out, "I can see you! Come out of the dark. We know you're there."

Thunder John and Thunder James rose to their feet and stepped in front of Yeshu. Mama Ana stood also and slowly raised her arms just above her waist, palms turned outward.

Mama Maria made her way around the fire ring saying gently, "You are welcome here. Introduce yourself."

Out of the corner of my eye, I saw Judah reach down for a stone the size of his foot. Maria Magdalena had turned aside and was tucking her hair under her shawl, and quickly slipping into Thunder John's fallen cloak. Later she told me she had used that trick many times, ever since she had been attacked in the night as a young girl.

But the dark figure was not going anywhere, neither toward us nor away.

Yeshu pushed between Thunder John and Thunder James, and stood beside his mother.

"Come closer, whoever you are," he said to the figure. "We have room for many more."

"I'm alone," the figure said in a hush.

"I know you're alone," Yeshu answered. "But here you are among friends."

"You will not greet *me* as a friend!" said the figure.

"Try us," answered Yeshu. "We have no enemies here. Only friends and family."

At first there was no movement. I could hear people near me breathing. I even thought I heard my own heartbeat speeding up.

The figure took one step forward, and a moment later another; then several more, slowly placing him within the light of the campfire. He was dressed in a shepherd's hooded cloak, but no Jewish shepherd I ever knew was that tall, and with shoulders the breadth of two men's!

"Come," Yeshu stretched out his arms. "Please."

Mama Maria reached for the cloaked hand. The man let himself be pulled forward into our circle, all the while keeping his chin on his chest so his face stayed hidden. But not from me. I was still sitting, and I looked directly up into that face. Our eyes met, and in the flickering firelight I caught a glimpse of his nose.

A gush of air escaped my lips and I shouted out, "Holy Moses! It's the Roman soldier who nearly killed me yesterday!"

The Mount Tabor nose was a dead giveaway.

Suddenly to my right there was a lurching movement. It was Judah, stone held high in his left hand, aimed toward the soldier's head.

"Spy!" he screamed. "Assassin!"

With a dancer's grace, Yeshu spun and leapt between Judah and the soldier. Just as the rock was about to come crashing down, Yeshu wrapped his arms around Judah in a great bear hug, and lifted him off the ground. The rock glanced off the side of Yeshu's head, and soon blood gushed down his cheek. Frantically, Judah dropped the rock to the ground and began wiping the blood from Yeshu's face with his freed hand.

"I'm sorry, Yeshu! I'm so sorry," he said, his dark, bushy eyebrows furrowing toward the bridge of his nose.

"I wanted to protect you. That's all..."

"I know that was your intention," Yeshu answered. "But weren't you there with us yesterday? Didn't you realize that you were about to do exactly what I would not want done? When are you going to stand beside me, rather than surging out front to do what I stand against?"

Judah hung his head. "I've hurt you." His lip was trembling.

Yeshu held him by the arm and said, "Don't despair, Judah. I forgive you, my friend. This is a scratch."

Yeshu looked deep into Judah's eyes. "One day the wound will be greater. And I forgive you for that, too,"

Judah stared back, utterly bewildered.

No one spoke until finally Mama Maria broke the silence, asking us to please sit down again, all the while holding tight to the soldier's hand. Her forearm was trembling, but I noticed her face was serene.

It was the soldier's arm that was doing the shaking.

Yeshu turned from Judah, who was wiping his blood-covered hand on the side of his cloak. He seemed like a lost boy.

Twisting first this way, then that, Judah finally he sunk down on a log and sat mutely.

Yeshu approached the soldier and reached out to grip both shoulders.

"Welcome," he told him. "I know why you've come."

The soldier looked even more shocked than when Maria Magdalena had appeared on the field of battle the day before. Perhaps even *he* didn't know why he had come. But I wasn't surprised, even though I had no idea why he was there, either. Yeshu often seemed to know each of us better than we knew ourselves.

Now Mama Ana spoke up. Leaning toward the soldier she said, "Friend, sit down. Tell us your story."

A smile crossed her face like moonlight softening a weathered cliff, and the soldier seemed to melt. He sat down slowly, cleared his throat once, twice, then yet again, and at last began to speak.

"My name is Cornelius. I was born in a hilltop village five days walk to the north of Rome. You see! I'm not even a Roman, even though you people hate me for being one."

"Your sword and spear are Roman," muttered Judah under his breath.

Yeshu shot a hard look at him and he went still.

"We hate no one here," said Yeshu.

The soldier took a breath and resumed. "My family is poor. My father and uncles once had a few sheep, though, and I was a shepherd boy."

Hearing that, I sat up straight.

"One day many years ago, a detachment from a legion set up camp near my village. Men came to our house and took half our sheep, giving my father nothing in payment. He protested that they were taking food from his children's mouths and clothes off our backs.

"When he heard this, the officer smirked and said, 'For your insolence, I'm taking your eldest son as well, the big one over there. That way you'll have one less mouth to feed.'

"Pointing at me, he said, 'Stand up straight, you're now a recruit in the Roman Army.'

"My mother began to weep. She pleaded with the officer, but to no avail.

"As for me, the first chance I got, I ran, leaping the stone fence that surrounded our corral and fleeing into the hills. The foot soldiers—seven of them—soon caught me, tied me up like a pig to go to slaughter. And here I am."

"May I see your sword?" asked Yeshu.

We all flinched, hearing that. Yes, a Roman soldier was in our campsite, but it hadn't really registered, once we'd taken him in, that he was likely to be armed.

Cornelius pulled off his shepherd's cloak and revealed himself in full military dress, complete with sword and scabbard. He unbuckled the sword from his belt and handed it to Yeshu.

"Well done!" roared Judah, shaking his dark curls vigorously. "You've tricked him out of his weapon. Now he's ours."

Yeshu just shook his head at Judah and looked disappointed. Then he unsheathed the sword, and turning it this way and that in his hands to inspect it, he raised his eyes to meet those of the Roman soldier.

"This is a very fine sword, Cornelius," he said. "It would be perfect for clearing weeds out of the garden and even working the soil before planting flowers and herbs." Grasping the sword by the handle, Yeshu pulled the point along the ground as if he were plowing a furrow for seeds.

"In our holy scrolls, Brother Cornelius, the prophet Isaiah received a vision."

> They shall hammer their swords into plowshares
> and their spears into pruning knives.
> Nation shall not lift sword against nation
> and never again will they learn war.

Then turning the sword around and holding the pointed end between thumb and forefinger, with the blade balanced flat on the back of his left forearm, Yeshu returned the weapon to Cornelius.

"That's crazy!" yelled Judah. "Now he'll kill you for sure."

Yeshu looked directly into the eyes of Cornelius, but spoke to Judah.

"This man has not come here to hurt us. He has come here because *he* is hurt. We will cure his wounds. Hatred, suspicion, fear; all of them."

"And what about his crimes?" asked Judah.

Turning to the soldier, he spit in the dirt. "So, how many Jews have you killed?"

Cornelius stared at the moist spot on the ground and shook his head. "I don't know."

Our silence was total.

Except for Yeshu, that is, who said, "We forgive you. I know your wish is to never kill again. That's why you're here."

"But what about the people he has already slain?" demanded Judah.

We all held our breath, waiting for Yeshu's reply.

"He will ask God for forgiveness, and he will receive it," Yeshu answered forcefully. "God is generous and compassionate, and redemption happens in God's time, which we must make our own."

He looked around at us. "Haven't I told you that God is in all of us? So, God is here, too," he said, patting the soldier's chest, "in Cornelius. The God in him can be cultivated like a garden, and the thorny rose bush will burst into bloom."

Yeshu turned back to Cornelius and then glanced at the sword and said, "That's why you came to visit us, yes?"

Cornelius' jaw dropped like a rock, and he nodded almost imperceptibly, as if he were acknowledging for the first time something he'd known only when dreaming.

Yeshu held out the scabbard to the quieted soldier, saying "Sheath your sword, Brother Cornelius."

Then he turned to Mama Maria. "Do we have any bread left over?"

She headed for the food pack. When she came back with a loaf, Yeshu said, "Break it in half, please. Give the larger half to our new friend, Cornelius, and divide the rest into pieces—one for each of us. We're going to eat with him."

As she did this, Yeshu smiled at Judah.

"And my brother Judah will receive his piece from Cornelius and take the first bite."

Judah looked at Yeshu, then at the soldier, and back again.

He shrugged, but extended his hand. Now his eyebrows were arched upward, like a man raising his arms in surrender.

God Is Love

Late the next morning, on the way to Emmaus, we stopped to quench our thirst at a village well. After drinking our fill and washing the dust from our eyes and faces, we sat in the shade of an old mulberry tree, surrounded by local children.

"Tell us a story! Tell us a story!" they implored.

People had started calling us the wandering storytellers. And the name fit. All of us taught through stories; even I knew how.

One of the kids present that day was extra keen. He had heard of Yeshu and figured him to be the master storyteller, with the rest of us merely his apprentices. So the boy insisted that Yeshu be the teller, and the other kids chimed in until Yeshu laughingly agreed. The boy pressed on, insisting that Yeshu tell a story he had never told before. This young fellow reminded me a bit of myself when I was small.

Yeshu looked at him hard, as if sizing him up, then smiled and winked.

"All right," he said, "but first I want all of you here to consider a line from the Nevi'im. Those scrolls may have been written by people our grandfathers' grandfathers were too young to know, but they have a lot to say about our lives right now. Today."

The boy appeared a bit doubtful, as if maybe Yeshu were putting him off. But he had a curious look on his face, as well, waiting to see what the storytelling carpenter might come up with.

"In the Debhārîm, the Book of Deuteronomy," Yeshu began, "we are told how to love God."

> You must love your God
>
> with all your heart,

> and all your soul;
> all your strength,
> and all your mind.

"Come to think of it, that's the way I loved my Abba Yosef and my Mama Maria when I was your age," Yeshu said, his eyes moving from child to child.

"Still do," he affirmed with a nod.

I caught myself looking away and quickly returned my eyes to Yeshu. He went on, "In the *Vayikra*, the Book of Leviticus, we are given additional instruction."

> You must love your neighbor
> as yourself.

"On these two commandments hang all the laws and proclamations of the prophets. You'll find all this in the Torah and the Nevi'im."

Yeshu paused to let his words sink in, like raindrops on parched earth. Suddenly, he slapped the back of one open hand into the palm of the other.

"So, who can tell me who their neighbor is?"

The sharp kid piped up, "My pal Yakob, who lives next door to me!"

"Pretty good answer," said Yeshu. "What about folks who live in one of the nearby villages, or in a land that is next door to ours? Are they still neighbors...or are they foreigners?"

No one made a peep. Even the quizzical boy seemed stumped.

Finally he ventured, barely above a whisper, "Both?"

"There are no flies walking on you, my friend," Yeshu said, chuckling, and the boy grinned, looking around at his companions.

"Okay, last question," said Yeshu. "Then the story; I promise."

His eyes met those of each child. "Do you recall what the scrolls say about how we deal with strangers?"

This one was tougher because almost no kids could read, and the rabbi and older men didn't cover everything in their services. You could feel the entire group, including the sharp young kid, waiting to see if Yeshu might rephrase the question in a way that would hint at the answer.

Similar to sniffing the air the way one does before a squall on Lake Galilee, Yeshu could tell what his audience wanted. He smiled and relented.

"The Book of Vayikra also states the following," he said.

> If strangers live with you in your land,
> do not mistreat them.
> Count them as your own people
> and love them as yourselves.

"Do you find this easy to do, or hard?" Yeshu asked.

No one spoke. But their somber faces gave them away.

"Well, just listen to my story. It's about how a stranger in *our* land dealt with one of *us*. This was not just any stranger; it was a man from the neighboring land of Samaria.

"Now, as many Samaritans do, this man actually lived among us, which is not as easy as you may think. Just imagine what it would feel like to be a Jew living in the land of Samaria. Troubles between Jews and Samaritans are very old. Surely, each of us could tell a story about how a family member, or someone in our village or a neighboring one, looks down on Samaritans in Galilee and Judea.

"Well, the Samaritan I'm talking about knew what it felt like to be treated poorly by others, including the very youngest of us."

Yeshu checked the children's faces to see if everyone was following along. Noticing two older boys smirking, he gazed at them steadily, not saying a word, until their faces were wiped clean. Only then did he begin his story.

"It was a very fine day, not so long ago. The sun stood high in a clear blue sky. A man who had been on a pilgrimage to the Temple was journeying home along a deserted road that wound down from the heights of Jerusalem to the lowlands around Jericho.

"Turning a bend in the road, the man was suddenly attacked by thieves. They did a real job on him, stripping and beating him, and leaving him lying in the dust by the roadside, half dead.

"Not long after, a priest came around the bend, striding purposefully toward Jericho. Seeing a bleeding man huddled on the ground in what seemed to be rags, the priest lowered his gaze to his feet and crossed to the far side of the road, muttering to himself, 'No use borrowing trouble.'

"He was recalling the 'purity laws' and he was determined to adhere to them in this situation, as he saw it.

"To himself he thought, don't go soiling yourself by unnecessary contact with the sick or injured. He shook his head, still deliberating. This evening you must unroll the scrolls by hand and read from the Book of Psalms.

"Without looking back, the priest mumbled, 'God be with you,' and hurried on.

"Next to come trudging along," Yeshu continued, "was a singer from the Temple choir returning from the lowlands. He actually paused for a moment, considering his present dilemma. Finally he went close and peered at the man. A convenient thought occurred to him: I can't be late getting back to Jerusalem, there's so much to do before evening prayers.

"Pulling a brass coin from his purse and dropping it by the man's head, he said, 'Have heart,' and walked on, humming to himself.

"Next along the road was a merchant leading a camel piled high with a load of hemp. He walked straight by, humming a tune, steeling himself for the haggling to be done in the market next day."

A young girl sitting near the front of the group couldn't stay quiet any longer. She blurted out, "But Yeshu, was the hurt man dead yet?"

"No," answered Yeshu, "but he was badly injured and the sun was burning hot.

"Then of all people, a Samaritan approached on a donkey. Seeing the battered man lying beside the road, he dismounted and hurried over for a closer look. Like all of us, he knew how pain and suffering felt, and his heart went out to the crumpled figure.

"It's a Judean, he thought to himself, but so what? It could easily be me lying there. I must help.

"He went back to his donkey, returning with two small flasks. He set about carefully cleaning the man's wounds with wine and oil, apologizing to the moaning figure because that was all he had at the moment. Next he took a large red cloth from his pack, tore it into shreds, and bandaged the Judean's head and arms. Wrapping his own cloak around the now shivering man, the Samaritan lifted him astride his donkey and walked him as quickly and gingerly as the road allowed, to the nearest inn, where he tended to him for the rest of the day.

"The following morning, the Samaritan dug into his leather money pouch for two silver coins, which he placed in the innkeeper's hand, saying, 'Take good care of this man until he is well enough to travel on. When I pass back by here on my way home, I will pay you for anything extra that you've had to spend on him.' And with that the Samaritan continued on his journey to Jericho.

"The injured man recovered fully and returned to his family and village, a new person. This act of kindness had transformed the Judean. For the first time, he understood that Samaritans were human beings, too, and deserved the same helping hand when in need."

The same young girl asked, "But how did the good-neighbor Samaritan know to act that way?"

"That's a good question," answered Yeshu. "Because no one on the road had ever helped *him* out, especially a Judean. And of course nobody in charge was there telling him what to do."

Yeshu cocked his head to one side. "If the priest and the Temple singer are a clue—those two fellows who passed by earlier and did nothing—then having such a person around might not have helped much at all."

Yeshu noticed two older girls had thrown knowing looks at one another, and he went on with his story.

"With most people I know, you see, power and superiority end up muddling the mind. Power muffles our hearing and blinds our sight to the troubles of others. Superiority whispers in our ears how good we are, how we deserve the best."

As always, Yeshu's eyes scanned his listeners' faces.

"How easy it is to turn away once we convince ourselves that if someone is in trouble, well, they must deserve to be. We may even puff ourselves up with distaste at being victimized by unjust demands for help from someone who is apparently so unworthy of our charity.

"And if the person should be as innocent as a wounded lamb, so what? Isn't saving that creature really the job of its shepherd over there, or the other members of its flock, wherever they might be?

"So, you see, if a person in need has no clear claim on us, too often we feel free to pass by."

A boy in the middle of the group piped up, "Maybe someone helped the Samaritan in the past, and that's why he did what he did."

"Actually, no," said Yeshu, shaking his head, "and that's what's so remarkable about him.

"Our Samaritan wasn't returning a favor. His life had never depended on a gift from someone else that now had to be repaid in kind. And he wasn't concerned about doing good to seem good. No one was watching. Nor, was he negotiating a bribe with his conscience.

"No, something else was at work that day, something welling up from deep inside. It spoke not through words but through actions. You see, the Samaritan expressed love for the injured Judean because he loved God. He knew without a doubt, as you and I do, that each person has that of God within them.

"And because we are all asked to love our God with all our strength, and with all our heart and soul and mind, that's exactly what he did. He showed love to that of God in the other man, without asking or caring *who* that man was in this world."

Yeshu looked around at the gathered children, one by one, letting his story settle. The eyes of all but two were on him. The boys who had been smirking earlier were staring at their hands.

When the boys glanced back up, Yeshu smiled and said, "God is love.

"Know that. Practice that. And you will need to know none of the other laws, because you'll be following all of them."

Heaven and Hell

A number of the kids in the group listening to Yeshu were wide-eyed over that last statement. We were all still for a few moments. Yeshu started to gather his things together to leave. Suddenly, the sharp boy in the front row turned around to me and said, "You're part of Yeshu's group, and you're not much older than my big brother. Can you tell stories, too?"

Before I could answer, Yeshu gestured in my direction with a quick motion of his forehead and said, "Of course he can, and he's going to tell one right now. Perhaps yet another one that you all will be hearing today for the first time."

My face turned red: with pride, but also alarm. Yeshu thought I was up to the challenge, but was I? It can be harder to tell stories to kids than to adults. Which one should I choose?

I considered a twist on the frog-in-the-well, but that's a long tale and I could see the kids were growing weary. And besides, I wanted to give them something that felt fresh and new to me also.

Mama Ana used to say that new stories often had old stories as their parents. So I decided to take a small piece of the story Yeshu had just told, and weave in strands from one my Gramma Ruth had long ago told Shoshana, Aaron, and me. It was when we sat around the hearth at her house one night right after supper, waiting with delicious anticipation.

For a while I sat gazing into my lap and slowly rubbing my forehead with the heel of one hand, so those present would know I needed some time to reflect. More important, I wanted them all to settle into the silence. When I felt that everyone one was centered, I looked up and began to speak.

"There was a bandit," I started out, "who at times was also a warrior. His past made him increasingly troubled about what would happen when his life ended. He had robbed and he had killed. But he was nobody's fool; he had seen death in many guises and knew it could come for him any day. Those who live by the sword, after all, can never be sure when they might die by it."

Yeshu's eyes met mine.

"The warrior knew of heaven and hell, but was unsure what either was like. Or exactly how a person ended up in one or the other. So after asking around for the wisest, holiest man anyone knew, he journeyed off to see him.

"Arriving at the man's hut, faraway in the parched sand country of the Sinai, the warrior knocked on the rickety door. From inside, the gravelly whisper of an ancient voice answered, 'The door is unbolted. I know why you are here. If you also know, come in and ask what you will.'

"The warrior pushed the door open and stepped in. His eyes swept the room. It was lit sparingly by open windows on the left and right. The space was mostly empty, with just a single table and stool on one side and a long bench along the back wall. At one end of the bench sat a small old man in a simple homespun tunic. A braided strip of goatskin gathered his hair away from his face. His eyes stared out impassively like two dark caves in a cliff.

"The warrior bowed his head ever so slightly to signify respect because, after all, he had come here seeking something; something he wanted very badly.

"'Wise sir,' he said, 'tell me if you will, what is the difference between heaven and hell?'

"The holy man gazed at him for a long time. His eyes brushed over the warrior's sword, his broad leather belt, and his spear, before finally settling on his face.

"Finally the holy man said: 'A professional killer like the one standing before me—such a person is most likely blind to any light I might shine on what separates heaven from hell.'

"'In fact, I question whether someone like you can even *begin* to comprehend such a difference.'

"The warrior felt the blood rush to his head as he swiftly drew a long, thin dagger from his belt and charged across the room with fury burning in his eyes.

"Raising the gleaming blade high to thrust it into his tormentor, he screamed at the holy man, '*No* one slurs my honor so rudely without paying for it! Beg for your life or *die*, you stupid old warthog!'

"The holy man smiled faintly. But just before the warrior could plunge the dagger into his eye, the holy one raised a weathered finger and pointed straight into the warrior's raging face.

"He spoke softly but firmly: '*That*, my son, is hell.'

"The warrior froze, as if smacked in the forehead with an oak club. In the next instant his stunned face melted, his arm fell, and the dagger clattered to the floor.

Slowly the warrior sank to his knees. Raising his hands to his chest, he pressed them together beseechingly as if in prayer.

"'Oh, holy master,' he said with a tremor, 'I have acted so stupidly and rashly; worse than a wild boar. I am so ashamed. A soldier should know how to hold himself in, and listen to what's been said before striking. My pride and anger almost ended your life in a flash!

"'And without realizing,' he added, 'that you were answering what I most wanted to know.

"'Please, wise sir,' the warrior went on, his eyes glistening, 'if your heart can find any way to do so, please forgive me. I beg you.

"'Here,' he gestured with open palms, 'I'll lay down my dagger and sword—right here, right now—and humbly serve the poor for a year as penance. Two years if you say so. Or a lifetime.'

"The holy man stopped the warrior from speaking further by lightly touching the man's trembling lips. He then placed his palm on the warrior's forehead.

"'And *that*,' said the holy man, 'is heaven.'

"He paused, nodding ever so slightly, as the man gazed up into his face.

"'Deep down, you knew the difference all along.

"'And now you *know* that you knew.'"

~ ~ ~

Finishing my story of heaven and hell, I lowered my eyes just a bit and heard the children let out an "aaah."

I stole a look at Yeshu. He was beaming at me like a proud older brother! I felt my face burning and my chest begin to swell.

For the first time in my life it seemed I had given something of value to Yeshu through a story that was mine. I was walking in step with a friend who was no longer slowing down so I could keep up. And my own journey as an authentic storyteller had truly begun.

She Is the Wisest

The next day I sat on a hillside above the River Jordan, working on a new pair of sandals for an old fishing partner of the Thunder Brothers. That very morning we had been walking along the Sea of Galilee near the town of Capernaum, when Yeshu spotted two men knee-deep in the water just offshore, casting a large net together.

Yeshu stopped in his tracks, turned toward the fishermen, and called out, "Come with us, and I will make you fishers of men."

The two of them, named Andrew and Shimón Petros, strode out of the water, dropped their net at the shore, and agreed to join us right there on the spot.

Imagine that.

When I looked at their feet—a habit of sandal makers, I guess—I could see that Shimón Petros had walked right through the bottoms of his sandals. After traveling with him for only a single day, I realized for the first time that I could tell how a person walked by how they wore out their soles. It was as if he wanted to push the road down into the ground and behind him.

Andrew, on the other hand, was not so intense and driven. As fisherfolk often say, he had a steady hand on the tiller and no need to blow air into the sail.

While I worked on Shimón's sandal, I watched Maria Magdalena and Yeshu far below me, where they strolled along the riverbank, back and forth, back and forth. Most of the time they walked arm in arm, talking intently. Occasionally they would stop and gesture with their hands, and then resume walking together.

Early that evening, I approached Yeshu when he was alone. Sitting with his legs stretched out, he was leaning back against a low stone fence and watching the night sky emerge overhead.

I stood next to his shoulder, my head tilted downward. "Yeshu, is Maria a disciple?"

"One of the three main ones," he answered, turning his head up in my direction. "And she is the wisest of all. The one who knows most."

"Then why do you argue so?"

Yeshu looked at me closely.

"You saw us at the river?"

I nodded. "I was watching from the hillside. I went up to where those three boulders sit, to sharpen my tools on the hard stone."

"We were not exactly arguing," he said, smiling. "We were discussing God's will for human beings. The Greeks who live among us call this *theologia*, the study of God."

"Is theologia what the rabbis do in the synagogues," I asked, "and the priests in the Temple in Jerusalem?"

Yeshu pulled at one end of his mustache and then the other.

"Some of the time," he said. "But in those places, all of us who are in attendance are also involved in the actual practice of worshipping God, what the Romans call *religio*. That word comes from *religare*," he explained, "which means 'to reconnect.'

"When we do it right, this worship brings us closer to God, and it leads us to serve God's will and to care for God's people."

He patted the ground for me to sit down beside him.

Now it was becoming clearer to me than ever, why some people were starting to call Yeshu not just "Teacher," but "Rabbi." And it pleased me that he felt I was capable of understanding the complicated ideas he was talking about.

Yeshu continued. "Unfortunately, sometimes religio descends into struggles for power," he said, "with practitioners at the top conspiring for positions and scheming to win the allegiance of others. It can end up dividing people rather than connecting them to one another and to God."

I nodded and an image flashed before me: of Yohanan and his truth-telling about the High Priest and the King, in crowded markets and wherever there was water for baptizing people. That sermonizing had led to his murder, by supposedly God-loving people.

Not noticing me bite my lip, Yeshu went on. "Like a sturdy foundation of stones, theologia is the deliberation that lies underneath the rules and practices of religio. It covers everything having to do with the human soul: its suffering and its joy; its past and its future. As well as what God is like, and how we should live in accord with God's will."

"And has Maria studied theologia?" I asked.

He answered slowly, "Well, no. She hasn't exactly studied it. But she teaches it. She knows the human spirit from the inside. Not from books and authorities, but from living deeply herself, and from really knowing other people.

"You've noticed this before and spoken about it," he said. "Am I right?"

I nodded my concurrence and asked, "Does she know all about Micah and Sara and Elisha?" I took a moment. "And Hagar, Annot, and Hillel?"

"Yes, she knows about them all," Yeshu said, "and about the other prophets, and of course, the laws, too.

"Daavi, I know you're aware," he continued, "that according to the ways of our Jewish faith, women are not allowed to study formally or to become rabbis. But with our journeying group, out here among the people, it's different. Everyone teaches; and everyone learns.

"I love talking to Maria about matters of the spirit," he said, "because she challenges me. Just like Yohanan did. They've both helped me sharpen my own understanding."

I gathered up my tool bag and said, "Then I'm going to talk to her about these things, too."

"You do that," said Yeshu. "But know something else."

I held my breath in anticipation.

"Maria also stands out among the others," he said, "because of her courage. She's as brave as your father!"

"My father?" I said, letting out a gasp of surprise.

"Yes," said Yeshu. "Surely you know. All the younger men in Nazareth have long revered your father for his resistance, especially for how he refused to do the Romans' evil work.

"We admired his heart, and his steel."

It was a good thing I was still sitting because hearing those words made me feel as if someone had grasped the back of my tunic and spun me around. I didn't have far to fall but I was falling nonetheless.

~ ~ ~

A week or so later, Maria Magdalena and I took a long stroll along the shores of the Sea of Galilee. We talked and talked, about Yeshu and about God.

Suddenly, I asked, "So Maria, when you imagine what God is like, do you envision a person? Some kind of man?" Then I quickly added, "Or maybe even a woman?"

She stopped abruptly, took hold of my arm like I was still a boy, and gazed into my eyes for a long time. I began to feel I'd maybe asked the wrong question.

Then she looked off over the still water. When she finally spoke, her voice did not waver. I listened keenly.

"God is inside of *you*," she said, "God is inside of *me*. "There is that of God in everyone." And she stretched her arms wide, like Yeshu would do. "So is God like a man?" She turned her head toward one of her hands. "Or is God like a woman?" She faced the other one.

I stared at her mouth, waiting.

"Is it God the Father? Or God the Mother?" She paused so long, I thought maybe she couldn't decide quite how to proceed.

Finally she dropped both hands and spoke with no hesitation. "I believe the answer to all these questions is: Yes!" Her voice shot across the water like a sea eagle.

"God is man...woman...father...mother."

Just when it seemed I was grasping her point, her eyes flashed. "And I also believe," she exclaimed, "that the answer to your question is, No!"

I flinched, recovering quickly.

"You are male. I am female. God is God."

She smiled. And the smile vanished as quickly as it had come.

Then she turned and walked away, leaving me there alone, pondering the vast sea. The sea in front of me and the sea within.

Teaching from the Mountainside

In the spring of the following year, when it was still too early to begin plowing and planting, we sent word around to local villages, farms, and encampments of travelers. The message was that Yeshu was going to speak the next day in an expansive meadow at the foot of a hill. As the hour approached, an enormous crowd had already gathered, several thousand strong, and he had to climb up the slope to be fully seen and heard.

Yeshu waited for folks to find a place and spread their cloaks on the ground. When they quieted down, he reached his arms out as if to embrace them all. After nearly three years of journeying, his own cloak was patched like a quilt, of every earth tone from wheat to loam. It hung straight from his shoulders, almost reaching the ground.

I myself had sewn on several of those patches.

Whenever we urged Yeshu to accept people's offers of a new cloak, he said it wasn't necessary, that this one was just fine because it was like the cloaks that people wore who came to hear his messages.

"When preparing to plow, would you hitch up a peacock next to an ox?" he laughed.

After taking a while to get settled, the crowd fell silent in Yeshu's abundant presence. With no introduction, he began to speak. Much of what he said that day I had heard many times before. All of us close to him had, but this time was special. The phrases rolled out like the broad Jordan waters of early springtime that course through forest, field, and meadow only an hour's walk from where we sat.

Yeshu spoke as if he were almost singing. And like rhyme and melody can do, this helped us recall for years to come the words and beliefs he passed to us—by breathing life into his lessons. The chanters in the synagogues and the Temple do something similar to seal words into the minds of those who are gathered there. Maybe that's where Yeshu had picked up his way of speaking in public. Except that *his* teaching to a crowd could lift you even higher than a Shabbat song.

What those present heard that morning they would retell to their children and grandchildren, who would someday retell it to theirs. It was that kind of lesson.

Yeshu spoke intently, pausing for long moments to let each piece of his message sink in until the words and the silence were conversing in harmony.

> Blessed are those who know their need of God,
> for theirs is the kingdom of heaven.
> Blessed are those who weep and are sorrowful,
> for they shall find laughter and consolation.

His voice carried to the farthest reaches of the field, without him hollering at the people as some are inclined to do. And it was infused with an inner rhythm, like a lute's song, that Yeshu drew upon whenever he spoke to so many.

> Blessed are those of a gentle spirit,
> for they shall inherit the earth.

The magic of his voice lifted us up, carried us along, dancing in time with each phrase.

> Blessed are those who hunger and thirst to do right
> and to see right prevail,
> for they shall be satisfied.

The words from his mouth flew right into your heart and made you soar so that your soul could sing.

> Blessed are those who show mercy,
> for mercy shall be shown to them.

> Blessed are those whose hearts are pure,
>   for they shall see God.

As the carpenter spoke, his eyes scanned the crowd tenderly. It felt to those present as if he were looking inside each one of us; as if he were pressing each word personally into our outstretched hands.

> Blessed are the peacemakers,
>   for God shall call them 'my children.'

Yeshu lifted his face to the sky and inhaled deeply. He was allowing us time to consider what we were being given. He seemed to be gazing into the beyond.

Slowly he raised his hands to us, arms outstretched.

> Blessed are those who have suffered persecution
>   for the cause of justice,
>   for the kingdom of heaven is theirs.

Then he stopped. His hands descended steadily to his sides.

Yeshu stood straight and still, leaning slightly forward like a shepherd poised to jump a crevice to rescue a lost lamb. His face shone and all eyes were fastened on him.

He knew at that moment his heart and ours were connected by one vibrant string. It seemed as if we had all stopped breathing at the same time.

Extending both hands wide again, he plucked the string, and our breathing returned, attuned to his words.

> You are the salt of the earth.
> You are light for all the world.
> A town that stands on a hill cannot be hidden.
> When a lamp is lit, it is not put under a basket
>   but on the lampstand,
>   where it gives light to everyone in the house.

Then he pointed a finger and gradually moved it across the expanse of the crowd, seemingly person by person, as he added further guidance.

> And you, like the lamp,
> must shed light among your fellow companions,
> so that when they see the good you do,
> they may be moved to praise your God in heaven.

Yeshu clasped both hands together in front of his chest. I thought for sure he had finished.

At that very moment, a child broke away from his parents and began running up the hillside. He climbed a large rock near Yeshu to get a better view but soon lost his balance and began to teeter. The crowd, now distracted, watched intently. A man, probably the child's father, scrambled up the hill, but lost his footing and slid backward in the loose earth.

Yeshu was quick. With a leopard's agility he sprang to the base of the large rock and caught the boy as he fell. The crowd roared its approval, and Yeshu grinned like a new dad holding his first child. Finally, the boy's father clambered up the hill and Yeshu handed him the stunned child. With that taken care of, Yeshu turned and called for the mother to come forward, too, so they could all see better together.

Just when it seemed that he was about to resume speaking, he halted abruptly and requested, "Let all the little children come unto me, and their parents with them."

Soon several hundred people had clambered forward, the crowd making way for them. While this was going on, Yeshu climbed a dozen steps further up the slope, to make more room for the newcomers.

Several men near the front of the seated crowd became concerned that he might be overrun, and reaching out, began to stop the children and even push them back.

Yeshu reacted strongly, "I implore you to allow the children to come to me. Do not hinder them, for the kingdom of heaven belongs to such as these."

Having stated his piece, he laid his hands on several of the youngest ones. Deep in thought, he looked over the gathering, giving everyone time to fully arrive. When all had calmed like a lake after a brief thundershower, he spread his arms once more and spoke.

> Life is more than food, the body more than clothing.
> Consider the lilies of the field, how they grow.
> They don't work, nor do they spin;
> but I say to you that not even Solomon in all his glory
> was arrayed as one of these.

He turned to his left toward the descending sun. I thought he might be preparing to leave but he turned back again, to clarify.

> Do not suppose that I have come to abolish the Law and the Prophets.
> I did not come to set aside, but to complete!

Then he remained facing the crowd for a long moment, completely immobile except for the glow on his face and the pulsating warmth in his eyes.

> My friends, never forget this:
> Love your enemies and pray for your persecutors.
> There must be no limit to your goodness.
> If someone slaps you on your right cheek,
> turn and offer him your left.

Through my mind flashed an image of Yeshu teaching me how to do the right thing after my nearly disastrous confrontation with a Roman sword. My thoughts were interrupted by the sound of Yeshu's voice. There was more he wanted to say.

> If a man wants to sue you for your tunic,
> let him have your cloak as well.
> Give when you are asked to give,
> for certain, to the least of your brothers and sisters.

Yeshu closed his eyes, raising his face. He stood that way for some time, as we waited. It seemed he was waiting, as well. Finally he looked back at us, spread his arms wide one last time—once again, as if to embrace us all—and offered a final instruction.

Always do unto others
as you would have them do unto you.
This is the law and the prophets.

Smiling out at the crowd, he brought both hands together in front of his heart, fingertips barely touching. He ended by sharing with all who were present that favorite prayer he had taught his wandering band, long ago in the cedars of Lebanon, the one he had prayed with us many times since.

"Our father who art in heaven..."

When he finished, he bowed his head to his chest, and the crowd stood as one and cheered him with arms lifted high above their heads, palms facing the teacher. As the roar of voices slowly subsided, many pushed forward in hopes of touching him, beseeching him.

~ ~ ~

That evening, Maria Magdalena and I went walking in the hills to talk.

"Yeshu was at his best today," she said, joy ringing in her voice.

I gripped both hands together in front of my chest, and pumped them twice in agreement.

"It felt like he was speaking just to me," I said, "even though I was in the middle of all those thousands of people."

"Mmm-hmm," she responded. "He does that."

We walked on in silence.

My eyes attended to the path, so that I would not stub a toe on a rock or step on any lingering caterpillar. The setting sun lit the greenness of all the small living things clinging so tenaciously to this rocky slope, and my heart welled up with love for the beauty of the world. And with compassion for all that lives within it.

Oh, how I missed Yohanan!

After a long while, Maria said, "You know...if Yohanan were still here among us, sitting on that hillside today, he would have offered up a strong conviction of his own."

I glanced sideways at her and felt my eyebrows crawling up my forehead in anticipation. She stopped walking and stared at her cupped hands as she deliberated on just how to say it.

"I believe," she said, "our gentle, wilderness prophet would have added a single assertion."

> Blessed are those who love the earth:
> who nurture her, do not abuse her,
> and give back her care for us.
> They shall be called 'stewards of God.'

She looked straight into my eyes. I clapped my hands together, this time above my head, and returned her gaze. I was awed by how she had captured what I was feeling just then. And even more, that she had so deftly found the words I lacked to express it.

Shepherd's Night

By noon the next day, at least a thousand more people had appeared to hear Yeshu. It was as though a flock of ravens had scattered and flown to every town and village in the region with word that a messenger of God was camped on a hillside nearby.

Many of these villages had no more than a few dozen inhabitants, and it seemed that in some cases, not one of them remained back at home. What was certain was that those who arrived came with a great longing, the way flowers reach for sunlight and roots thirst for rain.

But Yeshu was drained, and well before sundown he turned and walked to the side of the crowd to signal that the lesson sharing for that day was over. A few of us stepped forth and gathered round him. Scooping up our belongings, we hustled him off, and soon we were headed south, back around the shores of Lake Galilee.

As we walked, the sun slowly sank into the lake, burning a hole in its surface, turning it from bright blue to crimson, and finally disappearing.

Only an occasional utterance intruded on the quiet.

Then Yeshu stopped. Squinting his eyes, he looked up a hillside. On the very top, silhouetted against a sky that was azure with the gathering twilight, was a band of shepherds.

For as long as I had known him, Yeshu had been drawn to shepherds. Perhaps he felt close to their simplicity and solitude as they roamed the hills through all kinds of weather, protecting their animals from loss and injury. And surely he carried with him the tales Mama Maria had told him so many times of the night he was born.

With his eyes fixed on the hilltop band, Yeshu told us to rest where we were. Swift as a mountain goat, he climbed the slope to where the shepherds sat. From a distance we saw them rise up and crowd around him, most likely shy at first, then touching his sleeve and pushing forward to hug him, talking and laughing. Finally, Yeshu looked down toward where we waited, gave a whoop, and waved us up.

The shepherds had recognized him from months before when they heard him speak on another hillside, and they had insisted that all of us join them in their camp for an evening meal. We climbed the hill to where they stood waiting, and then kept climbing with them as they ascended along the ridge toward the high valley where they had pitched their tents and fashioned makeshift corrals from rocks and dry brush.

As the first wandering star appeared above the darkening horizon to the east, we all fell silent, concentrating on walking along the path without stumbling. Each of us was lost in thought.

We were all tired from the drawn-out day and the long climb at the end of it. Plus I was fixated on the warm meal that awaited us, and the hovering shepherd mothers who would serve it up like a blessing.

All around me I could hear the soft rustle of woven clothing and the light tread of sandaled feet, and up ahead of us the scattered hoof beats and bleating of the sheep. I felt the warmth of the shepherds' bodies, their shoulders wrapped in animal skins, as they moved beside me, in front of me, and behind me. In the faint afterglow of the departed sun, I could see their outlines against the now purple sky flecked with multitudes of emerging stars.

All of a sudden, the shepherds' quiet closeness made me think of Yohanan wrapped in his animal skins. Tears slipped down my cheeks. I was reluctant to look at Yeshu; somehow I knew he must be reflecting on Yohanan, too.

At that moment, I fully understood what it was that drew Yeshu to the simple people of the world, to those without power and those lacking in earthly wealth who stood with a single foot resting on the bottom rung of society's ladder. I saw that Yeshu was one of them, as was I. He was a child of parents who were salt of the earth, and so he felt a true brotherhood of brothers.

It was a feeling of deep belonging, and of being accepted for who rather than what we were. I held it inside me like a candle flame cupped against the night breeze.

~ ~ ~

The spell broke as quickly as it was cast, when a tall young shepherd at the front of the pack hollered out a long, haunting call of arrival.

Startled, I stumbled over a root, and two men directly behind me leapt to catch my sleeves. They swiftly lifted me up with their strong hands beneath my arms, and I seemed to float on light feet down the hillside toward the narrow, protected valley below—the valley from which a silvery answering call was now returning.

As we approached, I could see the women and children huddled around the campfire, looking in our direction. Before we reached the camp, the pungent fragrance of mutton simmering in a stew reached my nostrils, making my mouth water.

Soon we were embracing the others, who stood to meet us. We added food of our own to the evening meal: wild herbs picked that morning in a spring-fed ravine, and dried fish given to us by old friends of Andrew and Shimón Petros from the days when they were fishermen.

Everyone sat in a circle, shoulder-to-shoulder, and waited for Yeshu to bless the food and pray. When he finished, Nathanyel spoke up, "Thank you sheep. Thank you fish. Thank you God."

And we ate our fill.

After we finished, Yeshu talked about how it reminded him of the meals at home in Nazareth before his father died. "My Abba," he said, "would make everyone laugh, telling his tales and riddles. Mostly ones he made up."

"Give us one," a young girl begged. "Just one."

"Just one?" Yeshu said. "Then it had better be a good one."

He tapped his brow with a finger for a few moments and then smiled. "How is a tree known?" he asked.

We all shook our heads, even though several of us already knew the answer, since Yeshu had told this one many times. A small girl piped up, "By its name! Just like my name is Rachel!"

Yeshu laughed. "Well, you're very close," he said. "A tree is known by its fruit. And sometimes that's even in its name: apple tree; olive tree; mulberry; almond."

He paused and then said, "Here's a sister riddle, but I'll give you no answer: Are *people* known by their fruits, as well? Just like trees?"

The only sound was the fire popping and cracking. Then Yeshu pointed at me, "Your turn, Daavi!"

I was ready. With a clap of my hands, I tossed out, "What falls down but is run right back up?" No one could answer me, so I said, "An acorn that ends up in the mouth of a squirrel!" That one got a big laugh.

Then Yeshu shared his favorite one about the rich man entering heaven being more difficult than a camel passing through the eye of the needle. Everyone enjoyed that one except for a fellow named Matthew whom we had met in Emmaus. He had asked if he could travel with us for a while, telling us he had once worked as a tax collector.

"But Yeshu, don't forget," Matthew countered, "it's rich men who often feed your band as you travel."

Yeshu cocked his head. "I didn't say it was impossible, Matthew," he quipped. "Just difficult."

Everyone chuckled again. I smiled to see Yeshu so happy. It was clear how much he loved these moments of warmth and playful exchange among common folk that he either knew or was coming to know.

Turning his head slowly to the side, he sighed long and low, as though he were suddenly contemplating us from a great distance. Even as I looked over at him apprehensively, he seemed to be moving farther away, wrestling with thoughts none of us could see.

I rose to join the others cleaning up after the meal. Several of us helped the women and children break dead branches into kindling for the next day's cooking fire. Reaching for a branch, I noticed in the firelight all the strong hands, sleeves rolled up revealing bare brown arms.

I was especially taken by one of the younger women, with straight dark hair hanging to her waist. Her eyes flashed when she saw me watching her. She tossed her head to clear the hair from her face. She reminded me of someone I had once seen, but who could it be?

A notion pushed its way into my mind: I could marry someone like her, and live in a place like this on hillsides like these. Among shepherds and sheep and dogs.

As we worked, I began telling them about my lost sister, how she loved animals, especially songbirds. Finally I sang Shoshana's lullaby in hopes that one of them might have once heard it sung, or might somehow have heard word of her.

None of them had. But they found the song lovely, and they made me repeat it several times until they learned the words and the melody. Afterward they thanked me for my gift, and to my great joy, in the middle of the night I awoke to hear a young mother crooning the lullaby softly to her child.

After we were done with the chores, the older women banked the fire and everyone who was still awake stretched out on the soft, thick grass, feeling warm and tired and well fed. One of the sheep dogs snuggled up to me, followed by his master, a young shepherd no more than five years old. We used our fingers to comb the burrs out of the coat of the dog that lay happily between us, and we stared up at the great night sky along with all the others who lay there.

The shepherd boy pointed at the wandering star that by now had climbed through the constellations and stood high above us, glowing red like a tiny ember in a bed of ashes.

"Mars," the boy leaned over and whispered toward me. As there was no moon up yet, I nodded my head several times so that he would be sure to see. That boy knew his night sky better than any town inhabitant sleeping under thatch.

Then I heard Yeshu murmur that stars wander just like people.

He was back from wherever he had gone. His energy restored. Staring into the fire, he began telling a favorite teaching tale, just one of many he told deep into that expanding night.

"A woman," he started out pensively, "had just ten drachma coins to cover the needs of her family. To her dismay, she lost one of them.

"Immediately she lit a lamp and swept out the house with a stiff grass broom. When the coin did not turn up in the pile of sweepings, she dropped down on her hands and knees and searched for it until she discovered where it had rolled under a pine bench that sat against the wall.

"Joyfully she called together her friends and neighbors, saying, 'Celebrate with me, for I've found the drachma that was lost. Now my children will not go hungry.'"

Yeshu gave us time before going on.

"I tell you this story, because it's just how God searches for any one of us who becomes lost."

The youngest children among the shepherds stared up at Yeshu, presumably preoccupied with that lost coin and with God sweeping and kneeling on the Temple floor.

The little ones were now hustled off to their bedrolls, and Yeshu went on with several stories about travelers and workers he had known since his early childhood in Egypt, and others about ancient holy women like Esther, who saved her people from death, and the prophetess Deborah, who was a judge and a gifted poet.

"Esther's name," he said, "means 'star,' though at birth she was named Hadassah. Never forget, it's her act of courage that we Jews celebrate every year at the Feast of *Purim*."

Of Deborah, he recounted how she encouraged Jews to affirm their ties to God, and how she wrote the "Song of Deborah," that later became part of the *Shophtim*, the Book of Judges. I noticed Joanna and Maria Magdalena listening intently to Yeshu when he recounted this.

On he rolled with other stories. One was full of the particulars of Moses freeing the Jews from slavery in Egypt. Another featured the prophet Samuel, the great judge of Israel, who chose Saul as king.

He also told tales of young people, which caught the interest of the older children present. This was especially so when the story characters learned what is truly at the center of life by opening their hearts and risking danger and failure.

Those were some of my favorites, particularly the ones about David. He was the shepherd-boy who was my namesake. When older he went on to compose many of the Psalms in the Tehillim, some of the most beautiful poetry anyone has ever written.

As the night wore on, Yeshu's stories seemed to braid themselves together in my mind as I struggled valiantly to follow their various threads, drifting in and out of sleep. In and out of dreams.

Finally I fell into a slumber as peaceful as the ones I knew before Shoshana vanished.

Become Like Children!

At dawn we returned to Lake Galilee and found fishing boats that took us across to Capernaum, where Yeshu had sometimes stayed in the family home of Shimón Petros. This time we settled into the house of a wealthy man who greatly admired Yeshu. In a flash we finished off a simple midday meal of sliced millet bread, cheese curds sprinkled with almonds, and new wine. Afterwards, Yeshu went out for a walk through town with Petros and Nathanyel while several of us stayed behind to do some chores around our host's place.

When Yeshu returned, Joanna said to him, "Philippos and I have been debating something, and we want your opinion."

Yeshu cocked an ear and waited.

It was Joanna who stated the question, "Who is the greatest in the kingdom of heaven?"

Yeshu looked at her and at Philippos. Then he turned his eyes toward the doorway where a child was standing, peering around the doorjamb at us. Yeshu smiled at the girl and waved.

"Could you come here for a moment?" he asked.

She trotted over to him, and he picked her up and sat her on the table where we had eaten earlier. Without hesitation, he broke off a piece of bread from a basket on the sideboard, spooned on date honey from the adjacent pot, and gave it to her. She squealed with glee and stuffed the entire hunk into her mouth, peering up at Yeshu through long eyelashes.

"My answer is this," said Yeshu. "Unless you become like children," he said, "you will never enter the kingdom of heaven. Those who humble themselves to be like a child will stand tallest in the eyes of God."

With one hand, Yeshu rubbed the child's shoulders, and she giggled and arched backwards. Swiftly he scooped up a handful of raisins from a bowl and tossed them into his mouth. A second handful was deposited in his new friend's palm.

When the two of them were done munching, he made a face like a camel chewing its cud—sideways, of course—and they both giggled.

At that he turned to the rest of us and said, "Whoever receives *one* such child in my name receives me. But anyone who causes to stumble one of these little ones who have faith, would be better off having a millstone hung round their neck and being thrown into the sea. The world weeps that there are those who would cause such stumbling. Well, come they must, but woe unto them."

I looked around the room. I knew everyone in our band well enough by now to know who would be flummoxed by Yeshu's words and who was in step with what he meant. The Thunder Brothers, for example, were already digging their elbows into each other's ribs, one reminding the other not to be so serious.

When Thunder John finally keeled over and lay perfectly still, the young girl let out a laugh like a ringing bell. Thunder James stood over his fallen brother and nudged him gently with a toe.

Turning to us, he said, "Playing dead doesn't work unless you're dead serious about it."

While he waited for our reaction, his toe was tickling John without mercy. Soon John was tittering madly while James frowned. Then John was on his feet quicker than a donkey can sneeze, and James was laughing!

I guess being close brothers is like living with a mirror that you take turns peering into or out of. Maybe that's what helped the two of them to almost always see the double-sidedness in Yeshu's teaching.

Meanwhile Judah and Shimón Petros looked perturbed. They glared at the Thunder Brothers with furrowed brows. Judah's scowl wasn't directed only at James and John. From what I could read on his lips, he was muttering something about Yeshu needing to put his foot down to squelch such obvious disrespect.

Petros seemed more bewildered than angry. You could see him wondering yet again why Yeshu was always talking in riddles. Isn't it better to just say what you mean if you really mean what you say?

My eyes returned to Yeshu and saw that he'd been looking around the room, too, sizing up our reactions. He paused to closely watch Judah, trying to catch those guarded eyes under the tumble of matted curls. Having failed, he shook his head so softly I think I'm the only one who noticed.

Turning instead toward Petros, Yeshu smiled encouragingly. Shimón loved him like a young son would his father, with a simple faith yet to be tested. He couldn't imagine any situation that could call that faith into question, but eventually we learn that a life lived without questions can be full of surprises. It leaves one unprepared not only for unexpected challenges coming from outside, but also those from within.

As I sat watching all this, my mind drifted back home. My father used to tell Aaron and me, "A stone house built on solid ground can weather the fiercest storm, but it can shake apart in an earthquake because it's just too rigid."

I wondered how many of us were stone houses.

And then I remembered how my mother would add a lesson of her own, "Life's choices are not always obvious," she would tell us. "There are times when you have to be ready to follow the aimless meanderings of a bee despite the danger of being stung—or just numbed by tedium—if you want to eventually find the comb and its tasty honey."

Maybe that's why, I mused silently, that I felt little need to understand Yeshu immediately and easily.

Next my mind wandered over to the house next door to my parents. There was Mama Ana, I thought to myself, who always said the best stories were the ones that left room for the future to answer them more fully. Yeshu had learned that lesson well. He wanted us to know that the shortest route to a mountaintop wasn't straight up, not unless you had hawk wings and an eagle's eyes like Yohanan, and could fly. Most of us were more like mountain goats; we needed to pick our way along switchbacks and carefully find our footing in terrain that seemed to lead us to dead ends beneath tall cliffs.

Someone coughed loudly, and with a jolt I returned to the present. Once again I looked over at where the Thunder Brothers now sat, and it seemed as if they hadn't been listening either. They were completely focused on a tiny butterfly that had meandered through the doorway and was flitting here and there.

Thunder James cocked his head and heaved a sigh.

"That must be what God's eyelids are like when thousands of us humans are doing many crazy things all at once."

Thunder John grinned his agreement, but soon he was distracted by two sparrows that were snapping up bright green beetles outside in the courtyard. After each catch the successful hunter flew up to a nest in a hazelnut tree where its open-mouthed fledglings were waiting for their supper. Fascinating.

Gesturing toward the feasting place, John spouted, "Whenever I watch them, I feel like I'm winging through the sky, too!"

Yeshu gestured toward the brothers with his head. "Consider these two," he said. "Their windows are wide open for God to fly right in."

"Or locusts," someone muttered.

I glanced over at Judah. He was staring at the ground.

Shimón, looking annoyed, groused, "Maybe. But those brothers will end up with bug eyes, if they eyeball every crawling creature in town."

Everyone but Judah and Shimón enjoyed a rousing laugh.

As for me, I vowed that one day I would be a gigantic child, too. Although maybe I would vary it just a bit. Who can say where his life will lead him?

Just when it seemed we might be sliding from sense into nonsense, Yeshu's voice pierced my thoughts. He was returning to the genesis of our discussion.

"The great prophet Isaiah peered far into the future," he said, "and brought back a stirring vision for us to ponder.

> The wolf also shall dwell with the lamb,
> and the leopard shall lie down with the suckling goat;
> and the calf and the young lion

> and the fatted animal together...
> and a little child shall lead them.

He paused before asking, “Which of you will be that little child?”

There must have been a long silence. I’m not sure how long, because I was lost in my ruminating on the lamb and the leopard. Finally looking up into Yeshu’s face, I was startled to see a storm rising in his eyes. I gazed deeper and deeper into that gathering darkness. I imagined a howling wind amid the sheets of raindrops I saw there, when suddenly there was a flash.

It wasn’t lightning but people’s heels. A crowd was scattering. They were running from something and carrying infants. As I continued to stare into Yeshu’s eyes, I caught a glimpse of what was happening. The streets and alleys were littered with small bundles of blood-stained rags that wrapped the baby boys of Bethlehem who had been butchered on the orders of a cowardly king, the father of the one who had torn Yohanan from us.

Abruptly, Yeshu turned his head aside. I lowered my gaze to his hands. They were gripping his arms crossed over his chest. The scars from all those years of working with wood stood out, having turned white from the force of his grasp.

Before I could say anything, Yeshu had risen and was walking toward the door into a harsh glare like the blade of a knife.

I looked quickly at the others in the room, then back toward Yeshu. Silhouetted in the bright doorway was the figure of the small girl, waiting there, her hand reaching out to take hold of his.

Who Touched Me?

Often after preaching, Yeshu was besieged by crowds of sick people so desperate for help that we would form a protective ring to keep him from being crushed as he reached out to touch them. We would slowly edge him out toward the road until a way was clear and we were off to the next gathering. But sometimes the crush was overwhelming and the only choice was to make a hasty exit wherever we could. That's what happened a few days after we left Capernaum, at a spot along the lakeshore from which the only safe escape was onto the Sea of Galilee itself.

Fortunately the Thunder Brothers and Shimón Petros had many old fishing mates in these parts, and we were able to find boats. We set sail under a high sun across the lake toward the territory of the Gerasenes. The fishermen, whose boats these were, told us of a wild man living there, a man reputedly possessed by an unclean force. People said he lived in the cemetery on a hillside and walked unclothed among the tombs, howling and roaring with all his might and cutting himself with any jagged stone he found lying about.

The villagers had tried to keep him from hurting himself by tying him up. But it was no use. He broke the ropes and snapped the chains. Now he roamed the area day and night, frightening everyone, whipped this way and that by the implacable demands of his own miserable spirit.

As Yeshu stepped out of the boat and walked ashore through the shining water, the wild man came rushing down the hillside from the tombs and ran straight toward him. Villagers who had gathered at the shore to meet us fell back in alarm, yelling to Yeshu to prepare himself for an attack.

Instead the wild man threw himself into the shallow water at Yeshu's feet and began screaming, "What do you want with me, Yeshua, born of God most high? By all that is holy do not torment me!"

Clearly the man was full to the brim with inner demons, because when Yeshu asked his name, the anguished reply was, "Just call me 'Mob'—there are so many of us!"

Yeshu knelt in the water and took the man's dripping face in his hands. Looking steadily into his eyes, he shook the poor soul's head firmly, once, twice. Then he commanded loudly, "Out, demons. Leave this man in peace!"

The man collapsed in Yeshu's arms. His eyes, which a moment before had been filmy were now as clear as the sky over Galilee. He said nothing, quiet for the first time in ages and content as a newly fed child. His arms, no longer twitching uncontrollably, were once again his own.

Maria Magdalena hurried over, exclaiming, "Oh, yes!"

While Yeshu helped the man to his feet, Maria wrapped him in a spare cloak, holding him carefully so that he would not shatter. Now that we could see him clearly he was little more than a sack of bones. Who knows how long it had been since he had eaten properly?

Maria took him by the hand and led him to the shore. Sitting down, she dipped some bread into water poured from a flask and fed him a piece at a time. The local people watched wordlessly.

At that moment, a young girl pushed her way through the crowd and emerged to stand before the man.

"Daddy?" she said to him incredulously.

He leapt to his feet and the crowd fell back, but the girl did not move the width of a hair. On the contrary, she immediately reached out to him with trembling hands and they both fell into one another's arms.

"Is it really you, Daddy?" she asked, her voice quavering.

"Yes," he replied with a gasp. "It's your father, my dear. I'm home for sure." He smiled broadly.

"Let's go see Mama," the girl responded. "She's been waiting for you for years."

And she took his hand and led him through the throng of people, none of whom shrank from him this time, now that they saw he had found his peace.

At the water's edge stood Philippos, transfixed, closely observing all that was taking place, while gentle waves washed over his feet.

As the girl and her father walked off hand-in-hand, she abruptly stopped and turned back toward Yeshu.

"You're a nice man," she declared. "You made my daddy all calm and warm inside again. You should go do that for other people!"

There were gasps from the crowd, at the apparent impudence of the little girl. But Yeshu looked back in delight and I noticed his chest had lifted. He stood there till the girl turned back to her father and led him away toward home. The curious crowd tagged along behind them at a distance.

Pensively, Yeshu strolled along the beach, his feet also becoming sandy and wet. As soon as he was certain that the villagers had wandered off, he turned and waded out to the boat so we could re-cross the lake. Philippos, Maria, and the others who had followed him ashore, crawled over the gunwales after him, and I followed suit. Soon the skiff was skipping across the water.

Once we were under way I stretched out, laying my head back on a coil of rope. Up above me the billowing sails were snap! snapping! as the wind whipped the canvas.

All was right with the world.

Far overhead, long-winged birds sailed across the sky. I imagined fish flying beneath us, dodging the boat's curved hull at the last possible moment. Birds of the sea and fish of the sky—cousins in one marvelous family! What I wouldn't give to be one of these sleek gliding creatures.

~ ~ ~

The next thing I heard was a loud splash, and the feathers and scales dropped away. I was awake on the other side of the Sea of Galilee, watching James who had just cast anchor. We walked ashore through the cool water to find the great crowd we had fled was still waiting, hours after we had left. In fact, if anything, it was even larger. Yeshu was getting famous and people were now pouring in from nearby villages.

Pushing through the crowd came Jairus, head of the local synagogue.

He was nearly weeping. His young daughter—"the jewel of my life"—was dying. He begged Yeshu to come home with him and save her.

We set off together through the huge crowd, which began to re-form behind us like the tail of the great comet my mother once pointed out to me. We had only trudged a short distance when Yeshu stopped abruptly and turned around.

"Who touched me?" he said.

We all looked at him incredulously.

"You see this crowd pushing and pressing against you," Petros said, "and you ask, 'Who touched me?'"

Yeshu explained that he had stopped walking the moment he felt power going out of him.

He was still looking around, searching people's faces when a woman stepped forward. "It was I," she admitted. "I touched you."

She raised her hands to her face and then went on, "I'm sorry. I was so desperate. I've been sick for twelve years with bleeding that comes and goes but never stops altogether. I've spent all I have on doctors, but nothing's helped."

Momentarily, her voice caught in her throat. "When I heard what people were saying about you, I knew that even if I could just touch your clothing, I'd be healed."

Her voice rose. "And it's happened. I feel well again!"

Yeshu smiled warmly and responded, "Your faith has cured you, not I. Go in peace, free forever from this trouble."

As we walked on, he explained to the rest of us, "I turned and sought her out so she would know that she was whole."

I noticed Philippos walking next to Yeshu, his brow furrowed in thought. Looking back at where the woman had vanished into the crowd swarming after us, I puzzled over how Yeshu knew she had deliberately touched him. I was still chewing on that concern when we arrived at the home of Jairus.

We entered a small courtyard while the crowd milled around outside like a flood filling up the low ground around a hill. Relatives and friends in the courtyard were wailing Kaddish and sobbing. They cried out that the little girl was dead; hence the mourning chant.

Yeshu snapped around to catch Jairus' eye and said firmly, "Father, have faith."

Then he parted the curtain in the doorway and stepped into the house. Philippos and I pressed forward to follow him. Inside, Jairus' wife was being comforted by her mother and sisters, her aunts and cousins. She sat on the edge of a bed, wringing the useless hands in her lap as she gazed down in disbelief at the little three-year-old who lay there as still as stone.

Yeshu drew close, leaning over the girl. Then he asked, "Why all this lamentation? The child is not dead; she is deeply asleep."

Many of the women didn't know who Yeshu was. Turning to one another they laughed mockingly, almost angrily. Firmly, he asked everyone to step outside except for Jairus and his wife, plus Philippos and me.

Then he took the girl's small, pale hand in his own and said, "*Talitha koum*: Get up, my child."

The girl stirred and opened her eyes a crack. My own eyes gaped wide as the sky above Galilee.

Yawning, the girl sat up and looked first at Yeshu, then at Philippos and me, and finally at her stunned parents. Puzzled by all the attention, she rolled out of bed and began tottering around the room, looking for her favorite toy, perhaps to make sure it hadn't gotten lost with so many people around.

Her mother and father ran over and scooped her up in their arms. While we stood by, watching, the three of them laughed and talked as if just reunited after a long journey.

When the couple finally put their daughter down, Yeshu called them over, saying, "I ask only one thing of you: Tell no one what happened here today."

They looked at each other, then back toward Yeshu. He was already lowering his head to pass through the doorway.

Sensing their gaze, he turned around and said, "And be sure to give her something good to eat. She must be hungry."

Homecoming

Months on the road had left Yeshu drained as flat as a goatskin pouch that had once bulged with fine wine. Since we were not far from Nazareth, we went there to rest up. The home of Mama Ana and Mama Maria couldn't begin to hold everyone, even for a meal, so our band dispersed to houses throughout the village.

After putting it off as long as possible, I finally walked over to my parents' house. They were waiting, wondering if I would come. I suppose their anxiety pleased me. Certainly their attention made me happy. My father threw off his cloak, folded it into a cushion, and placed it on the wood bench for me to sit on. Meanwhile my mother bustled about, putting together my two favorite dishes: blackberries smothered with date honey atop a slab of spongy, unaged cheese; followed by fish stew with chopped olives and peas and a large slice of warmed bread.

As I munched, I felt my anger draining away. But that only made me call it back. It was like walking barefoot through a field of sharp stones.

We searched for something safe to talk about. The weather was over in a minute, so we talked for a while about my adventures with Yeshu and the others. I didn't say so, but it must have been clear I now had a new family. The unspoken question was whether I still had the old one.

I asked where my brother Aaron was, and my father explained that he was tending sheep in the high country and would be there for the next two weeks. Hearing that, I was pleased that my brother had taken over my old work.

Finally, my mother came and sat beside me. She took my hands in hers, and I looked down at our entwined fingers. From the corner of my eye, I could see my father leaning forward.

"Daavi, my son," my mother said softly. "People tell us that Yeshu is bringing many shining messages to the world. They say the one that most distinguishes him from all other messengers is his call for forgiveness."

My breathing stopped.

I was staring at my feet but I could tell she was looking straight at me.

"Daavi," she went on. "There's no simple way to say this. But it's the only way I can ask. Can you forgive your father and me?" she squeezed my hand imploringly. "We didn't act out of selfishness. We had nowhere else to turn. We talked about what to do for so long. Believe us, we thought at the time it was the right thing to do; really, our only recourse." She sighed heavily.

"Even now, I don't know another way," she said. "Please don't ask to know everything. It's not our place to tell you more than the little we know. There's already enough hurt as it is."

She paused.

"The important question is: Will you ever be able to forgive us?"

I stared at her hands holding mine. I wanted to pull mine away, but I simply could not. My father knelt beside my mother and placed his hands over hers. A tear spilled down my cheek, and I dared not look up into their faces, but I could hear their breath catching in their throats.

After a long while, I inhaled and exhaled deeply. Looking up at last, I said, "I'll do what I can to forgive you."

They nodded, and my mother said, "That's good enough for now." She smiled softly but sadly.

Tears welled up again in my eyes. I hugged my mother, then my father, but neither very tightly. Totally exhausted, I lay down in my old bed and soon tumbled into uneasy dreams.

~ ~ ~

The next day there were Shabbat services, so Yeshu went to the synagogue to teach. A large group gathered, most of them people I had known my whole life.

I was excited because I was not only Yeshu's friend, but a companion in his travels. I was sure people would greet him joyously, and that all my old pals would welcome me as a returning hero. I could not have been more wrong.

I took my seat among the congregation. From the start, I could hear the whispering, from one side and then another. "What makes *him* so special? How come he thinks he's so smart? What kind of tricks is he playing in these healings?

"He's just the village carpenter who ambled off whenever work got slow. What's this talk about some special calling? Wasn't being a laborer good enough for his father Yosef, whom everyone loved?

"And why would he leave his mother, who still has her home here among us? Is he somehow more special than his brothers Yehuda and Iacobus and Yosef and young Shimo?

"Shouldn't he be looking after his nephews by his sister, Netanya? Aren't they going to need to learn a trade soon? We could sure use someone new around here who would take care of our carpentry needs."

From my point of view, they were all acting like complete fools. Cautiously I looked around for my father. I knew he felt differently about Yeshu, but maybe he didn't want to show it in public. It was then I spotted him in the front row to the side, among the village leaders. I thought I saw a steely glint in his eye as he ignored the whispering, concentrating on what Yeshu had to say.

My mother sat across the room from him. When she looked in my direction, her eyes shone like Venus and Jupiter. I stared down at my feet, not sure what to think or do.

Later that day, Yeshu and I were walking along a path outside of town, looking for a spot we had often gone to with Yohanan to watch the first butterflies of spring and listen to the songbirds singing to their new hatchlings. Who knew that birds too had lullabies?

I gazed at the dried-up thistle Yeshu had plucked from the field. He was studying it, and turning it this way and that, touching it gingerly with his fingertips.

"He who might be a prophet, he said quietly, may eventually be held in honor elsewhere, but not among the people who should know him best, his neighbors and sometimes even members of his own family."

Not knowing what to say to him, I felt my jaws tighten. In the week of our stay, few Nazarenes were cured, and the crowds dwindled. Watching Yeshu closely during those days, wanting so badly to stick up for him, I felt powerless. I could see that in spite of his understanding he was disheartened by his neighbors' lack of faith, not in him but in God's plan for him.

Was it jealousy? Incredulity? Disavowal?

I felt confused and lost for lack of clarity, like that day the large cloud had enveloped us in dense fog on the way to the cedars of Lebanon.

Soon enough, our band packed up and moved on. I carried a heavy sadness away from there, as if I had just left a place I never totally belonged to.

I wondered if I would ever be back.

Mist and Embers

Early one sunny morning not long after leaving Nazareth, we approached a shallow stream and began to cross. Philippos went first, stepping carefully, as was his habit, from stone to stone. Unfortunately the stones were mossy, and still damp from last night's dew. When he had nearly reached the other side of the stream, Philippos slipped and lost his balance, regained it, then lost it again. His arms began swinging in ever widening circles as he desperately tried to get his slick sandal soles back under control.

We all stopped and watched, aghast. As his gargantuan feet slid completely out from under him on the wet stones, he arched backwards, his legs running momentarily in midair. Seeing serious Philippos so flailingly close to a total soaking sent the rest of us over the edge. We exploded with laughter.

That caused Philippos to twist his upper body around as he bore down on the water, looking sidelong at us with a puzzled anguish that seemed hopelessly funny. We roared even louder.

Philippos landed with an explosion of flying water and spray—no lightweight was he! For a moment we were all quiet, waiting to see what would happen next.

Up he popped in a frenzy of arms and legs, leaping to his feet as if trying to somehow avoid becoming completely soaked by standing upright as quickly as possible. The water only reached his knees, which punctuated the hilarious uselessness of it all. He could have hiked up his cloak and waded across the stream, remaining almost totally dry. He stood glaring at us, and whatever was left of our composure was swept away by another wave of laughter.

Philippos' eyes, wide as soldiers' shields, searched our faces with a fierce resolve to salvage what remained of his dignity. Maybe there was someone who hadn't noticed. We were a band of daydreamers, after all. And if a few of the people present were the caring type, at least one or more faces should be throwing out a line of support by showing sympathy for his plight.

To his obvious amazement even the gigglers were now hooting. His face reddening with shame, fury washed over Philippos. He shook his arms like a bear fighting a swarm of angry bees and let out a growl between clenched teeth. This only served to feed our laughter. In spite of ourselves, not a single one of us could regain control.

"Stop it!" he yelled. "And get me out of here, now!"

Poor Philippos stood waiting, hands on hips, his dripping head cocked to one side. His hopes were now dashed for erasing his misery by pretending that nothing had happened, so he was offering to accept our apology if we came to his rescue.

Weak with laughter, we fell to our knees, howling helplessly. Philippos made no move to finish the last few feet of his crossing. Looking like a wet cat climbing out of a cistern into which it's fallen, he was staring in disbelief at Yeshu.

Even as he stammered nonsensically, Philippos' unspoken thoughts were written plainly across his face: Can't you control your own naughty children?

The dripping bear looked away and right back again, still seeming to chew on his distress: what ever happened to compassion for all, no matter what?

Since Philippos had too much respect for authority to voice his hurt directly to Yeshu, he did the next best thing. Seeing his brother Nathanyel, Philippos scrambled over to the muddy bank where he filled both hands with rich, brown muck.

"Now stop that, Brother," he howled, "or I'll let this fly at you!"

Nathanyel was powerless to stop anything for the moment. All he could do was call out to Philippos, between spurts of laughter, "As a boy you could never...hit a lake with a rock...so why should I think...your aim is any better now?"

That did it. Peaceful, staid Philippos bawled out, "You were always the golden one. Let's see how shining you are this time!" And he let fly with both hands at once.

All eyes followed the two muddy globs sailing toward Nathanyel. One smacked into his forehead and began rapidly slithering down, and the other hit him right in the paunch, forming a great oval stain on his robe.

The gallery cheered wildly. Suddenly the tables had been turned. But a sense of doom colored our voices as each of us looked about for safe position and foothold. Everyone knew the unavoidable was nearly upon us. Pandemonium!

And so it happened. Nathanyel leapt into the water and ducked his head under to wash the brown slime from his brow and eyes. Once he was finished he glanced over at Philippos, and as family will often do, the two of them turned toward us as if we were all hooligans.

It was too late to flee, but we tried anyway. Mud and water rained down on us before we could stop crashing into each other in our vain attempts to scramble far from the bank.

There was nothing left to do: we all leapt into the stream. The women were in before the men, and we proceeded to thoroughly soak and cover one another with handfuls, and sometimes robes full, of muck and water.

Whooping and a fine spray rose skyward. A thin rainbow formed in the rising mist, which not one soul even noticed, except for a lone shepherd boy who passed nearby and stopped to gape at the free sideshow.

As often happens, exhaustion was the only force able to bring chaos to an end. On hands and knees we crawled out of the water onto the opposite bank, dog-tired and panting like oxen.

Stripping to our undergarments—women upstream, men downstream—we gave everything a good washing, laid it all out on the massive boulders lining the stream, and sunned ourselves dry.

That night we sat unusually close to one another around the campfire. Everyone, including Yeshu, went over to Philippos, put an arm around him, and begged forgiveness. With each of us, he let his lower lip creep out, as he was accustomed to do, and looking away, nodded ever so slightly. But gradually a smile that only children know lit his face as he basked in our attention while we rewrote history, agreeing what a good sport he had been.

Then Martha began singing. One ancient Hebrew song followed another. A ballad of two brothers made me think of Nathanyel storming to Philippos' aid. Caught off guard, tears came to my eyes, and I stared hard into the fire so no one would notice.

My mind was dwelling upon my own brother Aaron, and what I wouldn't give to somehow help my sister. Usually I thought of her only before falling asleep, but here she was, even though I was still wide-awake. I imagined slipping my hand into hers, and saw her smile. Then she rose and vanished into the smoke as it spiraled upward in the darkness.

After a while, I looked around at the others. The Thunder Brothers sat back to back, leaning against one another like two trees growing out of one stump. Martha and Shimón Petros, who for days had been nagging each other like an itch they couldn't stop scratching, perched next to one another, telling jokes and trading stories about their childhoods. We all listened in, as they knew we would.

Yeshu lay stretched out on his back, staring at the night sky, his head on Maria Magdalena's knapsack, while she sat nearby, combing the knots out of her hair with long brush strokes. I watched the comb sweep slowly down and outward...down and outward...and felt my eyes close. In my mind I followed sparks from the fire as they flew upward, salting the sky with even more constellations.

After a time, I realized the talking had stopped.

Then I heard a rustling and opened my eyes. Yeshu was sitting up; next he was on his knees and rising slowly to his feet. He stood there silently, gazing at the embers in the dying blaze. I could see that everyone was awake, watching him. His chest rhythmically rose and fell as he gathered his thoughts.

When he finally spoke, tiredness tinged his voice. Thinking back on this later, I can see how he must have been weighing what he was about to say ever since we left Nazareth. Probably waiting for the right time, when we were ready to grapple with it.

The morning's fun at the stream had brought us closer together. It had made us stronger, more open to hearing the news he was bringing, which turned out to be unsettling, even a little scary.

Yeshu inhaled one more time, at length. He folded his arms over his chest and began.

"A time of testing is near," he said. "Some will find a way through, others will stray." He paused.

"All of you will live lives that make a difference in the hearts and minds of others, but not in the ways you might imagine. You will be afraid in the days to come, but the only thing to fear, when all is said and done, is your own wavering."

He gave us time before going on. "Those who keep their eyes on the center of our path, and their heads up, will survive and thrive."

A stunned silence hung over us, broken only by the crackling and hissing as the last of the wood slowly burned down to glowing coals and ash.

Yeshu's face was no longer visible when Martha asked, "But Yeshu, why do you tell us this?" Her voice trembled. "Have you had a premonition, a vision?"

He would say no more.

~ ~ ~

All of us were troubled but also very tired. As our exhaustion slid down around us like a dark curtain, we dropped into a sound sleep. Several had dreams worth sharing the next morning.

For my part, I spent the night falling in and out of a tangle of what were actually nightmares. I was running from house to house, trying to warn mothers that soldiers were coming for their newborn boys, but no matter how hard I knocked, no one opened their doors. Then I was waving goodbye to Yohanan as he disappeared into the wilderness and greeting him as he came out again to preach his message. I spotted Temple guards in the crowd wearing cloaks over their armor and tried to point them out, but no matter how hard I tried, my arm wouldn't lift.

At that I saw Yeshu, radiant, teaching a mass of people covering a hillside like so many lilies. A great storm cloud arose and Yeshu stealthily vanished into the flowering crowd. I tried to follow to make sure he was safe, but I couldn't find his face among the many that were waving wildly on their stems in the howling wind.

For a long while after waking up, I wondered: when it was my time to be called out, would I turn and flee? Would I run from the oppressors of the spirit? Or would I hide away deep inside of me, running from the spirit itself? And if I did, would the spirit remember me when it was safe to emerge again?

I decided that somehow I would have to find ground to stand on and defend. I'd already lost enough with Shoshana and Yohanan to know that I couldn't save myself if I couldn't protect those I loved.

I knew now what I would do. I would follow right behind Yeshu wherever he went and help him share his far-reaching message with all who stood ready for it.

The Wedding Feast

The following day our journey resumed. As I walked, I brooded on my life and how insignificant it seemed. What could a young and homeless leatherworker ever amount to? Would I manage to grow into someone able to make a mark on the world around me, or even my village? Could I truly be of any service to Yeshu?

I felt so many deep rivers flowing within and around me. But what could I do today—right now—to help my soul grow richer? How could I perhaps feel I was riding those rivers to some brighter destination?

The answer seemed beyond my reach. Like grasping for a fistful of smoke.

That afternoon, as we were approaching a small village, we heard what sounded like a wedding feast. Yeshu never missed a chance to go to a party—he loved to dance and to talk—so he sent Joanna and Martha ahead to ask if visitors were welcome. They came hurrying back urging us to come along; the celebration was warming up and we were heartily invited. Luckily a wealthy wheat farmer had recently given us twenty loaves of barley bread, so we didn't arrive empty-handed.

As soon as we got to the village square, three couples recognized Yeshu and hurried over with young children for him to bless. Several people from the wedding party scolded them for bothering such a prominent guest, and that got him riled.

"Let me see these children up close," he said reproachfully. "As I have said many times before, don't ever block a child's way. Remember, God is one with beings such as these."

That said, Yeshu led the children over to a mulberry tree and took turns lifting them into the branches so they could pluck and eat the ripe, purple fruit.

One small boy, when it was his turn, began stuffing mulberries into Yeshu's mouth. Yeshu gobbled them down, smiling broadly and opening his mouth for more, like a fledgling partridge being fed by its mother. His mouth was soon stained a dark purple.

Then all at once I heard a song starting up, so I left Yeshu and strolled over to listen. Several women were singing with their backs toward me. The one with the sweetest voice turned slightly and looked to the side. My heart leapt in my chest like that same partridge fleeing its leafy hideaway. The profile of the chin and the nose—could it be Shoshana? Could I even hope?

I rushed over to get a closer view. My eagerness must have startled her because she turned and looked me full in the face. I stopped short, my eyes wide in anticipation, which made her smile.

Instantly my heart plummeted farther than it had dared to soar only moments before. Her smile was broken by large gaps between her front teeth, larger than any I had ever seen in someone so young, and totally unlike how Shoshana would look, even after all this time.

Clearly she was not my sister, and I was a fool.

And then it hit me. Would I know Shoshana if I saw her? Would she know me? I was such a pup when she left. She was young, too. How had life changed *her*?

The woman stared at me questioningly, but kept on singing. I turned aside, took in a gulp of air, and let it out gradually.

In an attempt to clear my mind, I strolled around and chatted aimlessly with the other guests. One of them told me about an ancient man who was present at the feast. He was over one-hundred-and-ten years old and had accomplished many things for his family and village. After telling this to Joanna and the Thunder Brothers, the four of us decided to search him out.

We found the elder under a tall, majestic poplar tree, near the garden wall. Sitting by his side was a small girl, probably his great-great-granddaughter. She was cooling him with a cotton fan that she dipped in water whenever it became dry.

The old man was smiling broadly, eyes closed, enjoying the breeze.

Thunder James had brought along a small pottery cup brimming with new wine. Before we could speak, the old man opened his eyes. He must have felt us approach. James leaned down and handed him the wine. The old man bowed his head in thanks.

He drank from the cup with closed eyes, letting the final drop slide off the lip of the lifted vessel and onto the tip of his tongue. Then he opened his eyes again, to see what we had come for.

Thunder John said, "We have a question for you, grandfather. That is, if it wouldn't be a bother?"

The old man leaned forward slightly and raised a single eyebrow in anticipation.

John looked at James who looked at Joanna and me. I looked back at John.

It was Joanna who finally said something. "We want to know what we should do to live a life as long and full as yours."

The old man said nothing for quite a while. Most likely he had been asked this before and knew his prolonged pause would whet our thirst for the answer.

Finally he spoke, with a voice that sounded like a saw passing slowly through a green log.

"Three things," he said. "First, drink nothing but herbal teas, day and night. Second, have five wives and no children. And third, if you sleep with an olive in your mouth, time stops."

We all just stared at one another. When finally the little girl stifled a giggle, the Thunder Brothers burst into laughter, and Joanna joined them. I quickly looked at the old man's eyes and saw the twinkle there.

As the hilarity subsided, he grinned—three teeth—and gradually turned serious. His face was calm and a tender radiance emanated from beneath the skin. A faraway look crossed his eyes like a thin curtain of mist.

We waited.

After what seemed like an eternity of silence, the curtain parted and he raised a single finger, looked up at us, and smiled.

Then he spoke again, selecting his words carefully.

Every day,
    see God,
    feel love.

Run! Yeshu, Run!

During the weeks that ensued, I wondered whether the old man's few words had given us enough to really munch on. But the more I pondered his counsel, the more I realized if I only did what he said, then like blooms opening up after spring rain, everything else would flower.

See God. Feel love. Each and every day. The harvest would be armfuls of bountiful action.

There was never enough time for mulling over such things, however. Towards the end of a long string of teaching and healing visits, we arrived at the edge of yet another village. Yeshu had just begun speaking in an open field that was waiting to be planted in wheat, when we spotted a column of soldiers heading straight toward us from around a bend just down the road. Surely they were coming after him.

The crowd he was preaching to suddenly opened up, and a boy several years my junior burst out. He grabbed Yeshu by the sleeve, tugged him toward the gap in the crowd, and the two of them began to run. Somehow Yeshu wordlessly knew he should pay attention to this young messenger.

Since I was standing right beside Yeshu as he preached that morning, I ran with them, believing today was my chance to help save him. People quickly parted and just as quickly closed ranks behind us as we ran.

It was not long before we came to the edge of a cliff. We stood staring down at least a hundred feet to a rocky stream.

"Now we're goners," I muttered under my breath.

However, someone quickly handed a rope to Yeshu, and in a flash he jumped over the side! I saw that the taut rope was tied securely around a nearby boulder, and when the rope went slightly slack, a man I had never seen before knelt down, untied it, and threw it over the cliff just as the soldiers arrived.

I was sure they were going to take me away like they did my father and try to make me tell them where Yeshu and his other supporters were. But strong hands grabbed me by the shoulders, pulling me away from the cliff's edge. Suddenly I found myself wrapped in a woman's shawl and headdress and forced into a sitting position in the middle of a group of ancient grandmothers. In unison, they all began hugging me and wailing the Kaddish prayer as if someone had died.

Hunkering down there among these women, I felt as vulnerable as the wriggling caterpillars Yohanan had rescued from the road years before, to save them from being flattened by so many heavy feet tramping by.

Later that evening, back in the wealthy farmer's stable where most of us were staying, I lay on my back staring up at the sliver of moon that shone through a high window. I was still trying to calm my heartbeat.

Had I aided the carpenter or not? It seemed doubtful. Perhaps I could have done more. But what...?

With luck, our celebration of Rosh Hodesh would bring me answers, but I wished this time the crescent moon were rising, not setting. Asleep in the hay that night, I dreamt of another time, running through crowded streets in Jerusalem, with people signaling us to turn down a narrow alley...duck into a doorway...cross a courtyard...go over a wall. There we lay stock still for hours in complete silence. After that escape, I began shaking and couldn't stop. In the dream, I quaked so hard I woke myself up.

The next morning Yeshu showed up at the stable, and I told him how afraid I had been, how afraid I still was.

"We could lose you just like we lost Yohanan!"

There, I'd said it.

Yeshu studied me for a long time.

Then he took me by the shoulders, and looking deep into my eyes as only he could, he said softly, "But Daavi, you will never lose me. Don't be afraid. I'll always be in here," and he laid his hand on my chest.

I felt the warmth.

"Fear is a viper," he said. "Staring into its eyes too long will paralyze you. You have wings, my friend. Never forget that you can soar because your soul is free. The sky is vast but a bird on the wind always knows the way home."

Removing his hand and lightly tapping himself on the chest twice, he added, "You will always be welcome *here* my young friend, my companion in work and in travel."

I nodded faintly, but rather than a winging thrush, my mind was a swarm of pestering crows. Losing Yeshu was unthinkable, not just for me but for all of us. Someone had to keep watch.

I fixed my gaze and once more silently swore I would never allow what I feared most to *ever* come to pass.

Clown of God

Our band never missed Pesakh week in Jerusalem, and since the time was fast approaching, we headed off in that direction. All of us loved going to the Temple and sharing the Passover meal together. I was especially looking forward to our Seder feast that year, the third one we had celebrated since Yeshu set out with us on his mission of teaching and healing.

Having just turned seventeen, I finally felt I was no longer the kid in the group but simply a young member. Our work was laid out before us; the way had opened, and I looked forward to growing into the prime of my life like Yeshu. At thirty-three years of age, he had accumulated vast storehouses of wisdom and experience, and he was poised to devote thirty-three more to serving our people and all humanity.

Only a day away from Jerusalem, I was sitting with the Thunder Brothers by a brook next to our campsite. Mama Maria was there, too, having joined the last leg of the journey to observe Pesakh with us. We had all kicked off our sandals and were soaking our hot feet in the water. We talked quietly. Every so often someone laughed, at times for no apparent reason. It's easy to laugh when you're dangling your feet in a cool stream.

Staring at the water, I became lost in my musings. I can't even recall where my mind was wandering. Most likely I was backtracking through time.

Just think about it: Four years ago I was in the cedars of Lebanon. Nine years ago I saw Shoshana for the last time. Ten years back I talked to Yeshu standing in a field of wheat. How far I had come, and yet how far there was to go.

An unknowable amount of burbling water had flowed past my feet by the time a butterfly landed on my hand, walked the length of my thumb, and flew off. I looked up to see Thunder James studying me.

"Back from the dream world?" he asked.

Then he smiled that huge smile, down inside his fiery beard. His smile had a way of broadening so wide that it pushed his cheeks out and his bronze eyebrows up until he looked like an owl settling in a tree at sunrise. He winked, and I chuckled at the thought of an owl dreaming while the sun came wide-awake.

James always made me laugh and he saw a chance to do it again. Laughter is one of the few treasures that can lift our burdens, and James loved to fill others with it. In an eyeblink, he raised a hand to the sky, his baggy sleeve sliding down below his elbow, and he was off on a roll. But this time his object of attention was someone harder to set off.

"Once there was a woman," he began, "I believe her name was Marona or Mahalia, or maybe Maria. No matter; it was some bunch of sounds between an M and an A."

He glanced sideways at Mama Maria, who sat on a rock, staring off into the distance, biting fixedly on her lower lip.

"Anyway..." he shook his head in mock exasperation, "once upon a time, there was this *nameless* woman who dreamt that she was traveling down a long, dusty road, when all of a sudden she saw a dazzling butterfly approaching her, beating the air with light, diaphanous wings...."

Suddenly his brow wrinkled and he began rubbing his hairy chin. "Humph," he grunted, "or was it the other way around?"

Thunder James leaned over and looked at Mama Maria. She was trying hard not to laugh, but finally she could contain herself no longer and sputtered into the back of her hand. "Just you wait," she said. "When you least expect it, I'll put *you* in a backwards story."

As she reached over and tugged on his rusty beard with both hands, they each knew he had won this round, dragging her away for a bit from her worries.

It was hard to believe that before meeting Yeshu, Thunder James was a fearfully violent man. Thunder John, too. Both of them always getting into scraps, and trying to wriggle out of them by wrestling opponents to the ground. These two boisterous fishermen were among my favorites. They had turned their lives completely around the day they uncovered what Yeshu had to offer them.

Just like he'd done with Andrew and Shimón Petros, Yeshu had walked up to the two brothers one evening as they dried their nets by Lake Galilee. After the three of them chatted for a while, staring languidly out at the swells in the water, Yeshu suddenly turned to clap each of them on the shoulder at once, saying:

"Fishermen brothers, join with me and be fishers of men. You will cast your nets into a sea of faces listening to us on the hillsides. There you will capture hearts and souls, and pull in their minds."

Today, however, James had a singular audience on his mind. He was determined to seize his advantage and make Yeshu's mother laugh freely. He knew she was still preoccupied by concern for her eldest son, and he wanted to whisk away the curtain of darkness.

In a flash, Thunder James sprang to his feet and began to walk around the campsite like a seasick sailor, his knees and legs becoming as pliable as wet ropes. Mama Maria collapsed in laughter.

Rather than lie back and bask in such an easy victory, James piled on. He began by mimicking specific people's walks. First, he did *her* walk, shouting out, "Okay, who's *this*?"

And off he went around the campfire, taking small mincing steps. "Like a red fox on hot rocks," he chirped.

Recognizing herself, Mama Maria raised her hands to cover her face, and her shoulders shook with laughter.

Next he did Maria Magdalena, legs treading firmly, left arm swinging way, way back, then stopping on the downswing right in front of her hip.

Just when I hoped I might escape unscathed, he really laid it on me, trotting like a puppy behind an imaginary Yeshu. And, of course, he topped it off doing Yeshu himself: huge stride, both arms swinging like the boom of a sailboat.

James mimicked animals, too. He did a pregnant camel that got everyone howling. Especially when it thrust its nose under the side of a tent, looking for food, and brought the entire thing down to the ground, wrapping up the camel and the people inside.

His mouse was hysterical, in every way imaginable.

Of course, he didn't just do others—his best stuff was aimed at himself.

"This is *me* doing Yeshu," Thunder James said.

And somehow he looked only half Yeshu's size, but his stride was twice as long. We all laughed even louder.

Egged on, he got more creative.

"Here I am disappearing into the distance," he whinnied, seeming to become a small figure on the horizon.

"And now I'm returning," he bellowed, miraculously marching back, all within the space of the campsite.

Judah stood up, as if to leave. "How about one where you disappear into the distance and *never* return?"

A hush fell over all of us.

Then it was Judah's turn to shake with laughter, combing his fingers through his tangled hair, and we saw that he was only joking. Everyone joined in, and we felt closeness again.

Thunder James continued, with renewed enthusiasm.

"Here's me going uphill," and a mountain seemed to rise up in front of him.

"Me going downhill," and he was scrambling down an incline, nearly falling.

"With the wind in my face," and he slowed almost to a stop.

"With the wind at my back," and he hustled right out of the campsite.

Yeshu, wiping his eyes and convulsed with laughter, cheered and clapped, along with the rest of us. Thunder James reentered the campsite, making theatrical gestures for all of us to halt our display of adulation.

Slowly, Philippos stood up.

"Why is this funny?" he asked.

And everyone roared again.

When the hullabaloo finally died down, James abruptly became serious. He made a sweeping gesture with his hands to indicate that he was finished for the moment with foolishness. Then he looked back toward me, made his way over, and sat down.

"So, Daavi, tell us about dreamtime."

"Some people say I dream too much," I answered hesitantly, "and laugh too often."

"I, for one, am happy to know you're dreaming," James replied.

"People who are starved of dreams see little," he went on. "They have trouble imagining the future. It's hard for them to visualize themselves as different. Or the world as anything other than what it is right now. Consider this: these folks can be like bows with no bowstring, their arrows going nowhere.

"We need dreamers, Daavi. Our people need dreamers."

At that, Judah came over, sat down, and began listening closely.

Thunder James kept talking. "We need laugh-makers too. Laugh-makers bring joy. They open the cage so the rest of us can extend our wings and fly, free of care. But birds have to land somewhere, right? Laugh-makers nudge and poke and tickle and relax us, until *poof!* Suddenly, in a flash we see ourselves, and where we fit into this world, differently."

He paused and grabbed a fistful of beard, pulling on it pensively.

"I believe that's one way people grow. And hearts expand."

He looked around at all of us and sighed.

"And then there is heartache. Dreaming and laughing are lifeboats that carry us over the dark waves of what can seem like unending pain."

At that point, Judah broke in, "Grow up, James! Struggle is how we move into the future. And endurance—better yet, rebellion—is how we survive pain. But you...you choose to act like a clown before God.

"*When,*" he demanded, bushy eyebrows pumping, "are you ever going to get serious? Don't you know we are being watched? Judged?" Judah was all but yelling.

"Can't you get it through your head that we're locked in a life-or-death struggle?" now he was pacing back and forth.

"There are people out there—*our* people—who are suffering." He threw up his hands and gasped."And you spend your time, and ours, joking!"

James stared at Judah until I thought he was going to hand him a quick fist for lunch.

Finally, James spoke. "Okay, Mister Martyr. You, who know better and therefore haven't listened to a single thing Yeshu has said. Just keep pushing your boulder up the mountainside. But try not to get crushed when you slip and it comes crashing down again, rolling right over the top of you." James halted for emphasis. "And maybe over Yeshu and the rest of us, too."

Judah glared. At everyone and no one.

James shook his head. "I hope I never ever get serious," he sputtered, "the way you want. Our true struggle is to clear a path that makes us fully alive, rather than offering a false choice between life and death. Our way allows people to be vibrant, by affirming life in one another. The other way, Judah, the way the people you meet with at night are choosing, turns life *into* death.

"You people are turning your hearts into pieces of granite for crushing the Romans and their toads, and you don't even see what you're doing to yourselves. Someday you, Judah, may need that heart, warm and full of lifeblood, and what will it be?"

I looked quickly across the brook, where Yeshu was starting the cooking fire for our evening meal. He was listening intently, but saying nothing.

Judah turned away from Thunder James and spit into the water. "It's no boulder I'm pushing against," he said. "No, it's rockheads like you."

And he walked off.

Without even getting up, Thunder James momentarily mimed Judah's walk—all shoulders and hips. We burst into a brief guffaw. Judah didn't look back.

Then James returned his attention to the rest of us and resumed speaking. "Some people," he winked, "just don't get it. I'm usually being most serious when I'm being funny."

He looked away for a moment. "And the more serious things get, the more we need to laugh!"

"Besides," he went on, "Remember what it says in the *Mishlei*, the Book of Proverbs.

> Even in laughter the heart may grieve,
> and mirth may end in sorrow.

He fell silent for a bit, looking down at his hands, which lay palms up on his massive thighs. When he finally spoke, it was quietly, with no joking.

"God put me on this earth to make people laugh.

"Every time I make someone laugh—a child, a sick person, someone who is afraid or in pain—God gets happy. It's a very straight path.

"But it's more than that," he went on. "Laughter and love are twin sisters, like two fast friends facing one another. I always laugh before and after I hug someone.

"And you know something else?" He looked at each of us again.

"Laughter defines the moment just before spiritual awakening. Someone laughs: a window opens in heaven."

He looked upward and shrugged lightly. "Those are the reasons why I clown around," he said. "It's that simple." He shrugged again. "Someone's laughing. God gets happy." He smacked both hands down on his knees. He was done.

My thoughts sailed back into my childhood, seeking out my Gramma Ruth and how we laughed with her: Aaron, Shoshana, and I. And, I now realized, with God.

Yeshu stood up from the campfire, and made his way across the stream.

"Well, you brothers sure make me laugh. Boanerges, oh Sons of Thunder, you sons of Zebedee, I love you for it." He leaned down, wrapping his arms around Thunder James, and squeezed. We could hear the breath rush out of both of them.

"It's a gift," Yeshu said, "and for that I thank you."

James sat there with his face lit up like a contented five-year-old. John, too. If I hadn't loved them both so much, I would have been jealous.

The Aged Rabbi

Having arrived in Jerusalem the night before, we were up early in the morning, my favorite time in the city. But once again, every street corner was full of Roman legionnaires. Clearly, the commanders reasoned that the weeks before and during Passover were dangerous times, for they always sent extra soldiers at Pesakh. They would never ever understand us, it seems.

Keeping to the back streets, our ragtag band made its way to the Temple to pray. Just inside the main door, we saw a rabbi sitting on a wooden stool, wearing long black robes, his white beard falling all the way to his lap. He was smiling as if he had been waiting for us. He nodded our way several times.

Yeshu went over and sat at his feet. We all followed suit.

"Rabbi," Yeshu asked, "given what is going on in the world today, what advice do you have for our Jewish people?"

Yeshu was looking into the rabbi's eyes and returning his smile. "Teach us," he implored.

"I do not believe myself worthy to teach to you," the rabbi answered. "You are the master here."

"Nonsense," said Yeshu, laughing. "You're either mistaken, or you're being too modest."

"Look at Daavi." He pointed my way. "Even the youngest among us teach the others."

"As a boy, Daavi taught me about shepherding: How to feed an orphaned baby lamb by soaking the tip of your sleeve in milk and letting the newborn suckle. How the shepherd always cares for the lambs first.

How he never fails to seek out a lost sheep, no matter what."

The old rabbi tilted his head, and his eyes twinkled.

Yeshu implored him again, "Teach us, Rabbi."

The rabbi smiled broadly at Yeshu, and then became serious.

"There are two great challenges facing us as a people," he said, his hands drifting up out of his dark sleeves like morning mist from a pair of rain barrels.

"The first is to maintain our spiritual roots in right living and love."

We all murmured our agreement. I saw Judah reach out to touch the rabbi's robe. Shimón Petros was beaming as he awaited the next morsel of counsel.

I stole a look at Yeshu. His eyes were locked on the rabbi's face, and he had touched his fingertips together as though in prayer.

The rabbi continued, "The second is to struggle against all oppression without becoming like our oppressors."

He emphasized the final word by pressing a fist into his open hand.

"For if our struggle turns us into people like our oppressors, then" he said, pointing at his heart, "then we are not only defeated, but lost!"

His gaze brushed over each face in our band.

"When your persecutor is dead and your heart has become a stone, who is left to hurl it against? One another? A new enemy?"

In the hush that followed, he turned both palms toward us and lowered his hands. Remembering what James had said, I glanced over at Judah who was now staring into his lap and chewing on a thumb.

Yeshu bowed his head and whispered earnestly, "Thank you, Rabbi."

Then gesturing toward himself and the rest of us, Yeshu said, "You have taught us with great wisdom, Abba. We should always listen closely to wise fathers like you. You have blessed us."

The rabbi's smile returned. He continued gazing at Yeshu.

"I know you," he said simply.

Yeshu looked back at him quizzically.

"Yes, I know you, Yeshu of Nazareth, son of Yosef and Maria.

"At the moment you are teaching by listening. But you made quite an impression in this very place with your words, some twenty years ago. You held a dozen of us rabbis captive for three days with your questions about the Laws and the Prophets—most of which you had answers for yourself!"

A smile flickered across Yeshu's face. He placed one hand high on his forehead and closed his eyes.

"We talked about you for some time after that." The old man smiled broadly. "I called you the 'boy rabbi.' What were you, twelve years old?"

Yeshu nodded. "My father was still alive then."

His eyes opened again and wandered around the Temple walls, then back to the aged rabbi.

"You called him Abba Yosef," said the rabbi. He was so proud of you when he finally found you with us, holding a circle of us rabbis spellbound. I thought his face was going to float off his head and soar right up into the dome of the Temple."

Yeshu glanced upward and his eyes shown like the first crocuses of springtime.

I Dream

That night I dreamt that Yeshu was challenged by two figures. First it was a Roman magistrate. Then came the High Priest of the Temple. The Roman accused him of forming a mob to spread dissent, which was forbidden by the Empire. The High Priest recited holy law to prove Yeshu was wrong to eat with unwashed sinners and to heal people on the Sabbath.

Yeshu stood his ground firmly, shaking his head back and forth at each accusation. He turned full round to face the crowd that had gathered and resumed his teaching, as though this day was any other day. This place, any place.

At that, a short, lean man stepped out and stood smiling in front of Yeshu. His head was completely bald, and his ears stuck out like Jerusalem's main gates when they're open. He carried a simple staff, and he had large, liquid eyes.

This man wore only a white cloth wrapped round his waist and loins, with the end of it thrown over one shoulder. His arms and legs were thin as apple saplings, and his skin was smooth and tawny like the clay bottom of the creek that ran through the olive grove behind my uncle's house.

In my dream, I was puzzled. This diminutive man did not look like a Jew or a member of any of the other peoples that I'd met on our travels. Maybe he was a fourth Magi!

He stood quietly with slightly bowed head, holding his hands in front of his chest, palms facing each other and pressed together. Then he slowly lowered his head until his two pointer fingers lightly touched his forehead.

I looked to see what Yeshu made of it. He took a step forward, and his lips formed an even broader smile. The two embraced.

I said to Yeshu, "You greeted him like a close friend, but he's a complete stranger."

"He's a brother," Yeshu responded. "My brother in peace. He struggles against injustice, and for freedom. Against a giant empire, while armed only with love and soul force."

My dream shifted to a crowded city square. The small, clay-colored stranger was lying on a raised bed in the open air, his body covered with sweet-smelling flowers. I saw a round, red spot on his forehead, between the eyes that were now closed. Pressing around him were thousands of weeping people. Suddenly the flowers burst into flame, and the people let out a gasp. The man must have been a king or a great hero.

Then I caught sight of a tiny woman in a long white robe, moving slowly through the crowd. She wore a headscarf of the same cloth, with blue stripes across the forehead. There were many hungry and shivering people in the crowd, and she gave each of them water from a cup and poured what smelled like steaming barley porridge into their bowls. When they had wounds, she put ointments on them and applied bandages.

She hugged every person she touched, but very gently as if to preserve her strength. Each time she fed or touched or tended to someone, she looked toward Yeshu.

Finally, she sat on a small stool that another woman, dressed just like her, had placed behind her. Immediately she was surrounded by children, who played with her hands and tucked wisps of her gray hair back underneath her white headscarf. Whether tending to others, or letting herself be tended to, she never stopped smiling.

I turned to Yeshu. "Is she some kind of a servant? Or healer?"

He answered swiftly, "Both."

Then the crowed parted and out stepped a man who looked like an Ethiopian. He had large, dark eyes, a gracefully sloping forehead, and close-cropped hair. He reached his hands out, and so did Yeshu. Their palms touched.

I stared at the muscular wrists of the ebony-skinned man. They were encircled by welts like my father's. But the hands moved freely, like sunlight on water. And at his feet lay broken links of chain.

The man had a face that dreams seemed to dance across. He leaned his head back and closed his eyes as if deep in a distant reverie. His mouth appeared to be singing.

When I turned to look at the crowd, I saw Yeshu standing, pressed within the masses, radiant with the hues of the three figures.

My dream ended like a water pot crashing to the floor. I saw that I had overslept; the sun was already climbing the sky.

I was completely confused, so I went looking for Yeshu and found him with Thunder John. I immediately told the two of them my dream, complete with all the details I could recall.

They both listened intently, never once taking their eyes from my face. When I finished, they looked at each other for a long time. Yeshu gestured toward John with a hand, and John shrugged his shoulders slightly.

Yeshu turned back to me. "That's a wonderful dream."

"But what does it mean?" I asked.

"I'm not sure I know," said Yeshu, with a pensive smile on his lips. "Each time one person steps off the path, another steps on."

He looked over at Thunder John. "John, you usually understand dreams better than anyone. What do you think?"

Thunder John responded, "I confess, I'm also baffled."

While John ruminated, he rubbed his chin and scratched the nape of his neck. "I do know when dreams are vivid but difficult to understand, they often turn out to be about the future. Dreams about the past are easier to read. But ones from the future can stump the wisest among us because we recognize so little of what we're seeing."

He looked up at a white egret soaring over our heads, then back at me.

"What I see in the images you've painted for us is a thread between Yeshu and three special people: a linkage of peacemakers. Perhaps you were dreaming of dreamers! Be sure to tell us if they return."

"Or whenever you have dreams as striking as this one, Daavi," added Yeshu." Never forget what Thunder James said at the campsite on our journey to Jerusalem, about the importance of envisioning.

"A soul like yours," Yeshu said, "is an answer to the warning that rings out in the Mishlei, the Book of Proverbs."

> Where there is no vision,
>
> the people perish.

I was elated. Rarely had anyone taken this much interest in my dreaming. When I was a kid, most of the adults in Nazareth had called me absent-minded or a breezy-head. So usually I just kept my dreams to myself. But this was different.

Yeshu, in the days to come, and Thunder John for years after, continued to be interested in what I dreamt about. They believed I had the power to travel into other times and places and see things others didn't see, all inside my mind.

I Am Called Daavi

Less than a week before Passover was to begin, we left the city once more. The representatives of several villages to the east of Jerusalem had made a fervent request for Yeshu to visit them and continue with his teachings. Interest in Yeshu's message was reaching a crescendo. Every day people knocked at Joanna's door to make similar requests. But this invitation was special. Many people had already gathered in anticipation of hearing Yeshu speak. We would have to hurry; the Sabbath would begin just before sundown.

Once there, Yeshu taught the crowd with stories for hours, asking and answering questions in between lessons. Completely drained of strength, he took his leave just as the sun disappeared below the hills.

The villagers lodged us in their mud brick homes, and the next day we prayed and rested until Shabbat ended at sundown.

At dawn on the following day, we arose and ate a simple breakfast of sweetened goat's milk, parched corn, and lentils. Upon finishing, we said our good-byes and headed back to Jerusalem.

Arriving at the city gates at midday, we were just completing our ritual purification in the mikveh when we discovered that a wealthy farmer had a donkey waiting to carry Yeshu into the city.

A bit bemused by this overture, Yeshu offered it to each of us in turn, but everyone demurred. So, finally he gave in, mounted the animal and rode through the gates, touching the mezuzah on the wall as he passed by.

Then almost immediately he halted the donkey and insisted that we all walk ahead of him.

"That way no one will suffer the indignity," he said, "of stepping in any of several gifts our brother donkey might leave behind him in the road."

Chuckling, we all complied. But then something totally unexpected happened. People began to pour out of their shops and homes to welcome Yeshu. Word seemed to race ahead of us that the carpenter-preacher, cousin to the murdered Yohanan, had arrived in Jerusalem.

Soon throngs of people lined the streets. Some were pushing and shoving, just to get a glimpse at Yeshu or touch his arm or shoulder. Many of them appeared to be craftsmen and mothers of small children, but there also were quite a few travelers on their Pesakh pilgrimages. They shouted greetings to Yeshu, and some of them even lay palm fronds in front of him for the donkey to walk over.

Looking through the crowds, I thought I caught a glimpse of the back of Judah's head bobbing this way and that, down the road in front of us. I couldn't be sure, but I wondered what he might be up to.

The soldiers on the street corners stuck close together. They had strained looks on their faces, and some cast glances over their shoulders as if to look for troublemakers or reinforcements. I felt my stomach knotting up.

At one point, I looked back at Yeshu's face, that face I was so familiar with. I could see in his eyes he was both surprised and perplexed. I knew his intent had always been to inspire and challenge people, not to rile them up, and never to draw adulation. His expression said to me that he wanted this ride to end, so as to get on with his real work.

That evening Yeshu sat by himself in Joanna's courtyard, braiding and rebraiding a leather strap that had fallen from the donkey. At times his hands stopped and his lips began to move. A while later, he would begin to braid again.

We left him with his thoughts.

~ ~ ~

The very next day, we again exited the city and were walking a footpath just outside the walls. We ended up sitting under a spreading oak by yet another village well. The more I traveled, the more I realized the well was truly the center of village life; the fountain of its sustenance.

We had just drunk our fill of cool water and were casually talking to the local women as they filled their clay pots. I sat beside an ancient grandmother, who asked me my name.

"I'm called Daavi," I said. "But of course, my birth name is David."

A smile broke across her face, smoothing out most of the wrinkles. "That's a very good name," she said. "A strong name. It was my father's."

She smiled again and gestured toward my chest with an open hand. "It means 'beloved' in Hebrew." Her face was bathed in sunlight.

"So," she asked, "how did you come to have that name?"

I was bewildered. I sat staring at the horizon, as if perhaps knowledge from the past could be found written there. No one had ever told me how I had gotten my name, and apparently I had never asked my parents.

The old woman patted me on the hand.

"Don't worry about it," she said. "You will know soon enough why you have your "beloved' name."

Then she stood, lifted her water pot, and walked off. I stared at her back until she rounded the corner.

I remained seated, a bit stunned and lost in thought, picturing my parents and the looks on their faces when I last left Nazareth.

Suddenly I snapped out of my daydream and noticed that Yeshu's gaze was fixed on me. He had a strange look on his face, and his eyes seemed to be grieving. He moved over and sat beside me.

"I'm the one to tell you why your name is Daavi," he said. "It's time..." and his voice trailed off.

Totally surprised by his statement, I stared at him, waiting.

"When my Abba died," Yeshu began slowly, "several years before you were born, my Mama Maria was expecting a child. Not long after, a baby boy was born, and she named him after my Abba's ancient ancestor, who as you know was King David.

"We all called the baby, Daavi," he said, watching me.

My breathing stopped.

"As often happens with the last-born child," Yeshu went on, "he became everyone's favorite. Of all the sisters and brothers I had, I felt most like a father to him.

"Your mother was sweet on him, too, because when he grew to be a toddler, he would often meander over to your house and sit with her in the kitchen corner as she prepared the evening meal."

Yeshu looked away and was quiet for a long while. When he finally spoke, there was a quaver in his voice.

"Our Daavi died when he was just three years old."

I sucked in a sudden breath. Yeshu looked at me and fell silent again.

"We were all heartbroken," he resumed after a while. "Your mother was especially so." His face had clouded over.

"She was expecting you at the time and was having a very difficult pregnancy. Together we all prayed for you. Every sunrise at morning prayers; and every sunset at evening prayers."

My eyes widened.

"When you were born—between two claps of thunder—she named you David. From the beginning we all called you 'Daavi.'"

Yeshu bowed his head for a moment. I reached over and touched his hand. I felt as if I had just discovered an older brother I didn't know I had.

He looked into my eyes and smiled. "I secretly hoped that you would become the Daavi we lost."

He cleared his throat and went on. "Then one day Yohanan saw us together playing a thumb-wrestling game I used to play with our own Daavi.

"Later, he pulled me aside and said, 'Yeshu, you must let the departed Daavi rest in peace in your heart. Allow this boy to grow into the Daavi he's meant to be.'

"He was right. And Mama Maria and I have proudly watched you grow into the man you are."

He squeezed my arm, his face radiant. "We are both grateful for the healing you brought us," he said, holding my gaze.

I smiled back at him.

Then he stood up abruptly and announced to everyone and to no one, "It's time for us to return."

We all rose to our feet, brushed ourselves off, and headed back toward Jerusalem's gates.

~ ~ ~

On the way to the city, we met up with some Greek travelers who happened to be heading to the Jerusalem bazaar, and we fell into conversation with them. I ended up talking with several younger people around my age. I told them about the Greek friend who taught me to say 'Eureka!' And then, as I often did, I told them I was looking for my sister, and described what a melodic voice she had.

Suddenly one of them brightened.

"Perhaps she's the woman who sells flowers in the central market," he said. "The one who gives a song with every bunch of flowers she sells. One of those songs is a very special lullaby."

He glanced at his companions, and I saw each of them nodding a tentative agreement.

As always, my heart began racing. Could this be the answer to my prayers?

"Can you sing me the lullaby?" I pleaded.

They all looked at one another and shook their heads.

"Sorry," said the boy. It was really beautiful, though."

I thanked them and hurried over to tell Yeshu and the others that I was going ahead.

I began walking, then broke into a run, became winded, and walked again. I was back at the main gates of Jerusalem in half the normal time, touched the mezuzah, but rushed by the mikveh, skipping the ritual bath. I was determined to head straight for the central market. Would I get there before the flower seller left?

Rounding the last corner, I heard her voice through the din of merchants and customers. Following the sweet sound, I finally spotted her sitting under a cloth awning that shielded her and her flowers from the hot sun. I couldn't see her face, but how beautifully she sang! Now my heart was racing with my feet as I pushed through the throng of people in the street to get a closer look.

Before I could get to her, she stood and stepped out from under the awning. She was nearly as old as my mother. This could not be Shoshana. Catching sight of me, she came over and grasped at my sleeve.

"Buy my last bunch of flowers, you handsome young man!" she implored. "Take them home to your dear mother for Pesakh."

My voice came out so low she had to lean close to hear. "I have no money," I whispered, "and my mother is far from here."

Anxious to leave, I started to pull away.

Holding fast to my wrist, she looked me straight in the eyes.

"You may have no money," she said, "but here is a flower for the hope I see in your heart." And she offered me a single red bloom.

I took it, thanked her, then turned and rushed off.

By the time I reached Joanna's house where we would again spend the night, the flower lay crushed in the palm of my hand.

Yeshu and the Red-Legged Lion

Of all those who had traveled this far with Yeshu, Judah was by far the most volcanic. What may not have been so clear to those who barely knew him was how much he could fascinate you, but also make you yearn to shake him. Or at other times to hug him.

Judah knew what he wanted. And when.

Liberation! Now!

He was driven by a fierce love of righteousness. And his passion for it fueled a heated anger with any tyrant.

Here's an example. One day in the Jerusalem market, Judah stopped to chat with an old woman who sat beside a doorway. She was selling five solitary lemons that were placed neatly on a worn cloth spread out in front of her. She and Judah whiled away the time by talking and joking.

Judah was so charmed by this market lady, he asked her how much it would cost him to buy all five lemons.

"Well I won't let you," she answered.

"But why on earth not?" Judah asked, his eyes widening.

"If I sell you the last of my lemons," she replied matter-of-factly, "then there would be no good reason for me to stay here at the market for the rest of the day."

Judah, for once, was speechless. He stared at the woman with his mouth agape, until finally he shook his head, stretched out his arms, and laughed to the sun.

An image of Yohanan laughing that way passed before my eyes like a diving hawk and just as quickly swooped up and out of sight.

To show his concurrence, Judah bought two lemons at twice the asking price. With that he thanked the smiling old woman, turned on his heel, and started off. Before he had walked ten paces, a rich merchant—the one who owned the shop in front of which the old woman had seated herself—rushed out his doorway and accused her of spoiling his business. He began kicking her remaining lemons in every direction.

Had Yeshu been there, he would have quieted the merchant, placed a hand on the old woman's shoulder, and searched for a way to settle differences by appealing to hearts so that no one would lose. Later he might have used the incident in a story, to teach a lesson about struggling for right justice, or about making peace under pressure.

Not Judah. He quickly lost his head and charged straight through the crowd at the merchant. It took four of us to keep him from pulverizing the man. The old woman gathered up the last three lemons in her skirt and ran off weeping. Wasting no time, we disappeared into the crowd before the authorities could be summoned.

That was Judah: always thinking with his fists.

He reserved his keenest rage, of course, for the occupying armies of Rome. Judah—like his father and his father's father, and countless ancestors before them—had one wish in life, one goal, and that was to live to see the messiah who would save Israel from all its subjugators. That messiah would be a liberator who broke the chains binding the land and its people.

Well, Yeshu wanted to remove those chains, too. Maybe that's why Judah was so attracted to him. Maybe he thought Yeshu simply needed to be guided, set straight. But Yeshu's carpentry skills weren't wasted. He knew by eyesight whether a plank or a foundation was true or not.

And he was a builder not a demolisher.

His vision was to start by breaking the mental chains that bind us, and the shackles of violence and vengeance. Without accomplishing this—he told us over and over—one set of masters would simply be replaced by another. As a result, the poor, the excluded, and the downtrodden would be robbed of their dearest possession: the hope that their lives could be changed.

Times were hard, and a month did not pass without rumors of a new messiah who had come to free us. A year rarely ended without at least one mad rush toward some self-proclaimed prophet. And always people's expectations collapsed like logs in a hearth when they turn to ash.

But hope itself ran as deep as a peat fire that blazes anew each time it finds another dried out root.

Judah was not alone in wanting to break this vicious cycle by finishing it. He and others, in their misdirected love and longing, wanted to spark a conflagration that burnt all falsehood away, thereby demolishing the prison house to the ground. Above all they wanted nothing to do with striving for a calming of the spirit that might promise certain individuals a doorway to heaven, but at the same time would surely dampen popular rage, leaving everyone else hungry and bound. For Judah and his companions, peacefulness was nothing but a midwife for victims and more victims.

My Uncle Bartholomaios felt the same. He wanted a modern-day Joshua or David, chosen by God, who would lead our people to freedom. In all the noise it was hard for them to hear Yeshu's steady call for action that fused justice and compassion with liberation of body *and* soul.

More than once Judah put his arm around my shoulder and said, "Mark my words, Daavi: the spirit is worth nothing—nothing!—if the back and the mind are like two sand gnats crushed under a soldier's foot."

For emphasis he would give me a squeeze that made the breath rush from my chest.

But never ever did I imagine what else he was turning over and over in his mind.

~ ~ ~

Two days before the Passover supper, Yeshu asked Judah to travel to Arimathea to invite a man named Yosef to join us at the large Pesakh Seder we were planning. Preferring not to make the long trek there and back alone, Judah invited me to go along. Perhaps he merely wanted a captive audience, but I prefer to think it pleased him to have me around.

It would be an all-day walk. Even so, I looked forward to being with Judah. I knew he would talk during most of the journey, and that everything he said would be provocative and interesting. But little did I know what he would reveal to me that day.

Walking in the road and rounding a curve, I could see that our path headed up a steep hill. To my surprise, Judah had been very quiet since we'd set out. On our climb up the hill, he let go.

"Where is Yeshu's thirst for liberation? His hope for a different future? A future in which we Jews are free to worship in our own way, free to gather together and openly express our beliefs and longings, free to govern ourselves and benefit fully from our own labor!" I wasn't sure if Judah was talking to me or to himself.

"You were there the day after last Sabbath," he went on. (Maybe he actually *was* talking to me....) "Wasn't Yeshu's triumphant entry into Jerusalem the most thrilling thing you ever saw?"

He threw both arms skyward.

"Holy Moses! Almost everyone in the whole city was lining the streets to greet this towering preacher as their hero: their Almighty Savior!"

Judah clapped loudly and whooped. Up shot the bushy eyebrows.

"It was astounding," he said. "He had the masses right in the palms of his hands." And Judah held his own broad hands straight out, palms toward the heavens.

"All Yeshu has to do now—I'm convinced of it—all he has to do is shout out the command. Yes! And the Jews will rise up against the Roman legions."

He was nearly bellowing now.

"Then the other leaders—I can mobilize them—they'll quickly fall in behind Yeshu to organize the long-term resistance. That way it won't be just a momentary uprising, a single ember exploding from the fire and quickly dying out.

"But Yeshu is the key," he rolled on, "because only he can fire up the people as a whole. I'm sure of it."

And he slapped the knuckles of his right hand into the palm of his left.

I dared say nothing. I didn't believe things would happen at all the way Judah was imagining them. But before I could turn over my thoughts any further, he suddenly stopped in the middle of the road and stared over my head up the hill.

When he spoke again, his voice had changed. He began expounding in a low, relentless manner, his eyes burning with a hard, bright light. Never once did he look down at me, so again I was uncertain whether he was talking to me at all.

"There's a dream I have," he said. "It comes night after night, sometimes for an entire week, before disappearing for months. But it always returns.

"In this dream Yeshu has become an imposing general, the finest in the history of our people. Greater even than King David."

Judah set his jaw and nodded for emphasis.

"An enormous army has formed under his command, an army that is unbeatable because it fights for freedom, not for riches or plunder. Yeshu's soldiers willingly lay down their lives because they care more for victory than for life. Because they would rather be dead than be enslaved again.

"I am this grand general's second in command. I am always a single step behind him, advising on how to wield this mighty force to free not just the Jews, but all nations!

"How dazzling is Yeshu in his golden armor. Imagine the sun shining a single beam with just one purpose."

Judah whistled a single note through his teeth. "His men do anything he asks."

His words began tumbling out now. "And he himself leads them into battle, invincible and terrifying, his shining sword cutting great arcs through the sky, slashing down again and again upon the Roman armies."

Judah's eyes gleamed as they flew from hill to hill around us.

"In my dream," he went on, "Yeshu is always right in front of me. My eyes are on his back and shoulders as he leaps and swings, leaps and swings, felling the fields of soldiers that stand in his way, like a scythe cutting wheat.

"But the biggest thrill comes just before I awaken. As the Romans fall back, scattering like leaves before the storm, Yeshu calls into the shadows and a great, shaggy-maned lion glides from its hiding place. He leaps to the lion's back, grasping its mane with one hand, his sword with the other, and together they charge forward at a dead run, straight through the gates of Rome itself.

"As they race along the streets of the imperial city, soldiers are left lying like so many stalks of wheat waiting to be gathered into sheaves.

"The lion's legs glisten scarlet with Roman blood.

"One by one, Yeshu pulls the temples, palaces, and ruling houses of Rome to the ground until all seven hills are flattened.

"Yeshu and the red-legged lion!"

~ ~ ~

Judah went silent again. He marched resolutely on, staring fixedly ahead from under those eyebrows of his, now emblazoned like two daggers crossing his broad forehead.

I was thunderstruck. How could he have so misunderstood Yeshu? He missed it all: Yeshu's vision; how it was to come about; everything!

We walked on. At the top of the hill, I brushed tears from my eyes with the backs of my fists, though Judah didn't seem to notice.

When I finally found my voice again, I said, "But Judah, Yeshu would never lead an army into war. I know we can't choose what we dream about, but how can this...this nightmare make you so happy?"

Judah snorted in disgust, but I couldn't keep quiet. "Yeshu says 'to live by the sword is to die by the sword.' He implores us to not become what we despise in our enemy."

I couldn't believe how I was talking back, but I just kept going. "Yeshu challenges us to struggle for peace and for justice. He teaches us how to fight with spirit force, not with physical force. And if we do that, if we use the tools of love instead of the weapons of hatred, some day Rome will belong to us. All of Rome will truly fall on bended knee."

Judah just laughed derisively and looked away.

I shook my head vigorously back and forth. "I'm sorry Judah, but I think you're wrong. Yeshu will never be your general."

Judah only walked faster, staring straight ahead. "Oh, yes he will," he said. "You'll see, soon enough."

It would not be long before I would realize how much Yeshu understood Judah and his fiery yearnings. He knew that he and Judah shared the same devotion to our people; the same desire to lift them up. And in spite of what Judah would do, Yeshu would love him to the end.

Disobedience

It didn't take much prodding to get Yosef of Arimathea to join us in Jerusalem for our Pesakh supper. In fact, he returned that same day with Judah and me, and brought his two young daughters with him. They were both thrilled to be included in the celebration.

The day before Passover began, we all stood and watched a knotted group of Pharisees stalk off from where Yeshu was teaching. Their accusations and threats had tightened our faces. My heart was a pounding drum.

Later, I gathered the courage to approach him.

"Yeshu, why do you break the rules?" I asked. "You know them better than anyone. And you know how angry the Pharisees get, and what they are capable of doing. So why do you provoke them? And in front of crowds, too."

He saw how agitated I was, but let me babble on.

"You talk back to the Pharisees and the Sadducees and the priests. You hold public meetings even when the Romans say not to. I asked Mama Maria if you were always this defiant, and she said no, you were very obedient as a child! Why are you *so* disobedient now?"

Yeshu broke into laughter. He actually liked it when I challenged him.

"So that's what she told you, is it?"

Reaching out, he touched my shoulder. "I'm sorry," he said. "I shouldn't laugh. I know you worry that someone will try to hurt me. Or worse...." He looked down at his hands, his feet, thinking.

At last he lifted his head back up. "It crosses my mind, too."

He returned to my original question.

"What Mama Maria knows, but didn't mention, is that I had no reason to disobey her. She always acted out of love.

"She also knows why I openly break the rules now," he went on. "It's because they are wrong." He crossed his arms.

"Rules that are wrong need to be changed. Take, for instance, the ban against healing on the day of Shabbat. Or the one against associating with so-called 'sinners' or the poor because they are supposedly 'unclean.' Sometimes the only way to finally change rules is to turn your back on them, and apply other rules, of a higher order."

He leaned toward me. "Listen closely, Daavi. I have always obeyed two authorities: God and my heart, my internal guide. Always. In the end, that's all anyone is obligated to do.

"Of course, I consult the community elders and the scriptures," he said, "and you should, too."

A dark cloud crossed his face. "But if a worldly authority—one of our priests or a Roman centurion—tells you to do something you know is wrong, you might have to disobey them. If a law is unjust, you may have no choice but to break that law. Not by acting like a common thief, though, who sneaks about for personal gain and then lies when he is caught."

I listened to him intently.

"No, you must draw together the courage to admit what you've done, announce why you did it, and take your punishment if necessary. That's one way to make wrong-headed rules visible to others," he said, "so that eventually they can be transformed.

"This is tricky work,' he added, "and if you take it on, you had best ask for God's help in examining your own motives.

"Here on earth, laws, even ones that seem to be good ones, are made by humans and can be mistaken. Moreover, what once appeared to be right can become old hat and ready to be left behind—for a new hat! Or it can favor the powerful and be unfair to the common folk. He raised a forefinger for emphasis. Never forget that just as these rules are invented by humans, they can also be put aside or changed by humans.

"Sometimes the only way to tell is to test the rule. You break it to draw attention to its uselessness or unfairness. That's how you get people to reconsider the rules. Because once people as a whole stop believing in them, or in the power that enforces them, they collapse like a house of reeds built on sand."

Yeshu's hands became a building falling to the ground.

"So, my friend, follow your God and your heart, your two inner guides, making sure they are in constant conversation with one another.

"Beyond that, don't obey anyone blindly." He paused.

"Not even me!" And he laughed.

When he saw me looking quizzical, he said, "We'll talk more about this another day. Let's put it to rest for now."

Unfortunately, that chance to talk further never came.

~ ~ ~

That evening I could not contain myself any longer. I decided I had to warn Yeshu. He was sitting by himself in the garden of the house in which we were guests.

"Yeshu," I insisted. "We have to run, tonight. Something terrible is going to happen. I just know it.

"You rode into Jerusalem. Thousands of people were cheering, laying palm leaves on the road in front of you. This is dangerous; you know that. The Roman authorities and the chief priests will never stand for it. They jailed Yohanan and killed him in cold blood for less. They are waiting for you, too. I'm sure of it."

Yeshu just looked at me, for the longest time.

"Oh, dear God..." I said, my hands leaping to press against the sides of my head. "You know all this, don't you? You see it coming, too!"

He kept looking directly into my eyes. Moments passed.

"What I'm doing is right." He spoke softly. "And the truth sets me free."

He gazed up at the great dome of night sky, and his voice rose a step as he said, "I'm ready for whatever may come." And he set his jaw. "My heart is at peace."

He nodded several times before going on. "I feel as if I'm soaring on the winds, my wings stretched out like a stork heading home after a long winter."

Then he pointed with an upward gesture of his forehead. "Along the starpath up there." His eyes lifted. "Do you remember that day, Daavi, long ago in the wheat field, when we had our first deep talk?"

I nodded. "As if it were yesterday."

He continued to stare at the firmament. "I cannot turn back now. I cannot stop."

Slowly he shook his head. "I can only go on," he said. "I am doing what I must do."

As for me, I was so engulfed by Yeshu's words, I couldn't come up with a single thing to say. And I wouldn't have had the breath to utter it anyway.

The inescapable weight of the future was crushing me.

The Last Seder

The next day, Pesakh began. As always, we had arranged for a large Passover meal together. When we arrived at the inn, we climbed the stairs and entered a room with a single, long table of polished cedar. As we took our places on the benches that lined both sides, Yeshu crouched down to closely inspect the way the table was put together. Running a hand over the wood, he noted how perfectly the legs were joined to the smooth, burnished tabletop.

When he looked up, the only seat remaining was at the head of the table, just inside the door. Everyone insisted he take it because it was the seat of honor.

He laughed gently, shaking his head. Yeshu loved to play Abba, our loving father. We were his family since he had never started one of his own. I knew he secretly missed those days when he was part of his birth family, and then after his father had died, when he had to be responsible for his seven younger sisters and brothers. Yes, Yeshu was our Abba.

He made his way slowly down the table, touching each person on the shoulders. Joanna and Maria Magdalena. Andrew and Shimón Petros. Mama Maria. The Thunder Brothers and their devoted mother, Maria Shulamit. Yosef of Arimathea and his two daughters, Ruth and Deborah. Judah.

Putting his hands under Judah's arms, Yeshu gently lifted him. Judah twisted his head around and looked up at him questioningly.

"Judah will sit near the door, at the head of the table," Yeshu said. "Because he may have to leave early."

Judah shuddered and his face tightened like he was choking. Yeshu steadied him until he found his balance, then helped him down the narrow room to his seat by the door.

I noticed Judah's hair seemed slightly less curly than it used to be. He sat looking straight ahead as if he were not seeing.

Yeshu circled the table's end and began working his way back along the other side, hugging each one of us from behind and saying a word or two. First Martha and her sister Miriam, followed by Philippos and his brother Nathanyel. Our attention shifted away from Judah.

When Yeshu had finished his rounds, all of us watched wide-eyed as he poured water into a washbasin, took off his cloak, and wrapped a large cloth around his waist. He went around the room once again, washing the feet of each one of us and drying them with the towel. There were more than twenty people in all. Nearly every one of them protested when he began his task, especially Shimón Petros.

Yeshu responded to Petros in a voice that all of us present could hear. "I am an example for you. I have been your teacher. Now, as a servant would, I have washed your feet. In the future you should wash one another's feet. That is what happens in a community of equals."

I felt humble and a little embarrassed when it was my turn to be washed. But Yeshu's presence warmed me, and I found my hand resting lightly on his shoulder. I could sense his muscles working as he washed, and I secretly enjoyed his care.

When he had finished with everyone, Yeshu made his way back around the table, halfway down, and squeezed in between Mama Maria and Shimón Petros. Sitting down, he put his arms around both their shoulders and hugged them.

Miriam leaned across the table and asked Mama Maria, "Is your mother coming tonight?" Hearing the question, I promptly turned my head toward them to listen.

"Mama Ana travels no more with her feet," said Mama Maria, "only in her mind and heart. I know she's thinking of us here tonight, and probably weaving a story for us to share the next time we're together."

All of us in earshot smiled and nodded at one another, sadness clouding our eyes. I turned my head toward Yeshu. His hands were sliding over the tabletop to find one another, as if to fall into prayer.

Moments later, gesturing to the youngest guests present—that would be Yosef of Arimathea's daughters—Yeshu began a series of questions and answers about why Jews gather for a Seder on the first day of Passover, and how the supper they share commemorates the exodus from Egypt when our people were liberated from slavery.

"The history of the Jews," said Yeshu, "like the history of all trodden-upon peoples, is marked by repeated struggles for liberation. And each time freedom is truly achieved, in particular when violence is avoided, then *all* people are the better for it. That's our special role. God has chosen this hard struggle for Jews so that we can be inspiring examples for humankind."

He clasped his hands together, glancing down at them. "Until all people are free," he said, "none of us is free."

His face was the color of dawn and dusk all at once. One by one, he looked each of us present in the eye, as was his custom.

"Hold in your hearts what I have taught you," he said. "We must also have compassion for the tyrants of the world because they too are enslaved and degraded by their own evil deeds. We shall show them our love, even as we oppose their actions. We shall liberate them from hatred and evil, as we liberate ourselves from their dominion."

He stopped.

"That way everyone benefits." Yeshu smiled. His beard seemed to stir as if a breeze had caught it.

"This is why the very measures we choose for freeing ourselves are so important. Those who use violence against violence, breed only more of it. And soon they become the mirror image of the oppressors who kindle such brutality." He pressed one fist against the other and held them up in front of us.

"We must learn to love like God loves." He clasped his hands together again.

I looked down the table to catch a glimpse of how Judah was reacting, only to discover that he had disappeared.

Yeshu continued, "Only when we allow God's temple to be created within our hearts and our minds will we humans be free forever."

As he looked around to see if we understood, his gaze paused for a moment on the partially open door.

Then his eyes returned to Mama Maria, and he asked her, "Remember the Seders we celebrated when I was a child, when the whole family was still together? How we always gathered with relatives in Jerusalem?"

"Yes, I recall it all as if it were tonight!" she answered, her face lit by more than oil lamps.

"And I would guess," she said, "that the earliest Seder you can remember, Yeshua, was just after our family's return from Egypt. My cousin Elisheva was present with her husband Zachariah, even then one of the most beloved priests at the Temple."

Yeshu picked up the narrative. "And they arrived towing a high-spirited five-year-old named Yohanan!" He shook his head, a wistful smile tugging at his lips. "All I can recall clearly of that event is Yohanan's unruly locks and large lively eyes. And the pet mouse that slept in his pocket! He couldn't stop giggling when he took me aside to show me that particular treasure. He even let me feed it a few corn kernels, fished from another pocket."

Briefly, Mama Maria took the reins of the tale back into her hands, "And many more Seders followed, most of them happy gatherings...until Yosef passed on." She dropped her gaze.

Yeshu spoke again. "There was a wholeness, a completeness to those early meals," he agreed. "No seat was empty back then." He glanced at Judah's vacant spot. "Hands that were joined together formed a circle. It was a celebration—of family and life—just like this one." He threw a look sideways toward his mother. "A meal together, any meal, can be sacred," he went on. "In spite of all our problems and differences, we can pause and break bread together: family, friends, even enemies.

"I remember, when my Abba was still alive, how everyone at the table called down God's blessing as one voice. And then how we went quiet, tasting each mouthful with pleasure." Yeshu's tongue ran lightly over his lips. "Just like tonight, there would be roasted lamb hock, unleavened bread, bitter herbs, and lettuce and other greens dipped in sauces and salted water."

Although Yeshu was addressing us all, he directed his reflections primarily toward Mama Maria, who was still gazing at the table and smiling a little sadly.

"After a while," Yeshu went on, "as our stomachs filled, we would begin to talk and joke. Mama Ana told wonderful old stories. She saved her best for the Seders, don't you think, Mama?"

Mama Maria's face brightened again. "And she always seemed to find at least one that no one had heard before."

Both of them fell into a nostalgic silence. Finally, Yeshu reached toward the platter of unleavened Pesakh bread that I had bought at the central market only that morning. The rounded piece he lifted up seemed as large as the wheel of a donkey cart. He blessed it and broke it into ample portions, passing them up and down the table until everyone had a piece. Then he lifted the pitcher of wine and poured each of us a cup, passing them, one by one, down the line as well. So, there he was, playing father again, providing food and drink for his large family.

Of course, he was aware of this. Looking around the table, he smiled and said, "To me, God is like the best of fathers and mothers. Consider what that means."

Then Nathanyel lifted a hand toward Yeshu and after clearing his throat, began to speak, "Master..."

"I'm not your master," interrupted Yeshu, leaning toward Nathanyel. "And I'm no longer your leader."

With warmth on his face, he looked at the rest of us. We were all quiet, listening closely. "You are not my servants," he said, "nor my followers. Followers do not know what their leader knows, but I have now taught you everything I know of God and God's will for you."

He looked down at his hands and then raised his eyes again. "And never forget, not only did you choose me; I chose you, and I challenged you to go out and bear fruit that will remain.

"So, for all of these reasons," he said, "I now simply call you *friends.*"

Yeshu leaned forward, pushing the wooden plate in front of him toward the middle of the table. He rested his forearms on the place he had cleared, looked toward one end of the gathered group of friends, then the other.

No one made a sound, waiting.

Then he spoke. "This is what I ask of you: love one another as I love you."

I looked at Maria Magdalena. Her eyes had widened slightly. We both glanced at the other members of our band of followers. Even the chewing and swallowing had halted.

Next Yeshu put his left hand on the center of his chest, fingers spread wide. "No one has greater love than to lay down their life for their friends."

I felt my breath catch in my throat, and I sensed those close by me had stiffened.

"So, you are my friends if you do what I am asking."

My breathing resumed.

"You may use this name 'friends' among yourselves."

Everyone nodded, as one person. I noticed out of the side of one eye, then the other, that we were all looking at Yeshu, not at one another.

Then Yeshu reached out to Shimón Petros and Mama Maria, and the rest of us understood we were to follow suit. We all joined hands, raising them together and praying the prayer he had first led us in years ago, among the towering cedars.

> Our God in heaven,
>   hallowed be your name.
> Your kingdom come,
>   your will be done,
>   on earth as it is in heaven.
> Give us this day our daily bread.
> Forgive us the wrongs we have done,
>   as we forgive those
>   who wrong us.
> And spare us from being put to the test,
>   but keep us safe us from evil.
> For yours is the kingdom,
>   and the power,

and the glory,
forever and ever.
Amen.

After the prayer ended, all was quiet until several people gradually began conversing softly with those sitting next to them.

Without warning Yeshu spoke. "When I am no longer among you, I want you to regularly share meals like this together...and remember me."

The table fell silent again, even more eerily than before. I could not hear a breath being drawn. It reminded me of flowers that close up when they are touched. We had heard Yeshu's words, but we resisted fitting them all together. Who would want to face life without him? So, we just nodded weakly in agreement and hunkered down over our plates.

"And always keep in mind," he went on, his voice quavering almost imperceptibly, "that whenever two or more of you are gathered, I will be there among you."

As I looked around at the others, first Shoshana's face and then Yohanan's darted through my mind and I flinched, wondering, who else will be missing?

"My last gift to you is this new commandment that I've just shared," said Yeshu. "That you love one another. Love one another as I've loved you!"

Finally, in response to Yeshu's gesture, both hands stretched out, palms up, everyone resumed eating.

I stole a sideways look at him to see if he was enjoying more of the bread I had brought to the table. But Yeshu sat still as still could be, his head bowed. Looking at him closely, I saw that his eyes were glistening above his beard. Once more, just like back when I was a boy, I held my questions in.

Perhaps he was thinking about his Abba Yosef. And Yohanan.

Or maybe he was looking ahead at what was soon to unfold.

And God Died

The Seder ended with a song, and we all stood as one and walked downstairs and out into the darkness. Yeshu asked a number of us to accompany him, first to the Mount of Olives, then to the Garden of Gethsemane.

While he was praying there, a crowd of strangers arrived, carrying torches. Some were armed soldiers in uniform, others were men in cloaks. One pulled the hood back from his head, and in the flickering light I could see it was Judah. He greeted Yeshu with a kiss on the cheek. Their gazes locked for a moment before two soldiers pushed Judah aside and seized Yeshu, each one grasping an arm.

Shimón Petros flew to Yeshu's side, drawn blade in hand. But Yeshu cried out, "Stop! Put down that sword!"

He stood with one hand up, palm facing outward.

"Put it away," Yeshu said firmly. There will be no violence from any of us. We do not live by the sword, but by the word. And the word is love."

Petros froze and I could hear the sound of other swords slipping back into their sheathes. No one else moved.

We watched silently as Yeshu was dragged off to be tried by men who already knew the verdict and the sentence—sedition against Rome and death by crucifixion—only the Empire could mete out that abomination. What kind of court could rename this travesty justice?

Later, I heard from someone who was present that Yeshu had been turned over to a gang of soldiers who pummeled and whipped him without mercy. Ah, torture! It's nothing but the tool of a rat's nest of cowards and tyrants attempting to twist the truth with terror.

To further humiliate Yeshu, they covered his shoulders with a torn sack stained purple from the grapes it had carried, and they pressed a plaited crown of thorns on his head. They finished by placing in his right hand a staff made from the dead branch of an olive tree.

Then his tormentors fell to their knees, mocking him, chanting, "Hail, hail, King of the Jews!"

The witness described how the soldiers rose from bended knees, laughing, to spit on him. One grabbed the staff from his hand and hit him over the head, driving the crown of thorns in deeper.

As day broke, a heavy cross was loaded on Yeshu's back. He was forced to carry it through the same streets along which people had laid down hundreds upon hundreds of palm fronds to greet him only days before. This time the journey was not to Jerusalem's heart, but just outside the city walls to the dreaded *Gol'gotha*—the "Place of the Skull"—the hill of death.

Fretfully I stood by the roadside along the way, waiting for my friend Yeshu to pass. Just before he reached me, I saw him stumble and fall, the enormous wooden cross crushing his knees into the pavement stones. He struggled to his feet, weakened by the beating and deprivation of the night before, and staggered on a bit before falling again.

I stepped forward to go to him but the surging crowd pressed in, pushing me aside. Soon finding myself at the back of the swarm of people lining the street, I edged along trying to break through to help whenever he fell, only to be vigorously shoved back, time and again.

The soldiers eventually grew impatient with the lack of progress. To speed things along, one grabbed an Ethiopian onlooker by the arm and pulled him out from the crowd, into the road.

From his knees, Yeshu looked up into the frightened face of this man, who was called Shimón of Cyrene. The instant their eyes met, Shimón's face calmed. He stepped behind the carpenter and, leaning down, thrust a shoulder under the cross, hoisting most of its weight onto his own back.

Yeshu straightened noticeably and they pressed on together, black man and Jew.

The gait picked up speed and I raced along the outer edges of the throng, trying to keep pace, jumping see over the heads of the jeering mob in front of me. Where were the people who had cheered Yeshu just days before? Where had this sea of angry faces come from?

No longer able to catch sight of Yeshu, I glanced upward at a movement that attracted my attention. Soaring high above were two great birds, circling and circling at the top of the sky.

With that I got tangled in a knot of people, hopped up on a wooden bench, searching again for Yeshu, and saw the top of the cross slipping from sight. Desperately, I jumped down and elbowed my way through. Finally clear, I started to run, only to trip over the jagged edge of a paving stone and fall forward to the ground. I bounced to my feet and rushed on.

How I longed to see Yeshu's face! To know his heart at that moment. I ached to stretch out an arm and touch him, tell him what was in *my* heart. But no matter how hard I tried, it was hopeless. He was always beyond my reach.

I noticed my hands felt like they were on fire. My right palm was scraped and the left one badly gashed from the fall. I felt oddly distant looking at them, as if they were a stranger's. Nothing else mattered other than what was happening to my closest friend and teacher whom I had sworn to protect at all costs.

When I finally made it through the city gates and arrived at the foot of Gol'gotha, the spectators had thinned. I walked uphill beside a cart carrying food and water for the men standing guard. Yeshu was already visible at the top, hoisted high on the crossed timbers.

Making my way to the base of the cross, I stood breathing in jagged gasps. Slowly sinking to my knees, my forehead pressed to the ground, I shut my eyes, telling myself this could not be happening.

When they opened, Joanna and the three Marias were there. Mama Maria was weeping soundlessly, hands clutching her elbows, while Maria Shulamit comforted her. Maria Magdalena and Joanna knelt on each side of me, pressing their shoulders against mine, protecting me from the soldiers who were looking on, eying us suspiciously.

Soldiers were everywhere and people were afraid of standing out. Usually, prisoners crucified by the Romans were left to hang in solitude—but this one was special.

A threat to public order.

A commander of peace.

Maybe Judah was right, I thought. Perhaps Yeshu dying could pull down an empire. Or at least a priestly dominion. Maybe all those people who had greeted him a week ago would rise up now to rescue him, in spite of his admonitions against violence.

Who knows, he might even perform a miracle. Climb down from the cross and save himself.

The sky had been cloudless all day, and a red sun blazed high above us, hammering all sense from my head. Exhausted, I even wondered if it might not have been better had Yeshu departed this life the night before, during the torture. At least he would have been spared the thirst and pain and public humiliation of this day.

But I pushed that twisted thought away. So long as life quivered in Yeshu's breast, we had hope. And we clung to that hope like a sparrow clings to a single sprig of trembling wheat.

At midday, storm clouds began piling up in the east. Soon they had stampeded over the plain toward the city, covering the sun, rocking the heavens with thunder, turning the firmament into a roiling cauldron. Great spears of lightning flashed, stabbing sky and earth, advancing ever closer to where we crouched.

Each burst caused Mama Maria to flinch and let out a small groan that was swept away by the wind and thunder. Every time, her stricken face wrestled itself back to calmness.

I saw her lips moving but could not hear what she said. Then I realized it was her son's name. Yeshua, "God is salvation." She was reminding them both that this was their bedrock. It was their gift to each other.

When I stole a closer look at Mama Maria's eyes, it seemed as though the rock might break up into sand. My gaze dropped and I saw her hands, folded at her breast. These were hands that had cradled Baby Yeshu as he nursed, hands that later had kneaded dough and fed him his daily bread as a boy. They were hands that had, laboring alongside his, fed the poor and nursed the sick to health when he was a man. Hands that had deftly guided untold newborns into the light of day and the shine of their parents' eyes.

Now they gripped one another in prayer as her son left the world.

While the tumult heightened, the three Marias and Joanna formed an ever-tighter circle around me, shielding me from harm and joining our hearts together. Looking up at Yeshu, it felt like a rope was being pulled taut around my chest. I could barely breathe. None of us could.

Pressing my knees to my chest, arm gripping arm, over and over I hoarsely whispered a prayer I had learned from the storyteller in childhood, "Dear God, Amen. Dear God, Amen."

As hard as it was to look, my eyes couldn't turn away. I could see his lips slowly forming word after word. With effort I realized he was reciting one last time from the scrolls.

Straining to follow the slightest movements of his mouth, I pieced together what he was saying.

> Love your God...
>
> with all your soul...
>
> Love your neighbor as yourself....

Yeshu—the boy rabbi, the wandering carpenter who had walked with the poor in spirit and comforted the afflicted, who had warmed those in need with his cloak—was now wrapping himself in the Torah.

Again and again, I whispered into my tightly clenched hands.

> Blessed are those who hunger and thirst to do right...
>
> Blessed are the peacemakers...

When my gaze lifted, he was repeating just two words, over and over. I strained again to determine what was so vital to him, but at first I couldn't. Then it became clear.

> Forgive them...
>
> Forgive them...
>
> Forgive them....

Before I knew it, not even a single word was discernible. His lips were barely moving.

Locking my eyes on his, I poured out all my strength. Pain wracked his face like squalls over a grey sea. His eyes stayed calm, and I stared deep into them. Eyes that I knew so well, that had seen so much beauty in the world, so much light in human souls.

Then I recalled that day long ago. "Yeshu," I said slowly, emphasizing each word with my mouth, "Give *me* your pain." His eyes seemed to flicker slightly. I watched him enter that silent space we had so often shared.

My head crashed with the thunder overhead, as the fire in those eyes faded like the last embers in a nearly cold hearth. In desperation I pulled at my hair, trying to hold him here by feeling his pain.

Swiftly the sky got darker until it was almost night in the middle of day. So dark, the world shrank till it could fit in a thimble. I tried to shout, enraged, but the rope constricting my chest wouldn't let me.

Yeshu's head sank lower.

"Please don't die," I whispered, my teeth pressed against the knuckles of my closed fist.

Moments later, the darkness of the day filled his eyes. They were pools reflecting a starless, moonless night. Yeshu's chin slumped on his chest.

He was dead.

And the sky had died with him...turning blacker than black. As the light vanished, a great gust of wind stung our eyes with dust. Later I would hear how it tore through the city, ripping the Temple curtain in half.

Life itself seemed over.

Humanity had died.

All the birds and animals had died.

God died.

I did not want to live in a world that could snuff out Yeshu's life in an eyeblink. A world dominated by a beast with an insatiable appetite for lambs led to slaughter. Such a world was odious and reeking with dread.

In a blinding rage I reached up like Samson to pull the sky down on top of me. Failing, I buried my head beneath my arms to shut out the terrible truth. My chest throbbed with the thunder roaring in my ears. Torrents of rain hammered my back.

I was dimly aware of the three Marias and Joanna struggling to their feet, then falling to their knees, wailing Kaddish in their grief.

The world, our world, had ended. Could it be true?

Oh yes, my eyes said, it is.

But no! no! my heart protested, it cannot be.

The sky over the hill was now crackling with lightning. Yeshu's motionless body was silhouetted eerily against that sky by each bolt. All around us, the Roman soldiers were dropping their spears and fleeing in panic.

I wanted to climb up to where Yeshu hung and embrace him one last time. Instead, I hunkered down closer to the four wailing, swaying women. At last, I comprehended Mama Maria's dread of thunderstorms.

Clinging to the earth like a mouse mired in thick mud, I stared blankly down, my eyes straining to focus. Tiny rivulets ran over my hands and gathered into torrents that poured downhill.

A dung beetle floated by, hit a stone, and was flipped onto its back. I watched it madly twist its legs in a vain attempt to right itself. A mere finger reaching out would be enough to turn it over. But just as I tried to do so, a gush of water washed it away. I couldn't even save an insect.

Far away I heard someone weeping. Or was it a crying out? A face like Judah's silently stared at me out of the darkness. Despite all my vows and three years of unflagging vigilance, I had been powerless to stop anything.

There was nothing left to do.

Nothing at all.

Nothing.

IV. Found

Ashes

Following Yeshu's death, I took to the road. For months, all I did was walk. Eating little, talking to almost no one. I was bereft, blowing wherever passing gusts carried me, wretched and wrung out. My life was unraveling like the ragged sleeve of a wind-whipped cloak.

A hole had opened in the center of my chest that felt unfillable. For the moment, I didn't want to see the face of anyone I knew, anyone who would remind me of who I was and where I'd been.

I slept under footbridges and in open fields, eating whatever the day provided, even if it was scraps people threw out for their dogs.

Once, I turned when I thought I had caught sight of a dove under a rocky ledge staring out at me. But when I drew closer, nothing was there.

I tried my best not to think, which only made me chew harder on the losses. My dear sister Shoshana—vanished. My friend Yohanan, the voice from the wilderness nourished by honey and locusts—murdered. And now Yeshu the carpenter, the storyteller, my teacher, my friend, my brother in life—executed. Wherever I looked, whether it was at the clouds, the bark of a tree, a whitewashed wall, I saw his face as life drained out of it.

Bitterness filled my mouth that could not be spit out.

Day followed day as I drifted along, anchorless and rudderless. I couldn't imagine that I had ever belonged to a place called home. I was barely seventeen and my life seemed over. The idea of going back to Nazareth and my parents—picking up the threads of my old life—felt unbearable. Constant, throbbing pain scattered my thoughts, flogging me along.

With this final crashing blow, I had lost myself.

My grief was so numbing I couldn't speak; all I could do was tear keriah. With a knife I slit a gash in my cloak, over my heart, for all to see. I stared at it hard, then slashed it again and again, waiting for it to bleed. Of course it didn't. How could it? The world had already been bled dry.

I vowed to wear that cloak as long as I breathed and after. It would be my burial shroud. Everything that had been lost beyond recovery, I swore never to forget. I would carry the unmendable ripping within my being till my very last footstep.

Like a shipwrecked fisherman clinging to a broken mast, staring upward and slowly turning in open water night after starless night, my soul was caught in the grip of an irresistible tide. Occasionally it would wash me up in a village where I'd seek out work. But as soon as a few coins jangled in my pocket, I'd push off again, usually after dark, telling no one.

I trekked mile after hungry mile, my aching feet trudging along until I was exhausted enough to find a hole to curl up and sleep in.

I was always gnawing on the same questions.

Why did Yeshu have to die?

Every person in our group needed him. The world needed him even more. Why couldn't he have been spared?

And then my heart would begin its incessant drumming. Maybe the stories spreading like wildfire were true. Rumors were everywhere of people saying they had seen him again. But how could that be? If Yeshu were still here, surely he would've found me. I'd been his friend since I was a toddler exploring his workshop. He'd carried me on his broad shoulders. And I carried the name of the young brother he'd lost.

Thoughts such as these pelted me like stones. My soul felt bruised and battered, and my body unclean. It was as if I were rolling in cinders till ashes covered my face, my chest, my hands and feet.

Finally I got angry; angrier than I knew was possible. How could God let this happen? To Yeshu, to all of us!

Shaking my fist at the stars I told God I would stop following the Laws and never step into another synagogue. But this only left me feeling worse. Whatever I said, nothing changed. It was all gestures, and gestures were futile.

That's when the real darkness descended. Instead of blaming God I blamed myself. None of this would've happened had I not failed Yeshu. I'm clever enough, and loyal. Everyone says so. I've been told this since I was a child. So why *didn't* I find a way to put myself in Yeshu's place and exchange my life for his?

I should've warned him and the others about Judah: about his awful bag of dreams; about the red-legged lion. This nightmare did not have to happen.

Some days I couldn't shake Judah's voice that was pursuing me like an agitated hornet. "Could have, should have, can't be turned into would have," the voice would insinuate.

Then it would say, "Now that it's too late to alter anything, what's left for you in this world? Come join me."

Countless times that pestering buzz took me off the path and nearly led me over a cliff. What saved me were the other voices. As the sun beat down I felt myself evaporate. I withered and shrank until all the small creatures seemed exalted above me. At last I could hear them speak.

In the voice of the toad and the cricket I heard Yohanan whispering. It washed over me and through me till the words became distinct.

> I have no food but tears, day and night.
> Deep calls to deep in the roar of your cataracts,
> and all your waves, all your breakers, roll over me.

In the song of the willow wren I listened to Yeshu reciting from the Psalms.

> I say to God, my rock,
> why have you forsaken me?
> You are the God in whom I take refuge,
> why have you cast me off?
> Why must I walk about as a mourner
> because the enemy oppresses me?

If Yohanan and Yeshu were here again in the flesh, I thought, they would understand this pain. They had gone through so much more. When

I lay in the dark at night, I could see their sad smiles as they cocked their heads, appraising me.

"Don't you know, Daavi," their eyes said, "that leaving this world won't halt its suffering?"

Every morning I sighed heavily and looked around me. I was bound to this world although it was entirely drained of color. A year after that terrible day on Gol'gotha, food still tasted like sawdust, and a wild iris had no more scent than a rock in a dry riverbed. The warbler sounded flat, and I myself could not sing – not even Shoshana's lullaby.

Sleep provided no rest, and even worse, it came and went mostly devoid of dreaming. At times I'd awaken suddenly in the dead of night feeling like a tiny vole cowering in the grass, trying to hide from the owl swooping overhead, hunting for prey under the torchlight of a full moon.

Then I would see the torches being carried by the phalanx of men who had come to arrest Yeshu. And all that followed came flooding back. Any likelihood of falling asleep again was gone. The nameless sadness that bent my back like a load of stone during the day crushed my chest to the ground on those sleepless nights; so much so that every breath screamed Yeshu's name.

To lessen the anguish, I rummaged around for a scapegoat. I started with Rome, an empire that had cheated us and would hold us enslaved forever. I wanted to throw myself hard against the Roman army—one at a time or in legions—followed by our priests and our legal authorities and all the other jackals. I felt Judah rising up inside me. And I shivered.

So I tried to shift my blaming to him, but when I learned how he had ended up, I surprised myself.

I wept.

I didn't know I had any tears left.

Oh, Judah. Realizing how utterly he had failed, how reckless and foolhardy he'd been to conspire with the authorities to hand Yeshu over, he had thrown a rope over the thick branch of an ancient olive tree, tied a noose around his neck, and hung himself.

Some were happy to hear of the fiery Judah swinging there, all alone.

But it made me feel worse than ever. He was so rash, and he believed everything began and ended with *him*. But his thrashing about was like a whip gripped at the wrong end by a hand that was inept, yet sincere.

And did Rome even need this hapless Judah? Hadn't Yeshu often told us that the soldiers could find him any time they really wanted to? Pluck him from the vine just as they had Yohanan. Yes, Judah was a handy pruning knife but others were available.

My father always said that Yohanan's vision reached a century into the future while Yeshu's spanned a thousand years or more. Judah considered both these cousins to be too much like dreamy boys. Yet in trying to shake them awake, he saw no farther than his own nose. The white-hot prophecy he boasted of on that day we walked together to Arimathea had blinded him. Staring into the light, he was unaware of the shadow he cast.

During those endless nights, I had plenty of time to think about Judah and how things could've changed. What was puzzling to me was why Yeshu brought him close and let him stay. I tried to see things through the carpenter's eyes and began to understand how Judah was not without virtue.

He was flint against obsidian—our Jewish fire starter. His longing for justice was a spark our people needed as they shivered in the unending darkness of Roman bondage and occupation. His fierce determination was a pulsing ember in the ashes of dawn, calling out for the breath of eager blacksmiths to rekindle the hearth fire for reforging our broken nation.

But Judah forgot that fire has no friends. Without a cradle of rock, it will burn down the house. Enraptured by its power, he turned to the flame of armed rebellion. He vowed to put Yeshu in a position that would force him to act. But alas, as always the results were not what Judah had foreseen. The blaze that was lit burned back toward Yeshu and consumed him, leaving Judah staring at the charred ruins of his convictions and passing cold judgment on himself.

Once again he mistook punishment for justice. He could not imagine the possibility of someone guilty ever being redeemed. It was too late to save Judah's life, but I wished I could tell him that his death and my struggle to understand it had helped save mine. It was the thin reed that kept me from drowning.

I knew now what I would not do. But I hadn't the vaguest idea of what *to* do.

Master Teacher, Final Lesson

Although I still couldn't understand why Yeshu had to die, or how to make his loss hurt any less, I was gradually able to stop floundering. What helped most was my finally deciding to stop fleeing and go looking for answers. Two days of trudging up a steep path took me to the tiny mountain village where Maria Magdalena was said to have gone into hiding from the authorities, following Yeshu's death.

None of the villagers admitted to knowing her or anyone like her. Exhausted I plopped down beside the well in the dusty plaza, leaned my head back, and told myself this was perhaps where I would expire.

I must have dropped into slumber because someone was gently shaking me awake. It was Maria leaning over me, smiling. She took my hand and helped me to my feet. For a long while we embraced wordlessly.

"My neighbors came to tell me a young man was trying to find me," she finally said. "They added that he wasn't dressed like a soldier and seemed too desperate to be a spy, but these days, who knew for sure? So I pulled the hood of my cloak up over my head, and came to see for myself."

She paused then, squeezing my arms, and said, "Daavi, my friend, I can't tell you how good it is to see you!" She gave me one last squeeze, hard.

"I miss...oh, how I miss...." and she halted, unable to go on.

I tried to speak but couldn't get a word out. We both sighed heavily, shaking our heads. Despite the sadness in our eyes, we couldn't restrain the smiles.

Taking me by the elbow, Maria led me back to the house where she was staying. She served up a meal of smoked fish and parched corn, followed by raisin cakes smothered with goat cheese.

After so long on the road, how good it tasted! I gulped it down like a famished wolf pup. Meanwhile, I was bursting with questions about Yeshu but couldn't figure out how to ask them. I suppose I feared the answers. Or perhaps I was afraid there would *be* no answers. In my mind, I heard my voice cracking like the wall of an irrigation ditch and spilling out a flood of emotion, so I sat there, empty spoon in my hand, empty plate in my lap, staring in awkward silence.

Finally I summoned the courage to ask how she was holding up.

At first she said nothing. Finally, staring down at her hands, she began, "For months I was an open wound constantly being poked." She sighed. "Looking at someone seemed to hurt as much as being looked at."

Hearing that, I felt my back stiffen.

She went on. "Keeping to myself didn't help, either. The wind touching my cheek or my hands breaking a loaf of bread – the slightest thing would make me think of Yeshu. My knees would go wobbly, and I'd be unable to stand." She took a breath. "For a while I was terrified of sliding back into the black pit he had pulled me from, a slippery pit with no handhold or foothold for climbing out."

She raised her face to catch my eye. "So I held onto the words that Yeshu gave us, knowing he must be here somewhere, present as always.

She raised her face to catch my eye.

"So I held onto the words that Yeshu gave us, knowing he must be here somewhere, present as always.

"I searched everywhere—inside the words, between the words—waiting for him to come. I wasn't saying just morning prayers and evening prayers; I found myself praying all day long."

She shifted her gaze to a distant spot before continuing. "I imagined his face. Inhaling, I looked into his eyes. Exhaling, I brushed them shut. Inhaling, I saw his eyelids open. Exhaling, I felt them close. And then I would awaken and it would be the next morning.

"I learned to do this even while taking care of the chores my hosts needed to have done. I did my work by turning the day into prayer. Soon I was so full it spilled over, and I began tending to the aches and sorrows of the people of this village, good folk who were kind enough to take me in.

"My praying became an expanding circle that enclosed not just Yeshu and myself, but moved outward to enfold the villagers and our band of followers. And it very much included you."

Her words were like a plowshare at winter's end, opening up my soul for the sowing of seed whose sprouting was yet to come.

Suddenly aware of her eyes fixing on mine, I felt my mouth fly open.

Words sprang out like bats winging from a cave, as I asked over and over, "Why did he have to die? Why? Why?" I gasped. "Why did he let them kill him? He could have saved himself. I'm sure of it. I just know he could."

Maria let me spill it all out: all the confusion and anger rushing like water through a dry gulch after a downpour.

I pounded my fist into my hand. "The schemers and connivers should be punished in the fires of hell. Or at the very least, they deserve to be haunted by guilt."

Staring at the earthen floor under me, I muttered, "The thunder and lightning that dreadful day must have left them quavering. The heavens opened up and rained down, trying to wash the world clean. It should have washed them all away!"

I raised my closed hand and covered my mouth with my knuckles. I had said enough.

Maria rose and leaned down to take my arm. Tugging me to my feet she led me outside and down a rutted path to a lemon grove. Loosening her grip, she forged ahead among the gnarled trees, turning around occasionally to be sure I was keeping up. Finally she sat.

We were all alone except for the sound of sparrows in the highest limbs. I understood from Maria's face that she had something to say that she didn't want repeated if the walls of her house had ears.

At first she was quiet. Then she began to sing words from the Psalms so softly she was nearly humming them.

> He will come down like rain
> on early wheat and mown hay,
> like showers watering the earth.

Several times she sang the verse, then stopped her singing as abruptly as she had started it.

I looked into her eyes and saw the drops of rain: Falling, softly falling. Glistening there and on her cheeks.

"Yes, Daavi..." she said tenderly, stopping for a time as if out of breath, "certainly Yeshu's death was completely senseless. Unspeakable. Only a monster would think otherwise."

She pressed the back of her hand against her teeth. I waited for her to go on, and before long, she did. "And yet—how can I say this?—when I'm feeling brave, I try putting myself inside Yeshu's head, seeing what he sees on that dreadful day, the atrocities coldly being carried out.

"Gazing down I find myself watching all of us peering up at him, hanging there, caught between life and death.

"Then I remember myself in that moment, being touched by the softness of his eyes in all his pain and misery. And I'm overwhelmed by the concern he shows, the love he feels, for *us*!"

She sighed.

"Listen, my friend. Yeshu's death was not meaningless, unless we make it so. He lived his life as a gift, and I will not forsake that offering. I've come to understand that in dying he teaches us a lesson that lives as long as we embrace it."

I straightened.

Her hands rose to her cheek. "The light of his face brought me out of the darkness, and I will follow where it leads."

She looked away, through the thicket of limbs and leaves.

"Don't get me wrong. I'm sure he didn't want to die yet. There was so much left to do. But he saw clearly how death is our companion. Every moment of every day he could feel the light touch of its breath on his neck.

"Daavi, do you remember the night around the fire when he almost as much as told us so?"

I nodded.

"I still shiver," she went on, "thinking about it. And yet he was so calm. I believe he was telling us that how we *live* defines our death. He wasn't afraid of dying because he wasn't afraid of living. He knew his own heart better than the shape and purpose of each of his father's tools. He had chosen this journey, and would not turn aside."

I nodded again, my memories intertwining with hers as she paused for a really long time. When she spoke again, her voice was strong.

"Daavi, I believe that Yeshu knew he was about to die...that he would be killed."

She gazed straight into my eyes. "And so he chose to make his death his last and finest act of teaching."

I became still as rock.

"He would face his dying without resistance; without inciting those who loved him to take up the sword in his defense; without dragging hundreds or thousands of people to pointless deaths alongside him. The folly of that would have extinguished them all," she swallowed hard, "while breaking and diminishing those of us who remained."

My eyes were fixed on her lips, following every word.

"But *one* death in place of many," she went on, "would light a flame that will burn forever in the hearts of those who can see it.

"He acted just as he taught us to act. He would die as he had lived, with love and compassion. He was telling us that others can snatch away our bodies, but only we can lose our souls."

Her eyes were no longer damp; they were glowing.

"I know your anger, Daavi. I lived in eternal torment before Yeshu freed me. But can you still hear his final words? I can.

> Forgive them.
> They know not what they do.
> Forgive them. Forgive them.

"He whispered those same words into my ear, years before, when we were walking back from the Cedars. I had asked him what was I to do if, while walking in the world, I met the demons that had been cast out of me. There were so many people in my village who had hurt me, and sometimes I saw those same demonic looks in the eyes of others, elsewhere.

"He leaned close and answered me without hesitation, "Forgive them!"

Maria formed her words slowly now. "I know how hard this forgiving is to do. I remember how long and hard I worked on it. But Yeshu's life shows us it can be done."

She peered through the trees and into the distance, then back at me.

"Daavi, Yeshu desired only one thing for himself at the end of his life." She filled her lungs with air.

"He wished to die into God."

With a start, I realized Maria and I were once again of the same mind.

Her eyes closed for a long while. Then opened.

"And so he did."

As I reached out to grip her hand, Maria fell silent, parted her lips to speak, halted. Then she added, "Consider carefully all that I have just said and I believe you will agree with me. Our Yeshu could not have lived—or died—otherwise."

I stood immobilized within the grasp of her words. I looked away, and caught sight of a leaf on a branch, being buffeted to and fro by the wind.

Much of what she was saying echoed in my heart. I had wrestled with this dilemma in different forms many times, always with the carpenter as my guide. Now the pole star had flickered and gone out. So it soothed me to hear Maria speaking these thoughts with such conviction. I trusted her judgment. But there was something else.

I could tell that she saw Yeshu as clearly today as when he walked the earth. My sense of him had grown shaky because I no longer trusted myself. Trusting Maria made me feel I might yet find my way back to the beloved lamb of God that I'd let wander off.

I cleared my throat; then murmured, "But Maria, aren't you furious with Judah?"

"Judah?" she said. "No."

Her eyes flitted away and I turned to see a swift-weaving akkabish lowering itself from a branch by a single thread of webbing. When I turned back, she had resumed speaking.

"Poor Judah was an actor with no lines, in a Greek tragedy scripted from the outset by others, for murder. It was murder ordered by thugs who sat astride thrones only to be vanquished by a dove that could not be caged."

She was staring straight at me. "Yeshu loved him, you know."

I nodded mutely.

"He loved him," she said, "like the shepherd loves the sheep that has strayed from the flock, out of sight and beyond earshot."

I winced. My mouth opened and a cry escaped like a bleating lamb's, closely followed by another and another in a chain of bound-up sobbing.

Maria's hand touched my shoulder, staying there until my breathing evened out.

"Yeshu forgave the worst of blunders by those he loved, even before they were committed," she said, continuing to look at me. "Can you forgive afterwards?"

I was trembling. Bowing my head, I allowed her question to settle in. So much had happened to so many people I cared about. So much had happened to me. Once I started forgiving, where would it end?

We sat there quietly in the thickness of the lemon grove until the sun dropped from sight and the stars sprang out.

Soul Shepherd: A Friend Among Friends

The next morning we ate our breakfast in silence. When we were cleaning up afterward, I finally spoke. "Maria," I said, "Judah wasn't the only one who became lost. Since Yeshu's death I've been wandering the hills and valleys of Judea like a vagrant. I tried to outrun the pain but couldn't."

I stopped speaking and started over, "I didn't know where else to turn so I came here."

I noticed a flicker in her eyes as I talked. "When Yeshu was alive, I found my life in following him. When he died, it seemed like I had died. Life itself had died.

"Yesterday I felt him close again, being with you."

I took a deep breath. "I want to be your disciple."

Maria stared at me, saying nothing, till I started to blush. Was she angry with me? Maybe I'd waited too long to search for her.

Finally she took me by both shoulders. Bringing her face close to mine, she leaned forward, the ends of her wavy, glistening hair brushing my chest. I couldn't move or speak. Had she shouted, I would have jumped out of my skin!

But she didn't shout. She just began to talk, her voice firm and without hesitation. "You will not follow me," she said. "No one will follow me. I won't allow it. Nor will I follow anyone else. You must decide for yourself what to do. I know you feel stuck. But you didn't come here for me to tell you that, did you?"

She paused to let her words sink in, then resumed, "You came here for help in remembering something you already know. We've walked many roads together, shared laughter and heartache, and I've watched you grow into the young man Yeshu hoped you would be.

"I know you may not feel ready. But you are. You're the helmsman of your own spirit and the shepherd of your own soul. Just as now we all are.

That's what Yeshu was trying to tell us the night before he was snatched away. He has led us to the edge of the cliff. And we must fly.

"You no longer need to be told what to believe, or how to shape those beliefs. Yeshu has taught you the scriptures and the laws. Some of them he cast a new light upon. He has shown you how to seek out your own truth; how to struggle for peace. How to love your friends, your enemies, and yourself.

"Yeshu and Yohanan have taught you how to pray, how to meditate, how to hold all life sacred. They taught you how to listen for God's voice within you, how to better know God. And how to love God—in your heart and your actions.

"Mama Maria has taught you how to endure; and Martha how to sing through joys and sorrows. Mama Ana has given you the history of our people, and of your village and your family. And she has taught you a very, very powerful skill: how to tell stories that move people, light them up, giving them maps to use in finding the way through their lives.

"Joanna has taught you how to be a loyal friend and to serve others.

"You have been well prepared, Daavi. *No* one could be better prepared for the journey each of us must one day take through their own inner world, and through the world around us."

Maria released my shoulders and took hold of my hands. Her face softened. "If you want to walk *with* me through this world of ours for a time, then I accept the offer of your good company. I'm happy that you would overlook the faults of a scorned and resented woman, dragging her mistakes behind her like the bells of those suffering with leprosy."

I started to speak, but she laughed quietly, way down in her chest. Her eyes twinkled as she made it clear she recalled my story from the riverbank long ago, when I told her about the drifting band of afflicted souls intoning their cries of "Unclean!"

Then she went on, "But you will not follow me. And I will not lead you."

My mouth started to open, but she put her fingers to my lips to stop me from speaking.

"If you agree too quickly, we might both lack faith in what you say. Daavi, the hour has come for you to go back into the wilderness. This time because you choose to, and because you have the right questions.

"You mustn't go to ask, 'whom shall I follow?'" she added. "But instead to ask, 'do I need to follow anyone at all?' Not to find 'who's on the right path?' But 'what path am *I* on?' And 'where would God have me journey now?'

"The next time you see me," she said, "we'll both know without speaking a word if you still want to join me, shoulder to shoulder, in taking up the work that needs to be done in this world."

She smiled. "God and Yeshu will be there helping guide our plowshares, of course..." Her eyes flicked down momentarily, then returned to mine. "Fair enough?"

I nodded.

~ ~ ~

That very afternoon I set off, without really knowing where I was going. I opened myself up as Maria advised, and trusted that my feet would find the way. It felt odd at first because aimlessness had gotten me lost after Yeshu's murder. But this was a different kind of wandering. It was wandering with purpose.

The first thing I discover—I should say rediscover—is that wilderness isn't far away but all around. It isn't just a place but a way of thinking and feeling. Just like Yohanan said, it can be but a single step from where you stand.

I begin by walking, counting each stride, hoping to fall into a certain rhythm. Day follows day until eventually my heartbeat keeps pace with my feet and my mind slowly clears like a vast sky, empty except for the questions I've brought along. Those questions float like clouds above me, and like clouds they change shape as I walk and watch.

Things that early on strike me as utterly strange begin to seem familiar, until finally I feel a name pressing at the end of my tongue. But I resist the naming, waiting to see if the changing is done.

I sit by a passing stream for hours, among stands of weeping willows and sycamores that so love the water they can never get too close. What might this living water tell me about life and the spirit? The stream won't stop talking, though I comprehend not a word of what it says.

Yohanan and Yeshu and Maria Magdalena went into the wilderness in search of soul and spirit. Did they sit by this same stream, or another, and right away understand its song? In my memory the three of them seem twice as tall and four times as wise as I.

Biting my lip, I wonder: will I ever grow to the level of their eyes? I stare deeper into the water, and finally the stream stands still; and it is I who am moving unrelentingly by.

I rise to my feet and walk in, crossing the stream with its chilly rapids, feeling the water splashing my legs above the knees. On the other side, I turn to look back, reaching out to trace my finger along the boulder-strewn hillside and down the willow branch and over the wings of heron and swan.

Moments later, lying face down to drink from a spring feeding the stream, I draw in the scent of cedar bark and lilacs on the wind. The moaning song of the turtledove nestles softly in my ears. Unexpectedly, I long for my earliest childhood, when all was right and safe and close to the hearth.

Heart in hand, I walk and walk into the night, laying myself upon a bed of soft grasses when I can no longer see to lift up my feet and set them down.

The next day at sunrise I awaken near a gentle hillside, surrounded by crimson poppies and purple hyacinths. The rays of new light turn the petals nearly transparent, each overlapping its neighbor like the tiles of a roof. The ants and I gape in awe. My nostrils twitch from the mix of scents.

Downwind, butterflies flutter among a clump of junipers. The trembling needles whisper what my tongue hasn't been able to say. Rolling over onto my back, I watch a dozen hawks above wheel in tight circles, hunting for their breakfast. It seems that everyone is up and about but me.

My eyes turn inward—also hunting—and I ponder a line of scripture, measuring it against the mysteries of the hungry heart.

> Is it by your wisdom that the hawk soars
>   and spreads its wings toward the south?

Sitting up and reaching into my pouch, I pull out my own breakfast, a handful of nuts gathered the day before. I chew them now, one by one, to make them last. They crunch between my teeth like the sound of an adz on a surrendering pine log.

Resting my head on my folded cloak, I imagine the curling woodchips flying this way and that, and then I recall my father telling us, after his return home from Roman imprisonment, the story of Job from the Book of *Iyov*. Burnt in my mind are several lines from the narrative.

> If a tree is cut down,
>   there is hope that it will sprout again
>   and that fresh shoots will not fail.
> Though its roots grow old in the earth,
>   and its stump is dying in the ground,
>   yet at the scent of water it may break into bud
>   and make new growth like a young plant.
> But a man dies and he disappears;
>   humans expire, and where are they?
> As the waters dwindle from a lake,
>   or as a river shrinks and runs dry,
>   so mortals lie down never to rise again
>   until the very sky splits open.

Oh Yeshu, beloved storyteller! You once ushered me into Yohanan's presence long after he had been slain. Though his life was severed by the murderer's axe, the waters of his spirit flowed on and did not run dry. Surely Yeshu, you must be here, too.

But where are you?

I push myself to my feet and begin climbing the hill. Every step feels steeper than the last. All day I trudge upward, staring at the ground rising in front of me, watching each foot gain its tentative toehold in the rocky soil. Thoughts spin behind my eyes like maple seeds in a windstorm.

My head is pounding.

Reaching the top at last, I lie down and curl into a ball, exhausted. When my eyes open again, it is dusk. The stars rise, and the night chill descends with its sharp talons. My teeth clatter as I huddle under my thin blanket like a mole in a nest of leaves. From a nearby tree an owl hoots enigmatically.

Is it calling me?

Or did I summon its call?

Lips quivering, I silently mouth words from the Psalms, seeking solace in the comfort of my own arms that are now encircling me.

> I am like a vulture of the wilderness,
>   like an owl of the waste places.
> I lie awake.
> I am no different from a lonely bird on the housetop.

At the first graying of dawn, bleary-eyed and sleepless, I roll up my blanket, sling it around my shoulders, and wander off down a long, dry streambed, trying to shake the chill from my bones. The ground is soft and littered with stones and soon I am wheezing like a lost sheep bleating for its shepherd.

"If Yeshu is alive," I whisper, "he will come looking for me."

Several miles later, a whiff of sweet-smelling gum from a myrrh tree tickles my nose like gnats seeking moisture in the blazing noonday sun. Thoughts so small I can hardly hear them whizz through my mind. I stagger on, barely keeping ahead of the day's turning wheel, desperate to avoid being crushed.

I stop.

Enough! This wilderness is endless. I'm done with walking. Perhaps I shall run! If Maria won't accept me, maybe Petros will?

Frustrated I kick a rock and screech as my toe begins to throb.

"You are so hard-headed, Petros," I holler out.

Listening to the words rattle through my head and echo off the stones, I explode with wild giggles and can't stop until it turns to sobbing.

Finally, I crumple over, sitting down and rocking back and forth, holding my forehead in my hands.

After a bit, my breath stills and an inner voice tells me, "No, you must stay in the barrens until your task is finished—or you are."

So I get up and go on, farther away now from anyone I know, and farther down inside myself than I've ever been. Embarking on a total fast, I scatter what nuts and berries I've found, to the birds and ground squirrels around me. My only food is what enters my eyes as the scurrying creatures eat their fill.

Soon these eyes learn to feast on their own. One afternoon I pause by a patch of lavender and kneel to peer deep into a fragrant blossom. I'm swept back to the day when Yohanan pointed out creation and eternity in a single flower.

Once again, my mind halts as it struggles to grasp an idea so intertwined, so vast.

The golden dust of a nearby narcissus rides the breezes circling my head. I wait, cocking an ear to listen. Languorously the dry wind sings with Yohanan's lilting voice a passage from Solomon's Song of Songs, the book known in Hebrew as the *Šîr HaŠîrîm.*

> The flowers appear on the earth.
> The time of the singing of birds is come,
>   and the voice of the turtle is heard in our land.

But as quickly as the breeze lifts me up, it dies away. For a moment, gliding high above, I catch sight of a dark cloud that resembles the hem of a familiar robe, yet when I reach out to touch it, it's empty and I lose my balance, tumbling down out of control. My head spins and the earth opens like a pit.

With my face pressed to the ground, I awaken and hear a familiar voice reciting more words from the Book of Job, recounting the trials of Iyov.

> A man blossoms like a flower,
> 	withers, and is slashed down.
> He slips away like a shadow,
> 	and continues not.

I sit up and open my hands, watching crushed petals fluttering to the ground. They are words forming phrases I don't want to see.

Yohanan lives. Yeshu lives not.

Yeshu lives, Yohanan lives not.

I touch Yeshu and Yohanan; I touch them not.

I shake my head in disbelief while my mind races in circles like an angry dog chasing its tail. Finally, completely spent, I swear I will leave.

And I do.

At the edge of a village I smell fresh bread being pulled out of the oven as children laugh in delight, and suddenly I whip around and hasten back the way I came, asking myself: where do I belong?

At long last a day dawns when I know every creature and every plant by heart. I concentrate on a thistle for a minute, an hour, wondering if *it* is watching me and pondering.

Fervently wishing I knew the thistle's language, I hear echoes of Yeshu's voice, singing the Psalms to me when I fell from the tree.

> As a deer yearns for the running streams,
> 	So does my soul long for you, oh Yahweh.
> With my whole being I thirst for God, the living God.
> 	"Where is your God?" they ask me all day long...

I can feel Yeshu there, resting on the throne of that thistle. But I can't see his face. It's turned away from me.

That evening, soon after falling asleep, I dream vividly. Things are like they were before Yeshu died. I know he's happy I'm dreaming; that it's important.

I can feel him walking a half step behind me. I try to slow down so he can get in front and I can see him squarely. Yet each time I cut my pace, so does he. Why does he hide his face from me?

Over the nights that follow, the dream keeps recurring. Soon the days seem endless as I wait to fall asleep. Each night we walk side by side—this presence and I—until I wonder at last where we are. I try to ask but hear only the sound our sandals make gliding through the grass.

Then one night I close the door on the day and enter the dream again and find myself alone on a plain high in the mountains. The silence is vast, and I think this must be the solitude of the wandering stars. I can't hear myself breathe and for an instant the notion crosses my mind that I might be dead. But then far away a figure that at first glance seemed to be a tree, leans forward and begins to walk directly toward me.

I strain my eyes but can't make out who it could be. As the figure nears, I notice another one approaching from my right. And then a third appears from the left. Instinctively I glance over my shoulder, only to find a fourth hurrying to catch up with me. I don't recognize a single face, even when they are almost upon me.

Before I can ask who they are and what they want, the four step together and merge into one. In a flash I know it's Yeshu. It doesn't look like Yeshu, but without a doubt it is he.

The figure floats like mist and shines with all the colors of the rainbow. I'm not afraid. I want to reach out and embrace it.

Instead I begin to walk. It walks with me. I stop and it stops. I retrace my steps. It follows along. I leap into the air, and it leaps right beside me, turning once before floating down.

Suddenly this all strikes me as hilariously funny, and I burst out laughing. The figure laughs too until both of us are bending over and dropping weakly to the ground.

For a moment, I lie there, staring at the star-flecked heavens, slowly catching my breath. When finally I try staggering to my feet, the figure offers me a hand.

As I stand up, in a flash it steps inside me. I feel it from the crown of my head to the soles of my feet.

Briefly, I awaken, filled now with a new sense of oneness, of peace and completeness.

Yes, this is how the crisp air tasted as our small band knelt together under the canopy of the cedars of Lebanon. We knelt and watched the invisible hand inscribing our story with sun and breeze on the scroll of lacey ferns covering the forest floor. It's how the light shone in our eyes when Yeshu broke bread on that long ago night before the world snapped in two. It's how I felt when my family had formed its own perfect circle at the dinner table and Shoshana sat beside me.

I hold this feeling inside me as preciously as earlier this morning I cradled in the palm of my hand a lone downy feather from a bluebird's breast, my breath causing it to quiver.

A wordless humming floods my soul, and I think, so this is how the opened thistle speaks: In silence. With silence. In God. With God.

I tumble back into sleep and reenter the dream. Before I know it, I'm walking, striding, making my way across the plain and down to a village I've never been to before. I walk to the village center to find the well that is always there. Peering over the side, I look far down at the shimmering water below. There I find my face glowing like a paper lantern with a lit candle within. It flickers but will not go out. I can't stop smiling.

My eyes spring open, and this time I'm fully awake.

I know what to do.

Maria Magdalena was right. It will not be easy to give up the comfort of a wise master—a beacon in the night, right here on earth, directly in front of me. Someone who could fix my confusions, tell me what to think, what to believe, what to do. Someone who would put my doubts to rest.

But I realize now, Yeshu has always been my guide. And he still is, even though I cannot reach out and touch him. He goes where I go. He lives inside, teaching me every day.

Because he touches *me*.

He transformed us the night before he died when he said, "I am no longer your master or your leader; you are no longer my followers."

I just didn't know how to hear it then. How to hear silence when it speaks. So I didn't fully grasp his message when he added, "I now simply call you *friends*."

Yes, Yeshu, a friend is what I am. A friend among friends.

I See the Face of God and I'm Not Afraid

I feel my desolation slipping away as night fades and day begins to bloom. But my wilderness work is not done. I know it, though I cannot quite put my finger on what is missing. I lie there staring up at the sky, trying mightily to make the mist blow away—or at least swirl into patterns that will bring my world into focus. Unannounced, the bird of dawn flies out of the sun and into my breast. It brings not clarity but uncertainty.

If I am a friend among friends, where are they? Yeshu's band of followers is splintered. Judah is dead. Petros, who knows? There's Maria, but she sent me off. The Thunder Brothers are mute. Wherever on this lonely earth can I be at home?

I stand and begin to walk. The ground again slopes in a gradual rise. My legs feel steadily stronger the higher I go. An unseen hand on the small of my back is pressing me onward. My entire being moves with it. I will go where it takes me until daylight ends.

At last the ground levels out and I stop to look around. The plain stretches out on all sides, as far as the eye can see. Which way should I head? I count off a hundred deliberate steps to the north. Then I stop for my chest to rise and fall several times, wheel around, and walk another way.

I know without deliberation that where I want to go can't be found by walking straight, so I keep swerving slightly and rarely make a perfect turn right or left, but angle off. My aim is to have no aim, discovering where my feet, and my thoughts, may lead me. Letting heel and toe find the path that creates and recreates itself as it is walked.

During all of this meandering my mind floats high above, watching like an eagle riding a current, so I know that I'm not lost. The tiny figure below isn't forlorn or stumbling about quite the way he was before finding his friend Maria again. Back then he was pushed and pulled by agony and despair, unable to escape the long shadow of Gol'gotha.

I walk and spread my wings to catch the breeze, waiting patiently to see where and how the way opens up, where God's breath may carry me. I'm in no hurry. I mull over a notion, an image, a few paces at a time or for as long as it holds me.

I begin with the scarred backs of Yeshu's hands holding tools; Mama Ana's story voice; Judah's set jaw.

Walking, slowly walking: Yohanan's Psalm singing; my parents standing silently side by side; Mama Maria's warm bread.

Step following step: Gramma Ruth's infectious laugh; the sparkle in Shoshana's eyes as she sang to me.

Heel, toe, heel, toe: The Thunder Brothers' sacred clowning; the shepherd girl's singing into the roar of falling water.

Inhaling, exhaling, with each rising leg and footfall. On I go, culminating with Yeshu's words—love your God, love your enemy, love your neighbor as yourself.

After the sun sets, I stop and watch the gloaming settle down around me. I take the fading light in and let the darkness out. Breath after breath, watching and waiting. In one quiet motion, I spread out my blanket and follow it to the ground.

There I lie without stirring, inhaling the darkness and exhaling the light. Lifting my face upward I seek the first wandering star to appear, trying not to look straight at it, but just to its side as Yohanan taught me to do. As the night lowers its expansive dome over me, I gaze deep into the gaping holes in the Via Lactea, letting my mind go still.

Rather than sleeping, I catnap. Focused not so much on the dreams to come as on the moments when I'm balanced at the fringe of plunging into slumber...and then focusing again when I'm climbing out of the pool. Entering and leaving, the images are hazy and the words unformed; smells are nameless; sounds are muffled by mist.

That's when the least expected notions show themselves: A stream, all burbling and no water. Clouds stretching out on the ground, turning in their sleep. Lions lying down with lambs.

In those moments, even more startling brother-sister pairs lock arms: Judah in love. Children leading their parents by the hand through a thunderstorm. A melting sword.

A valley of black flowers, their petals brushing my ankles, exuding the scent of memories from others who walked this way before.

Tattered shepherds' cloaks covering a throne. A Jew lifting a wounded Roman to carry him home. A tiny, bent woman heaping lilies of the field into the bowls of hungry landowners lined up on her doorstep.

Rather than search for meanings, I simply watch, open up, and let the night sky turn. Does a blade of grass refuse to drink until it understands why the raindrop strikes the earth just above its roots? Does the wind hold its breath until it knows just where its blown trail is meant to end?

I move forward with faith that without my finger directing them, all the colors of the dawn will form rainbows in dew clinging to grass.

The next morning, I resume walking. Easily distracted as always—perhaps as I should be—I pause next to a small pond surrounded by reeds. Gently I kneel down on the mossy bank and stare into the still water under high clear skies. Time passes, as it is wont to do, so I let it. Can I do otherwise?

Without warning, I hear a sound like a single raindrop plunging through the surface of the pond. My head snaps up in time to see only ripples circling outward. On the opposite edge of the pond, just above those circles, grows a plant with broad, waxy leaves as large as stepping stones. One lone immense leaf hangs over the water, and it is speckled with drops of dew.

Gazing at this leaf, I notice that the dewdrops occasionally creep down toward its sloping middle, timidly joining one another in the trough formed by the central vein, until at last they gather enough weight to cause the leaf-tip to gently descend...just enough to release the gathered drop for its plummet to the water's waiting surface.

The sound of the impact of droplet on pond is like the muted plucking of a single lute string. Sweetly melodious and clear. Nonetheless, to avert the next note from redirecting my contemplative stream, I resolve to teach myself to answer the sound with an ever deeper quietness. Each splash will be a reminder to become even more still than I already am. Thereby ceasing all stirring, from my scalp to my toes; hushing the endless curiosity of me talking about what I perceive; stopping everything but my soundless breath.

In this manner, one moment extends to touch the next moment falling in. In between, I discover the silence inside of silence. The bell ringing inside a bell.

All that surrounds this still center becomes as golden as sunshine after a squall.

Continuing to stare into the water, I bend closer and puff across the surface. In the ripples that crease my reflection, I see Yohanan's weathered face. I puff again and see Yeshu's. Here and gone and here again.

Inadvertently, I lean forward so far my nose touches its twin and I feel myself rippling outward until I am the pond looking up into a bottomless blue sky. Suddenly a frog leaps out of nowhere—out of me?—into the very center of its splash, sending more pronounced circles expanding outward. They roll over the ripples my nose has made, combining to form new interlocking circles.

As the colliding rings gradually disappear, I catch sight of a blur out of the corner of my eye, a tiny creature zipping by that startles me. I swing my head to solve the mystery. Much to my surprise, not one but dozens of dragonflies have suddenly materialized and are darting back and forth just above the surface of the water. The frog's leap must have stirred up some minuscule source of food.

I'm mesmerized by the flurry of diaphanous wings beating the air, each one reflecting all colors of the rainbow, every color on earth. Effortlessly, these tiny flying beings are weaving a tapestry of sparkling hues hanging just above the water.

All the while my mind flits along in time, trailing its own visions: of Yeshu singing; of the myriad hues in Yohanan's eyes; and of God's shimmering covenant with men and women and all creatures, a covenant which extends watchfully over the earth, as the rainbow.

The subtle melody made by the dragonflies' wings lingers when I close my eyes, assuring me that no crazed monarch can demolish what Yohanan and Yeshu stood and died for. Love embodied cannot be simply snuffed out and wiped from sight and memory.

Opening my eyes, I breathe from my waist up to my throat and feel the tones and colors swelling in my chest. Then, as quickly as they came the dragonflies are gone, and out of the corner of my eye I notice a long-legged bird, an egret, standing motionless at the other side of the pond. I hadn't seen or heard it arrive. Perhaps it was always there, blending with the reeds.

Staring intently down its long, golden beak, the tall white bird lifts one leg out of the water, swings it forward, and steps through the pond's shining surface to re-anchor its fanned-out toes in the mud below. It pauses, legs angled apart, and then carefully withdraws its rear foot from the water to swing it forward another step.

This slow dance proceeds along the shoreline: Lift...step...pause. Lift... step...pause. Until the bird finally arrives at a new hunting spot, heralded by a sudden cock of its head.

This is my cue to arise and resume my own unhurried walk. With new knowledge, I slow my pace until I'm rhythmically lifting one foot with a long inhalation, swinging it out and placing it back on the earth as that same breath slowly leaves me. In time, the other foot follows. Steadily I move forward through a canopy of trees, eyes fixed unwaveringly on a spot three paces ahead of me, the air under my feet like shallow pond water.

I contemplate the steadfast presence of the stalking egret, forever seeking the silver flash of a lone fish nibbling at a root, or the unwary frog swimming blissfully within beak-spearing distance. But what is it that *I* am seeking? No image rises to the surface. I've been walking for days now, my thoughts suspended in still water. Doing what? Fishing for a thin glimmer of understanding?

By late morning I arrive at a thicket of brambles that I can traverse only by crawling through very cautiously on hands and knees. Momentarily I am back in the Cedars of Lebanon, observing the ponderous but somehow graceful lumbering of a watchful, helmeted creature making its way forward. As it advances, Yohanan recalls Rabbi Abraham's pronouncement:

"And when I see a turtle walk, I've never seen a turtle walk before."

Soundlessly, on the thicket's other side I climb back to my feet. Ahead is a gnarled mulberry tree. With relish, I grasp the lowest limb in one hand, swing myself up, and proceed to climb the tree with care, in hopes of getting a better view of what lies beyond. However, when I arrive at only the second limb, the leaves above me explode as a thousand roosting blackbirds whoosh up and off toward the hill to my right, suddenly banking to the left and then veering off to the right again as if propelled by a single set of wings.

How do they all know just when to do that?

Is some otherworldly puppeteer pulling their strings? Sending them simultaneously soaring and diving, twisting and turning? Yet it can't be that. Soldiers under the sway of tyrants go to war like dangling puppets, but not the winged creatures of God's earthly kingdom.

Then I feel the threads attaching to my own shoulders and knees, feet and head, and I see how each human life resembles a lone gnat pinned in a spider's webbing. How we long to be free as blackbirds, those masters of instant togetherness, each following the lead of the one beside it as they write themselves across the sky.

I begin to clamber down from the tree, without even a mulberry to make my effort worthwhile. Fruiting season is long past.

When I lower myself gently back to the ground, it feels soft and welcoming and I long to lie down and sleep. My legs have become as heavy as my eyelids, so I sit where I land and begin to practice a deliberate inner walking—step by nameless step—down a gradual slope toward the valley of profound silence that lies at my center. At one breath per pace, I steadily descend.

Soundless...
quiet...
still...
silent...
deeply silent...
deeper...
deepest....

I practice this form of wandering in the days that follow until I finally grasp that the longer I stay still in any one place, the more the local creatures reveal themselves to me.

I vow to learn to move carrying that stillness within me.

One afternoon I find myself walking my prayers through a wooded glen, inhaling on each footstep as always. Ahead, an ancient tree lies on its side in the clearing it made when it calamitously toppled in some long-ago storm. Now a nurse log, it is selflessly giving back to the very forest that bestowed it with life.

I slow to a halt and my gaze gradually takes in the abundance of saplings, ferns, and mosses that have grown up over the years out of the breast of this disintegrating mother. As she humbly lies there steadily returning to the earth, I congratulate her on her brood and thank her for her gifts, all with subtle movements of my eyelids and fingertips. In reverence I stand for an hour, rooted to the ground, watching the circle of life and death dancing under the sun.

I blink and the sun is setting. As dusk settles in around me, I notice darker forms emerging from the depths of the forest. One by one they take shape, and a herd of deer is moving toward me. Four fawns are in the center, with three bucks of varying ages at the periphery. The rest are does. The mothers pause to gently rub noses with their fawns, then separate slightly to survey the clearing. Moments later they drop their heads and begin grazing, while the bucks hold theirs high, eyes ever alert, sweeping the surrounding trees for signs of danger.

If a branch snaps or two leaning trunks groan against one another in the wind, all grazing heads rise as one to join those of the sentinels. Ears stand up, all pointing in the same direction like sunflowers facing the fiery shield. Legs and bodies are immobile for what seems like half an eternity. Until finally some undetectable signal sends first a few heads back to grazing, then all the rest but those of the sentinel.

As I watch, not moving a finger or an eyebrow, a powerful yearning tugs at my heart. If only I could be a deer within a herd of deer.

The forest shadows steadily lengthen as night settles down around us like a drowsy grey cat. Not wishing to leave, I kneel to spread out my blanket and curl up inside it. The nurse log has put her children down as well, and they disappear into the darkness.

Just before falling asleep, I hear a nightingale call in the distance. Is it time for evening prayers? I try my best to answer, but sleep vanquishes me and my response lingers on the edge of my lips.

When dawn arrives, the deer have vanished. I say my morning prayers where I sit, and then, breaking my fast, wolf down a palmful of berries from the low-lying bushes nearby. Waving a single, grateful farewell to the nurse log and her family, I resume my slow walk through the forest.

All day long I wander through wonder.

The following morning, lying beneath my blanket and staring up at the birdless, cloudless sky, I know there's little left for me to accomplish in the wilderness for now. It's time to return to the world of people. Even though there are still knotty puzzles weighing down my pockets that sway as I walk.

Chewing on one last handful of nuts and berries, I roll up my bedroll and begin making my way down a parched gulch toward the path below that leads to the nearest village.

After a few minutes, I round a bend and freeze in my tracks. Some twenty paces ahead stands a leopard, also motionless. Our eyes lock and the great beast drops into a crouch, ready to spring, the fur along its spine raised and the long tawny tail twitching nervously back and forth.

Total silence envelops and holds the two of us tight.

My mind speeds from thought to thought, searching for a tunnel to open up to squeeze through and escape. Surely the beast must have heard my footsteps as I kicked a pebble along, lost in reflection. But it did not slip away as wild animals normally do. A cat this size isn't seen unless it wants to be.

I know I shouldn't run—no human could be fast enough—and turning my back would invite attack. That would be it, and I would never find Shoshana, never see my parents and Aaron again, never have a wife and child.

For some reason I remember how Yeshu once grasped me by the collar, pulling me behind him, and slowly backing us away from the Roman soldier who meant to do me harm. So I carefully step backward, watching the cat as I move.

Its eyes are an intense gold, with burning stars at their centers. Its face is terrifying but fiercely handsome. One large paw lifts and steps forward. Matching my retreat with its advance, the cat never leaves its crouch. I continue stepping back and feel my knees trembling.

With a sudden powerful uncoiling, the cat leaps. Up the side of the gulch it scrambles and is gone.

I gasp for air, suddenly aware my breathing had stopped. My heart pounds and I order my feet to walk. Eventually they do and I pass the spot where the cat had been crouching.

I cannot push those two gleaming eyes from my mind. They seem so familiar, but I cannot place them. I had frozen in the great cat's path, yet it didn't growl in warning or even curl a lip. Had it wanted to devour me, I wouldn't have seen it till it struck. Had I not stumbled upon it...but, no, it must have been waiting.

I shiver, realizing it could have been shadowing me for days. But why would it show itself only to release me and vanish?

I skip, kicking my heels in the air, and let out a yip.

"Oh, Mama Ana!" I cry out. "So *this* is what it's like to be caught in a raging river and pulled out by the jaws of a beast who deposits you safely at the feet of your mother."

Arms outstretched, sailing down the slope on the wings of a kite, I count my blessings. My heartbeat and breathing return to normal by the time I reach the valley floor and step onto the footpath to the waiting village.

Walking briskly, I follow the crisp echo of footsteps not yet taken.

In this way I leave one wilderness for another; a single heart seeking its place among many.

~ ~ ~

A fortnight later I stood at the edge of Maria Magdalena's village. Approaching the well, I saw her pulling water up with a leather bucket. For a moment I wondered if I was still dreaming.

But that notion vanished when she looked up. I ran to her and we hugged wordlessly. When we finally stepped back, our eyes were brimming with tears. And the light from our smiles filled every shadow.

Maria's gaze locked on my face, as if she could see words forming on my lips. I had no warning of what I might say until what was in my heart flew out.

"Maria," I said, my body tingling from toes to tip of tongue, "I saw the face of God!"

Her eyes shone. In a near whisper she said, "Let's walk."

I picked up the overflowing bucket, and we strolled arm in arm, talking, sometimes at once, until we arrived at her house. I put the bucket down inside the door, and we set off for the river on the outskirts of town. There we found a massive rock, worn smooth by the currents.

Kicking off our sandals, we sat quietly side by side on the rock for a long time, shoulders pressed together, soaking our feet in the cool running water. Gratefully letting the river wash our feet, and the sounds wash over us.

Each of us traveling new currents that were opening up far down inside.

The Silence of Rope Walker

Maria Magdalena always seemed to know what to say to me, just the right thing at just the right time. Lost in thought as we sat watching the water roll deliciously over our feet and splash against our ankles and calves, after a while it seemed to me as if the river itself was speaking. Startled I looked up to see that it was Maria telling me a story.

"When I was a young girl in Magdala," she had begun, "before my path broke up and I lost myself..." she swallowed hard, "a man lived alone at the edge of town, on the same lane as my family. Everyone called him 'Rope Walker.' He was stone deaf, and he made every foot of rope used by the village households.

"We kids would stand and watch Rope Walker slowly backing away from the weeping willow near the well in the center of town, rhythmically twining strands of cactus and date-palm fibers into a long rope securely tied to the willow's trunk. The others would run around him screaming bloody murder, saying whatever came into their heads because they knew he couldn't hear them. But I could, of course, and it made me blush.

"Sometimes from the way he studied them I wondered if maybe he could hear, but was just too busy rope-making to pay any heed. He wasn't blind after all and could see clearly in the faces and gestures what was being expressed. Whatever he was thinking, his gaze mostly stayed fixed on his work as he methodically advanced backwards till the strand stretched past five, ten, or even twenty houses, sometimes requiring him to lean way, way back, using his weight and strength, plus the occasional forked pole, to keep his serpentine product from dragging through the dust or mud.

"This was serious business. He depended upon these carefully plaited ropes to barter with townspeople for food, or to sell in the weekly market for a brass coin. That's how he got by. To be sure, every family needed rope: to tie off grain sacks for storage, tether a donkey, or fasten new thatching securely to roof beams to keep out the wind and rain. Carefully crafted and sturdy as the ropes were though, I never once heard anyone say they needed the man who actually made them.

"I often wondered if Rope Walker was miserable or happy, lonely or content. He ignored the kids' antics, as I said, dismissing them with a wave at times, wordlessly accepting their company at others.

"The adults of Magdala must have been harder for him to ignore because they treated him like one of their donkeys. His deafness and muteness were taken as signs of stupidity.

"I knew better. I could see the flicker in his eyes, as if his mind were preoccupied by something far away. I imagined him weaving his thoughts and dreams together as he edged gradually backward, twisting textured storylines into surprising endings that would leave anyone who was able to follow with mouth wide open. How I would have loved to grasp hold of *that* strand of rope—one end double-knotted, the other tied to the trunk of the weeping willow—and swing from it high into the air.

"Once, Rope Walker stopped his arduous twining to rest a bit right in front of our house. I stood in the doorway, peering directly into his eyes. He gazed back and smiled softly. I didn't turn away. I was unafraid, and I hadn't the slightest urge to jeer or scream. For this he rewarded me with the only message I ever saw him give anyone.

"He gently let down his rope and laid his armload of cactus and palm fibers in the grass beside the lane. Fixing his eyes again on mine, he raised his hands and cupped them completely over his ears. Next he squinted his eyelids nearly shut. A second later he opened his eyes wide till they seemed about to pop, raising them to the sky while an awestruck smile erupted over his face and both hands floated upward. His long fingers fluttered like butterflies as they reached high above his head.

"Soon his hands lowered and his gaze dropped down to meet mine again.

"I nodded forcefully and said to him, even though he couldn't hear, much less understand me, 'Yes, silence *is* wonderful.'

"And then, as if I was hearing it for the first time, I whispered to myself, 'Silence is absolutely full of wonder!'

"How I knew this was what he meant, I can't say. Yet I was certain. It felt as if I had just witnessed a wordless Psalm.

"Silence had been hidden to me before that day, like a shadowy void, but it's been an overflowing pool to explore ever since, thanks to Rope Walker.

"On that day, I began to notice that I felt calmest and most secure and creative when being still and quiet. Snug in my blanket before falling asleep or sitting on a sundrenched hilltop or resting after gathering berries, I would let my mind fly like a leaf wherever the breezes might carry it.

"As I got older, the silence sharpened and grew brighter. Every day I basked in it, reflecting on what people were wordlessly saying when they talked, and what they meant when they said nothing at all. And in between those thoughts I learned to pray in profound silence. To offer up my soundless attention like God's mirror.

"This was before the demons entered and shattered my soul.

"And here's the funny part," Maria said. "I learned to do this quiet contemplating mostly because the men at the synagogue would not teach me or any other girl how to pray. So, I decided to teach myself. Since the ancient Hebrew words were hidden from me, I had to look elsewhere. I would sit alone, waiting for my mind to fill with the air of God's breathing. Waiting for the sounds of God's own language, which was like no tongue ever spoken by men in a synagogue.

"The more I did so, the more I learned about the rainbow of silence. How its hues were woven from countless, invisible threads; each one leading to a different human heart."

As Maria spoke, I found myself nodding at her words, trying to relate them to the dream I'd had, in which I saw my face in the well. I must have drifted away because all of a sudden I noticed she was not talking, but just smiling at me.

Noticing me catch up, she continued her story.

"Often silence is so common we don't give it a second thought," she said. "For instance, there's the transfixed stillness of a hungry family sitting around their table, eating a loaf of bread fresh from the village oven. Or there's the hushed connection of two friends together on the road, plopping down under a tree and leaning back against the trunk in the shade to escape the afternoon sun.

"Then there's the nearly noiseless absorption of Rope Walker," she said, "and many others like him, toiling away."

With that I stepped into Maria's song, "And what about the calmness just before a storm, as you wait for it to break over you, all tingly in your fingertips and along the back of your neck!"

"That's *so* true." She laughed quietly, as her shoulders crawled up her neck to quiet down the tingling.

"Plus the vast silence of the wilderness," she went on, "when you've left the last village far behind, and you're trekking into a distant forest or a desert canyon. A wren trills—and suddenly you know there is no other person to speak to but yourself, and this is what you've been doing the entire time you've been wrapped in contemplation."

I smiled in recognition, then said, "Let's not forget the silence of loneliness. And..." I took a breath, "of death."

Maria nodded and we were quiet for a while.

"Silence at midnight," she suddenly offered, "is not quite the same as what it is at noon. Just like feeling stillness and peace in your heart when there's noise and chaos around you, is not equal to sitting on a hillside above the village, gazing over the rooftops, being quiet within quiet."

Maria paused to brush the hair away from her eyes. In my head I was trotting back over my years of shepherding.

"For sure," she continued, "all these forms of silence shape the spirit, and they inform our feet for their journeys, and our hands for their tasks."

I pictured Yeshu carefully sighting along the edge of a plank. And then wordlessly planing it smooth while his mind's eye soared like a golden eagle surveying the valley floor from high up and way far away.

For sure Maria was eavesdropping on my thoughts because she added, "But of all the trees in the orchard of stillness, one is special. The longer I knew Yeshu and Yohanan, the more I saw, in spite of their wondrous words, how embedded they were in the deepest silence. Just like ancient olive trees rooted in rich soil, they welcomed the surrounding hush. Its depth carried them far, allowing them to explore their own souls so as to find and travel those pathways, inside and out, that connect to God."

She folded her hands in prayer in her lap, studying them, then looked up at me.

"Do you remember how Yohanan nudged us into silence in the cedars of Lebanon? How time seemed to stand still while the unabashed old turtle trudged through the legs of God?"

I nodded.

"And how Yeshu, speaking to thousands on a hillside, would stay quiet for many breaths between each affirmation of who are the blessed?"

I nodded again.

"I learned the *beauty* of silence from Rope Walker, and then the *power* of silence from our storytelling teacher," she went on, "and from the man whose voice cried out in the wilderness.

"Of course," she raised a single finger high, "Yeshu and Yohanan also taught me with their words and actions. And yet, those who overlook the depth of their stillness miss so much. These two taught us bushels and more about sitting quietly alert, without expectations, waiting for a message from that of God within us."

She reached a hand down and dangled her fingers in the bubbling water, then dried them absentmindedly on her robe where it stretched over her knee.

"I'll never forget the day that Yeshu talked about wordless prayer," she said. "Telling me how he loved to sit alone for hours with God, saying nothing, thinking nothing in particular, waiting to be spoken to, to be slowly filled up."

"You'll recall that he told us, 'Long ago I learned in prayer how at times we need to stop talking so much to God, and just listen.'"

I sat up straight, remembering that moment.

"I wish now," Maria continued, "that I had asked if this is how he cultivated his singular beliefs about forgiving others for their harmful actions, loving our enemies, and never striking back when struck. Who, before Yeshu, was teaching such lessons?"

She shook her head softly.

"And who, before Yohanan, was showing others how to love all living things on earth? He entreated folks not to harm God's creatures. And even more surprising, that we should treat every one of them as sacred. All those years of stillness in the wilderness seem to have filled him with reverence as well as awe, the way spring rains fill an arid water hole after a long, dry winter."

Listening to Maria, the certainty I felt while dreaming edged closer, like a thrush poking out from under a low bush to show its head in the clear light of day. The song was there, inside me, but its intricate notes had to be woven with life as it's lived. Just as Rope Walker's nimble fingers patiently braided in silence, I needed to work at the vision that comes with eyes closed.

I was still young, and at first I thought dream work and contemplation had to do only with what my own life meant. Maria's story suggested something more. The final purpose of silence and solitude, she seemed to be saying, was not solitary.

This message was present in everything she spoke about, but unless a person already suspected it, her words were very hard to hear. Think about it: thirsty souls preoccupied with finding water too often remain blind about the true nature of its source, even as they drink their fill.

I still had lots to do in mastering my craft. To mention just one thing, I had to hone the differences between dreaming asleep and dreaming awake.

Nevertheless, more than once Maria had reminded me of the tools I, too, had been given by Yeshu and Yohanan. I'd misplaced them for a year or more. Then, one by one I'd uncovered them in the wilderness. How they'd gotten there, so far from where I'd dropped them, is another of God's great mysteries. But now that I had them in my hands again, I would sharpen what had gone dull. I swore I'd master how best to employ them, though I didn't yet know what their uses would be.

Powered by Love

That evening after a light supper, Maria and I talked about Yeshu's last week alive: from the triumphal ride into Jerusalem to the unspeakable execution. It weighed upon her that people she talked with were so fixated on his days of suffering, and not thinking deeply enough about his years of teaching and comforting. Of course his agony was dreadful, yet the possibility of what he wanted for us was still there, close enough to touch.

Talking about how near and far away that was finally took its toll on both of us. With shoulders slumping we retired to our sleeping pads.

Deep in the night I dreamt, and what occurred will stay with me forever. In the dream, I'm walking a path at the base of a darkened hill, dragging Yeshu's cloak. Or is it Judah's?

The sky is threatening and I gaze up the shadowy hill and gradually make out that it's crowned by a cross. The cross is empty, but the hill reminds me of Gol'gotha.

A chill flows over me as I round a curve in the path and realize I was wrong. A figure *is* there, on the opposite side of the cross. Approaching from behind, I couldn't see it.

Circling the hill, staring upward, I see that it's Yeshu. He's standing on a narrow ledge half-way up the vertical beam, his arms reaching wide in front of the horizontal one. But not nailed to it.

In my mind I hear Yeshu singing out long ago from the mountainside, "Blessed are the lovers of justice and the pure of heart...the merciful and those who weep.

"Blessed are they who hunger and thirst to do right...and those of a gentle spirit."

"Blessed are the peacemakers, whom God shall call 'my children.'"

His arms are stretched out not by soldiers but by Yeshu himself. There he stands, welcoming everyone in, as if we were travelers weary from the road, walking through the doorway. I feel warmed by his unanticipated hug, and the cloak slips from my hand.

With a start, I awaken in the darkest corner of those moments just before dawn.

Aching to beg Yeshu to forgive me for being unable to protect him, I try to slip back into my dream, but cannot.

My eyes open and I watch the stars dissolve as the thin light pours in. Lying prone on the earth I pray that the carpenter be remembered for how he lived rather than how he died. What comes last is not always what's final.

And alas, who would imagine that a death could ever sum up the mystery, the wonder, of an entire life!

Thousands died that year on two crossed timbers; only one lived like Yeshu. His death was a dark curtain through which his life shines still.

My eyes close tightly and when I reopen them, dawn's rays are streaking through the mist. If I strain, I can still catch sight of him teaching to the crowds, loving hands extended from patchwork robes and lifted to the sky. I watch him step forward, offering relief to those burdened by illness and anguish, those who are flung to the edges of society to live as outcasts, wailing "Unclean! Unclean!"

I even see him conferring love and forgiveness not just upon the poor and downtrodden of our world, but also upon those who consider themselves his enemies.

This is the Yeshu I know and will always hold in my heart.

Alive. Reaching out. Embracing.

Powered by love!

Heartsong

Ever since Maria told me the story of her time in the wilderness, a question had nagged at me. Finally one day, while we were taking a basket of melons to a bedridden widow who lived in a hut outside the village, the words spilled out.

"Maria," I said. "That fox, you know the one that led you to the underground stream when you were off looking for Yohanan?"

She glanced at me sideways.

"Did you ever see it again?" I shifted the heavy basket to my other hand.

"No," she sighed, "never." She tugged on her ear for a few moments.

"Well, not exactly..." she said. "A curious thing happened that I don't suppose I've ever told anyone about." She scratched the other ear. "One morning, several days after following the fox and finding the life-giving water that would quench my deep thirst, I returned to refill my goatskin. The pool that formed after I had rolled the large stones away and scooped out the earth was still there. Kneeling at the water's edge, I noticed a smooth patch of moist clay. And indented there were two perfectly formed paw prints of a fox."

I smiled.

Maria continued, "My breath caught in my chest as I looked around, but I was totally alone. No matter," she said. "At that moment, words that Yohanan so often spoke to us darted through my head: 'You help me. I help you. We all belong to one another.'"

Pausing to smooth the wrinkles from her skirt, Maria smiled softly. "Since that day, the fox visits me often. But only in dreamtime."

I stared at her for the longest while, saying nothing. Although I'd vowed to work hard on it, the fact was my own dreaming had gone mostly dry again since discovering Yeshu inside me while I slumbered. I no longer felt despair but there was still a persistent and sharp longing. Something essential was forever missing.

I turned over in my mind the thought that it must be Yeshu himself that was missing. What I wouldn't have given just to spend an hour walking beside him. We'd talk about whatever came into our heads. Which fruits were our very favorites, and what was tickled the most when biting into them: the tongue or the nose? Or how Mama Ana could read a man's eyes when he was telling a story, to see if he really believed what he was recounting. And how Gramma Ruth cracked jokes with people to discover what they were like when they weren't being so darned serious.

Yeshu inspired such love and loyalty in all of us, and in many different ways. In the months after his death, several of our former band reported that he had come back to life and walked the earth again. The Pharisees and lots of pious people said these were lies being spread by desperate followers who had stolen the body to create a myth that would make Yeshu, and perhaps themselves, immortal.

I didn't know what to believe. But I knew what I *wished* to be true. I wanted everything to be like before. I wanted lots of time with Yeshu, just like in the old days. To be sure, I could now feel his spirit moving inside me, but was there something more?

During those days and weeks, dreams came occasionally, and unexpectedly, then vanished. Waking, watching Yeshu's back disappear into the night shadows, was agony. Being left alone in the light of day felt as if I were crossing a desert with no more than a memory. It was much like having only the corner of a cloth dipped in water to wet my tongue. I was thirstier than ever.

When people claimed to have actually seen Yeshu—like Thomas, the greatest doubter of all—it bothered me. *Why* would he not show himself to me, his loyal friend, face to face?

Maybe I had been looking for him the whole time in the wrong places. Finally I'd woken from the stunned daze I'd been in following his death.

Locating Maria and then spending time in the wilderness had brought me back into the peopled world. This is where Yeshu chose to be, so perhaps I would find him here.

~ ~ ~

One morning, at the outskirts of the village, I was weeding in a garden belonging to a family that was giving me a corner of their plow shed to sleep in. When the sun got high, I took a break and went to a nearby spring for water. I wasn't the only one. The blistering heat had brought several farmers there.

Stooping down and lifting cupped hands to my lips, I listened as a man asked his neighbor, "Your brother, the one with the injured back, how's he doing?

"Oh, much better," the neighbor said, "ever since he met that healer Joanna who's been going from village to village tending to folks who are sick or injured."

When the man called out the name Joanna, I glanced up sharply. Could it be our Joanna?

Despite my insistent questions, the man couldn't say much more. He didn't know what she looked like since they'd never met, and his brother hadn't described her. I asked where this brother lived. Maybe he could tell me more, maybe even where she was going next. With almost no forethought, I had already decided to trace the healer's steps until I found her.

That night at supper I told Maria Magdalena all about it. She gave me a sideways look as if a notion had suddenly struck her that she had been trying to recall.

"Seeing Joanna again would be splendid," she said. "And if you want help, I know how to find her."

Maria's eyes said she knew I was thrilled to have her help. She grasped my hand.

"Give me a week," she said.

Three days later, she told me she'd tracked Joanna down through relatives. The next morning we ate breakfast and packed food for the journey.

Watching Maria fill my goatskin with water, my eyes followed the stray drops as they dripped one by one onto the hardened dirt floor, each spreading a bit as it soaked in. It reminded me of something, but what? Ah, the footprints of the fox gradually evaporating from the stone.

I found myself ruminating on how paths that cross never really end.

Then we were off. We easily found the healer in Bethsaida. How good it was to see Joanna again!

She and I embraced, Maria hugged her too, and I asked if the stories about her were true.

She smiled impishly and said, "That depends on which story you mean. I don't turn grapes into wine or copper into gold, though I might know how to do one and am not much interested in the other."

Then turning more serious she added, "But if you mean recapturing Yeshu's touch, the answer is yes. For the three years we walked together, I watched how he helped people heal themselves."

She inhaled deeply.

"So that's what I do. And I've learned that healing is a calling, not work. Every morning I awaken anxious to start. My old bones may creak, but I never feel tired even though there seem to be more wounds than people."

She was staring straight at me as if waiting for something.

"But, Joanna," I said, "isn't it hard to see so much suffering and illness? You talk as if it just goes on and on. With no respite ever." I shook my head. "So, how can you not be sad and worn out? Don't you just want to be free from it sometimes?"

"No, not really," she answered. "Whenever I see a need, I feel like a bee drawn to a hyacinth." She smiled and her eyes wandered off as if gazing over a vast field of purple blossoms.

"I must have gotten *that* from Yeshu, too. And Yohanan."

Her words rang clear as a hammer striking a bell.

"So," she said. "I've found my purpose."

She paused, studying my face. "You could join me, you know? I could use the help. And your company."

What else can a bell do after being struck? And struck twice, no less.

Before I knew it, I was nodding yes.

"That's tremendous!" she exclaimed. "We have so much to catch up on and do together, you and I."

Suddenly her hand flew to her cheekbone.

"Oh, that reminds me, Daavi, guess who else will be traveling along with us, sharing our work?"

Puzzled, I glanced at Maria, then back to Joanna, and shook my head.

"Come," she said to us both, "his lodging is just down the road."

We approached a low-slung house of reeds and daub. Joanna stood discreetly to one side of the door and called out a greeting. A moment later a man emerged from the low doorway, bent over from the waist to avoid hitting his head on the cedar-plank lintel. When he straightened up, my jaw dropped.

"Philippos!"

"Hello, Daavi," he laughed.

I hardly recognized him. His dark, curly hair tumbled to his shoulders and he now sported a full beard. But his eyes were what had changed most. They sparkled like wet, black mica after the sun emerges from a cloudburst. And they were deep as any village well.

"Say, weren't you always going on about wanting to tend horses?" he asked me abruptly. "So, how's that going for you?"

Flabbergasted, this time I barely caught my jaw before it hit the ground.

Staring back at him, I mumbled, "Uh, no..." then louder but still hesitantly, "no, that was you: *Philippos,* 'lover of horses.'"

His eyebrows leapt up as he stifled a guffaw behind his sleeved wrist.

I slapped my hand to my forehead. I'd been lured into a fool's trap!

All four of us laughed and hugged and exchanged proper hellos. Grasping Philippos by the shoulder I congratulated him on his newfound sense of humor. "Philippos, I fell just like winter wheat before a sharpened scythe," I said.

He shrugged, then answered, "Everywhere one looks there's pain, so why add more by being a pain in the neck?

"Besides," he added, "laughter helps lance the boil. It clears the bile from the liver. It's better than wine for rinsing the bitter taste from your mouth, and much less likely to make you retort with something you will later regret."

He winked at me. "See how much I learned from those insufferable Thunder Brothers?"

Listening to him spin out his patter, I was reminded of the herbal cure sellers at the bazaar in Jerusalem, with their tiny packets of wonder potions and their gift of gab.

Just as I was trying to figure whether Philippos was being serious or satirical, he stepped closer, and patting me on the back, whispered in my ear, "Daavi, you're a sight for sore eyes."

He must have felt me wince because he stepped back quickly and said, "What I mean to say is my eyes are sore from weeping, and just looking at you soothes the burning and takes the sting out."

Noticing me tilting my head sideways, watching him closely, he added, "Seriously, friend Daavi, I hope you're here to join us. We cure when we can. We comfort always. And above all—as the Greek doctors counseled long ago—above all, we try to do no harm."

Philippos smiled warmly at me. "I always knew this was my calling, Daavi, and now I'm more certain than ever. As Yeshu taught us: doing good does one good."

He paused before going on, "But doing *well*? Ah, that's where the rich physicians are really experts."

I couldn't believe it was the same person. How agilely he danced between being serious and being funny. Clearly he had not been lying down collecting dust since I had last seen him.

Then suddenly Philippos grew genuinely solemn, taking hold of my hand. "Daavi, Yeshu's death knocked me flat. I tasted soil and blood. I wanted to lie there, roll in the dirt, rub my hair with it." His gazed dropped to the ground.

I listened intently as he continued.

"But over many months I slowly climbed to my knees. Looking around, I saw I wasn't alone. How many others had seen their life laid low through no fault of their own; some of them completely unable to rise. How could I have forgotten? Wasn't this what brought me to Yeshu in the first place?

"I found the courage to stand and I vowed to be a healer like he was." His voice trembled. "His killers wanted us to forget him, and thereby, all who suffer in this land. Carrying on his work with the least among us keeps his spirit alive."

Joanna clapped her hands together.

And under my breath I uttered a fervent "Yes!"

"Well stated, Philippos," Maria chimed in.

Gravely he turned to her, his head tilted downward, speaking humbly. "What advice could you offer me, Maria, for reaching the summit I have my eyes on?"

Pleased at being asked, Maria responded, "Yeshu is still your teacher, my friend. You only need to listen to him."

She pointed at the center of his chest. "His voice speaks not just in the work you do, but here in your heart." She lowered her arm and paused.

Then looking off in the distance—and into the past—she added, "Oh, and don't forget to smile at every person who comes searching for you."

His face instantly brightened, opening like a tiger lily facing the midday sun. "I'm ready," he said. "I've been practicing for months at the edge of a pond."

Maria stared at him for a long time. "Philippos, you amaze me. The once gangly creature with multiple legs has transformed into a striking dragonfly with two fine-looking, gossamer wings!"

I thought his smile, after he heard that, would lift him right off the ground.

~ ~ ~

That evening we sat around the hearth where Joanna had found lodging; just four old friends catching each other up on news about the other members of Yeshu's band.

I told them about Judah confronting the disaster he'd made and trying to escape it by sentencing himself to death.

Visibly shaken by my grim report, Philippos then recounted how the Thunder Brothers had been touched by visions of tongues of fire and were now preaching to huge crowds.

"Sometimes they even speak in a language no one knows," he said, "but that everyone seems to understand anyway."

"I'm not surprised," said Maria, shaking her head and chuckling. "Those gargantuan brothers are forever pushing forward. And as for speaking in mysterious tongues, Yeshu always said, 'words never get in the way when John and James have something important to say.'"

Joanna poked at a smoldering log with a stick, pushing it back into the fire. "Maria," she said, "have you heard anything about Petros?"

"Ah, yes, poor Petros," Maria responded, her voice lowering. "That's another story."

She stared into the flames for a long while. "Daavi has told you about the waste of Judah. Well, it seems Petros spends much of his time," she said, shaking her head, "railing at that shattered man for betraying Yeshu."

She smoothed out her skirt. "Sometimes Petros acts like a horse thief on his mount, shouting 'Robber!' at the pickpocket in the market. He fumes and blusters to forget how he shares the agony of betrayal.

"Well, you all know what folks say," she laughed quietly. "The camel cannot see the crookedness of its own neck."

My ears felt like they were standing straight up, and the others shifted in their seats. Maria noticed instantly.

"You heard me right," she said, eyes flashing. "I said 'betrayal.'"

She took a deep breath, and I saw her face settle.

"On the night Yeshu was taken prisoner," Maria said, "Petros was hanging around the gates of the palace of the High Priest. Inside they were torturing our Yeshu—orders from above—when a woman saw Petros and demanded: 'Aren't you one of the followers of that false King of the Jews who is going to his death?'

"'No way,' Petros shot back. 'Never heard of him.'

"And that was just the first of three times that night he denied having anything to do with Yeshu," Maria said.

She set her jaw.

"Now he has to live with himself, reconcile his self disgust with the memories of the one he loved."

A crow cawed in a distant field. Maria ignored it.

"Our good friend Petros," she added, "desperately wants to see Judah's betrayal as so enormous that it erases his own. He believes that with luck he can hide behind Judah's shadow, and that it will always be larger than the shadow he himself casts."

She scooped up a handful of sand and let it slowly filter out, building a small pyramid grain by grain as she talked.

"A few weeks after we..." her voice failed her, "after we lost Yeshu, I crossed paths with Petros on the road to Bethany.

"Actually I was walking, and he was sitting in the shade of a tree at the edge of a field, staring down the road as if it weren't even there. His pack lay beside him, its contents spilling over the ground.

"He seemed shipwrecked—not surprisingly considering what we all went through." She glanced at me, then went on. "His back was to me, his head tilted to one side. But I knew it was him from the color of the collar on his cloak.

"I mended that collar for him once," Maria said, smiling wanly.

As she went on with her story, no one stirred a finger or made a sound.

"I quietly approached poor Petros from behind and laid my hand on his shoulder.

"'Master?' he whispered hoarsely, lifting his head slightly toward my resting hand.

"'No,' I answered, 'it's Maria. Of Magdala.' His shoulder jerked away from my hand.

"I gave him a moment, then spoke his name, gently. He didn't look up, but his neck stiffened, then relaxed. We talked for a bit, about this and that, but he never once raised his face to me. His eyes seemed not to see. I could recall times with Yeshu when it seemed that Petros had moments of deafness, but this latest was brand new.

"As I watched him sitting there, I felt my heart softening. He was hurting; that was undeniable. So, I took a loaf of bread out of my bag, tore it in half, and laid it in his lap. His hands went to it, but not his eyes.

"I left him sitting there, saying to him softly, 'Look down inside, friend. Seek your vision. And listen. Listen for your heartsong, Petros. Yeshu is within you.'

"His head twitched. Then I detected a faint nod.

"I straightened, turned, and stepped back onto the road to continue on my way, feeling a sadness so profound that my feet felt like they were carrying a great stone laid across my shoulders."

Maria stared into the embers, and she bit on her lower lip.

I surprised myself by saying, "Petros may be more lost than any of us." Maria looked up.

"Why do I say that?" I asked. "Well, because...because he doesn't yet know he's lost."

Maria, Joanna, and Philippos signaled their agreement by softly intoning, "Hmm."

We all became quiet until finally Joanna said, "There is nothing lonelier than being spiritually alone. Petros seems to have lost his community."

She looked down at her clasped hands. Let's hope he can rediscover it." She poked at the embers again. "And that we can welcome him, if he chooses us."

She paused.

"As Yeshu would want us to."

She lowered her head, as if looking inward. When she raised her eyes back to us, we all three nodded. With that we banked the fire, spread out our bedrolls, and went to sleep.

In the middle of the night, I dreamt of Judah weeping.

When I Was Thirsty, Flowers Bloomed

A few days later, Maria Magdalena announced it was time to return home to her adopted village. We all tried to convince her to stay, knowing full well that her mind was made up. She thanked us, shifted her eyes to the path outside the door, and said simply, "I've a task to complete."

All through the planting season and beyond the harvest that followed, I traveled with Joanna and Philippos and labored as their assistant. Together we made compresses and soothed babies burning with fever. We bathed the festering wound of a shepherd girl who had cut her foot on a sharp rock, and bound it in herbs we had picked from the field. We used a poultice to soak the aching hands of an elderly weaver so she could finish her tapestry. We prepared an ointment and carefully applied it to a toddler who had stumbled into the cooking fire.

Sometimes at dusk, figures would emerge from the shadows, beseeching us to treat sores that were the telltale signs of leprosy. They were people just like the rest of us, but whom no one else dared to touch. More than once, Yeshu had shown both Joanna and me what touch meant to those who suffered from this malady, and the power that could be released. So we welcomed them and did what we could to provide comfort if not a cure.

Then there were those who were locked not only in the maladies of their bodies but in prisons made of stone. Because Joanna's deceased husband had been part of Herod's court, she knew which names to whisper to get us inside the jails of Jerusalem to care for sick inmates. Sometimes there were children lingering at the prison gates, or even living inside with their mothers. I played with them and made them dolls and toy animals out of scraps of leather.

Once we came across an orphaned street boy, and Joanna went door to door seeking someone to take him in, not as a servant, but as a family member. She located a barren couple and watched their eyes fill at last with the bounty of having a child of their own to love and raise up.

Throughout the year that I spent with Joanna, she taught Philippos and me all that she knew about ministering to the sick and the disabled. One of her lessons that has served me best she called the "healing circle."

"No one ever heals alone," she said. Others are always drawn to a person who lies ill or injured: family, friends, even strangers. Yeshu.

"Using whatever means are at their disposal—touch, special foods, prayer, herbal remedies, stories and song—each caring person reaches out to the sufferer. Each set of hands, palms toward the sky, slides under the one in need. It's as if together they lift that soul up, encircled within a ring of caring."

While speaking, Joanna had been extending her hands, palms up, illustrating what she meant.

"When the urgency is past," she said, "one by one those who came to help remove their hands, step back, and return to their daily lives. And the person who is still recovering is left supported by love, as if still suspended within the circle of healing left behind."

I could hear in the timbre of her voice how much Joanna loved painting this picture.

"Daavi," she said, "did you ever hear the story about Yeshu and the paralyzed man who was lowered through the roof?"

I blinked hard. When would that have happened?

"It was the day you and Judah walked to Arimathea," she said, answering my question before I could ask it.

"Yeshu was in a village caring for the sick, having borrowed a house that soon became so jammed with people seeking a blessing that no one else could fit in. People were even craning for a view from the doorway and windows. In early afternoon, four men appeared on the adjacent hillside, carrying a fifth man upon a mat woven from reeds. The man could not move, not even a finger.

"The four bearers saw the crowd," Joanna said, "but didn't give up hope. They circled round the back and climbed onto the roof of the house. After opening a hole by removing the tiles one at a time, they used ropes to carefully lower their friend—it could have been their brother—down toward Yeshu, who was in the center of the room doing his healing work."

Joanna made a hand-over-hand motion, as if she were lowering a weight from above its intended resting spot.

"Yeshu looked up and saw the mat twirling as it lowered. He stood up to steer it to the floor with hands made strong by years of labor. With those same hands, Yeshu lifted the immobile figure into a sitting position. Then he told him in a warm tone of voice to stand, fold up the mat under his arm, and walk from the house. And that's just what the man did," she exclaimed.

"I've never forgotten that day. The paralyzed man's faith, multiplied by the faithful circle of his friends, had made him whole again."

~ ~ ~

Joanna also passed on a skill that would serve me well later in life. She taught me to write. I already knew how to read. Yeshu had made sure of that when I told him I wanted to study the scrolls. But writing was quite another matter.

Joanna had herself learned to write by convincing her husband to teach her how so she could better manage their household and assist him with the inventories he was instructed to keep for his job. At heart though, what she really wanted was to preserve the words to the songs she composed, and the poetry that tumbled from her head like an endless brook.

As my lessons progressed, Joanna praised me for being a fast learner. And when I asked, with some trepidation, "But what am I going to write down, once I learn how?" she laughed and laughed.

"Daavi," she said, "You're already a marvelous storyteller. Just pluck the words out of your mind, stick them on the end of your quill pen, and string them on the papyrus that I will give you, like a camel caravan carrying valuable spices and gems across the desert." She laughed and I joined in.

As I've said before, Joanna's husband had left her plenty of money, and now she used it not only for covering our daily needs, but a portion went to buy old clothing that I mended to give away to the families that came to us.

Since we had more than enough food, guests were always at our table sharing a meal. Joanna and I would regale our guests for hours with Yeshu stories, while Philippos studiously picked out notes on the zither that a wealthy wine merchant had gifted him.

A surprising number of people knew about Yeshu. And almost all who had gotten a nibble wanted to sample more.

Yet Joanna's stories tasted bittersweet to me. I missed Yeshu terribly. Her tales evoked his presence, but hearing them was no more satisfying than eating lemons when you're starving. And hearing his name, or seeing his image shimmer in my mind, felt like touching a bruise.

Joanna knew I was still searching for something more. She was patient with me and compassionate, and she extended the same kind of loyalty to me that she had given Yeshu.

One sun-drenched day, after treating victims of an earthquake that had rocked a nearby peasant village, toppling houses, I was resting by a stream, listening to the song of the living water. From out of the past, face after nameless broken face floated by my mind while I gazed up at the sky where a great white egret with long, slender wings soared high above, circling effortlessly, legs stretched out behind.

A gentle breeze caressed me, and the hair on the back of my neck prickled as if I were growing feathers. How peaceful the earth must look from that height, I thought.

In the next second, I was yanked back to earth by a man yelling and running toward me cradling a child in his arms. The girl wept inconsolably, her left leg dangling oddly and bleeding.

While the father gently cupped the girl's head with his hands, I bent over her on my knees and went to work. First I cleaned the wound and made a poultice from herbs in my packet mixed with mud from the stream. Then I fashioned a splint from a spare stick of firewood, and using strips of old cloth, bound it gently but securely to her broken leg. The child sobbed and sobbed, clenching her hands into tiny fists that shook in pain.

"Look into my eyes," I said, brushing the hair back from her face and gently rubbing her shoulders to release the tension from muscles tight as knotted ropes.

"Give *me* your pain."

Her gaze locked onto mine and her breathing steadied as if a storm at sea were subsiding. I could detect her entire body relaxing as I stared deep into her eyes.

Something in her look beckoned, and drew me even closer, until all of a sudden a massive wave welled up and washed over me. I gasped and my shoulders began to heave and shake. *I* was now the one weeping inconsolably.

I had just seen Yeshu.

Joanna noticed what was happening and hurried over. She knelt behind me, and gripping me by the shoulders, leaned close to quietly recite something Yeshu had told us long ago.

> When I was hungry, you gave me food.
> When thirsty, you gave me drink.
> When I was a stranger, you took me into your home.
> When naked you clothed me.
> When I was in prison, you visited me.
> When ill, you came to my help.

Then Joanna asked, still speaking into the nape of my neck, "Do you remember what happened next? How Martha protested: 'But Yeshu, when did we see you hungry and feed you, or thirsty and give you drink, or a stranger to be taken home, or naked so we clothed you?'"

Philippos must have overhead the commotion because he was right there, kneeling beside us, chiming in, "And remember how I asked, 'And when did we see you imprisoned or ill and come to help you?'"

I stared down at the resting child, letting the words wash over me.

"And I'm sure you recall," Philippos added, "how Yeshu looked around at each of us and answered, each word ringing like a golden temple bell.

He said, 'I tell you this: anything you did for one of my sisters or brothers, however humble, you did for me.'"

Joanna gently nudged me till I turned round to face her.

"Daavi, listen closely. You have found Yeshu. He is here. For years you've searched far and wide, calling his name and waiting for him to appear. And he has been right in front of you all along!"

"Yeshu lives," I whispered. "He lives."

Kol Ami

For years my home had been the road. Had the time come to resume my journey? Or perhaps it was time to conclude it. Weighing this I got up and joined the others in morning prayers. When we finished, Joanna took me aside to let me know she would be moving on soon. She was heading back to Jerusalem for several months to take care of matters that needed attention.

Or perhaps conclude it?

Philippos was considering spending some time in Capernaum. He had heard that a mysterious disease was cutting down large numbers of young children there, like stalks of barley before the curving scythe. He had a special soft spot for sick kids, and absolutely no fear of whatever was afflicting them.

I wondered what I was to do now. Should I go with one of these friends?

I felt compelled and yet bewildered. There was a mysterious pressure at my shoulder, nudging me forward. But another tugged at my heels, bidding me to stay. I felt that I was edging around something too big to see, like a blind pilgrim tracing an endless wall with all his fingers, hunting for a gate to see if a city lay inside.

But above all, here's what I knew as well as I knew my own name and the sound of my voice: I had at last found Yeshu alive, first within me, and now—when I comforted the small girl in pain—within others. Each time I found him I felt a burden had been lifted.

But looking inward I saw a sentinel fire burning on a distant hill, calling me toward something I could not begin to fathom.

Was my journey endless? Would I walk and walk until one day, aged legs simply stopped working? What was the sense of that?

Joanna noticed me staring at the ground and asked, "So, Daavi, what is it you will do?"

"Maybe, I answered haltingly, "I'll return to the road."

She looked at me askance. Then spoke with measured clarity. "Daavi, you've found Yeshu," she said, "within you and within that little girl. Why do you need to keep wandering?"

I couldn't help stiffening. Her words felt like a slap.

"Just what are you saying?" I snapped. "That the quest is over and I should give up searching?"

"I said no such thing," Joanna snorted, her hands on her hips.

"Daavi, move beyond what you've heard, or haven't heard. You need to answer for yourself why you keep looking. Exactly what is it you have not yet found?"

I just shook my head. If I knew that, we wouldn't be having this back-and-forth.

Joanna kept her eyes fixed on me, with a faint smile tugging at the corners of her mouth.

Her voice softened. "I know you, Daavi. And I can feel the heat of your unrest. Whatever it is you are searching for, I believe it will surprise you when you find it. You won't be at peace until you do, so your place is not here anymore. Nor is it with me or Philippos."

She reached out a hand and touched my elbow with her fingertips. "Yeshu told us, 'Seek and you shall find,'" she said.

"So what are you waiting for?"

Her smile broadened.

~ ~ ~

There was still much to do that day, not just tending the wounds of the earthquake survivors but comforting the family members of those who had died. By midafternoon my work was winding down because so many helpers had stepped forward. It reminded me of Yeshu's story about his time with his Abba in the village of Ludum.

Nearby, I caught sight of Joanna taking a rest, so I went over to ask if I could share something with her privately.

"Certainly," she answered. We went walking in the fields.

"I've decided to go home," I said.

I expected her to be surprised, but she wasn't.

"Of course," she responded. "Your time has arrived and you are ready. I'll miss you, but we'll see one another again."

She had said everything for me. I stopped walking and threw my arms around her. "Thank you, Joanna. You saved my life."

"Yes, I know," she said.

Then she laughed and shook her head.

"Actually, no," she said, looking me straight in the eyes while I waited nervously for the verdict of her second thought.

"Neither I nor anyone else saved you. You found your life by giving it away. Just as Yeshu said it would happen.

I felt light as a bird on the wing.

"And Daavi, something tells me it won't be the last time." She dropped her arms to her side and took a half step back.

Lowering her gaze and cupping her hands within a golden splash of sunshine, she said softly, "I will be holding you in the light."

I cupped my own hands inside of hers.

"And I, you...."

We hugged again and laughed—to thwart the sorrow.

The next morning I took my leave from Philippos, who rose at dawn to see me off. Stepping onto the road I walked out of Bethsaida a different person. One more time I had changed.

Yes, my name was still Daavi and that's who I looked like. Yet I was more. Much more.

Joanna was right to push me. I had found myself by finding Yeshu.

Whoever I would become, however my life ended up, wherever my true home turned out to be, I would not be alone. With every step I took I could feel Yeshu's heart beating inside mine. Vowing to follow wherever it led me, I walked along without care, reveling in the breeze at my back and the new sense of purpose I had to chew on.

Even so, I felt a twinge inside me from having said good-bye to my friends, and I shifted my thoughts to the joys and trepidations of going home. It was quite early in the morning and the road remained deserted as I approached a crossroads. Off in the distance a lone figure was approaching. From his hobbled and bent gait, at first I thought it was an aged man. Then I saw it was just a man carrying what appeared to be a foot plow and two scythes on his shoulder. But as he grew closer, I couldn't help noticing his hands and head, which were covered with cloth.

His hands were wrapped past the wrists, almost to the elbows, and his head cover wrapped across his face and around his neck. I marveled silently: In this heat?

Nearing one another, we exchanged the customary nod and words that are due when meeting a stranger on the road. But before he could trudge past, a voice inside urged me to go further.

So I stopped and said, "That's a lot of farm tools for one man."

He laughed and halted, too. "They're for the people in my village."

He was looking at the ground as he spoke. "We all work together."

I wondered if he was just painfully shy, or was he hiding something. Or maybe both?

I offered him a drink from my water flask, but he quickly replied, "Oh, no thank you. I shouldn't."

I insisted, and with his free hand he held out a gourd that was attached to his belt by a cord. "Well, I am quite thirsty," he said. "Could you pour me some?"

For an instant, I was offended. Why wouldn't he drink from my flask? Was he afraid I was somehow polluted or diseased and therefore he didn't want to touch anything of mine?

But the same inner voice calmed me, and I waited to learn more. "Sure," I said, and filled the gourd.

Something in my voice must have won his trust because slowly he raised his head. Through the loosely wrapped cloth peered a handsome, bearded face. Straight off I noticed the beard was tattered, with patches exposed where the skin was severely scarred.

Leprosy! I thought, gripping my elbows under my cloak.

Our eyes locked and I gasped. My hands flew out from my cloak like startled doves. Just as swiftly I yanked them back, slapping my thighs.

He stared wide-eyed as I grabbed him by the shoulders, sending the plow and scythes crashing to the ground. I *knew* him.

The shock on his face revealed his fear of being thrashed, so I tried to explain by shouting out, "You have one brown eye and one blue!"

He stared back in alarm, certain that I was crazy.

"You were in Nazareth," I said, biting off each word to calm my voice, "almost ten years ago. Yeshu gave you and your companions water. We kids collected bread for you. Am I right?"

"Yes," he broke in, pumping his head vigorously. "Yes, I remember!"

Suddenly he stepped backwards. "Be careful," he stammered. "I don't want to harm you."

Refusing to let go, I said, "Yeshu hugged each of you, and received only blessings."

I shook my head firmly. "No," I said, "I'm not afraid."

To myself, I thought: At last. At last.

As if able to read my mind he blurted out, "You must be the boy who almost hugged me."

"But how did you know that?" I said.

"I just did," he replied. "We get pretty good at reading people: How someone stands. Does he lean away; do his hands disappear into his sleeves; his lips curl or tighten. Does his voice crack when he speaks; or perhaps he doesn't speak at all."

He glanced aside. "We learn to tell whether a person might be angry or ashamed." Then he looked straight back into my eyes. "So I saw both your forward leaning *and* your hesitancy."

He was right. And I was so young. That day was one of the proudest of my life to that point, and yet it left me disappointed. I felt like an arrow that had just missed its mark.

He continued talking, "What Yeshu did that day was astonishing, not just to you Nazarenes but to us. No one had done that before. And of everyone there, you seemed most ready to follow his lead."

With that, the two of us began looking around for a shade tree. We stretched out on the ground under a nearby sycamore and talked for a long while. He was called Ezrah, and just like the meaning of his name in Hebrew, he was in fact a very generous person. Always lending a hand to his neighbors and his friends.

He told me about his childhood and what happened when he first got sick, how the entire village shunned him. He was excluded from everything, not just games with the other children but even extended family meals and worship services on the day of Shabbat. Finally, the villagers forced him onto the open road, where he scavenged like a wild animal, until eventually he came upon others in the same predicament.

"Our group of cast-offs was led by wise and compassionate elders," he said, "women and men who welcomed me even though I was one more mouth to feed. When I found them, they explained they were wandering like the early Israelites in the desert.

"Their leader, our leader, was an older woman whom we affectionately, maybe even a little jokingly, called Mama Moses." He chuckled.

"I remember her!" I cried out.

He smiled broadly and went on. "They all urged me to join them and pledged to help me. Lucky for us, we didn't have to journey for forty years before Yeshu helped us discover a land of goat's milk and forest honey where we could put down roots."

He let out a lingering sigh.

"And that's how I found a new home. I was barely nine years old."

Ezrah went on to tell me things about Yeshu I had never heard.

"Yeshu came to our camp," he said, "the evening you saw us at the well. We talked all night about what to do, about how to stop our constant flight. People we met on the road were more frightened and ignorant than mean. But their fear often burst out as hatred and rebuke. We were shunned and driven away as certain as smoke pours from a doused fire. We made our home in the affection and care we offered one another, but we needed someplace safe to put down roots. Even migrating storks can't fly forever.

"With Yeshu's encouragement, and his promise to help, we decided to hunt for an out of the way parcel of land no one was using to settle down on and start a community. It would probably be thorny and dry, but it would be ours, and with time we would make it green. Everyone would be welcome, regardless of their misfortune or past mistakes or the family connections they were born into.

"The promise we poured into it would make it our Promised Land. No more begging! No more rocks or taunts! No more bells.

"Yeshu suggested we call our new village *Kol Ami*—which in Hebrew means 'all of my people.' We liked the sound of it.

"He told us, 'The inner and outer healing of each person in Kol Ami will spring from the collective embrace of love from all those who live there.'

"A few weeks later our small band of men, women, and children suffering from leprosy traveled to the base of Mt. Horeb. There we came across others who joined up with us: two Samaritans who had been falsely charged with sedition and had escaped from prison; a blind flute-playing weaver; and three deaf woodcutters who quickly learned you can't chop firewood at dawn without making someone very, very unhappy."

I laughed and Ezrah joined in. Then he went on with his story. "Yeshu arrived soon after with Yohanan and a friend since childhood, a woman named Martha."

I brightened.

"The three of them explained how our new community could work together and make decisions; what we might grow; how we could safely barter for things we needed, like tools and seed, by seeking out good people in other towns. And, of course, how we would worship God. Since no rabbi or priest was available, we would do all the ceremonies ourselves.

"For that reason, there was no need to build a synagogue. We could simply meet in one another's homes."

He smiled when he said this. "Imagine that—we actually had homes," he said. "For us it was a miracle. We lived and worked together as a community, growing closer and stronger. And over time, others found us and also settled down in Kol Ami.

One day, a few months later, a new band of outcasts appeared out of a windstorm at the edge of town. They also suffered from leprosy and looked as ragged and broken as we did when you saw us in Nazareth. Maybe more so, because their wandering had gone on even longer than ours. Happily, among them were a handful of young men and women about my age. That turned out to be a true godsend for me."

His smile broadened.

"And Mama Moses?" I asked. "Did she make it to the Promised Land?"

Ezrah's face fell. "It seems that groundbreakers often don't get to see the fruits of their labors harvested," he said. "She died on the road, just before we arrived. Her eyes sparkled till the end."

As the sun approached its zenith, Ezrah explained he had to go. His family was waiting in Kol Ami. "Why don't you come along and spend the night?" he urged. "The walk isn't long."

Without hesitation I was up by his side and walking briskly, anxious to meet these people who had known and been touched by Yeshu when I was just a boy. I offered to carry the foot plow or the scythes, but Ezrah declined. Probably he felt safer, better hidden underneath that jumbled load when others passed us by.

Finally we came to a place where three white stones were stacked on top of each other by the side of the road. Ezrah gestured with his chin that we would turn onto the lightly traveled footpath marked by the stones.

He led and I followed. After several miles we entered a shallow valley. The farther we walked, the higher the hills rose on either side, until eventually the path ended at a wall of mature willows.

But Ezrah was not deterred. Handing me the scythes, he adjusted the plow on his shoulder and set off, weaving his way through the trees, turning and ducking as he went, with me close behind. I took great care not to hook a scythe blade on a tree branch.

Crossing a shallow brook on stepping-stones, we heard two song sparrows exchanging alarmed calls and responses. The spicy scent of watercress momentarily tweaked my nose.

Soon we broke out of the stand of willows and headed down into a valley deeper than the one before. We descended along a seasonal streambed until one earth-colored house appeared, then another, and finally all the rest.

We had arrived at Kol Ami.

Worn out from our journey, we went straight to Ezrah's homestead and threw ourselves on the grass under an apple tree to rest. His family was out.

"Probably they're visiting neighbors," he said.

After we'd had some water—me from my flask, he from his gourd—we rose to store the foot plow and scythes in the house. As I entered the doorway, words in Hebrew caught my eye. Leaning on the foot plow, I stopped to read them.

Carved into the right doorjamb, just below the mezuzah, it said:

ACT JUSTLY

On the wooden lintel up above were the words:

LOVE TENDERLY

And on the left jamb, beginning at eye level:

WALK HUMBLY WITH YOUR GOD

Ezrah saw me studying the phrases. I turned to him, gestured toward the door, and said, "Yeshu's favorite lines from the scrolls."

He smiled and nodded.

Come Back Home

Grabbing a handful of almonds and dried figs for the two of us, Ezrah invited me to take a walk around Kol Ami. We strolled slowly, munching on our repast. I was very impressed by how well kept everything looked. The fences, the corrals, the home gardens, the fields: all were carefully tended and in good repair. Though clearly poor, the villagers had made the best of their misfortune.

Ezrah paused outside a house, stuck his head in the doorway, and announced to those inside that their new scythe was waiting back at his place.

Someone said something I couldn't quite hear that made Ezrah laugh, and soon he was locked in conversation. Not wanting to intrude, I wandered along the lane a bit on my own. Up ahead was a woman sitting on a fallen log. Rocking a baby in her arms, she was gazing into its face and singing softly. I tried to hear the song but couldn't.

My lips silently mouthed words of my own that began ringing in my mind as I walked. 'Go to sleep, my little wanderer...'

As I came closer, the woman paused and looked slowly up. Our eyes met briefly and she smiled. Her face was noticeably scarred, and I sighed.

As always, not Shoshana.

I stood there enveloped in a cloud of longing and sorrow, smiling back weakly and watching her press her nose to the baby's, then laugh and resume her muffled singing.

"Travel safely through..."

With a start, I cocked my head to try to make out the faint strains of the melody—even though I was still capturing very few of the words—when suddenly the song thrust deep inside me like a hand grasping for treasure at the bottom of a pool.

The hand squeezed so tight I could barely breathe.

My feet began moving forward on their own, and I drew nearer.

"Come back home..."

In a flash the entire world closed in.

My lips were whispering along, "a wiser and more loving being."

As the words washed over me, I pressed my hands together to stop their trembling. Where had this woman learned our song? Had she met my sister on the road perhaps?

When the woman looked up again, my head was shaking no. It wasn't the words but that voice.

And those eyes.

Shoshana!

I tried to utter, "Dear God. You're found!" But not even a puff of breath escaped.

With that, my knees gave way, and I sank to the ground and sat leaning to one side, a single hand anchoring me to the earth.

Shoshana's head jerked in alarm and she asked, "Are you all right?"

My free hand reached out to her, then fell back in my lap.

I still couldn't get my tongue to work, so I gulped a mouthful of air and slowly let it out. "Come back..." I managed, but my voice broke.

I tried again, "Come back home..." then stopped. Someone was weeping very close by.

I didn't realize it was me until Shoshana rose with the baby, came close, and knelt by my side. Using the edge of her sleeve, she brushed away the tears streaming down my face.

Finally I loosened the knot in my throat enough to whisper, "Shoshana."

Then louder, my arms reaching out in a blind embrace, "Shoshana!"

Startled, she leaned back, clutching her baby closer, raising her shawl to her face. "How do you know my name?" she blurted. "Who are you?"

I just kept nodding in joyful amazement, saying that dear name over and over.

Shoshana stared at me, wide-eyed. "God in heaven!" she gasped.

Now *she* was trembling. Her shawl slipped from her face, and her scarred hand flew to cover her mouth.

"Daavi...?" She struggled for air.

"Daavi!"

I groaned.

Her hand reached forward as if to touch my cheek. "Dear God within," she cried out. "My prayers are answered. My family!"

I reached for her hand.

Flinching, she pulled it away, exclaiming, "Be careful, the sickness!"

Rising to my knees, I touched her lips to quiet her. My head shook from side to side with wonder, as my palm moved to lightly stroke her hair.

"It's all right," I insisted. "I'm not afraid."

Soon I was sitting beside her, wrapping my arms around her shoulders, our foreheads touching. She pressed closer, her breath coming in small gasps, the gurgling baby cradled in her lap.

I held my dear sister tightly, afraid to let go lest she vanish again. Her free hand clutched one of mine just as fast, her shoulders heaving every few seconds.

I could feel my heart flutter vigorously, like a large white bird about to rise up out of my chest and into the sky above us.

Yeshu felt very close.

"Shoshana," I murmured—to the carpenter as much as to her—"Yeshu taught me to not be so fearful that I'd give up what was dearest to me. What good is it to save one's life and lose one's soul?"

She tilted her head back to look at me. Then she said, eyes widening again, "Yeshu became your teacher?"

"And my friend and brother," I smiled, pumping my head vigorously. "He watched over me after you were gone. I even traveled with him later on!"

I'd hardly gotten that out when memories flooded in. It's so odd how a person you're close to can die and still be there, or be lost and found all at once. My eyes welled up once more, blurring my vision. I stared at Shoshana as if she were a ghost.

She squeezed my hand. "Oh, Daavi," she said, "I know. I know. For me it was like the world went dark when I heard. Cold and dark. I wept for weeks."

She looked down at her tunic. "All Kol Ami wept." Her voice caught. "We all did our keriah."

My eyes dropped to where her tunic was torn. I couldn't speak.

"But you," she added, "you're so lucky to have had so much time with Yeshu. I barely got to know him before I was spirited away."

She sighed. "Still, he's given me so much." Then she brightened. "And not just me," she said. "Before I arrived, he gave my husband and the others the idea for Kol Ami!"

"Your husband?" I asked.

Shoshana pointed behind me with her chin. Rising to my feet I turned to see my newfound friend, Ezrah, standing there, his head-wrap off, his curly hair silhouetted against the azure sky. He was smiling broadly at the marvel of it all.

I turned back to face Shoshana, a tinge of disbelief still tugging at my sleeve. Blinking, I gazed into her eyes, set deep in a face a dozen hard years older than the unweathered girl's that I remembered. Scarred now but still beautiful.

Like the moon.

In a flash it all came back. I suddenly understood, down inside, what must have happened those many years ago: My parents talking loudly but indistinctly out in the courtyard at night. Then the long silence that they descended into, signaling their decision. The door creaking open so softly only a mouse could hear, while Shoshana and I slept soundly in the corner. The silhouette of a figure bending down, putting a hand over her mouth to keep her from shouting out, picking her up and carrying her outside while I slept on. I, waking the next morning to find her gone, perhaps forever, both of us terrified of what could happen when one's eyes are closed.

How awful it must have been for her. Soon enough, the townspeople would have found out she was sick, and my parents couldn't protect her every minute. She would have been driven off, like Ezrah. Maybe even stoned.

And in the meantime, how would Mother and Father protect Aaron and me from Shoshana unintentionally spreading the dreaded illness. It was hard enough losing a child, but to lose one's whole family?

A small angry voice in my head asked, "But isn't that what Shoshana lost, her whole family?"

And then the anger stopped the way a hailstorm stops—the clamor subsides and the sky clears. I was wrong. Our parents had not thrown Shoshana out. They had arranged for her to go with others who were also afflicted. They had given her over to a new family and hoped for the best. To save her. To save us all.

Finally grasping this—the heartbreak Mother and Father must have felt—was for me nearly unbearable. No wonder they didn't try explaining any of it. It was too terrible for words.

I tried getting to my feet, but once again my knees gave way. I could not stand up under the weight of such thoughts and feelings. Closing my eyes I began to pray, listening for Yeshu and taking one halting breath after another.

"Our God in heaven, hallowed be your name..."

Shoshana sat beside me, and began stroking my hair. I heard her lips moving with mine, barely whispering.

When I finished and opened my eyes, she looked at me for the longest time. She nodded repeatedly, biting her upper lip, her fingertips lightly touching my cheek. She knew what was happening inside me. And I knew what must have been swirling around inside her.

We were together again at last. Forever.

"And the baby?" I asked suddenly.

"Ezrah's and mine," she replied, smiling at her husband, who was cradling the infant in his arms.

"Your nephew Daniel!" he exclaimed.

I threw up my hands and cheered. "Number one!"

~ ~ ~

For the rest of the afternoon Shoshana caught me up on her life, at times talking ever louder, her voice racing as if her chance to share might end as suddenly as it had arrived.

Story followed story, gradually bringing me closer to Kol Ami, Ezrah, and of course Daniel. Eventually she stopped talking and we were quiet for a long while. At last, taking my hands in hers, she looked into my eyes.

"Daavi," she said, "Put your heart at ease. Mother and Father did the best they could. Having Daniel has taught me that. I hold him up to the light and ask myself if I could ever give *him* up, and every part of my being screams no. It would be worse than losing an arm or a leg; more like having my heart torn out. But then I ask myself if that means I would be putting my life before his.

"You know the story in the scrolls? I'm thinking of the one about the mother who was brought before King Solomon and who chose to give her baby away rather than have him cut in half? Unfortunately the test Mother and Father faced had no monarch to referee it. There was no one to save them from the choice they made, by restoring me to them. At least not at that time."

I tried to speak but again I couldn't.

"And yet see where my life has led me?" Sweeping her hand in a broad arc, she insisted, "Look around you."

I looked left and right, nodding tentatively.

"Daavi, I've learned life is a rocky path up a rugged mountain. From the bottom staring upward, it appears one way. But near the top gazing down, sometimes through thin clouds of memories," her eyes stared ahead pensively, "things can look quite different.

"During those final months of mine in Nazareth, though I was only a child, I was afraid and ashamed. People glared at me with stony eyes. It was like being on the edge of a cliff without really knowing why."

She raised a fist to her mouth. "All I knew was there was something terribly wrong with me."

She cleared her throat and went on. "Then came the night visit: hands reaching toward me out of the shadows, covering my mouth, lifting me up, whisking me away. The next thing I knew, I was on the road, alone, in the company of people I didn't know."

Her arm drifted back to her lap.

"We wandered for years, sometimes fearing that our meandering search might never end. But finally we found Kol Ami, found it by building it! We were only the second of several groups to settle down here."

Once more she sighed deeply.

"But think about my life now, Daavi," she said softly, gazing down at Daniel. "I have a baby. I have a husband and a home. I've helped plant and grow a new village. Imagine that!

"So, I ask myself," she said, looking straight at me, "had Mother and Father not entrusted me to the good people who brought me here, where would I be today? What would my life be like had I stayed in Nazareth?"

She gestured with both hands. "I might have none of this."

I closed my eyes. Closed them because I was seeing stones slowly raining down on Shoshana. When I opened them again, her face was blurred in my vision. And my heart had softened one more time.

As dusk finally surrounded us in its embrace, we walked back to Shoshana and Ezrah's house. We sat in the tiny courtyard while she talked, on and on, and I listened.

Using dark barley bread to soak up the warm sheep curds and chopped olives in a bowl between us, we leaned forward and stuffed the dripping treat into our mouths. Finished, we washed it down with a few swallows of newly fermented apple wine.

"Your cup is overflowing?" I asked at last, during a lull. "The way has opened for you?"

"Yes," she laughed in joy. "It's a good life here in Kol Ami. Ezrah calls it the first of many Yeshu villages to come!" She looked over at her husband, her face radiant.

I See Your Father

The very next day, Shoshana and I resumed our catching up. We asked one another dozens of questions, and gave dozens of answers: about Mother, Father, Aaron, our uncles and aunts and cousins. And about all that had happened to her, and to me, including the local history we had seen being made, had even sometimes helped to make. Most of all we talked about Yohanan and Yeshu and the band of friends who walked together. She wanted to hear even the tiniest detail about our journey to the cedars of Lebanon. Starting with each of us carrying a small stone to and from, following Yohanan's lead.

And of course she was hungry to hear about my three years on the road with Yeshu and the others. Carrying Yohanan in our hearts. And on our chests.

In the afternoon, Shoshana and I took a long walk together, hunting for wild berries. We began reminiscing about our earliest memories back home in Nazareth. I told her all about my first clear recollection of Yeshu: standing in the wheat field at sunset, showing me the path to the moon and the stars.

"He knew already, didn't he?" she said. "It's the path he traveled."

"Yohanan, too," I answered with a nod.

"And Daavi, are you on it?

"Well," I said, "yes, I am."

She smiled, then abruptly asked, "Would you like to hear *my* earliest memory of Yeshu?"

"Absolutely," I replied, nearly rising up out of my seat. "Please tell me."

"Well, I was five or six years old," she began. "You were born already.

Looking back, I realize that Yeshu was a young man then, maybe a dozen years older than me, although I remember him being as ancient as Father and Mother!

"He was already working in the carpentry shop, supporting Mama Maria and his sister and brothers. His father had died a few years before. Mother told me that following his death, the singing and laughter stopped floating over to our house from the windows next door for quite a long while."

Shoshana looked down at her hands, then returned to her storytelling.

"I used to like to dip a gourd into the water pot after I had walked with Mother to the well, and then carry it carefully over to the doorway of Yeshu's workshop and stand against the wall, just outside.

"I would listen attentively for the sound of him working, which would sometimes be punctuated by a wood chip or two flying through the open door. Only when I knew for sure he was there would I call toward the opening: 'Water delivery! Fresh, cool water! All you can drink!'

"This always got a big laugh out of Yeshu, who would call back: 'Oh, it's my thirst-quencher-girl! Come in, Shoshana. Come in.'

"Stepping over the door sill, I'd hand him the brimming gourd and watch him drink with relish.

"Once done, he'd burst out with an exaggerated 'Aaah, best water I ever tasted! Thank you, young maiden named for a blossom!'

"Then he would hand the gourd back, and reach out a closed fist toward me, saying, 'Here's your pay: two pine curls and half a palmful of sawdust.'

"I never tired of that exchange. It was back when he began telling the occasional story to village children who visited his workshop. Did he keep on doing that?"

"Did he ever!" I answered. "Tonight I'll tell you several of his best ones."

"Oh, yes!" Shoshana exclaimed. Then she resumed her tale.

"Often Yeshu and I touched foreheads as I was leaving his workshop, pausing for just a few moments to be quiet together. He sitting on his work stool; me standing in front of him."

She smiled and glanced away for a moment.

"This one time I remember as clearly as a summer moon in the window above my bed."

She lifted her eyes.

"I looked straight at him as our foreheads slowly came closer and closer together. Impulsively I blurted out, 'You have big dark eyes like a camel.'

"Yeshu almost choked with laughter. It momentarily broke the spell as he leaned back on his stool, stomping one foot on the sawdust floor, followed by the other.

"Soon his face grew serious and again our foreheads came closer, my eyes staring deep into his.

"'What do you see in there?' he asked.

"'It's like looking into the well,' I answered, 'when my mother lifts me up to peek over the edge.'

"My gaze parted from his for a moment, and I could see a smile gently tugging at the corners of his mouth.

"'Look deeper,' he urged.

"I did, taking a long breath in and letting it out slowly. At last I spoke, but very softly.

"'I see your father.'

"Yeshu fell backward against the workbench, a startled look in his eyes. He sat there staring at me, his mouth slightly open. His face took on the colors of the time-polished bench he leaned against, as he balanced there on the stool.

"I froze right where I stood.

"Drawing in a single breath, he raised his eyes toward the rafters of his workshop, where sweet-smelling cedar boards lay drying. Then without warning he pitched forward, elbows propped on his knees, and buried his face in his hands.

"I was so frightened I couldn't speak. After what seemed forever, Yeshu slowly raised his face back up. Believing I had said something terribly wrong, I couldn't meet his eye. My gaze dropped to his hands and I noticed that his palms were wet with tears.

"How had I lowered this large, wonderful man into misery?

"Finally, pressing my lips together, I summoned the courage to squeeze out the words: 'Yeshu, I'm so sorry. I wish I hadn't said that.'

"I took a small step closer, put my hand on his broad shoulder, and implored him, 'Please forgive me for making you sad.'

"I cleared my throat. "'Are you mad at me?'

"'No, Shoshana,' he said. 'I'm not sad and I'm not angry.'

"He took hold of me by the shoulders. 'You've given me something very precious. It's so big, that for a moment I couldn't bear the weight of it. Thank you, my little friend. Thank you!'

"I stared at him, not understanding.

"'Children take in things,' he said softly, 'that big people often miss. In my eyes you saw that my Abba's not lost. He's still here, deep inside.' Yeshu placed his hand upon his chest, fingers spread wide. 'This is a powerful truth, Shoshana. It gives me heart. And I'm forever grateful.'

"He squeezed my shoulders," she said, "and I smiled with relief."

The telling paused as an echo of that beautiful smile swept across her face the way sunlight at daybreak illuminates a hillside of wild roses.

Shaking her head, Shoshana resumed her story. "Then I said to him, 'I should go home now,' and took a step toward the door.

"'You are home,' he answered, with a twinkle in his eye.

"I nodded.

"'Go now, to your mother and father,' he said.

"I nodded once more.

"'And thank you again, dear lily flower.'

"Slowly I turned and left him there at his workbench, reaching for his father's mallet and chisel."

Clasping Hands in God's Circle

After Shoshana finished her story, we quietly filled a satchel to the brim with berries. As soon as we were done, we turned and set out for home. We walked so slowly it seemed we were trying to catch hold of the present and not let loose. Otherwise it might escape into the past and be lost to us except in memories that fade with time. Those moments were bites of sweet honey loaf we held in our mouths to savor the taste as long as possible.

I cherished the tales my sister spun for me. They were bright flashes filling in large gaps of her life that I had missed out on—and was ravenous to know about.

Listening reminded me of what it's like on a cloudy night looking up at the sky, the firmament completely hidden, until without warning some lofty wind opens the dark curtain to reveal patches of stars looking down from above.

And with luck, one gets a glimpse of silvery moon!

The following Sabbath, Shoshana, Ezrah, baby Daniel, and I spent much of the day wandering alongside a river near the village. We strolled, then stretched out as it suited us, all the while talking and talking. However far it meandered, the conversation always returned to Kol Ami.

Ezrah explained how Yeshu, Martha, and Yohanan had advised the new community to ground itself in love—not just in principle but in practice. What he was saying was of course not new to me. I had heard the gist of these lessons countless times listening to stories in Yeshu's workshop and on the road with Yohanan to and from Lebanon. They were the banner our ragged band waved as we crisscrossed Judea and Galilee, preaching and healing, carrying the message that God is love; God's creatures are sacred; God is in each person and within every family and village.

But something in Ezrah's voice suggested the Kol Ami experience was also different. He could barely contain his excitement, and I began to feel as if I were watching the sun rise for the first time all over again.

"Martha told us," he said, "that being cast out from our former lives could be a blessing. It gave us the chance to remake life not only for ourselves but for others still on their way. And this could only be accomplished as a group, pulling together.

How we treated one another, day by day, would be as important as the labor we did to earn a living. By holding each other in tender light as we cleared fields, sowed seed, and built our houses, we would not only survive, we would thrive.

"Kol Ami can become a beacon for the world," she insisted.

Shoshana added wistfully, "I wish I'd been here when those ideas were first sprouting. But my little band was still on its way. They were waiting while I lay burning with fever in a healer's hut, far up in the mountains to the west of here. So I didn't see Yeshu then. Or ever again."

She stared down at the scarred and furrowed hands that gripped one another in her lap.

Then she looked up and brightened. "But I still carry his stories from the carpentry shop, and from Mama Ana's fireside, too. Mama Maria often talked to me, you know, while she worked in her house. She would go on and on about people in Nazareth and how they stumbled into and then clambered out of their many problems and conflicts. I thought then that it was just gossip about how amusing and quirky people can be, but now I realize she was teaching me. In one way or another, the stories were always about finding ways of making peace and showing compassion.

"When my band of wanderers finally arrived in Kol Ami months after its founding, I grasped Yeshu's message immediately. Or at least I knew as much as those already there, young as I was."

She glanced at Ezrah, who smiled in agreement.

"Now I'm the village storyteller and historian," she continued, trying not to smile too broadly. "Whenever a story is needed to shine light on one of our truths, people call on me."

She looked away again, then brought her eyes back to mine.

I lifted both eyebrows high, to get her to tell such a tale. Shoshana swallowed the bait and the hook, like any good storyteller would, and began her telling with a teaser. "My favorites are the fables about how animals learn life's lessons, while in the meantime teaching people a thing or two." She winked mischievously.

"You know," she began, "like the one that was already old when Father's father was just beginning to grow a beard."

Now I was the one who was hooked.

"It's about a long-eared rabbit," she went on, "who one fine morning meets a colossal, cinnamon-coated bear on the path that crosses the meadow. Bear is limping and whimpering with each step.

"Rabbit knows she should run while she can but curiosity gets the better of her. So she asks Bear, 'Why are you crying and hobbling along like a giant grasshopper with a front leg missing?'

"Bear woefully lifts a swollen paw to show a large cactus thorn stuck between two of his toes. Rabbit wants to run before Bear turns her into breakfast, but something inside her nudges her forward. Creeping toward the wounded paw, she gingerly closes her buck teeth around the thorn, and yanks it out.

"Bear roars with relief and licks his throbbing paw over and over, while Rabbit runs like the wind before she can be fallen upon and devoured.

"Four seasons later, in a nearby stand of pines, Rabbit is hopelessly caught in a hunter's trap of green willow branches bound up tightly with sinewy vines. Along comes Bear who recognizes his savior from yesteryear but doesn't let on that he knows.

"Playfully, Bear tells Rabbit, 'I could eat you or I could set you free! And you know, at the moment, I'm a very hungry bear.'

"Rabbit shivers in her skin. Then Bear laughs uproariously—which is how bears laugh, isn't it?

"And with that, Rabbit recognizes him.

"'Save me!' she implores.

"'But I'm a bear,' says the beast. 'And bears eat everything.'

"With that he attacks the trap, swinging mightily with his huge paws and tearing it to pieces. Out tumbles Rabbit, desperately trying to figure out how to outrun a bear that is so close his hot breath threatens to singe her long ears.

"Then Bear rises up on his hind legs, blocking out the sun, and slaps his thighs, guffawing so hard he loses his breath. When at last he stops wheezing, he says, 'Have a happy life, my dear little hoppy friend.' And once more he roars.

"Finally he gives Rabbit a nudge with his once-wounded paw.

"She blinks, flaps her ears in thanks, and scrambles headfirst into a nearby patch of briars to count her blessings.

Shoshana tossed her head and smiled knowingly. "Friends, it seems, come in every size. And where you meet them is always a surprise."

She laughed.

"And that, *my* friends, is how my rabbit tale ends!"

I clapped my hands together, beaming in delight at Shoshana's clever telling. Just as quickly, she steered the subject back to Kol Ami.

"Daavi, all villages are close-knit," she said, "but ours is special. We are bears and rabbits of all the same dimension, seeing one another for what each of us is deep down inside.

"But it's more. Who we are isn't based on who's been kept out, but on those that have been drawn in. People here discover who they are in how they're connected to one another. The smallest children live this truth from the beginning but forget it as they age unless all of us looking after them see it and remember."

She looked down at Daniel and smiled wryly.

"We've learned that a community isn't something readymade that you're just born into," she went on. "It's built and strengthened, or weakened, day by day." She straightened again.

"Kol Ami is our child and we've grown as she has, from years of patient attention applying seven practices that Yeshu, Martha, and Yohanan shared with us. Everyone in Kol Ami strives to follow them. And here they are."

> I take your hand, you take mine;
> we walk forward together.
> Treat others as you would have them treat you;
> serve your neighbors as you would your family.
> Build up your community by discovering and sharing your gifts –
> we are all responsible for one another.
> Rage is a blister to be lanced and healed with acts of love.

Daniel suddenly arched his back and Shoshana halted to reposition him. Without missing a beat Ezrah chimed in, saying, "We take every opportunity to remind ourselves and our children about these shared lessons."

> A community is a boat, and everyone in it a lifeline.
> Take from the earth only what you need,
> leaving the seeds and the roots imbedded
> and the soil richer than before.
> Day in, day out, always make time to
> laugh, dream, show love, seek God.

Little Daniel burbled his agreement. Shoshana and Ezrah both looked at him affectionately and giggled. Smiling along, I couldn't help wondering what it would be like to live in such a place. I was hearing echoes of Yohanan and Yeshu in all they had said.

By late afternoon we were turning homeward. There we shared a meal before putting Daniel to bed. Our talk went on till the room became dusky and the fire burned down. Finally, each of us followed the example of the dozing child and crawled into our own little nest of blankets.

The next morning I awoke early and stole outside to watch the embered crescent moon, and the sparks of the wandering stars, as they gradually vanished with the night.

It was Rosh Hodesh. A new month was beginning, and as I welcomed the sun rising like a phoenix out of the horizon's fiery rim, I knew clearly what I would do.

I stood and walked back into the house. I couldn't wait to tell Shoshana and Ezrah my news. Kneeling by the side of the family bed, I shook Shoshana gently. She sat up with a start, and Ezrah rolled over on his elbow, blinking, to see what was going on. Shoshana's eyes scanned my clothing, before looking back into my face.

"Are you leaving?" she asked, her voice faltering.

"Actually, no. I'm staying!" I whispered. That is, if the Kol Ami Yeshu village will have me."

Shoshana threw a glance toward Ezrah, then back at me, her face glowing just like the dawn outside.

"But that's not in question," she insisted. "New people choose us; we don't choose them."

"Okay. I choose you!" I said, so loudly that little Daniel woke up howling.

Shoshana swept him up in her arms, rose, and did a little dance. Soon she and Ezrah and I were hugging and laughing so deliriously that Daniel stopped crying and stared at us with large, round eyes.

After things quieted down a bit, I looked at my sister.

"Shoshana," I said, reaching out to grasp her hand, "before I can settle in here, there is something I must do."

I paused, then asked, "And I want to know if you will join me."

She stared back quizzically.

"When I met Ezrah on the road," I explained, "I was on my way somewhere, somewhere I hadn't been in a long while." I stopped speaking as I searched for the right words, "Because I'd been smoldering and fuming."

I paused again.

"You haven't been there in a long time, either."

She tilted her head, looking intently at me and nodding softly.

"I must go to Nazareth," I said, "to make peace with Father and Mother. To tell them how sorry I am for blaming them for sending you away. All those years, I stewed in anger over what seemed like their betrayal of us.

"At the time I couldn't understand what on earth they were thinking. Nor was I capable of even imagining that they had done all they could to save Aaron and me, and *you*.

"Finally I see it clearly. I want my parents back and I want them to have their family back, their whole family."

I fought back tears. "It's time for the circle to be unbroken."

Shoshana squeezed my hand. Her lower lip trembled.

"Yeshu pointed the way," I went on, "when he taught the beatitudes on the mountainside. He repeated that message many times afterward. But I never quite got how it applied to me."

Shoshana had learned the words, too, so we recited them together.

> If, when you are bringing your gift to the altar,
> you suddenly recall that your brother or sister
> has a grievance against you, leave your gift
> where it is before reaching the altar.
> First go and make your peace with your brother or sister,
> and only then come back and offer your gift.

"Think about it. Seen in a different light," I said, "Father is my brother, no? And Mother, is my sister. Yet for years I was so lost in my *own* grievance that I misread the signs right there in front of me. I mistook Mother and Father's silence as proof of guilt when it was really grief.

"I cannot and will not build a new life for myself while what's left of theirs is in ruins. They've been living in silence for so long," I went on. "It's how they honored you. I think it's time to give the silence back its name. Not shame but sorrow. Sorrow and sacrificial love—the hardest kind."

Then I wrapped Shoshana's hands in mine. "But I shouldn't be speaking for you. Do you feel at peace about joining me? Maybe you need more time."

Shoshana moved one hand from mine and pressed a finger to my lips.

"Hush. I've been ready to return from the moment I left," she replied. "But I was never sure my desire was right. Nor certain I was wanted." Her eyes were glistening.

"Now I know. My dear brother Daavi, all grown up, has convinced me. We'll leave as soon as you like."

I smiled in agreement. "I'll need a day or so to pull my thoughts together. That will also give me a chance to introduce myself to my new neighbors."

I'd already met many of the people of Kol Ami with Ezrah, but most hadn't yet had a chance to get to know me. Not that I had much to do, as it turned out. Already word was racing around about the new resident who was not only Shoshana's long-lost brother, but one of the few who had actually walked with Yohanan and Yeshu.

~ ~ ~

The very next morning a curious crowd gathered under the oak tree in front of Shoshana and Ezrah's house. Greeting me with polite murmurs and here and there a wave of the hand, they sat down in a semicircle and motioned for me to sit at its center, facing them.

I sat down, quite nervous, not knowing what to do or say. It surprised me, given all the villages I'd walked into unknown, along with Yeshu and the others. Of course my friends then had been my elders, and now I was doing this alone. So I looked out at this sea of folks, kind as they were, unsure of what I should tell them, or just how to put it.

Eventually, a man with graying hair, who rested a basket of fresh fish on one hip, broke the spell and put me at ease.

Smiling broadly he implored, "Brother of Shoshana and friend of Yohanan and Yeshu, speak to us! You walked beside our dear teacher. You've heard his words and stories since childhood. How many times we tried to hear him..." the man lowered his eyes to the ground, and shook his head as if to steady his cracking voice, "only to be driven from the back row of crowds by frightened people! Cursed by those who listened to Yeshu with open ears and closed hearts."

He coughed, clearing his throat, while his fellow villagers looked on and nodded in agreement.

Finally he resumed, "Tell us, friend, what was it Yeshu said that most moved you? Were there teachings of his that brought you here to join us in Kol Ami?"

I opened my mouth to speak, then closed it in an attempt to gather my thoughts. "Friend," I began, "I will tell you what I know, or at least try to."

Before going on, I extended my hands, palms up, and asked all who sat with me to share my silence. Shutting my eyes I let my mind slowly descend like a leather pail, spinning on its rope, as I gradually dropped deep into my well.

The crowd waited patiently, using the time to search through their own silences.

At last, the hand of God lifted me to my feet and words came. The voice was mine. And not mine.

"Dear friends, old and new," I said, my arms reaching out in greeting, then falling to my sides. "Here are some precious words I learned from Yeshu..." Inhaling steadily, I felt my chest fill up. Only then did I feel ready to speak. "Let us love one another. For love is from God, and everyone who loves is a child of God and knows God.

"But the unloving know nothing of God. For God *is* love."

I felt Yeshu's presence moving through my heart. I listened to the words spilling from my mouth and remembered them as those he spoke—almost singing—to that cluster of shepherds and field hands in the village on the outskirts of Jerusalem. It was soon after we left the Temple and its moneychangers and his formal teaching began.

It was only the start, yet it was also a culmination. "Because God loves us, we are bound in turn to love one another. As long as we do so, God resides in us and God's love comes to perfection in us."

These were possibly the first words I heard Yeshu preach that day. In my mind I saw us all seated under a village oak much like the one I was sitting under with the people of Kol Ami today. I thought along with Yeshu as he found his voice.

"This is the proof that we remain in God and God in us. It's the proof that each of us has been given a share in God's spirit."

The lyrics kept spiraling and encircling, my voice feeling stronger with each refrain.

"Though God has never been seen by anyone, we see that of God every day because those who dwell in love are dwelling in God, and God in them."

I gestured with both hands toward those gathered under the tree, and also at the village beyond.

It was then I noticed a woman in the front row, sitting beside what had to be her granddaughter. The grandmother's face was heavily lined, her eyes on fire. When those eyes met mine, a broad smile smoothed her face. Straight away, she lifted and flicked a quivering hand to urge me on.

I complied. "If a person says, 'I love God,' while hating or harming his neighbor, that person is not speaking truth."

I saw a number of heads nodding.

"If one does not love the neighbor who can be seen, then how can one love God who is unseen?"

As I spoke each phrase, my eyes scanned the gathered villagers.

"Those who love God love their neighbors, and do not raise a hand against them."

I paused.

"They clasp hands to help form God's circle."

With that, I stopped speaking and bowed my head, falling back into silence like a pebble tossed in a pond. A hush rippled over the group. Once smooth, the quiet went undisturbed for a long while.

"All that I have just spoken," I said finally, my voice quavering, "has brought me to Kol Ami. Brought me to this place after a long, long journey in my own wilderness."

"Yeshu led me here like he led you here. All of us were astray." I was blinking away the dampness in my eyes.

I cleared my throat and then said, "Rising before dawn the other day, I saw written across the great dome of sky: Kol Ami is rooted in God. The invisible made visible.

"Kol Ami is a flower blooming in the desert during a drought. Heaven where once there was hell."

I waited. Listening. All faces were turned toward me, all eyes locked on mine.

"This is why I've joined you," I said, bowing my head.

The ancient grandmother slowly rose to her feet and walked to where

I stood. Curving her arm around my back without touching me, she tilted her head slightly to the side and bent close to my chest. I realized I was being embraced while being kept safe.

My arms followed her lead, and I bowed my head toward hers, knowing that other occasions for closer embraces would come.

One after another each person approached and gave me the same hug. I've never in my life been so deeply touched without touching.

By the time they finished, I was breathless. Then one by one they left me there surrounded by their lasting presence.

Forgiveness

At dawn the next morning Shoshana and I set out for Nazareth. Daniel was too large by now to be carried such a distance, and there was no donkey to be borrowed. Besides, this was a trip best taken by Shoshana and me alone. So Daniel and Ezrah stayed home.

For hours we journeyed arm in arm, sister and brother, sharing childhood memories and hopes for the future. Walking at the fast pace of the young and joyful, we reached Nazareth in the late afternoon. When we walked in the door of our old house, mother turned from the hearth and promptly dropped a bowl of figs that crashed to the floor, spilling plump fruits in every direction.

Shoshana and I caught her before she could join them. She clung to the two of us as if she were being rescued from drowning.

Father was in his workshop. Hearing the earthenware smash and mother's mournful wail, he rushed in. Spotting us in a single glance, he raised his hands to cover the top of his head, his lips moving silently in prayer.

I stepped over and placed my arm around his quaking shoulders. How small he seemed to have grown. He took my free hand in one of his and held it to his heart, reaching around with the other to pull me near.

"My son," he whispered, "Daavi, my dear son."

I hugged him awkwardly, trying to stifle a sob, then still hanging on to him, turned and reached out for Shoshana.

Taking her hand I pulled her close and pressed it into his, saying, "Father, look who is found! It's your daughter Shoshana, come home at last."

With a cry like an owl's, Father threw his arms around Shoshana and drew her close. She gasped and buried her head in his shoulder.

Eagerly, Mother took my hand and Father's, and he clung tightly to Shoshana's who held mine. We all said Yeshu's prayer together.

> Our God in heaven...
> forgive us our wrongs,
> for we too will forgive
> all who have wronged us....

When we finished, we fell into an ever-deepening silence, each one holding the others up. At last the circle was whole. Our hand-squeezing said more than any words could have right then.

My head still bowed, I softly asked, "Mother, Father, remember when you asked for my forgiveness? And I said I would try?"

Their faces lifted toward mine, shining with light like the hearth behind them.

"Yes. Oh yes, I forgive you," I said. "But can you forgive *me* for taking so long?"

Mother let loose of my hand and pressed her fingers to my lips, while Father said, "The past is done. Long gone. No more words."

And we all embraced. How good that felt. How long that hug was in coming.

Mother quickly put food on the table: smoked lake sardines and barley bread, the figs she had dropped and rinsed off, and a pitcher of wine. We held hands again, said a silent blessing, and then merrily set upon the food like a starving band of thieves.

At that moment, Aaron walked in. He had been scouring the hilltop villages for just the right animal skins to make saddles and, of course, sandals. He roared with delight seeing me, and I rushed over, only to be pounded on the back and swept into an embrace worthy of a wild bear. I gave as good as I got, though he was nearly a head taller.

Then Aaron turned toward Shoshana, his face a question mark.

"Our *sister!*" I burst out, gripping Aaron's arm just above the elbow.

Aaron's jaw plummeted in disbelief as he threw a glance at me and then back to Shoshana, who was in his arms in a second. For him it was as if meeting her for the first time. He was just a toddler when she had left, and he had no firm recollection of her at all. Now a flesh-and-blood person stood before him, filling what had been an aching void.

I eagerly watched their faces and saw the tears spring to their eyes. Mother and Father's cheeks were also wet, as were mine.

Finally, with a drawn-out sigh, Aaron pulled up a bench that Yeshu had made for us back when I was a young boy bringing him drinking water and handing him tools. We all sat and returned to our eating, gabbling like geese in a small pond.

Aaron ate with one hand and held fast to Shoshana's arm with the other. Mother even disappeared and returned with a fresh melon slice and a handful of grapes for each of us to celebrate with.

As soon as we finished, Mother asked to use Aaron's bench. She clambered up on it to open a cupboard just beneath the roof. Reaching in as far as she could, she pulled out a small cloth bundle bound with a leather cord. Father helped her down and she began untying the packet. I came close and stared at her hands, while she teased and tugged at the knot. Soon, she addressed me.

"Daavi, I've been saving this for you since you left. It was made by someone dear to your heart."

While I tried to guess, my mother's trembling fingers finally loosened the knot so that it came undone, partly opening the cloth wrap. Smiling, mother stole a look at me as shyly as a young girl hiding behind her hand.

"You better finish," she said, thrusting the bundle toward me.

As soon as it fell into the palm of my hand, my heart leapt inexplicably. I tore open the wrap. Shalom! Shalom! There in my hand lay the toy dog and faithful companion Yeshu had carved and polished for me, just before the whole world cracked open.

Once, I thought I had lost Shalom forever.

Childlike joy swept over me, followed by wrenching sadness. Holding Shalom to my heart, I inhaled slowly and powerfully, letting peace flow in just like I used to.

Once more the gentle carpenter had lifted me high in the air and then set me lightly down again. I felt like a fledgling falcon and its ancient ancestor, in a single moment. How can love for another be so sweet and at the same time, so painful?

I looked at Mother through misty eyes and hugged her tightly.

"Oh, Mama," was all I could say.

Dropping onto the stool, I began stroking Shalom's smooth coat over and over before tucking him into the heartside pocket inside my tunic. Just after I pulled my hand out, a jolt lifted me off my seat. Everyone looked at me goggle-eyed, as if afraid I'd been stung by a hornet. I ran to the sagging ladder that leaned against the loft, scrambled up, and thrust my hand under the rafters. Finding what I was searching for, I gently eased it out.

The old leather bag was falling apart but still intact. Edging back down the ladder, I turned to Shoshana.

"Now *you* get to discover a treasure," I said.

Looking back at me quizzically, she hastily pulled the knotted tie-thongs apart and dumped the contents into her lap. She squealed with delight.

"My leather pots and platters! I played with these for *hours* when I was child. How did you know where they were?"

"That's simple," I answered. "I hid them soon after you were lost because I knew the very day you returned, you'd want them."

"How right you were," she exclaimed. "I'm taking them home for Daniel, and his sister if she comes."

She paused for a moment, before adding, "Oh yes, and for myself!"

Turning the small treasures over and over in her hands, she spoke pensively. "So much that was lost is found."

Then she grew quiet and continued staring into her lap.

We spent the rest of the evening catching up. Mother and Father just couldn't hear enough about their first grandchild. Gradually, however, the conversation drifted to old times, back when Mother and Father were beginning a family and Gramma Ruth was still alive. We all wisely skipped over Shoshana's absence and the reasons for it—there would be far better moments to touch that healing wound.

Finally Father's imprisonment came up. As Mother shared what it was like to wait all those months with two small boys who needed to be fed, I studied the faces of my sister and brother. Almost every detail Shoshana was hearing was new to her, whereas Aaron had been so young during this calamity that he remembered only Father's homecoming.

Slowly it began to dawn on me that I myself knew only fragments of the story: the shouting from the rear of the house; the soldiers dragging Father away; my waiting on the doorstep, day after day, staring down the road; and finally, my being the first one to see Father approaching in the distance, large raindrops plummeting past him into the dust. But below the surface of this story? Everything was a mystery to me.

So, I listened intently when Father told how he had been freed, his voice cracking even after all these many years. His captors had humiliated and tortured him, relentlessly trying to force him to produce the wretched leather bindings for their prisoners. As time passed, they were no longer even needed—months earlier, the Romans had forced others to do their bidding. The danger for them was not a shortage of leather manacles for tying the wrists of resistant Jews; the danger was what might happen if someone could say "No!" to Rome and get away with it. Who knew where that might lead!

When Father continued to resist his captors' demands, they shifted from his body to his spirit. This we learned when after waiting patiently, Mother said with a soft voice, "My husband, there's just one thing I've never understood for sure." Clearing her throat, she looked down and back up again. "I've been afraid to ask..." she said, "but can you tell me now..." she reached out and touched his hand, "what was it that finally made you agree?"

Father looked at her and sighed. For a long time he said nothing. Finally, he answered in a near whisper, "I was told that if I continued to refuse, they would set me free." He took in a long breath. "And replace me with you."

I sat pinned to my seat as if a tree had fallen on me. My breath caught, trapped in my chest. One more time, memories spun backwards in my mind, and when at last they stopped their spiraling, they had been altered forever. I would never again see my father, or think of my father's abduction, in the same light.

Just before turning in, my mother took me into the courtyard and thanked me over and over for coming. She said my father had been unwell and had begun to talk of dying.

In the middle of the night, I heard him coughing. I rolled out of bed, lit a lamp, and went over to where he lay. Mother stirred, but I gestured for her to go back to sleep.

Kneeling beside Father, I asked, "Do you need a drink of water?"

He nodded faintly. When I brought his cup, he drank deeply and then smiled.

"The father has become the son," he said hoarsely, "and the son, the father."

His silvery hair reflected the low blaze of the flickering lamp. The skin that stretched across his forehead and cheekbones seemed nearly transparent. How fragile he appeared now.

"No, Abba," I said to him, my eyes widening upon hearing myself speak that name.

I lay my hand in his and saw Yeshu with *his* Abba. With that, I thought to myself: how much alike we fathers and sons are. If only we could have the patience and good fortune to see it.

Looking earnestly into his eyes, I added, "The father hasn't become the son; the son longs to someday become the father."

He squeezed my hand. I glanced over at Mother. Eyes open, her face glistened like starlight.

"And like my mother, too," I said.

A soft smile flew across her face.

I turned the lamp down low and sat quietly beside the bed, watching them both until they fell back asleep. In the flickering light, they did indeed look like slumbering children. Even their skin seemed smoother.

My eyes wandered back and forth from face to face, alighting on Father's brow before settling on the strong bridge of his nose. Only since finding Shoshana had I been able to grasp what Yeshu meant when he told me he and the other young men of Nazareth considered my father heroic. Anger had clouded my eyes.

My father, at great cost, had refused to collaborate with the most powerful army on earth. For weeks and months he had refused to help them tie the hands of the resistance—one slight man facing off against steel and stone.

And Mother had been just as strong. I could see that now in the quiet determination with which she had lived her life watching over us. She knew that *doing* was the ablest teacher: The she-hawk walks the edges of its nest with sure foot; vigilant eye scanning limb and horizon. Her young follow her every move. Fledgling hawks learn to soar by watching their mother leap from the edge of the nest, beating her wings time after time against the buffeting winds. It's certainly not by listening to pleading cries from on high, urging them to "Fly! Fly!"

With a full heart, I leaned forward, blew out the lamp with a puff, and returned to my bedroll. Closing my eyes, I saw the rest of my family also tucked under their blankets—all five of us under one roof for the first time in more than fifteen years.

~ ~ ~

The following morning I went over to see Mama Ana and Mama Maria, as I always did whenever I was in Nazareth. Mama Maria rushed to the door and, with a shout, hugged me warmly. She seemed to know already that I was coming to visit and who I'd brought to Nazareth with me. Grasping my sleeve, she led me into the home where she had raised Yeshu and his sisters and brothers.

The house had always been full to the brim, and still felt that way, even though she now lived in the lone room with only Mama Ana. As my eyes adjusted to the dim light, I could see the aging matriarch lying in bed in the corner. Her white hair spilled over the pillow like a shimmering crown. She seemed asleep.

As I tiptoed over and sat on the edge of the bed, she opened her eyes. "Does your mother know where you are?" she whispered. "You'd better run along home or you'll have hot water and hard bread crusts for dinner!"

My heart sank. How diminished she had become.

Seeing my crestfallen face, she abruptly grabbed my hand with a firm grip and became convulsed with laughter.

Soon she quieted. "Hello, Daavi," she said with the unwavering voice I remembered, giving me the wink of an accomplished trickster.

"I've been keeping close track of you since the last time we saw one another," she said. "You've been teaming up with Joanna, haven't you? Doing the good work you two learned from Yeshu."

I nodded excitedly.

"Well, that's good," she said. "And you've done the right thing now, coming home."

Her brow furrowed and her voice dropped slightly. "A little late, I suppose, but definitely the right thing." She squeezed my hand even harder.

"And best of all, a small bird told me that you've found Shoshana!"

Then she pulled me toward her, and we hugged. "Now we are all set free," she sighed into my ear, "after years of lips pressed together, years of heartstrings pulled taut."

There was much I wanted to say, but my voice was caught in my throat.

~ ~ ~

Shoshana and I spent the next several days trading stories with our parents about each of our lives apart from one another over these past years. Interwoven with new accounts were shared reminiscences about our times together long ago. We also told them about Kol Ami, and haltingly I let them know I was joining the community. Their faces sagged a bit with disappointment, but they knew that Shoshana and I belonged together and they were pleased we could look out for each other.

We left Nazareth a few days later to return to Kol Ami, but not before Shoshana went next door to visit with Mama Maria and Mama Ana. I had been instructed by both to send her over as soon as possible.

Mama Ana had grasped me by the shoulders as I sat by her bed and said with a catch in her voice, "I want to look into Shoshana's eyes, hold her hands. It's what my grandson would want."

Her face radiated from within. "And it's what *I* want."

The day of our departure Mother and Father were hovering over us like two shorebirds prancing around the edges of a reed nest full of hatchlings. All they could say was, "Shoshana this..." and "Shoshana that...."

It was clear that they could not speak her name often enough, and the room filled to the roof beams with the sounds of "Shoshana" floating about like so many spring butterflies in a meadow of delight. So many joyful hosannas.

Finally, the long silence was broken.

Then it became time to part. We all promised to visit back and forth, and shared plans to do so after trading hugs and kisses. Ushered off by tearful good-byes with our parents at the door, Shoshana and I started out for Kol Ami, our home.

But after only a dozen paces, something made me stop and wheel around. Mother and Father were standing shoulder to shoulder in the doorway, lit up by the early dawn light. I caught Father's eye.

"Abba!" I called out.

His face brightened and his eyebrows lifted in anticipation. I had to swallow hard before going on.

"Abba, thanks for fetching Shalom back to me that time I left him in the wedding village."

A smile wide as the sky crossed his face and his eyes sparkled with sun.

"This time," he called back, his voice husky, "it was *your* turn to bring peace to this home."

His hands enfolded one another. "At last our family has found shalom."

Hill of Sorrow; Wellspring of Joy

Journeying back to Kol Ami, Shoshana and I talked about our parents' promise to come visit for our next Passover celebration. They and Aaron would stay a month beyond the Pesakh Seder, building a solid bridge to Daniel, and to Ezrah, as well as getting to know a village like no other they had ever known.

Shoshana and I had lots to think about that day as we trekked from home to home. My mind raced to keep up with my feet. I kept returning to what Mama Ana had said during my bedside visit, and I wondered just how much of my own story I understood.

All these years I had been searching far and wide to rescue someone lost, first my sister, then Yohanan, and finally, crushingly, Yeshu. And what about my father who had disappeared into prison almost before I could talk? And later there was our confiscated flock of sheep that I could not protect. But what about me? Trying to save Yeshu made me think of him as the lost sheep in his parable. And I was the failed shepherd. But he was right there in my heart the whole time. Wasn't it I who had been lost?

Then came the thunderclap. In all my searching, *I* was the one being found. Ezrah found me and brought me to Shoshana, who found the brother she'd lost, now grown into a man. Mother and Father found their prodigal son. And I fell into the outstretched arms of Daniel, who found the uncle who didn't know till then what it was like to have a nephew. I had found myself, over and over again. And I had learned how Yeshu had found me as a child and had never let me go.

Glancing sideways at Shoshana walking beside me, I realized my story mirrored hers. She was lost to her family, but found by her community;

and then her husband, and now her child.

Perhaps lost and found are simply opposite sides of the same doorway. Knock and it shall be opened. Seek and you shall find. Open...and there, with a hand on the other side of the door, is someone who has been seeking *you*.

Suddenly, Shoshana's voice broke into my thoughts. "Daavi," she said, "I'm not sure how to say this, but I'm haunted by the memory of Mama Maria's face when I visited her yesterday. I can't imagine what it must have been like for her to witness the death of her son, to have her beloved 'Yeshua' torn from her. Of course I would never ask her. You were there though; what was it like for her?"

I said nothing for many paces, and Shoshana knew why. Then I tried answering. "We were engulfed that day in a violent storm. And not just from the sky but on the road all the way to that awful hill. Afterward I became separated from everybody—by my own fault. So unfortunately, I'm not sure I can answer your question well, Shoshana."

We walked a little farther, and then I said, "Would you like to hear about a dream I had a month or so ago? Your question made me remember it." I looked over and saw the keen interest in her face.

"That night," I began, gazing straight down the road ahead, "I had retired early, after a long day of hard labor. I lay in bed watching through the open window as one by one the stars presented themselves and then gathered like a minyan of ten ancient men coming together to intone their eternal prayers in unison."

I sighed. "Slumber soon brushed its fingertips over my eyelids, and I plunged into a dark pool, bursting to the surface into dreamtime, out of breath, back on dark Gol'gotha where Yeshu hangs from a crudely built cross. The storm has passed, and the soldiers are lowering his broken body into Mama Maria's outstretched arms.

"The weight of the body leaves her no choice but to ease herself down onto the large rock directly below the tree of sorrow. There she sits, silently cradling his broken body, her head bowed from the unfathomable grief of being alive while her child lies dead. Her face is so still you can't tell if it's anguish or compassion. Maybe both?

"As for Yeshu, he could be an infant asleep in his mama's lap, totally at peace, back at the center of his being. Yet he seems cold, his skin white as the marble statues of fallen soldiers I've walked by in the Greek-built towns of Dekapolis, near the River Jordan."

From the side of my eye, I could see Shoshana's gaze fixed on me as I talked. "In my dream," I continued, "I, too, am immobile as stone, unable to move my eyes from mother and son. Mama Maria sits with her knees apart to support Yeshu's weight, holding him from behind with one hand under his right arm, her other hand suspended, palm up beside his legs, but not quite touching him. Is it surrender or bewildered questioning?

"Or perhaps it's a hand held there in reserve to catch him, as she always has, if he begins to descend further.

"Yeshu's right arm hangs down gently over her skirts, a single fold of cloth running between the first and second fingers of his hand...as if in this small way, he still holds onto his mother. His left arm, the one he so often stretched high above his head to hold the attention of the crowds, now lies still at his side.

"Eyes nearly closed, it's as if he's dropping off to sleep. The curls of his mustache and beard frame his slightly parted lips, silenced for now by our oppressors. His head lies back, resting in the crook of Mama Maria's elbow.

"I dwell upon the breadth and strength of Yeshu's neck, and yet how exposed it is, vulnerable to those who would do him harm. His face seems unconcerned—certain of having achieved his journey's end with no need for alarm about menacing threats. Unafraid of repose.

"Looking into that face, does Mama Maria see the baby she held, just like this, more than thirty years before in the makeshift hillside stable in Bethlehem? Shepherd families crowded around back then. Now I am the lone shepherd bearing witness.

"I want to step closer and embrace her, but I dare not intrude upon these final moments with her son, she who delivered him to the world and first introduced him to love. Never having learned to hate or to wound, she was incapable of teaching another to do so. Love would suffice for all times and all troubles.

"My hands shake with the urge to reach out and touch Yeshu, as well, lift him up. But I simply stand there watching, fully aware of how I had touched him only one day before when I knelt down by a wounded child and asked her to give me her pain.

"Now I understand, better than ever, what he meant when he said to us, 'I will make you shepherds of God's children.'

"Like a child, I stare aghast as the scene changes. Women are laying Yeshu in a tomb in the side of a hill. It's the crypt that Joseph of Arimathea offered up. Born in a cave, Yeshu is being laid to rest in a cave.

"I hear words from Genesis sighing in my ear:

> Dust you are,
> to dust you shall return.

"Just as I wonder—is this all there is to our earthly sojourn?—I'm jolted awake."

Turning my head, I looked at Shoshana. "At that moment, the words of your lullaby were ringing like bells in my ears: 'Travel safely through your dreams...a wiser and more loving being.'"

Shoshana stopped walking, as did I. She stood with her hands covering her face, weeping silently. When she could speak again, all she said was, "Mama Maria. Oh, Mama Maria."

I put my arms around her and together we softly whispered Yeshu's prayer.

~ ~ ~

Striding back into Kol Ami, late that afternoon, I felt elated. I clapped my hands and began to plan the house I would build as near as possible to Ezrah, Shoshana, and little Daniel. In the meantime, I would live with them and share the chores.

After supper, as the shadows grew long, the four of us strolled around the village. Shoshana pointed out the very first house built here. She then told the story of how it took all the men *and* all the women to excavate their village well and line it with stone.

"The founders of Kol Ami,' she recounted, "at first fetched their water from the creek on the edge of town. By the time my band arrived some months later, our harvests were ample enough that we could think about building more than houses. Our first project was to dig a well, one deep enough that it would never run dry in late summer like the creek did. And of course it would be far cleaner than a creek filled with silt during flooding.

"Since I was the smallest and lightest of all the early settlers," she said, "when the well was nearly finished, they lowered me to the bottom, strapped into a sling attached to a long, thick rope. I carried an oil lamp to check all the stonework, row by row as I was pulled back up. My hands were nimble and sure, and I was known for being a careful, diligent worker.

"I wasn't much more than twelve, and the foreman in charge was afraid I'd panic, but the opposite proved true. As they slowly lowered me, I peered up at the sky-blue disc above my head and watched with a smile as it shrunk smaller and smaller to the size of a coin.

"The deeper I went, the richer I felt. I could hear the men's voices as they leaned over the edge to keep track of me in case I tugged on the rope or called out. It sounded just like the prayers they murmured in low voices during Shabbat services.

"When I finally reached the bottom of the well, a profound peace came over me. The air was cool; the scent of the water, fresh. I felt protected and alive. It was like being a cloud: able to become whatever the next moment made me."

A smile slowly crossed Shoshana's face as her gaze drifted through the past. "I regretted there was work to do," she went on, "because what I really wanted was to just sit there, quietly suspended, turning slowly in my sling and waiting to see what God's breath had in store for me.

"But I knew there was a job people were depending on me to complete. 'Clouds bring water to moisten parched tongues and fields,' I whispered to myself. 'And that's what I was sent here for—water.'

"Nevertheless, I couldn't help once in a while taking a break from my inspections, letting my eyelids close softly, and listening to the music the water-drops made as they trickled from the sides of the well and struck the surface of the pool below. It was like listening to the language of miniature bells.

"I felt sure that our village was blessed, and that we were finally safe from harm or threat. This source of life-giving water was the keystone of our living synagogue, Kol Ami."

By then, Shoshana, Ezrah, Daniel, and I had reached the wall of the well. Leaning over it and looking down I could picture my sister, still a child, being lowered into the deep, and I was grateful for having received her story, her history.

In a single breath, my vision changed as I vividly recalled the time Yohanan told me about hearing God's voice by going 'into the well.' And how as a child I had pictured him, mistakenly, lowering himself by a sturdy rope. It could have been at the very moment that Shoshana was being lowered into *this* well!

The anguished sob that escaped my chest was indistinguishable from a triumphal laugh.

Closing my eyes I breathed in the memory of my own descent into the cool silent well within me during my visit to the cedars of Lebanon. I felt my hands rising to my heart as if on braided cords pulled from above.

My eyes popped open and I noticed Shoshana looking at me oddly, but I waved her away with a twist of my wrist to signal I'd explain it all later. Right now I simply wanted to allow my gaze to penetrate deep into the heart of this real well of mortared stones, and to pay heed to the reverberating beat of its silence.

I listened for the whispers of Yohanan teaching the child I was; listened for Yeshu's humming as he prepared a story for my young ears and eyes. I was intent on deciphering if I could, within the intertwining harmonies the two of them made, the ever more luminous voice of God.

Goosey

Before long, Ezrah took Daniel home to wash up for bedtime while Shoshana and I resumed our stroll around Kol Ami. Once more, it seemed to me that a puff of night wind had cleared a space in solid clouds, uncovering a piece of the firmament, a shining moment in my sister's early life after leaving us.

At one point in our walking we stopped for Shoshana to tighten her sandal straps, when I saw a figure approaching down the path from the river. I could tell it was a woman about my sister's age, but that's all. I kept watching as she came closer with her strong stride, toting a large basket of freshly washed clothes on one shoulder.

Leaning toward Shoshana, I whispered, "That woman," I gestured with my chin, "so, what's wrong with her?"

Quickly Shoshana followed my gaze, then looked straight back at me. Shaking her head, she laughed softly.

"Daavi," she said, "there is nothing *wrong* with anyone who lives in Kol Ami. We are all just people. Some may be different from most people in other places, but they're still as human as anyone."

She paused. "Just like our blind Uncle Bartholomaios is different."

I gazed at the ground, coughed, and nodded several times.

Then she said, "People choose to live here for many reasons, some of which are not visible to the eye."

I felt my cheeks getting hot and stared at my feet, unable to meet Shoshana's eye.

"I feel so ashamed," I said finally.

"Daavi, Daavi." she responded, "I know you meant no harm. Forget about it. And now look at who you saw coming!"

Grasping my arm she turned me toward the river path. Gradually I could see the woman's face. It was another Shoshana—Yeshu's sister! His "lily of the field," as he always called her. The one the rest of us called Shaani.

"Several years ago," Shoshana added, "childless and widowed, Shaani went to live with relatives in a village not far from here, to start life over. A few months back she married Ezrah's cousin, and they decided to move here where land was available for them.

"Next week they begin building their house." Shoshana hesitated. "I'm sure they could use some help."

I was already rushing ahead to greet Shaani. At first she had no clue who I was. But after I fed her enough hints, she guessed. Hastily putting down her clothes basket, she rewarded me with a great hug.

When she stepped back, I found myself staring at her torn cloak. And she was staring at mine.

"We are joined, you and I," she said, "by the rip across our chests."

I sighed, audibly, and reached out to take her hand.

"Every piece of torn fabric," I answered, "someday, with care, will be mended."

I dropped my gaze momentarily before looking up. "I promise to trade you stitch for stitch."

She signaled her agreement with shining eyes and a set jaw.

I couldn't wait five heartbeats to mend with the first stitch. I told her the story about Yeshu greeting every lily he saw on our journeys with a "Hello, Shoshana! Your brother welcomes you!"

She blushed and giggled while I beamed. If I was Yeshu's long-lost brother, I now had two sisters.

~ ~ ~

One morning a week later, Shoshana told Ezrah she was going to visit her good friend "Goosey" who had just returned to Kol Ami after a long visit with her aging parents. Shoshana smiled in a way that made me curious.

"Would you like to come along?" she asked. "Goosey wasn't here when you introduced yourself to the rest of the village and this would be a good chance to meet her."

My reply was a bit jocular. "How could you call a friend 'Goosey'?" I said, feigning disbelief. "It sounds like a name kids would use to tease someone."

She just smiled and said, "You'll find out soon enough."

"Fine," I said. "So, Goosey-woosey..."

Throwing a sandal at me, she answered, "Well, put yourself to usey. My sandal's gotten loosey."

Ezrah rolled his eyes. Feeling like kids again joking with Gramma Ruth, Shoshana and I made no effort to stifle our riotous giggling.

Arriving at Goosey's later that morning, we found her sitting on the ground in front of the house, her backstrap loom stretching from the trunk of a lemon tree to her lap. She was leaning over, immersed in the task of weaving a shawl, her dark hair falling around her shoulders, her legs covered with a blanket. Looking up she smiled shyly and her eyes flashed at me.

And lightning struck. My heart began to pound, and my jaw seemed to flop up and down like a broken hinge as I tried in vain to speak to her. I had not been so taken by anyone in this way since that girl in the shepherds' camp years before. Either I was in serious trouble—or in great luck.

Goosey invited us to have a seat on two stools nearby. Because I sat and only stared, Shoshana had to do all the talking. After introducing me, she excitedly recounted how she had just been reunited with this dear brother of hers, then she leapfrogged on as the two of them wondered what Daniel would say first, "Mama" or "Abba."

Strangely, whereas I was too paralyzed to do more than breathe, Shoshana couldn't seem to sit still. Every minute or so she would pop up to fetch something for her friend. It left me wondering why this Goosey didn't just paddle over and get her own shank of weaving yarn or cup of water. At one point Shoshana even ducked into the house and emerged with a basket of apples.

Meanwhile, I was sneaking occasional peeks at Goosey, intent on guessing her age and settling on fifteen or sixteen.

The thought flitted by that Mama Maria was married before then, and so was Mother.

"Daavi!" Shoshana burst out. "I just asked if you wanted to know how Goosey got her name. She loves to tell the story."

I nodded mutely, and Goosey smiled at me again, less shyly this time.

Bam! Another bolt of lightning.

By the time I had recovered my wits she was into her story.

"Years ago, not long before my tenth birthday," she said, "my father took me to where a large crowd had gathered to witness a holy man healing people." She tilted her head, a wry look crossing her face. "It was impossible to get close, and of course I couldn't walk." She pointed at her legs under the blanket. I stared in that direction.

"So out of kindness," she went on, "people took me from my father and passed me over their heads, from hand to hand, until I reached the healer."

The scene began gradually materializing in my mind, first slowly then more swiftly, like wind before rain.

Goosey was still talking, "He was a village carpenter named Yeshu." She looked at me. "I've heard that you knew him." And she batted her eyes.

Wham! A third bolt of lightning.

Goosey and Shoshana both stared at me. Noticing the expressions on their faces, I pulled myself together, limb by limb.

"I know why you're called Goosey," I sputtered. "I was there."

Now it was her turn to look surprised. Shoshana, too.

"You must be..." I stalled, searching my memory, while I held one palm up toward her, to signal that she shouldn't answer quite yet. Then I got it.

"Rebekah! Right? You're the one Yeshu lifted up and told the story to. It was the legend of the Goose Girl."

Now it was Rebekah who gazed fixedly at *me*, blinking several times. A smile slowly crossed her face.

"Well, I was listening and watching, too," I went on, feeling bolder by the minute. "I can remember wishing you were older. I found you so bright and charming."

I couldn't believe I was saying these things.

She smiled again. A welcoming smile. So I moved my stool over closer to her.

My sister Shoshana has always been quick to catch the drift, so in a flash she knew enough to invent some errand she had forgotten to run. The next thing I knew, Rebekah and I were alone and deep in conversation.

I called her Rebekah and she seemed to like that.

We talked about Yeshu and my travels with him and how this gentle wandering storyteller had changed each of our lives. We talked about our favorite tastes and smells, and ancient parables, and the art of weaving.

Oh, and Daniel's sweet laugh.

Six months later, we were married. My parents came to the wedding along with Aaron, who had by now taken over my father's workshop. Mama Maria and Mama Ana came with them, one with graying hair, the other white.

Joanna and Martha showed up, too, and of course Maria Magdalena was there, more striking than ever with a thumb-wide streak of silver in her hair that was not there before. And I have to mention the Thunder Brothers, who confirmed the story that they had been visited by tongues of fire and become traveling preachers, sometimes speaking strings of words they themselves could not translate but could still comprehend.

I wasn't surprised because if anyone could speak sense without sense, it would be the two Boanerges.

Even Cornelius arrived! He was in full soldier's uniform. The Thunder Brothers were elated. They rushed at him and lifted him into the air, one of them grabbing his legs, the other his shoulders. "Now we've got you!" they bellowed. "Where's that cliff!"

Then they lowered him back to the ground, and all three clapped one another on the back, punched each other's arms, and then pretended to wrestle together in circles, each man against the other two.

The Kol Ami villagers were astounded. *What* were these crazy brothers doing? An entire Roman regiment might arrive tomorrow to punish us all.

Those of us who caught what was happening laughed until we cried. When we got our wind back, we explained. Everyone else smiled a bit weakly and shook their heads. They would have to get to know Thunder James and Thunder John better before hoping to understand.

As for me, I couldn't have been happier with the antics. And Cornelius flashed a huge grin. This was probably one of those rare instances when he could fully forget he was a prisoner in armor.

Immediately our soldier friend wanted to know the latest news on everyone he knew who might be coming to the wedding, as well as those who would not. One of them was Petros, who was known to be preaching from town to town throughout Galilee, with a band of followers, and was most certainly too busy to get away.

Finally, looking around, Cornelius asked, "Where's Judah?"

We told him about Judah's wave of remorse and how he had taken his own life in retribution. For a brief moment, Cornelius looked away, his face a mask. Then he suddenly sat on the ground where he had been standing and buried his face in the crook of his arm.

Several of us moved close, encircling him. After a while, he lifted his eyes back up and spoke softly. "Yeshu made him apologize that night by the campfire, but I'm sure he still thought I was his enemy. I'd hoped to tell him how much Yeshu has meant to me, so he'd know otherwise."

Those who had drawn round smiled at him warmly. Several of us were biting our lower lips.

Then Cornelius rose to his feet and told us how he had been jailed for refusing to guard Yeshu's death cross. Now he was free, of a cell that is, though not free to return to his home village far to the north. We were so proud of him when we learned why he had disappeared.

When we asked him how he had heard about the wedding, he pointed toward Joanna. "We crossed paths in the Jerusalem market a month ago. She gave me the news."

At that, I noticed that my mother was laughing and playing string games with Daniel and several other children. It struck me that while mothers are plenty busy raising their children and caring for an entire family, grandmothers have the luxury, after many hard years, of reaping the laughter and play they've sown.

Meanwhile, my father was sitting in a circle with several village elders, wrapped in animated discussion. Later I learned that he was sharing everything he knew about tanning leather. Before that day, Kol Ami herders had been trading their animal skins to caravan merchants for next to nothing, maybe a few sacks of dates for a large bundle of hides.

From that day forward, all skins were cured in the village, employing a concoction made from local tree bark. Once tanned, they were used for carrying water, storing wine, and of course, for the fruits of my leatherworking trade: sandals, satchels, ox collars and plow harnesses, donkey reins and bridles, and the occasional well bucket.

With more plentiful and affordable materials, I was eventually able to take on an apprentice, and no longer did I have to make long journeys to fetch the skins I needed. I scolded myself that I'd never learned this skill from my father, and felt grateful that he'd brought it to us now, a redeeming present on my wedding day.

After a bit, several Kol Ami elders gathered the wedding party together and one of them, Ezrah's mother Sarah, turned to me and spoke.

"Son Daavi," she said, "you have adopted us as your home village, and you have chosen one of our most special young women to be your wife. We want to honor you with a gift. We have no money, or we would buy you something costly like an ox or a new workbench. But is there something we could provide that might warm your heart forever?"

Even though I was taken completely by surprise, I knew immediately what I wanted, because the possibility had poked its way into my mind some time back. I'd been deliberating about it off and on ever since, so now I answered without hesitation.

"I would like you to welcome a certain person here in Kol Ami to live out the rest of his life. That would make me happy."

"Is he family?" an elder asked, spreading his arms out in the direction of Father and Aaron. "Your family is always welcome here."

Before I could answer, another villager interjected, "Or perhaps he's a friend?"

"Not quite yet," I responded.

"So, where does he live?" asked a third voice. "Tell us his name."

"If he is still alive," I said, "he lives in Magdala. I don't know his birth name, but everyone calls him Rope Walker."

I glanced at Maria Magdalena, whose eyes had turned inward.

"But why would he leave his home?" asked Mama Sarah.

"Where he lives now," I answered, "he does have a small house. But I happen to believe he lacks a home. For him, Kol Ami would be like arms reaching out in a friendly embrace."

I hesitated, giving my stricken friend time to deliberate.

"Of course, someone special is needed to invite him," I went on. "You see, he hears nothing, though he understands a lot. Drawing pictures in the dust beside the road would be enough, I think, but he'd have to fully trust the person doing the drawing."

I was still looking Maria's way. Her hand rose from her side, fingers slightly curved as if she were reaching up to gather a young bird from its nest.

"I will go," she said quietly.

All heads turned toward her.

"Where Rope Walker dwells now is nowhere he should be. Like me, he has no family. And although it won't be easy for me to return to Magdala, I shall do it." She coughed hard into her hand. "I need to do it."

Then she straightened. "And when I return, I feel certain Rope Walker will be with me." A wistful look crossed her face. "Just as an elderly father might follow his daughter home through the night."

Smiling, I looked directly at Maria now. That's how I caught sight of her mouthing the words, "Thank you, Daavi."

Then we sat down to eat, after which we danced all night. Even Rebekah danced, wrists locked round my neck, legs swinging through the air as I swirled her in my arms. I have never seen a face so happy.

Maria told me later that it was mirroring mine.

Story Blankets, Yeshu Villages

Kol Ami was the hub of my life now. One spirit journey was concluding, and the next had begun. I had grown from a boy into a man; from a follower into a pioneer. My first task was to build a home for Rebekah and for the children that we hoped would fill it. All the villagers pitched in, day after day till it was finished. This is how every dwelling is constructed here.

With a deep sense of joy, I put the final touch on our house by carving my favorite words from Yeshu into the massive cedar lintel above the doorway. In Aramaic it read:

LOVE THY NEIGHBOR AS THYSELF
FORGIVE THOSE WHO WRONG YOU
BLESSED ARE THE PEACEMAKERS

These were words Rebekah and I had vowed to live by. And we wanted to place them on our door for ourselves to see every day, and for others, who had never known Yeshu, to gather into their hearts.

A mezuzah was also affixed to the right doorjamb, following the well-known instructions from Deuteronomy, the Book of Debhārîm. As I've mentioned before, this way, every time we entered our home we reached out with our right hand to touch the small scroll inscribed with words reminding us there is just one God, whom we shall love with all our hearts, soul, and strength.

Departing somewhat from tradition, we placed the mezuzah waist-high instead of the proscribed shoulder height, so that from an early age, our children to come could all touch it.

Often during that first spring in Kol Ami, as night turned from purple to blue gray to rose and orange, I stood in the garden in front of our house, reflecting on Yeshu and my time with him.

When the sun crested the hill above the valley, I would begin to turn over the earth with a foot plow and kneel down to plant vegetables for our table, plus repeating rows of sunflowers to shelter the singing wrens and the sparrows. It was a new way I'd found to pray with my hands.

Although I didn't realize it at first, I was also busy back then with another kind of tilling and tending. Rebekah and I took to traveling the countryside to sell our wares, but also to carry Yeshu's words along with us. Those journeys uncovered other Yeshu villages, and when we could, we would help them grow and blossom.

As soon as villagers learned that both of us had not only known Yeshu, but also lived in a community he had lovingly helped establish, they would invite us into their homes and give us honored seats by their hearths. There they would eagerly quiz us about all that we knew and thought. We shared our stories and observations, each of which grew sharper the more probingly we were questioned.

Many a mile I walked beside my beloved, her bundles of weavings strapped behind her as she sat astride "Thunder." This sweet old donkey had been my wedding gift to Rebekah so that she could get out and about. James and John had roared heartily when they heard of their namesake.

The evening of our wedding, Rebekah sat proudly perched on Thunder, her lap covered with an enormous spray of wildflowers that my mother had picked that morning and arranged on a wooden platter. My father kept the blooms fresh through the blistering day by lightly sprinkling water on them every so often.

When the brothers walked up for their turn to congratulate the bride, Thunder John could not contain himself.

He proclaimed to the heavens with a flourish of the hand, "Mounted on your mighty steed, Rebekah, may Thunder carry your flashing light through the skies!"

Rebekah smiled, one eyebrow arched guardedly.

John rambled on, undeterred. "And may God's grace descend on you like the rain that falls not just on the fields of the rich or the well-born, but that slakes the thirst of *every* person and *every* plant and animal under the sky. Hallelujah!"

Out of the corner of my eye, I saw Thunder James shifting from one foot to the other, as anxious as a staked camel chomping at the bit.

Unable to wait any longer, James jumped into the conversation feet first, landing atop a thick log nearby.

"But woe be it!" he boomed, hand held high, "that anyone should be caught peering upward, mouth agape, as this mighty steed flies over."

My bride shot a hasty look at James; she was clearly apprehensive about where this was going.

"Because when a donkey thunders, my dear Rebekah," he cried out, "it's not rain that falls but something far more pungent."

Laughter thundered from James' wide-open mouth and rolled through all the bystanders watching nearby. Without missing a beat, Rebekah dispensed her grace, flinging her spray of drenched flowers straight at James. It smacked him in the jowls with a blow that so jarred the precarious balance of his sandaled feet, he was felled like a tree receiving the final chop of the ax.

As he descended, James spun round and crashed to the ground, face down. John commenced to dance about his prostrate brother in a tight circle, with a fist stuffed in his mouth, only pretending to stifle the loud chortles cascading out. With his free hand, he snatched up the flowers and handed them back to Rebekah.

"That, my dear," he declared, "is what we in the elocution trade call a well-placed retort!"

~ ~ ~

On the journeys with Thunder that followed, we made a modest living. I sold leather goods produced in my workshop, and I repaired anything crafted from animal skins that had worn out. Rebekah made sales straight from the saddle of her sturdy and loyal donkey. Stacked behind her on Thunder's back were woven shawls and tunics, grain sacks, swaddling clothes for newborns, and blankets to keep children and adults warm on cool nights.

One item, however, was not for sale: her Yeshu story blanket. It was the most beautiful and intricate weaving I'd ever seen, leaving me speechless each time she unrolled it. Rebekah had carded and spun the wool herself, carefully grinding and mashing and mixing roots and berries and leaves from special plants, for the purpose of hand-dying the threads in a rainbow of colors.

Just the right threads were then juxtaposed and interwoven, so that an admirer could follow the patterns and tales with an eye or a finger, even with eyelids shut, allowing the images to become etched in one's memory.

Each story was laid out along its own band of colored threads that had been woven on her loom, one tale flowing into the next, the story paths lying side by side so they could be viewed across time, from right to left, just like the scrolls.

Rebekah's story blanket caught the attention of all who saw it. Over here in an upper corner, you could find wise Melchior and the incense he brought for an infant king. Over there you saw a clutch of rabbis, staring in wonder at a boy answering riddles. To one side, a bearded man bent over a cricket, nudging it along; on the other, the living waters and the Cedars of Lebanon. Up there a man waking a child from a sleep as deep as death.

And look right here, a goose flying with a girl on its back. There were enough stories to warm the coldest night all the way through.

Anyone who wished to do so was welcome to touch the blanket, lift it up and over their shoulders, and lose themselves for a bit, even take it home overnight to cover their children. And of course we were often asked to come along to the house, to share a meal and tell a story that the children could sail upon into the dream world.

Rebekah was soon renowned throughout the region for her skill, and my work was in demand, as well. We would spend part of each day toiling with our hands. The rest of the day we devoted to extending our hearts to help neighbors mend and stitch together their differences, and weave their community into a stronger fabric.

We also brought along the latest news of other communities, thereby tying one together with another. Slowly but surely the net of God's grace took shape. And all of it was ultimately the product of Yeshu's labor: Yeshu, the fisher of men and of women.

Remember, it was he who had proposed the name of Kol Ami, well before his mission time had formally begun. Its meaning, "all of my people," continually reminded the villagers of their common bond and their need to pull together to heal and build stronger lives.

The villages that emerged after Yeshu's passing took charge of naming themselves, usually in Hebrew, to honor our heritage. These names nearly always turned out to be melodious ones. But not everyone knows what the lyrics mean because most of us, especially the youngest, haven't been schooled in Hebrew. So at times I translate the names into the Aramaic we speak every day.

Let me see, first there's our neighboring town, *Tikkun Olam,* "repairing the world." The next one over is *K'lal Avodah,* "devoted community serving God." Then there's *Ru'ach,* "spirit wind." Oh yes, and I shouldn't leave out two others: *Rachamim,* "compassion" and *Kehillat Refuah,* "community of healing."

In the end, it's not the name that makes these places special. What's most telling is that the carpenter lives in each village, as its beating heart.

Of course, sometimes memories of what he taught dim and need rekindling. On one occasion, Rebekah and I entered a village and found the elders arguing about what to do with their neighbors down the valley. A stream passed nearby and connected the two towns, but half the year it narrowed to a trickle.

It was dry season and this group of struggling farmers was reluctant to let even a dribble go by to reach the farmers downstream while their own fields were so parched. Of course that village downstream had fields that were even drier, and increasingly its farmers grumbled about coming upstream to make off with a share of the crops that "their water" was causing to grow and ripen.

The women told Rebekah that during times when water was plentiful, they and the women from the other village all used a large rock slab at a bend in the stream, for washing clothes. Their children played together while the mothers rinsed clothing and wrung it out to dry on tree limbs and rocks. Laughing and sharing stories about their families, these women had formed real friendships and knew each other by name.

It was the men who didn't seem to recognize that the others they eyed so suspiciously across the shallow stream were but their own reflections in the water. Rebekah urged the women to speak with their husbands about the water problem they had in common and see if they could come together and all pull the same wagonload with a single rope.

When the time seemed right, I asked ten men, five from each village, to accompany me on a walk. At first they assumed I was leading them into the desert to pray for rain, since it takes ten men to make a minyan. But when I asked if anyone knew where to get a camel, they stared at one another and shook their heads, tacitly agreeing that this well-meaning fool must be light-headed from the heat. When I reminded them that nothing is better for sniffing out water than a camel's nose, their eyes lit up.

As I expected, no one in either village had a camel; however, an earnest discussion started about what substitute might be available. The goatherd who was hosting Rebekah and me in his home said that the sniffing animal, whatever it was, had best be a female because they tend to have better senses of smell than the males do. And a pig farmer from the other village added that if it could be a new mother, well that would be ideal, because her nose would be better attuned to bodily needs. Finally we settled on a young goat, one that had just dropped her first litter of kids.

So off we went with our nanny in tow. In less than an hour of exploring the hillsides and ravines above the creek, the heat drove that momma straight to a small sinkhole, where she began to dig furiously with her hooves, even using her snout. Before long, her nose was covered in mud and wet gravel. We pulled her away, and soon rewarded her with the tip of a pig's bladder, filled with water bubbling from the spring that had just opened up.

Then everyone ran home, tunics flapping in the wind, to fetch picks, foot plows, or whatever other tools were handy. For the next week, we worked in teams to broaden and deepen the spring and build a large, ground-level cistern from earth and rock to hold its waters. During the wet season, when the spring was really gushing, the cistern would fill to the brim, allowing the two villages to later siphon off what was needed during the dry season and keep the stream running steadily.

Our project became the talk of the region, and other Yeshu villages asked me to assist them in following suit.

Of course, things were rarely so cut and dried. In some cases, springs simply weren't there to be found. Yet that didn't mean a village was arid of resources or didn't have other needs. I always began by sitting down with people and talking.

"Before we start," I'd say, "we should get to know one another better."

The talking might commence with water, but I always listened for what other needs were perhaps more pressing, as well as to identify who the most interested folks were and what skills they had.

Sometimes the result was another cistern or a well. Other times the stream of talking took a different course, and water was transformed into something totally unexpected. Perhaps planting a new orchard to be shared by all, or searching out an itinerant healer, such as Joanna or Philippos, who would be willing to pass through town once a month.

Clearly, I was being stretched far beyond leather working. But this new work was also a craft. I learned by doing, hoping that the materials at hand were strong enough not to tear apart; then patching up things as best I could when they did. Even when our efforts failed to meet expectations, the village always ended up a bit stronger and prepared to swim up alternative streams.

It was all such a surprise—just as my whole life has turned out to be. My calling was neither to preach nor to heal, but to help guide communities along their path through the human wilderness. What we found was amazing. People no one paid much attention to turned their baskets upright and revealed hidden candles that burned like torches.

Meanwhile other folks who passed us by without a thought, blinded by their good fortune, turned out to be hoarding only ashes. And along the way, my becoming a good teacher taught me how to be a better pupil. The Yeshu villages I guided were guiding *me* as well, opening me up with their light and ripening me like a juicy peach.

~ ~ ~

After doing this work for some time, I sat down beside Rebekah at our table one evening. First spreading open my hands, I then closed them around hers. "Look at your husband," I said softly. "Once again, he's gained his life by giving it away, just like Yeshu promised."

She raised my hands to her lips and kissed them.

"I strive to practice the art of sharing selflessly," I said, shaking my head, "and all the while my own life grows richer and deeper."

Rebekah's eyes shone. "I feel the same," she said. "No matter how hard I try, at the end of the day it always seems like my receiving far surpasses my giving."

And then she added in a near whisper, "Yeshu lives!"

Workshops of Wonder

As soon as Rebekah and I had a little money saved, I gathered Ezrah and a few others to help build a cozy workshop next to our house, with a separate door that faced the road. At one end I set up my leatherworking bench, and at the other Rebekah sat at the new upright loom that Yeshu's brother Yehuda had made for her during a visit to Kol Ami to see his sister Shaani.

It was the first such loom he had ever built, but after inspecting her old one and listening carefully as she explained what was needed, together they figured it out. Watching his hands deftly wield the tools that had been Yeshu's and Yosef's—and Yakob's before them—I swelled with the pride his brother, father, and grandfather would have felt. And I told him so.

One day when we were hard at work, a small girl showed up at the door to watch. We asked her in for a treat of figs dipped in date honey, and while she ate, I served up a story that I concocted on the spot. It was about the day the sun burned so fiercely, it melted a rainbow, covering all the birds and flowers of the earth with color.

The next morning the girl was back, with her little brother in tow. Soon there were other small friends as well. Just like that, it had become a morning tradition. My hopes for the workshop door facing the road had come to fruition.

So, that's when the next idea struck me. Packing several, large, empty grain sacks on Thunder, I bolted off to Nazareth to visit my parents and Aaron and ask a favor of Yehuda.

Stepping into his workshop at Mama Maria and Mama Ana's—the very one where I had spent so many hours as a child—released a flood of memories. For a moment I was light as a leaf sailing in the endless breeze of Yeshu telling a story; one like the saga of the butterfly and the bee who became fast friends in spite of their differences.

I noticed how dim the room seemed with the curtains drawn across the window to keep out the afternoon heat. The quiet grew heavy and my expectations sank like a stone in a dark cistern. My lips tasted salt from the tears crawling one-by-one down my cheeks.

I breathed slowly and steadily, letting my eyes get accustomed to the gloom. Finally they fastened on the jumble of stools stacked in a corner. They were so tiny! And made with such care by Yeshu, just for us kids. Now they were coated with dust and laced together by myriad webs of concealed akkabishim, those swift weavers who create their lacework day and night.

At that, something stirred behind me and I jumped. Yehuda was standing there, coughing softly into his hand. Wordlessly he walked over and embraced me. Still holding my shoulders with his hands, he stepped back to look into my eyes.

"Is everything okay?" he asked. "Has the loom broken; do you need anything?"

"Maybe three or four bags of wood shavings?" I stammered.

Laughing, he handed me the broom to gather up all I wanted. So I did. He watched in puzzlement while I silently swept and filled. As I toiled, we made small talk, chatting about my family and his.

Each of us noticed the keriah tear still on the other's chest. Our eyes met and said everything there was to say.

As I was making ready to leave, Yehuda suddenly walked over to the corner and pulled a stool off the pile.

"Long ago he made this for you," he said, "and I expect you'll need it again soon enough."

I was thrilled, but now it was my turn to express puzzlement. "Just look at it," I said. "Each one's so small, and yet how big they made all of us kids feel to sit on them. Like kings!" I exclaimed.

Then I was bowing once, twice, and thanking Yehuda profusely without knowing exactly why.

He chuckled and added, "Yeshu wanted them used by children, and my wife and I have had none," he glanced at the roof beams, "nor am I able to recall a single story well enough to tell it." Shrugging his shoulders, he let out a sigh.

Suddenly his expression changed, his brow wrinkling as if he had just remembered something. He rushed back into the main part of the house. Hearing a clatter, I poked my head through the doorway and watched him rummage through a wooden box stashed against the far wall. In a few moments he returned to thrust a thick leather bag into my hands. It looked a bit like the Eureka! tool pouch I used for storing leatherworking tools: the one I had carried as a boy without fail whenever I tended sheep.

This was the third and final treasure to be unearthed that year in Nazareth. My head was spinning. Although it was half again as large and much heavier than my leatherworking tool pouch, this one had obviously been made by my father and engraved by my mother. Tugging open the cord that tied it shut, I saw Yeshu's woodcarving tools inside.

My heart leapt.

Scooting over to Yehuda's workbench, I took out each tool, held it up to the light, felt its heft in my hand, and laid it out on the benchtop where Yeshu, Yosef, and Yakob had all labored. Finally I put each tool carefully back in the pouch and held it out to Yehuda.

"No," he said, "please take them for yourself, or for Rebekah. My hands have lost their nimbleness after years of handling logs and stone. All my energy goes into building roofs and jambs and windows and tables. There's no time for fine carving or engraving. And no sons or daughters to pass them on to."

Yehuda glanced down at the worn threshold that lay across the family's doorway.

"Are you sure?" I asked, extending my hand again to return the pouch.

But once again he insisted, "Take them. Tools long handled with love should not remain idle. You and Rebekah knew Yeshu. You're craftspeople. You'll put them to good use, I'm certain of it."

Carefully, I tucked the bag in the chest pocket inside my cloak. "Thank you, Yehuda," I said in a whisper, a lump constricting my throat.

He dipped his head slightly, then added, "And let me know how the stool fits. If Kol Ami has need of the rest, I'll send them along with Aaron the next time he visits."

With that he insisted that I take two more right then.

A few days later, fresh back from Nazareth, I pulled the pouch out of my cloak and spilled its contents onto our table to show Rebekah.

A splash of light burst across her face. "I watched Yeshu carve two geese with these," she exclaimed. "They were on an ebony bracelet he gave me. I never took it off until..." She bowed her head, propping her elbows on the table and pressing the heels of her hands against her eyes.

A long while passed before she resumed.

"The day I heard that Yeshu had been killed," she lowered her hands to look at me, "I put the bracelet in a box and buried it. I couldn't bear seeing it anymore."

She stopped to clear her throat. "It's time to unearth the box and wear my bracelet again."

Treasure number four! I lifted Rebekah onto Thunder and we went to the house where she had resided before we were married. I explained to the family living there now that my wife had left behind a keepsake and we'd come to retrieve it, with their permission.

Hopefully the box was still where Rebekah had buried it, under a peg on the rear wall outside where she used to tie up her old backstrap loom. In no time at all we had dug up the box and pried it open. Rebekah removed the bracelet and rubbed it on her sleeve until it shone. Then she slipped her hand through the bracelet and beneath the outstretched wings, and she raised the geese to the sky.

"I will learn to wood carve," she cried out. "I know I can."

And so she did, beginning with a miniature dog, modeled on Shalom. Next came camels with hilarious, oversized faces that she gave to neighborhood boys to play with. They loved getting down on their hands and knees in the dirt and forming caravans to take them on adventures to the far ends of the earth.

For the girls she crafted magical wild geese so that each child could learn to fly through her dreams. The geese were small and slender and had wings that moved when a leather cord was pulled, and the girls flew with them, racing from one end of the courtyard to the other.

Then of course there were treasures for Shoshana and Ezrah's children. They loved her story about Bear and Rabbit rescuing one another, and mine about the tiny frog that got all the animals scaring themselves by booming out with his echoing voice from the bottom of a well.

> I MAKE THE LION TURN TAIL AND RUN!
> I *CRUSH* THE CAMEL UNDER ONE FOOT!
> I CLEAN MY *TEETH* WITH THE EAGLE'S BEAK!

Rebekah carved a replica of each of the characters: the rooster with the ruffled feathers, the goat with its bulging eyes, the braying donkey, even the self-assured monkey with her infinite calm.

We spent hours with our nephews and nieces, reenacting the story with the barnyard menagerie that Rebekah had provided, tickling ourselves silly the way Shoshana and I once had with Gramma Ruth. Shoshana and Ezrah joined in.

It got me thinking about how stories really are magic carpets.

Looking at Shoshana's kids, I could see their mother, and Aaron and me, and feel our grandmother smile.

Although Rebekah had not been able to meet Gramma Ruth, or watch my sister and brother and me playing and joking with her, she harbored similar sentiments. That night she asked me, "Do you know why I like carving these figures? It's not just the fun of storytelling with the children, watching them play at make-believe." Her eyes sparkled as she reflected on it. "I do it mostly because I believe that every time a child smiles...God smiles!"

I recalled at once the day Thunder James said, "Every time I make someone laugh, God gets happy!" And I wished that Rebekah could also have gotten to know both Thunder Brothers well.

With no regrets, Rebekah passed the animal troupe on to Shoshana.

Nearly everything she carved she gave away. Everything except the miniature dog.

I assumed it was because it was her first, and modeled after the work of a master craftsman. Finally curiosity got the better of me, and one day I asked her why.

"But Daavi," she replied, "you wouldn't want your Shalom to be alone."

I hesitated, then said, "Well, Shalom will want to know: what's his new friend's name?"

"We'll have to wait," Rebekah smiled wistfully, "for her *owner* to tell us."

That was how I found out Rebekah was with child.

Hurrah!

~ ~ ~

At the same time our child was making a larger and larger bulge in Rebekah's midriff, something mysterious was growing inside me, too. Indistinct notions took wing in my head as if the wood shavings in my newly carpeted workshop had soaked up Yeshu's voice long ago and now they were talking to me.

No matter how hard I concentrated on working a piece of leather, these notions buzzed in my head like bees in a hive. Finally one day, just after our noon meal, I told Rebekah I was going for a walk to clear my mind.

I headed off down the lane behind our house. Avoiding this and that trip-weed, I trudged over the loose gravel and rain-softened soil. Soon the barking dogs of Kol Ami had faded in the distance behind me, but whatever was nagging at my thoughts kept at it like a playful puppy relentlessly tugging the hem of my cloak. After climbing in the hills for a while, I could tell this wasn't something I could outrun. Those pesky little teeth were not going to release their hold easily.

So I found a large rounded rock, and sat with my back pressed against it to rest for a bit. The sun was still strong overhead and there was no shade to speak of. My head bobbed once, twice, till my chin dropped to my chest. Fighting sleep, my eyes popped open and looked up. But the lids had ideas of their own and grew heavy again. Soon I was repeatedly nodding off without falling into full slumber. Vague images flitted in and out of my mind like the shadows a bird casts on the forest floor when winging from branch to branch.

I saw Yohanan striding from one end of a meadow to the other, singing out the Psalms. Yeshu reciting stories from the Torah from memory as he helped me circle the sheep the day the big cat came. Rebekah flying over the heads of the crowd just like the goose girl. Rebekah dancing at our wedding, her arms around my neck. Rebekah dancing! Leaning against me; laughing and breathing hard when the music stopped; surrounded by the celebrants, and standing in front of me.

Yes, standing! Somehow. But how?

The answer exploded in my head like a sea eagle hitting the water talons first to scoop up a fish. But this fish was feet made of wood. New feet and legs—crafted by her devoted husband. That's how Rebekah was standing.

It matters not whether the eagle arrived when I was asleep or awake. All I can say is I was fully alive, nurturing my hatching fingerlings as they swam in ever larger circles. Readying themselves to someday be fished out by a diving mind.

But could I turn my imaginings into reality? All those years I'd spent with Yeshu in his carpentry shop, like a cloth soaking up spilled water, led me to believe I could surely do it!

Jumping to my feet, I began half walking, half trotting back to the house. When finally I arrived, I rushed through the door and told Rebekah straight off, "I'm doing no more jobs for the next couple of weeks."

Her eyes widened in alarm, so I quickly explained that nothing was wrong. In fact, something was right. "I'll be laboring hard," I said, "just not on orders for leather."

Of course that mystified her even more. But she soon saw for herself, with increasing excitement, what I was up to. That's because her help was essential, in the weeks that followed, for the experiment to work.

I started off by scouring the hillsides and valleys for the strongest, most resilient wood I could find. I finally selected several sturdy limbs from an old olive tree that had blown down in a windstorm. Tipped over perhaps by providence.

The grain of olive trees is more tightly packed than that of any other wood. This requires the sharpest tools possible. So, first I borrowed an adz, draw knife, chisel, and mallet from a carpenter friend in Tikkun Olam; much later I bought my own. At the start, I had to make attempt after attempt, rough hewing, chiseling, carving, polishing, until at last a pair of workable legs was ready.

Carefully I attached the two new limbs to Rebekah with soft leather straps encircling her upper thighs. Then I laced these broad straps into a braided deerskin belt that rode just over her hip bones. After days of trying, Rebekah finally stood on her own and painstakingly crossed the room using two strong canes made of ebony. Bracing her back against the far wall, she let go of the canes and clapped her hands, her face shining. She was standing.

I smiled back, asking her, "What do you suppose Yeshu would say?"

"He would shout with joy," she responded.

"Then he'd closely inspect each leg and cane," she added, "turning them this way and that, and exclaim, 'Oh what fine labor you've done: your head, your heart, your hands working as one. Bravo for you, Daavi.'"

From that day on, I had a new life's work. People streamed to our door, young and old from near and far. Some had been born without limbs below the knee, just like Rebekah. Others had suffered calamitous injuries in falls or rockslides. All arrived requesting walking aids of their own. I felt honored to be able to help. And always I began by stepping into the wild for a bit of quiet pondering. How could I solve this new brain puzzler?

One of the first to come was Ephraim, from Rachamim. At the age of twelve, he had been walking home from Jerusalem when he was run down outside the city walls by a Roman chariot speeding to a village that had threatened to rise up in rebellion. The wheels severed his legs at the knees.

Arriving at my shop three years later, carried on his father's back, his face was gray and expressionless. Two months later, he rocked through our doorway—after having been taught double-cane walking by Rebekah—his face afire with triumph.

When the boy's father, Yitzhak, came the next day to say good-bye, he gripped my forearms tightly in his hands. Seeing that he was lost for words, I nodded and tried to fill the silence, "I know. You're grateful. Well, it was my privilege. I wish you a safe and peaceful journey home, friends."

Still Yitzhak would not let go. But neither could he speak. Finally, he squeezed out just two words, barely audible, that still roar in my ears after all this time.

Leaning close to my shoulder, he whispered, "Yeshu-work!"

This is the highest compliment anyone could have given me. As soon as Yitzhak and Ephraim left, I turned and pressed my forehead against the doorway, above our mezuzah, for the longest time.

Blessed beyond measure, I kept doing this Yeshu-work for many years whenever called upon, accepting only what people were able to pay.

Yitzhak left us a coin that day, earned from harvesting olives from his family's grove. But Ephraim's smile was already more than enough.

Father Child, Little Wanderer

After Rebekah shared with me the wondrous news that she was expecting our first child, I began noticing things that had formerly passed me by. Spotting a bird's nest in a thicket made me hustle over to see if there were chicks, and if so, what was going on. The smallest children in Kol Ami had my full attention: what they asked for; how the changeable weather on a father's face made them giggle or whimper; or how they lost themselves playing with a twig and a pebble, the same way God is immersed in love.

It felt as if I had opened a curtain at daybreak and been delighted by a sunbeam knifing through the darkened room, igniting a Via Lactea of dust particles where a moment before there had been nothing.

Many nights, Rebekah and I would lie in bed in the dark and plan how we wanted to raise our children, how to enchant them and surround them with love while teaching lessons like right living and sharing, spontaneity and self-control. Oh, and we decided we shouldn't forget nonsense and playfulness. Maybe we would even raise Thunder children.

Serious anticipation of becoming parents made us forget momentarily that no one needs to teach spontaneity or play to a child. It's actually more like an exchange. The adult shows the child how inner control can nurture wisdom while the child helps her elders relearn the skill of being open to the world and curious about everything.

But finding that out required a real child, not the made up one of our imagination. I could hardly wait. Talking side by side with Rebekah deep into the night, every so often I would lay my hand on her growing belly to see if at that moment I might be so lucky as to sense the quickening.

Early one morning, my eyes still shut, I awoke to the sound Mama Ana once described as the dreamcatcher at her loom. Reaching out in the darkness to alert Rebekah, I discovered her side of the bed was empty. Turning and propping myself on an elbow, I peeked through the slightly cracked door to the workshop and detected the flickering of an oil lamp. The clickety-clack I had heard was from Rebekah up early and already earnestly weaving, tightening each new row of hand-spun yarn with the smooth and rounded edges of the cross-board.

Rolling out of bed, I padded barefoot into the workshop, wearing only my sleeping garments. In an instant I noticed that taking shape on the loom was a tiny blanket in earth colors. I knew it must be for warming our child. Suddenly I realized I could use a covering myself against the brisk morning air.

As I moved closer and gently squeezed Rebekah's shoulder with my hand, my eyes found the cedar storage chest that now sat near her knee with its lid propped open. Inside was a woolen piece I didn't recognize. When she turned to look up at me, I inquired with a gesture from my free hand if it would be okay to inspect it. She flashed a smile that said of course I could. The lamp didn't cast much light, but just touching the cloth as I lifted it told me how fine it was. I spread it out on my workbench and lit two more lamps. I saw it was a second blanket, larger than the one on her loom.

"Oh, Rebekah...." was all I could utter.

It was a new Yeshu story blanket, even more beautiful than her original one, and I felt warmed already. The first three woven bands I knew quite well. Over there was a boy, perched on the shoulders of a bearded giant striding toward the village well. And here was a girl, being lifted off the ground by the same giant to glide over outstretched hands on the wings of a goose. And there was the same boy and girl only older now, sitting side by side, clasping hands, their faces lost in conversation.

That's when it got really interesting. As my eye reached the bottom of the blanket, I could see that it ran out, ending in scores of twisted threads trailing off toward the floor.

Perhaps seeing doubt rippling across my face, Rebekah smiled again, saying, "It's not finished yet. It's a gift for when our child turns thirteen."

She pointed to the end of the blanket. "The other stories, the ones yet to be lived, are still unwritten. When our young one is old enough to pick a story I'll weave it, unless of course the child wants to help. That I would welcome because eventually each of us must take over the weaving of our own lives, choose our own designs, colors, and themes.

"I can even imagine how one might choose to leave the piece unfinished just as Yeshu's life opened a way with no end in sight. But all of this is for the youngster to work out. That's the inheritance I'll bequeath.

"I'd like to do a blanket," she added, "for each child that comes to us." Her eyes fastened on the loose threads of yarn.

"And, if God wills it, for every grandchild, as well." She paused to run her fingers over the strands of the small baby comforter on the loom in front of her.

I sank down onto the bench that was just behind me and closed my eyes. Soon, the smell of Yeshu's hair as I bobbed along on his shoulders, the squeal of delight as Rebekah flew for the first time, the touch of her hand as we talked all aglow about the child we had yet to meet, all of this filled me to the brim. Sometime later—minutes that could have been hours—my eyes opened, and I pushed myself to my feet. With a few short steps I crossed the workshop.

Wrapping my beloved wife and the mother of my child in my arms, all I was able to say was, "Oh, Rebekah...dearest Rebekah."

Later that afternoon some neighbors asked if I could drop by their house to help patch a leaky roof. The task took longer than I expected, and as I walked home through the twilight, letting the rich, shadowy blues of the gloaming gather round me like a woolen shawl, I spotted the distant flicker of an oil lamp in our window. A moment later, I realized I could hear someone singing. Drawing closer I made out it was actually two voices, not one. The lilting melody was my sister teaching Rebekah her lullaby!

I stood there listening for what seemed like forever, barely breathing, when it struck me. For most of my life, humming this song to myself took me backwards, to a piercing loss I could not forget. Now hearing it sung was turning me around and lofting me into a future whose bounty I could only guess. Overwhelmed, I sighed so deeply that the singing stopped.

When the two voices resumed, I suddenly wished they would sing the lullaby once again, just for me. And by doing so magically sing me into a wiser and more loving Abba!

Listening to those two voices fill the silence I understood they *were* singing to me. With my sister and my wife beside me, surely, I thought to myself, I must grow into the parent I so much wanted to be.

In the coming weeks Rebekah and I began talking about names. She shared with me that if the baby turned out to be a boy, in spite of tradition she wanted his second name to be Daavi.

Noticing me stiffen a bit, she said, "Do you see a problem?"

Shaking my head I replied, "I'm less worried about our child's name and more concerned about living up to its expectations."

"Mmmm," she agreed. "Sometimes I get anxious, too, anticipating becoming a mother. I didn't know there were so many worries over what could go wrong."

She closed her eyes for a moment, then looked over at me. "Sometimes it feels like I'm walking with my canes through a meadow of tall grasses, accidentally collecting burrs on my skirt."

She fingered her hem. "Every time I pause to pick one off, three more stick on."

We both laughed. Strangely enough, we found comfort in the idea that no one is ever prepared to be a parent for the first time. You go to sleep in a sandy creek bed during a drought and wake up on a high grassy plain, stretched out on a thin slab of warm, dry stone, blanketed by fog.

You wonder, just how did *that* happen?

Then you go on living as if this were where you had always been. Or at least I hoped so.

Of course, Rebekah was way ahead of me, as is often the case with women and family matters. For example, it turns out she not only had a name picked out, she had three! "If we're blessed often enough, that is," she quickly added.

"The three names," she said, "are Emunah, Tikvah, and Chesed, because faith, hope, and love were the three strings of the lute that played Yeshu's heart!"

Rebekah suggested I pick the one we would begin with, so I chose Chesed, "because for Yeshu," I said, "love always came first."

As the time neared for the baby to be born, Rebekah and I sat down together and agreed on one thing, for sure. Rebekah put it best, saying, "No more travel for a while. Whoever wants our wares and our advice will have to come to us."

And come they did. We had more requests for work than time to fill the orders.

Meanwhile, we basked in the luxury of busily tending our humble nest in Kol Ami where we would raise the first of several young goslings.

Though we had abandoned the road for the moment, we still visited our nearby neighbors whenever we could. One day Shaani invited us to a Shabbat meal with her family. At the appointed hour, I helped Rebekah onto Thunder and began to lead the two of them down the path to Shaani's home. Glancing over my shoulder to check on things, I halted, staring in wonder.

There, for just a moment in my mind's eye, it seemed as if we were Mama Maria on a borrowed donkey being led by Yosef on the way to Bethlehem, long ago. Our child would not be born in a stable, laid in a manger, or visited by a family of shepherds. But there would indeed be animals nearby, and a village of friends arriving at our doorstep to shepherd *us*.

That got me thinking: what after all is the difference between Baby Yeshu and the miracle of every infant born on this earth? Well, none that would have mattered to the storyteller from Nazareth.

I didn't mention any of this aloud. I just gave Thunder's bridle a tug, and we walked on to Shaani's where we would share our swelling anticipations with Yeshu's sister and her husband.

~ ~ ~

During those days, I often prayed to be given the strength of the prophets as a guide to protecting my own wife and child. But in truth I really wanted to see my own father; and soon enough, there were my parents, walking through our door.

Father clapped me on the shoulder and said, "You will be a *fine* Abba."

Looking into my eyes he smiled broadly as if seeing someone he once knew, while I wondered about just who I would soon become.

And become I did. There are no words to describe the soul-shaking awe that accompanied Chesed's arrival. It seemed like an eighth day of creation. Afterward I felt tired to my bones, prompting my mother to ask, "Just who has given birth here?"

I smiled but didn't know what to say. The house was overflowing with people tending to the new mother and the newborn, including Rebekah's mother and father who had travelled from their home village. My head was turning this way and that. Standing there in the middle of the crowded room, I felt like a third thumb.

Later I was sent by the two new grandmothers to sleep in the workshop. The next morning I awoke early to discover it was Rosh Hodesh. I had poked my head out the doorway and saw that the sliver of crescent moon was rising. I also heard several voices chirping already in the main room of the house where Rebekah and Chesed lay.

After dressing, I gingerly elbowed my way in to kiss mother and child. Tiny Chesed was adorable and gorgeous and enchanting. And her father was repeatedly smitten.

Glancing at Rebekah, it was clear that though her face was lit up from within, her brow was creased with concern. The concern, it turns out, was for me.

"Daavi," she asked softly, "what is it you always do when you're mystified by a question, or when something's brewing and you don't know what it might be?"

I immediately understood what she was getting at and kissed her again on the cheek. Giving our baby in her arms a pat on the belly, I stuffed a pocket with nuts and dried fruit from the cupboard and headed out the door for a long, meandering walk in the hills.

Was I dreaming, or had I actually woken up?

Recalling once more Yohanan's instruction that wilderness can be just one step away, I let out a joyful roar for no reason and then laughed, knowing that no one could ask, "Now what was *that* for?"

I walked till it felt right to stop. Looking around me just to be certain, I let out a long, low whistle of delight and plopped down on the sun-drenched hilltop, facing the spot where the slightly wider crescent moon would set that very evening.

Just above the distant horizon, it was already black as night, with massive clouds relentlessly piling up. Filled with joy, I watched the thunderhead build till it covered a piece of sky taller than my two open hands held up at arms length, one above the other.

Staring into this mounting darkness above the horizon, I tried to decipher what the crackling lightning was saying, listening to the Greek chorus thunder out its unintelligible message. The sound rumbled across the sky and the plain like a stampeding herd. I breathed it in, letting it roll up and over my chest and shake my shoulders on its way by.

Still, I couldn't tear my eyes away, and then in a flash a she-wolf streaked over the roiling clouds, vanishing into the blackening wall as swiftly as it appeared. A few moments later a lion's head and shoulders pushed through the center of the dark curtain. Glancing in the direction of my hilly perch, the beast turned full round and glided off on ebony legs.

Lightning flashed again, followed by a roar that almost sent me to my feet before I reasoned that the storm was too far away to threaten me. Still, I gasped when a leopard's eyes and spotted muzzle materialized at the very top of the thunderhead. The great cat stared out, swinging its sleek head back and forth, then dissolved into the blackness as new rumbling built to a crescendo.

Exhilarated, I lifted my face toward the swirling horsetail clouds above me, then buried it deep between my knees, my eyes shut. A silent breeze slowly ran its fingers through my hair and down the nape of my neck. Presently, warm rain gently drummed up and down my back. My life was turning over like those tumbling clouds.

Once a father's child, I was now a child's father.

I wondered silently: Whatever is a fellow to do! We fall into the world upside down and then find ourselves being lifted by another right-side up. And just think about it, I was born in a storm not unlike this one, a tumult that terrified my mother. And Mama Maria, who comforted her, was equally shaken. Did they glimpse in that celestial mayhem what one day would rip the curtain of the Temple asunder and drive whimpering soldiers away? Scattering these men far from a cross of jagged fire and stabbing rain on a desolate hillside?

Gasping, I opened my eyes to look up, feeling a mighty surge coursing through my body like a torrent down a dry gully—to discover instead an overwhelming stillness.

The storm had abated and sunlight was pressing against my face like the tender fingertips of a lover.

Quietly I reflected: Everything passes, leaving that which abides. I'd found my center again, my wellspring of peace.

A sudden gust of wind at my back urged me to my feet. Throwing my cloak over one shoulder, I headed home, softly singing Shoshana's lullaby... over and over...like falling water.

Gospel According to Maria

From that day to this, with God's blessing, two more sweet babies have followed the first, and our lives have grown deeper and taller like a new grove of date palms sending roots down and fronds up. Before long, the green canopy reaches across the sky and the ground is covered with moving shadows and mouth-watering fruits of a labor that is also at times full of play. These savory dates tweak the nose as well as the tongue and teasingly brush the eyes with visions of tasty delight. Palms rise, great leaves fall, and one day the distant memory of a time when there were no palms at all begins to seem far-fetched. This is how it has been with our children.

Over the years, needing no excuse but always proffering one, Maria Magdalena has honored us with regular visits: on birthdays, special anniversaries, religious feast days, or simply times when rainbows or the absence of them feed her nostalgia.

For decades now, she has been walking from village to village, telling her Yeshu stories to all who wish to listen. She has made certain that at least once a season she passes through Kol Ami for a week or so to teach and storytell to the villagers, young and old. Her real purpose is to visit our family and, of course, to check on the well-being of Rope Walker, her adopted Abba.

Now nearly a century old, Rope Walker lives in a tiny cottage that our village built for him in the middle of a walnut grove, surrounded by a myriad of tree limbs that long served for tying up his latest bit of work, to keep it taut. He doesn't need the limbs any more but he welcomes the shade. No longer able-bodied enough to spin the fibers and braid the long thick ropes he once did, he sits under a favorite tree, enveloped in his infinite silence, plaiting lengths of twine. These he then weaves into chair seats and patterned window shades that keep the chilly night air from our homes, cooling the interiors from the daytime heat when doused with water.

In return we, the people of Kol Ami, bring him the food and clothing he needs to live free of the misery he knew in his birth village of Magdala.

Still enchanted by his craft, Rope Walker rises early every morning and toils till midday, using materials brought by the children of Kol Ami from the marshes and fields. They never let his supply dwindle, knowing the reward for every armload of rushes and reeds is a sweet date or a shelled walnut for popping into one's mouth. Most would do it for no treat at all—this is how our village raises its children. And though his lips are silent, you can see his love for each child dancing across his face. And so can they.

Every time Maria visits, we talk from dawn to dusk about everything and anything, past and present. We never tire of laughing and giggling like the children around us who can't sit still till we've fed them another story. The years have only strengthened the bond between us, and in our talking we follow Rope Walker's lead, spinning and braiding and weaving together all that a lifetime of seeking has revealed. The tapestry we unroll is broad, resilient, and colorful.

And I suppose we are, too. Well, broad at least. My knees are getting creaky and with Maria's slowing pace, she seems to float over the stones in the road. As we sail arm in arm together around Kol Ami, lost in conversation, we doubtless look like the dual-masted boat that once carried us across the Sea of Galilee with Yeshu.

After our sailing is done, Maria goes straight home to Rope Walker, who weeps to see her come. And then weeps again when she leaves. They are family now, and this is how families are.

When I ask her if she is ready to quit the road and enjoy a well-deserved rest, Maria just smiles. "I'm following my star, Daavi," she says, "with Yeshu a step in front, a step behind, and always at my side. Were I to stop, it would mean the journey is over."

Truth be told, Yeshu's light has illuminated a new path for many of us.

His words have flowered inside folks such as Maria. They bloom and bear fruit like a spreading mulberry tree.

Now and then, she and I ponder it all aloud on our walks. Over time we've decided that our way of seeking God is like a tree rather than a majestic building. Its height mirrors the depth of its roots rather than being an edifice of stone covering a darkened cellar. Our worship is like being back in the cedars with Yeshu and Yohanan. Our temple is a forest in which God lives in the broadest trunk and the tiniest leaf. Locking our arms and souls together we form a green canopy for song and prayer, for shelter, and for shading and serving those stricken by misfortune.

Just as each family in Kol Ami is a wooded community, each village in the vicinity is a communing of families. And one day, long after Maria and I and the others in Yeshu's band of wanderers are gone, the family of humankind will be seen as the community of communities. Of this we feel certain.

But there are moments as Maria and I are sharing our deepest concerns, when other themes spill from our mouths, trailing behind them swirling flavors and aromas of mystery and wonder.

Only recently I told Maria, "There's a part of humanity's core that I reflect upon often, having spent all those years on the road, and even more time at home welcoming pilgrims in for a hot meal and a bed."

I raised both palms and made motions as if I were inspecting them closely. "It appears that despite all our differences, we are also the same. Fruits and flowers."

She smiled, and I went on. "Consider the many forms we take in our search for love: how hard we try; how long we look!

"And just think how we all seek God. Some of us pray prostrated on the ground with arms and legs outstretched, or chant dawn after dawn and dusk after dusk. Others sit meditating by a river as it passes endlessly by, or on the edge of a cliff at sunrise." I pointed toward the horizon. "Some kneel on a rug to pray, hands extending rhythmically over the space in front of them." I pointed now to the earth at our feet. "Or chant the Songs of Solomon in a synagogue."

Not missing a beat, Maria joined in, "Then there are those who circle like gentle whirlwinds becoming the still point in the axis of heaven and earth. Still others sit in silence as you and I so love to do, eyes turned inward, souls turned outward." She bowed her head and said, "All of us are passengers on the ark of this world, voyaging under the same sun in the same sky." She sighed cheerfully.

I stepped back in. "But there are also those who lose their bearings and fall victim to despair. They mistake the sea for a desert, forgetting that both are wilderness; that what seems barren or alien is alive with possibility for those who take care to observe and to learn.

"Water awaits within the thorny cactus," I added, "for all who know where to look. And the minnow by the shore must linger in the eddies to grow large and wise enough to be caught in the net cast by the fisher of men and women.

"Maria," I said to her, "I'm sure you've observed those who cannot see or hear what village and wilderness can teach us; you've seen how they can grow sad and impatient and chase false gods in wineskins, potions, and magic powders."

She nodded, but I wasn't finished. "They may soothe their thirst for a night, but the day makes them parched again. The thirst that torments them, that they would do anything to escape, is God calling out to them. But for these lost lambs—as they stumble this way and that, never quenched, never satisfied—God is always somewhere else, watching in grief."

Maria nodded again as I finished speaking, and she raised one hand to lightly touch the center of her chest. "And yet all the while that we seek, each in our own way," she said, "God waits inside us, and among us. Serenely present, with open arms, to be discovered and embraced.

"Finding and being found is not the end of the journey; I know you agree, Daavi. *We* are the journey and each turn of the road brings something new and intriguing."

"Yes," I said softly. It felt like we had just sung a song together.

Bidding her a peaceful evening I found my way back home, as if I were still a boy following close behind the wilderness walker and the carpenter.

Only now was it clear to me that I haven't one home but many. As do we all who live in community, in one Yeshu village or another. Those of us who are able to do so are open to carrying the spirit wherever the wind may blow us and to wherever the earth may receive us.

Some soil is fertile and the seeds quickly take hold; other ground seems barren and the seed must wait. We have learned to be patient, dwelling in the silence that is our friend.

Sitting and joining hands in each other's homes or around the beds of the ill and elderly, we form our circles of support and love, and our circles of healing. We take counsel from Yeshu's teachings, which we have committed to heart. And we do our best to emulate him in living honorable lives by loving one another. Especially when that's hard.

Yeshu lives on because we have welcomed the gift he gave us by his dying as he lived.

But not everyone feels about Yeshu the same way we do. Once, Maria smiled wryly and said to me, "Some people wear their traditional way of seeing the world like armor, covering themselves from head to foot. Blindly they accuse us of abandoning our Jewish roots, but this misses the point entirely. It isn't about whether or not we should be Jews. Yeshu lived and died a Jew," she shrugged, "so why not us?"

I slapped a knee in agreement.

"The important question," she added, "is how to fulfill his mission of being Jewish, of serving God, with all souls standing on a level plain, arms interlocking."

From the outset, Maria has wished only to tell Yeshu's story, but never to lead. She has wanted our Yeshu villages to be open to the spirit of each of its voices. More than once, she has reminded us of his counsel that answers are often lacking because the people with the keys for unlocking them have been left out.

More than once in our strolling talks, Maria has insisted, "For those of us who happen to be women, all I've ever wanted is that we take part in teaching, in making decisions, and in carrying out our ancient traditions as well as the new practices that Yohanan and Yeshu bequeathed us.

"It's just common sense," she adds, "that *both* legs are needed, side by side, if human beings are to walk a Yeshu path."

So Maria simply goes her own way. As she travels from village to village, she builds a history of Yeshu's life and teachings. And now word is spreading that she is composing her own gospel.

There was a time when you could hear this gospel of Maria's only from her lips, or those of people who knew her. Now it's on scrolls of papyrus, inscribed by the hand of someone whom I cannot name. What I can reveal is who crafted the leather bindings and embossed the intricate designs on the pouches the scrolls were inserted into. I can speak their names because they are no longer among us to suffer persecution. It was my father and mother who added their work to Maria's. And thus to Yeshu's. Now it is I.

As each scroll is finished, it's hidden along with others like it, to keep them all safe. Those like myself, who know where they are, have sworn not to reveal the place.

This gospel is Maria's gift to the future. On a day when it's safe again, her scrolls will be unrolled once more, so that everyone can know her story and her thoughts.

Often I ask myself what that distant day will be like. I picture a shepherd not unlike the ones I know, seeking shelter from a downpour, stumbling upon a large earthenware jar hidden in a cave. He opens it up, and out spills dust-covered scrolls written in ancient words. Learned scholars show up like the Magi did, to see for themselves, and they find a message inscribed in a language as eternally young as the human heart.

Stories Can Change the World

Even as the years roll by, my storytelling goes on. Just as it has every day since I returned to Kol Ami from Yehuda's and spread the wood shavings onto the floor for our village children to wriggle their toes down into. The scent of the shavings seems to bring out the best in my Yeshu tales. It appears that the kids agree because they keep coming back for more.

However, more than a few of their parents find it odd that a leather-worker and a weaver would have such a strange floor for their workplace. Even Shoshana, when she brings her grandchildren over to listen, teasingly inquires if we are still weaving tables and stitching benches. Rebekah and I just smile, and share a wink.

Actually the children got into the spirit of things from the start. Their shyness rapidly turned to giggles until the girl who was our very first listener hushed them and then turned to ask me a question.

"Where did all these wood curls come from?"

Straight-faced I answered, "From the heads of tree giants who live in Lebanon!"

The entire gang of kids laughed in delight. "Tell us a story of the wooded giants!" they insisted.

So I did. And what a story it was, too. It had a wilderness tramper, his friend and cousin the tale-spinning carpenter, and a shepherdess singing into a waterfall. Then there was a wild woman who was very wise, two brothers made of thunder, and a song walker who hummed to their heels. There was also a horse lover with a huge heart, a wise turtle as old as the trees, and a lost girl with a lullaby for a compass who was there and not there.

Oh, what adventures they had!

Of course, I shouldn't leave out the shepherd boy traveling endlessly through his dreams. He was made of moonlight and rainbow mist, of birdsong and the scent of the Torah when it's carried by old men. And after all, he's the one who toted this tree giant story back home, tucked away in a corner of his heart.

As I spun out the saga, I sat looking around the circle of rapt faces. Out of the corner of my eye I could see the small toes digging deeper into the shavings, and I smiled inwardly.

Speaking slowly and softly, drawing the children onto the front edges of their stools, I allowed my eyes to travel from face to face.

I wondered which ones were most moved by my Yeshu stories, and by the tales I had learned from Shoshana and Rebekah that I now told, as well. Might it be the tiny girl next to me, whose eyes stayed locked on mine from beginning to end? Or was it maybe the wistful one over there, gazing out the doorway?

Once when this dreamy child was leaving with the others, I caught her hand and tugged her back. "Which story did you like best, today?" I asked, fully expecting her to stare up at me blankly, in light of her hour or two of private whimsy while I held forth.

"Oh, I loved the one about Yeshu and the Goose Girl!" she answered.

And much to my astonishment, she proceeded to recount the entire story to me, word for word. Then she thrust a wood curl close to my nostrils for a sharp whiff, and ran out the door flapping her arms like wings.

This made me extra happy I had told the children Yeshu stories that day, and it reminded me that I not only tell these stories but I listen to them as well. All who knew him or heard him speak have tales to share, and I'm always eager to hear them.

Sometimes—particularly when it's Maria Magdalena on one of her periodic respites in the walnut grove just round the bend—the stories concern events I've lived through.

Then there are ones I heard first from Yeshu, but it's always intriguing to listen to the version retold by some other person who was touched by it in a special way. On occasion it seems to be a different recounting altogether.

That's what stories are like. That's what life is like.

~ ~ ~

And then there are moments, sitting in the sun or in the starlight, when I turn to Yeshu himself for more stories, closing my eyes to listen deeply. Just yesterday evening it happened to be one that he'd told me long ago, but this time his listener was not quite the same person.

Wandering unhurried through the stars, I heard his voice break into my thoughts.

"In my twelfth year," he began, just before our annual Passover journey to Jerusalem, my Abba and I were in the village of Ludum on a building job."

I nodded, in recognition.

"One morning we heard a low and distant rumble and then a thunderous clamor coming from the mountain above the village. Soon, a chorus of shouts rang out, calling for everyone to 'run to the river!'

"We all ran like deer, older children and adults scooping up younger ones in their arms. There was a hill by the river that we scurried to the top of, and as we turned to look back we saw a massive landslide smash into the village. Boulders rushed through the lanes, courtyards, and houses like so many stampeding horses.

"The slide was over as quickly as it started, except for the settling dust. We all raced back to the village and spent hours searching for injured and trapped people and animals. Every one of the fleet sheepdogs had survived and they were able to sniff out three elderly women, two men even older, and several oxen, all of them clinging to life under partially collapsed roofs and walls.

"Next, at the urging of their leaders, all the Ludum families gathered near the edge of the village, in a high, fallow field that had been untouched by the slide. There they formed into groups by household. Praise God it was joyfully determined that no one was missing."

I nodded again. It sounded just like what shepherds would do, making sure all the sheep of the flock are accounted for.

"As best we could," he continued, "we calmed the weeping and offered encouragement to those who stood transfixed, with eyes glazed.

"Then we began to assess the damage. There was rubble everywhere, in a great tangle of toppled mud-and-cane walls, caved-in thatch and timbered roofs, and the debris from the slide.

"I turned to say something to Abba, but he was gone. Startled, my eyes scanned the gathering until I saw him not far from where I stood, wrapping his arms around a husband and wife. I ran over to join in the embrace.

"That's when I heard my father speaking in a soft and soothing tone that reminded me of the serenity I heard in my Mama Maria's singing while she brushed the tangles and burrs out of my hair when I was a young child."

Drawing in a long, deep breath, I smiled.

"What Abba was telling the couple was this. 'God is going to do extraordinary things in the weeks to come. You must allow God to bless and guide you through these days and nights. You will be blanketed with the grace and generosity of others, and you must accept it without protest or attempts to repay. Just surrender to the light within, and let it bring about its wonders.'

"Abba paused and we all breathed as one for a few moments.

"Then he said in a clear, strong voice, 'Know that you are going to be touched and lifted not by a God who is separate, but the God who is present; who dwells in the hearts and hands of your friends and neighbors here in Ludum.'

"Abba turned and moved on with his message to the next family, and then another and another till it was done. I followed, always standing beside him.

"At last a Ludum elder moved through the crowd with a lifted hand. As he walked he spoke out, calling everyone to return to the river to wash off the dust and cleanse any wounds that had been sustained.

"While this was transpiring, as if struck by a premonition Abba scrambled back up the hill, but this time he looked away from the broken village and out over the valley below. Suddenly he waved his arms in circles and motioned for the villagers to reclimb the hill and join him. When they got there, he raised his right arm and pointed."

My back straightened and I leaned forward to see where Yosef might be pointing.

"Coming toward us, across the fields and along the riverbanks were scores and scores of people, some walking, others running. Those who walked toted ladders and roof poles and tools. The few runners arrived first, rushing up to the Ludum elders to ask how much damage there was, and what did the village need. Then they left hurriedly to fetch more hands and materials.

"Soon hundreds of people from neighboring villages were camped in tents on the outskirts of town, with more tents set up for the homeless locals. Food and cooking pots arrived on donkeys led by women and children, and makeshift kitchens were set up and stocked with firewood.

"Work crews swiftly organized and the rubble clearing began. Walls were rebuilt, roof beams set, and thatch woven over the beams and tied down with thick ropes made of hemp fiber. Women and children helped carry materials in and debris out.

"That evening, in front of a lean-to hut that my father and I had fashioned from uprooted trees and broken beams, Abba stared into the fire, running his fingers pensively through his beard.

"I studied his face and saw that his eyes were brimming.

"Finally, he said, 'My son, today we saw God—the God that resides within us and ties our communities together like strong roofs tied by ropes able to withstand all types of weather. I was certain the people of Ludum would rise to protect one another, but what I could not have predicted was that from surrounding villages so many who hardly knew the victims, or knew them not at all, would drop whatever they were doing and rush here as soon as they heard.'

"Abba's face was radiant."

My smile matched Yosef's. My eyes were brimming, as well.

"I continued gazing at Abba," Yeshu went on. "The restoration of Ludum was an illumination. For me it was as if every window of the Temple in Jerusalem had been thrown open at once, letting light stream in from the heavens. You could see the glow in the faces of all the people of Ludum, and in those of their neighbors who were standing there by them in their hour of peril."

Yeshu's story ended, and my thoughts left him there mingling with the people of Ludum. I knew he would return some other evening, after his work was done, and he and I would continue where our conversation left off, as we meandered in my mind through the ancient fields of my childhood.

~ ~ ~

How close I am now to the youngster I was and to the lasting friend who took me under his wing. I'm able to call them both now from a place deep inside. Each passing year has made this easier to do, even as my joints stiffen and other tasks get harder.

Storytelling, of course, is no task at all. It flows on and on like the River Jordan. So much so that recently a pair of very stuffy village elders dropped in at our family workshop to complain about the flooding.

"Why do you insist on filling the children's heads with those old stories?" they demanded. "These youngsters should be learning their numbers and letters and a practical trade."

From my workbench, I peered up into their faces, feeling suddenly boyish again. I pictured myself back on the dusty streets of Nazareth, being lectured by my gruff Uncle Bartholomaios outside Yeshu's carpentry shop. My uncle's blank eyes moved to and fro as he tried to set me straight.

For a moment, I could say nothing to these two men standing in the middle of the workshop, glaring sternly at me with my uncle's eyes. As my mind jumped back and forth in time searching for an answer, I reached down to scoop up a handful of cedar shavings, and holding them under my nose I inhaled their fragrance.

Then the answer came, as it always does when I wait for it.

My shoulders rose. "You ask me why I tell these stories?"

I look at each visitor full in the face. "The reason is simple, my friends. It's because Yeshu taught us that by telling stories, we can change ourselves and others."

I gave them a moment to consider.

"By telling stories, we can change the world!"

Garden in the Sun

As for my own story, though I feel young as a sapling with its first nest full of hatching eggs, the reflection staring up from the stone mikveh where I bathe daily shows otherwise. It seems I've grown broad-trunked and wizened and the nest is in need of new straw.

The child has given birth to the man—who will one day return to the child, and beyond. The young ones Rebekah and I ushered into the world are now raising families of their own. And our Yeshu villages continue to grow and multiply, as well.

Although the time is dark for the people of our land, I've already seen the darkest day and have come to know that love is an enduring flame. Like Yeshu this light lives on by being passed to others. So I go on telling my tales for those who will take up the torch after I'm no longer here.

Of all the listeners, my favorites are the grandchildren who gather round like bees drawn to nectar. They come looking for me every day, some very close to having young ones themselves, others only walking and talking a few years now. After considerable flutter and bustle, they finally nestle down.

Then one of them says, "Grandfather, begin the stories the way you always do!"

I sit silently for a while, gathering my thoughts and memories about me just as I have gathered my brood. When I've had time to find my peaceful center, when each eager youngster has had a chance to settle in, and the quiet is truly quiet, with a turn of the wrist and a sweep of the hand I signal them to imagine me back in the day.

With that, we all fly through time, and I begin with the early evening long ago when I saw Yeshu standing in a field of wheat, the sun and the moon shining on him from opposite sides of the sky. I spin tale after tale for my fledglings, until in due course they feel sated and I release them to wing away till another day's storytelling resumes.

Alone, I turn my mind in other directions and cut my restless thoughts loose to wander and soar wherever they take me.

But of late I do so with a purpose. It was perhaps a year ago that my youngest grandson suddenly asked as the day's storytelling ended, "Grandfather, when you die, will your Yeshu stories die with you?"

I sat there stunned as the stump of a tree struck by lightning. Speechless, I wondered how many words were left in my hourglass.

That evening after Rebekah had turned in, I stood alone in the courtyard, pondering the child's question. The night breeze carried Yeshu's words as he invoked Isaiah long ago. "And a little child shall lead you."

Instantly I resolved to do whatever must be done to preserve my stories. I would write them down on scraps of leather left over from past jobs. Scraps that couldn't be turned into ox collars or donkey halters or even sandal thongs would carry my words forward.

I turned and strode inside. Beginning with a single leather strip, I sat at the table in our workshop, staring at the small oil lamp flickering in front of me. Looking up, I watched the flame cast a different shadow on each wall!

With so many strands to grasp and braid, I understood that the writing wouldn't be easy. For a while my mind was a churning cauldron. Then a quiet stirring began deep inside...and swelled all around me. Surrounded by Yeshu's presence, I found my voice in the stillness and dipped my pen into the mica dye. Carefully I began to mark the leather, like Joanna had taught me years before.

I counseled myself to write the stories just the way I tell them to my grandchildren. In this way, others will be able to know Yeshu as I did. And what is read and remembered will be passed on to generations yet unborn who will learn what he lived for, what he taught with words and action. It is my wish that those who truly hear will be moved to turn their hearts and minds into hearths for keeping Yeshu's fire burning brightly.

Gripping my quill with renewed purpose, I let the words flow. And flow they have, like rolling streams, until finally my story has nearly reached the sea.

In this ominous time for the Jewish people, when I'm finished I will take the same step as Maria Magdalena and hide my writings behind the eyes of those who read them, waiting for those who care and who long to bring the heart's truth to light.

This is my midrash and my living prayer.

~ ~ ~

In the daytime I sit in my garden, engrossed in reverie. Rebekah comes and unfolds her Yeshu blanket for me to sit upon and contemplate, or to stretch out on and daydream. After supper, before dozing off, she reminds me to spread it over my lap while working at the table, so that I keep warm and the past stays close at hand.

I write late into the night—my family slumbering nearby, my sister and her family at rest down the lane—bringing to life the deepening shadows that the flickering oil lamp casts about me.

Always, the carpenter and the wilderness walker guide my hand.

When my scribbling stops and I can't think what to say, my fingers roam over those woven stories or hunt for a hem to hold between two knuckles, waiting for the spirit to resume its whispering in my ear.

Night after night, I step out our door and find a spot to lie down for a while in the starlight. There I gaze up at the heavens and let my soul wander through the dark and the bright, the distant and the near. And in the reliving and retelling, I continue, even now, to search for answers.

Time is a boundless plain that I shepherd my thoughts across, moving from present to past and back again, looking for green pastures. I know the landscape better and better. Nothing gets lost. When thoughts stray, it's so something can be found. Sometimes, what's found is not the object the quest began with.

Stories full of truth and heart settle easily into their place as history and the ages unroll in front of me as if inscribed on a never-ending scroll.

My white hair may spill down past my shoulders like water over a cataract, and my legs may be too stiff to walk again to the cedars of Lebanon, or even to Jerusalem for Passover. But I'm spirited enough to journey to those places and beyond through the Yeshu stories my grandchildren clamor for in our workshop.

Every day I watch questing reignite in the fire of their eyes. I can almost hear the tales of Yeshu they will tell when I'm no longer on this earth.

I can hardly wait.

Just before I sent them off today, one child shouted out, "Don't ever end your story, Grandfather!"

So I wove a new beginning into the ending of the one I was sharing.

This is how the vine grows. And the generations.

The End Is the Beginning

We are never too old to dream.

I still journey in that winding way and do so as often as I can, a distant lullaby echoing in my ears. With the sun warming my cheeks, or the moonlight brightening the way, I travel into the depths of my being, enveloped within my beloved silence. Still seeking truth, hand in hand with Yeshu, moving ever closer to God as I unfold God's plan for me.

My eyes may be dim, but my vision is bright as ever!

I sit quietly among my sunflowers and roses, leaning against the tree that fits my back so perfectly. And I travel through my mind, my heart, my soul: contemplating what has been and what is still to be, forever crafting and polishing all that I have yet to tell.

This is where I also greet visitors from Yeshu villages who come to talk about how to resolve old hurts and quarrels, and embrace new challenges, thereby strengthening their web of life. Rebekah and I help as we can, but the fact is these folks have by now become master crafters of community, spinning their own vibrant histories out of plain wool and wheat shafts.

My tale is only a fragment of the much larger book we are all writing together. One day soon I'll tie together the ends of the narrative I'm recounting, lay down my quill on the workbench, sigh gently, and smile.

I'll stand and step into the garden where the moon will be rising in front of me, the sun setting behind. With a long, deep breath, I'll grasp the cloak of the gathering night, wrap it round my shoulders, and continue on the pathway to the stars.

But first I'll face back for a moment to see who's following. Who's waving goodbye. Then I'll turn around and step off again.

Yeshu is already waiting up ahead, ready to renew our conversation.

In an eyeblink, I'm at the carpenter's side, walking with him stride for stride, basking in his smile of welcome.

His eyes sparkling like the stars that we walk toward, he says, "Do you remember?"

I meet his gaze, in anticipation.

"Long ago," he says, "I stood in a field of wheat at sunset and moonrise, when a shepherd boy, perhaps a tenth your age, joined me. We waited patiently, as the quietness filled us.

Out of the expanding silence the lad asks, 'Why are you looking at the moon?'

"'Because it marks the path to the stars,' I reply.

"'Is there a path to the stars?' he wonders. 'Can you really travel there?'

"'Yes,' I assure him. 'And so can you, Daavi.'"

Yeshu falls silent as we stroll up the path, each of us enfolded in the wings of his own thoughts.

I see clearly the mountains and valleys of my life, its shadowed forests and sun-dappled streams. I weigh the decades in the palms of my hands. Nagging questions still linger in one cupped hand, but the outstretched palm of the other is overflowing with cherished convictions. In the fullness of time they have flourished within my swelling heart, each one a bright note of comfort, hope, and joy. To my delight, the passing years have turned them into song.

Like a bird I carry this song in my throat, where it is poised to fly from my lips, telling the world what I've always longed to say—whether on the brightest or darkest of days.

I sing it out for my storyteller friend and all others who are listening:

I know that God is love.
And all living things are sacred.
I know that God is within us, and among us.

And from beginning to end...and end to beginning,

I know that I love Yeshu.
And Yeshu loves me.

Made in the USA
Charleston, SC
20 September 2013